***** T H E   C O V E R *****

Peter put his arms around her. "Jeneil...," " his voice cracked.

Jeneil choked up. "Don't say it, Peter, Please. Just I love you, that's all nothing else. Save everything for our reunion. Please keep remembering our reunion." Tears started and she wiped them away quickly. He held her to him and she heard him shallow. "I have something for you to take with you. It is important." She said, pulling away gently, "It shows the kind of trust I have in you, so don't let me down." She reached into her robe pocket and pulled out the glass unicorn. "Take it on your quest. When the prince returns it, the princess will keep her promise to marry him."

He looked at her sadly. "Oh, baby, this isn't fiction. This is real. It's zero hour." He took a deep breath to calm his emotions.

She nodded. "I know Peter, but I want to be with you so much, giving it to you makes me feel like I'm going with you. The glass unicorn is my hope for us. She took the unicorn and kissed it gently, then handed it to him. "Now you'll always have my kiss with you, too."

He took the unicorn and put his arms around her. "Crazy kid." He said, lovingly. He kissed her on the cheek and walked out the door unable to speak or shallow. She closed the door gently and gave into the tears that fell.

Peter stood at the top of the stairs and turned around. Looking at the Camelot sign, he remembered the first time he'd seen it. His throat was in pain. He reached into his jacket and took out the unicorn. "Don't worry," he said, looking at it, "I'll be back to claim the beautiful princess. That's a promise."

- The Songbird / Volume Three

*****T H A N K   Y O U*****

This is a "Author's Edition" of "The Songbird / Volume Three" This "unedited" version of the story is complete just as Beverly intended it to be read.

Only a limited number will be printed for family and friends. "The Songbird / Volume Three" is the third of a five volume series. This should make this a treasured keepsake for those friends who have continued to support our efforts to bring recognition to a truly gifted writing talent.   Your help is so very essential to "The Songbird" success.

Beverly Louise Oliver-Farrell was never given the opportunity to show her incredible writing and storytelling gift to the world. She represents all of those with exceptional talent who are bypassed in life simply because the every-day existence of life's struggles never affords that opportunity to be recognized and showcased. Beverly talks about this "Conveyor Belt" of responsibility in "The Songbird".*(Page 4 / Volume 1)* To all gifted talents out there who never get the opportunity to jump off. This is for you.

The original manuscript was handwritten in twelve five-subject notebooks over an twelve year period. I just couldn't allow such talent to be lost in a box in the attic.

Thank you so very, very, very much for supporting "The Songbird."

2/10/2014

Brian B. Farrell

The Songbird

Volume Three

By

Beverly Louise Oliver-Farrell

***** A C K N O W L E D G E M E N T S *****

Getting "The Songbird" Published would never have happened had it not been for the efforts of some very special people. They make up "The Songbird" team. It took me two weeks to type the first twenty-nine pages into the computer. I hit the wrong button and lost it all. I realized then that I couldn't do this myself. I'll be eternally grateful for each of their contributions.

A "Very Special Thank You" to "The Songbird" Editorial team.

Brian J. Farrell
Benjamin G. Farrell
Amber Massie
Karalee Shawcroft
Lisa Cramer
Kimberly Niven
Virginia Rabun

*****

I have had fantastic support from some very learned technical people. The patience and efforts they have shown in dealing with such a computer klutz as me and keeping my equipment running and meeting the needs of "The Songbird" project is greatly appreciated by all of us.

A "Very Special Thank You" To "The Songbird" Technical team

Benn Farrell at Dockrat Entertainment (Website)
Lee Sanchez at PC & Mac Repairs (Computers)
Bill & Sharon Price at Laserpro II (Printers)
Jean-Claude Picard at Microcrafts (Lamination)
Jon Best (Graphic Designer/Cover Assembly)
Wishing Well Glass Blowers (Unicorns)

***** A C K N O W L E D G E M E N T S *****

Every Wednesday night I go to an "Independent/Assisted Living" facility and read and share "The Songbird" with a group of "Very Special" people who have become my close friends.

I don't think they will ever fully understand how much they have taught me and caused me to grow. I thank them so very much for their support and encouragement.

A "Very Special Thank You" to "The Songbird Book Club"
at "Viewpointe"

Virginia Rabun	Harriet Spangenberg
Ruth Goetzman	Genevieve Campbell
Chet Derezinski	Leo Van De Water
Bertha Lang	Eleanor Wright
Bob Thompson	Beverly Osburn
Phyllis Mueller	Elizabeth Nichols
Gladys Mercier	Carol Barrett

*****

A "Very Special Thank you" to members of the Viewpointe Staff for their valuable assistance in gathering our group together each Wednesday night.

Judine Carkner   Natalie Mutch   Peggy Striplin   Patty Wright

*****

One person deserves "Special Recognition." His encouragement and living example has shown me that "you never give up your dreams."

A "Very Special Thank You" to my "Best Friend"

Robert Louis Tyler

***** S Y N O P S I S *****

"The Songbird" is a love story about a young woman named Jeneil who believed in fairy tales, a prince charming, and happy endings. She goes on a quest to find herself before the "conveyor belt" of responsibility forces her to accept a lesser existence. In her quest for superlative, she almost destroys herself and the lives of some of those people around her.

Jeneil, a white girl from Nebraska, finds her Prince Charming in Peter, a Chinese gang kid from the streets of New York's Chinatown, who is in his last year as a residence in a New England hospital where they meet. "The Songbird" is their story. Add Steve, Peter's best friend, whose life began as a baby left on the doorsteps of an upper New York state orphanage, to the mix and life will never be the same for this triad of friends

.

It is a story of love, communication, murder, mystery, danger, betrayal, suspense, honesty and dignity, personal achievements, and a look at life which covers the trials of human relationships. It is steeped in a reality that will cause everyone who reads "The Songbird" to identify with their own life experiences.

COMMENT: *The complete story of the "The Songbird" is a five volume series. Beverly Louise Oliver-Farrell has laid out "The Songbird" from beginning to end, stacking one incident on top of another like a set of logo blocks, carefully interlocking the past, present, and future together in a not-so-perfect world. Beverly holds the reader's interest by leaving clues and dangling unanswered questions throughout "The Songbird" and just when you think you have it all figured out....... She is very successful tying it all together and being able to keep the end of the story a secret until the closing pages.*

I love you, Baby

I'm going to miss you

***** F O R E W A R D *****

To my knowledge there is only one piece of writing in existence which expressed Beverly Louise Oliver-Farrell's's own view of what it was she was trying to convey in The Songbird story. It is contained in a letter Beverly wrote to her step-daughter,(my daughter). Part of that letter appears on the back cover of each volume of "The Songbird." I would like to present the entire letter to you as a way of giving you a greater understanding of the thought process of this outstanding writer.

*****

Dear Mary,

You are a sweetheart! You are living through what I address in my novel! I had asked Dad if I might read your Emails, because I'm totally fascinated!

A line to my novel is: "We bring out the beast or the best in others."

The principles and philosophies I put in my novel are based in reality. However, the protagonist is fiction, based on a compilation of many qualities and characteristics of several women I've known and admire. To see my protagonist personified is a kick.......my younger sister suffers from a brain chemical imbalance that has made her life torture. I've told her that we are all running ahead of the man with the net. She just happens to trip and get caught in it. I deeply believe that about mankind.

Everyone seems entwined in Jekyll/Hyde functions. Henry David Thoreau in 'Walden Pond' maintains that all people are leading lives of deep desperation. As sad and even depressing as that sounds, I believe it.

The precept that we carry generational baggage and live partially in the shadow of our parents seems observably true. George Bernard Shaw in 'The Importance of Being Ernest' said a girl's curse in life is that she will be like her mother. A boy's curse in life is that he won't.

In my novel I try to show the importance of communication in our lives. I propose that we are all cocooned in four-sided Plexiglas cubicles. We see each other and we faintly hear each other, so we think we are living. Yet, until we struggle to rise above the Plexiglas, we don't experience actual seeing and feeling in the dimension of reality. It's a bittersweet experience filled with joys and sorrows. Those who are victorious seem to be an intelligent, sensitive, and courageous people.

You and your dad are going at the Plexiglas. You go girl! You go! All the best to you as you climb above all four sides of the cubicle.

*****

I have been asked on many occasions if Beverly was in fact Jeneil in The Songbird. The answer is best given by Beverly herself in the above letter. '*....a compilation of many qualities and characteristics of several women I've known and admire.*' I have found this to be true, in essence Jeneil represents the best in all women whether it be what they are or what they desire to be which is why so many women will identify with Jeneil, and also why so many men will see parts of themselves in both Peter and Steve.

Brian B. Farrell

The Songbird

One

The holiday decorations were put away and life returned to its usual routine. Jeneil said she liked life's pace returning to normal even though she missed all the colors of the season. Peter had tried to settle the situation with his mother, and she was fine if he visited alone which he did the weekend Jeneil went to Nebraska, but he couldn't stand the ice in his mother's voice when Jeneil visited with him. He had nearly been destroyed when Jeneil cried on the drive home from one very short visit. Jeneil couldn't take long visits there and Peter was concerned. He hadn't seen the acceptance from his family his grandfather had mentioned regarding their relationship. His mother saw to it that he never saw the rest of the family and it was obvious to him that she was afraid of Jeneil.

Both Peter and his grandfather were at a loss over how to deal with the situation, and Peter was at a loss over a few things that were happening. Once, Ron had stopped in while Peter and Jeneil were visiting. Ron was planning his wedding and had stopped in to pick up something for his mother. His careful scrutiny of Jeneil had annoyed Peter and with the situation between Jeneil and his mother as it was, Ron's staring caused Jeneil to be twice as upset after they left.

But the one person Peter couldn't understand at all was Karen. She went out of her way to be nice to him. That reacted negatively to Jeneil too, since Karen was as icy to Jeneil as his mother was. He was beginning to think he shouldn't take Jeneil to visit at all. Visits left her upset for days and it was affecting their relationship. She would become distant and cry a lot, and those days were hell to get through. He was tired of it. There seemed to be only one solution to the whole mess, marriage. It seemed like the best answer. He thought about that as he stopped to pick up Karen. She had called and asked him for a ride to college. He agreed only after she pleaded, insisting he was her last hope.

"There you are," Peter said, pulling up to the Student Union.

"Thanks, Pete. Thanks a lot," Karen beamed. "Come in and I'll buy you a coffee. I'd like to be seen with a knockout guy in there. It'll get me noticed."

"What happened to the romance?" Peter asked, surprised by the compliment and the absent mention of Greg.

Karen shrugged. "I'm not ready to be as serious as he wanted to be."

"Well, wait until you are then, smart move."

"You see, Pete. Chinese girls are taught morality."

He bristled at the obvious slam to Jeneil. "Get out, Karen."

"Pete, don't get mad."

"Karen, out."

"I'm sorry, Pete, but I'd like to see you with a Chinese girl."

"My life's none of your business. Get out." He reached over and opened her door.

"Mouth, Karen, all mouth. Learn to shut it," she berated herself as she watched Peter drive away. "What's that girl got!" She stomped her foot then walked into the Student Union, planning to take him a peace offering at the hospital.

Karen looked around the large room as she waited in line to pay for her coffee. In the far corner sat Uette Wong reading a book. Karen grimaced. Because of her mouth, Peter had missed meeting Uette. How easy it would have been to walk past her. Peter was good looking and a doctor. Even if Uette didn't want him, there were others there who would be interested. There must be. But Uette was his type. Karen was sure of it. Uette was like Jeneil, but she was Chinese, had better standards, and was beautiful. Now it would be tougher to get the two to meet. Karen just hoped Uette would want to.

Karen found Uette to be moody. Sometimes she'd smile and at others she'd walk right past you like you were invisible. Karen had spent days smiling at Uette in order to seem approachable. She sighed to herself. She was going to be the maid of honor at Peter's wedding and she was going to earn it. Uette looked up as Karen approached her table.

"Karen, how are you?"

"Just fine, Uette. Mind some company?" Karen asked, relaxing.

"No, not at all, sit. You look a little undone around the edges." She looked at Karen with beautiful brown eyes that were perfectly made up and filled with sympathy. Her teeth were perfectly even and incredibly white. Karen decided to gamble it all. There wasn't much time; Peter wouldn't put up with the bad treatment towards Jeneil for much longer and his mother was frightened of his total withdrawal from the family.

Karen sighed. "I am a little under. I just had a run in with my stepbrother."

Uette smiled. "I was spared the brother business, but I can understand the stress. Life with three perfect sisters isn't easy, especially when you're the youngest and expected to follow their perfect examples. Relax. The tension isn't worth it."

Karen was impressed with Uette's insight and felt more encouraged. "I'm only interested in his welfare, but he can't see it." Karen drank some coffee.

"Is he in trouble?"

"The family thinks he is. His mother's worried sick about the girl he's dating. She's white."

Uette smiled. "Karen, this isn't ancient China. It happens to decent people."

"No, it isn't that. We happen to know that the girl is interested in his best friend who's white. She's going to drop him, but he can't see it. He's totally wrapped up in her, completely blind."

Uette sat back in her chair. "Uh-oh, that sounds like trouble but what can you do if he won't listen?"

Karen took a deep breath. "This sounds pitiful, but his mother and I were hoping to find someone Chinese who would take his mind off her."

Uette smiled slowly. "And you're approaching me?"

Karen fidgeted. "Don't be insulted. Your beauty alone would do it. The girl has nothing going for her. She could almost be a zero if she slipped the other way a few numbers."

Uette laughed. "Well, she must have something going for her if she has your stepbrother completely blinded."

Karen drank some coffee. "She does, S-E-X."

Uette raised her eyebrows. "Oh, your stepbrother likes to have fun."

Karen sighed. "Unfortunately, it's his middle name." Karen felt good about being so honest with Uette. She really liked her.

Uette looked at Karen seriously. "Why do you think I can compete with a girl who's offering that kind of fun?"

Karen realized the insult. "Oh gosh, I didn't mean that. He's Chinese and we feel he'll go back to Chinese girls with the right start. He had a bad beginning, that's all. He was always in trouble as a kid, but he's grown up. He's studying to be a doctor. He's sane at least."

Uette wrinkled her eyebrows, obviously curious. "What your stepbrother's name?"

"Peter Chang." Karen held her breath and watched Uette. From the look on her face it was obvious she had heard of him and Karen's courage dropped, dragging her hope with it. Karen sighed. "I can see that you've heard of him."

Uette smiled. "Karen, every Chinese father has warned his daughters about Peter Chang. All my sisters had nightmares about him from the things my father would warn us about." She laughed.

Karen nodded. "I know. That's why he's turned to white trash." She covered her mouth, embarrassed by the tasteless slip. "I'm sorry."

Uette sat forward. "He has really changed?"

Karen stared, wondering. "Yes, Uette, he has. He really has. He's really sane. He has to be, he's studying to be an orthopedic surgeon. And he's good at it, really good. He couldn't have made it to his second year of residency and not have changed could he?"

Uette shook her head. "I don't know. He's a legend in some circles. It's hard to imagine the guy I've heard about settling into the routine of a doctor. He must be a character."

Karen giggled. "Oh, he's a character, but he has really changed. The family can't believe it either. Actually, we're proud of him."

Uette shrugged. "Well, he hasn't changed completely. He's still involved with girls and sex."

"No, Uette, one girl, and she has him completely turned around. He thinks he's going to marry her." Karen was surprised her defense of Peter was genuine. "But when this girl switches to his white friend," Karen sighed, "boy, I don't know if Peter could take that."

Uette looked puzzled. "How do you know she's interested in his friend?"

"We've seen the three of them together. Peter's friend can't keep his hands off her and she lets him, even snuggles to him. It's a mess, a disgusting mess." Karen shook her head as she finished her coffee. "Peter can't see it. He's completely blind to her faults. His mother claims he's just ready to settle down, it happens to all men, but he clings to this girl because a Chinese girl won't give him a chance."

Uette looked sympathetic. "Karen, if what I've heard about Peter Chang is true, I have serious doubts that I'm his type at all."

Karen shook her head. "Uette, you're wrong. You're cool, intelligent, and beautiful, with a subtle sexiness. That's Dr. Chang's type. I told you he's changed. You should see his girl. We're talking major nothing here."

Uette sat back in thought. "Karen, this all has me very curious. I'll do it."

Karen's face showed her excitement. "You will? Oh, Uette, you don't know how happy my stepmother will be, but what about your family?"

Uette smiled. "I'll handle them. If I even let them find out at all. I've dated boys my father didn't like before. He forgets women have the option of saying no. He's really prehistoric. He'd arrange our marriages if we let him. I'll handle it. Right now, I feel this is a situation that needs help. Chinese should stick together."

Karen sighed. "Uette, you really cheered up my day. This is the biggest hurdle."

Uette laughed pleasantly. "Don't be so sure. We still have a zero who has Peter Chang and his best friend totally turned around. Maybe it's time she had some competition."

Karen smiled broadly. "I just knew you were the right person to ask. Thank you so much. You are just what we need, believe me."

Uette held up her coffee cup in a toast. "To the rescue of Peter Chang." Karen smiled and nodded.

*****

As class let out, Karen picked up her books and rushed out of her sociology class. She usually took her time leaving since there was a guy in class she wanted to get to know better, but today was different. As she rushed to the parking lot, she smiled. Peter better appreciate the sacrifice she was making for him. As she waited for Uette, she saw a white Corvette slow down as it approached her and was surprised to see Uette behind the wheel. The interior of the car was real leather and Karen was completely overwhelmed. "Oh, Pete's not going to believe this. His girl gets him a three hundred dollar car and he thinks she's wonderful. You are going to make her look sick. The family thinks she has a little bit of money because her father left her a small investment company. Little bit is right compared to you."

"I bought this car for myself."

Karen was shocked. "Wow! I'm really impressed."

Uette laughed. "My father thought it was too showy so I saved money from a modeling job in New York. It makes my father nervous, but he knows he can't hold me too tight. I'm not my sisters, so he allows me little things like the car and modeling. Did you get the brownies for Peter?"

Karen was surprised. "You call him Peter, so does his girl."

"Well, he's a doctor now. Pete was a troublesome street kid, Peter sounds like a doctor."

Karen smiled, very pleased. "Oh, Jeneil, you don't stand a chance." She giggled.

"Jeneil, that's odd; it has a tone of masculinity to it."

Karen shook her head. "She'd make a great boy. She beat Pete, I mean Peter, and his friend at basketball then got behind Steve and knocked him over and pushed Peter onto the ground. She could be a football player, she's so tough, and they eat it up. I'll never understand it. She never wears nail polish, her lipstick always needs touched up, her hair's always falling out of place, and yet they're all around her like she could break, like she's delicate. Ugh!" she screamed. "The girl drives me crazy. Even Peter's grandfather is taken with her and he's old. You can forgive him being senile, but Peter and Steve? Two great guys being fooled by her. She's a magician, a sorceress. She must be."

Uette smiled. "Well, here's the hospital. I'm really nervous. The great Peter Chang. I hope I don't trip over my tongue or remember my father's warning and start to shake."

Karen laughed. "Pete's very serious when he's at the hospital. He takes his career very seriously."

They went to the elevator and headed for the fifth floor. A nurse looked up when they got to the nurse's station and Karen cleared her throat nervously. "Would it be possible to see Dr. Chang for a minute?"

"Of course, I'll locate him for you." The nurse smiled broadly as she leaned over to another nurse then both nurses looked at the girls and smiled.

"What are they grinning about?" Uette asked.

Karen shrugged. "I don't know."

"Dr. Peter Chang, that's so impressive," Uette said, smiling as she heard Peter being paged then stared as he came from a room and headed toward the desk. "Oh my gosh, Karen, he's absolutely gorgeous. What a total hunk. I'm getting weak."

Karen giggled. "Don't fail me now, Uette, please."

Peter was shocked to see Karen and he looked Uette over as he got closer. "Karen, what are you doing here?"

Karen fidgeted. "I felt bad about our argument this morning, so I brought a peace offering, two brownies." She handed him the bag and he took it looking very puzzled. The two nurses who were watching looked at each other and nodded.

"How did you get here? I thought your car broke down."

"Uette brought me. Uette, this is my stepbrother, Peter Chang. Peter, this is Uette Wong." Peter looked at Uette, trying to place the name.

"Hi, Peter." Uette smiled warmly at him.

He returned the smile. "Uette, you drove Karen all the way across town to bring me two brownies? And you're going to drive her home? You must be some friend."

Uette studied his eyes. "I was free. She needed help." He nodded, matching her stare.

"Thank you." Peter looked at Karen. "Really Karen, your conscience impresses me. Does this mean you had Uette drive all the way here because you're sorry for what you said?"

"Well, I uh, I'm sorry I made you angry," Karen stammered, realizing she was caught in the pretense.

Peter grinned. "Thank you for the brownies."

Karen smiled; relieved he wasn't going to make things tough for her. The elevator doors opened and Steve stepped off, walking over to them. He looked at Karen and studied Uette.

"Hi, Karen," Steve said. "Excuse me, Pete. Do you have the scans and printouts on the explosion case?"

"Dr. Turner has them."

Steve nodded. "You're in on the conference with Maxwell and Sprague, aren't you?"

"Yeah, I'm on my way."

"Okay, I'll see you there."

"No, wait Steve. I'll walk over with you. I need some briefing on it. I'm through here." He looked at Karen. "Aren't I?"

"Sure," she said, fidgeting. "I just wanted to bring you the brownies."

Peter grinned and nodded. "Thanks again." He looked at Uette. "Nice meeting you and thanks for driving Karen all over town."

Uette watched as Peter walked away with Steve. "Boy, you were right. I heard he had the mind and nerves of a steel trap," she commented, thinking out loud.

Karen looked at her. "Who said that?"

Uette returned to the moment. "I'm not sure, someone, somewhere. Karen, he's shrewd. We can't be this obvious anymore. It'll work against us."

Karen looked pleased. "You mean you're not discouraged? He wasn't very personable."

Uette grinned. "I'm not discouraged. I find him interesting, very interesting indeed. I think he's gorgeous and very much maligned by my family."

Karen sighed. "This is a dream. It must be. Thanks, Uette. Can you imagine the girl I described with those two?"

Uette turned her head quickly, surprised. "That's the friend you were talking about?"

Karen nodded. "Unbelievable, isn't it? One girl latches onto the both of them."

Uette pushed the elevator button. "Karen, then you've added wrong, zeros don't attract and then blind jungle animals."

"Jungle animals?" Karen asked, puzzled.

Uette smiled as they got on the elevator. "Karen, those two are men. I'm talking real men. The girl's not a zero. This is getting more fascinating."

*****

Peter and Steve walked to the conference room. Peter opened the bag. "Karen brought brownies because she felt bad about making me mad this morning." Peter laughed as Steve made an expression of total disbelief.

"What's she up to?"

Two

Peter drove home feeling exhausted, grateful his shift hadn't been extended. He had called Ron during a slow period and had been surprised when Ron invited him and Jeneil to the wedding. Apparently Sue felt bad about the mess and insisted Ron call knowing word would never reach them if trusted to the usual family line of Ron's mother to Peter's mother. Peter had sighed with relief; the invitation he had received earlier was in his name only. Ron's mother had sent them out, afraid to oppose her sister. Peter looked forward to telling Jeneil the news. She needed to hear something cheerful from his family.

Jeneil was really pleased and excited. Not knowing Ron or Sue, she decided on a gift of money feeling they would make better use of it than a gift that was all wrong for their tastes. Peter relaxed, encouraged by her excitement.

The wedding was at one-thirty on Saturday. Jeneil changed her outfit three times then finally settled on a black dress. She paced as Peter got dressed. It was a disappointment that they wouldn't be able to attend the reception because he had to be on duty at four, but she was pleased to at least be going to the ceremony. She handed him the envelope with the money and let him help her slip on the grey fake fur jacket.

Peter held her by her shoulders. "You look fantastic, honey, really, really great. The bride's in trouble. You're going to outshine her."

Jeneil sighed. "I just want everything to go smoothly."

Peter kissed her cheek. "It will, honey. Let's go." She stopped at the mirror and put her hat on then her leather gloves. She turned and Peter shook his head. "Jeneil, when you look like this I wonder what the hell you're doing with the likes of me."

Jeneil touched his cheek. "We look like we belong together. Let's show 'dis crowd we gots class, bud. Let's knock 'em dead." He laughed and put his arm around her shoulder.

*****

Parking was tight and they had to walk half a block to the church. Peter recognized people from his childhood as they stared in shock as he walked by with Jeneil. He wasn't sure if they were stunned because she wasn't Chinese or that he wasn't there in handcuffs with a police escort. Jeneil looked money and was attracting attention, and he was glad he had worn his blazer with a fashionable overcoat. It struck him at that moment how important clothes were and how good they could make a person feel. He walked tall with Jeneil on his arm and he could tell people were impressed.

Peter and Jeneil climbed the steps to the church and stopped inside the large foyer. His mother was smiling and talking with Malien, her color draining as she caught sight of them. Peter's spine stiffened and he prepared himself. She marched right to them followed nervously by Tom, who was trying to stop her. Malien put her hand to her mouth as she watched. His mother's face was contorted by the time she got to them, her eyes on fire. Peter felt Jeneil's hand squeezing his arm and he pulled her closer to him.

"What do you think you are doing?" She looked at Peter, speaking in a low whisper.

"Ron and Sue called and invited the both of us," Peter answered quietly.

"I don't care! They were being polite. You should have enough sense of decency to realize that. She doesn't have a place here, especially in a church. Don't either of you have any conscience at all?" She glared at Jeneil. "Get out of here before you embarrass the whole family. Sue's family is decent, they care about morality." Peter felt sick. The shock and hurt on Jeneil's face was unmistakable and he could feel her shaking.

"Let's go, Peter," Jeneil whispered, her voice trembling.

Peter's mother held his other arm. "This is his family, he belongs here."

"Fine, I'll leave." Jeneil let go of his arm.

Peter took Jeneil's hand and looked straight at his mother. "We'll leave. She stays or we both go."

"Peter, no," Jeneil interrupted, "I understand. Please, I don't want a scene. People are starting to stare. Please, I want to leave."

Peter and Jeneil walked toward the exit. "Wait for me here. I'll give the envelope to Ron and be right back." He kissed her cheek and went toward the door at the far end of the foyer.

His mother glared at Jeneil, shaking her head in disgust. "My only hope was that he'd find a nice girl and settle down, instead he finds someone as crazy as he is. Look around you. In case you haven't been taught these things, decent people come here to this building. They get married properly before their families and friends so everybody is proud. Can you even understand any of this?"

Jeneil stared directly at her, frightened by the words that were on her tongue straining to be said, anger rising higher and higher within her. She swallowed, struggling with her voice. "Tell Peter I said he should stay." She turned and left, walking quickly down the stairs. She crossed the street blinded by the tears that filled her eyes and spilled down her cheeks. Running the half block to the car, she unlocked the door and got behind the wheel, sobbing. She pulled her hat off and threw it across the seat. Pulling herself together, she started the engine, afraid Peter would catch up to her. She drove away wanting desperately to erase the whole scene from her mind.

Peter knocked gently on the highly polished mahogany door. A young man in dark grey cut away tuxedo opened it. "Could I see Ron for a second?"

"Yeah," Ron said from inside, smiling as Peter walked in. "Hey, Pete, great to see you."

Peter put his head down then looked at Ron. "Listen, Jeneil and I can't get past my mother." He took out the envelope. "Here, we'd like you to have this." He handed Ron the envelope then held out his hand. "Best of everything to the both of you."

Ron looked serious as he shook Peter's hand. "Let me talk to her."

"No, Ron. It's better if we leave, really. She's on fire out there. You don't need it today."

Ron sighed. "I'm really sorry, Pete."

Peter smiled. "Don't even think about it. You've got a bride and a church full of people waiting for you. Concentrate on that. I'll see you later." Peter left, heading quickly for the foyer. He looked around; Jeneil wasn't there.

Peter's mother came to him. "She left. She told me to tell you that she'd like you to stay." He turned toward the door but she grabbed his arm. "Peter, this is your cousin's wedding. You have to stay. What will people say?"

He looked at her. "They'll find something, I'm sure." He opened the door and left, running toward the car, angry to find it was gone. "Damn it, Jeneil. Damn it." He walked to the end of the street, counting his change. Unfamiliar with the bus system, he arrived at the apartment at three-fifteen. He walked up the stairs trying to calm down, realizing Jeneil must be just as upset. Finding the apartment empty, he threw his overcoat on the sofa. "Shit, just what I need now, disappearing games from her." He sighed and ran his fingers through his hair. Going to the bedroom to change for work, his telephone rang and he took a deep breath. "So help me, Mom, you won't like my language if this is you."

"Pete, Morietti."

"Hi, Dan, what's up?"

"We've been trying to reach you. Can you come in as soon as possible? This place is bedlam. Three doctors are out with the flu, all calling at the last minute. We even called Steve in from his day off. He worked first shift."

"Sure," Peter said. "I'll be right in."

"Thanks, Pete. I'm telling you things are really happening here. Even the girl from Records was brought into the ER."

Peter's heart stopped and his head began to buzz. "What girl from Records?"

"The young one with the long hair, Jeneil."

Peter had trouble breathing. "What happened to her?"

"I don't know. When she was brought in, I thought Steve went into shock but he insisted on taking the case, so I don't know anything about it."

Peter's throat was tight and he had trouble swallowing. "I'm on my way."

"Thanks again, Pete."

Peter raced around and was out the door on his way to the hospital. He rushed to the ER, slowing down as he got closer so he wouldn't attract attention.

"Where's Dr. Bradley?" Peter asked a nurse.

"I don't know." The nurse looked around. "We haven't had time to breathe since noon. I saw him in earlier."

Peter went to the records basket and leafed through the reports. Jeneil's wasn't there. He wondered if she had been admitted. He went to the head nurse. "The girl from Records, Alden-Connors, where is she?"

The nurse closed her eyes, thinking. "Released, yes, she was released."

"It wasn't serious then?" he asked, beginning to breathe normally.

She shrugged. "The police brought her in then Dr. Bradley handled everything."

"Where is he now?"

She checked the list. "He signed out. That's odd; I thought he'd be working a double since we're so short handed."

"Thanks." Peter headed for the phone booth and dialed Jeneil. There was no answer. Worried, he went to the desk to sign in.

"Dr. Chang, telephone." Peter looked up and the nurse sent him to the viewing room to answer.

"Pete."

"Steve." Peter sighed. "Where's Jeneil, what happened to her?"

"I brought her home. We just got in. She misjudged the speed of a truck and pulled out in front of it. She realized the mistake in time and swerved off the street and hit a tree."

Peter's stomach knotted. "What are the injuries?"

"Minor bruises to her head and left forearm, and a possible sprained muscle in her back. The cops brought her in because she was hysterical. She couldn't stop shaking and crying. She was a wreck, Pete. What happened? Do you know? I can't believe it was just the accident that did that to her."

"She ran into my mother at my cousin's wedding. She drove off upset. That's probably how it happened."

Steve sighed. "Well, I hope your mother is satisfied. She almost killed her. What's her problem, Pete? Really, is it worth the kid's life?"

Peter didn't answer. "Can I talk to Jeneil?"

"She's changing for bed. I hit her with a strong sedative. She won't be awake too much longer. Hold on." Steve knocked on the bedroom door but there was no answer. Opening the door, the lights were on and Jeneil was under the covers. She was out. He went back to the phone. "Pete, she's out cold. I arranged to have her car towed to a garage. I put a few painkillers in her purse but I can't be sure she even remembers so I'm telling you." Steve sighed. "I'm supposed to work a double but I don't want to leave her alone. Even the bruise on her head is minor but she looks so helpless lying there."

Peter rubbed his forehead. "I know, I don't want to stay here either but they'll never let me go." He sighed. "And what reason could I give them? Shit," he said, frustrated. "Wait a minute, Steve. I'll call the woman upstairs. She's Jeneil's friend."

"Oh, great." Steve relaxed. "I'll stay until she gets here."

"Thanks, Steve. Thanks a lot."

"Sure, I'll probably see you soon." Steve hung up and went to the bedroom. Turning off the lights, he went to the side of the bed and leaned over Jeneil. "Aw kid, nothing's worth jeopardizing your life, even accidentally. Tell the bitch to go to hell and be done with her." He shook his head and smiled, touching her cheek gently. "You're so beautiful." He kissed her hand that rested near her chin. He hesitated then kissed her lips lightly. "I love you, Jeneil. You'll never know it. You're too dense." He smiled and touched her hair. "Pete deserves you anyway. He took the time to find you. I didn't, but I'll tell you, I think he's so damn lucky. You're so crazy about him. He's not sane where you're concerned either." He shook his head, smiled and kissed her cheek. The door buzzer sounded and he went to answer it.

"Hi, I'm Adrienne. Peter just called about Jeneil. Is she really okay?" Adrienne wrung her hands nervously. "Should we call her uncle?"

"No, she's out cold from a sedative, let her rest. She has some minor bruises and she'll be hurting worse tomorrow. I just didn't want to leave her alone. I feel better knowing someone will be checking on her until Pete gets in."

"I sure will," Adrienne replied. "I'm so glad you guys thought of me. Why was she in the car alone? She went to a wedding with Peter. What happened?"

Steve hesitated then decided she was a close friend so why not. "His mother happened."

Adrienne angrily shook her head. "That narrow-minded bitch won't be happy until she completely wrecks her life. Where's the car?"

"Tony's Garage on Bond Street. I told him to hold off working on it until he hears from somebody."

She smiled. "Thank you for being there for her. You like her, don't you?"

Steve nodded. "She's a great kid."

Adrienne smiled and nodded, agreeing. "She gets to you where you live. I never thought I would have a white soul sister." She chuckled.

Charlie opened the door upstairs. "Is Jeneil okay?"

Adrienne nodded. "She's shaken up but resting now." Charlie sighed with relief.

Jeff stopped as he was passing by. "Is something wrong?"

"Jeneil had a car accident. She's resting now."

"Does she need someone to stay with her? Does she need help? I certainly owe her enough favors besides being a concerned friend."

Adrienne smiled. "I'm covering until Peter gets home. We'll see about tomorrow."

Jeff nodded. "Remember me if she needs anything."

"I will." Adrienne smiled. "Thanks, Jeff."

"Sure," he answered, and left.

Steve was impressed. He felt more relaxed knowing Jeneil wasn't as alone as he first thought. The telephone rang. It was Peter asking Adrienne to turn the sound off on his telephone and unplug Jeneil's telephone next to the bed.

"How is she?" Peter asked Steve.

"She's still out and will be for awhile. She was a wreck when they brought her in. Her body needs to rest from that alone. I'm coming in now. Adrienne's all set to take over."

"Thanks again, Steve. I mean it."

"It's okay, Pete. She's a friend. I'll see you shortly."

Peter was very quiet during his shift, badly shaken by the accident. As Steve watched, he could see anger growing within Peter. During a slow period at ten, Steve slapped Peter gently on the back. "Come on, I'll get us some coffee." Peter nodded and followed Steve out of the ER. As they walked past a row of telephones, Peter stopped. Steve looked as he stood there.

Peter went to a telephone and called Adrienne. Jeneil was still out but looked peaceful. Peter hung up and sighed as he reached into his pocket for some change. "Steve, stick around and watch Chang's revenge." He inserted the coins and dialed. "Karen, where's my mother?"

"She's at Aunt Risa's. Everyone's there. You know the family. Are you okay?"

Peter ignored the question. "I'll call her there, thanks." He hung up. "Steve, how would you like to lend me some money to end this war?" Steve handed him some change. "I might as well go down in a blaze of gunfire. She's so damn worried about her image. Let's see what the truth will do. She always has her way. It's over." Peter dialed and Risa answered. "This is Pete; could I talk to my mother?"

"Pete," Risa said, "I'm sorry you had to work."

Peter decided to go for it. "Ron and Sue invited me and Jeneil to the wedding. We were at the church, Aunt Risa, but my mother wouldn't let us in. I'm sure she said I had to work. I thought you should know the truth. Then, to add to that, the nice Christian lady insults Jeneil so bad she takes off upset in her car. Well, I would like my mother to know her mouth put Jeneil in the hospital. She was in an accident right after she left the church."

Risa gasped. "Oh my goodness, she is badly hurt?"

"The last time I was able to talk to her was at the church before the accident." Steve smiled, listening to Peter lay it on thick. Peter could hear everyone in the background asking what was wrong, and then he heard his mother's voice. "Tell them, Aunt Risa, just the way I told you."

Risa faced the family. "Lien, you apparently were so rude to Jeneil at the church today that she was very upset. After she left, she was in a serious accident." There were gasps and several oh-nos.

Peter could hear Malien. "Lien, we've been trying to tell you to stop pushing, but no, you couldn't see past your own pride. Well, look what you've done now. Is she all right, Risa?" Peter listened as Risa told them that Jeneil was unconscious and Peter hadn't spoken to her since she left the church. Peter's grandfather grabbed the phone.

"Peter." The old man could barely talk he was so badly shaken.

"Grandfather, she's going to be okay. No thanks to my mother. Jeneil could have been killed." Peter could hear his grandfather clear his throat and sigh. "I want to talk to my mother."

"Of course. Lien, Peter wants to talk to you." His mother took the phone; Peter knew it even though she didn't talk.

"Mrs. Lee, listen carefully to what I'm about to say. It's over. Is that clear? I've warned you and warned you about this. Well, today you nearly killed Jeneil." He heard his mother sniffle. "I won't give you another chance to finish the job. I don't intend to see any of you again, ever. My name's not Chang anymore. You are not my mother. Leave me alone and stay away from Jeneil. I hope that's clear enough."

Steve whistled as Peter hung up. "That was heavy, Pete."

"So is what Jeneil went through. Let's get some coffee."

Peter was asked to work a double. He hated the idea but they were so shorthanded that everyone was working a double so he stayed. Steve came to him before he signed out at eleven. "Pete, would you like me to stay at the apartment tonight to check on her?"

Peter sighed with relief. "That would be great. Steve, really I don't know how to thank you."

Steve shook his head, resisting the sentiment. "I love you both."

Peter had called Adrienne to let her know Steve was on his way. Expecting him, she left to get some rest. When Steve arrived, he checked on Jeneil; she was sleeping. He took her pulse. Her cheeks were flushed and she felt a little warm so he decided to let her sleep. She stirred and he relaxed thinking she was good on her own. He went to the sofa and stretched out just as the telephone rang; it was Peter.

"What's she like now?"

"She's out of the effect of the sedative and sleeping on her own. She looks flushed but her pulse is normalizing, and she stirs when she's touched. My guess is she's in pain. I gave her the sedative figuring shock had dulled the pain but I expect I'll give her a painkiller. She'd probably go right back to sleep. Everything else looks normal. I'll check her eyes when she wakes up, but I know the head injury was very slight."

Peter sighed with relief. "I'm glad you're there. Help yourself to whatever's around. I don't think anybody here has had a proper meal. We're all living on coffee."

"Thanks, Pete. I'm getting hungry now that I'm slowing down. I think I'll raid the refrigerator."

"Thanks again, Steve."

Steve went to the kitchen and poured himself some milk. Seeing grapes, he took some and sliced some cheese. There was nut bread wrapped in clear plastic. He sliced some of that too and leaned against the counter as he ate.

"Peter?" Jeneil called. "Ouch!" Hearing her, Steve got a glass of water and went to her. She squinted from the light as he approached the bed. "Steve? Where's Peter?"

He sat on the edge of the bed. "The hospital's shorthanded. He had to work a double, honey. I just finished mine. How do you feel?"

"I ache all over and my back feels tight. Am I all right?"

"You're all right for having hit a tree. You'd feel better if you'd hit a big marshmallow."

She tried to laugh. "Ouch!" She lifted her head quickly. "The truck! Was the driver okay?"

Steve shook his head. "He's fine. You moved out of the way and so did he. He was luckier than you were. You were the only one hurt."

She sighed and put her head back on the pillow then began to cry. "I shouldn't have been driving. I wasn't thinking straight. I could've caused a serious accident." Steve went to her purse for the pills and handed her two with the glass of water. "I'm worried about my back. It doesn't feel right."

"It's a muscle strain. They can be pretty painful. We x-rayed your spine and your ribs. I had Pete check the films when they were ready and they were clear. He knows spines."

She nodded and smiled. "It pays to know doctors. What about my car? Did the city tow it?"

"The cops realized I knew you and talked me through the process. The car had to be towed away, but only because the fender was pushed against the wheel. You landed it pretty good, even using the tree instead of brakes." He took her hand and got serious. "Don't drive when you're upset anymore. Pull over." She nodded and bit her lip. "Better still, don't get upset anymore. Tell her to go to hell from now on."

Jeneil started to cry again. "It's so hopeless. She thinks I'm trash."

"Who the hell cares what she thinks," he said, reaching for the tissue box, and then he put his hand beside her on the bed and leaned toward her. "Come on, no more crying. I can perform surgery but I'm not sure I can save you from drowning. I was never a lifeguard, so please, no more tears."

She laughed lightly, trying not to hurt, and then she touched his cheek gently. "Thanks for getting me through it and for being here now."

He rubbed her arm gently. "You scared me pretty good, kid."

She sighed. "I scared myself. I don't like feeling out of control. I always let her get to me. She wants to hurt me. I know that and I still put myself under her feet. That's masochistic. It's going to stop."

Steve smiled. "Now you're making sense. Maybe the tree did you a favor. It bumped some sense into that head of yours."

She nodded. "In a way, it did. Mandra taught me not to run scared after my father died. I had forgotten but the accident just reminded me. Mandra would say, 'You've got you, Jeneil. You'll always have you. That's a lot, so you don't need to run scared.' Well, I ran scared and almost lost myself. No more."

Impressed by her strength and spirit, Steve leaned down and kissed her cheek. "Can I get anything for you?"

"Some warm milk?"

"Sure." He squeezed her hand. "But first," he said, plugging in the telephone and dialing. "This is Dr. Bradley; I'd like to talk to Dr. Chang."

Jeneil smiled as he handed her the receiver. "Steve?" Peter answered, concerned. "Is Jeneil okay?"

"She's fine," Jeneil answered.

Peter sighed as he heard Jeneil. "Oh, baby, it's so good to hear your voice. Are you really okay?"

"Well, like Steve said, I hit a tree not a marshmallow. I have to expect some pain." She laughed, and Steve smiled and went to the kitchen.

"How's your head?" Peter asked.

"I guess the accident jostled my brain a bit. I could have sworn you were here. You kissed me and told me you love me. You called me dense. Why would you call me dense? But it didn't sound like you either." She shrugged. "Everything was hazy. It was all a confused dream obviously because you're there."

"Believe me, honey, I wish I was there with you."

"I'm fine, Peter. Sir Steven the Loyal is on duty. He's heating some milk for me. I'm feeling tired again, but the pain is easing up. I'll sleep so Steve can get some rest."

"I'm glad you called or Steve called or whoever called. I haven't been near you through this whole thing. I've been worried about you and tied here. I love you, Jeneil. This is just what I needed."

"Me, too." Jeneil smiled. "I'll let you get back on duty."

"I'll get out of here as fast as I can."

"Good. I miss you."

"Bye, honey."

Jeneil reached for the base of the telephone. Her back tightened and she dropped the receiver. Walking in and seeing her helpless, Steve was filled with tenderness for her. "Lay back, sweetheart. I'll get it. Here's your milk." She stared at him, his voice suddenly sounding familiar to her as the voice from her dream. He noticed her staring. "What's the matter?"

She shook her head. "I can't believe what drugs can do to a person's mind," she said, and sipped her milk.

*****

Steve and Peter were both assigned second shift for Sunday to give them a chance to sleep. Jeneil looked at them as they sat on her bed having breakfast with her. "I think you both should sleep at the dorms today or you won't rest. Adrienne will be with me. She's been so great about stopping in. She was here early this morning. I'm like this with her help." Peter smiled knowing Jeneil meant she was showered and refreshed, but he had never seen what she was wearing before.

"What's this, honey?" he asked, tugging at the sleeve.

"It's a bed-jacket. My great grandmother made them for my mother. That woman seemed to have had more to do with my mother than my grandmother. Isn't that odd? I like the jackets." Peter liked them too since they covered her nightgown. He kissed her cheek, appreciating her desire to be covered. "Please go to the dorms and sleep. I'll probably spend most of the day sleeping, too. You'll rest better there."

Jeneil settled in after they left. She tired easily and sleep felt good, so she slipped under the covers and gave into it. She startled awake when Adrienne called her hours later. She lifted her head, gathering her thoughts and focusing on the moment. Peter's grandfather was standing at the bedroom door.

"Mr. Chang?" she questioned, sitting up groggily.

"I'm sorry, Jeneil. It's a bad time to visit," he said uncomfortably.

Adrienne smoothed Jeneil's hair back. "No, it isn't. I was going to give her some lunch soon."

Jeneil rubbed her temple. "Lunch? I've slept all morning?"

Adrienne smiled. "You did, girl." Jeneil turned to fix her pillows. Her back tightened and she grimaced in pain. "Time for a pain pill, too." Adrienne left the room after helping Jeneil sit up.

Jeneil sighed from the strain. "Please, Mr. Chang, bring that chair closer and sit down."

"You're having a bad time of it," he said, sitting down.

"No, it's time for a pain pill." Her voice indicated the pain she was in. "How did you get here?"

"By bus," he answered quietly.

"Bus? It's cold out there. Why didn't you call Peter?"

He stared at her, realizing she didn't know about Peter's phone call. He smiled, appreciating her concern for him even now and he felt terrible that his family should be causing this gentle, caring girl so much misery. Adrienne came in with water and medication, and Jeneil took it willingly.

"My meatloaf will be ready in a half hour," Adrienne said. "I'll bring you some."

Jeneil hesitated. "Adrienne, would you mind if I had some chicken soup? I have a container in the freezer. The microwave will heat it in seconds. Mr. Chang, will you help me eat it? You must be chilled from taking the bus."

"Jeneil, it'll be ready in seconds. I'll bring two bowls," Adrienne said understandingly, and went to the kitchen knowing Jeneil was worried about the old man's comfort.

The soup tasted good to Jeneil. She was hungrier than she had realized. Peter's grandfather finished his and sat back in his chair. "Thank you, Jeneil. I feel better now."

"I wouldn't mind some tea. Would you be able to find your way around my kitchen?"

"I'll get it with no trouble."

"Thank you, Mr. Chang. With my back today, I'd have tea ready by spring."

"What's wrong with your back?"

"It's just a muscle sprain but it hurts."

He patted her arm. "I'll get tea for us."

Jeneil was enjoying his visit. He was easy to talk to and pleasant, and he had brought pictures from China with him, along with a very peaceful spirit. "Mr. Chang, will you do me another favor and let me send you home in a taxi? I'm enjoying your visit so much. Don't worry about bus schedules."

"Jeneil, that's an extravagance. I don't live a block away."

"Yin and Yang, Mr. Chang. I can't appreciate frugality if I don't understand extravagance."

He laughed. "You grasp Yin and Yang easily."

"It makes real sense to me." She smiled.

The apartment door opened and Peter and Steve walked in. "Hey, baby," Peter called, holding up a white paper bag. "I brought a surprise."

"How are you doing, sweetheart?" Steve asked, following Peter to the bedroom.

"Pretty fair," Jeneil called. The grandfather put his head down, wondering what Peter would say about his visit. Peter and Steve stopped when they saw him, surprising Jeneil with their reaction.

"Grandfather," Peter said quietly.

The grandfather looked at his grandson. "Peter, I was concerned about Jeneil. I needed to visit and reassure myself that she was fine."

Jeneil was puzzled. "Mr. Chang, you don't need to explain visiting us. Peter, he came by bus with the temperature near twenty degrees."

He looked at the old man but couldn't be angry. Going to him, Peter put his hand out. "Grandfather, that's too dangerous. I'll drive you home. Thank you for caring so much about Jeneil."

The old man sighed and grasped Peter's hand in a firm handshake and smiled, relieved Peter would accept him back in their lives. There would be another time to tell him how badly his mother felt about Jeneil's accident. For now, he'd wait.

"What treat did you bring?" Jeneil asked.

Peter held up the bag. "A strawberry frappe."

"Ooo I love those, but I've just had lunch and I'm having tea. It'll keep in the refrigerator. Where did you have lunch?"

"Dave's Creamery."

She laughed. "Who was fish fillet hungry?"

Steve grinned. "I was. Pete had…."

Jeneil interrupted. "A cheeseburger and French fries."

Peter shrugged. "What can I say?" They all laughed.

The grandfather watched as both Peter and Steve sat on the bed comfortably with Jeneil. They were all very close and it could be seen easily. But he didn't sense any undercurrent that he thought would be present if there was any hint of deception among them. He saw the innocence. They all liked each other. They all trusted each other. Theirs was a different relationship, even odd or strange, but it was definitely not immoral. He knew Jeneil and she wasn't capable of cunning deception. He would risk his life on that. He smiled to himself. The three were actually very refreshing to watch. Their trust, their love, made a person relax just being around them. They seemed to understand the relationship and it worked for them.

He marveled at how difficult a relationship of this type would be to achieve just by the very nature of their closeness, but they had achieved a healthy balance and he felt the credit belonged to all three. They understood friendship and love and were keeping both separate. They were strong energies but again his concern was for Jeneil. Of the three, she was the most fragile. She was also the most open and the most innocent. That made her the most vulnerable. As he watched, he knew even the slightest change in that balance would ultimately change the relationship, and he knew the relationship as it existed now couldn't last. It was like a person's childhood; it would pass. That's exactly what these three were involved in at the moment, a relationship as innocent as a childhood. They were a triad, three closely related things. He wondered who would be most affected by the eventual change. In studying them, it was difficult to tell. They were so closely related. Jeneil's voice broke through his thoughts.

"Your grandfather was telling me that Ron and Sue went to the Bahamas."

Peter looked at his grandfather. "The Bahamas? They don't have that kind of money. He hasn't been out of college that long and she just graduated. Is she teaching school yet?"

The grandfather shrugged. "They want the debt now they said, while they'll both be working."

"I guess it's stylish to go to the Bahamas for a honeymoon." Peter shook his head unimpressed.

Jeneil looked at him. "Well, everyone is different."

Peter and Steve looked at each other and nodded. "That's why Crayola makes different color crayons," they both recited the phrase she liked to use so often.

"Go take some vitamin C and stop teasing. I hear that flu is nasty. I don't want it near me. Go." She pointed to the kitchen.

"When was she appointed boss?" Steve asked, both he and Peter looking at each other.

Peter smiled. "We should sell her to the Pentagon. They could slip her over enemy lines in the dark of the night and by morning they'd have a full surrender, just to get away from her," he said, and his grandfather laughed.

"I'm not kidding about the vitamin C with the hours you're both keeping and with it all around you. Vitamin C, now! Before you go to work, four tablets each."

Steve smiled at her. "Hey, Pete, let's take her vitamin C and still catch the flu. Maybe it'll teach her a lesson."

"I love you," she said, grinning. "And take dinner; I put some in the freezer from Thanksgiving. There should be turkey and two or three roast beefs."

"Any brownies?" Peter asked.

"In the freezer, too," she replied. "Why, are you brownie hungry?"

"Yeah, Karen brought two to the hospital the other day that almost gagged us. I've wanted brownies ever since."

The grandfather looked puzzled. "Karen doesn't bake and why has she started bringing you food?"

Steve looked at Peter and grinned. Peter stopped at the door. "I gave her a ride to school. We ended up arguing and she brought them as a peace offering."

The grandfather shook his head. "Anything's possible I guess." Jeneil watched, mentally assessing the information.

Three

By Tuesday, Jeneil was back to work. She was stiff and achy, but functioning. Jerry Tollman came by the office with a small bouquet of pink carnations. Jeneil was completely surprised and the women she worked with smiled at the romantic gesture. Jeneil wished Jerry wouldn't be so brazen. He barely knew her and she couldn't understand this campaign of his.

"Are you pain-free yet?" he asked, sitting on the edge of her desk.

"It's mostly aches now." She could feel herself flush as the other four women grinned as they watched.

"You looked terrific when they brought you in, except for the hysteria of course. That was one classy outfit." She stared at him and felt herself becoming redder as she heard a giggle from the women. Jerry smiled, noticing. "I guess your boyfriend was a wreck when he heard about the accident. I was hoping to meet him. I thought he'd be by to pick you up."

"He's out of town," she lied.

"On business?" Jerry asked, and she nodded. "What does he do that he needs to leave town?"

Jeneil was getting impatient with the interrogation. "He's a hit man for the mafia."

"What?" Jerry laughed.

Jeneil came to her senses. "I'm just kidding. He's a welder. He specializes in bridges and guardrails." She was starting to feel uneasy.

"It's kind of cold for that work now, isn't it?"

"Not down south."

"Boy, he's really far away. Aren't you lonely?"

Jeneil looked at him and shrugged, wondering where he was going with his questions. "He has to work. It's part of life." She nervously folded and unfolded the corner of the green tissue paper of the bouquet.

Jerry smiled. "Do you know Dr. Bradley personally?"

"What?" Jeneil snapped her neck, looking up quickly. "What do you mean?"

"He hovered over you when you were in the ER. I saw him take you home."

Jeneil felt cornered. "I, uh…he, uh…his girlfriend's grandmother is my neighbor. He knew I didn't have a ride home." Her throat was aching.

Jerry nodded. "I just wondered. He seemed so concerned."

Jeneil was nearing panic. "Oh please, don't read anything more into that."

Jerry laughed. "Relax. I'm not his girl's spy."

"Isn't that what you would say if you were?"

He laughed. "That damn girl has everybody in here paranoid, can't get a decent story about the guy anymore. He was real fun before he fell in love. I guess we'll have to be satisfied watching Dr. Chang's love life."

Jeneil's heart stopped and she wondered if Jerry's questioning was because he knew about her and Peter. "Dr. Chang?"

Jerry smiled. "Yeah, we finally saw him with his girl."

"You did?" Jeneil asked cautiously.

"Yeah, she brought him some food a few days ago. He's sure lucky. He and Steve eat pretty good because of her."

Jeneil almost broke into laughter. Her mind screamed with relief. Karen, they saw Karen. She smiled at the thought.

Jerry grinned. "Some guys have all the luck; Chang, Bradley, and your boyfriend. Well, I guess I'd better get back on duty."

Jeneil nodded as Jerry stood up. "I was out yesterday. I need to catch up here, too. Thank you for the flowers. Pink is a cheerful color."

"You're welcome. Stay well now."

"I plan to," she said, and he smiled at her warmly and left.

Mrs. Sousa brought a vase over to Jeneil's desk. "I'd say your boyfriend should worry about him." She chuckled. "You can use this so your flowers won't wilt. How are you holding up?"

"I'm a bit tired, but I'll be fine."

"Dr. Chang's girlfriend should worry, too," Sarah chimed in, joining them at the desk. Jeneil would've asked why but Mrs. Sousa beat her to it. "I heard she brought a friend with her the day she stopped by. Word is the girl was very, very beautiful. I heard she looked like a model, dressed really high style and looking Dr. Chang over very closely, very interested if you know what I mean."

Mrs. Sousa shook her head. "Boy, you don't know who to trust these days, your best friend on the prowl for your guy." She went back to her desk and Sarah went to help an intern who walked in. Jeneil went to get some water at the cooler in the hallway. She caught a glimpse of Peter as he got on the elevator and she thought about what she had just heard.

*****

Peter stepped off the elevator on the fifth floor and caught sight of Uette Wong sitting on the corridor bench. She smiled and waved to him, and he walked over to her.

"Hi." She smiled.

"Hi," Peter answered.

"I stopped in to donate blood. I felt a little woozy so I decided I'd say hello if you were around while I waited to feel stronger before I drive home."

Peter nodded, studying her face. "Is someone you know having surgery?"

"No, why?" she asked, puzzled by the question.

"You donated blood. Usually people donate if someone they know needs it for surgery."

She shrugged and turned her head at a studied angle. She smiled, making the most of her perfect teeth. "No, I donated mine to the general public. Anyone is welcomed to it."

Peter watched her. "Do you give blood regularly?"

"I don't have a steady income from it if that's what you mean," she said, sensing his suspicion.

He smiled. "How are you feeling now, still woozy?" She raised her eyebrows and then wrinkled her nose.

"Just a bit lightheaded, I'm improving. I don't suppose you have time for a cup of coffee?"

"I'm due to make rounds."

She made a disappointed but cute face. "I didn't think so. Karen told me you're very serious about your work. Someday you'll have to tell me why you decided to become a doctor."

He stared at her. "Well, right now I have to make rounds. Be sure you're stable before you drive...," he faltered. "I'm sorry; I've forgotten your first name. I know your last name is Wong."

"Uette." She smiled.

"Sorry Uette."

She waved her hand indicating it wasn't anything major. "It's all right, Peter. You have other things to concern yourself with that are more important than my name. I'm not insulted."

He nodded. "Good, and be careful driving home."

"I will." She flashed her teeth again as he turned and walked to the nurse's desk. She went to the elevators and grinned as she waited. "You'll remember my name, Dr. Chang. I'm not insulted or worried, I just need to erase that ten you're in love with and make her a zero. And I obviously have to erase your memory of my family's attitude toward you. You remembered Wong easily enough. But it's a beginning." She got on the elevator as the doors opened. Turning, she saw Peter watching her. She smiled and waved. He stared unsmiling and unwaving as the doors closed. "That's okay, Dr. Chang. I love a good challenge." She smiled. "I would love to know what that ten of yours looks like. I need to find out just what your type is. Karen isn't objective about her that's for sure."

Peter watched the doors close then dialed the blood clinic. "Can you tell me if a girl named Wong donated blood today?" He waited. "That's the one. Okay. Thanks." He hung up and headed off to start rounds. "Well, well, well, why is my Dragon blood beginning to signal me?"

*****

The elevator doors opened and Jeneil walked off carrying manila envelopes as she headed toward the desk. Barbara Stanton shook her head. "I feel sorry for his girlfriend. That shark is out for blood."

"You know it," the other nurse agreed.

"Who?" Jeneil asked, overhearing the remark, curious about somebody who would be called a shark.

"Dr. Chang's girlfriend," Barbara answered.

"She's a shark?" she asked, wondering if they meant Karen.

"No, her friend is. She just happened to stop in here a few minutes ago and spent some time flashing enticing smiles at Dr. Chang."

"I heard she was very beautiful," Jeneil said quietly.

The nurses laughed. "She's a knockout."

"And she knows it," Barbara sneered.

Jeneil leafed through the envelopes and sighed. "Well, what matters is if Dr. Chang notices it."

Barbara laughed. "Jeneil, you should see this barracuda in action. No man stands a chance. She looks like she gets what she wants. His poor girlfriend, I'll be really mad if he dumps her for that girl. After all that food; she even knitted a sweater for him and Dr. Bradley for Christmas." She shook her head. "It never seems to fail; that nice homebody type gets left behind when something like this shark swims around. Ooo, I hate her type."

"What's her type?" Jeneil asked.

Barbara thought for a moment and another nurse answered. "She's an actress, must be a whole other person behind that perfect smile."

"Yes," Barbara agreed, "that's it. You can't believe she's real, a sweet innocent smile that hides somebody else behind it." Jeneil left the envelopes and went back to the elevator, once again assessing the new information.

*****

The door to the records department opened and Mrs. Sousa went to the counter. "I seem to be lost," the girl said. "Where is X-ray from here?"

Mrs. Sousa thought for a minute. "Wait, I'll get my directory so I won't get you even more lost. That's not an area familiar to me."

Jeneil glanced up and noticed the girl was staring at her. Jeneil also noticed she was Chinese and very beautiful. A chill went through her. She looked back at her work. Something deep inside of her knew this was Karen's friend, the one the nurses called the shark. Jeneil made one correction to their description; the girl wasn't just beautiful, she was incredibly beautiful. Jeneil could tell the girl was still staring at her while Mrs. Sousa gave directions. The girl politely thanked her but stayed at the counter.

"Excuse me, Jeneil," the girl called. Jeneil looked up, surprised to hear her name. The girl smiled. "You are Jeneil? That's what your nameplate says." Jeneil nodded, wondering what was happening. "Are you related to Vicki Muldare?"

"No, I'm not. Why?" Jeneil sensed there was more than what was being asked.

The girl shook her head. "It's incredible; you look enough like her to be her sister."

"Do I?" Jeneil smiled her facade smile. "I don't have any relatives named Muldare."

The girl shrugged. "Well, I guess what I've heard about there being a double for all of us might be true, my mistake." She laughed and looked at Mrs. Sousa. "Thanks for your help." Mrs. Sousa smiled and nodded as the girl left.

Sarah looked up from her desk. "Why didn't she use the directory in the corridor?"

Jeneil reached for a leaf that had fallen from the bouquet Jerry had given her. Why didn't she indeed Jeneil asked herself.

Uette walked quickly to the elevator and got on when the doors opened. The car stopped at the next floor. She watched fascinated as Steve got on with two older doctors and listened to their conversation carefully, noting Steve's comments. The doors opened and everyone got off. Uette went to the exit and pulled up her collar against the cold wind. The whole situation was very curious. How could that mousey girl possibly have Peter Chang crawling on his knees? Goodness, Karen was right, no polish on her nails or herself, and no personality. She didn't even seem bright. Peter's mother must be right, he wanted to get married and this girl would have him. It must be. There couldn't possibly be a real attraction. She even had a tasteless bouquet of pink carnations on her desk. Good grief. This was going to be easier than she had thought. Move over Miss Mouse, the Chinese were there to reclaim their own. Dr. Chang was theirs; Jeneil could have Steve. Uette laughed to herself. Karen must have added wrong for sure. It was too farfetched that Steve would look twice at her. No way did Jeneil have him. Karen had been right about one thing though, she wasn't far past zero.

*****

Jeneil put a cassette into the stereo and paced as she listened to soothing classical music. Everything she had heard at the hospital was filtering through her brain. She wished she could go to the ocean and face the wind. She needed to examine her feelings about what happened at the wedding, the accident, Karen's behavior change, and the new very beautiful and very brazen Chinese girl. Jeneil sighed; she wasn't feeling up to driving to the beach. She was tired and her back was still tight from the accident, so she removed her hairpins and let her hair fall freely. The apartment door opened and Peter walked in. Looking at him, she thought how handsome he was and how sexy he looked. Then, she thought of the beautiful Chinese girl.

"Hi, honey," he said, smiling at her. He went to her and touched her face gently. "You look tired, baby."

Jeneil grinned. "Peter, when a woman looks tired that's when a man should lie and tell her she's beautiful." She slipped her arms around his waist. "Hold me."

"Let me put my mail down," he said, putting the envelopes on a chair and then held her.

"No, really hold me," she said, "like you can't do without me."

He looked at her and grinned. "I have to do without you remember; you're recovering from an accident. I might hurt your back."

She chuckled. "I need compassion, you give me comedy. Some days you make a lousy teddy bear, Chang."

He kissed her cheek. "What's the matter, honey? Where's Irish? Nebraska's really low."

She swayed gently in his arms. "You can't appreciate high if you've never been low; opposites, Yin and Yang."

He smiled. "I love you, you crazy kid."

"A lot?" she asked, staring at him.

"Oh please, baby! Change for bed. I'll make us some Ovaltine. You need to rest. You've got a whine in your voice." He let her go and removed his jacket, hanging it up, and then headed to the kitchen.

She sighed. She was great competition for the girl; a whiny, crazy kid with a backache who could only share warm flavored milk with him in bed. She shook her head and sighed then reached to straighten out his mail. She noticed her name on the top envelope; *Jeneil-Alden Connors c/o Dr. Peter Chang.* It was addressed to Peter's P.O. Box. She picked it up. There was no return address.

"Peter, why did my mail go to your P.O. Box?"

He rushed out of the kitchen. "Put it down!" he snapped, shocking her.

"But it's addressed to me."

"It's from my mother. It's her handwriting. Put it down. I'll throw it out with the other junk mail." His anger surprised her.

"Why did she write? Why didn't she call? She usually calls." He took the envelope from her, surprising her even more. "What am I missing? What aren't you telling me? I don't want to throw it away."

"Jeneil, no, I don't care what she has to say. Damn it, I told her to leave me alone and stay away from you, and three days later you get this."

"You told her that?" Jeneil was shocked then the pieces began to fit. "Your grandfather was uncomfortable when you came in Sunday. You told him that, too."

"I told them all to stay away from us."

Jeneil was having trouble remaining calm. "Give me that envelope."

"It's just more of her shit, Jeneil."

Jeneil held out her hand angrily. "Peter Chang, give me that envelope now! I have a rule; I open whatever somebody sends me. One day I found my mother crying. When I asked her why, she hugged me and told me to open any letter I ever received. It didn't make any sense but she was hurt about something, deeply hurt. She said, 'you can't settle anything if you don't face it.' Give me that letter, Peter. Even if it's an angry letter, she'll reveal something about why in her words. I want to read it."

He held it a moment longer and then sighing handed it to her. "I'll check on the milk." He went back to the kitchen while Jeneil opened the letter. It was short. She sat down on the sofa and covered her mouth. Peter returned quietly. Seeing her reaction, he took the letter from her. "I told you not to read it."

Jeneil stood up. "You told her I could have been killed and it was her fault! I can't believe it! You did that?"

Peter read the letter. It was different in tone from anything he had ever heard from his mother before. He read the ending out loud. "*I thought I was doing the right thing, but nothing is ever right if somebody is badly hurt. It upsets me to know that I was the cause of your accident. I don't know how I would face myself if you had been killed. Peter was right. It would have been my fault. As it is, the loss has been very great. It cost me my son. I won't recover from that loss either. I'm sure it's too late, but to live with myself, I need to say I'm sorry, Lien Lee.*"

Peter was impressed the apology sounded so sincere. He couldn't believe it was from his mother and it completely surprised him that she would care about losing him. He had always felt that she didn't care about him but since he was part of her, she expected him to meet her standards in order to protect her pride and image. He looked at Jeneil, who was watching him in silent anger. "I wanted to hit her as hard as she hit you. You were lying here sedated. I was upset."

Jeneil covered her eyes, feeling the strain of everything at that moment. She sighed heavily. "I don't understand your relationship with your mother. I find myself in the middle all the time, one of you accusing me unfairly and the other defending me unfairly. I'm worn out, Peter. It's overkill. The whole situation has shaken my deep belief in talking peace, in caring, in never giving up. I feel like I'm in a maze and there's no way through to the end. It's all a sick joke and there's no end to it. It's not funny, Peter, it's not funny at all; the shouting, the hurt toward me, toward her, toward you, toward your grandfather. The list goes on and on." She cried softly. "Life has to have values in order to have quality. Peace is a quality I need in my life. I thought it was achieved through caring and loving, trying to understand people, wanting to understand people. And yet, those values don't work in this. They don't even make a dent and I'm tired of the battle." She paced then turned to him. "I can see one thing clearly anyway, I need to correct an injustice just as clearly as your mother needed to write that note. I need to do this." She walked to the bedroom, picked up her telephone and dialed.

Karen answered, shocked at hearing Jeneil's voice. "Jeneil, are you feeling any better?" she asked, just for something to say.

"Much better, thank you, Karen. Is Mrs. Lee there?"

"She's right here. Hold on." Jeneil was surprised at the warmth in Karen's voice.

Jeneil could tell Peter's mother was on the line. She held her stomach as the old fear began to surface, the silence making her feel insecure. "Mrs. Lee, I received your letter today. Thank you for writing it, but I need to make something clear. I don't blame you for my accident. I don't want you accepting the guilt. Yes, you upset me and hurt me deeply, but I drove the car knowing I wasn't in control. I did that, not you. My being hurt physically is my fault, so if that's why you wanted to say you're sorry then you don't need to. It feels very good that you wanted to though." There was silence then Jeneil could hear quiet crying. "That's all I called to say, Mrs. Lee. I'll let you go."

The woman cleared her throat. "Jeneil, my father told me that he visited you and that Peter accepted him. Is it possible…," she began to cry again but Jeneil understood.

Jeneil turned to Peter and pointed to the phone. He shook his head. Jeneil put her hand to her throat nervously. "Mrs. Lee, anything is possible even if it isn't at this moment. I want you to know that I'd like it to happen." Jeneil heard more crying and she sighed. "I'm sorry, Mrs. Lee. I didn't call to upset you. Maybe I should have written too, but my style is person to person. I'll let you go now, goodbye."

As Jeneil hung up, she thought of something Mandra had said to her often; Jeneil, when you're right and you act on it everything in you tells you you've done the right thing. Every cell in you shouts it. Jeneil understood what Mandra had meant. Her father called it the capsule of truth, the nucleolus. It wasn't easy to see without effort, but the high was worth it. She smiled; they had known what they were talking about.

Peter came up behind her and kissed her shoulder. "You have a braver heart than I have. You have more love, too. I really admire you, Jeneil."

Jeneil turned and faced him. At that moment the compliment meant more to her than him telling her she was beautiful. She put her arms around him. "I needed to say that to your mother. You do what you need to once you discover what that is."

"I know," he whispered, holding her to him. "Thank you for understanding."

Four

Jeneil continued to improve but she was concerned about Karen and the Chinese girl. The fact that the girl was brazen enough to come to her office unsettled Jeneil. It reminded her of the way Amy Farber had operated, but at the moment there was nothing to be done about it. Life continued making its demands and Jeneil was scheduled to fly to Nebraska; she wished she wasn't. Peter was working a double Thursday and she was leaving Friday before he got home from work. She reviewed the whole situation while she packed Friday morning. She could feel herself becoming insecure. The beautiful Chinese girl had done that to her. Everything in her told her there was an undercurrent and she felt insecure because relationships weren't easy for her to grasp. But the Chinese girl looked like she understood them. Jeneil had thought about discussing it with Peter, but there was never time with his tight schedule and when there was, the subject seemed ridiculous so she had concentrated on her business in Nebraska.

Jeneil called the apartment several times Saturday but Peter was never there. It added to her insecurity, and she was becoming tense and it was noticeable. Uncle Hollis asked if everything was all right with her and Peter and it annoyed her that he'd assume it wasn't. She brought herself into line and vowed to face the wind as soon as she got the chance.

*****

Peter headed to Ron and Sue's apartment Sunday wondering why he had been invited for lunch. Ron hadn't invited Jeneil and had told him that Sue would be at a bridal shower all afternoon so it would be just the two of them. Peter parked in the visitor's area and smiled. He hadn't recognized the address but he recognized the building. It was one of two large apartment buildings Jeneil owned, and he wondered if she knew she was Ron and Sue's landlady. He had been there once with Jeneil to check the new carpet that had been installed in the lobby and the remodeled laundry room. He remembered being impressed. He knew Jeneil was in business, but until her different businesses surfaced from time to time he never thought about it. Business was how she earned money, but it wasn't her life. He pushed the security buzzer. Ron answered and Peter took the elevator to his floor. The building was different from before, it looked nicer, more cheerful. Ron was waiting in the hallway.

"This seems like a nice building." Peter smiled, taking off his jacket, looking around the apartment.

"It is," Ron answered. "I hope it's everything we've found it to be so far. The owners seem to care."

"Who are the owners?"

"I don't know names. It's one of those deals where it's a corporation, not an individual."

Peter grinned, that sounded familiar. "Who do you pay rent to?" he asked, wondering why Alden-Connors Corporation hadn't surfaced. Ron would recognize that.

"J.A.C. Management Associates," Ron answered, and Peter wanted to laugh. J.A.C. was Jeneil Alden-Connors, he thought, connecting the dots. Ron pulled out a chair from the table. "I'm impressed so far. Usually when the owner gets lost in a corporation it means you have trouble finding people to deal with anything, but so far this group is okay. We even found a small fruit basket and a note welcoming us to the building. Other tenants we talked to said there's been a big change since the new owners took over. It's becoming an 'in' building to live in because of the extras and great treatment." Ron went to the refrigerator and brought out two deli sandwiches. "Sit down, Pete. I picked up lunch. Sue isn't into the routine of married life yet. The cupboard is bare. She's still not back from the Bahamas mentally."

"Did you enjoy the island?" Peter asked, and then felt stupid reminding himself nobody who had just gotten married would want to look at an island.

Ron shrugged. "It's an island, expensive sand and surf."

They ate, not really talking about anything and Peter wondered why he was even there. They had never been close and he couldn't figure out the new interest Ron was showing in him. Ron poured more coffee and sat down again, rolling his paper napkin nervously.

"Ron, why am I here?"

Ron smiled. "I've always liked that about you, Pete. You go straight from point A to point B. It's also what gets you in trouble."

"What do you mean?" Peter asked, adding sugar to his coffee.

"You never developed political savvy and you were always in trouble because of it."

"Political savvy?"

"Yes, the art of fitting in."

Peter laughed. "That's sure true."

"You also don't get mad when I preach to you anymore. I'd be roughed up by now if we were younger."

Peter shrugged. "What can I say? I didn't want to be you so why copy what you said."

Ron laughed. "I always liked that about you, too. I'm Peter Chang. You don't like it, don't look."

Peter shook his head. "If you liked it, why the hell were you always preaching?"

Ron smiled. "At first, it was because my mother and your mother asked me to. When I got older, it was to try to help you avoid trouble."

"I never knew that." Peter chuckled, surprised. "And boy, you sure knew how to avoid trouble. You were never in it. Didn't it drive you crazy being so good?"

Ron stared at him. "Pete, you're here today because I'm trying to keep you out of trouble."

"What trouble?" Peter asked, puzzled. Ron rolled his napkin again.

"I invited you and Jeneil to the wedding because Sue insisted. I didn't agree."

Peter stiffened. "Ron, if you're going to put Jeneil down, I can't promise I won't rough you up."

"I'm not going to put her down. She's a very nice girl. She has great taste in clothes and she seems like more than a clerk in the records department of a hospital. I heard she looked like a million dollars at the wedding. Some of my office friends wanted to know who she was. She turns heads when she wants to, but Pete, she's white."

Peter stared, not believing his ears. "Oh shit, Ron, I didn't expect that from you."

Ron put his head back and sighed. "Pete, I'm going to put my life in your hands. I really want to help you. I'm not a bigot." He paused. "When I was in college, I was crazy over a white girl. It was heavy. I think I made it through college because of her." Peter was shocked and Ron smiled. "I'm telling you, my life's in your hands now. She kept me sane. The pressure, the tension, we were good for each other; physically, too."

"Why did you give her up?" Peter asked, shocked by the confession.

"In our junior year, she got pregnant. When we began asking ourselves what to do, we decided that what we had wasn't going to stand up to marriage. Neither of us wanted to get married at that time. I paid for half of the abortion fee."

Peter drank some coffee, trying not to choke on the news. Was this guy really his cousin who had never been in trouble? The family's Mr. Perfect?

"After that, the relationship cooled. It wasn't the abortion, we had just never looked at our relationship closely before. We broke it off and shortly after that I met Sue. I finished college and now I'm working and married."

"How come I never heard the family talk about this?" Peter asked. "Damn it, they're always talking about my life."

Ron looked at him. "Pete, no one knew. No one knows. They thought I was a serious student who didn't have time for relationships. I didn't live with that girl." He shrugged. "That's what I mean about political savvy and the art of fitting in. I had my own personal life and the family was happy because I provided them with the image they wanted."

Peter had trouble grasping what Ron was saying. "Are you comparing that girl and you to me and Jeneil? Ron, Jeneil and I are going to be married. We both want that."

"Pete, ask yourself if she can keep up with your life once you're a doctor. She's a records clerk. You're going to have social demands. She has a social sense though and I hear she's into cultural things, the Arts League, The Rep, but Pete, her education level is not equivalent to yours." Peter covered his eyes with his hands, struggling to believe someone who knew him and Jeneil could say that. Ron sat forward. "Pete, don't turn off. It might not mean anything now, but it will when you're trying to fit into your career."

Ron fidgeted. "Pete, the world doesn't trust races that mix. They don't trust races. I've found that I have to be very careful in my career. I'm a damn good corporate tax accountant, one of the best, and another guy got assigned to a big account instead of me. He's not really as good as I am, but he's white. I notice the accounts I get; shirt sleeve, blue collar businesses. The Chinese are in business too, so I staff for that; factories, laundries, and restaurants. Oh, it's not just Chinese I handle, but I never get the brown blood corporate office crowd either. We grew up with it in school and it's still out there, believe me. And I'm talking fitting in. You have to constantly prove yourself."

Ron laughed sadly. "I'm not sure what the hell they want me to prove. That I'm not a communist? But you know what drives me the craziest? If I went to China, I could name my price, all I'd need is to master international corporate tax and business law." Ron hit the tabletop with his hand. "But I don't speak the damn language. I'm an American. I don't know anything about China or Chinese ways. I don't even know how to use chopsticks. So I fit in here, and Pete, you fit in by not being different. They trust you if you know you're Chinese. You prove you know that by marrying Chinese, by having Chinese children. You can't marry white or black or pink or plaid. You marry Chinese. I'm not a bigot. Pete, I think you know that now."

Peter nodded. "Yeah, I've seen the fine line we're expected to walk because we're different." He had to admit it was walking that fine line that was making him crazy. And it was Jeneil who was getting him through his residency. He knew what Ron meant.

"Pete, you're asking for trouble when you confuse race in a career."

Peter sighed. "Ron, you're married so you know what Sue means to you. That's what Jeneil means to me. You fell in love with Chinese, I didn't. I can't ignore that anymore than you could give up Sue."

Ron studied his cousin. "Pete, we've been honest here. Right now I feel like your brother, so please let's keep what's said here between us, okay?" Peter nodded and Ron sighed. "I think the world of Sue. She's a terrific girl, but she's not Lori."

"The white girl?"

Ron nodded. "You know, Pete, I even understood you and Lin Chi. Sue and I didn't begin a sexual relationship until six months ago. After Lori, life was the pits even while I dated Sue. Then I ran into Denise. She was my Lin Chi. Maybe not a professional, but man she was something. Lori became a fond memory after her."

Peter wondered and wanted to know. "Was Denise Chinese?"

"She sure was."

Peter was confused. He felt Sue didn't measure up to Denise either. He risked it. "Ron, why didn't you marry Denise?"

Ron smiled. "Pete, life is so simple to you, but life isn't really simple. Denise makes me come alive and I have to concentrate to not toss everything aside for her, but she'd never make it in my world. I even love her bawdy taste. I can't believe it myself that this girl can chew a piece of bubble gum, blow bubbles constantly, and it makes me want to throw her down on a busy highway in front of the world and take her. She gets to me. I know it's crazy." He sighed. "But my life won't fit her in it. Her grammar alone is outrageous and she doesn't care. One day I mentioned it to her and she said, 'so what, you understand me, don't you.'" Ron leaned back and shook his head. "Man, I could just imagine her at the company Christmas party. Her outfits alone would shake up the senior partners. The damn girl has given me some of the best daydreams I've ever had."

"So you broke it off with Denise for Sue?"

Ron looked at Peter. "I can't. I know she'll get married someday and I'll have to give her up, but I'll take every last second I can with her, and boy I know I'll envy that guy." Ron put his head down. "Are you in shock yet, Pete? You're awfully quiet."

Peter laughed. "No, I'm just wondering how the hell I was called the Chinese Stud with you around."

Ron laughed. "Pete, you're okay. You really are. And this has been good. I've never kicked my shoes off and talked like this. I've never trusted anyone enough. Can you just imagine what the family would say if they found out."

"Oh shit, Ron, don't tell them. They'll blame me. It's bad enough I'm carrying the blame for Rick and his clothes."

Ron laughed harder. "Poor Pete, you were always in trouble and just for being honest. Sue and I felt bad about Thanksgiving. Jeneil didn't deserve that. She's not what I expected. None of the pieces I hear about her fit."

"Ron, you don't know her," Peter said seriously. "You talk about education level. She makes me look sick. She knows more than I'll ever learn about certain things."

Ron was puzzled. "She's a clerk."

"By choice, she likes the job and the people. She's not into image. She wants to find herself so it's a nice place to hide. She's a lit major and any other damn thing she decides to be."

Ron was puzzled. "She's been to college?"

Peter nodded. "She dropped out after her junior year to find her missing pieces. She's a crazy kid with a very odd way of looking at life."

Ron smiled. "She sure doesn't look like Denise, but she sounds like her."

Peter grinned. "I guess you could say she has political savvy."

Ron laughed. "Yeah, practiced to a fine art."

"Ron, she's all those girls in one for me. I think it shits that men can't have women all in one combination. Why are they so rare?"

Ron rolled his paper napkin again. "No, Jeneil's not all of them, Pete. She's not Chinese."

Peter leaned on one elbow and grinned. "Tell me I should care having gotten so damn close."

"You're gonna go for it, aren't you? You don't give a damn. Son of a bitch, you'll never change." He threw the napkin at Peter and laughed good-naturedly.

Peter put the napkin on his empty plate along with his own. "I know my career will make demands, but it can't demand Jeneil."

Ron shook his head in awe. "Hey, I'm Peter Chang."

Peter smiled. "Don't like it, don't look."

Later, Peter drove to work trying to absorb everything he had learned. He thought of all the trouble he had with the family; Peter is a delinquent, Peter has a problem, Peter is disgusting. He sighed and thought of Jeneil in the foyer of the church. His mother had insulted her for having loose morals. Peter's throat tightened as he realized she was no different than the bride in the white gown receiving all the praise, except Jeneil was being more honest and receiving all the insults, and all because of him, because she loved him. In that moment, she became more special to him. Give her up? Ron wouldn't either if he had gotten so close to this combination.

*****

Jeneil's plane landed after what seemed months in the air. She put her luggage in the car and drove away, anxious to get home. She hadn't been able to get a hold of Peter all weekend and all the problems cropping up in her life settled on her as she got to the apartment. She unpacked quickly then ate dinner alone at the dining table by candlelight as she listened to music. It all reminded her of Peter. Their whole week had been turned upside down by her accident and a flu outbreak at work. She missed him. Looking at her watch, she decided she needed to face the wind. All her insecurities were returning as she thought about the Chinese girl. Jeneil rinsed the dishes thinking she'd rather ignore the girl than rationalize her, but everything told her the girl shouldn't be ignored. Except hopefully by Peter, she thought, smiling at the idea. Jeneil wrapped herself in warm layers of clothes, put on her toggle coat, and left the apartment.

Parking in the public lot, Jeneil got out of her car. The sky was speckled with twinkling stars and with the exception of a few small cumulus clouds, the sky was clear, the moon at half phase. The beach wasn't its usual brilliance of grey light dusting over the sand and reflecting off the water, but there was light. She strolled along the beach getting used to its feel. It was time to put her thoughts together and see what they spelled.

The wind wasn't as biting as she expected it to be and she took her hair down and danced. She began to feel free as she renewed her friendship with the earth and wind. The full moon was missing and she reminded herself that it wasn't missing, just in shadow. Breathing deeply, she closed her eyes and felt the exhilaration of being in that spot at that precise moment in time. The feeling made her realize she couldn't do anything about the irritations in her life until she put herself in touch with everything that was real and concrete. The phase dimensions of reality filled her. The irritations were a reality; the elements were also a reality. She smiled and was filled with a sense of purity, oneness with her surroundings. It had a cleansing effect on her and she knew who she was. She was Jeneil. She was a being of life. The memory of those words at sunset when she was cosmic filled her with electricity, warmth radiating through her.

Jeneil thought of the Chinese girl. How had the girl come into her life; through Karen, but why? The bits and pieces she had been storing slipped into place like a puzzle. Karen and Peter's mother had been very close lately. Of all the family those two had made their disapproval clear. Karen bridged a bond to Peter bringing the beautiful Chinese girl with her. His mother had said all she wanted was for Peter to meet a nice girl. Jeneil shivered as the thought went through her, but it was real and she knew it. His mother and Karen were providing Peter with the opportunity to meet a nice Chinese girl. Two facts struck Jeneil forcefully; the girl was interested and they had achieved this out of Jeneil's realm of control at the hospital. Jeneil's mind riveted on the two very strong positive facts and she compared her own energy to it. Her relationship with Peter at the hospital was weak; they were a secret, a negative energy flow. Their relationship at home was also weakened by the energy-draining battle with his mother; it was also negative. Jeneil shuddered to her very core and it frightened her, recognizing it as a negative flow of energy.

Jeneil moved from the spot where she was standing and breathed deeply. She forced herself to concentrate on who she was; a being of life. There were positives in her relationship with Peter; one in particular was their love. Snatched bits of sacred writings came to her mind; *Love was the propellant of positive energy, the force by which everything worked. All of life as we know it flowed from the positive love force.* It made sense and warmth radiated through her again. She was left with one clear thought; the force of love must be at a level so strong that it was unmistakably positive, pure love. Where was it? How was it achieved? What was it? How did she know it? Her mind was becoming clouded so she turned her head and let the wind brush her hair. She closed her eyes and tilted her head to one side, feeling the wind roll across her face. She opened her eyes quickly, startled by the sound it made as it blew past her ear. It almost sounded like a word. Jeneil smiled and held up her hands, enjoying the feeling of the wind against them. She knew the word—soul.

Jeneil walked the beach and looked up at the house. It had been months since she had been there. She remembered the night she and Peter had met on the beach, and remembered he had liked the house. Turning, she ran the length of the beach to her car. Checking her watch, she estimated that she'd get home just as Peter would. A thrill passed through her. She wanted to see him, to be with him. She turned the key and headed to the highway. Thoughts of Yin and Yang ran through her mind. All things had opposites. Life was a matter of balance. Was balance achieved by control? How much control did they have over their lives? There were answers to those questions, but where were they? The wind had left her exhilarated and the drive seemed too long.

Peter had tried several times to call Jeneil during his shift. He called Adrienne and was relieved to hear she had seen Jeneil come in. It satisfied him to know she had landed safely. He drove home thinking about her and missing her like crazy. He had special feelings for her ever since lunch with Ron. He wanted to hold her just to feel her in his arms. He smiled, thinking how terrific she was. The apartment lights were on but her car was gone. "Where is she? Am I the only one anxious for this reunion?" he asked, disappointed as he sat in his car. The wind tore at his jacket as he hurried to the front door, the warmth of the hallway feeling good against his face. He went to the kitchen to prepare Ovaltine. He got as far as putting milk in a saucepan when the door opened. He put everything down and went to see her. He stopped. She took his breath away. Her hair was down and windblown, her cheeks flushed and her face had a beautiful glow. That look always stopped him cold and played havoc with his ribs.

"Hi, Chang." She smiled, undoing her scarf slowly.

"Irish, where have you been?" he asked softly.

"Facing the wind," she answered, slipping off her coat. He took it from her and felt her warmth just being near her. Her eyes were on fire.

"You're cosmic," he said, and she smiled. "How's your back?"

"Completely recovered."

Peter smiled and slipped his arms around Jeneil's waist. He felt her relax against him. The warmth of her skin was incredible, her face feeling warm and soft against his cheek. He wanted to kiss her but knew that would ignite the spark so he held back. She clung to him and she felt so good.

"Why were you facing the wind?"

"To renew old friendships."

"Looks like it worked. You look incredibly beautiful."

"The beach brought back old memories." She kissed his neck softly and he felt her breath near his ear. He swallowed hard as she moved her lips to his. He got lost in the electricity. Every part of him, every fiber, knew she was right there. He kissed her passionately then held her to give himself a chance to breathe. He smoothed kisses across her cheek, not wanting to stop. "Chang, I love you so much," she said, and kissed him passionately.

He pulled away and took a deep breath. "I've got to slow down. I want this done right."

She smiled. "I'll change for bed."

He kissed her gently then released her. "Welcome home."

She smiled that gentle smile of hers. "I missed you."

He touched her cheek. "I missed you too, baby."

Afterwards, Jeneil was glad they hadn't rushed. She nestled into his arms, completely happy. Peter looked at her. She was radiant. "Jeneil, you're so beautiful."

She smiled and snuggled closer. "Hold me close all night."

Peter thought about his lunch with Ron. He didn't know why he'd been so lucky to find Jeneil, but he was glad she was his. She was everything in his life that was good and exciting. Ron's life surprised Peter, not morally, but finding out he was human was unexpected. It shocked him. He couldn't imagine himself marrying somebody he wasn't crazy about. "Jeneil," he said, not having a complete thought ready.

"What?"

"I'm glad you're in my life, really glad. It's more than just I love you."

She kissed his cheek. "I'm glad I'm in your life, too."

Five

Peter got to the hospital early. He wished his reunion with Jeneil had been on a first shift week. He felt especially close to her and it was the kind of reunion he'd like to keep repeating. Second shift was a killer schedule and they rarely saw each other. A new disadvantage was Steve was exclusively on first shift until he completed his residency which was a few weeks away. Peter began to realize the effect that would have on their friendship and the triad. Steve would begin his own life in a world that wouldn't involve the triad as much. As Peter walked toward the East Wing, he knew he would miss Steve.

"Paging Dr. Peter Chang." Peter heard the voice behind him and turned. "Hi." Uette Wong beamed her beautiful smile as she ran to catch up.

"Another blood donation?" he asked, continuing to walk.

"No, I'm visiting a friend who's here, a bad case of the flu. She's doing much better."

Peter put the printout he had been looking at in his lab coat pocket. "We're running in all directions trying to keep up. Most of our cases are bronchial problems and Pediatrics is filled with asthma sufferers."

"I hope you're being careful," Uette said seriously. "You're around nasty germs all day."

Jeneil got off the elevator and turned toward the nurse's station, stopping in her tracks as she saw Peter and the beautiful Chinese girl walking together. The girl smiled at him and Jeneil's heart stopped beating. It was an Amy Farber smile. She had seen it dozens of times in Loma. Peter and the girl stopped at the cross corridor.

Uette opened her purse and held out an apple. "Here." She smiled, handing it to Peter. "An apple a day keeps the flu germ away."

"Thanks," Peter said, studying her for a second before taking the apple.

She nodded and grinned. "It's supposed to be an apple a day keeps the doctor away, but I don't want to keep you away, just the flu." She touched his hand gently. "Bye, it's nice seeing you, even in passing." She made sure her smile was beautiful as she squeezed his hand, and then she turned and walked down the corridor to the exit.

Jeneil watched and a feeling of panic passed through her. At that moment she sensed real danger. She choked back tears as surprise and disappointment replaced the panic. Peter watched the girl walk away for a few seconds before he continued toward the East Wing. Jeneil leaned against a counter as she leafed through the memo envelopes.

Barbara Stanton came up to her. "Well, did you see the vulture? She's past using just her fangs; she's touchy freely now. I hope she picked up something while she was here."

Jeneil looked at her. "Why does she get to you?"

"I don't know." Barbara shrugged then she sighed. "Yes, I do. I was aced out by one like her once. It hurt."

Jeneil swallowed. "Did you get back together?"

"No, but this far in life and a marriage to another guy, I'm glad it happened before I married the gutless wonder instead of after. I could be divorced with kids right now."

"You're a positive thinker," Jeneil commented softly.

Barbara smiled. "That's the only thing about her type, you get to have your guy's love tested. Win or lose it's better to find out before marriage."

"I guess," Jeneil sighed, and continued on her delivery route feeling very discouraged.

Arriving home after work, Jeneil realized Barbara was right but it didn't make the test easier to endure. Sorting through her mail, she saw a small package from Robert Danzieg, who was working in New York for two weeks. Curious, she opened it. It was a Rossini tape. Jeneil smiled. He was really something to be thinking of her even while he was in one of the busiest cities in the world. Going to the stereo, she inserted the tape and read the note. *Sweetheart, wish you were here. It's a fun city. Promise to visit it with me sometime. Enjoy Rossini and think of me. Love, R.D.* Jeneil smiled again. The gift cheered her up and made her feel better. She felt like a nothing whenever she saw the Chinese girl. She put her head back and sighed. The girl was so beautiful, and she and Peter made a stunning couple. Looking at Robert's note, she folded it.

"Thank you for calling me sweetheart, Robert. It makes me feel feminine. Next to the Chinese girl that's tough for most women. What's your name? And what has your beauty done for you? Is it only skin deep?" She sighed. "Jeneil, don't let the negative energy destroy you. Meet the challenge. You have a great advantage. He has to deal with Robert and his notes and gifts." She shrugged. "But he's a friend, a very good friend. That girl is interested in Peter. It's obvious she's attracted to him. And why not, he's gorgeous." She missed him. "Why does this have to happen on a second shift week? Wait for him, Jeneil, until the final choice is made." She groaned. "And when will that be?"

Her telephone rang and she answered quickly, thinking it might be Peter. "Jeneil; it's Steve."

She smiled. "Hi, do you feel like a pro yet?"

"Closer, I had lunch with Dr. Sprague and the group's attorney today."

"Papers all signed?"

"Not yet. I'm reading them and then we'll meet again with Dr's. Turner and Young."

"That's really exciting, Steve."

"Yeah, I'm getting excited and I feel like celebrating. I asked Peter if I could borrow his girl for dinner. Can you deal with only two parts of the triad? I'd like to have dinner at a nice restaurant. Have dinner with me, high gear as you call it."

She wasn't in the mood for a celebration, but she heard Steve's excitement. She owed it to him. This was a special time in his life and she reminded herself that he'd always been there for her. "All right, where are we going?"

"The Chateau."

"Steve, you really mean high gear."

He laughed. "Still interested?"

"Count me in." She threw herself into his excitement. "What time will you be here? How did you get reservations?"

"It's not a Friday or Saturday night. I'll leave the hospital at six-thirty and be at your place after I change."

"That's fine. This is sounding like fun."

"See you later," Steve said, glad she sounded excited.

"Okay and thanks," she said. "I hate living through second shift weeks."

Steve chuckled. "What's a second shift week?"

She laughed. "Ooo, you're that much closer to the end. Let me get to putting my finery together."

"See you later," Steve said. She hung up and smiled, her excitement growing.

*****

The feeling of completing his residency was more special to Steve than he thought it would be and there were times when a family would be a handy item; graduations, holidays, and special moments. Peter and Jeneil felt like family. He rang the front bell and heard footsteps. Jeneil opened the door wearing a long lounge dress.

"I'm almost together. You look so doctor," she said, noticing his dark suit. "Come on." She ran up the stairs and he walked in after her, sitting on the sofa as she disappeared into the bedroom. "Now, I'm ready," she said, rushing back into the room carrying her grey fur jacket, handing it to him.

He smiled. "Jeneil, when you go high gear, you leave the kid image way in the past. That blue dress is beautiful on you." He held her jacket for her and she slipped into it. He always loved the way she smelled. "Let's go to dinner."

The restaurant wasn't crowded, but there were enough people to make it social. Steve held her chair for her. "Good, we won't have to rush," he said, sitting down. The waiter brought the wine list and Jeneil watched as Steve ordered without hesitation, including club soda for her. He had real polish when he wanted it. He smiled as the waiter left. "I'm glad we're in this room. It's a cozier atmosphere."

She raised her eyebrows. "Oh, and we have been here often enough to know the rooms?"

He grinned. "Enough."

"Steve, I think I should be treating you to dinner."

He shook his head. "This is a celebration. Invite me to dinner at your house when I'm finally into my office."

"A party for the triad then."

"Good." He looked at the effect candlelight had on her face. "That blue is a great color on you. You look beautiful."

She smiled. "Thank you, Steve, thank you very much. Those are pleasant words. I needed them."

He looked puzzled. "You needed them?"

She waved her hand to make nothing of the remark and sipped some water. "We need to hear it some days more than others. That's all."

He smiled as he studied her and wondered if it was tension he was noticing. Seeing the waiter coming their way, Steve asked her what she'd like. After ordering, they were left alone again. "Jeneil, when will the secrecy end?"

"What secrecy?" she asked, his question catching her unaware.

"That you're with Peter. That we're friends."

She shrugged slightly. "I don't know. Does it matter?"

He moved his spoon a little and returned it. "Quite frankly, it does to me."

"Why?"

"Because I'm being assigned an office and I'd like you to come and see it. Come help me put it together."

She was taken aback by the remark and she sighed. "There are changes in the air. I can feel them." She rested her chin on her hands.

"You sound scared."

"No," she lied, "the triad's changing, Steve." She paused. "But change is part of life I suppose."

He touched her arm. "Hey, I didn't mean to bring in the heavy mood. I just want you to come to my office. I want a few plants. Choose them with me."

She brightened. "I can do that from behind the scenes."

"Jeneil, you look like a woman tonight, a beautiful, sophisticated woman. Maybe it's time to let everyone know you like Pete and I do."

She shook her head. "I'm not ready. I'm not always a sophisticated woman."

"Do you enjoy leading a double life?"

"It's only at the hospital."

"But why should it have to be anywhere?"

She unfolded her napkin. "I need to see who I am without pressure. I thought you knew that. I thought you understood." She laughed lightly. "You're making me think I'm crazy."

He smiled and touched her hand. "No, you're okay, eccentric for sure. I guess I'm being selfish. Come and see my office and help me." He took her hand. "Let's dance and put the serious stuff aside."

She smiled. "I'd like that." Steve led her to the dance floor and as they danced her mind drifted to Peter and the girl.

"Jeneil, what is it?"

"What do you mean?"

"Something's bothering you. I can see it."

Jeneil felt weepy. She swallowed hard. "Will you hold me?" He was shocked, but held her tighter as she leaned against him, sensing how fragile she was.

"What's the matter, honey?" he asked, kissing her temple.

"Just insecure about change."

"Don't be, sweetheart, you've got Peter and me." He squeezed her gently, wanting to comfort her.

She grinned. "Oh, Steve, you and Peter deal in more fiction than I'd ever touch."

He laughed gently. "Are you insulting me?"

She kissed his cheek. "No, no, I'm not. I love you both. But you remind me of something. I think I'll have it printed on a card as a reminder. *I don't need to run scared. I'll always have me.*" Jeneil noticed the waiter at their table. "Your steak and my swordfish are waiting."

He looked at her. "Are you okay now?"

She nodded. "Yes, I have me right here. I'm always nearby and handy. I'd like to dance with you again. I follow you easily. Where'd you learn to dance?"

"A girl I dated was a dance instructor."

"Oh, do you know how to ballroom dance?"

"I'd have to brush up, but I got as far as the Rumba." He pulled her chair out for her.

"Oh, teach me. I can Cha-Cha but that's it. Please teach me."

He laughed as he sat down. "Anything to keep that fire dancing in your eyes, beautiful."

After dinner, they arrived home laughing. Jeneil's mood had lifted from all their dancing. Peter had just gotten in and was hanging up his jacket when they walked in. He smiled. "You're both up late for a work night." Jeneil went to him and hugged him.

"Did you know your buddy here can dance? I mean really dance? I thought I knew the Cha-Cha until I danced with him."

Peter laughed. "Oh, yes, that was the year of Sharon." He put his arm around Jeneil's shoulder. "She looks like she had a lot of fun. Thanks, Steve."

Jeneil hugged Steve. "I did have fun. Can you come and teach me those dance steps."

"That's a deal. Just tell me when."

"Ooo." She kissed his cheek. "How about all this week?"

"You're on."

"Dinner, too," Jeneil held the door for him, "and we can go to the florist and get your plants."

He smiled. "Thanks, kid." He kissed her cheek and waved to Peter as he left.

Jeneil slipped her jacket off and Peter looked her over and whistled. "I'm glad you were with Steve." She kissed him enticingly then slipped away to hang up her coat in the bedroom. He raised his eyebrows and grinned. "I'll get the lights."

Jeneil had come home in a good mood and finished brushing her hair and got into bed. Leaning on one elbow, she stared at Peter.

"What's wrong?"

She grinned. "I'm trying to decide if I should seduce you or rape you."

He laughed. "What the hell did you drink tonight?"

"Club soda," she whispered, snuggling to him and kissing his neck.

"So you decided on seduction, did you?" He pushed her arm from under her and pinned her down. Leaning over her, he grinned. "I decided on rape."

She touched his face, running her finger along his jaw line. "Better hurry before I beat you to it, Chang."

He chuckled and kissed her gently. "Irish, you're beautiful."

She choked up. "Do you really think I'm beautiful?"

He nodded. "In more ways than I ever thought possible in one person."

Tears rolled from the corner of her eyes. Swallowing hard to stop more, she shrugged. "Um, I'm just being silly. Sometimes women like to hear men say they're beautiful. It helps on those days when we don't feel pretty."

He kissed the back of her hand. "You are beautiful," he whispered, and moved his mouth slowly along her arm toward her shoulder. "You are incredibly beautiful," he whispered, his words thrilling her as much as his caress.

Peter was in the shower when his telephone rang. Jeneil covered the mouthpiece and answered by giving the telephone number.

"Hello. Is Dr. Chang in? This is his aunt."

Jeneil uncovered the mouthpiece and sighed with relief. "Peter's in the shower. I can have him call you."

"Thank you. Have him call Risa."

Peter walked into the room and Jeneil signaled to him. "Hold on, Peter just walked in." Peter saw Risa written on the paper.

"Hello, Aunt Risa. This is Peter."

"Peter, can you stop by today?"

"Is something wrong?"

"I don't know. Grandfather is here with me. He caught a bad cold last week and he's not over it yet. In fact, I think he looks worse. The medicine doesn't seem to work."

"Is it a prescription?"

"No, it's just what we bought at the pharmacy."

"Okay, I'll be right over."

"Oh, thank you, Peter. I knew you wouldn't turn your back on us in this. Thank you. Grandfather told me to call you." Peter was pleased to hear that. It was good to have his family's trust and respect after so many years of criticism.

"What is it?" Jeneil asked, after Peter had hung up.

"My grandfather caught a bad cold. My aunt wants me to check on him."

Jeneil frowned. "Uh-oh, he's had that cold for a while."

"You know about it?"

"Yes, I talked to him last week. He had just caught it and it was the heavy in the chest kind."

Peter untied his robe. "I'll get dressed and get over there."

Jeneil kissed him. "I've got to get to work."

"Bye, baby." He hugged her with one arm.

"Remember me to your grandfather." Peter nodded.

*****

Peter saw the car as he parked in front of Risa's house. His mother was there. He got out carrying his bag. Risa met him at the door. "Peter, I guess you know your mother's here."

"It's okay Aunt Risa. I'm more concerned for Grandfather."

"Thank you, Peter. She came after I called you." Peter went to Ron's bedroom. His grandfather looked grey and his breathing was labored.

"Oh my gosh." He went to the bed and took out his stethoscope. His aunts gathered closer to the bed. "Why didn't you call Dr. Slater?"

"I insisted," his grandfather said, gasping for air.

"What is it?" Malien asked.

Peter listened to his grandfather's chest then took his pulse. He checked his eyes and hands. "Any vomiting or diarrhea?"

"Yes, it began yesterday," Risa answered.

"Bad?" Peter asked.

"For most of the day. Peter, what is it?"

Peter sighed. "Checking quickly, I'd say he's got a lot going on. Anemia, pneumonia, dehydration, and I hope not the flu. I'll call for an ambulance." As he left the room, Risa began to cry and Malien hugged her. Lien paced. Peter returned. "The ambulance is on its way. Get his overcoat and bundle him as warmly as possible, but don't over tax him." Peter sat on the bed. "Grandfather, you've been told about ignoring symptoms. This isn't the old days. We can afford doctors. You have insurance. I'm taking you to the hospital. Do you feel strong enough to put on your coat?" The old man shook his head.

"But it's below freezing outside!" Peter's mother spoke up.

"The paramedics will handle it," Peter said, worried. "Damn it, Grandfather."

"Peter!" his mother gasped.

"I'll call the hospital. Get his insurance information for me." Peter left the room and was in the kitchen on the telephone when the ambulance arrived. He hung up and turned. His mother was standing before him.

"Peter, will he be all right?" She began to cry. Without thinking, he went to her and put his arms around her. She was shocked and began sobbing.

"He's been in good health, Mom. Let's see what happens. He's strong; I've seen worse cases of the flu." Malien and Risa stopped crying, shocked at seeing Peter holding his crying mother in his arms.

A paramedic came to him. "Dr. Chang, will you be in the ambulance or following?"

"I'll follow." Peter let go of his mother.

"Then we're ready."

"I'd like to go in the ambulance," Malien said.

"That's fine," the paramedic answered.

"Aunt Risa, drive my mother to the hospital. She's too upset to drive," Peter said. "We don't need something else." Risa nodded and Peter left, walking by his grandfather's gurney with Malien.

The hospital was ready for the admission. Peter went to his locker to change into his lab coat and then met the orderlies as they brought his grandfather to his room. "Go get some coffee or something," Peter told his family. "Let the techs do a workup on him. It'll be awhile. I'll be with him anyway."

The three sisters sat in the cafeteria with their cups of coffee collecting their nerves. Malien noticed Jeneil walk in counting coins from her wallet. Jeneil had begun dressing more stylishly since the Chinese girl had stopped at her office and she wore a softer hairstyle now. She was letting more of the real her be seen and it was being noticed. Some of the men looked her over as she went toward the cafeteria line. Jerry Tollman ran to catch up to her. Slipping his arm around her shoulder, he squeezed her and smiled.

"Take your break with me, my treat."

She thought quickly. "Jerry, people might begin to talk, flowers, breaks together, you know how this place is."

"Who listens?" He studied her face admiringly. "You are gorgeous," he said bluntly.

She smiled. "You should have been a salesman. You're wasting your persistence in medicine."

Risa and Peter's mother had followed Malien's stare and witnessed the review Jeneil had gotten from Jerry.

"She's very pretty." Malien smiled. "Men like her."

Lien frowned as she watched Jeneil with Jerry. "He's dressed like Peter; that must mean he's a doctor, too. I don't understand these men today. He must know she's Peter's girl."

Risa smiled. "It's a different world today, Lien. I worried about Ron for years, I'm glad he's married now."

"Ron?" Malien and Lien were both surprised.

Risa nodded. "He's was too perfect. I had my suspicions."

Malien raised her eyebrows. "It's a miracle sons survive their mothers."

Peter walked in looking for them and went to their table. "Grandfather is settled in his room. We don't have tests results yet, but Dr. Slater will be in to see him soon. He'll be on medication and at least comfortable after that."

"What do you think, Peter?" Malien asked.

"He's on an IV for the dehydration. We'll work on these secondary problems and see what happens. Seeing him in a hospital makes me less nervous. I was shocked when I saw him earlier. He's very weak from going through this for so many days, but I've seen people look worse than he does leave here smiling and waving so I'm hopeful. His health is unusually good. That helps."

His mother looked toward Jeneil. "Peter, do you know the man with Jeneil?" Peter turned to follow his mother's gaze.

He laughed. "That's Jerry Tollman. He likes her. He makes her nervous, too."

"I don't understand why he would do that to your girl."

Peter held onto his stethoscope. "No one at the hospital knows about us except Steve."

His mother looked puzzled by his answer. "Why not?"

"Gossip, people would make too much of it. It could interfere with our jobs. I don't like everyone nosing into our business." His mother shook her head.

Risa smiled. "It's a different world today, Lien. That makes sense to me."

Peter wanted to end the conversation. "You can see Grandfather now." All three of them got up and followed him out.

Jeneil noticed them leaving. "Dr. Chang's surrounded today."

Jerry looked toward them. "His grandfather was just admitted. That must be his family."

"What's wrong?" she asked, concerned.

"He's waiting for test results. It looks like flu and complications."

"Complications?" She didn't like the sound of that.

"It looks like pneumonia too, amongst other things."

Jeneil wanted to see him. The hospital kept a patient busy when they were first admitted, and with the family there she thought better of it. Maybe at lunch break, she thought. The news put a pall on her. At lunch, she rushed to the gift shop, picked up a card and headed to the grandfather's room. He was asleep and her heart sank. He looked so sick. She signed the card and left it on his table in a sealed envelope.

The sisters came back from lunch and Lien noticed the card lying on the table. "Shall I open it for him?"

"He's too weak right now. Go ahead."

Lien opened the envelope, pulled out the card, and read it out loud. "*Mr. Chang, I stopped by. You were asleep which is more important for you than cheering me up with your stories. Please get well very soon. I really love listening to your stories. All my love, Jeneil.*" Lien smiled.

Risa took the card, smiling at the words. "Father really loves her. There's gentleness about her. She seems younger than she is, too."

Malien took the card. "Peter is very lucky. She's a nice girl. Have you noticed that he…," she searched for words, "…fusses over her? I think it's cute. It's odd to see him do that; he never showed emotion toward girls. They trailed around waiting on him like slaves. With Jeneil, he's always by her, holding her hand, putting his arm around her, just showing her attention. It's so nice to watch. He honestly loves her. I've never seen him so open with anyone before. He even hugs now." She laughed. "I always had to hug him."

Risa nodded. "It is nice to watch. He acts like she belongs to him, like he's in charge of watching over her, and he's happy to do it."

Peter walked in and went to his grandfather to take his pulse. The old man woke and smiled when he saw his grandson. Peter smiled and patted his arm. "I'm glad you're in here." The old man nodded, agreeing with Peter.

"Have you eaten lunch?" Lien asked Peter.

"No, Jeneil usually leaves it in the refrigerator for me. I'll be going home for lunch and to rest. I'll probably work into third shift tonight. This place has been really hit by the flu."

Malien looked at him. "Well, you really look healthy."

"Jeneil believes in vitamin C. She gives it to every living thing around her whether they believe in it or not. She requires it in order to be in her life."

Everyone laughed and Lien picked up the envelope. "Father, you have a card. Would you like me to read it?" He nodded and Lien read the card. Peter smiled broadly, pleased with Jeneil's words. The grandfather held out his hand and Lien handed the card to him. He read it quietly and smiled. The effort tired him and he sighed, resting the card on his chest. Peter took it from him and he closed his eyes again to sleep.

"He looks weaker," Risa said.

"He's getting better, Aunt Risa. At home, he struggled against the pain. He's on medication now and his body is making up for the stress it was under. He is better. His pulse is stronger already. In fact, it might be wise if you all went home now. He'll probably sleep most of the afternoon. You get some rest yourselves. He'll need to be looked after when he leaves here, so don't let yourselves get tired. You need to stay healthy now. Get ready for his homecoming."

Risa's eyes filled with tears and she blotted them with a tissue. "Peter, that sounds so good. You've made me relax just saying that. I'll take some vitamin C, too. It's been working for you."

Peter smiled. "Good. All of you need some rest. It would be better to work out a schedule for family visits. He needs a lot of rest. Not too many at once is a rule to protect the patient." They nodded understandingly. "Well, I'll go home too and follow my own advice." They smiled as he walked out.

"Lien, you can be very proud of him. He has changed his life so much."

Lien smiled. "I am very proud of him. I want the best for him. He deserves it."

*****

Jeneil walked by the room on her break. Seeing it empty, she went in. The grandfather was still sleeping, seeming more relaxed and she felt more at ease having seen him this way. She left a note for him and left the room.

Peter got to work early and went to his grandfather's room. He was awake. Peter smiled. "I thought you'd sleep all afternoon."

"The nurse woke me for medication. Peter, there's a note. I've been too tired to reach that far." Peter handed it to his grandfather, smiling, recognizing Jeneil's handwriting. The old man opened it. *Hello, I stopped by again. I'm glad I did. You seemed so much improved. The visit did me a world of good. I'm glad you take orders well and got better quickly. Thank you. Love again, Jeneil.* The grandfather chuckled then coughed. Peter took the note and laughed. It was Jeneil's odd sense of humor. The grandfather smiled. "I'm sorry I missed her."

"Me, too," Peter replied. "We rarely see each other."

"You have a good relationship. You can take the tension."

Peter nodded. "It's all her doing. She's into relationships as a lifestyle."

"Your mother was very touched that Jeneil called to say she didn't blame her. It meant a lot to her. I think things may go more smoothly now."

Peter sighed. "I sure hope so."

Six

Jeneil heard the apartment buzzer sound and got up from the table being careful not to smear the paint on the clown. "Hi, Steve." She smiled. "You got through the front door."

"Jeff was going out."

"Come in." She closed the door with her foot and held her hands carefully to not get paint everywhere.

"Am I wrong? Was I invited to dinner?" Steve asked, looking at her paint-speckled jeans and long men's shirt.

"No," she said, looking at him seriously, "but I guess I can put something together if you're desperate." Steve looked puzzled and she smiled. "I'm kidding. Come and sit with me while I finish this project. Will you get two wine goblets? There's a bottle chilling in the refrigerator. I'll have apple juice."

Steve found his way around the kitchen while Jeneil waited at the kitchen door and then they went to her office. She smiled noticing he wore the sweater she had made for him.

"What have you got going here?" Steve looked at the clown face and yarn.

"It's a card for Mr. Chang."

"You're dressing it in clothes?"

"Yes, I made a clown outfit from scraps. These Styrofoam balls are going to be balloons. It's three-dimensional."

He smiled. "You're cute."

"No, I'm a big kid. That's why I can't be a sophisticated woman all the time." She bent over the clown and outlined details with a fine point brush. Some of her hair was tied back with a ribbon and the rest hung loosely, thick in waves and curls. She had a smear of red paint on her jaw.

Steve got lost in the details of her and noticed the wisp of hair curled gently over her ear. Damn those ears, he thought, studying their structure. Delicate pearl earrings rested in the center of each small earlobe. It was her earlobes that actually made him crazy. He couldn't believe he'd ever get hung up on a girl's ears.

Jeneil turned and saw him staring. "What? Have I painted myself, too?"

"Just a little red," he answered, uncomfortable having been caught.

She smiled. "Not to worry, Sir Steven. I prepared dinner before starting this so your dinner is free of any art debris."

He laughed. "Where did I get Sir Steven?"

"You're in our Camelot. We call you Sir Steven, the Loyal Knight with Shining Honor."

"Hell that sounds real dull."

Jeneil choked on a laugh and smeared the paint. Taking a cotton swab, she dabbed at it quickly, giggling as she worked. Steve smiled watching her. She turned quickly and smeared the swab of black paint across his cheek.

"Hey!" He laughed, wiping it with his hand.

"Don't mess with my artistic temperament." She grinned, wiping his face with a tissue. "Get a piece of paper and draw a floor plan of your office. I have some paper there." She nodded toward a grey box on the shelf unit against the wall. Getting a sheet, he saw the letterhead was from Alden-Connors Corporation.

"Oh, look at that logo. I like the way it's done."

"I like it, too." She began cutting pieces of yarn.

Steve laughed. "Tell me something. What would your business associates say if they found out you were spending your evening cutting yarn for a clown."

She chuckled. "They'd probably say I showed good judgment surrounding myself with doctors."

"Jeneil, why do you work at the hospital?"

"So I won't be dealing with that letterhead all day. Besides, of all the things I do, being a clerk is the most soothing. I keep things in order. It's not a neon job, but it's a necessary one and I like it. The people are real and the work has a beginning, a middle and an end; an instant sense of achievement. Don't lecture me. My uncle is about to freak out over my staying there. My days are numbered. Since the apartment buildings, he lectures regularly. Poor Uncle Hollis, I guess I give him nightmares."

"Apartment buildings? Where?"

"Fairview 1217 and 911."

Steve whistled. "Those are 'in' places. Some of the doctors have looked into it. So did I."

She smiled. "Did you choose one?"

Steve shook his head. "Not this year. I decided on a less expensive building. I've got to build up my bank account. Those other guys have families and wives who have helped them through. I've had scholarships, but I'm not free from student loans. I'd like some money behind me." He laughed. "I had more spending money when I picked pockets than I do now. I decided to take over John Radzinick's lease. He can afford Fairview 1217 now. He's a bachelor. We go the bachelor pad route. Married doctors go to Glenview."

Jeneil smiled. "The development of homes heading south?" He nodded, and she sang, "Little boxes, little boxes, they're all made out of ticky tacky. Little boxes, little boxes standing all in a row."

He grinned. "They're expensive ticky tackies."

"It isn't the price," Jeneil replied. "They're all the same. Have you seen them?"

"No, but that's the game in town."

"Are minorities allowed?"

"I would guess so. Those are professional people in there." Steve watched her. "Worried that Pete will have trouble?"

"It doesn't worry me. I was just curious about where my future lies." The oven buzzer rang and she stood up. "Dinner's ready. I'll clean these brushes while you draw your office floor plan." Steve was just finishing when Jeneil walked back in. "Dinner's on the table. You can bring your goblet." She picked up hers. "Have you finished the sketch?" He nodded and looked at her. She had changed her outfit to a nice dress and leather boots. Her hair was tied up loosely.

Steve grinned as he looked her over. "How many people do you become in a given night?"

"This is my shopping for plants costume. Let's eat. Dinner's getting cold." She turned and he followed her out of the office.

They studied the sketch during dinner and decided on the number and types of plants to get. Steve enjoyed the whole idea of putting his office together and it was fun to be sharing it with Jeneil. He knew he was going to miss her. There was no doubt in his mind that if she wasn't Peter's, he'd be campaigning to take her away from whoever she was with. Admitting that to himself didn't even move his conscience anymore. Peter was a brother to him. Jeneil needed to become more of a sister-in-law. He'd handle it. He had to. There was no way he could imagine life without them. He had removed Marcia from his emotions; he was familiar with the process. What amazed him was that he should need to do that with Jeneil. Considering the level of their relationship, he found it odd. At least he wouldn't have to get over a physical memory of her. That would be unbearable. It would have to be. She was wildfire. He saw it between her and Peter.

"What about paintings?" she asked, looking up to find him staring. "What now? I removed the paint."

He smiled. "You're gorgeous. That's all."

She squeezed his hand. "Keep that compliment coming often, Sir Steven. I think you're gorgeous, too."

He laughed and watched her study the sketch again. His mind wrestled his conscience. *Jeneil, I'm in love with you. I sit here staring at you like a lovesick schoolboy and you don't see it. I don't even know how I fell in love with you. How'd you like to know that about Sir Steven the Loyal, gorgeous?* He smiled at his plate as he thought.

"Does Dr. Sprague have any paintings in his office? What are you smiling at?"

"I can't remember if he has any. Why?"

She held up the sketch. "I was just picturing myself in your office. Putting your diplomas on the wall behind your desk leaves other walls completely open. Have you ever seen my mother's seascapes?" He shook his head. "I have one in my bedroom. Come on." Flipping the light switch, she took him to the chair near Peter's desk where a painting in blues, grays, and white was hanging. "My mother did this as an anniversary gift for my father. He liked powerful surfs. But she has a painting of an ocean at dusk. Its shadow tones and the surf rolls gently onto the beach. It offers a calming, peaceful image. That one might be nice in your office."

"Jeneil, I can't go for much more than plants, at least not right now."

"It's a gift from me."

He shook his head. "That wouldn't be fair."

"And why not, my mother left it to me. I would love for you to have it. It's sitting in a storage room on the estate," she blurted.

"Estate?"

"I, uh, grew up on one. I thought I had mentioned that. We lived in a guest house. Some of my things are still there. It would be no problem to bring the painting back the next weekend I fly to Nebraska."

"An estate, Jeneil? I knew you grew up around money, but estate sounds like big money."

She touched his arm. "Don't forget I lived in the guest cottage. It was small and cozy. Am I pushing this painting on you? Is that it? Maybe you don't like my mother's style."

"No," he insisted, "it's a nice painting. It's just that I wanted you to help me get plants and now you're giving me paintings."

"When I get the fever, you need to watch me." She laughed and hugged his arm. "You're going into private practice, Dr. Bradley, that's exciting." She gave his cheek a quick kiss.

"Come on, let's go get those plants." She dragged him from the bedroom. "That long wall opposite your desk would make a great display for medical artifacts. You know, masks of a medicine man from an American Indian tribe, stuff like that, voodoo ornaments. What do you think? Maybe you could go to Tahiti and bring some things back."

He watched her as she walked backwards and chattered on. "When you said fever, you meant fever." He laughed. "Tahiti!"

She smiled. "Well, who knows?" She got her coat and handed it to him. It was caramel colored cashmere. She added a wool crepe scarf in a pattern of varied colors that sparked the outfit.

"Jeneil, you're dressing money. Why?" he asked, looking at her as he put on his jacket.

"I do that when I shop. People take me more seriously. Mandra taught me." Jeneil added brown leather gloves and smiled. "This place will give you a very good price. I've done business with them before."

Steve pulled into the parking lot of a greenhouse someone had added to. The cold wind snapped at them and they walked quickly to the front entrance. Steve held the door for Jeneil and she put her coat collar back into place when they got inside and smoothed her hair a bit. A woman smiled at her from the register. "Aren't New England winters fun?"

Jeneil laughed. "Like dentistry without anesthesia. Is Glenn here tonight?"

The woman nodded. "I'll get him for you."

An older woman came up to them. "Jeneil, a shipment of herb seedlings arrived. Do you want some verbena?"

"Ooo, yes I do. Did you get any crab apple blossoms?"

The woman smiled. "On the shelf in bay four, I'll put a box at the register for you."

"Thanks. And two cherry tomatoes plants, they must be ready to leaf now aren't they?"

The woman shrugged. "Just about, I'd treat them like hot house orchids until the end of February."

"Well then forget them. I'll come back. I'm going to grow some indoors this year."

"Oh," the woman replied, "then try a packet of seeds. There's a variety that hangs in baskets and grow fruit until you can't stand them anymore, and the low temperatures outside won't hurt them."

Jeneil laughed. "But a packet has so many seeds. If I waste them, I feel guilty." She thought a minute. "Okay, I'll take a packet. I can pot them all and give them to friends. It'll pay them back for their supply of zucchini every summer." The woman laughed and walked away. Steve smiled, liking Jeneil's simple interests. Jeneil walked into a section with baskets and pots and groaned. "Slap my wrists if I pick up anything. I love baskets. This place loves to see me come in. I can't resist leaving with something."

Steve noticed people looking at them. Clerks would smile at him, too. He smiled, realizing they must think he and Jeneil were a couple. He liked it. Jeneil picked up a basket and he slapped her hand, surprising her. "You told me to do that."

She laughed. "Just this one, it would be nice on the bookshelf holding the peperomia plant."

He bumped her arm with his elbow. "You're hopeless."

She smiled at him. "But I'm still gorgeous right?"

A man in a shirt and tie with graying sideburns walked to them quickly, smiling broadly. "Jeneil, I'm sorry to keep you waiting."

"It's a good business tactic, Glenn. I've been buying while I'm waiting, which hasn't seemed very long." The man laughed and Jeneil turned to Steve. "This is Dr. Bradley. He's putting his office together and he's decided on these plants." She handed him a list.

Glenn shook his head. "Jeneil, I love doing business with you. I get a list and we're done. I couldn't get to you sooner because I was trailing a patron around trying to help her decide what to replace a rubber plant with." He looked at the list. "Since there are only a few, I can't give a special price break. I can give you a discount though. Is that okay?"

Jeneil looked at him. "How about including them on the Fairview list and delivering them to his office which isn't too far from there."

Glenn smiled. "I should have thought of that myself. You've got it. Thanks for bringing the business here."

She nodded. "Include Dr. Bradley's bill with mine and my office will handle it."

Glenn nodded. "The pots and baskets for them are on me." He held his hand out to Steve. "Congratulations. A new practice, huh?" Steve nodded. "What field?"

"Neurosurgery."

"Well, remember us as you expand."

Jeneil smiled. "Glenn, he's joining with Medical and Surgical Associates."

Glenn raised his eyebrows and gasped. "Young, Turner and Sprague, wow! Thank you, Jeneil, a free plant for the receptionist then, too. It was very nice meeting you, Dr. Bradley. I'll get this order going. You'll have it tomorrow. Thanks Jeneil, Dr. Bradley."

Steve looked at Jeneil as Glenn walked away. "You're a pretty slick name dropper."

She smiled. "Your name will someday open doors, too."

He chuckled. "Is that a promise?"

"Count on it. Dr. Steven Bradley's name will be special. Life owes it to you."

He grinned. "You're cute."

"No, gorgeous remember, gorgeous."

They went back to the apartment for dessert and coffee. Jeneil brought the tray to the sofa and put it on the low table just as her telephone rang.

"Hi, honey."

"Peter." She smiled. "How is your grandfather?"

"Trying to recuperate from visiting hours, the whole family came when they heard. They didn't stay long but the flow was constant all evening. Tomorrow will be friends and neighbors probably. I should have put him in ICU."

Jeneil laughed. "Is he improving?"

"Yes, he's responding well to medication. What have you been up to? I called earlier, no one answered."

"Steve and I went shopping for plants. We're having dessert and coffee now."

Peter groaned. "That sounds so good. I have to work third shift tonight, too. It's crazy here. When the doctors who are sick get back to work, they get assigned double shifts. They're still a little weak so I hope they don't relapse." He sighed. "I miss you, baby."

"Me, too," she answered. "How have you been holding up?"

He chuckled. "By not thinking about it and having a great woman looking after me. Can I talk to Steve?"

"Sure, hold on." She handed the receiver to Steve, surprising him.

"Hey, Pete, I won't ask how things are going," Steve said, and Jeneil wondered why he seemed embarrassed.

"Steve, how come you're not catching doubles?"

Steve sighed. "Because I'm in surgery most of the day with Young, Turner, or Sprague. I knew people would notice. I'm all but out of the hospital schedule now. I feel bad; I'm wandering around there and it's different. I don't like it either. I can see how shorthanded things are. I'm sorry, Pete."

"No, it's okay. I just haven't seen much of you lately and I suddenly realized that you have regular hours now."

"I know. It isn't easy to watch you guys live through this mess."

Jeneil smiled, understanding why he sounded embarrassed. Peter stretched his back. "Forget it. You've served your time. Jeneil said you bought some plants."

"Yeah, she got a special price for me. She's been great about helping me put my office together."

Peter smiled. "She's great like that. I've got to get back, put Jeneil back on so can I say goodbye. I'm on third tonight and she works tomorrow. This schedule is wonderful."

"She's right here." Steve smiled and returned the receiver to Jeneil.

"Peter, are you taking your vitamin C?"

"Faithfully, believe me. I love you, Jeneil."

"I do too, Peter. I'll miss you."

"Thanks, honey, that'll get me through. Maybe we'll see each other sometime."

"I hope so, Peter. Bye." She sighed as she replaced the receiver.

Steve looked at her. "I feel guilty. He's pulling doubles and I'm sitting here enjoying the evening with his girl."

"It's not your fault. But I don't like this turmoil. It's unsettling. It's also interfering with my life plan. The energy flow is clouded and mixed, and I feel lost and helpless."

Steve laughed. "Lit majors are a real kick! Most people would just say I miss him."

Jeneil forced a smile. "It's beyond that kind of simplicity, Steve. Changes are in the wind."

He put his coffee cup down. "I'm scheduled for early surgery and all day surgery, too. I'd better leave." He got up to put his jacket on.

She nodded. "Stay on your vitamin C."

He smiled. "Just to prove you wrong." He noticed the drop in her mood and put his hands on her shoulders. "Jeneil, what's with you and changes lately?"

She shook her head. "I'm just sensitive. I'm too cautious sometimes. I worry a lot about some things." He sensed her fragility and put his arms around her. She relaxed in his arms and it felt good to him. He wanted to protect her from whatever she was worried about even though he didn't understand it. "Thank you for holding me. I feel safe."

He kissed her temple lightly. "Hospital schedules can play havoc on a relationship. Hang tough, sweetheart. This flu outbreak will pass and Pete will be on his normal schedule again. I feel like a traitor watching it all happen around me."

Jeneil stood back and smiled. "You're in surgery all day, that's hardly easy."

"But I don't get tired from it. In fact, it makes me relax."

She nodded. "I can understand that. That's what happens to me in the theater."

"Jeneil, I think you found your place there."

She laughed. "I found a big piece there. Now if I can only zero in on what particular thing about theater does it for me."

"You can't find out just playing at it, honey. It sounds like the hospital is in the way."

"Yes, I know, Uncle Hollis," she teased, and took his hand. "Are you free tomorrow?" He nodded. "Come and teach me to dance."

"Sure." He smiled and kissed her cheek. "I'll see you tomorrow."

Jeneil locked the door and looked around the empty apartment. She didn't like what she was sensing. The changes were mounting in greater numbers and the triad was almost over, she could feel it. She had known it would happen but had hoped it wouldn't so soon. Steve was going into private practice and that would remove him from the triad. She would be leaving the hospital soon and surrounding all the change was the Chinese girl. Like a fragrance, that change was rolling in unstoppable and steady, a change she could see but couldn't hold or touch. "I don't even know your name," Jeneil said, "but you know mine. And much, much more, I'm certain of that. You're more prepared for this battle than I am." The word battle vibrated through her as she spoke, stunning her, and a cold shiver passed through her. She felt like she was standing in a cold, damp, penetrating fog, totally unprotected. "Soul, Jeneil. Soul, remember? But where is the time? The elements are not combining in my favor. Why? I'm getting answers but no help." She went to heat more Ovaltine, hoping to shake the mood and get warm again.

*****

Jeneil went into work early and headed to Peter's grandfather's room. He smiled when he saw her. She went to him quickly, hugging him gently and kissing his cheek. "I've been worried about you."

He patted her hand. "I'm much better today."

Taking a thermos from her carryall, she smiled. "Freshly squeezed orange juice, can you manage with a straw?" He nodded. Pouring the water from his glass and rinsing it, she filled it with juice and held it for him to drink. "Don't rush; I came in early to bring this to you. It's good to hear your voice." She felt his forehead as he sipped his juice.

Peter walked in and stopped, shocked by the sight of Jeneil looking after his grandfather. He smiled, touched by her concern and caring. He closed the door for privacy and went to stand by her. She looked at him and smiled gently. He studied her face; she was more beautiful than he remembered. It seemed longer than twenty-four hours since he had seen her. He kissed her cheek. The grandfather smiled as he watched the two of them then settled his head back. Jeneil put the glass aside. She brought the clown card out of her carryall and handed it to the grandfather. The clown's face had a cheerful smile and there was a card hanging from its hand that read, '*Without sickness can we really know health?*' The grandfather smiled, recognizing her reminder of Yin and Yang.

Peter took the card. "I've never seen a card like this. Where did you get it?"

"I made it."

Peter smiled and shook his head. The grandfather was touched by her work. "Jeneil, it's very nice. You've gone out of your way on my account."

"I enjoyed it, Mr. Chang. We made our own cards in our family. It felt good to get back to it."

A nurse walked in as Peter put the clown on the vanity table. She showed surprise at seeing Jeneil in the room. Jeneil noticed her reaction. "Mr. Chang and I know each other. We belong to the International Arts League."

"Oh," the nurse answered, looking from Peter to Jeneil. Seeing the nurse look them over, Jeneil was surprised that inside herself, she didn't care. It didn't seem to matter anymore. She was there for his grandfather. That was all that really mattered.

"Oh, what an adorable card." The nurse picked up the clown. "Styrofoam balls on pipe cleaners as balloons. That's clever. Where did this come from?"

"I made it," Jeneil answered, hesitating for a second.

"This is really nice. I'd like to show it to the other nurses. Would you mind?"

Jeneil shrugged. "It's Mr. Chang's."

The old man nodded and the nurse left promising to bring it right back. Peter and Jeneil looked at each other, and Peter took her hand. "I think you've risked your privacy on all this, honey."

She nodded, agreeing with him. "It doesn't seem to matter, there are changes surrounding me anyway. Oddly enough, every circumstance now seems to remind me whatever happens, happens. The clock seems to be chiming at an odd hour. Que sera," she said quietly, sighing.

The grandfather watched her, sensing the concern in her voice. He looked at Peter. They should get married, he thought, and soon.

Jeneil took her hand from Peter's. "I'd better get to work." She went to the grandfather. "I plan to be by as often as I can. It's good for my health. I need to see you improving."

He smiled. "Thank you, Jeneil."

She nodded and kissed his cheek. Picking up her purse and carryall, she looked at Peter. "See ya 'round soon, Chang. Just don't git to forgettin' me, ya hear now?"

Peter laughed. "No chance of it, Irish. No way in hell."

The grandfather smiled, enjoying their ability to express their love so easily. Jeneil smiled at Peter as she left. The grandfather looked at Peter seriously. "Peter, get married. Get married soon. I'll help if you need it." Peter was surprised by his grandfather's directness and wondered why he seemed so concerned.

*****

The hospital buzzed about Jeneil knowing Mr. Chang and her artistic ability. The card had gotten a lot of notice and it brought unwanted attention as people remembered different things about her, but never did they talk about her and Peter. They might have tried because they asked about Jeneil's boyfriend a lot, asking why he was out of town, but the gossip was he was an engineer on a construction job in a foreign country. Jeneil smiled as the gossip returned to her and she assumed having seen Karen with Peter, people refused to budge from that story line. It also came back to her that there had been two more visits by the Chinese girl and that she had brought him food. Barbara Stanton was enraged over that. Jeneil wondered what Peter did with the food since she was still providing him with lunches and dinners, but she couldn't believe she was even interested in where the food went since the girl was so obviously brazen about her interest in him. Peter never mentioned her to Jeneil and Jeneil never asked. With the few hours they had together, Jeneil didn't want them wasted on negative energy.

Jeneil and Steve had begun dancing lessons. That was a bright spot in her life. He was fun and she liked spending time with him. Her moods and insecurities never took hold with him around, and she felt safe and comforted. The evenings they shared were genuine and she discovered she really loved dancing, especially Latin dances, and Steve was impressed with her enthusiasm. Sharon had been a dancer and had taught him to dance because he had asked as part of a campaign to improve himself and to fit in socially. Dancing hadn't been any more than that to him until Jeneil. She had a fire for it, like other things she enjoyed. She considered it exercise and therapy, and he agreed with her.

Their evenings together were fun for Steve, too. He even resented the invitation to Dr. Sprague's house for dinner because he had to give up his evening with Jeneil. He also knew that if Jeneil went with him to Sprague's that would be fine too, proving to him that dancing was the secondary interest. He was becoming concerned about his feelings for her, not being as easy to put aside as he had thought. He was totally shocked that she didn't see his interest in her. His emotions for her felt so near the surface, so obvious, but she didn't have a clue about how he felt. That fact was clear to him. It was hopeless to try and withdraw now.

Something was happening between them. It was never discussed but he felt strongly that she needed him. At times, she would lean toward him and reach out to him, and those moments were pure magic. It didn't matter to his conscience anymore; he was entangled in the electricity of her. What did begin to pain his conscience was that if she ever showed any romantic interest in him at all, he would take her even though she was Peter's. The idea hurt him and his friendship with Peter. Guilt surfaced when he'd run into Peter and Peter would jokingly ask how his girl was. Steve forced himself to keep his conscience in check and his guilt brought him back in line about his feelings toward Jeneil. Something had to change. He knew it. He felt hopelessly drawn into something he was feeling, something he couldn't unravel or do without. As warped as it seemed, he spent every minute he could with his best friend's girl, wishing she was his. He forced himself to say those words out loud. They sounded adolescent but they kept him in check. He liked looking after her and for whatever the reason, she needed him, and he wanted to be there for her.

Seven

Winter felt long and cold, and Jeneil's internal clock was ready for spring. She liked the idea of growing something, to be part of life, and so decided to prepare bulbs to force bloom. After putting the bulbs in slightly moistened soil and wrapping them in plastic bags, she put them in the bottom of the refrigerator and hoped Peter would never find them. She laughed as she imagined his reaction to finding soil so near his food, even protected in plastic. She closed the refrigerator door and wondered what to do next. There were several nonfiction books she was reading. She also had some new knotted yarn to make herself a sweater with. The pattern was simple and she had liked the texture the yarn had given the display sweater in the store. She had also bought some material in pastel blue with plans to make a skirt to match for spring. When her father died, Mandra taught her to keep planning, working, and dreaming. "Create," Mandra kept telling her, "study and create. It's the fiber of life, Jeneil. Envelope yourself with it and you'll survive anything."

Jeneil smiled to herself realizing how triads had affected her life. From her parents, she had learned about the quality of life. From Mandra, she had learned preparation and survival. Mandra had been heroic at it as far as Jeneil was concerned. From all three, she had learned love. And now in her own triad, she was learning other sides to love; the deep emotional and romantic, and the strong steadying friendship. She smiled and wondered why she was so frightened of the changes ahead. In looking through the past year, change had brought her Peter and Steve, good solid friends, and business associates.

"I know what it is, Nebraska," Jeneil said to herself, "you're the one who likes order so much. Transitions aren't orderly so you're insecure. Okay girls; let's get together on this shall we? There's only one body for all three of us. Be fair. Jeneil, you're the strong-minded one, you decide. Irish has energy to spare and can't bear the thought of sitting still to read or knit, and Nebraska is insecure and needs comfort. What do we do?" Jeneil smiled. "Simple, dust those books and the shelves, you'll use Irish's energy and cater to Nebraska's sense of order." Jeneil went to the bedroom to change into work clothes. "Jeneil, you're good. We knew we could count on you."

Jeneil started on the top shelf, dusting and stacking each book. The shelf was then dusted and polished. The project gave the room a look of upheaval and Nebraska was bordering hysteria but kept concentrating on one shelf at a time for motivation. Inserting the Rossini tape into the stereo, Jeneil climbed the stepladder to continue dusting. The apartment door opened and Peter stood staring at the mess. Stunned to see him, Jeneil jumped off the last step of the ladder and went to him.

"You didn't tell me you'd be coming home." She hugged him looking puzzled. "Why are you home, it's the middle of a shift?"

He smiled at her. "They want me to double again so they gave me a couple hours off to sleep and rest." He sighed. "And I'll take it." He held her close to him. "Baby, remind me of all the reasons I've said I wanted to be a doctor. I seem to have forgotten why I'm living like this."

She rubbed his back gently. "Because you like feeling half dead and zombie-like?" He snickered. "Not it, huh? I know why, it's because you really enjoy paying high rates for malpractice insurance and worrying about law suits. That's real fun." He chuckled. "Not that either, I guess," she responded. "Then it must be that you like prescribing plastibycycline. Am I right?"

He laughed and straightened up. "Plasti-what?"

"Bycycline. It sounds like an acrylic pill, doesn't it?" She smiled then became serious as she studied his face. "Peter, you're incubating something!" She looked at him more intently. "Oh my gosh, you most certainly are. You're not taking C are you?"

"Honey, I'm okay. No, I haven't taken C lately. I keep forgetting."

She sighed. "Well, you've got something in your system now."

"Baby, I'm okay. Just damn tired, that's all."

"No, Peter, it's showing in your eyes and your coloring. I can see it plainly." She went to the kitchen and he followed.

"Oh shit, baby. I get a few hours off and you talk quarantine. Am I the only one missing us being together?"

She handed him a glass of cloudy liquid and opened the cupboard. "I'll make an herbal infusion."

"Oh gosh, honey, really, that's wonderful," he pouted.

She worked quickly, ignoring his bad humor. She opened the refrigerator and took out some things that she put into a strange looking device. Then, emptying it, she stirred it into a cup she had strained some liquid in. Opening a jar, she added a teaspoon of glop to the liquid and stirred it then handed the cup to Peter.

"Drink it quickly."

"What is it?" he asked, and she just stared at him. "Tell me or I won't drink."

"It's only fennel tea, black horseradish, and crushed garlic."

Peter put the cup down. "Garlic, Jeneil? That's going to be real fun for you."

She handed the cup to him again. "Drink it, Peter, please. It'll be fine. Please drink it." He shook his head then drank the weird tasting mess. "Take a shower," she said, "but I want to regulate the water temperature."

"You're serious," he said, staring at her.

She nodded. "And hurry." She left the room.

Peter rubbed his forehead. "I spend all these years studying medicine and then fall in love with a girl who wants to play witch with roots and mud water. Jeneil!" he called, heading to the bedroom. "I don't want you crazy. You hearing me? I want you sexy, baby. Is that plain enough to get through cerebral? Are you listening?"

She met him in the hallway carrying his robe. "Do you honestly think you are capable right now? It isn't what you need most."

"Oh, that's a nasty swipe." He laughed. "Cut out all this shit and get into bed. We'll see, okay."

She smiled. "Chang, give the Chinese stud a break, please. Get that macho body of his to the shower."

He grinned as he began undoing his shirt. "Gladly, sweetheart, you need to be taught a lesson. I leave you alone a few nights and you become a cerebral bitch. The shower will cure us both. Let's go." He took her by the wrist and led her to the shower. As he got in, she said she would as soon as she adjusted the temperature. "Hey, Jeneil, that's getting seriously hot now, come on."

"Please, Peter," she pleaded. "Cooperate will you?"

"That's hot!" he yelled from behind the shower curtain.

"Stay under it!" Jeneil watched the secondhand on her watch then turned up the cold and lowered the hot tap.

"Oh shit!" he groaned. "What the hell are you doing to me! Pneumonia is more treatable than a cold. Is that what you're after in this game? Jeneil, I'm freezing." She changed to tepid and heard him sigh with relief. "Are you coming in now?"

"No, towel dry and I'll meet you in bed."

He laughed. "Well, that's okay, too. Jeneil, I've seen kinky in my day, some of it was even fun, but baby, this kinky you're into is strange."

She smiled. "I'll turn off the water. Be grateful it's not leather and chains."

He laughed and reached for a towel. "Ooo, Jeneil, have you been reading trashy novels while I've been away?"

"I'm going to bed now," she answered seductively.

He grinned. "You better keep your promise. I hear that tone of voice."

"Bye, Chang," she said in a sultry whisper, and then closed the door behind her.

He laughed and shook his head. "I'm quitting medicine. Who needs that shit with her at home ready for fun?"

Jeneil was standing by his side of the bed rubbing her hands together when he came in. "What's this?" he asked, putting his arms around her. "You're not even undressed yet. Jeneil, enough of this, c'mon."

"Just a body massage, Peter, and then I'll crawl into bed with you."

"Hey, now that sounds really good." He got under the covers and lay on his back. She rubbed her hands briskly to warm them and then took some cream and smoothed it onto her palms. "Cream, too? Jeneil, you have been reading trashy novels," he said, laughing. She smoothed her hands over his chest, rubbing the cream onto his body. "Oh man, that does feel great," he said, closing his eyes. "It smells nice, too."

"Turn onto your stomach," she said, and then began massaging his back.

"Oh, baby, this is fantastic." He stretched and was silent as she continued rubbing his back, shoulders, and upper arms. "Jeneil, what's in that cream?"

"Why?" she asked cautiously, raising her eyebrows.

"Because my skin is beginning to feel warm, what's in it?"

"Only essence of wintergreen, the heat will be good for your body."

He groaned. "Jeneil, baby, I'm going to give you essence of bruises. This is more witchcraft shit. And here I thought you were into sexy." He sighed.

She bent down and kissed the back of his head. "Chang, I'm into sexy. I promise I'll crawl under the covers with you after I finish this."

He laughed into his pillow then lifted his head. "I'm going to make you keep that promise."

"Here, put this on," she said, handing him a dark shirt.

"Jeneil, are you kidding? In sexy, the clothes come off, not on. I remember that much."

She laughed. "Put the shirt on, Peter." He felt relaxed and refreshed so decided to go along with it to put an end to her ritual. The material felt warm and soft as he slipped it on. "Lie on your stomach."

He yawned. "Promise me you'll get under the covers."

"I promise." She kissed his back and began massaging it gently.

"Talk to me, honey. I want to hear your voice."

"What shall we talk about?" She smiled, hearing the restful tone in his voice.

"I don't care. Recite the telephone book, just talk."

"Okay, let's see. Page one, Aaron, Abercrombie, Alice, Arthur."

He laughed. "I missed you and us and this."

She kissed his back. "I missed you, too." She dropped her voice an octave and spoke more softly. "Steve and I have been dancing. I got a book from the library and we're following the step patterns from it. Can you believe him, a full-fledged neurosurgeon doing that in his free time? He's a lot of fun. We're trying to do the Bossa Nova. For being called a star, it was a fad that faded fast. Just its sparkle, I guess. It's fun though."

She stopped and listened, and could tell by his breathing that he had fallen asleep. She smiled and covered him with a warm quilt. Rubbing her hand over the quilt gently, she grinned. "This wasn't witchcraft, Peter. It's some of what I learned from studying to be part of the Sultan's harem. The women were taught to know what the Sultan needed when he came to her. It wasn't always sex." She stood up, went to her side of the bed and carefully got under the covers. "I'm keeping my promise, Chang. I crawled under the covers with you."

She looked at his hair. He needed a haircut. She loved his hair on the long side. It was so thick and dark and seldom stayed in place when it got longer. It reminded her of Chang; wild and free. She wanted to run her fingers through it and snuggle to him. "Well, I promised I'd get under the covers but I didn't promise I'd stay. Harem girls must have learned to be cerebral, too. All that massaging and feeling your skin is tough on cerebral." She got out of bed slowly to not wake him and left the room, turning out the lights and closing the door.

She finished dusting the books, putting everything back in place. Smelling her hands, she grinned. "How romantic, essence of wintergreen and furniture polish. Let's get ready for Chang to wake up."

Jeneil turned on the shower. The bedroom was still quiet when she went in to dress. She slipped out quietly again, going to the kitchen to put chicken soup together. She heard Peter's telephone ring and sighed. Taking a bottle from the herb shelf, she poured a glass of warm water into a teacup and squeezed lemon in it. Knocking on the bedroom door, she walked in. Peter was just finishing his conversation.

"This isn't vitamin C," he said, looking at the teacup and two tablets.

"No, it's cell salt."

"Now, what's cell salt," he asked sharply. "I need my head clear."

"Trust me, Peter. I haven't given you anything narcotic." He sighed and took the tablets, drinking the water from the teacup. He almost gagged as the sourness from the lemon reached his taste buds. "Geez, warn a guy will you," he snapped, reaching for his robe. "Still playing witch, are you?"

"Peter, don't," she said gently. "You're getting angry at me."

He stood up. "I'm not angry at you. You don't want sex, that's your business. Just say no next time instead of knocking me out. I don't like being tricked. You manipulated me. That makes me crazy." She could see he was hurt.

"Peter, look at me. Am I dressed like this because I don't want sex?" He looked her over; she looked great and sexy. "I was planning to wake you so we could be together but I think the telephone call messed that up. Do you have to go in right now?"

"There's been an accident. I'm needed in surgery."

She sighed and nodded, and he put his arms around her. "I'm sorry, baby. I guess I'm disappointed. I should be thanking you. My body feels like its rested eight hours and I've only slept two and a half."

"I know." She smiled. "At the time, that's what you needed most. You look much better."

He kissed her. "You and your witchcraft are okay."

Jeneil laughed. "You'd make a lousy sultan, Chang."

"What does that mean?"

"Nothing, except I love you." She smiled and hugged him. "Get ready for work."

Jeneil went to the kitchen. She had warm chicken soup waiting so he could eat quickly and some vitamin C. She packed him some goodies for snacking and warned him to take C at work and drink fruit juice instead of coffee. He stopped at the door to kiss her.

He sighed. "That kiss feels so good."

She smiled. "The weekend's coming and shift change."

"It better hurry." He smiled and kissed her again. "This weekend we're staying in bed and if you go anywhere near your herbs, I'll break your arm." She laughed, and he kissed her and left.

*****

Peter ran into Jeneil in his grandfather's room regularly. Her little jars and thermoses accompanied her. Apparently she had him drinking herbal solutions, too. Peter watched his grandfather closely for signs that her medicine was conflicting with the hospital's, but his grandfather only improved. Jeneil disguised the smell of garlic on people using lemon and the nurses couldn't figure out why there was a smell of garlic from the sink. The grandfather loved homeopathy, Jeneil had made a convert of him, and he looked forward to her visits. Each day she brought a new sign to hang on the clown's hand with a message written on it. The family loved it, but Peter noticed that Jeneil was very careful to avoid them. He wondered, but he didn't worry. His grandfather was scheduled to leave the hospital on Saturday morning and Peter noticed a handmade booklet hanging from the clown's hand. The title was *Rx*. Curious, he opened it and laughed as he read the recipes for Jeneil's herbal drinks.

The grandfather sat on the edge of the bed, waiting to be discharged. "She brought me enough herbs for a month," he said. "She's worked hard to get me healed."

"I think the hospital helped too, Grandfather."

"Jeneil and I both know that, but she's right, with so many patients the food is going to be boiled instead of steamed. She is interested in so many things." The old man smiled. "She loves learning. She loves life."

Peter grinned. He was scheduled to work a double but had been given Sunday off. Drs. Sprague, Maxwell, and Fisher had made it a point to congratulate him on his steadiness and good health through the crisis. New cases were leveling off, but the staff had been hit hard. Peter had added Jeneil's garlic concoctions to his list of herbal preparations and had noticed a difference in stamina. She suggested he give up coffee while he was under stress but he had doubted her, feeling he needed the caffeine kick when his schedule was tight. She had also started him on what she called an herbal cleansing program to clear his blood of toxins and he noticed the difference. He wasn't as irritable and he lasted for longer periods of time under pressure. He also noticed that he could take a nap for an hour or two and he awoke refreshed. He was becoming more open-minded about herbs.

Peter went to the entrance with his family and watched while his grandfather got settled into the car, and then he went back to the fifth floor. It was near noon and he was covering for Dan Morietti, who wanted to sleep for an hour and a half. Peter was looking through the rack of medical charts when he heard tapping on the window. Looking up, he saw Uette. She smiled and signed to him to talk. Peter left the medical room.

"Hi, Peter. Will you have lunch with me?"

"We're short staffed, Uette," he said, taken aback by her directness. "In fact, I'm covering for a doctor who's gone to catch up on some rest. I'm not sure when I'll eat. Was there something in particular you wanted?"

"No, just a chicken sandwich and coffee, I guess." He looked at her, wondering about her answer. "That's a joke, Peter."

"Uette, maybe you were too young to remember, but your father gave strict orders for you girls to avoid me. If he knew you just asked me to lunch, you'd be under guard until you're forty." She stared at him, totally surprised by his directness, and then she regained her footing. "I'm not that young, Peter. I remember, and since you brought it up, I'd like to apologize for my family's treatment of you. Obviously it's undeserved."

Peter studied her. "It wasn't at the time and I doubt your father would approve now."

"I don't care what he thinks. I make up my own mind about my life and I'd like to have lunch. I'd like to know you better. You're a difficult man to get subtle messages to so maybe I should be more direct. Please have lunch or dinner with me sometime soon."

This was a different type of Wong, Peter thought. He gave her a slight smile. "Uette, you might not know this, but I'm serious about a girl. We're planning to be married."

Uette raised her eyebrows, pretending to hear it for the first time. "What? Without having gotten to know me better? That's not fair." She made a deliberate pout.

Peter laughed, stunned by her statement. "Are you sure your name is Wong?"

She flashed a beautiful smile and tilted her head. "You can't do this to me when I've only just met you. Break my heart gently at least, you brute." She fixed his lapel but he had a feeling it didn't need fixing.

He shook his head. "Uette, I'm not sure what this is all about, but really, I've found what I want in my life with my girl. I'm not looking around, and I should be checking on some patients, so if you'll excuse me."

She smiled. "I understand, and she's really a lucky girl. I hope she knows that. Well, maybe just a casual lunch sometime. You certainly aren't what my father described."

He looked at her steadily before walking away. "I've got to check on some patients. Nice seeing you again."

Uette went to the elevators. What did that mousey girl have? She couldn't believe it. This wasn't really happening. He actually set her blood racing and she couldn't even get him to look twice at her. She usually pushed boys away. There must be some way to deal with this. He just wasn't giving her a chance. Karen would help though, she was sure of it. The door opened and she got on the elevator. "Jeneil, have I misread you? I couldn't have. Karen and her stepmother see you the same way. He's mine, Jeneil. I'll even defend him to my family if I have to, and it's so odd that I feel this strongly about him. It must be chemistry or something. Dr. Chang is mine, Jeneil."

*****

At ten-thirty that night, Peter went to the telephone booth. "Jeneil."

"Oh no, Peter, not a shift extension," Jeneil groaned, hearing his voice.

"I just called to tell you that I'll be taking a quick shower here and then I'll be leaving."

"You're serious! It's real! Oh, Peter, I love you! Hang up and get moving."

"See you soon, baby."

Driving home, Peter smiled as he recalled Jeneil's excitement. He could feel his excitement build as he unlocked the apartment door and went to the bedroom. Jeneil came from behind the dressing screen wearing her fluffy blue robe. "Why the robe, honey?" he asked, having expected a nightgown.

She grinned. "Because it's cold without clothes on."

He hugged her to him and kissed her gently. Lifting her off the floor, he carried her to the bed. He kissed her powerfully as he began to undo her robe. There were no words between them, just passion. And a strong desire to satisfy each other.

Jeneil awoke and was surprised to find herself still in Peter's arms. She felt rested and wondered what time it was. The room was still in darkness, but the light filtering through the window shade indicated it was early morning. Peter's arm was around her so she didn't move knowing she'd wake him if she stirred. She lay enjoying the feel of his skin against hers. She wanted to touch him, the passion she still had within her surprising her. Their lovemaking the previous night had been so satisfying but she wanted him now, too.

"What are you doing awake?" Peter asked, the deepness of his voice vibrating through her. She jumped, and he squeezed her gently and kissed her forehead. "Are you okay?"

She nodded. "Are you?"

"Yeah, except for wanting a rerun of last night."

Jeneil smiled and kissed his chest. Moving her lips to his mouth, she kissed him passionately. They lost each other in their kisses, allowing passion to overtake them as the feeling of being together fascinated their senses again. Jeneil smothered him with kisses when they had finished. He smiled, lying back in bed and enjoying her. She snuggled against him, clinging to him.

"Jeneil, I like this better than herbs."

She laughed lightly. "So do I." He smoothed his hand across her back in a light massage. She relaxed, enjoying the sensation. "What time is it?"

"Why? Does it matter?"

"Steve's coming to breakfast."

"What? Honey, I thought we'd be alone today," he said, disappointed.

"I'm sorry, Peter. You getting the day off was a surprise. I expected you to work first shift so I asked Steve to come over."

Peter sighed. "Let's call and cancel."

She lifted her head quickly. "No, Peter!"

"Why?"

"What would we tell him?"

He chuckled. "I don't think we'd have to explain to Steve."

She sighed. "Well, you call him, I can't. I'd have trouble facing him after that." His telephone rang and they both groaned as he answered.

"Peter, it's Risa."

"Hi, how's Grandfather?"

"Well, I'm worried about him. Could you come over before work? That's why I'm calling so early."

"What's the problem? Is he worse?"

"He looks flushed."

"Did you take his temperature?"

"It's only one hundred, but after last time I'd feel better if you made sure he was all right."

"Okay, Aunt Risa. I have the day off. Is it all right if I get there after breakfast?"

"That's fine, Peter. The family's coming here for dinner. Why don't you and Jeneil come, too?" He smiled; that sounded good to him.

"Okay, Aunt Risa. See you later." He hung up. Jeneil waited anxiously.

"Is your grandfather worse?"

"I don't know. His temperature's up a little, but he's on an antibiotic so what can he pick up?"

Jeneil thought for a minute. "Peter, it might be the family. When my mother went to the hospital for a hysterectomy, we fussed over her so much when she got home that she got weaker. So we restricted her visiting hours and tried to duplicate the hospital setting. We were wearing her out with our love. Maybe that's what your family is doing?"

Peter laughed. "It's possible with that bunch, but I'll check on him anyway. It makes sense though, what else could he have picked up so soon except family." He laughed again. Jeneil had gotten up and was tying her robe. "They're even having dinner there today. That's a significant symptom, I think."

Jeneil smiled. "They really love him."

"Honey, Aunt Risa invited us over." Jeneil closed her eyes and breathed deeply. Peter didn't notice. "We can go over after breakfast, okay?"

She turned away. "Well, I hadn't thought about it and right now I have to get breakfast started." He watched her leave and wondered about her lack of interest in the invitation.

Jeneil answered the front door as Peter finished dressing. She walked in with Steve as Peter came from the bedroom.

"Hey, you're home," Steve said, shocked to see Peter.

Peter smiled. "Time off for good behavior."

Steve grinned. "Sprague is in awe of your performance. You are getting yourself some pretty great reviews." He looked at Jeneil. "So what am I doing here? You two should be alone." Peter smiled at her, reminding her that Steve would understand.

"Well, he has to check on his grandfather anyway. Breakfast is almost ready." Jeneil went back to the kitchen.

"I'm sorry, Pete."

Peter shrugged. "Don't be silly. We haven't seen each other long enough lately to hold a conversation. This is a good time." Steve noticed the dining table wasn't set, and went to the buffet drawer for placemats and silverware.

"I heard you were a whiz in OR the other day even after they called you back with only a couple hours of sleep." Peter watched Steve setting the table, surprised that he knew where things were and that he was comfortable doing it. "Hey Pete, did you find a miracle cure?"

"Uh, what? Oh, no." Peter laughed. "Things were so bad they thought anyone who could stand up for more than five minutes without coughing was a whiz. Jeneil gave me her herbs. That's all." Steve grinned and opened the drawer for napkins. Peter watched, still surprised.

Jeneil came from the kitchen. "Oh, thanks, Steve. That's what I was going to do." She returned to the kitchen. Peter noticed they seemed to understand each other and work together. He assumed it was from having dinner together so often, but it was a jolt seeing how close they had become. Jeneil brought out the food and Steve took the tray from her, knowing where the serving dishes were to be placed.

"I'm starved," Steve said, putting the empty tray aside. Steve and Jeneil sat down.

Jeneil looked at Peter. "Aren't you joining us?"

"Yeah," Peter said, and took his place at the table. They finished serving themselves and conversation flowed easily as they ate. Jeneil had learned Steve's likes and dislikes. She had strawberry jam for Steve's biscuits and butter for Peter's, which was his preference, but there was a difference. Peter felt it. Steve and Jeneil seemed closer and even talked about things Peter didn't even know about or hadn't caught up with yet.

Jeneil turned to Peter. "Steve is taking over a lease in Wallace Towers," she explained to help him understand the conversation.

Steve swallowed a bit of egg. "John Radzinick's moving to Fairview 1217."

Peter nodded. "When are you moving?"

Steve shrugged. "I don't know. I still have the dorm for another quarter. I'm sure to get caught in the middle though. There won't be that many checks before the first of March and I'll need furniture." He sighed. "More money. No wonder families hold parties for these guys. They get a pretty good start from them."

Jeneil smiled and patted Steve's hand. "Well, your family's right here. The demo apartment at Fairview 1230 is getting a facelift. All the furniture comes from Blacknell's. It's there for the advertising and they want to update the rooms with newer furniture. They'll sell what's there now at less than a floor display price. It's good quality merchandise. I'll see that you get it. They'll even move it for you."

"Jeneil, that's great," Steve said, overwhelmed.

She smiled. "What's a family for?"

Steve sighed. "Damn, I'd be in a big mess right now without you." He sat back and looked at Peter. "You won't believe the money she's saved me, hidden expenses I never expected. I've just concentrated on getting my education, now I need to learn about life and Jeneil's been there with all the answers." He shook his head. "I don't know how I've gotten this far without you." He squeezed her hand.

Peter watched then smiled, realizing how they had gotten closer. Steve needed help. Jeneil was helping. It was the triad.

Jeneil held up the coffee butler. "Who wants more coffee?"

"I do," Steve answered.

"Me, too," Peter added. "And then we've got to get to my aunt's house." Jeneil poured coffee without answering.

"What's happening there?" Steve asked.

"My grandfather's recuperating there. I'm going to check on him and make sure he hasn't had an overdose of family." Steve laughed as Peter finished his coffee. "They're having a dinner so it's possible he's got too much going on around him. Hey, why don't you come with us? There's always enough food."

Jeneil fidgeted and cleared her throat. "That's not a very good idea." They both looked at her.

"Why not?" Peter asked.

Jeneil put her fork down. "Because the invitation didn't come from your mother, she might not approve. I'm not planning on going."

Peter was stunned as he stared at her. "Jeneil, my mother is really high about you lately."

"Is she?" Jeneil answered politely but disbelieving, feeling his mother's change of heart had only come after he disowned the family. Jeneil saw it as a necessary tactic to get Peter back where his mother and Karen could control his contact with the Chinese girl. There was no way Jeneil wanted to risk running into all three of them and being humiliated again.

Steve looked from one to the other. Gathering his plates, he got up and went to the kitchen. Peter watched Jeneil as she sat staring at her plate. "What is this all about?"

She didn't look up. "Peter, I'm not comfortable being with your family. I'm sorry, but life seems to run more smoothly if I stay away from them."

"So what do I tell them?"

"I don't know. Is the truth too harsh?" She turned her juice glass several times.

"Then I won't stay for dinner."

She looked up quickly. "I think you should."

He stood up. "No, we're there together or not at all."

She sighed. "Life is so cut and dried for you. It's either or neither, maybe or possibly. Your mother will be angry if you don't stay."

"Then come with me."

"No." She remained resolute. "I can't." Tears rolled down her cheeks and she wiped them quickly.

"You're wrong about this. My mother has had a change of heart. She's different since the accident." Jeneil remained silent. Peter shook his head and went to get his jacket. Standing at the door, he looked at her. "What do I tell my grandfather?" Jeneil remained silent. He opened the door and left, slamming it behind him.

She got up and began clearing the table, tears streaming down her cheeks. Steve came to her side and seeing the tears, touched her arm gently. "What is it, kid?"

She covered her face and sobbed, and he slipped his arms around her. Responding to his gentleness, she snuggled to him and cried. "They frighten me."

"But Pete's in the middle now."

She cried harder. "There's no end to it. I can't win no matter what I do."

He rubbed her back gently. "Maybe it's still too new since the accident. Give it a rest for a while then see what surfaces on both sides." He kissed her temple. "Come on, honey. Get hold of it for your own sake." She nodded and began to control her breathing. He held her, puzzled over what was happening. There was a major screw up somewhere, he thought to himself, and she was already paying for it. He put his head against hers and continued to hold her, enjoying her need for him.

*****

Several of the family was already there when Peter arrived. His mother watched him as he took his jacket off. "Where's Jeneil? Risa said she invited her."

Peter looked at her, wondering what to say. "She's not feeling well." He decided to lie. "I won't be staying for dinner."

"Well, she's looked after your grandfather so much this week it's only fair she has her turn." Peter was both shocked and pleased by her attitude.

He nodded. "I'll check on Grandfather."

The old man smiled when Peter walked into the bedroom. Peter pulled a chair to the bed and sat down, studying his grandfather's face. "What's happening? Too much love?" He warmed his stethoscope before checking his grandfather's chest and back. "You're clear but you look very tired."

"I am." The old man sighed. "The hospital was more peaceful."

Peter nodded. "I can take care of that. We'll use Jeneil's prescription and restrict visiting hours and the number of visitors." The talking and laughing in the other room was getting louder, and Peter closed the bedroom door and saw the old man relax as it got quieter. "Are you taking a lot of liquids?" His grandfather nodded. "What about sleep, any trouble?"

"Only when people come in."

Peter smiled. "And I'll bet that's often."

"They mean well."

"I know."

"Where's Jeneil?"

Peter fidgeted with his stethoscope. "She's at home. I told my mother she was sick."

The grandfather watched him steadily. "What's the truth?"

Peter wrestled with the words. "She didn't want to come."

The grandfather studied his grandson. "Peter, what's wrong?"

Peter shrugged. "She didn't say, but with the way she's been treated it's not hard to guess."

The old man was concerned. "Jeneil isn't unforgiving."

"Then I don't know, Grandfather."

"How are things between you?"

Peter looked up from his stethoscope. "Just fine, great."

"Is that the truth?"

"Yes, we're okay. She's been terrific about my hours, and she's been busy helping Steve get his office together and settled into an apartment. Steve Bradley needing help, that's something to see. She's great with him, Grandfather, and she couldn't stand him a few months ago. She changed her attitude for me because he's a close friend of mine. That's why I don't understand her resistance to the family. You're right, it's not like Jeneil."

"Peter, get married."

Peter sighed. "I can't force her."

"Let her know how important it is." Peter looked steadily at the old man wondering again about his genuine concern.

There was a knock on the bedroom door and Ron stuck his head in. "Hey, Dr. Pete, can Sue and I visit Grandfather?"

Peter stood up. "Yes, but don't stay too long and the visit should be a quiet one. He's still recuperating. Get another chair. Sitting on the bed isn't allowed."

Ron laughed. "Yes sir, Dr. Pete. Where's Jeneil?"

"She's sick," the grandfather answered quickly. "Peter, go home to her now." Peter smiled, appreciating his grandfather's handling of Jeneil's absence.

Eight

Peter could hear laughter as he put the key in the apartment door lock. He walked in; Jeneil and Steve were sitting on the sofa. She was knitting; he had a newspaper resting on his lap. They were discussing something he had read and had found funny. Peter went to them. "What are you knitting? Christmas is over."

Steve smiled. "She's feeling like spring. It's a sweater for her." Peter felt his annoyance growing. He resented Steve for knowing how Jeneil was feeling and what she was doing, but he pulled himself together.

"It's a pretty color," he said, and went to hang up his jacket. Steve followed him.

"Hand me my jacket while you're hanging yours."

"You're leaving?"

"Yes."

Jeneil looked up. "You're not staying for dinner?" She was disappointed. "The three of us haven't been together in a long time. The triad's losing its strength." She got up and wrung her hands nervously.

Steve smiled at her. "When Pete's schedule gets back to normal, we'll have a bumming out night." Jeneil nodded and went to the stereo while Steve put on his jacket.

"Pete, I heard that you assisted Maxwell in a nose reconstruction. Word is the job was brilliant. I wish I had been around, I'd have sat in."

Peter smiled. "Maxwell is brilliant. He used a technique I just read about in a medical journal. When I read the article, I couldn't believe the procedure could be performed successfully, but Maxwell almost followed it by the book. I put the article aside. Do you want to read it?

"Yeah, I really would. I'm sorry I missed that job. It'll go down in the annuals of OR. I heard the patient was badly crushed. He fell down concrete stairs at the civic center and hit the wall."

Peter nodded. "If I hadn't read the article, I'd have said give up when I saw the patient. Maxwell came alive on that one. The guy is something else. His mind displaces everything else and he almost wills the operation to work. His steadiness and stamina made me feel like I was just out of med school. I'll get the journal."

Jeneil put a cassette in the stereo and undid her hair, shaking it free. Steve watched her and could see she was getting fragile again. He wondered what was happening. Peter returned with four magazines and sat at the small table. Steve sat opposite him facing Jeneil, concerned as he watched her pace.

"It's in one of these," Peter said, thumbing quickly through the top one. "I put magazines aside when I find an article I want to copy. I haven't gotten around to it lately with my schedule. I've got to learn to be steadier. Maxwell's a rock. I don't think he ever unravels. Nothing affects him." Peter thumbed through the next one. "It's here somewhere."

Peter picked up the third and smiled as he opened it to the article. He looked up at Steve and his heart froze. A wave of panic passed through him, numbing his chest as he saw Steve watching Jeneil. Never in all the time Steve had been around had Peter seen him look at Jeneil like that. His chest tightened and his throat began to hurt. He forced himself to swallow. He looked toward Jeneil; she was swaying to the music, caught up in the rhythm, totally oblivious to them. Peter fought what was surfacing in him, but the words screamed through his mind. Steve was in love with Jeneil. There was a physical attraction between them. It was more than friendship. Peter hated when Danzieg looked at Jeneil like that but Steve's look was worse, much worse, and Peter wanted to hit him. He wanted to grab him and punch his face in. He looked down at the blurred article, forcing himself to control his anger.

"Did you find it?" Steve asked.

"Uh, yeah." Peter breathed deeply.

Steve reached for the magazine. Peter wanted to throw it at him. He wanted to grab his arm and drag him across the table to strangle him. Rage was building, dragging feelings of betrayal with it into Peter's stomach, right to the center of him. Peter forced himself to sit silently. It was an effort that actually hurt his chest muscles.

"Can I take the magazine with me?" Steve asked. "I promise I'll return it tomorrow."

"Sure," Peter answered, surprised his voice worked.

"Thanks, Pete. Did somebody tape it?"

"I'm not sure," Peter answered, not looking at him.

"Well, thanks. I better leave." Steve walked over to Jeneil. She stood up and hugged him. He kissed her cheek. Peter felt a pulse beat in his temples as he watched. Walking to the door, Steve waved to him. "See ya, Pete." Peter nodded as the door closed.

Taking the magazines, he went to the bedroom. He threw them on the desk and paced. He wished he could calm down. He couldn't think straight. Lying across the bed, he sighed then sat up quickly. How far had they gone? He looked at the bed then stood up. Oh shit, his mind screamed as pain passed through his chest. His stomach felt sick.

Jeneil came into the room. "How's your grandfather?"

Peter turned away and puttered at his desk to avoid looking at her. "Worn out, the family's overdoing it."

She laughed. "We did, too. At least it's easy to correct."

Peter held onto the desk for strength as a thought entered his mind. "Jeneil, I think I'll stay at the house to make sure the family eases up on him."

Jeneil was surprised. "You're that concerned?" Peter nodded, and she went to him and put her arms around him. "Okay, I understand. How long will you stay?"

He looked at her and wondered why she wanted to know. He shrugged. "I'm not sure."

She kissed his lips lightly. He was rigid. "Are you all right?" she asked, and he nodded. "When are you going?"

"Right now," he said, and he saw her surprise.

Disappointed, she sighed. "Okay, if you're that worried. I'll get your luggage and help you pack."

She sat on the bed across from him, watching as he put shirts in the brown canvas bag. She sensed something between them, a distance, a wall. The Chinese girl's face flashed before her and her throat tightened. She breathed deeply. "Who was at the house?"

"My mother, Tom, John, my uncle, I'm not too sure. Ron and Sue were there." He continued packing, not looking up.

"Was Karen there?"

"I don't know. I didn't see her."

"Were any friends there or was it all family?"

He looked at her. "If you were so damn interested in who was there, why the hell didn't you go with me?"

His anger had slipped out and Jeneil was shocked by his tone. She tugged at a thread on the quilt to avoid looking at him. The outburst had hurt her since she already felt insecure. He left the room to get things from the bathroom and the uneasiness penetrated Jeneil more deeply. She struggled to not get emotional. Her telephone rang; it was Hollis.

Peter packed his shaving things and toothbrush. Closing the bag, he went to the living room while Jeneil talked on the telephone. He paced as confusion and hurt filled him. Stopping at the potted plant, he stooped down to look at the ceramic figures. Sir Steven the Loyal, my ass, he raged in his mind. You saw it Merlin, didn't you. Get married,

Peter, you told me. His throat tightened. He sighed, looking at Arthur. It shits, man. It eats at your gut. I wish I had read the book. How did you keep sane? How did you keep from killing him? He looked at Lancelot. You're a son of a bitch, you dirty bastard. Why don't I take care of him for you, Arthur? Make him hit the wall and explode into pieces. That'd help, but my good friend isn't that easy to deal with. My good friend, he sneered, there's your place, you asshole. He put Lancelot next to Guinevere. And you, he looked at Guinevere. His chest tightened sending pain clear to his throat. He stood up quickly. Grabbing his jacket and picking up his luggage, he opened the door and left.

Finishing her call, Jeneil went to the living room not believing what she knew had happened. She thought she had heard the door close but had trouble believing Peter would actually leave without saying goodbye. Her heart bordered hysteria as the sound of the door slamming remained inside her. The changes had begun. The echo of the slamming door brought back the cold, penetrating, damp fog. Tears rolled down her cheeks as confusion and hurt surrounded her. The apartment felt different and Jeneil cried softly, struggling with the feeling things would never quite feel the same again.

*****

By the time Peter got to his mother's house, he was feeling mean and ugly. Hearing the door slam, Karen came to see who it was. She stopped at the kitchen door, shocked to see Peter and his luggage. He looked fierce. "What happened to you?"

He was surprised she was there. "Nothing, I'm going to stay here for a while to keep an eye on my grandfather."

"Well, you look furious. What happened? Did the Princess resent you leaving the love nest? Be careful or she'll lock you out if you make her unhappy."

"Go to hell, Karen, and stay out of my way. Is that clear?"

Peter went downstairs to his old bedroom. Everything seemed different. Everything felt changed. Throwing his bag on the bed, he sighed. He had to think. His feelings were choking him. The look on Steve's face refused to leave his mind. He was in love with her. He was crazy about her. Peter thought of his mother and her warnings. Anger rose in him and rage poured through his system. He felt penned up, chained. Putting his jacket on, he left and began running. He wanted to wear himself out and spend the adrenaline that surged through him. He liked running, doing something he didn't have to think or feel. It was cold and he had to concentrate on running and breathing. He ran for blocks until his chest felt too tight and his legs stiffened. He turned to go back but there was no more energy for running so he walked quickly.

By the time he got to the house, he was freezing from having sweated and then walked so far in the bitterly cold wind. The kitchen air felt warm to his face, but his body was shivering. Throwing his jacket on a chair, he went to take a shower. Warm again, he dressed and left the bathroom. The house felt cold after the hot shower. He shivered again and sighed. Exhausted, all he wanted was to feel warm and lie down. Hot coffee steamed from the coffee maker. Ovaltine sounded better, but he poured some coffee. It wasn't quite doing the job. Going to the hutch in the dining room, he opened a bottle of whiskey and poured some into his coffee. He took a good sip and not being used to drinking felt the liquor hit his chest and penetrate his body. Finishing his coffee, he went to his bedroom and tossed the bag on the floor. He got under the covers and felt himself getting warmer. He was tired, very, very tired, mentally and physically, and he wanted to sleep.

*****

Jeneil got up from the chair where she sat wrapped in a quilt for warmth and turned off the cassette tape. It had been hours that she had been sitting there. At first, she had expected Peter to call and apologize for not saying goodbye. She even expected him to be back to say it in person. By the end of the second hour, that was set aside as a fantasy. What had resulted was the thought that Peter couldn't face her. That's why he avoided saying goodbye. Jeneil felt the Chinese girl had been successful in her campaign. Jeneil also had begun to reason that he wasn't saying anything about a separation because he wasn't sure of his feelings for the girl. The thought that he had feelings for the girl at all hurt Jeneil and tears spilled over her cheeks and blinded her.

By the end of the fourth hour, Jeneil forced herself to face a coldly realistic question. What if after this separation he decided he didn't want the other girl? What then? Jeneil tried to examine her feelings and was surprised what she felt was a very dull ache, a deep sadness. She had no idea what it meant. The whole situation was so new. She cried again, not believing she had spent hours thinking of those things. She kept telling herself he was taking care of his grandfather, but the cold fog kept telling her the separation was more serious or he'd have handled it differently. Forcing herself to make dinner, she thought of Mandra. "Keep a routine," she had said, "you'll feel like you have purpose in your life."

Jeneil picked at her food and was glad when it was gone so she could do dishes. The last cup was put away and time faced her again like a black tunnel. She thought of calling his aunt's house to talk to him and check on his grandfather, but the fog had driven a fear into her that he might not be there. She wasn't ready for that reality. She thought to call Steve, but it was getting late. What would she say to him? The separation wasn't even clear in her mind. She stared into the black tunnel of time knowing she had to do something. She decided to knit. It didn't require thought and it relaxed her. As she knitted, she enjoyed the shade of blue and watching the knotted yarn grow into a sweater.

By late evening, she was amazed the sweater had grown so much and she was ready to begin the neckline. Yawning, she put the knitting aside and stood up. The apartment felt empty and cold. She remembered Peter leaving. The finality of it caused her to choke up, and she cried as confusion and hurt surrounded her again. Sighing, she went to the bedroom to change, disgusted that she was back to the very emotions she had begun with hours earlier. None of her reasoning had worked. She was getting angry now, at herself and Peter. He owed her honesty and again the thought that he couldn't be honest because he wasn't sure of his feelings came to her. She cried as anger filled her. Changing into leotards instead of her nightgown, she danced and danced until she couldn't think anymore. She just wanted a break from it.

*****

Peter sat up quickly and looked around. He was in his old room at his mother's house. The old dream still bothered him, but only when he was exhausted. And the dream had changed. It was more violent and he always woke up sweating. He sighed and looked at his watch; it was five in the morning. He couldn't believe he had slept so long. Lying back, he thought of Jeneil and the pain began again. He thought of how close she and Steve had gotten, and realized he had helped by putting them together so much. Anger rose again as he remembered Steve volunteering to stay with Jeneil after the accident and asking permission to take her to dinner.

"Son of a bitch, Steve had marched right across my head with my eyes wide open," Peter said, and exhaled loudly as pain passed through him. He thought about Jeneil. He thought about them together Saturday night and Sunday morning, the pain and hurt nearly killing him. He heard Chang scream, "She's mine." Peter remembered Jeneil staring at him as she told him she would never do that to Chang. The memory of how sincere she had sounded returned to him. It had been a promise. He felt the tightness in his throat loosen and he breathed deeply a couple of times. She couldn't have faked Saturday and Sunday; she couldn't fake. She hadn't even noticed Steve watching her. It was Steve. He was overboard about her. Nothing had happened. Nothing!

"Oh, Jeneil, I'm sorry, baby. What a lousy thing to think." He sighed, breathed and laughed, believing deeply that nothing had happened between them. He knew it. But he was faced with Steve. That was a real problem. There was no mistaking the look on Steve's face; he was in love with her, he wanted her. Peter got angry thinking about it. "Get in line, Steve." Peter laughed then got serious. She was closer to Steve than anybody in her life so far; closer than Franklin, Robert and Dennis. He remembered her saying if she wasn't with him, she'd be closer to Dennis, and he wondered if that could be true of Steve. He sat up on the edge of the bed.

"This is it, Jeneil. It's going to be over. I can't keep going through this because of your lack of experience with men." The hurt returned but it wasn't as sharp. He knew what he had to do. She had to be allowed to know for sure it was him she wanted. He couldn't be married to her if he couldn't be sure. He closed his eyes as he faced the thought of staying away. "I have to do it." He sighed. "I have to, and then it's over. She'll be mine then I can feel free about it." He got up to get ready for work. It was six when he got to the kitchen. He was making toast and pouring some juice when his mother walked in.

"Peter, I heard you walking around. What's wrong? Why are you here? I went to your room last night and you were sound asleep and completely dressed. Karen said you moved in to check on Grandfather?" He nodded as she stared at him, studying his face. "Karen said you looked very angry."

"Karen likes life exciting. She looks for trouble where there isn't any," he said, finishing his juice.

His mother sat down. "Peter, it is strange that you're here. What did Jeneil say?"

"She understands," he insisted.

She shook her head. "You two are not normal. I'm not sure which of you is crazier. You're both so odd."

"That's why we get along so well." He smiled.

She cleaned the crumbs from the table while he put on his jacket. "Peter, it isn't Steve, is it? She hasn't decided that she needs time to decide between you?"

"Don't make a big deal of this. I'm here to be closer to Grandfather. That's it. I don't plan on staying long."

She nodded. "Shall I make a lunch?"

He shook his head. "No, thanks, I'm gone."

She sighed as he left. "Why can't you be like Ron? He leads a quiet life. No trouble, no headaches. Not you, you march through life exploding like fireworks." She prepared coffee for brewing and began the routine of a new day.

*****

Jeneil had gotten up at five to dance. She hadn't slept well and was tired and stiff, and dancing had been a chore. She went to the bathroom hoping a shower would help her mood. Looking in the mirror, she groaned. Her eyes were puffy from crying and she felt ugly. A tear rolled down her cheek. "Oh, stop it, Nebraska," she shouted, wiping the tear. "Pull it together, wimp. Where's the witch hazel?" She opened the medicine cabinet. Pouring witch hazel on two cotton balls, she squeezed the excess. Closing her eyes, she applied them onto her lids. Standing there, holding her head back, she heard Irish.

"What you've got here is a war Amy Farber style. Shape it up; the guy wasn't unhappy Saturday night or Sunday morning. You're at war, why give up your ammunition and hand over the spoils? Look good, girls. Turn his head. Make him mad he's not here. Remind him of what he gave up. Stop the lunches and the cookies. He goes without. Make him miss you."

Jeneil looked in the mirror and laughed. "Irish, you're mean and ugly. Well, Chang's mine. If Peter can't handle it, we don't need him." A serious look came over her face and tears fell. She wiped them and threw the cotton balls at the mirror. "Oh, put a cork in it, Nebraska. We've got work to do. We can't send Jeneil in there looking ugly. Come on, shine and glow." Jeneil turned on the shower, laughing. "Shine and glow? It sounds like a floor wax. Let's get with it girls, positive energy. Positive, hear me?"

Jeneil chose the yellow and black outfit knowing Peter liked it. She applied her makeup carefully to camouflage the puffiness. Adding gold earrings, she stepped back to look at herself. "There, you see," she said. "Who would ever guess that Nebraska is a marshmallow in this outfit?"

"Chloroform her and send Jeneil to work," Irish demanded.

Taking extra vitamin C, Jeneil drank lemon juice and water then packed a lunch. "Watch your energy. Choose your food carefully. It all adds up. What's her name will at least lose sleep over it when we're finished."

By the time Jeneil got to work, positive energy was flowing through her. She was well turned out for a Monday morning and people were looking twice as she headed toward the elevators. She couldn't wait for memo and record delivery time. She got to the fifth floor hoping to run into Peter, spotting him at the nurse's desk.

Jerry Tollman spotted her. "Holy shit, she's glowing. Damn it, her boyfriend's back, I'll just bet."

Peter turned to see who Jerry was talking about and was stunned to see Jeneil. His heart flipped. She looked terrific as she walked over and stood next to him, leafing through her envelopes. Her perfume reached him as she bumped his arm deliberately and excused herself. He was shocked by her boldness.

"Dr. Chang, how's your grandfather doing?"

"He's improving," he stammered.

"Good." She smiled. "Tell him I said hello. The Arts League misses him. Hi, Dr. Tollman," she said to the staring intern. "Barbara, are the weekend discs here?"

"Not all of them. I'll call you. Say, what's gotten into you? You're dazzling."

"Spring, I'm ready for spring. I'm forcing bulbs to bloom. I'll bring you a crocus," she said, as she walked away. Peter watched her. He didn't like it. She was too cheerful. Had she called Steve after he left?

Jeneil got on the elevator and leaned against the wall for support. Seeing Peter nearly ripped her apart. She breathed deeply. The elevator stopped and Steve got on wearing his surgical gown. He whistled. "Wow, kid. Who are you out to kill?"

She smiled. "I'm ready for spring."

He laughed. "You look like you're ready for anything."

"Too much?"

"For lesser men maybe, Pete can take it." He studied her face as she rubbed her temple. Her eyes looked different. "Jeneil, what's wrong?"

She closed her eyes. "Please, don't make me cry."

"Cry? Honey, what's wrong?"

She shook her head. "Peter and I are having problems."

He sighed. "I'm sorry. Still the family?"

"I'm not sure anymore. Are you free tonight?"

"I'm going to a medical association dinner. Besides, you and Pete really need the privacy if you're having trouble."

"He won't be home tonight." She nearly broke down as she said the words.

"I'll skip the dinner," he said, sensing her tension and fragility underneath all the sparkle.

She touched his arm. "No, please. Whenever you're free this week, let me know." The doors opened to her floor and she stepped off.

Steve wrinkled his brow as the doors closed. "Whenever I'm free? Where's Pete? What the hell is happening?"

*****

Peter got to Dr. Sprague's office a few minutes before his appointment. An intern left and Dr. Sprague held his hand out to Peter. Peter stood up and shook it. "Good to see you, Peter," Dr. Sprague said, sitting down. "You've been holding this place together I hear."

Peter sat. "I don't like being a hero. You're expected to be perfect. I can't be."

Dr. Sprague smiled warmly. "Then what brings you in here today if it's not for a trophy?"

Peter tensed. "I'd like to be put on the third for a weekend and have my doubles second and third. I'll take on extra doubles to compensate."

Dr. Sprague studied him closely. "Why?"

"I'd like to keep an eye on my grandfather," Peter answered, feeling warm.

Dr. Sprague continued studying him. "Peter, I'm twenty years older than you and you're not a kid just into med school. Now pass the real answer by me." Peter stared at the floor. "Well, it's obviously very personal," Dr. Sprague commented, and Peter nodded. "Let me ask you; is it more important than your career because that's what you'd be trading. You can't deal with something in your life so that must mean it's more important than your career. Rearranging your career won't go unnoticed, Peter. It's a bad time for that to happen. You've been so steady these past few months. What's wrong with the first shift?" Peter didn't answer. Dr. Sprague sighed. "Peter, this is so important to your career that I'd rather fire her than risk your mistake, and she's good at her job, too."

Peter looked up quickly. "It's only for a weekend and it's not her fault." Peter couldn't believe he said it and he rubbed his forehead.

Dr. Sprague sat back in his chair and looked at Peter closely. "It's only because of your great performance lately that I'm not sending you out of here. You've been very steady. It's remarkable. A schedule change won't be easy. We have you in strategic spots. It'll be a nuisance as well as a headache. You've been through enough lectures on displacing yourself from your personal life, so what's the struggle? Can't you put it aside?"

"Dr. Sprague, if I caught the flu and called in sick you'd have to work around me. I'm not asking that. I'm even offering to take extra hours. That's pretty steady, isn't it?"

"Peter, the flu is out of your control. Not everything else is. That's the issue here. Control in your life."

"Does your life always fit into a neat package?"

The older doctor smiled. "No, but I have to control its effect on me. It's the nature of the work, Peter. I'm sure you can see it without me talking about having other lives in your hands." Peter nodded. "I'm going to refuse your request to show you that you can work it out without compromising your career. If it gets difficult, I want you to come in and talk to me. I admire your stoicism, but sometimes a fresh look is all that's needed to find a solution. I leaned on the arm of my superior while I ironed out life and it's millennia of woes. I've either seen it or lived through it myself. You're too important in what you're doing to mess up now. You belong in surgery, Peter. You do. You've got the right stuff. Let me help keep life simple for you. Will you remember that?"

Peter nodded, stood up and extended his hand. Dr. Sprague stood up and shook it. "Thanks for the reminder."

Dr. Sprague smiled. "Change is part of life. That's why I refused your request, to show you sometimes life takes care of itself if we just wait for things to change. Come in if I'm wrong, Peter. Remember that."

Nine

Pedestrians moved quickly on campus, January bringing with it biting winds and frequent snowstorms. Karen rushed through the door of the Student Union, stomping snow from her feet and shaking it from her hair. Uette rushed in behind her, performing the same ritual. "Karen!" She smiled. "What luck running into you today, we need to talk."

Karen was surprised; she hadn't seen Uette since they went to the hospital together. "Okay, you find the table and I'll get the coffee."

They draped their wet coats on the other two chairs at their table and settled back for a visit. "Karen, I'm getting nowhere with Peter. He's all but told me to leave him alone. Nicely, of course, but he won't even think of looking past Jeneil."

Karen nodded. "Things have happened, Uette. The family loves her now."

"Did she dump Steve?" Uette asked, staring in disbelief.

Karen shrugged. "Pete's mom insulted her at a family wedding and she left so upset that she had a car accident. That started the change. Then, Pete's grandfather went into the hospital and she fussed up a storm over him, making cutesy cards and bringing juice squeezed by her own little hands. So now she's loved by all. Even Pete's mother is keeping quiet about her. Pete was furious after the accident and dumped the family because of it." Karen made a face in disgust. "Jeneil even used that to further her cause. She called Pete's mother and endeared herself by telling the grief stricken woman that she held no blame toward her for the accident. Now, Pete's mom thinks Jeneil's wonderful and responsible for Pete's change of heart so she's grateful." Karen sat back and exhaled. "That girl's a first class actress."

Uette sighed. "Well, he's mine, Karen."

Karen looked at her, puzzled. "Yours?"

"I like him a lot. He hasn't given me a chance at all."

Karen smiled. "Are you serious? You really like him?"

Uette grinned. "Karen, he's so masculine, so sexy. He's steady as a rock. He's beautiful."

Karen raised her eyebrows. "You've flipped over him!"

Uette nodded. "But if I don't see him away from the hospital, he'll never look twice. I'm sandwiched between diseases. Who can look her best? Can you help me get him away from there?"

Karen smiled broadly. "Uette, I think the gods are smiling favorably upon you. He's staying at my house for a few days to keep an eye on his grandfather, and if you ask me, that's not the whole story. I saw him the day he got there. He was furious. I think there's trouble in Loveland, but he's such a clam, we'll never know about it. So this is the week to visit me at my house."

Uette screamed quietly. "I always get what I want, ever since I was a kid! It's really uncanny how things fall into my lap. I love it! Tell me how I deal with this."

Karen thought for a minute. "It's tough. He never has regular hours and he visits his grandfather. Stay close to your phone and I'll try to find out when he'll be there. Doctors are lousy dates, Uette. That's the only thing I admire about Jeneil. She seems to put up with his schedule."

Uette raised an eyebrow. "Oh please, don't you get soft about her, too. She's probably filling in the other hours with Steve. I can't believe it, that mousey girl with those two!"

Karen stopped. "Mousey? How do you know she's mousey?"

Uette looked sheepish. "I stopped at her office to check her out."

Karen laughed. "I love it! I'll bet she doesn't even know."

Uette snickered. "I said I was lost and I even spoke to her. I couldn't believe her type would even turn Peter's head. I wanted to be sure it was her so I pretended she looked like someone I knew and asked if she was related." Karen laughed, enjoying Uette's boldness. "Oh, Karen, you were right about her. She looked tired and drab. She even had this stupid bouquet on her desk, pink carnations. The kind you buy at street vendors. It sat on her desk in a vase that was too short for them. She's pathetic, Karen, a nothing."

"Uette, something sounds wrong here. Jeneil has good taste and a sense of style. I heard she showed up at the wedding looking quite classy."

Uette laughed. "Well, she must have had help choosing the outfit because the girl I saw was tacky and tasteless. And those awful flowers. You were so right about her."

Karen looked puzzled. "Something doesn't make sense." She leaned back and laughed. "But nothing I hear about her ever makes sense. How can she look high class on a clerk's salary anyway? I've seen her in expensive outfits, but I think she bought them to impress the family. She probably emptied her bank account trying to look like a doctor's wife. She doesn't have any family, she's an orphan. She and Steve are right for each other."

Uette fixed her hair. "She's not a doctor's type, I am." She grinned. "Mrs. Peter Chang will sound much better on me anyway. She's not even Chinese."

Karen's face showed shock. "Mrs. Peter Chang! Are you serious?"

Uette stared steadily at Karen. "Get him away from the hospital and I'll have him trying out the name on me."

Karen shook her head. "You really do get what you want, don't you?"

Uette rested her chin on her hand and smiled. "Always, Karen, always. Jeneil had better hold onto Steve. Peter's mine. I like having the best and he's it."

Karen stared, not believing Uette's confidence. It was a different girl who sat across from her. A different girl entirely, but a doctor's wife shouldn't be mousey she reasoned. Mrs. Uette Chang, she thought, it sounded right. She was happy about it, for Peter.

*****

Steve called Jeneil after getting in from dinner. "Is Pete working a double?"

"I don't know," Jeneil answered, twisting a strand of hair around her finger.

"You don't know? Jeneil, what's going on?"

She held back tears. "I don't know that either, Steve."

He was silent for a minute. "Where is he?"

"Staying at his mother's so he can check on his grandfather."

Steve was silent again. "Did you two fight?"

"We hardly spoke after you left yesterday then he packed and left." She couldn't bring herself to tell Steve that Peter never said goodbye.

"Jeneil, this is strange. What's he saying about it? When is he coming back?"

"I don't know, Steve." A tear escaped, and she put her head back and held her breath.

"I'll call him," he said angrily.

"No, Steve. Please don't, I can only wait to see what he's doing."

"Wait for what?" he asked, puzzled.

"I don't know. Until he tells me what's going on I guess."

Steve ran his fingers through his hair. "Jeneil, he hasn't even called?"

"No, I haven't talked to him about it since he left."

Steve sighed. "Honey, this is weird. It's not like Pete at all. I want to talk to him."

"Not about what's happening, please. He has to tell me himself," she said, pacing as she talked.

"Tell you what? What aren't you telling me? You sound like you're waiting for something particular."

She sighed. "I don't know, Steve. I don't know anything really." She began to cry.

"I'm coming over." Her tears had reached him. She needed him. He knew it.

She caught her breath. "No, Steve. You have early surgery. I'll be fine. Talking about it made me weaken. I'll let you go. It's getting late."

"I'm meeting with Sprague and Turner for the papers tomorrow, but I'm free Thursday. If Pete isn't back, I'd like to come over. I want to help. There's something missing in all this. Don't let it go too long, honey. The silence isn't good for either of you."

"Steve, when Peter doesn't want to talk, I can't wrench anything from him." Jeneil sighed.

*****

Peter walked past the row of telephone booths then stopped. He turned and walked toward them. He stopped. He turned and walked away. He missed her and wanted to hear her voice. Then, he remembered Steve looking at her. If they had gotten so close with him around last week, he'd see what happened when he wasn't around. She had to be his completely. Chang couldn't take it any other way. He wasn't made like that. Peter walked back to the floor and the ache spread through his chest.

*****

Steve finished his OR schedule and changed quickly. Taking the magazine he borrowed from Peter, he went to look for him. He realized he hadn't seen Peter at all on Monday. Something was very wrong. He could feel it deep inside of him. He caught sight of Peter getting on the elevator.

"Hey, Pete, hold the elevator," he called, and he watched as Peter got on and the door closed. Steve stopped. He could have sworn he called loud enough for Peter to hear him. He pushed the button to signal another car. Stepping off on the fifth floor, he saw Peter in the viewing room. Peter looked at him when he walked in then went to the x-ray. Steve was puzzled. "Pete, here's the magazine I borrowed."

Taking the x-ray from the clips on the viewer, Peter put them in an envelope and started to walk out. "Put it in my mail slot," he said, and opened the door.

Steve was stunned by Peter's abruptness. "Pete, do you have a minute?"

Peter kept his back to him. "No, there's a case in ER waiting for these."

Steve watched Peter head toward the elevator. He leaned against the table, thinking about what had happened. Something had changed him. Peter was different. What the hell was happening?

Peter steadied himself against the wall of the elevator car. He couldn't believe the anger he felt toward Steve and it scared him. He still wanted to hit Steve, to strangle him. He swallowed hard, wondering what his reaction would be if Jeneil chose Steve. He rubbed his forehead and sighed. He thought about Dr. Sprague and concentrated on calming down. He was a doctor, a good one. He clung to that for steadiness.

Steve tried to see Peter a few times throughout the day, but he had either been in OR or involved in a case. Steve was surprised Peter was so noncommittal about finding time for him. They had always been able to find a minute or two, but Peter had walked past him saying they were short staffed and he was busy. Steve was very concerned. Whatever was wrong was serious and he decided something had to give. Someone had to tell him what was missing in the mess. He looked forward to seeing Jeneil as she seemed the more likely one to talk. He had seen Peter put up that wall before and nothing could be done until he decided to break it down. He sighed, shook his head and went to sign out.

*****

Wednesday night, Jeneil had a dinner meeting scheduled with her lawyer and Dr. Sprague had a few people to his house for a small dinner party for Steve. Dr. Sprague had been surprised when Peter refused to attend and took extra duty so Dan Morietti could go, and he had watched Peter walk away looking tired and drained. He didn't like what he was sensing and he hoped he was wrong.

*****

Karen dialed Uette's number quickly. "Uette, Pete's coming home for a few hours. He has to go back for the third shift but he'll be here at seven."

"Thanks, Karen. Will anyone be home?"

"No, Dad's at the restaurant with my stepmother and John is at a friend's. Mr. Chang is still at his daughter's."

Uette was delighted. "Karen, you have just helped me tip the scales of justice. Will you be home?"

Karen snickered. "No, I thought I'd go to the rally and leave you here with him. Then, you tell him you're waiting for me. He gets very suspicious."

"Thank you, Karen. Thank you."

Karen smiled. "When do you want me to come home?"

"How about ten or ten-thirty?"

Karen was surprised. "That late? Okay, I guess you do need the time. I hope you know what you're doing. Doctor's have an awful schedule, Uette."

"It can't be all bad, Karen. He finds time for Jeneil. I've got to go. Thanks for calling."

Karen held the receiver. "Yeah, but he lives with her," she said to the dial tone.

*****

Peter signed out and went to his car. He felt tired. It seemed like he felt tired a lot lately but today he felt drained. He had run into Jeneil earlier in the day wearing the blue sweater she had made. She had worn a skirt of the same color, a white blouse and pearls. Peter sighed as he remembered. She had looked terrific and everyone had commented on it, and the comment that she was going to make a great wife because of her ability to knit and sew had torn at his gut. Even Jerry Tollman's lovesickness irritated him. Peter missed her. They hadn't talked since Sunday and he had hoped she would have at least called. That fact made him nervous, as well as the fact Steve was trying so hard to talk to him. He gripped the steering wheel tightly. She would have to tell him herself. Peter put his head back on the seat and sighed.

Turning the ignition, Peter pulled away slowly and headed to his grandfather. He always stopped in and checked on him before going home. The visits relaxed him and he needed relaxing badly. He hated the thought of sleeping. The dream always interrupted his sleep now and he had started taking a shot of whiskey to knock him out before bed. It seemed to work and he had it figured like a prescription. At least he slept until early morning when the liquor wore off and the dream startled him awake. He never felt rested though. He thought of the dream he had this morning and shivered. Usually he broke away from the tubes and ran toward Reed, the realism of grabbing Reed's throat and pressing his thumbs against his windpipe making him wake up sick. In this morning's dream, he had lunged at Reed and grabbed his throat, feeling himself press harder and harder. He had awakened screaming when he had looked at Reed's face and seen Steve's instead.

Peter parked his car in front of his aunt's house and sighed, rubbing his face. He felt hot. Opening the car door, he breathed the cold air, welcoming the cleansing feeling it gave him. He and Jeneil always talked about the dream and it usually helped, but he was having it more frequently since leaving. He ran a few feet to the door to leave the thoughts behind.

Peter went to the bedroom. He laughed as he saw his grandfather with a small walkman. The grandfather took the headphones off when he saw Peter. "What, are you into rock?"

The old man laughed. "Jeneil sent two cassettes of books to keep me busy. It's a wonderful idea. I'm too tired to read, but I love listening to the stories. It relaxes me. They came in the mail yesterday." Peter was surprised to hear that. His grandfather looked at him. "Peter, are you getting sick? You don't look well at all."

Peter shook his head. "I'm tired, my schedule is tight. I have to go back for the third tonight."

"Then why aren't you home with Jeneil instead of here?"

Peter moved uneasily in his seat. He sighed. "Grandfather, I'm staying at my mother's."

"What is it, Peter?" Peter sat forward and rested his elbows on his legs. The grandfather watched, growing more concerned. "Peter, what happened?"

"Nothing really, well yeah, I guess it is something. My mother was right. Steve, uh, Steve," he swallowed, "Steve's in love with Jeneil."

His grandfather looked panicked. "How did you find out?"

Peter looked up at the ceiling. "I saw him watching her Sunday. It was written all over him." He sighed and rubbed his face.

"Why are you staying at your mother's?" The old man tensed, afraid to hear the answer.

Peter fidgeted. "Steve and Jeneil are really close, Grandfather. I want her to be sure she wants me, not him. She's very… very inexperienced. She's hardly dated at all."

The grandfather pressed his head deep into his pillow and groaned. "Oh my goodness, Peter, the Songbird is yours. She's yours. Can't you see that? Look at her. What did she say about this?"

"I haven't talked to her. She thinks I left to be here with you."

The grandfather was annoyed. "Peter, you're stupid. You left the Songbird unprotected." He began to cough.

"Calm down, Grandfather. If Songbirds are loyal, she'll be mine," Peter said, getting his grandfather some water.

The old man shook his head. "You don't understand. You don't listen. You don't leave a Songbird to chance. They're too delicate and fragile." The old man sighed. "Peter, Jeneil is yours. She doesn't see past that. Her commitment to you is very deep. She takes abuse from your family for you. She looks after me because she sees me as the patriarch and she's committed to family, family as the Chinese know it. Oh, Peter, of all the family not one thought to keep fresh flowers before your grandmother's picture like I do. Jeneil has sent a spring bouquet three times a week since I caught cold and couldn't get out. She's worked herself into the family for you. She's yours." He shook his head. "You need a lot of training to catch up to her. Go home, Peter. Go home before there's serious damage. Do you understand? Go home."

Peter was surprised to hear his grandfather's words. Suddenly his actions since Sunday felt very stupid.

"Peter, it doesn't matter if Steve loves Jeneil. She's yours and even he must know that because he hasn't told Jeneil about his love for her. Does she know about it?"

Peter shook his head. His grandfather had pointed out a fact he hadn't seen. Steve hadn't made a move toward Jeneil. Peter exhaled, feeling very stupid. He couldn't get past his shock and anger, and it had blinded him. Chang screamed in his mind, "Peter's too soft, too far from the streets." Ki had taught them about the danger of anger. Peter was guilty of losing it. "Oh shit!" he murmured and got up. "I don't deserve her." He sighed. "I'm the one not ready for marriage, not her."

"Peter, go home," the grandfather insisted. "I'm fine."

Peter nodded. "I'll pack and go home after third shift tonight." He got his jacket and left the bedroom. Stopping at the telephone in the kitchen, he dialed Jeneil. There was no answer. He hung up and went to his car.

As Peter walked into his mother's house, he realized he felt better. He was tired, but he felt better. He dialed Jeneil again. There was still no answer. He could tell he wouldn't get any sleep at the rate he was going. His mind was revving up about their situation. He went to the hutch and poured only two-thirds the amount of liquor into the glass and drank it fast. He was facing a double shift and needed sleep. He went to the telephone again; still no answer. He let it ring longer. The liquor began to hit him when there was a knock at the kitchen door. He opened it and Uette stood there, bundled against the cold.

"Is Karen home?" she asked, smiling.

"I don't know. Come in from the cold. I'll call her." He went to Karen's room and returned. "She's not here. Was she expecting you?"

"Yes, I'm sure she'll be here soon. Can I wait?"

Peter shrugged. "Sure. Take off your coat. The living room is probably more comfortable." He could feel his head getting numb.

"Can you sit and talk for a few minutes?" She flashed her eyes at him.

Peter sighed. "Uette, I'm exhausted and I'm facing a double. I've got to get some rest. I'm on duty again at eleven so I'll have to be rude and leave you alone to wait for Karen. Make yourself comfortable. There's hot coffee in the kitchen, help yourself, but I've got to get to bed. I'm done in." He turned and went downstairs.

Uette watched him leave and angrily folded her arms as she heard a door close. She paced. "This is not working. What do I have to do to get him to notice me?" she asked herself, going to get some coffee.

Peter got to his bedroom and felt his body getting weaker. He drank the liquor fast but he didn't mind, he needed to get to sleep and he could feel himself beginning to go out. He got as far as his underclothes then just piled into bed. Glad to be lying down and ready for a good rest, he could feel himself spin into the pillow and he was gone.

*****

Jeneil walked up the stairs and unlocked the apartment door quickly. Going to the answering machine to check for calls, she stomped her foot realizing she hadn't turned it on. "Oh, Peter, did you call? When will this end?" She took a deep breath, proud she had fought the tears, but the disappointment was painful. The empty apartment felt like a tomb. Some of his things were still there, but she hadn't seen him for three days except in passing at the hospital. Even that was rarer since Sunday. She sighed, her nerves rattled from the hours of waiting, wondering and not knowing. She got ready for bed. The telephone rang and she raced to answer it.

"Jeneil, it's Steve."

She fought disappointment and choked up. "Steve, how was the dinner party?"

"Overwhelming, the Sprague's treated me like a son. It totally shocked me; after all they've done for me, I didn't expect a thing, even the party, but he gave me a check to help get me started."

Jeneil could tell Steve was deeply moved. "They're terrific people," she said, sniffing.

"They sure are," Steve agreed, and then paused. "Jeneil, is Pete home?"

"No, he isn't." She had trouble saying it.

"Have you heard from him?"

"No, I haven't." That was even harder to say.

Steve exhaled loudly. "Honey, I'm really worried. Something is wrong. I can't get him to stay long enough to talk to me. I know he's avoiding me, Jeneil, but I don't know why."

Jeneil's heart sank as she heard Steve's observation. Peter couldn't face Steve either. That cemented her fears and she began to cry.

Steve held the receiver tighter. "Jeneil, what the hell is happening? What am I missing?"

She sighed and cleared her throat. "Steve, I have a guess, that's all, but each day my guess becomes more real."

"What is it?"

"Do you know anything about a Chinese girl who has been to the hospital to see Peter?"

"Uette?" Steve asked, puzzled.

Jeneil held her breath. She finally had a name. She collected her thoughts. "I guess that's her name. I don't know her, but I've heard she's interested in Peter. She's been to the hospital several times to see him."

"So what?" Steve answered, and then caught the meaning. "Jeneil," he laughed, "you don't honestly believe Pete's interested in her, do you?"

"You obviously know more than I do. I didn't even know her name, but I know she's serious about Peter. If it's not her then explain why he left here without saying goodbye, why I haven't heard from him, and why he can't face you either." The evidence rushed at her and she cried, overwhelmed by too many facts and fears.

Steve smiled. "Oh, baby, you're a wreck over her?"

"Then what is it, Steve, what?" Jeneil asked through tears.

"I don't know, but damn it, I'm going to find out. This is crazy. I'm sorry, Jeneil, but I'm not staying out of it anymore. He'll talk to me tomorrow or I'll hit him. I'm sick of him passing me off and you can't keep living like this, you're a wreck. What's the matter with him? I'm damn angry now. If I didn't have surgery in the morning, I'd go to the hospital now and deal with it. I know he's on third and first, but I'll pin him down tomorrow, honey. I promise. This will be over tomorrow."

Jeneil sighed. Steve's take charge attitude calmed her. She wanted it over and she began to see that she should have insisted on an explanation. Peter owed her one. She had to put aside her fear of the truth and face it.

"Baby, get a good rest tonight. This is settled. Consider it over."

She sighed. "Thanks, Steve. Your attitude alone has opened my eyes. He owes me an explanation."

"Of course he does. I know he's dog tired from his hours and the stress, and maybe he's not thinking clearly, but this isn't right either. Get some rest, kid. I mean it."

"I will." She sighed and sat on the bed, wishing she could feel positive about what was going to happen. This change was still a cold, penetrating, ominous fog.

Ten

Steve woke up angry the next morning. It was only four-thirty, but he was ready to see Peter. The memory of Jeneil crying stayed with him as he showered and dressed. What the hell was Peter doing to her? He drank some juice then headed to the hospital. He checked the fifth floor. Peter was in surgery. Steve went down to the OR to catch Peter when he came out before his own surgical schedule began. He waited in the scrub room. Some of the surgical team came out of OR before taking the patient to Recovery. Peter came out removing his mask and stopped abruptly when he saw Steve.

"I want to talk to you," Steve said sharply, standing up.

Peter wondered about Steve's tone and looked around. Several doctors were scrubbing and had looked up. "Not here," Peter said, walking past Steve.

Steve grabbed his arm. "Wait a minute, buddy. You're not passing this off. I want to talk to you now."

Peter was shocked. The surgical team was watching, as well as the doctors scrubbing. Steve's hostility was obvious. "Hey, Steve," Peter said, taking Steve's hand off his arm.

Steve shoved him toward the door. "Then outside now."

"Get off my back," Peter said, getting heated.

"After we talk," Steve snapped.

Dr. Sprague rushed over to them. "What are you two doing?" He held back his anger, looking around at the people watching, lowering his voice to a whisper. "Where the hell do you think you are? Both of you, outside."

The three of them walked out into the corridor. Dr. Sprague looked from one to the other and sighed. "I can't believe this. I expect this from new med students who have worked their first double. Even then it's rare. I want an explanation. What's happening here?"

"Nothing," Peter answered glumly.

Dr. Sprague took a deep breath. "Chang, tell me to butt out and mind my own business, at least that's honest, but don't insult my intelligence by saying nothing when I saw you two ready to have it out in the middle of OR. I want you in my office at nine." He looked at Steve. "And you take a walk. You're early for surgery, aren't you? I don't want you in there until you get it together. Can I trust your judgment? Be prepared to assist. There's no way you're driving the truck today. Shit, Bradley. Are you looking to blow it all now?" Dr. Sprague's face was red with anger.

"I need to talk to Pete," Steve said quietly.

Dr. Sprague nodded. "So I heard. Well, take a walk and talk to him later when you're not so likely to use your hands."

"I'm calm," Steve said.

Dr. Sprague glared at him. "You heard my decision. It wasn't open for discussion. I never thought you two would need a refresher course in self-control. Both of you were always too cool. I had hoped you would learn to feel a little, so you've shown me that you have. Now learn to balance it." He snapped his mask from around his neck. "I can't wait to hear what comes of this outburst." He held the door open for Peter.

Peter looked at Steve and sighed. "Steve, tonight at the dorm, I'm out at six."

Dr. Sprague closed the door. "Oh shit, that sounds like an invitation to rumble."

"I didn't see it that way," Steve said calmly.

"I didn't mean it that way," Peter added.

Dr. Sprague ran his hand across his face. "Why wasn't I born smart like my brother and buy a shoe store. He has decent hours, sensible employees, and people always need shoes. But I'm not that smart. I had a dream that I could help humanity and improve mankind's lot in life. So what's my job? I'm refereeing two of my best surgeons. Geez, I wonder if Bobby will give me a job counting shoelaces." He walked into the scrub room.

Peter finished in OR and headed for some coffee. He was numb. It was hard to believe he'd finished first shift. The night seemed hours away too long and he knew the day was going to be worse. He wasn't tired, but tense and wondered if he'd ever not be tense again. Standing at the window on the fifth floor, he waited for the familiar car to drive in. He looked at his watch. Looking up, he spotted it and felt the excitement in his chest. She got out of the car and walked quickly toward the building. He sighed. "Baby, we've got to talk." He choked up. "We've got a major bummer here." He closed his eyes and leaned against the wall, slowly drinking his coffee.

*****

Peter paced as he waited to see Dr. Sprague. The secretary called him and Peter settled himself in the chair before a watchful Dr. Sprague. "Well Peter, life sure changes quickly. Monday I was going to give you a trophy, today you're in here to get your butt kicked."

"That's why I don't like being a hero. Mistakes seem twice as bad when your halo falls."

The older doctor grinned. "Actually Peter, I'm going to kick your butt if you don't open up and tell me what's happening. There's a mess brewing and I hate messes, so sit back and share the burden with me." Dr. Sprague looked at Peter, who sat silently. "Okay, I'll start. You and Steve are having trouble dividing one girl." Peter fidgeted. "I'm not hearing any words, Peter."

Peter put his head back. "I'm handling it."

Dr. Sprague leaned forward. "Like hell you are. It didn't look that way this morning."

"That got ahead of me."

"Because you're not handling it. I've already talked to Steve. He doesn't know what you're uptight about. Who's holding all the pieces of the puzzle? The girl?"

"No, it's not her fault!" Peter answered quickly.

Dr. Sprague sighed. "So you keep telling me and yet two good surgeons are ready to beat each other in front of their colleagues. High school principals handle problems like this, not the Chief of Surgery. I told you to come in if life got complicated."

"It hasn't."

Dr. Sprague shook his head. "I hate hospital romances. They screw things up faster than computers. So how do we handle this? Maybe you don't think the ice is thin, but I hear it cracking. I've seen these situations before. There always has to become two for peace." Peter looked at him, not sure what he meant. "Something's got to give, Peter. What's it going to be?"

"What do you mean?"

"How do we make three into two here?"

Peter sat up straight. "Dr. Sprague, you once said that life will change things. Why can't we wait for life to solve this?"

The older doctor rubbed his eyes with his hand. "Chang, you are one tough nut to crack. You feed me my own advice." He sighed. "Okay, here it is. I want this settled. It's not and I'm staying in until it is. I represent the hospital and my decision is based on that fact. Now, I want to say this again, sometimes life gets too tough alone. We know that. We plan for it and we're here to help. I mean that sincerely. You're special, Peter. You're good and we like turning out good surgeons. I'm here to help. Understand?" Peter nodded. "Okay, if I can't help you then you'd better get out there and help others. But Peter, remember you can't help others too well if you can't learn to help yourself."

Peter shrugged. "No complaints so far. I lost control this morning. I'm okay now."

Dr. Sprague smiled. "Steve told me he started it. He said he woke up mean and ugly, and pushed too hard. It all came out wrong."

"I still let him rattle me. That's my fault."

Dr. Sprague smiled. "Okay, I'll always be here for you. I mean that."

Peter stood up. "Thanks," he said, and shook Dr. Sprague's hand, turned and walked out.

Dr. Sprague leaned back in his chair. "Peter, you must have been one hell of a street fighter. You're made of steel and that's what's going to make you one damn good surgeon, too. You've done wonders tempering the steel these past few months." He shook his head. "What is that quiet girl in Records really like that those two were willing to do each other in? And they both say the same thing; it's not her fault. Is she so helpless and fragile? So who's got the answer? One doesn't know and the other won't talk." He sighed. "And to think I could have been worrying about what color shoes would be in fashion this summer." He smiled. "And going stark raving mad counting shoelaces."

*****

Jeneil got home and put her things away. The day hadn't gone at all like she had hoped. She had planned on telling Peter she needed an explanation. On top of that, Steve had been nowhere to be found to settle the awful gossip about the two of them having a fight. It had frightened her, remembering Steve's promise to confront Peter. She breathed in deeply. It was just gossip. What would they have fought about? She heard Steve pushed Peter. She shook her head. The gossips had all kinds of explanations; Steve was upset about Peter's treatment of his girl, the beautiful Chinese girl was turning Peter's head and Steve was protecting Peter's girl. Jeneil wondered just how that one got started, but it was so close to why Steve was going to talk to Peter that she wondered how much had been said in front of witnesses. It was just crazy gossip. She was sure it had started because Steve had announced that his girl wouldn't accept the engagement ring and he couldn't take it anymore so they had ended things.

Jeneil felt surrounded by change; everything was different. Looking for something familiar to do, she went to the kitchen for her watering can. She poured water amongst the elves and realized how little attention she had given to that hobby lately. They didn't seem to mind. She smiled and went to the kitchen, returning with a refill. Going to the Camelot plant, she knelt down and realized the figurines had been rearranged. "That's odd," she said out loud. "Arthur, why is your back turned to Guinevere? Are you angry at her?" She smiled and fixed him, and then noticed Lancelot near Guinevere. She studied him. "What are you doing there? You belong with Arthur. No wonder he was angry. He got jealous!" She smiled, and taking her hand off Lancelot, she looked at all three and began to wonder. "Who changed you around? I didn't. It was Peter." She stared at the figurines. "Arthur was jealous and angry so he turned his back on them."

Jeneil covered her mouth and shook her head. "It can't be. There's no reason to be." She thought of her and Steve dancing. "Could it be?" She put the figurines back the way she had found them and looked at them again. "That's crazy. Oh, Peter, you couldn't. Why would you think that? How could you think that?" She stood up slowly and remembered the Sunday he left; she stayed with Steve instead of going with Peter to see his family. "Oh my gosh!" Turning, she went to the telephone and dialed, covering the mouthpiece. "Dr. Chang, please." Her heart beat rapidly and she fought to stay calm.

"This is Dr. Chang." His voice went through her, almost shaking her inside out as she uncovered the mouthpiece. "Hello," he said. "Hello."

"Peter." Her voice was barely audible from shaking.

"Jeneil?" he asked softly.

"Yes." She heard him sigh. At least he didn't hang up. "Peter, you've got to come home. We need to talk."

He was silent for a moment. "Okay, I'll be there tonight."

"Thank you, Peter." Her voice felt formal, but it was all she could say without losing control.

"Okay, I'll be there around seven-thirty."

Jeneil went back to Camelot and stared at the figurines. Her temples hurt from tension. Feelings raced through her, all sorts of feelings, opposite feelings. The turmoil made her temples throb and she went to the medicine cabinet for headache tablets.

*****

Peter parked his car in the dorm parking lot and noticed how strange the place felt to him. Living with Jeneil felt like home. He sighed and knocked on the door.

"What's with the knocking, this place is half yours, remember," Steve said, opening the door and looking Peter over as he stepped inside. "You look like hell. Sit before you drop. Want some coffee?"

Peter nodded and went to the kitchenette table. "Thanks for easing it with Dr. Sprague."

Steve poured two cups and joined him. "It was my fault. Are you hungry?" Peter shook his head. Steve watched him, thinking something was very wrong. "Pete, what's happening to you?"

Peter leaned back against the wall. "I think I've gotten myself into a mess of shit."

Steve wrinkled his eyebrows with concern. "What did you do?"

"Nothing, I swear." He sighed. "Remember Uette, the girl with Karen?" Steve nodded. Peter stirred his coffee. "She's been a real pain in the ass. She pops up everywhere. A few days ago at the hospital, she made a pitch. I told her I wasn't interested and I thought that was it. Last night, she came to the house to see Karen. I had three hours to sleep so I took a shot of bourbon before she got there. I left her in the living room and went to bed and was out cold." He sighed and rubbed his forehead. "My mother came home early to make sure I was awake. I woke up and Uette was in bed with me, absolutely naked."

Steve's eyes widened as he tried to absorb what he had just heard. "Set up?"

"From a Wong girl? Make a judge believe it." Peter sighed again and shook his head sadly. "You should have heard my mother scream and who could blame her? I'm in her house in bed with a girl and not just any girl, a Wong. My mother was so upset I swear she'd testify against me if the girl accused me of rape." He leaned forward.

"What's the girl saying, Pete? How does she explain being there?"

Peter sneered. "I gave her a drink to get warm. That's all she remembers."

"You didn't?"

Peter sat up, annoyed. "Steve, I've smelled her bait for weeks. I couldn't get away from her fast enough. I told her to get herself some coffee and I went to bed."

"Holy shit," Steve said, rubbing his face, "you're right. You've got yourself in a mess of shit, two completely different stories." He shook his head. "Are you ready for the other shoe to drop?" Peter stared at him, wondering. "Jeneil thought you'd left her for Uette. She's known about her from the hospital gossip."

Peter closed his eyes. "Oh shit!"

Steve got up and paced. "Pete, why the hell did you leave anyway? Was it really to take care of your grandfather?" Peter nodded, looking down at the floor. He couldn't tell Steve what he had thought. Steve walked back and forth with his hands in his pockets then stopped. "Okay, let's look at what we've got here. You're innocent. She's not. What's her game? Why do this?"

Peter took a long sip of coffee. "Steve, what if she's pregnant and the guy won't marry her so she holds me up for the crime?"

"Pete, would any guy not marry her? She's a knockout whose father's got money."

Peter sighed. "Shit, that's right. Then what? Why do it?"

Steve sat down. "Maybe she got the drink herself and wandered down to your bed. Maybe that's all there is to it."

Peter looked at Steve. "I don't trust it, Steve. She strikes me as not real, like she's playing a role. She reminds me of a snake. I've known two other girls who I felt like that about. They were both groupies for the Dragons, real scum, paid spies against their own kind."

"Pete, the girl is hardly at that level."

"I'm only saying what I feel inside, what my blood is saying."

"Did anything happen?"

Peter shook his head. "I was too tired to even stand up. The Chinese Stud was gossip, too. Well, not when I was younger, but with my hours all I was capable of last night was sleep, and I know, trust me, I never touched her."

"Then my guess is that it wasn't any more than that. She drank too much and ended up in your bed. What can you do anyway? It's her move now, isn't it?" Steve looked at Peter. "Are you going to tell Jeneil?"

Peter felt pain shoot through him. He nodded. "I promised myself I'd never keep anything from her again. After telling her about my father, I figured what could be worse?" He sneered. "This. This is worse."

"Well, you didn't sleep with her."

Peter sighed. "I know that but will Jeneil believe it? Especially thinking that's where I was?" He stood up and paced. "Shit, when I screw up its never small stuff. And my mother, you should've seen the look on her face. I felt like garbage, Steve. I honestly felt filthy and I didn't do anything. She's furious. Oh man, and when my grandfather hears it. I can't believe it, just when I'm beginning to get myself cleaned up in the family."

Steve sighed. "Yeah, I know, life pushes the button marked 'SHIT.' I'm sorry, Pete. I hope things go okay with you and Jeneil." Peter looked at him and could tell he meant it. Steve was a good friend and Peter felt lower for having thought Steve had betrayed him.

*****

Peter thought of how things had changed since he had last been to the apartment. In just three short days he had managed to accuse his girl and his best friend of betrayal, and let himself get so angry he had left himself wide open to Uette's nonsense. That hurt the most and it was the one thing he dreaded telling Jeneil, but he would tell her. One thing he'd learned from being with her was he liked life honest and simple. Life ran smoothly that way and he saw the difference. The minute he hid his feelings about her and Steve life had gotten complicated. The result was the chaos that surrounded him now. He had no idea how he would tell her or how she would deal with it. He sighed as he unlocked the apartment door and stepped inside. Of all the places he'd been the past few days, this was home. It felt good being back and he leaned against the door, enjoying the warm feeling of being home. He looked up as Jeneil came from the bedroom, neither of them speaking.

She wrung her hands nervously. "Peter, we really need to talk. I mean really talk." She was getting emotional, and she walked to the Camelot plant and stopped. "Peter, explain this to me." She pointed to the rearranged figurines.

"Jeneil." He went to touch her arm but she moved away.

"No, I want you to explain that, Peter." She looked at him with tears in her eyes. "I want to hear you tell me that you thought I was like Guinevere." She wiped her tears. Her hurt was killing him and he looked at the floor, vowing to never allow anger to lead him again. "Tell me, Peter," she cried softly.

"Jeneil, listen. When I saw how Steve felt about you I felt betrayed. I'm sorry."

She stopped crying and stared at him. "What do you mean, how Steve feels about me?"

He sighed and reminded himself that he wouldn't be going through this if he hadn't gotten angry. "Jeneil, Steve's in love with you."

Tears rolled down her cheeks again. "You've let your mother's irrational raging ruin a good friendship? Steve has been nothing but a good friend to both of us, the best. He doesn't deserve her accusations. It's ridiculous. Couldn't you even think to defend us? I'm not even Steve's type. Just a few months ago we were all but enemies." Peter could see she had no idea Steve loved her and was touched by her innocence. She didn't see it because she didn't want it. Her mind didn't work that way. Steve was a friend and that was as far as it went for her. She turned away. "I can't believe you'd think that about me. Where is our relationship? Our life? Have we built anything between us at all? We don't have trust or you wouldn't think that about me. And I thought you had left me for Uette."

"Baby, it's just that you're so inexperienced. I need to know that I'm what you really want. Not someone else. I don't want any doubts."

She turned to face him. "Tell me how I do that, Peter? How do I prove you are what I really want?" She went to him. "I know how, Peter. I just realized it for the first time." She touched his face. "Let's get married."

Peter felt his heart stop and wondered how she would react to the incident with Uette. He had to tell her. He took her hand and kissed it gently. His throat felt tight. Pulling her to him, he kissed her forehead.

"Jeneil, I have to talk to you." He went to the sofa and dropped onto it, discouraged. She looked at him, wondering what was wrong, thinking it was an odd reaction to the idea of marriage. Sitting beside him, she watched him steadily. He looked at her and took her hand. "Awhile ago, Karen brought Uette Wong to the hospital and introduced us. She kept coming back; I guess she thought I was available. I told her about us and that I wasn't interested in anyone else." Jeneil's eyes filled with tears. "Last night, she stopped by my mother's looking for Karen. I was home alone. Lately, I've been having trouble sleeping so I took a shot of bourbon before I went to bed. I left Uette in the living room."

Peter stopped and let go of her hand. Sitting forward, he leaned on his legs and rubbed his chin. "Jeneil, my mother came to wake me and Uette was in bed with me." Jeneil stared at him, completely numbed by what he had said and she felt herself begin to shake. Her hands felt cold and she rubbed them together, staring down at them. Tears dropped onto her thumb and she watched them spill over her skin. Peter leaned back against the sofa and sighed. "Jeneil, I was shocked to see her there. The last I saw her, she was in the living room waiting for Karen."

Jeneil stood up and paced. Removing her hairpins, she shook her hair loose and rubbed her temples. The tears wouldn't stop and she felt sick from shaking so much inside. Rushing to the bathroom, she lost what little was in her stomach. She bathed her face with cold water and brushed her teeth, hoping the peppermint flavor would settle her queasiness. Sips of water didn't help. She felt weak and went to the bedroom and sat on the bed, breathing carefully for control. Peter walked in and leaned against the bedpost.

"Jeneil, tell me what you're feeling," he said quietly. "I have to know."

"I'm confused," she sobbed, and curled up on the bed. He sat down and rubbed her arm gently. Slipping behind her, he put his arm around her. The pain in his throat was intense and he had trouble swallowing. She was hurt because of him and the guilt was killing him. He kissed her shoulder and she began to quiet down. "Peter, were you drunk?"

"No, I was asleep, out from exhaustion and the shot I swallowed too fast. I wasn't drunk and nothing happened. I didn't touch her."

She turned and looked up, wanting to believe him. "Nothing happened?"

"Nothing," he repeated. "I don't understand how she got there."

"Did she tell you?" She sniffled.

He breathed deeply. "She said the last thing she remembered was that I gave her a drink to warm her up." Jeneil raised her eyebrows, surprised. Peter responded quickly. "Honey, I told her there was coffee in the kitchen and I went to bed. I had my shot before she even got there and it started to hit me while I was talking to her. All I wanted to do was sleep. I left her in the living room."

"Then if she's lying, you're in trouble, Peter."

He kissed her forehead. "Am I in trouble with you? That's all that matters to me right now. What happens to us? I want you to believe me and I know my story sounds so damn weak." She was quiet as she watched him. "Jeneil, I love you. I never thought I'd be capable of feeling this much love for anyone. Seeing the hurt I've caused you has taught me a lesson about anger. I was hurt and angry when I thought about Steve and you. When I really thought about it, I knew you wouldn't do that. My anger affected my reasoning and it's caused all this." He sighed. "I always did mess up big when I blundered."

"Did you and Steve fight in the OR?"

"No, we lost more control than we should have, we got loud, but it wasn't a fight."

"Was it about me?"

"Yeah, he didn't like how I was handling this. He was concerned for you."

Jeneil sighed. "Did you tell him why you had left here?"

Peter shook his head. "No, I had come to my senses by then. I went to the dorm before I came here. Jeneil, what happens to us?"

She touched his cheek. "I believe you. I don't trust her, Peter. I've seen her and I don't trust her. I'm very frightened right now. You're so vulnerable, but I believe you."

Peter put his head next to hers and sighed. "Baby, I don't know what to say. Why do you believe me? Why?"

She thought for a minute. "Because I know Chang, I guess."

He smiled and touched his lips to hers lightly, barely kissing her. She felt so soft and warm. He could hear Chang whisper, *she's mine.* "I love you, Jeneil."

She nodded and met his lips. He was home now. She was there and he was relieved she believed him. She seemed fragile and he put his arm around her gently. His grandfather was right, Songbirds needed protecting and looking after, which was fine with him. That job had become a pleasure. He laid next to her, holding her hand in his. Her trust in him had left him speechless and he now understood what his grandfather meant. She was deeply committed to him and that made him love her more. Nobody would ever make him doubt himself with her again. Chang was right, she was his. He felt them getting closer; barriers and anger and hurt were dissolving. He sighed relieved the damage hadn't been more serious. He kissed her hand.

"Jeneil, did you mean it about getting married?"

She nodded. "I know it's not the right time but I want to get married now. Something about all this has me frightened. I don't want to lose you." She wiped her tears and he touched her cheek, wiping away one she had missed.

"Baby, you will never lose me, never. From the first time I kissed you, I could feel the difference and I knew you were going to change my life. After I made love to you the first time, I knew it was over for me. Looking back at that moment, I think I was already in love with you. I'll always be in love with you, Jeneil. It's like breathing to me."

Jeneil snuggled to him and kissed him passionately. His words had erased all her insecurities. She loved him deeply and she wanted him to know that. This was one of those times when things should be physical. When a higher level of communication failed and superlative was damaged, physical was a basic, a beginning, the starting point of renewal. She promised herself someday she'd learn why, but at the moment why didn't seem to matter, she and Peter did.

*****

Steve found Peter in the viewing room reading x-rays. Opening the door, he walked in slowly, concerned about what he might be dealing with. "Hey, Pete, I expected you at the dorms last night. Are you still at your mother's?"

Peter shook his head. "Steve, Jeneil believed me. It got a little tight, but it was fine, we're fine. We're getting married when the licenses and blood tests are completed."

Steve sat on the table completely shocked. "I can't believe it!" He had trouble breathing for a minute. "I mean that's great, but I can't believe it. I mean damn, she's got to be one of the most incredible women ever." He held his chest and laughed lightly. "Boy, that's not what I expected to hear. I guess she did believe you. Married? Wow!" He got up and paced. Peter saw Steve's struggle and he looked down at the floor, feeling bad. For a second, he had forgotten Steve's love for Jeneil. Steve came over to him, smiling. "That's really great, Pete. Am I going to be the best man?"

Peter looked up, surprised. "You want to be?"

"Of course, unless you wanted someone else."

Peter studied him. "No, you've been a great friend," he said quietly, impressed with how Steve was handling the news.

"Then let me know when. I've got to get back to OR." Steve opened the door. "I'm glad the situation worked out for you, Pete." Peter nodded and watched Steve close the door.

Steve stopped at the water cooler and took several sips of water. He rested his hand against his arm. His mind was whirling with thoughts and feelings. What had he expected? He knew it would happen someday. She believed Peter. She actually believed him. So did he, but he thought women were touchy about that stuff. He had never pegged her as a wife. Married! Jeneil, she couldn't! He loved her and he always would. It was so crazy that he should, he knew it, but he did. Jeneil couldn't be married. Everything in him felt like she was his, like they belonged together. He felt like he should take care of her. It felt like she belonged to him and that was crazy, too. He took another drink of water.

"Steve, are you okay? You look sick," Rita said, stopping as she passed by.

"I'm okay." He stood up straight and breathed deeply. "I'm just a little tired, that's all."

"I heard you and your girl decided to end it, sorry," she said, frowning deliberately.

"That's life. Payback for past sins, I guess," he joked.

"Then she's the one who ended it?"

He nodded. "She's going to marry someone else." His voice was strained and he wondered why he even said it.

Rita watched him. "Hey, you're really hurting about it, aren't you? You look like you just heard the news."

"This one was special Rita, really special."

Her face showed compassion. "Well, she's a fool, Steve. She never even got to know your best quality." She grinned and punched his chin gently. "You always did look fantastic in scrubs. And out of them." She winked. "There's a beer in my fridge for you any time you need it, guy."

Steve smiled. "We should fall in love Rita. We always did understand each other."

"Not me, darlin'! I've been married twice and they ended before the ink on the license dried. I'm not meant for love and marriage. They complicate life with feelings and pain.

Seeing you like this reminded me. It's a boo-boo sweetie and like any other boo-boo, it heals and goes away. Friendships last longer. Stop by for that beer, Steve. I mean that."

Steve smiled wearily. "Rita, I don't know if you'd like the new me. I don't even recognize myself lately. I've changed so much."

"I know. I heard about you shoving Pete. That was a total gag, nobody could believe it. Word is you're eyeing his girl and it's hurting the friendship."

"What?" Steve asked, stunned by the news. "How the hell did that get started?"

Rita touched his shoulder. "Relax, Steve. Seeing you like this proves it's only gossip. Anybody can see you're torn up over your loss. I'll fix the story, guy. Trust me."

Steve relaxed. "Thanks, Rita. I'd hate for Pete to hear that shit. Boy, this place hasn't changed. They've now got me betraying my best friend." He shook his head.

"Not to worry, Steve. You're out of here soon and into the world of stodgy offices and dull, dull, dull."

Steve laughed. "Thanks, Rita. You're a ray of sunshine."

She smiled. "I went that route for a year. I came back to hospital duty before rigor mortis set in. Congratulations on going with Sprague and good luck. We'll miss you around here, although for the past few months no one has seen you anyway. She's still a fool, sweetie." Rita smiled sincerely. "I've got to go." She patted his arm and walked away.

Steve rubbed the back of his neck and sighed. "She's not a fool, Rita. I am. She was there the whole time and I never noticed. No, I'm the fool, that's for sure."

*****

Jeneil was surprised when Dr. Sprague's secretary called. As she walked to his office, she tried to think of what he would want of her. She sat on a chair and waited. The secretary's phone buzzed. She answered and then hung up. Smiling at Jeneil, she told her to go in. Jeneil knocked, feeling a bit nervous and opened the door.

Dr. Sprague stood up, smiling, and Jeneil relaxed. "Come in and sit down." He pointed to a chair in which she sat and waited.

Jeneil watched as he paced, curious about his uneasiness. "Am I in that much trouble?"

He laughed and sat down. "No." He was quiet then stood up and paced again. "I could be though." He folded his arms and looked at her. She wrinkled her eyebrows, confused by his words. He sat at his desk and sighed. "Jeneil, this meeting doesn't fall under hospital business. I want you to know that. This is all unofficial."

Jeneil wondered if that meant it was personal, which confused her even more. She waited. He ran his hand over his mouth nervously then looked straight at her.

"Jeneil, you strike me as intelligent and sensible. I'm counting on that now. Actually, I'm gambling on it. I'm concerned about something. I have five very outstanding surgeons in my service. Steve Bradley and Peter Chang are two of them." Jeneil's stomach knotted. "I've watched them closely from the time they arrived, first Bradley then Chang. They were different. Their backgrounds weren't those of my usual students and I wondered if this was a game to them. They proved me wrong. I've nurtured them personally because I was impressed with what they had achieved just to get to med school. Our work has been rewarded. They're two of my best." He paused and looked down at his desk. "I've taken a personal interest in them, and as part of my job as a professional, I get involved in their lives as necessary."

"Yesterday, they turned on each other and I stepped in," Dr. Sprague said, looking up at Jeneil. She put her head down and swallowed. "Neither of them gave me details; Steve claimed he didn't know why Peter was uptight and Peter wouldn't talk at all. I happen to know it involves a girl." He watched as she clasped her hands and stared at them. "I've decided to ask the girl and I'm banking on her being intelligent and sensible enough to realize that I want to help. I want to know what I'm up against before I lose two outstanding surgeons. They're lives have been highly classified secrets for a few months and I've liked that, but I want to know what's happened to the peace. I'm asking as the man who's nurtured them like a father. That's where I'm coming from."

Jeneil wrung her hands. "This is unofficial and nothing gets written into records?"

"That's a promise," he assured her. "I'm asking for myself in order to be there for them."

She fidgeted. "How many others know about the three of us?"

"No one else that I've heard and I make it a rule to hear everything."

She sighed and began to relax. "Peter and Steve both have a tremendous respect for you as a man and a doctor. I'm banking on their good judgment now," she said directly, looking up. "Peter and I live together. We're planning to be married. When Steve was put on probation, he spent a lot of time with us to keep sane. I guess we were swept into each other's lives by our secrets and became bound together. The three of us became good friends. We're more like a family. At least that's how I feel. I'm not too clear about how this situation evolved, but Peter had mistaken my friendship with Steve as more serious. He moved out for a few days without an explanation leaving Steve and me wondering why. Yesterday, Peter told me that Steve was in love with me."

"Is he?"

"No," she insisted. "Steve has been nothing but a good friend to both of us. I'm not even Steve's type. That's what makes this situation so ridiculous, but real none the less. Once Peter and I talked about it, everything settled down. As far as I know, he and Steve are still good friends. Steve doesn't know Peter thought that about him and I don't want him to. It's senseless. It could only hurt, not help."

"Are you in love with Steve?"

"No!" she answered. "I love Steve, I care about him, he means a lot to me and he's a wonderful friend, but I'm in love with Peter. We're going to be married. Peter misread my friendship with Steve. He knows better now. That's what it was all about. Steve was concerned so he tried to get Peter to explain what was happening. Peter had been avoiding Steve, too. He was convinced I should have a chance to see if I wanted him or Steve. I know it sounds adolescent, but Peter and I were both surprised by our feelings for each other and we've been living together to test the relationship. Steve needed help, we're his family. It just got complicated. It'll be fine now that I'm aware of it. It's over and everything is settled. You don't need to worry. That brings you up to the minute."

Dr. Sprague was impressed with her openness. "Jeneil, thank you for being honest with me; it's worse not knowing and wondering what might happen next."

She nodded. "I can understand that in your position. Steve and Peter are professionals; they had already settled this between them. They're great friends and I'm annoyed at myself for causing that to change. I needed to be aware of the problem, too. I'm embarrassed the situation got this far. I'm sure they are, too. Our lives have been changing so rapidly lately, that's why this escaped us."

He smiled and stood up. "Thank you again for coming in and trusting me."

She stood up. "It wasn't easy to talk about and I can promise you I won't be back because I'm going to make sure it won't be necessary." He laughed, and she smiled and opened the door.

"Thanks, again." Dr. Sprague shook his head. Well, Bradley and Chang were telling the truth. It wasn't her fault. He thought she had all the pieces to the puzzle, but she didn't. Steve Bradley was in love with her. He really hoped this was settled. How were they going to make three into two in this case? They were like Siamese triplets. Was this over? He knew they would keep it out of the hospital, but who would lose? Somebody had to. It was inevitable. He wished Jeneil had a twin. He wouldn't mind seeing both of them with her as a wife. Payback was tough. Steve could have had any woman he wanted and now the one he really wanted belonged to his best friend. Life hadn't been easy on that guy, but with his amazing dogged determination and his fierce drive, he took the shit, turned it into fertilizer and grew rose gardens.

Dr. Sprague sat down and leaned back in his chair. He didn't know how Steve was going to spring a rose garden from this. Peter and Jeneil were going to be married. He thought about Peter and shook his head. That guy never so much as slipped, even believing his best friend and his girl...he stopped...and even now knew Steve loved her and yet he was standing amidst it all. It was Steve who cracked, not Peter. He was damn good; Dr. Maxwell was right.

Eleven

Jeneil paced as she waited for dinner to finish roasting. Uneasiness had settled in as she reviewed all the changes happening to her and Peter but she refused to panic. What she needed was a clear head and a sharp mind. Stopping at the Camelot plant, she sighed. "And keen insight. We need soul, Peter. I've always wanted our souls to be married. It's necessary." She sighed again. But he wasn't ready, not at a superlative level anyway. They'd been too busy for soul. The telephone rang.

"Hi, honey."

"Peter, dinner's almost ready. Do you have to stay late?" She needed to make every minute of their time together count.

"No, I've been given tomorrow off."

Jeneil was shocked. "How did that happen?"

"Dr. Sprague called me into his office and asked if I'd stay on days for another week in order to cover part of the third shift. He gave me tomorrow off because discharges were high today. He wanted to take advantage of that and give his toughest doctors a rest so they could get themselves renewed. He's always paid me compliments, but it's different now. He said he was really impressed with my steadiness and constancy."

"Did he say constancy, Peter? Not consistency?"

"Yes. Why, is it wrong?"

"No, it's just that there's a difference between the two. Consistency is steadiness like a habit; constancy is steadiness stemming from fidelity, a commitment. It's a superlative."

"That's what I mean about him, Jeneil. He acts like he's really impressed with me. I don't know why."

She smiled. "You deserve it. Like the grapevine that has produced a magnificent harvest at a certain growth level but it continues on unaware that the harvest is magnificent. The growth is its only awareness and concentration; that's constancy."

Peter laughed. "Sometimes there's no doubting you're a lit major. Dr. Maxwell speaks my language. It's not constancy or grapevines, it's, 'you're damn good, Chang.' That, I can grasp."

Jeneil laughed, loving his simplicity. "Why did you call then if you aren't working late?"

Peter leaned against the wall. "I was thinking since I have tomorrow off, let's get away. Maybe go to a motel and leave the world behind. I'd like to be alone away from everything except you."

An idea flashed through Jeneil's mind and excitement spread all through her. "Peter, let's go to the beach house!"

The idea excited Peter. "Oh yeah, baby! That's even better. What a great idea! I love that place. It'll be warmer than a motel room. Will it take much work? I need things to be simple right now, honey."

She smiled. "Leave it all to me, Peter. Just come home."

"Great." He sighed. "Jeneil, you're special. You really know how to make a guy appreciate life."

The compliment thrilled her. "It's really nothing, darling; we harem girls are very well trained." Her voice smoldered into the receiver.

He laughed. "The wires here are melting, honey, and my ribs along with them. Keep that thought though, beautiful. I'll be out of here at seven or sooner if I can."

Jeneil raced to the bedroom, rejuvenated by their plans. "This is a break, the elements have combined in my favor," she screamed with delight, gathering things quickly and following the lists her mind kept pouring forth. She stopped and wondered what day of the month it was. Running to the window, she looked up at the sky. Excitement filled her as she saw the large, brilliant, blue-white circle there. "It's fate," she screamed to herself. "Minister Moon is in town. He's here for the wedding!" She raced back to her preparations even more elated. By the time Peter arrived, she had their clothes packed in bags and dinner packed in a picnic basket.

Peter looked around. "This is it, just the luggage, picnic basket, cooler and box?"

"This is all of it." She smiled.

He grabbed her around the waist, holding her close, growling into her shoulder. "I love you. You belong in a jungle. Life is simple for you. Chang thinks you're the greatest."

She laughed, holding her head back while he kissed her several times. "Are Peter and the doctor having trouble with me?"

"Chang never asks him. He's in charge of being in love with you."

She laughed. "Good, he's all the man I want anyway."

"Come on," he said, holding her hands. "Let's move out. I can't wait to get to the house." He kissed each of her hands.

"Peter, I've decided I'd like to be married spiritually tonight."

"Okay, I'll get married to you any way I can. What's involved?"

She shrugged. "I don't know. Being so sudden I haven't studied it completely. We'll work up to it until our souls are united." She sighed. "Because this isn't the exact time for the ceremony, it probably won't be superlative."

*****

The house looked forlorn in its cold shadows. Jeneil turned on the power at the basement entrance. "I'm heating the house," she said, opening the kitchen door, turning on the light switch.

"For only a night?"

She turned to Peter. "It's not only one night. It's a special night. How many times have you been married spiritually?"

"In the past week?" he asked, teasingly.

She punched his stomach gently and he backed away laughing, following her to the living room. She stood in the darkness and turned on a switch, lighting the lamps. "Hi, house," she said. "Wake up, it's a celebration and you're invited. You'll need to look warm and festive, and shine with ambiance." Peter looked around the room. It had been months since he'd been there, but the house still had the same sense of warmth and comfort he had felt the very first time he was there. Jeneil turned up the thermostat and rubbed her arms. The cold dampness penetrated her coat and chilled her skin. "Let's build fires in all the fireplaces."

"All the fireplaces, you mean both don't you?"

She blew on her fingers to warm them. "No, there's another one off the living room by the front door."

"I never saw that part of the house."

"It's a library and there's a smaller room off that with its own entrance. I think it was an office. There's a small fireplace in there, too."

He smiled. "And in the master bedroom."

She nodded. "Let's just heat the first level though. There's no furniture in that bedroom." He heard the heat snapping through the house and he felt relaxed. It was a peaceful home.

"Jeneil, after we're married, let's live here."

"Here? Really?" Jeneil asked, turning suddenly, surprised by his remark.

"Well, after I'm in private practice of course. We couldn't afford it now." He noticed she smiled. "Why, don't you want to lose the summer money?"

She shook her head. "It's not that. I really bought this house for myself then I realized I needed to live amongst people if I was going to stop observing and start participating in life. But I love this house, so I rent it to keep it as a business. It kills me to rent it out. It feels like my house. My soul has always relaxed here." She put her arms around him. "Don't you want to live in Glenview?"

He held her. "That development we passed on our way here?"

She nodded. "I thought all the married doctors lived there."

"Maxwell doesn't. He has a small farm in Oakridge." Jeneil brightened, delighted not every doctor lived in Glenview. Peter kissed her forehead. "Drs. Sprague, Turner, and Young live in Marshfield."

"That little village on the bay?" Jeneil asked, surprised.

Peter nodded. "Why, are you afraid of Glenview?"

Jeneil looked embarrassed. "It reminds me of Loma."

Peter laughed. "Good, then it's settled. We'll live here."

She snuggled to him. "You're terrific."

"When do we get married legally?"

"You tell me," she replied, shrugging.

He smiled. "Then let's get our license on Monday as soon as the office opens. From there we'll get blood tests done and after that." He stopped and thought. "Who marries us?"

"A judge, I think."

"Okay, then we'll get the blood test first, then the license, and then we buttonhole a judge in the building."

"I think we have to wait a few days. The license is posted somewhere to make sure we're not committing bigamy."

Peter put his head back, annoyed. "What shit, if we were planning bigamy, would we be using the same names?"

She laughed. "Dems da rules, bud." She kissed his chin.

He sighed. "I guess I'll go through life never understanding rules."

Jeneil smiled. "Poor Chang, well it's only for a few days. If you'll take care of the fires, I'll put dinner together."

"That's a deal." He let her go after kissing her.

Peter started in the den and worked his way to the library. He wondered why a room would be called a library until he saw the bookshelves from floor to ceiling. A room for reading and to think some Americans used the room with the shower in it. He decided it was all in what a person was used to. Going to the fireplace, he noticed the room was all wood. Someone named Carl had carved his love for Julie into the beautiful paneling and Peter shook his head. The house showed signs of abuse, not much but enough to indicate it was a summer rental. The abuse annoyed him and he was surprised the house meant so much to him. He remembered the nail and his bedroom wall carvings; another apology owed to his mother.

As the newspaper fanned into strong flames and stretched toward the kindling, Peter stood up and looked around the room. He turned off the overhead light and the room dimmed, illuminated by the struggling fire and the moonlight streaming through the large double window. He went to the window and looked at the view. The surf was rough and dashed against the rocks in the inlet. He remembered Jeneil saying her soul relaxed here and he knew what she meant, feeling strongly that he belonged here, too. Jeneil walked in quietly and smiled as she saw him enjoying the view. He turned realizing she was there. "I'm already relaxing. I'm glad you thought of this place."

She joined him at the window and leaned against him. "We actually met here on the beach. I think I really saw you as a person for the first time that night."

He nodded and rubbed her arm gently. "Me too, I was aware of you but you became real to me that night."

She sighed. "Mrs. Peter Chang, another change. You've been changing my life since our beginning on this beach, in this house."

He kissed her neck lightly and held her closer. Looking across the inlet to the open meadow, he smiled and pointed. "Isn't that where we camped out?"

She nodded and smiled. "I grew up that night. It was a giant step toward becoming a woman. My parents told me making love to the right man was worth waiting for. They were right."

Jeneil squeezed the hand he held at her waist and as the moonlight surrounded her and memories of the house came back to him, the love he felt for her filled him. He kissed her shoulder as she leaned against him. "I love you, Jeneil. I always will."

"I love you too, Peter. I'm so excited you want us to live here. We do belong here. We met here. We made love for the first time here and we're going to be spiritually married here. It's our house, Peter. It feels right."

She turned and put her arms around his neck, pressing her lips against his with a gentle kiss. He understood its warmth and was caught up in the feeling they belonged there. He held her to him, enjoying the moment and was filled with the knowledge that all this was very right. She rested her head against his chest and he held her. There were no more doubts. She was his. Mrs. Peter Chang. It felt incredibly right to him and he held her closer, kissing her temples gently.

She sighed. "I really hate to end the moment but I'm sure dinner's ready." She kissed him and reluctantly moved away from the warmth, love, and security of his arms. He went to check on the other fires then joined her in the dining room. Several candles of different heights were clustered in the center of the table, silk daisies and ferns tucked amongst the thick white candle bases. He smiled, loving her care for details.

The house felt warmer as the fireplaces and heating system combined, making the night comfortable. Jeneil served the food and poured some wine as Peter began to eat then concentrated on her own plate. Moving her asparagus around uneasily, she looked at him. "Peter, if we're going to achieve a strong closeness tonight, I have to confess something." He looked up surprised and swallowed the piece of roast he was chewing.

"Okay," he said quietly and drank some wine, wondering what it could be.

She looked back at her plate and continued moving a piece of asparagus around slowly. "Dr. Sprague called me to his office. He was concerned about you and Steve. It was all unofficial. He really likes you two." Peter waited, wondering where she was going. She looked up at him. "I told him about the three of us and your suspicions. I really think he already knew or at least strongly suspected. He told me you never talked about it and Steve told him that he didn't know what was wrong."

"Why do you feel you have to confess that?"

She leaned her arms on the table. "Because soul is a very intimate encounter and I didn't like having that secret from you."

He looked down at his plate, feeling guilty having thought her capable of being unfaithful when she had trouble keeping even minor secrets from him. Feeling the moment was right and understanding about conferring and closeness, he decided to risk it. "Jeneil, I should tell you something. When I left on Sunday, I did think you and Steve had betrayed me. I ran for blocks to forget it then I slept until early the next morning. When I woke up, my mind was a lot clearer and I knew you couldn't do that to me. I'm sorry I even thought that about you. I was just as shocked to realize that Steve is in love with you."

She sighed surprised he still maintained Steve loved her. "I assured Dr. Sprague this was all settled. I guess it isn't."

He looked at her. "It's all settled, honey."

"Not with you thinking that about Steve."

He looked away. "I misjudged Steve, too. He would never betray me."

"Steve and I are close, like brother and sister. I can understand your mistake."

Peter decided to bury it for good. She couldn't see it and the two of them had obviously never gotten as close as he had imagined. He got up and stood beside her, touching her arm. "I can promise you that I'll never think that about you again. Chang has had trouble believing you could be his. He knows better now."

Jeneil smiled and shook her head. "You're wrong. Chang and Irish are fine together. It's Peter and Nebraska who have trouble. They're unstable because we're changing so much. We're in transition. It was Chang and Irish who met on this beach. They're devoted to each other." Peter rested his forehead on her arm and she touched his hair gently. "Why do you think I keep Chang alive? It's Chang who's holding the largest piece of my life. I don't know why yet but I know its Chang."

Hearing her words and her sincerity, he realized how deeply committed she was and what his grandfather had meant about the Songbird's loyalty and devotion, about looking after her carefully. Her deep love for him made her fragile. That's why she needed his protection. That's why he had to be sure he wanted the responsibility. Wanted the responsibility, he asked himself. Chang couldn't live without her. The responsibility was necessary for her survival. Peter lifted her head and kissed her.

"I'm crazy about you," he whispered.

"That's a good beginning for soul." She hugged him. "Your dinner is getting cold." She smiled, lovingly running her hand over his hair. He kissed her lips lightly then went back to his chair. There was a deeper connection between them and each felt it as they finished the meal. Peter was glad they had come. All the damage had been repaired and they were solidly together again. He sighed with relief and contentment as he finished his wine. "Peter, let's have coffee and dessert in the den. Remember, you made popcorn the first time we were here?" She got up and began gathering the dishes. "Let's see what the room feels like now."

He smiled and helped her. "Am I going to repeat the popcorn tonight?"

She laughed. "No, I made chocolate mousse. Well, I made it my way. Sienna would scream from shock at my quick mousse."

Peter laughed and followed her to the kitchen. They did the dishes together as they waited for the coffee to brew. The house felt warm now and Peter felt at home. The last time he was there, the damp chill had reminded him that he was just getting away from it all. Now with the house cozy and warm, he felt like he lived there. The last time he was only attracted to her and he laughed to himself as he realized now he was addicted to her. He thought about the major changes that had taken place in their lives since they had last visited the house.

"You were right about heating the house, honey. There's a more permanent feeling about us being here."

"I can feel it, too," she said, getting a tray and setting cups and saucers on it. "Ready for dessert?" He nodded and took the tray, and they walked together to the den. Jeneil drank warm water and lemon juice, tossing a twig into the fire. "Peter, after we're married, I think I'll leave the hospital."

He put a spoon into the creamy smooth chocolate. "That isn't necessary, is it? I like having you around where I can see you."

"I think it will be, Peter. I think it's time I moved on from the hospital anyway."

"Uncle Hollis?"

"Not completely. It's just a feeling. There's an opening at The Rep with Dennis. I think I should take it."

"What's the job?"

"A go-for of sorts, I think," she answered, shrugging.

"You're underselling yourself again."

Jeneil turned and leaned against the hearth. "Well maybe, but when you don't know where your place is it's hard to determine your value."

He took her hand. "You're having fun not fitting in, aren't you?"

She smiled impishly. "But I'm learning a lot about myself. That feels therapeutic. And it will keep me out of the corporation."

Peter leaned his elbow on the hearth. "Honey, what about your hours there? Will we have a conflict? I still have another year of residency. My hours are awful. You know that."

"Yes, but I'll be Mrs. Peter Chang. That's going to make a big difference in our relationship. I can see that now."

Peter raised his eyebrows. "Baby, let's not get too comfortable. There have been residents whose marriages have collapsed. I'm never going to take our marriage for granted." He put his empty dessert dish on the tray. She leaned toward him for a kiss and he was more than willing.

"You want me at the hospital, don't you?"

He kissed her cheek several times. "I don't want too many changes all at once, that's all. Until you, I'd never noticed how the slightest change could affect a person's life. We have a great formula going for us. Let's not change it just because some judge has the authority to tell us its okay to live together now."

She smiled. "I'll see what I can do about staying at the hospital but I feel stagnant. I haven't even enrolled for courses this year and it's already second semester. I don't even know what I'd take." She kissed his shoulder. "I'm ready for a change; I only wish I knew what."

"As long as it's not from me."

She smiled gently. "Never Chang, I belong to you and after tonight I'll be yours forever. So I hope you're sure I'm what you want; forever's a long, long time."

"I'll take it and beyond, too." He moved closer to her for a more serious kiss.

She pushed away and took a breath. "Let's go for a walk on the beach and cool off before the evening gets ahead of us. We'll make love after our souls are married."

Peter picked up the tray. "You didn't eat dessert."

She got up from the cushions and picked up her cup and saucer. "You eat it. Your incredible metabolism will burn it as you swallow. Mine won't." She took the tray and Peter ate the second dessert on the way to the kitchen.

"We might need to shovel the steps from the bluff," he said, getting their jackets then going out to check the steps. Returning, he helped her with her jacket. "They're clear."

Walking the winter beach felt different. The sand wasn't as comfortable and they walked slowly, avoiding the remnants of burnt wood from the end of summer parties. Jeneil sighed, disgusted by the debris.

"At first I thought we'd be married here on the beach, but one day I looked up and decided the patio at the house would be the right place for our souls to be married. Having been there tonight, I know now that's the right place." Jeneil stopped to look up at the house and pulled her collar up to protect herself from the wind. Peter put his arm around her shoulder. The house looked cheerful all lit up, the warm glow from the lower level seeming to take the chill from the biting wind.

"I'm glad we aren't getting married here. I can barely hear over the surf and the wind."

She nodded and turned to the ocean. "But these are our witnesses. These elements will combine in our favor so we'll be together forever." He watched her and smiled realizing how sincerely she believed what she was saying. He turned and held her close to him.

"You can count on me loving you forever, baby. That's a promise."

She stepped back quickly. "Hey, don't begin the ceremony yet." She smiled, and he smiled and kissed her cheek.

"Can we go back yet?" he asked, turning his back against the forceful wind.

She shook her head. "No. Face it, Peter. Face the wind in its fury so you can appreciate it in its gentility. We need to connect to its energies."

"Honey, that's your trip not mine."

She turned quickly and faced him. "No!" she shouted seriously, grabbing his arms. "No, you have to feel it too or we won't be married. Cooperate, Peter."

"Okay, okay," he said, holding her, sensing her intensity. "I'm with you on this. Don't panic."

She hugged him. "Be sure, Peter. It's our guarantee of success. Don't fake it, please. We'll wait until everything is right for the ceremony. Soul, not passion; promise me."

He nodded. "Okay, now what?"

She looked around. "Let's stand at an angle where we can see all the elements; moon, Earth, and water." She walked farther on the beach testing angles. She stopped then walked farther inland. "Right here," she said, standing steadily facing the wind. "Study the harmony, Peter. Study the strength of it." He stood beside her and agreed it was the best angle for viewing the three elements. Even the wind was less harsh at this angle. Jeneil slipped her hand in his and everything felt less silly to him. He knew he wasn't grasping it as clearly or as deeply as she was and that he needed to draw from her fire for whatever she wanted to happen.

"Honey, what do you want from me? I don't know what to look for or what to feel. You're clearer about this stuff than I am."

She looked at him and sighed. "What you need to achieve is," she thought about her words, "a feeling deep inside that you belong to this moment and this place." She smiled. "Something like you felt in the house."

He nodded and faced the view again. It felt peaceful, but he wasn't feeling part of it.

She watched him. "You're not grasping it, are you?"

"I'm sorry, baby. I don't deal in abstract as easily as you do." He could clearly see she was discouraged

She paced for a few steps. "Maybe through me, Peter, maybe I can carry it for us. Give me some time." She turned and studied the view, breathing in deeply. She closed her eyes and got lost in the wind. It welcomed her and Peter watched as she blended with it. He envied her ability to give herself over to something as abstract as a relationship with the wind. She opened her eyes and turned to him slowly. "Peter, take my hands." He removed his gloves like she had and took her outstretched hands in his. They were surprisingly warm. "Listen to me carefully," she paused, looking steadily into his eyes, "I am a being of life, energy flows through me. The Earth is alive, it possesses energy. Water has life, it pulses with energy. The sky and wind are forces of life. The moon moves, it possesses life. You are alive, Peter. You possess life. You are related to the energies. Feel it, Peter, as strongly as you feel the wind, as clearly as you see the moon, as surely as you hear the water and as solidly as you stand on the Earth. Give yourself to their energies. Experience them, Peter. Awaken your senses."

Her words created an awareness of what was around him and they became less passive. He saw more clearly. Even the water's rhythm seemed louder as it came in and went out. He was surprised by how abstract they actually felt once he used his senses.

"Contact," she said, smiling and squeezing his hand as she watched.

"That's clever."

"No, it's energy! You need me for contact, don't you?"

"I think so," he replied. "Your fire for all of it makes me see clearly. Touching you makes this feel less silly."

"Stand behind me." She leaned her back against his chest. "Now listen and follow." She placed his hands around her waist and closed her eyes. "As I mention each energy, hold it in your mind until it's as real as I am in your arms. If you need to open your eyes to use that sense then do it. Do whatever is necessary for you to connect." He wasn't sure what she meant. "Connect means feeling it strongly," she said, sensing his questioning, jolting him as her answer came so closely to his thought. She breathed in deeply and exhaled. "I am alive. I am a being of life. I am one with you. I am an absolute. I hear. I see. I feel. I am." She held his hands tighter. "I am energy. I possess life and energy flows from me. I use that energy now. Where I stand, my energy meets the energy of the Earth."

Peter opened his eyes. His connection to the Earth seemed stronger with his eyes open. Jeneil continued. "The Earth is alive, it possesses life; it is an energy. I am part of that energy as you are part of me as you hold me now." He began to follow and understand what she was doing. "The water is alive, it possesses life; it is an energy. It meets the energy of the Earth; the Earth meets my energy. I am part of their energies as you are with me now." Peter's eyes followed the water to the Earth then to her and to him. It began to make sense and become less abstract. "The wind is alive, it possesses life; it is an energy. It unites with water, water unites with Earth, and Earth unites with us so that we become one."

Peter began to link them as he listened and followed with his eyes and felt Jeneil in his arms. He could see the moon meet the sky and join its energy. The sky met the water as it pulsed to the Earth and joined its energy. Through Earth, they were connected to all as their energies passed through him and became part of him. It was how he knew he was one with them. Jeneil opened her eyes and let go of his hands, lifting hers up to the moon. From where they stood, it looked like she touched the moon connecting them to it. At that moment, Peter became aware of standing on a planet in a universe surrounded by life and a purpose. The moon's brightness shadowed Jeneil's hands and she became a shape, a bridge closing the cycle of energy he felt. It was getting too abstract and he held her close to him for reality. She lowered her arms and moved away. She turned to him smiling.

"You felt it. I know you did." She put her arms around him and kissed him. He felt the kiss. He felt her fire. She was life. She was his purpose and his meaning at that moment. He knew what she meant by energy. It was more than physical; it was a combination of everything that he was, all of him in one intense pulse of energy. The closeness he felt to her was incredible. She pulled away gently and touched his lips with her fingers. "We're almost ready for the ceremony. Let's go back now. Are you cold?"

He shook his head, surprised he actually felt warm. She put on her gloves and took his hand as they walked back to the house. They were silent, but Peter felt her within him. He could feel the Earth, the water, the sky and the moon, an awareness that made them very real to him and he liked it. Squeezing her hand, she looked at him and smiled. He wanted to pick her up and hold her, needing her to be as close to him as he felt to her inside. Letting go of her hand, he put his arm around her shoulder. It was better but not completely.

They reached the house and the heat pressed against their skin. Peter hung their coats and went to the kitchen. Jeneil had coffee warming on the stove. "Do you want more coffee?"

"I don't think so, honey. I'd just like to sit down with you in front of a fire."

She smiled as she watched him. "Will you put the fire out in the library?"

Peter went to the library where the fire had become glowing coals. He separated the pieces and turned off the lights. He noticed Jeneil had put candles on the mantel in the living room where they were burning brightly. There were also a few candles on the hearth and some clustered in trays on the floor along the baseboard. The French doors had green foliage on either side with a cluster of white candles before it. He wrinkled his eyebrows as he wondered what she had planned. He noticed the fire needed some attention and he rearranged the coals and added two more logs. Finishing, he decided to see what she was doing. He went to the kitchen but she wasn't there. All he wanted was to sit with her by a fire. Was that too much to ask? The encounter on the beach had left him with a longing to be near her, to have her so close, to continue their unity.

"Jeneil?" Peter called, knocking on the bedroom door. Opening the door, he was thunderstruck by her appearance. He hadn't expected to see her in a white dress with her hair down. He caught his breath as he stared at her. The dress was old fashioned and he remembered it along with rose petals and white candles from their apartment. "Oh man, you look sensational."

She put her arms loosely around his neck and sighed. "There are no flowers and all the extra touches I had hoped for are missing because this ceremony was too premature." She leaned against him for support through her discouragement. "I was planning for this night to be so special. Instead, it's thrown together because we were so pressured."

"Honey, trust me, it's special and you look fantastic." He kissed her as he held her in his arms. "That beach energy thing has me energized. I love you."

Easing away from him, she put her head down. "We need more time for soul. You don't quite understand cosmic." She wiped a tear. "This is supposed to be forever, something to keep us buoyed through the times when life runs amuck."

He held her shoulders. "Hey, baby, where's your fire Chang felt out there on the beach? You got him to realize he has a place in the universe, on a planet, near the ocean, in a house, with an incredible woman. Who's not understanding?"

She smiled, charmed by his effort to cheer her up. She kissed his cheek gently. "Thank you for trying."

"Try? Come on now, we're going to be married spiritually tonight, remember." He took her hand. "I guess the living room is the place. It looks special, too." He led her down the hallway to the sofa, facing the fire. "Now what?"

"Let's just sit for awhile to see if the atmosphere will improve."

He sat next to her. "Honey, the atmosphere is terrific. It's romantic and warm. I love the way you care that things be superlative. This is all special to me, even the idea of being married spiritually."

She looked at him and smiled. "You really mean that, don't you?"

"I do, baby. I really do." He ran his fingers through the hair that had fallen over her eye and brushed it back, and then kissed her forehead lovingly. "Oh, baby, you're special to me." He moved closer, putting his arm around her. She snuggled against him as they faced the fire, sitting together silently. "You look so terrific." It was the truth and the closeness he had felt earlier was returning. He was aware of her in his arms in their house and he knew he was ready to marry her. "Jeneil, I can't wait to be married to you. I want our life to begin. I want to be your husband. All those words that embarrass the hell out of me like love, honor and cherish, I want them in our lives." He looked down at her and kissed her lips.

Sitting up, she looked at him. "Peter, concentrate on what I mean to you. You've been telling me that I'm special to you. In your mind, list those reasons and concentrate on them." She got up and put a tape of classical music in the cassette player. Standing in front of the fire with the firelight and the candle glow surrounding her, she held her hand out to him.

Her dress, her hair, her total look rushed at him and he knew there would never be anything that compared to the love he felt for her at that moment. He went to her and kissed her, surprising her with its power. "Because you make me feel alive."

"Hold on to me. Concentrate the way I told you to." She looked steadily into his eyes as she rested her arms lightly on his shoulders. He held her gently around her waist. He was used to soul done this way and he actually enjoyed it. Focusing on the reasons she was special to him, it wasn't long before the moment began to feel different. The warmth and glow from the fire, the way she looked and his thoughts about her brought with them a feeling of closeness. It began as awareness and progressed to appreciation. When he achieved the desire for her to belong to him, his mind ran out of words. He wanted her. He wanted them to be together. All his feelings rushed at him.

"Jeneil, I want to marry you. I want us to belong to each other." He pulled her closer and held her to him. "I love you, Jeneil. It goes beyond words."

She nodded and smiled. "I feel the same things." She kissed him. "Let's get married right now." Taking his hand, she walked to the French doors. "I want us to be surrounded by the energies we felt on the beach."

"Honey, your dress is very light. Won't you be cold?" he asked, concerned.

"No, I'll be fine." She handed him the ring he had given her as a Christmas gift. "You can put it on my right hand. I read somewhere the wedding ring is usually worn on the left third finger because it's believed it goes directly to the heart. Maybe the right third finger leads to the soul." He held the ring and smiled at her.

Opening the doors, Jeneil took Peter's hand and walked onto the patio. It was warmer than expected as the wind encircled them. Looking into his eyes, she smiled. "I love you, Chang. With these energies as my witness, I ask permission to be with you forever. As all the energies in the universe combine in harmony, I ask for our souls to join in a marriage of spirit. As strongly and firmly as I know these energies to be real and absolute, so I firmly believe I belong to you and we can be married forever in spirit. I offer my soul to you forever with a love that will last with the stars, the moon and the sun for as long as they endure. Twinkling stars, moons, sunrises and sunsets will be symbols to you that I'm yours. The wind will remind you I belong to you and from you I can never be separated." She held her hand out to him. "I accept your symbol of our marriage."

He slipped the ring on her finger and swallowed. This all felt very real to him and he was deeply moved by her words. Putting the ring on her finger thrilled him and made words difficult. He concentrated on her and the moment. "Jeneil, I love you. I offer my soul to you to be married forever, never to be separated. This marriage is very real to me. I promise I will always love you."

She smiled as she hadn't expected words from him, his promise both surprising and pleasing her. Peter put his arms around her, holding her against him. His feelings were so strong they almost hurt. Moonlight surrounded them with brightness and he heard the ocean roar over the wind. It sounded like music to him.

"You are mine now, Jeneil, forever. We are married. I know we are."

She nodded. "We are married. I am yours forever."

He kissed her and the closeness he felt almost swallowed him entirely as he held her. She blended to him. The wind swirled about them, pushing at them, seeming to force them even closer. He took her hand, kissed the ring lightly, and walked indoors with his arm around her. Locking the doors, he then turned to her. "You must be cold, honey."

"A little but I'm so happy it doesn't matter." She held her hand in front of her and studied the ring.

He took her hand and kissed it. "Mrs. Peter Chang, I love you." She smiled, thrilled by the name. "Let's get you warmed up." He lifted her off the floor into his arms and carried her to the fire. Sitting on the hassock, she shivered. He knelt before her. "You did get chilled."

"I'm fine," she insisted. "There wasn't time to get champagne and the room service here is awful."

He kissed her lightly. "I've got connections in the kitchen. How does Ovaltine sound?"

"Oh, I'd like that," she said, moving closer to the fire.

He stood up, then bending, he kissed her forehead. "Be right back."

Peter heated the milk. Deciding cups and saucers were too small he filled two mugs and went back to the living room. Jeneil had gotten cushions and placed them on the floor near the fire. She leaned against the hassock, stretched out on the cushions. She looked up when she heard Peter. He stopped and stared at her.

"What's wrong?" she asked, noticing his expression.

"Not a thing," he said, settling onto one of the cushions. "Not a thing. You look incredibly beautiful. Your cheeks are deep pink and your face is glowing."

She took her mug. "The wind does that to me."

He leaned toward her and kissed her cheek. "You feel so soft and warm." Her eyes sparkled, and he smiled and held a handful of her hair. "You're the only girl I've ever met who makes good health a fine art."

She smiled. "Comes from living with a doctor."

Moving closer, he put his arm around her and stretched his legs out next to hers. He let his eyes follow the outline of her legs through the dress and continued over the rest of her. Kissing her temple, he smiled. "The first time I sat next to you in the records department, you got to me. I remember looking you over and being shocked I had let myself do that. You broke down barriers and it scared the hell out of me. But look at me now, husband to Mrs. Peter Chang. Not bad for a street kid."

She smiled and leaned her head against his shoulder, sighing. "There's something to be said for waiting to begin a physical relationship until after the marriage ceremony. This would be our own first time to make love. That would have made this more special."

He squeezed her shoulder gently. "This will be the first time. I'll be making love to Mrs. Peter Chang."

She turned her head and looked up at him, smiling. "So it will. You have a definite romantic streak to you."

He grinned. "Comes from living with a lit major."

She kissed his cheek and he put his mug down and took hers from her, placing it with his. He turned slightly to face her. "You look too good." He kissed her temple and ear gently, enjoying the smell of her hair. "This feels like a wedding night to me and I'm looking forward to making love to my wife." He kissed her lips, enjoying the sensation of their softness against his. Electricity stirred in his chest. "You're beautiful," he whispered, "incredibly beautiful." He rubbed his cheek against hers. "I love your softness." She closed her eyes, enjoying the excitement his touch stirred in her. She put her lips to his, and he responded, holding her closely and leaving her breathless. He smoothed his mouth to her neck with gentle kisses. "Let's go to bed, Mrs. Peter Chang." His whispered words passed through her as the name settled deep within her and became indelibly written in her heart.

Twelve

Peter faintly heard a rooster crowing. He opened his eyes. The blue walls were familiar and he remembered them from another weekend he had spent there. He also remembered tossing one pillow to the floor, angry at himself for thinking about Jeneil. He smiled and thought about the previous night. Turning over, he slipped his arm around Jeneil's waist and kissed her back.

"Hey, your husband's awake." She laughed softly at his remark. "What's so funny?" he asked, kissing her shoulder.

"You remind me of that rooster. He's awake so the hens have to get up."

He laughed. "Well, let's not waste my day off." He smiled as she turned onto her back. "You were already awake you sneak."

She grinned. "I was just waiting for the rooster."

Peter took her hand and kissed it. "Let him worry about the hens, I'll take care of my wife." He leaned closer to her and she let him slip into her arms. He growled and gently bit her shoulder. "I like weddings and honeymoons with you."

She held him to her. "You're crazy."

"About you, baby. I'm totally crazy about you." He kissed her, responding to the passion he sensed in her.

*****

They were having a no-fuss kind of day. Breakfast had been quick, cleaning even quicker. They walked to Settler's Point and Jeneil collected specimens from the shoreline, adding them to a plastic bag. The sun was almost overhead when they returned from their hike to the meadow across the inlet. Memories of their first time together added to the romance of the day. Jeneil confessed she had been trying desperately to interest him and had felt like a bag of sand when he hadn't responded. Digging out a kite, they went to the shore. The kite and the wind were great, but the temperature shortened the fun. Returning to the house, they sat in the kitchen with Ovaltine to warm themselves.

Jeneil sat up from a comfortable slouch. "You must be hungry. I have some deli-meat for sandwiches."

He took her hand. "Let's grab a cheeseburger on the road. We can drive the coastline."

"Mmm, that sounds good." She picked up her mug and went to the sink. "Shall we close up the house now?"

He groaned. "I hate to. The thought of leaving annoys me."

Going to him, she rested her hands gently on his shoulders. "I don't want to leave either. After we're married legally, let's move in. I can afford it."

He looked up at her. "I can't."

She sat on his lap. "But we both love this place. Until you're ready, I can cover the cost."

"No, baby, part of being your husband is looking after you. I can manage the apartment cost. Besides, this is farther from the hospital. It would be difficult with my hours. When I'm finished with my residency, we'll race to move in."

She smiled. "You're right. I know it, but so much of us and our beginning is here. I don't want to leave. Something inside of me wants to lock us away from the world in here."

He kissed her. "We can spend our days off here."

"Oh, let's do that. The summer season will start in a few months and we won't be able to get near this place. It lacks the beautiful solitude then anyway with the blistering bodies all over the sand."

He smiled. "If that kid Carl is coming back, he'd better leave his damn knife home or I'll carve his initials on him where he'd least like to have them. Damn it, that beautiful paneling ruined by his lovesickness. Tell him to stay home with Julie this year."

Jeneil laughed. "Julie is Agnes's daughter. I have Agnes come make sure the summer's mess doesn't get out of hand. She brought Julie with her and Carl hated to leave her behind when he left. That's his note to her on the paneling. Agnes felt terrible about it."

Peter shook his head. "She should. He ruined the room doing that."

She smiled and kissed him lightly. "You really do love this place the way I do."

He nodded. "It's our house." She kissed him warmly and he held her, enjoying it.

"I love you. I'll never forget all of this, never."

He rubbed her leg. "You'd better not. How many times have you been married spiritually?"

"This week?" she asked, teasing him. He smacked her buttock in response. "Ouch."

He kissed her gently and hugged her. "Let's go for a drive. We can stop in Upton for salt water taffy."

"Do you realize that we've spent our time here reminiscing?" she asked, getting up.

He picked up his mug and stood up. "That's what's so nice about great memories."

"That's almost poetic, Chang."

He kissed her and laughed. "You bring out the romantic in me."

She followed him to the sink. "Peter, let's go to Jarreau's tonight for dinner and champagne to celebrate our wedding."

"Can we get reservations?"

"We can try. We might not get a great table. Let's call from the motel. They won't mind."

He laughed and put his arm around her shoulder. "I guess they won't since the place is yours. Okay, let's put the house into hibernation." He sighed.

*****

They drove the coastline, enjoying the view and being together. The ceremony had made a difference and there was now an actual feeling of being married and a commitment to a life together. They stopped at the seaport town they had once visited to buy salt water taffy then headed back to the apartment.

Peter was doing his tie at the bureau mirror when Jeneil stepped from behind the dressing screen. Peter looked up into the mirror and turned around to look at her. "Hey, I get the blue dress." She held her hair to one side so he could do the small hook and eye for her. Finishing, he put his arms around her. "I love you in that dress. You look sensational. I'm even ready for Jarreau's small portions."

She laughed. "Okay, husband, I just need to do my hair." He sat on the bed and watched her twist strands and quickly pin them up. "Ready."

"No jewelry?"

"Just my ring." She smiled, holding her hand out and admiring the wedding ring.

He smiled, loving her simplicity, and went to her. "Boy, I know how to pick a wife. She has diamonds and pearls in her jewelry box, but she gets thrilled over a nondescript metal ring." He kissed her cheek.

"This is the symbol of my future, my forever," she said, and he held her fur jacket for her.

"Mrs. Chang, let's go celebrate our forever." He kissed her cheek as she slipped the jacket on.

Peter was beginning to feel like a veteran at Jarreau's having remembered what Steve had done the last time. He was ready to order from wine to dessert, and relaxed as the waiter left knowing he had passed the test of ordering without making a mistake.

Jeneil noticed and smiled lovingly at him. "You are definitely of the White Fang mold and a quick learner."

"I'm going to read that book one of these days. You must have given it to me for a reason, so I'd like to know what it's all about."

She touched his hand. "Before the flu outbreak, I had hoped we could read it together. My father enjoyed having my mother read to him. It was a pleasant relaxation after Sunday company left."

Peter shook his head. "Would those educated people believe this, their princess married to a street kid?"

She looked at him and studied his face seriously. "Don't underestimate yourself, Peter. You're made of pretty noble fiber. Chang has it all except the packaging. He's coated with a rough exterior. I admire him a lot. My parents would be proud of you as a son-in-law. I'm certain of that, for making their princess very happy if for no other reason."

Jeneil rubbed his hand, her words exactly what he needed to hear. He settled back in his chair feeling comfortable. He had ordered a complete meal at Jarreau's on his own and he was celebrating his marriage to a beautiful princess. Life felt great at that moment. Even Chang felt satisfied and Peter gently squeezed the hand she had resting on his.

*****

Peter waited in bed as Jeneil changed, holding his arm out for her to snuggle when she slipped under the covers. She gave a relaxed sigh. "Is this really the end of our beautiful marriage day?"

"No, it's the first day of the rest of our eternal marriage."

She turned to look at him, completely surprised. "You're just filled with beautiful remarks lately."

He laughed. "Marriage agrees with me."

Putting one arm around his waist, she snuggled to him. "You handled the restaurant extremely well."

Brushing her hair off her shoulder, he smiled. "Once I knew how little they give to eat, it's a matter of survival to order appetizers and catch the dessert cart. I'm wise to them now." She laughed, enjoying his positive attitude. His mouth looked sensuous and she kissed him warmly. "Well, is that what the sip of champagne did to you?"

Kissing his chin, she smiled. "No, the poached pears in claret sauce." She snuggled closer to him. "Mmm, I feel married and it feels wonderful. I knew it would, that's why I had to resist the idea. Now I don't care if I ever find Jeneil. Mrs. Peter Chang is very happy."

He smiled. "You'd better find Jeneil before my residency is over."

"Why?"

"Because after that we move to the ocean and fill the house with kids."

She smiled. "You're all settled in life, aren't you?"

He nodded. "Yes, I am. I see the whole thing clearly. A career I really enjoy, a wife I'm crazy about and children, that's it. There ain't no more after that, bud. That's the whole movie right to the credits."

She sighed. "You're so lucky to see it all so clearly."

He looked down at her, concerned. "Why, are you having trouble with the picture?"

"Only the career part."

"Wife and mother not enough? The corporation and foundation take up the rest of the time anyway."

It was her turn to be concerned. "Where's the theatre?"

"As a career? I thought that was just fun to give you a break from the corporation. I assumed the kids and I would replace it."

She settled back. "Gosh, I thought I was showing a serious interest in the theatre."

He chuckled. "As a go-for? Come on, baby, you've got more than that in you."

"I enjoy the theatre atmosphere Peter, like you enjoy medicine."

He squeezed her. "Hey, you're not having trouble imagining a bunch of Chinese sons, are you?"

She laughed mischievously. "No, especially with blue eyes."

He looked puzzled. "Slip that by me again."

She snickered. "Peter, my father had light blue Irish eyes. Dark wavy hair and blue, blue eyes. Will it shake up the Chang Dynasty too much if that genetic defect should surface in a son or two?"

He laughed. "Holy shit, I never even thought of that."

"You're not getting your ring back." He smiled and kissed her forehead. "Can we name one Neil Connors Chang?" she asked, falling into the idea of children.

He took her hand, enjoying planning. "And Liam for my grandfather."

"And there has to be a Peter."

"Honey, three kids already and we haven't even started on girls. Where do you plan on keeping the theatre? The last class I had in OB, the textbook said women gestate for nine months, and the little suckers need a lot of help once they're born."

"I'll do it," she boasted. "I'm a woman. We're invincible."

He laughed. "I'll remind you of that when you have three sons tugging at you and you want to go work in the theatre but you have morning sickness from carrying your first daughter."

She looked steadily into his eyes and grinned. "You can't scare me."

"Good." He smiled gently and kissed her with all the love that had been building in him all night.

*****

Peter rushed to the locker room then to the fifth floor, thinking he and Jeneil could have used a whole week for a wedding trip even though they had been living together. The excitement of being married was adding real zest to their lives. He smiled and put the last bite of breakfast cornbread in his mouth before reaching the nurse's station. Steve joined him at the medical charts. Peter was surprised to see Steve in on a Sunday. "Hey, what are you doing here, a refresher course on suffering?"

Steve laughed. "Admissions got heavy and you couldn't be reached, so I took the weekend to cover Sprague's ass. Where did you go?"

Peter almost mentioned the wedding in his excitement but stopped remembering Steve's feelings for Jeneil. "We decided to take a short break away from it all."

Steve smiled and nodded. "Sounds great, when's the ceremony?"

Peter shrugged and selected three charts. "Whenever we can. We're going for a license and blood tests tomorrow. I heard there's a few days waiting time."

"License and blood tests?" a nurse asked from behind them. "Peter, are you getting married?"

Peter held his breath, concerned about the slip up, and then realized the secret would be out soon. "Looks that way," he answered, enjoying being able to say it.

The nurse hugged him. "Oh, that's terrific! When?"

Peter smiled. "We don't know definitely, but very soon."

Peter watched Steve walk away as the nurse congratulated him enthusiastically then went to tell the other nurses. There was a difference in their friendship now; he saw it and he knew there wasn't anything he could do about it. He watched as Steve pushed the elevator button then put his head back and rubbed his neck. Peter wondered how he had missed noticing how deeply Steve had fallen and he sighed for the hurt of a good friend. It was a situation he never thought he'd be in but Jeneil was his; he couldn't give that up for anybody. It had taken the ceremony to cement that fact in his mind. She was his. Even thinking the words thrilled him and sent electricity through his chest. He took the charts and sat down to bring himself up to date on three particular patients.

The shift was that of a normal Sunday, peaceful and routine. Peter sat with coffee, enjoying his thoughts. Word was out about the wedding, and some of the interns and residents were coming up to him with congratulations. It felt good; it felt right. Peter basked in the normalcy of it; Chang couldn't believe normal could feel so good. Toward the end of the shift, time began to crawl. Peter began to look for busy work and was glad when his buzzer signaled. He called in to the operator, who transferred an incoming call to the viewing room.

"Grandfather," Peter said quietly, remembering his name was mud among the family. All the elation of his news with Jeneil was washed aside. "Are you still improving?"

"I'm back home, Peter, and much stronger."

"That's good," Peter answered, hoping to put off the real reason for the call. "Make sure you rest for at least another week. Relapses aren't any fun."

"I'll be careful," his grandfather replied. "When are you off work?"

"At seven." Peter thought he heard the greenhouse door slam. "I'll be there at seven-thirty," he said, with resignation to the unasked invitation.

"I'd appreciate that, Peter. Thank you."

"Can I bring anything for you?"

"No, the family is still fussing. Just come."

"Okay, I'll be there."

Peter left the viewing room dreading the end of his shift. It was difficult to get in his car and drive to his mother's house, and his stomach knotted as he drove up and saw her car in the driveway. It was worse than he expected and he knew there was going to be a confrontation. He braced himself and headed for the kitchen door. His mother was emptying the dishwasher and turned around when he walked in then quietly turned away.

"Grandfather called me," he explained, not sure of his place.

"He's in the greenhouse," she answered, not looking at him, her voice devoid of emotion.

"Are you okay?" he asked, hoping for a hint of how she was handling the incident with Uette.

"Your grandfather's waiting for you," she replied coldly.

"Mom, listen…."

"No," she answered sharply, turning around. "I will not listen to your explanation for filth. I don't want it in my life. Is that clear?"

He nodded, seeing the look of disgust on her face. "Yeah, it's clear."

Peter went to the greenhouse feeling sick to his stomach. He could swear he had seen, *you're just like your father*, in his mother's eyes. He closed the greenhouse door quickly and went to the back. His grandfather was sitting on his chair with headphones on. Peter sat on the bench. His grandfather opened his eyes. Taking the headphones off, he turned off the cassette player.

"Still listening to the stories Jeneil sent?"

The old man nodded. Holding onto the collar of his wool blend shirt, he added, "And this arrived Thursday. She said whenever her parents caught a bad winter cold they couldn't seem to get warm again until summer. She made this for me hoping it would help keep me warm until winter is past." He sighed. "She said it helped her parents to be wrapped in wool." The old man rubbed his forehead. "Peter, what happened?"

Peter rubbed his hands together. They were freezing even though the room was comfortable. "What did my mother say?"

"I asked you," he replied quietly, watching his grandson closely, studying every facial muscle, every eye movement. "The last time we talked you were going home to Jeneil. I heard that you didn't. Now, what happened?"

Peter rubbed his face, tension making his muscles stiff. "Grandfather, I had three hours before I had to be back on duty. That wasn't enough time to go home and explain to Jeneil and still rest. I tried calling but she was out. Lately, I've had trouble sleeping so I took a shot of bourbon. Uette Wong came here looking for Karen and asked if she could wait. I went to bed because I was exhausted and the bourbon was already hitting me, and I was asleep as soon as I got into bed. Mother woke me with her screaming and when I turned over," he paused, the words sickening him, "Uette was in bed with me. That's all I know, Grandfather. That's the entire story."

The grandfather watched Peter with a very serious expression. "Peter, your mother was in the kitchen when Uette left. She apologized several times and said she was freezing when she got here and you gave her a drink to warm her up. She said everything after that was a little blurred. She insisted you meant no harm, but you had been drinking and she's not used to liquor, that's how things got out of hand. She apologized again and left in tears."

Peter stood up and began pacing, not believing the story he was hearing. "Grandfather, I had my shot before she got here. I left her in the living room and told her there was hot coffee in the kitchen."

"Peter, were you drunk?"

Peter spun around. "No, I wasn't. I had three hours until duty; I didn't have time to get drunk. I don't even drink except for an occasional beer because I could be called in at any time, damn it. That girl is trying to save her ass."

"Peter, the Wong girls are decent, well brought up ladies. They are ladies, Peter. I know their grandfather. He has a family to be proud of. His son holds to the Chinese traditions even having been born here. The family is well respected by everyone myself included."

Peter sat down. "Grandfather, I may have given you trouble and I admit I ran around with girls, but I never got any drunk and took advantage of them. And I never forced any girl to be with me. I may be a bastard street kid, but I never used girls because I promised myself I wouldn't be like my father." Peter could feel himself begin to shake, the accusation hurting him deeply. He began to pace again and then stopped before his grandfather. "I may not have the respect of the Chinese community that the Wongs have, but damn it, I've worked hard to get where I am and no crazy girl is going to take that from me. She's no lady, Grandfather. Ladies don't lie. I'm a good doctor and I have the respect of my colleagues. I'm sure not going to risk that on some starry-eyed kid Karen's age. I never gave her a drink, I never took her to my bed, and I know I didn't touch her."

"You're sure?"

"Yes, I am," Peter insisted.

The grandfather was puzzled. "What did you mean she's a starry-eyed kid?"

Peter sat down again. "Karen brought her to the hospital and introduced us. She kept coming back alone and even asked me for a date." The grandfather raised his eyebrows. "I told her I was serious about Jeneil and I wasn't interested. The girl is a first class haunt. She's not like her sisters. She even said that to me."

The grandfather sighed. "But there's never been any word about her amongst our people. She's the most beautiful of the Wong girls and all the girls are thought of highly. They are well respected, decent, moral girls."

"I don't care what the word is on her; she's got a side she's not showing people, except me. Through this mess, I've gotten a glimpse at the most beautiful of the Wong girls and she's not that at all. Have we heard anything from her father?"

His grandfather shook his head. "No, I don't think she would tell him. Those girls are committed to upholding family honor. They've been taught the meaning of the word."

"Not her, she's lying, probably to protect her honor." Peter hit his leg with his fist. "Damn it! I can't believe I got suckered by this little girl looking for kicks. I'm twenty-four years old! Geez, my mother has thrown me back to the gutter because of this. That makes me the maddest of all." He got up and leaned against the potting table, exhaling heavily. His grandfather watched him closely. "Grandfather, do you believe me?"

"Yes, yes I do, Peter." The old man wondered about his next question. "Peter, did you tell all this to Jeneil?"

"I did. I learned a long time ago if I keep it straight with her, she can handle anything."

"You mean she believed you, too?" the old man asked, hopeful.

Peter smiled. "Songbird, Grandfather. She's one clear through, which is another reason to not get involved with that whacky kid. Why would I trade Jeneil for a night of kicks with a kid like Uette? I'm not dumb, Grandfather. I'm a little stupid at times, but not dumb."

The grandfather smiled. "Well, I can call Jeneil and thank her for my shirt. I wasn't sure what might be happening with you two."

Peter sat on the bench, smiling. "I'll tell you what's happening with us. Jeneil believes very strongly in soul, universal energies and cosmic forces. Friday night, she and I were married spiritually as she calls it and tomorrow morning we're getting our marriage license. By the end of the week, we'll probably be married. But I feel married already. She makes cosmic pretty strong."

The grandfather stared and then smiled. "That's really wonderful news. I'm glad to hear it. Are you planning anything?"

"No, just to find a judge to satisfy the law. She's already my wife. I know she is."

"So she believes in energies. Do you?"

Peter shrugged. "With her around I do. She has this thing she does. It's hard to explain, but she and the wind get along really well."

The grandfather nodded and grinned. "I'm quite sure she would. It's interesting that she discovered forces of energies."

Peter laughed. "Are you kidding, you should see her and sunsets."

The old man looked puzzled. "Sunsets?"

Peter sat forward, relaxing, glad the tension had passed. "I can't explain it Grandfather, but she does this thing. It's all tied up with energies, sunsets, and the wind. I don't claim to understand it. I just think it's damn cute."

The old man lifted his eyebrows. "She's mixed with two energies?"

"Ask her about it." Peter laughed. "I can't do it justice."

The old man was silent in his thoughts for a moment. "When will you get married?"

Peter shrugged. "Whenever the law says we can."

His grandfather nodded and smiled. "Good. Would you like some coffee?"

"No thanks, Grandfather. I'd better stay out of my mother's way and I haven't been home for dinner yet either. My wife's waiting for me."

The old man smiled at how easily Peter used the term. "Let's see what time will do to your mother. I'll see that she hears your version. Right now she's still very upset."

Peter drove away feeling much lighter than when he had arrived. His grandfather's opinion and trust meant a lot and he was grateful his grandfather had believed him.

Jeneil looked out of the kitchen door when she heard the key. Peter walked in and she threw him a kiss. He heard the oven door open as he removed his jacket and she walked out of the kitchen carrying a dish. "These chops will be leather pretty soon. I'm glad you called before going to your grandfather's. Did your visit ruin your appetite?" She placed the dish on a trivet on the table and went to him.

He held her to him. "No, my grandfather believes me." Jeneil sighed, relieved. "But my mother thinks I belong in the gutter." Jeneil heard the catch in his voice and sensed how deeply he was hurting. Her heart ached for him since his relationship with his mother had been so newly reconciled. She held him close, not having words to express how she felt. "Damn, I don't mind when I deserve it but when it's an outright lie I get furious. That little bitch left me holding the bag for her own mistake and I'm furious with myself for getting suckered."

"Has there been any word from her or her family?"

Peter shook his head. "My grandfather feels that Uette won't tell her father about it because family name and honor is so important to him."

"Then we'll just have to work on reconciling with your mother again."

Peter sighed. "Oh man, that's going to take awhile. She's disgusted with me."

"Then we'll work slowly," she commented, kissing his cheek.

He nodded, but not hopefully. "Let's have dinner." He pulled her chair out for her.

"You can sit down, Peter; I'll get the rice and put the green beans into a serving bowl."

Dinner began to renew him. He had learned to accept candlelight dinners and even enjoyed them now. It was a pleasant way to relax. Jeneil always found something or read something that she chatted about and all those things combined helped him to come around. It never failed to rejuvenate him.

Jeneil brought in dessert. "Steve's finishing his residency very soon. I'd like to have him to dinner this week. I promised him a homemade dinner to celebrate. Where is he lately? I haven't heard from him. He used to call often." She took a spoonful of fruit.

Peter didn't look up. "He's been very busy."

"He must be giving us some time to get ourselves in harmony. He was concerned about us. He's very thoughtful that way. What a great husband he'll make for some woman. I still think I should introduce him to Charlene. She's not just beautiful she's very smart, too. Beauty hasn't destroyed her."

Peter smiled. "I'd ask him first."

"I will," she assured him.

Peter couldn't answer for Steve anymore. The gap between them was evident. Maybe Steve wasn't aware of it but it was there, even Jeneil had noticed his absence. Peter felt sure it was a result of hearing about the marriage and he was glad he knew about Steve's feelings. At least now he could avoid situations that would hurt Steve more. Peter had trouble believing Steve could bring himself to be best man, but he decided to wait and see. He could always ask his grandfather, or Charlie since Jeneil was asking Adrienne to be a witness. Finishing his fruit, he sighed, hoping Steve would find a girl soon. That would help the friendship. Peter hadn't expected to feel so bad having been so angry, but he still trusted Steve with Jeneil. He looked up as Jeneil put her arm around his shoulders.

"I loves ya guy, even tho' the world's a kickin yo' dog around."

He laughed and patted her hand. "That's all I need, baby."

She hugged him and kissed his cheek. "Relax on the sofa. I can manage clean up alone tonight."

He stood up and put his arm around her, kissing her warmly. "I knew being married to you would be real fun," he said, releasing her.

"Ooo and for only doing dishes alone, wait until you see my other talents." She bumped his hip with hers. He smiled as she grinned at him then backed away carrying dishes.

He sighed to himself. "And she belongs to me. Chang, if you've done anything right, it's her and medicine."

*****

Jeneil got on the elevator and began to unbutton her coat. Two nurses got on giggling. "Are you sure?" one asked.

"He said it himself," the other answered.

Jeneil took a breath; Monday morning gossip.

"When?" The first asked excitedly.

"He said soon. They're going for their license today. How about that? Dr. Chang getting married."

Jeneil felt jolted as panic seized her. Peter told them? Her mind had trouble believing it.

"We can stop worrying about her friend the shark then. He was too shrewd for her."

Jeneil relaxed as she realized they didn't know about her. The gossip still had Peter tied to Karen. She breathed deeply, not looking forward to the hospital knowing about her personal life. It reminded her so much of Loma and that town never got any gossip right.

"I feel bad for Dr. Bradley though. Dr. Chang's news must remind him of his loss even more." Jeneil was puzzled by the remark. "Rita said he's really broken up about losing his girl." The elevator stopped at Jeneil's floor. She excused herself and the nurses stepped aside to let her off. The doors closed. "Steve told Rita she's getting married to someone else. Rita said her heart almost ached when he told her this one was special."

"Wow, he sure fell hard. My grandmother always says, 'Watch the one who kisses them all. When he finds someone special, he really falls.'"

"I guess she's right," the first nurse said.

The second nurse chuckled. "Don't tell that to my sister. Her husband was a kiss them all type. When he met her, he couldn't live without her. They got married and he still can't break the habit of kissing them all. I don't think she'd even mind if that's all he did. He likes the excitement of the chase; once they're his, he gives them up. I don't know what's wearing out faster, her patience or his hormones." She laughed then stopped. "I really shouldn't laugh. It's a very unhappy marriage. She threatens divorce and he pleads for forgiveness so she stays and he starts chasing skirts again. She's a complete wreck about the up and down of it." The nurse sighed. "Marriage is such a gamble; women should stop being part of the mess. No more marriage," she said, as if it was a campaign slogan.

The other nurse laughed. "Yeah, and we'll teach our kids to do the same."

*****

Jeneil was surprised how wild news of Peter's marriage had become. It was the talk on every floor she stopped on to deliver envelopes and she began to get nervous that the gossip would latch onto the fact it was her Peter was marrying. Stopping to analyze her anxiety, she realized it wasn't so much gossip knowing about her and Peter, it was more that she didn't want anyone knowing before they were actually married. It was part of her feeling unprotected. The fog hadn't disappeared.

During lunch hour, she and Peter met at the municipal building to apply for a marriage license. Peter left annoyed by bureaucratic red tape. They each needed birth certificates. Jeneil had hers at home and Peter was now forced to ask his mother about his. He made a promise to himself to keep all the stupid details society required him to prove such as birth and inoculations and school records in a special file like Jeneil had. They were both disappointed about the delay and discouraged about having to wait seven days after the application to be married. They ate the lunch Jeneil had packed at a small park nearby and talked each other back into positive thinking in order to brace themselves for the conveyor belts they faced before they could be married. They went back to work having enjoyed at least spending time together.

Jeneil saw Steve coming from the cafeteria as she returned to work. She watched as he stood apart from a group of doctors waiting for the elevator. He looked lost standing alone staring at the floor with his hands in his pockets. She wondered if he was sad or if he was playing the role for the gossips. Her heart filled with love for him and she could see he needed the triad.

Steve looked up to answer a question one of the doctors asked and caught sight of Jeneil. His ribs almost disintegrated as he saw her and he felt electricity pass through his chest as she smiled and subtlety mimed that she wanted to talk. He allowed the other doctors to get into the car and moved away from the traffic by the elevator, waiting for her in a private area of the dreary corridor. He smiled, looking her over. He had missed her.

"You're a stranger lately." She smiled. "I miss you."

He tried to ignore the electricity in the center of his chest. "You and Pete need some time alone. I hear you've set the date." The words drained his chest.

"Not really." She sighed. "We ran into problems at the license bureau. We weren't prepared for the red tape. I should have known better. I deal with it all the time in legal matters. So we have to go back again with our birth certificates."

Steve smiled. "We live for those damn computers lately."

"Seems that way," she agreed. "I keep perspective by remembering that if I ever get amnesia at least someone will have a record of my real identity."

He laughed. "Yeah, that happens in a person's lifetime."

She laughed then studied his eyes. "Is something going wrong in your life?"

"Why?" he asked, surprised by the question and curious about her interest.

"You seem down and the triad is lopsided lately. Everything is changing too fast for me, I guess."

"I feel it, too."

"Then why are we letting it happen if we're aware of it?"

He smiled, enjoying her simplicity. "Who can hold back time and tide?"

"No one, but we can offset their affect on our lives."

"Oh yeah, how?"

"Come to dinner. I owe you a celebration, remember? We need to rejuvenate the triad; it's being eroded by time and tide."

Steve wanted to hold her and make time stand still or better yet turn back time so she could be his. He wished he could shake the feeling that she was his, that she belonged in his life. The feeling played havoc with his nerves and it was that feeling alone that destroyed him whenever someone talked about Peter getting married. "Dinner sounds great. When?"

"How about Wednesday?"

"Alright, right after work."

She smiled. "I've lost touch with you lately. Is your 'after work' the same as Peter's?"

"Only for one more week."

The realization of Steve's career beginning so soon thrilled Jeneil. "I am so excited about your career. It actually puzzles me. Maybe I'm just delighted to be around someone who knows what he wants and has achieved it. Wednesday's dinner will be a real treat. We'll go the whole distance, champagne and a fattening dessert, too."

"Jeneil, I love you for caring." His heart pounded in his chest as the words left him, loving the excitement she showed for his life.

"I love you too, Steve. I think you know that. You're really special to me. It's a complete surprise that anyone could be closer to me than Bill. Gosh, I grew up with him. Don't slip away from our lives, please."

"You've got me, kid. My feelings puzzle me, too." He looked at her, touched by her words. "I need the triad."

She nodded. "We're family. I know we are."

He smiled. "I think so, too."

Morgan Rand was in the elevator when Steve and Jeneil stepped on and he watched them closely until the elevator stopped and Jeneil got off. "Bradley, tell me she hasn't fallen for you, not her."

Steve looked at Rand, annoyed by the intrusion into his business. "She's my ex-girlfriend's grandmother's neighbor. I was wondering what was new or different."

Rand studied Steve and felt sympathy for the sadness he saw. "Tough break about your ex. Any hope for a change?" Steve shook his head, surprised by Rand's sincerity. Morgan Rand leaned against the wall and sighed. "Better the mistake was caught before you got married. Marriage brings its own problems. A shaky relationship could be mangled by it." He stared at the floor in thought. Steve watched and it was the second time he'd seen a human side to Morgan P. Rand.

"Is the luster of the honeymoon getting dulled by life?"

Rand sighed. "No, Bradley, by details; mortgages, down payments, where to live, career disappointments."

"Career disappointments? You're in with Sprague. I'm sure of it."

Rand smiled. "Not my career, Sondra's. I'm going to stay here. She wants to write and feels all the opportunities are in New York. Her college degree is a source of achievement for her and she feels really cheated working at an ad agency. I compromised and decided to live in Glenview for Sondra's sake. It's her preference. I'd like to live at my grandfather's place, but it's not chic enough. My grandparents stayed on at their little acreage. To them, it was home. They were good unassuming people with tough values.

Sondra doesn't seem to care about family traditions. She finds them strangling. At least my brother will take my grandparent's place. I'd hate to see it leave the family."

"Glenview isn't your speed?"

"Not really, but it's a good real estate investment. It's going to stay protected, I'm sure of that. But I want a place where I can put my seven-year-old sweater on and ride the back roads on Raven. That mare's as old as my sweater." He laughed lightly. "The sweater unravels and I have it stitched again, and riding the back roads eases the tension. It's my way of kicking the tie and cuff links syndrome when I need to find myself."

Steve smiled to himself. A human Morgan Rand wasn't a half bad guy at all. "Sounds like great therapy."

"Exactly what it is," Rand sighed, "therapy, it lifts the spirit." They waited at the elevator door and parted ways when the doors opened.

*****

Peter had someone cover for him when Jeneil finished work and met her at a private medical laboratory since she didn't want to use the hospital for the blood test. Peter got into her car when they were finished, feeling better having that behind them. "One step closer." He smiled and kissed her hand, noticing she looked thoughtful. "What's running through your mind?"

"Nothing special. I just wonder why civilization has become such a zircon with people having to conform to such rigid standards; licenses, blood tests. Anyone would think we're striving to produce a super race, a radiant culture, a superlative. It doesn't seem to be working." Peter stared at her and laughed lightly. "What's so funny?"

"I'm sitting here thinking how beautiful you are while you're tripping through a theory on sociology. That's the difference between a street kid and a princess."

She touched his face and smiled. "Stop calling yourself a street kid. You're an outstanding orthopedic surgeon and I'm not a princess, I'm a person whose brain is rather lopsided and chases fantasy dust." She chuckled.

"What?" he asked, wondering what she found funny.

She sighed. "I'm glad bureaucratic red tape doesn't insist on a compatibility test for marriage. The computer would short circuit trying to figure out why an orthopedic surgeon is attracted to a college dropout who can't find herself." She laughed again. "I'm sure glad Peter was a street kid. Dr. Chang would never even look twice at me."

"Don't count on it." He kissed her with deep feeling.

She smiled. "I hope you like the finished Jeneil. She seems to be unraveling faster lately."

He grinned. "I told you, I think lopsided is cute."

She looked at him and became filled with love. "I think you're terrific, Chang."

"Keep that thought, beautiful. It's good for the marriage." He sighed. "I better get back to work."

She nodded. "I'll hold dinner for you."

"Good." He kissed her hand then reached for the door handle.

"Oh, Steve's coming to dinner tomorrow night."

Peter stopped. "He is?" He was surprised but smiled. "That's good, very good. I miss having him around." He got out of her car, waved to her from his and drove away.

"Mrs. Peter Chang." She smiled into the darkness. "It sounds completely right." She sighed and drove away.

Thirteen

Jeneil was excited all day at the thought of the triad being together again. She was planning to make a special dinner for that reason as well as to congratulate Steve. Visiting the liquor store on her way home from work, she bought French champagne and a red wine for dinner. Checking her list, she sighed pleased her plans were working well so far. The French pastries were in the car, the flowers had been picked up, and unless her oven malfunctioned the roast beef had begun cooking. All that was left was to get home, do the vegetables, prepare the appetizer, and put herself together.

Excitement filled her as she headed home. The oven cooperated, the roast was cooking, and the vegetables were ready for steaming so she went to take a shower. Putting on a long hostess dress, she did her hair, added jewelry, and went to check on the dinner rolls that were rising. Going to the laundry room sink to work on the flower arrangement for the shelf in the living room, she stepped back to check on the room. The table looked festive with silver and crystal. Her watch read six-thirty; only an hour to the triad's reunion. She smiled and went to check the roast.

*****

Steve met Peter on the fifth floor. "Do you want to meet in the parking lot?"

"No, I have to check a patient in Recovery. Leave when you're ready."

"Are you going to be late?"

Peter signed a medical chart. "No, I don't think so, but I've been so busy I'd rather not have another deadline to worry about. You go on ahead. You look ready to leave now."

"I am. My schedule this week is almost a joke."

Peter laughed. "Last week of school, huh?"

Steve smiled. "It feels like it, too."

"Congratulations, Steve. You did it. The exams and the sleepless nights are all behind you now."

Steve sighed. "You know, I've only concentrated on becoming a doctor. Being in practice is like a book of blank pages yet to be written. Other than learning more about what I'm doing in neurosurgery, my life is a complete blank. It feels odd."

Peter laughed. "Now you'll get married and have kids just like people who build bridges or fly airplanes. That's the scheme of things."

Steve stared at Peter. "It can't be that simple. There are a lot of days between just getting married and getting a wife pregnant."

Peter replaced the chart. "You'd better read the script, Steve. That's how the rest of the movie goes."

Steve leaned against the chart cabinet. "That's it? It's all cut and dried?"

Peter looked at Steve, wondering why he seemed to be just waking up. "What do you want, skyrockets and parades?"

"No, I don't think so but," he stopped. "I don't know. Is that all there is?"

"Steve, trust me, you'll leave here tired, go home to your mortgaged house and a pregnant wife fighting edema, look for crab grass on your lawn and check on college costs for your kids who aren't born yet."

Steve made a face of pain. "Geez, Pete, you're a killjoy. Damn, that sounds awful, a zombie life. Thanks for nothing. Man, cheer up before going home, okay?"

Peter laughed as his beeper sounded. "Meet you there." Steve nodded and walked away groaning. Peter picked up the telephone and the operator put the call through.

"Peter?"

"Grandfather." Peter smiled at the sound of his voice. "How are you feeling?"

"I'm pretty fair." The grandfather sighed. "Peter, I'd like you to come over after work." Peter noticed it didn't sound like an invitation.

"Is something wrong?"

"Yes, I'm afraid so." The old man cleared his throat and swallowed past a lump.

"What is it?"

"It's terrible, Peter, you'd better handle it here."

Peter hesitated. "Okay, I'm through at seven. I'll be over. Can you tell me what it is?"

"Not on the telephone Peter."

"Okay, I'll be there." Peter hung up, not liking his grandfather's tone. He sighed, thinking his mother must be raging.

*****

Steve arrived at the apartment early, wondering whether to go upstairs. Maybe she wasn't ready. He shivered as the wind howled past the car door. On second thought, he could read the newspaper. He went to the front door and rang the bell and heard her coming down the stairs.

"Hi," she beamed. "You're out early. Come in." He looked her over as she closed the door behind him.

"Jeneil, you are so beautiful."

"Well, thank you."

"How come you're so dressed up? I'm in jeans."

"That doesn't matter." She heard her telephone ring. "Oops, excuse me." She rushed up the stairs and he smiled as he watched her gracefully holding the long dress to avoid tripping. He followed slowly, pulling himself together. She was replacing the receiver as he walked in and he noticed the look on her face.

"What happened?" he asked, going to her.

She looked at him, slightly distracted, wringing her hands. "That was Peter. His grandfather called. He has to go to his mother's. He wants us to begin dinner."

"You're worried."

"Yes, yes I am. His mother must be upset."

"Over what?"

Jeneil sighed. "Uette and Peter."

"This many days later?"

Jeneil shrugged. "I don't know." She sighed. "What awful timing. The triad was supposed to have a night together."

Steve hugged her with his arm around her shoulder. "Come on, kid, she'll rage and he'll be here for dinner. That's how it works. She screams and he walks away. You'll see."

She smiled. "I hope so, but she's not ruining this dinner. It's too special." She took his hand. "Congratulations, Dr. Bradley. I'm really very proud of you." She kissed his cheek.

He smiled. "I think you're terrific for doing this. The table looks ready for a holiday and dinner smells great. What is it?"

"Roast beef."

"Oh, I expected pot roast!" He was disappointed.

"Pot roast! But this is a special dinner, a celebration."

"I love your pot roast"

She raised an eyebrow. "You're not ruining this evening either. Uncork the bottle of champagne please, so we can begin our celebration." He poured two glasses and handed one to her. She raised it to present a toast. "Congratulations, Dr. Bradley. You've earned all the glory surrounding you right now. I am really, really proud of you. What you have achieved leaves me embarrassed for my own pattern of drifting through life. It's an honor to be your friend and I hope some of your superlative will rub off on me. Your drive and determination have me overwhelmed. I mean that sincerely. I'm in awe of what you've done with your life. It's magnificent. You have a right to be proud."

Steve sipped his champagne then shook his head. "Jeneil, all that praise. How can I stay a simple doctor after that applause?"

She laughed. "I don't know, but I'm overwhelmed. I think you're wonderful. In fact, I want a hug from this magnificent neurosurgeon." She put her glass down and went to him. He put his glass down slowly and she put her arms around his neck and hugged him. He held her, closing his eyes to brace himself. Her words, her enthusiasm, her caring and warmth filled his chest, bursting with the love he had for her.

"Jeneil," he said, strangled by his feelings.

"What?" she asked, stepping back.

He took a deep breath. "Uh, thank you for all of this, for being such a good friend, for all of it. I've never met anyone like you before. You overwhelm me, too."

She smiled and picked up an envelope from the table. "Here, with my best wishes."

Opening the envelope, he saw a handmade card that read, *Congratulations*. Opening it, a check was inside. He read the verse in the card. *With best wishes to one of the most outstanding men I have ever met. This gift is my way of sharing the excitement for what's ahead of you. Thank you for being you. I'm crazy about superlative. Love, Jeneil.* He smiled. "I won't be able to settle for normal, Jeneil. Be careful."

She laughed. "You're not normal, believe me."

"Thank you for the check," he said, looking down at it. "What?" he gasped, seeing the amount. "Jeneil, I can't take this. You've already done so much." He handed it to her. "This doesn't feel right."

She touched his arm. "Steve, it's okay, honest. I had a bond mature and I needed to invest it somewhere so I want you to have it. Please don't be embarrassed. You're a great investment. We're family. Look at it that way. My father wouldn't mind me sharing my money. He'd be as proud of you as I am and give it to you himself. He planned on it maturing the year I graduated to help finance my career. It eases my conscience to see it go to your career since I don't have one."

Steve smiled. "Jeneil, you made life a career."

She kissed his cheek. "Please take it. It's just unexpected, that's why it seems too much."

"Whew!" he exhaled. "You're something else. Money doesn't tie you in knots, does it?"

"I respect it like any enormous power. It's always nice to see it work somewhere special." She squeezed his hand. "Dinner's about ready. You can relax." She sighed. "Darn that problem at Peter's mother's, he's missing all this." She shook her head and went to the kitchen.

Steve watched her walk away, totally stunned that she could turn over her father's gift like it was just a tie. The respect he already had for her grew deeper as he realized the scope of her generosity and her sincerity. He sighed. "She's not normal. She's definitely not normal. Pete, you're one damn lucky guy to have her."

*****

Peter parked his car in front of the house. The driveway was full and he didn't recognize the dark sedan parked behind his mother's. He opened the kitchen door and immediately knew there was trouble. His mother stood against the counter crying quietly while his grandfather and stepfather sat on one side of the kitchen table looking serious. Two other men sat across from them looking just as serious and at the head of the table was Uette. Peter walked in slowly, gathering his nerves. He didn't like how this felt. His mother left the room quickly, crying into a tissue.

His grandfather sighed. "Peter, this is Mr. Lu Wong, Uette's grandfather, and Roland Wong, Uette's father." Peter nodded to them since neither man extended a hand to him. He could sense the anger coming from Uette's father. "Sit down, Peter." His grandfather pointed to the empty chair opposite Uette, who kept her head down. Peter took the seat, his stomach tensing as memories from his boyhood surfaced. "Peter, we have a problem," his grandfather began, "Uette went to her father about what happened. It seems she's pregnant." Peter looked at Uette in complete shock and the back of his neck began to tingle as he watched her wipe her tears. He reminded himself that he was a doctor and ignored the look of disgust Roland Wong was giving him.

Peter gathered his nerves. "Uette, I don't know what you think you're doing. I hope you haven't named me as the father of your baby if you are pregnant because we both know that nothing happened. I never touched you." Uette looked up with tears streaming down her face. Peter was stunned by her look of shock and his stomach knotted.

"Pet…Peter," she faltered. "How can you say that?" she sobbed between words. "I'm pregnant and it's your fault. I know you didn't mean to harm me. It was my fault too, but how can you face me and lie like that?"

Peter caught his breath as panic spread through him. "Uette, are you crazy? I never touched you. I left you standing in the living room. I never gave you a drink." Peter noticed Uette's father getting red in the face.

"That's enough," her father snapped. "I had hoped becoming a doctor would have given you some pride and dignity. I can see I was wrong. You haven't changed. You still lack a sense of responsibility."

Peter sat up straight. "Wait a minute, Mr. Wong. I didn't touch your daughter. I've been telling her I'm not interested every time she's come to the hospital to see me."

Uette's father looked at his daughter, surprised by the news. "You've done that? You've been chasing him?" Uette nodded and cried into another tissue. Her grandfather lowered his head and shook it. Her father sighed and lowered his head in embarrassment, too.

Peter felt hopeful. "Mr. Wong, I'm not interested in your daughter. I'm married." Everyone at the table looked at Peter, shocked by the statement, except for his grandfather who knew what he meant.

"Married!" Uette gasped. "But Karen didn't tell me that!" She began to sob, nearing hysteria. "But I'm pregnant! I'm pregnant! It's your fault! Oh my goodness, what happens to me now?" Tom got up to get her a glass of water as she sobbed.

Uette's father shook his head and sighed. "I'm sorry for the mistake my daughter has made in this."

Uette looked up. "When did you get married?" she asked, her voice shaking. "I thought Jeneil was interested in Steve. Karen said you were going to be hurt by her. When did she marry you?" Tom raised his eyebrows, shocked hearing his daughter's name. Peter's grandfather began to remember bits and pieces, and frowned as they started to add up.

Peter stared at Uette, surprised she knew Jeneil's name and Steve's, as well as there being an attraction between them. Karen, he sighed to himself, Karen.

Uette's father looked at Peter. "Why were you here if you're married?"

Peter fidgeted. "My grandfather had been hospitalized; I wanted to stay nearby to check on him." Mr. Wong nodded his head understandingly then lowered it, embarrassed.

"When did you get married Peter? We never heard about it." Tom asked quietly, pleased Peter was coming out of this looking fairly decent.

"We were married spiritually last Friday and we're waiting for our license now."

Uette's father lifted his head slowly with a wrinkled brow. "You're getting your license? Then you're not married legally?"

Peter caught the insinuation. "I'm married, Mr. Wong. We've been living together and I am her husband."

Uette's grandfather looked puzzled. "You're living with a girl but not legally married?"

Uette's father stood up and paced as anger filled him. He stopped at his chair. "Mr. Chang," he looked at Peter's grandfather, "I'm sorry, I hate the thought of insulting you, but this no account grandson of yours is very shrewd. He almost had me believing my daughter was a lair. She's not lying, he is. He's not married," the man sneered, "he's only living with the girl. He's still taking advantage of girls. It's his way. It's in his blood."

Peter stood up. "Mr. Wong, I've never taken advantage of a girl, and I especially didn't take advantage of your daughter. I am not like my father. I resent that."

Uette's father was furious. "Oh sit down, you piece of scum. You have no honor to defend. You resent my attitude? Well let me tell you, you piece of vermin, what I resent."

Uette stood up. "Father, stop it! Stop calling him names. He didn't take advantage of me. I told you the drink I had made everything blurry. He had been drinking, too. I'm as much to blame as he is."

"Uette, he gave you the drink!" her father answered sharply.

"So I could get warm," she defended. "He wasn't trying to get me drunk to take advantage of me. We both felt the effect of the drinks and found we were attracted to each other." Peter sat down slowly, staring at Uette in total shock and disbelief. Her lie left him speechless and he wondered how or when she had worked out the details. Peter's grandfather watched him closely as the others watched Uette. Peter put his head down and took a deep breath, realizing he was in serious trouble as reality began to hit.

Peter looked up. "Uette, for gosh sake, tell the truth. You have no idea what you're doing. This is crazy! This is very serious. Tell the truth, please," he pleaded.

She looked at him compassionately. "Oh, Peter, I'm sorry, I really am. You obviously don't remember that night at all. I'm not lying. I can see that you're not lying either because you really don't remember what happened." She sat down, sighing. "What a mess." She began to cry again. "How do we settle this? What's fair?"

Her father touched her shoulder. "Uette, he's involved with someone else. He doesn't want you. That's the reality of this. And actually, I'm just as glad. I don't want him as a husband for you. You deserve better."

"Then what happens to me? I can't face the thought of an abortion," she sobbed, and both the grandfathers grimaced. "How can I face people being pregnant and unmarried? What about the family?" She put her head down and sobbed heavily.

Her father patted her arm compassionately. "What can we do about it? We'll have to face it. That's all."

Peter felt sick. This was a nightmare. He wanted to hit her for lying and that embarrassed him. He swallowed hard. Uette sat up and dried her tears. She looked at Peter. "Do you think you could marry me just for the sake of family honor, mine and yours? We could be divorced after the baby's born."

Peter sat up and almost choked on her words. He took a deep breath. She wasn't real. She reminded him of Jeneil playing gotcha, but he knew this girl was dangerously serious.

Her father sat down and looked at Peter's grandfather. "Mr. Chang, Uette's suggestion makes sense to me."

Peter looked at the man. "Mr. Wong, I never touched your daughter. If she's pregnant, it's not my baby."

Uette's father sat back and covered his eyes with his hand, shaking his head. "Uette, listen to him. He's not only calling you a liar but a tramp as well. Do you really want his name for the baby? He tramples family honor, Uette, it means nothing to him."

Peter sighed. "Mr. Wong, that's not true. But nobody's thinking about my wife in this. She's my family. I can't abandon her."

Large tears rolled down Uette's cheeks. "But she's not pregnant Peter, I am."

"And she's not your wife, stop lying," Uette's father shouted.

Peter looked him steadily in the eye. "She is my wife, Mr. Wong," he said calmly.

Uette got up and paced as she cried then sat down again. "Peter, I can't see any other way out. Please, I'm begging you to help me. Marry me so my family is spared the shame."

Uette's grandfather had been sitting quietly. He looked at Peter's grandfather. "Liam, Uette is making sense, especially since Peter can't prove she's not lying."

Peter stared at the old man in disbelief then looked at his grandfather for support, his chest draining of all his strength as he saw his grandfather nod his head in agreement.

Peter stood up quickly, his rage building. He turned away, reminding himself that he was a doctor not a street kid. He kept swallowing and breathing to calm himself. He turned and faced the group, sighing heavily under the weight of his anger. "Chinese are something else. I'd have more justice in the white man's court. At least she'd have to prove I'm lying. The white man would consider me innocent until I'm proven guilty."

Uette continued to cry. "Peter, I don't want a paternity suit in this. How will that protect anybody, my family or your career?"

Peter looked at her. "Uette, marry the real father. Please, tell the truth."

She cried, letting tears roll down her cheeks unchecked. "Peter, I'm really sorry about this. It's a shock to you, I can see that, but believe me, it's your baby."

Uette's father sat down. "That's it, Mr. Chang. I believe my daughter. I'm asking Peter to marry her. I doubt the marriage will last until the baby's born, but there should be a marriage. She doesn't deserve to face all the shame. He has a responsibility too, and I'm asking that you help her to save face."

Peter stood near the table with his hands in his pockets. "Hey, talk to me, not my grandfather. I'm not a kid," he shouted.

Mr. Wong stood up, knocking his chair backward. "Shut up, you white barbarian. I'm talking to your grandfather because I can see you really are a piece of scum. It sickens me to be begging your grandfather to intercede on Uette's behalf and pleading with you to marry her. If you had half his sense of dignity and honor, you'd know what I was doing. You have no idea what saving face really means. You've never cared what people said about you. Honor and saving face is a joke to you, so shut your mouth, you dung heap. If this was ancient China I'd do my best to have you executed."

Peter struggled to gain control as he felt Chang surfacing after being called a white barbarian but he couldn't resist. "With your kind of justice I can see why the empire fell."

Mr. Wong pointed at him angrily. "Shut your bastard mouth. I don't deal with trash. I'm talking to your grandfather."

Uette's grandfather touched his arm firmly. "Roland, please, your anger won't help anything. Please calm down and think of his grandfather." Mr. Wong lowered his head, obeying his father immediately.

Mr. Wong bowed to Peter's grandfather. "I humbly apologize for insulting you like I have. I'm deeply embarrassed for my anger before you. Peter's lack of conscience infuriates me, but I regret insulting you." Peter's grandfather bowed in acceptance of the apology.

Peter watched, completely taken in by the change in Uette's father and the deep and sincere respect he showed his grandfather. It stirred something deep within, a memory that brought him pride. It reminded him of Ki. Ki had insisted they show honor and respect to each other, and it was the first time Peter had seen it outside the Dragons. He was deeply touched and very impressed. Suddenly he saw the situation from Uette's father's eyes. Remembering Ki's training, Peter moved closer to the group.

"Excuse me, Grandfather. I'd like to say something. I promise I won't embarrass you." His grandfather was taken aback by Peter's keen understanding of authority and his show of respect. He nodded at Peter to speak. Peter lowered his head as an act of respect. "I don't want to insult anyone, but I'm innocent of Uette's accusation and the injustice isn't easy to accept." Uette's father stared at Peter, surprised by the dignity he showed and not infuriated because of the way he handled himself. Peter addressed his grandfather. "Can I at least ask how she knows she's pregnant?"

Peter's grandfather looked at Uette's grandfather, who nodded and turned to his son. "She should answer that Roland."

"Of course," her father agreed, and looked at Uette. She was confused by what was happening and turned to Peter. Peter noticed and turned his back to her, which confused her even more. Her father saw Peter's gesture and understood. "You'll answer to me," her father said, shocked by Peter's knowledge of old customs. Peter's grandfather breathed a sigh of relief hoping sanity might surface amidst the mayhem.

Uette wrinkled her eyebrows and obeyed. "I used a home pregnancy test. It turned out positive."

Peter turned to his grandfather. "Since the charge is so serious, do I have a right to ask for more professional tests, especially one for the term of pregnancy?" Peter's grandfather again looked at Uette's grandfather.

The older Wong nodded. "It's not unfair, Roland."

"I agree," Uette's father answered.

Uette looked from one to the other, not grasping what was happening. "What does that mean? Is he going to marry me?"

"You'll go for the tests he has requested," her father explained.

"Is this some trick, Peter?" she asked, confused by her father's acceptance of Peter's attitude. Peter didn't answer but once again turned his back to her. Mr. Wong understood Peter's silence, knowing he was letting them know how deeply insulted he was by Uette's charge.

Uette's father touched her arm. "You'll take the tests and we'll come back. It's fair, Uette." Peter's grandfather stood up. She looked at them, not knowing what to say.

Uette's grandfather stood, acknowledging his authority and bowed to Peter's grandfather. "Liam, I apologize for any insult to you and your family, and I thank you for hearing us." He bowed again. Peter's grandfather returned the bow.

"Accept my apology too, Mr. Chang. I'm deeply embarrassed my family has a part in this shame to you and your grandson." Mr. Wong looked directly at Peter and Peter realized the apology extended to him, too. He understood all this and it surprised him again to see it outside the Dragons. These were rules he understood.

Peter's grandfather bowed to the senior Mr. Wong. "Lu, thank you for the dignity and the respect you have shown me. I apologize too for the insult to you and your family. I'm sorry this shame has come to both our ancestors. Please, let's see that the tests get done quickly. I feel compassion for your granddaughter. The situation should be handled quickly for her sake. She lives daily with the greater burden."

Peter saw Ki's rules working again. Each worried about the honor and dignity of the other. The Wongs were responsible to worry about the Changs and the Changs to worry about the Wongs. He looked at Uette's grandfather. "Mr. Wong, I appreciate your understanding of the tests. I'm sorry this has happened, as sorry that it's happened to you and your son as I am about the embarrassment to my own grandfather. Thank you for allowing me some rights in this."

Both of the Wong men stared at Peter as he talked, impressed with his sense of dignity. Uette's grandfather spoke. "Peter, I believe you are sincere. Let's hope our combined wisdom will bring justice in this. Thank you for your concern."

Peter nodded, and his grandfather was filled with pride as he watched his grandson. Uette's father held her coat for her and she buttoned it watching Peter. She went to speak to him but he again turned away. Uette's father studied them closely. Shaking hands with Mr. Chang and Tom, he escorted his daughter to the door. The older Mr. Wong shook hands and followed them out.

The silence in the room settled on the three men who were left. Peter sat down weak and dazed. The weight of the silence and the seriousness of its message overwhelmed him. His grandfather watched him then sat down. Tom joined them. His grandfather patted his arm. "Peter, I hope you understand why I had to agree to their request for marriage."

Peter nodded. "I didn't at the time and I was angry, but seeing things from Mr. Wong's side." He shrugged. "I'm in deep trouble." He looked at his grandfather. "Do you still believe me?"

The old man nodded. "Yes, I do, Peter. I'm frightened for you. It doesn't look good."

Peter sighed. "How am I going to tell Jeneil?" He leaned his elbows on the table and covered his face with his hands. He exhaled a deep sigh of discouragement.

Peter's mother walked in slowly. "Why are you worried about Jeneil? Is she pregnant and unmarried? Will she have to explain why she has a baby and no husband? No, Peter, Jeneil is too educated in the ways of the world. She knows how to not get pregnant. It's poor Uette who got caught in her innocence. She needs our sympathy, not Jeneil. What you're really worried about is telling Jeneil you got Uette pregnant and betrayed her."

Peter sighed and shook his head. "I didn't get Uette pregnant. I never touched her."

"Oh, please. You ask Uette to tell the truth. I saw you in bed with her, remember? You can't maneuver me like your grandfather. I saw you."

"You saw nothing," Peter said strongly, "nothing. You saw her lying next to me. That doesn't prove anything."

She shook her head. "I don't understand it. You really have no conscience at all. You're disgusting, total filth. And you won't even marry the girl. You're dirt, complete scum."

"Lien, that's enough," Tom interrupted, annoyed.

She was surprised. "What? Has he got you believing him, too?"

"Yes, I believe him, Lien. I saw how he handled himself. I feel he's being honest. He could have gone along with the girl's request. She's only asking for marriage as an explanation for the baby. She never asked him to stay married. I think if he was guilty, he'd have taken the easy way out, marriage and then divorce. He isn't, he's maintaining he's innocent. It's a matter of honor to him. That's what makes me believe him."

Peter's mother shook her head. "I can understand the women's movement. No one sees our side on the issue except us. He should consider himself lucky that it wasn't Lin Chi he got pregnant. The most beautiful of the Wong girls is a decent marriage, a marriage you can hold your head up in."

Peter looked at her. "Not when she's passing someone's baby off as mine." He stood up and grabbed his jacket. "I've got to go home. I'll put instructions on what tests she should have done in the mail to her father."

His grandfather stood up. "Send it to me, Peter. I'll handle this. It's my place."

Peter nodded. "Thank you." Tom extended his hand and Peter shook it, appreciating Tom's defense and support. Avoiding his mother for the sake of peace, he left.

*****

The ride to the apartment was too short. Peter still had no idea how to tell Jeneil what happened. Walking up the stairs slowly, he could hear music and knew Jeneil and Steve were dancing since he had seen Jeneil practicing to that piece. He opened the door and went in, and Jeneil and Steve stopped dancing when they saw him. Jeneil went to the stereo and turned it off, her heart stopping as Peter leaned against the door and stared at her. Wringing her hands nervously, she went to him.

"What is it?" she asked, and Peter took her hands and squeezed them.

Steve cleared his throat and picked up his jacket, sensing something was very wrong. "I'll be going."

Peter looked at him. "Steve, I'd like you to stay." Peter put his arm around Jeneil and she watched him intently.

"What happened, Pete?"

Peter swallowed, having trouble telling them. Jeneil gasped. "Oh my gosh, Uette's pregnant." She covered her mouth. "That's it, isn't it?"

Steve was shocked. "Geez, Jeneil, don't even joke about that."

"Jeneil's right. Uette's claiming it's mine. She wants to get married to protect family honor. She said we can get divorced when the baby's born." Peter held Jeneil and she began to cry.

"Holy shit," Steve said, sitting down on the sofa, completely dazed. He rubbed the back of his neck. Jeneil had trouble steadying herself, her sobs uncontrollable, and Peter watched as she rushed to the bathroom. He held his stomach, the pain intense, and he sighed and rubbed his forehead. He dropped onto the hassock and leaned forward, folding his arms against his stomach. Steve exhaled loudly from shock. "Pete, I'd better leave. You and Jeneil need some time together. This is private."

"Steve, I'd like you to stay, maybe to have one clear mind in this. I don't know, I guess I need the triad."

Steve shook his head. "Pete, my mind's not clear. I'm in complete shock. I can't believe this." He got up and not hearing Jeneil, became concerned. He went to the bathroom door and knocked. "Jeneil, are you okay?"

"I'm okay," she said softly. Hearing the water run, he went back to the living room and stood before Peter.

"Man, I don't know what to tell you," Steve said, sitting in a chair next to Peter. They watched as Jeneil went into the kitchen and returned with a glass of ice water and sat on the sofa. She stared at the glass then sipped slowly. Peter got up and went to her, sitting beside her.

She looked at him. "We're in big trouble."

He nodded, choking up. "Yeah, I am. This is a beaut. Jeneil, if she's pregnant, it's not mine."

"Can you prove it?"

"I asked for some tests. Her father and grandfather agreed to them."

"This was a family conference kind of thing?"

Peter leaned back. "Oh yeah, Chinese style with honor and dignity and…." He put his head back. "…With a girl who's lying through her teeth and hiding behind Chinese traditions. She's a bitch, cold, calculating, stares right at you and lies. She's good. She was so convincing even I had trouble believing me."

Jeneil stared at him. "Peter, if you have any doubts about your innocence at all."

"I don't." He sat up quickly and took her hand. "Baby, I don't. I just meant she's so good at lying to your face you begin to wonder. You have to keep reminding yourself that she's lying."

Jeneil shivered. "She sounds ruthless."

"She's crazy, honey. She must be. Nobody pulls this trick in an age of tests and technology. I swear, if she's more than a week pregnant, I'll blow her away so fast."

"And if she's only a week pregnant?"

"I've got to believe the tests will prove I'm not lying."

Jeneil sighed and sipped some water. "I've made coffee. Would anyone like some?"

"I would," Steve groaned.

"Me, too," Peter answered.

Jeneil returned with a tray and set it on the low serving table. She fixed coffee for Peter and Steve, and sat back with her water. "Peter, did she panic at all about taking the tests?"

Peter swallowed some coffee. "No, she just asked if it was some kind of trick."

Jeneil got up and paced. "Then she's not worried. She's acting very confident."

Steve sighed. "She's right, Pete."

"I don't care," Peter said, holding his stomach. "I'm not lying." Jeneil watched him then went to the kitchen.

Steve rested his head back. "Jeneil," he called, "do you have any aspirin?"

Jeneil returned and handed him a bottle then went to Peter and sat down, handing him a small plate. "Your stomach is bothering you. You missed dinner. Eat something."

"I don't think I can," he groaned.

She touched his hair gently with her hand. "Try Peter, you can't get sick now. Eating a little always helps your stomach."

Steve watched, marveling at her concern. He sighed, thinking she was incredible; Peter came home and told her he'd been accused of being unfaithful and she fussed over him. Steve realized how deeply committed she was to Peter and he was concerned for her. She was so vulnerable and in the position of being badly hurt. His respect for her grew from his deep admiration for her. His feelings were beyond love and he wondered what the step beyond love was called.

"Better?" she asked, as Peter put the empty plate on the tray.

He nodded. "Yeah, thanks," he said, sitting back with his coffee.

Jeneil watched him. "Peter, how does she explain you denying the baby's yours?"

Peter shook his head. "Let's see. She got to the house freezing, I gave her a drink to get her warm, but I wasn't trying to get her drunk or take advantage of her. I had already been drinking, her drink made everything fuzzy, and we developed an attraction for each other. She defends me to her father, who wants to have me executed ancient Chinese style, by saying it's as much her fault as mine."

Steve watched Jeneil take a gulp of water and close her eyes. Putting the glass down, she got up and paced. She took her hairpins out and swung her hair free, and then began to cry softly. Steve wanted to hold her, she looked so fragile, but he watched as Peter got up and put his arms around her.

"Peter, she's deadly," Jeneil said, between sobs. "You're in super trouble. You might as well pack your things and leave me now." She broke away sobbing and ran to the bedroom, closing the door.

"Oh shit, what a thought. I couldn't face that," Peter groaned.

Steve leaned back, sighing from frustration. "Pete, go see Sprague about this."

"I can't," Peter said, pacing.

"You'd better, Pete. He might know about more tests. Let him help. This is serious. Do you realize what can happen if you fight this." Peter stared at him and Steve shrugged.

"Think about it. How appealing will you be if word's out that you got a girl drunk and pregnant and won't own up to it?"

"It isn't true."

"I didn't say it was. I'm just telling you how the gossip will sound. How's that going to look when Maxwell looks you over to join him? Sounds like my probation, doesn't it? Not all of that was true either."

Peter sighed and nodded. "Oh shit, what a mess."

Steve stood up. "Pete, go see Sprague, please. He hates surprises. If you tell him before anybody else does, he'll fight like a pit bull for you." He picked up his jacket and stopped at the door. "Jeneil needs you right now. See Sprague. And you know you've got me whenever you need me." He shook his head. "Damn, I'm sorry about this, Pete. I feel like it's me. Medicine can be a crock of shit, can't it? Doctor's can't be human. We can't make mistakes. We can't even be accused of making mistakes in our personal lives. She's a cunning bitch, Pete. Protect yourself with Sprague. He'll be able to help if the shit hits the fan."

Peter nodded. "Yeah, I guess you're right."

Steve patted his shoulder. "Take care of Jeneil. Tell her I said bye and thank her for everything for me. She's really terrific."

"I will. Thanks, Steve." Peter locked the door and rested against it. He looked at the closed bedroom door and closed his eyes. "Pack up and leave, baby? My life would be over if that happened." He sighed and went to the bedroom.

Jeneil was sitting on the edge of the bed. He sat beside her and rubbed her back, and she leaned against him. "Peter, I'm so frightened. The cold, damp fog is back."

He kissed her cheek. "I'm right here, baby. I'm right here. We were married forever, remember? Hold onto that."

Fourteen

Peter had called for an appointment with Dr. Sprague as soon as he was out of surgery and knew he would have trouble talking about his mess. Telling his personal business to anyone other than Steve or Jeneil was tough. He sat down and waited. Dr. Sprague walked in smiling. Taking the messages his secretary handed him, he stopped before Peter. "I'm going to get you a bunk for my office," he teased, smiling warmly. "Come on in." Peter followed and took his usual chair. Dr. Sprague sat down, studying Peter. "What's happening, Peter?"

Peter sighed. "I need to talk to you. It's personal."

Dr. Sprague's expression sobered and he picked up his phone. "Diane, hold my calls."

Peter fidgeted, not knowing how to begin. Dr. Sprague got a cup of coffee for Peter from his coffee-maker. Pouring one for himself, he sat down and waited. Peter drank some and shook his head. "Dr. Sprague, maybe I'll come back, I'm not quite ready to deal with this." Dr. Sprague felt for Peter and his pride. He'd never known him to come in and talk.

"Who's covering for you?"

"Dr. Morietti."

Dr. Sprague nodded. "Take your time, Peter. I'm free right now and I'll cancel my next appointment and excuse you from duty if necessary. What made you come in? Is there something I can do to help?"

Peter shrugged. "Not really. Steve said you hate surprises and told me to come."

"He's right, I do hate surprises but I know life's full of them so trust me. What can you surprise me with; car accident, lawsuit, problem with another doctor?"

"I've been accused of getting a girl pregnant."

Dr. Sprague was quiet. He sat forward. "A girl? A minor?"

Peter shook his head. "Geez no, that's all I need."

Dr. Sprague watched him steadily. "Is it true or even possibly true?"

"No, I never touched her."

"Give me your story."

"It was when I was staying at my mother's. This girl had been coming to the hospital and being a pest."

Dr. Sprague nodded. "I heard. They call her the shark."

Peter was surprised. "Well she is, I guess. She showed up at my mother's while I was there alone. I was due back here for the third and I only had three hours to rest so I took a shot of bourbon. I had worked a double, I was exhausted. The shot hit me before she even got there. I left her in the living room and went to bed. The next time I saw her was when my mother woke me with her screaming. The girl was in bed with me."

"Oh shit." Dr. Sprague sat back sighing. "You're sure you didn't touch her? And you weren't drunk?"

"I never touched her. I was sacked out, not drunk."

Dr. Sprague nodded. "What's her story?"

"She claims I gave her a drink, I was already drinking, things got fuzzy and we were attracted to each other. She's not mad. She knows it wasn't deliberate, but she's pregnant, it's mine, and she wants to marry me but we don't have to stay married."

"Why would she set you up? The real father won't marry her?"

"Dr. Sprague, she's a knockout and the family has money. I can't imagine anyone turning that down."

Dr. Sprague smirked. "You are. And if the baby's father is a married man, he might, too. What are her morals like?"

Peter shrugged. "Good family, never a hint of scandal. I don't know her but that's what I'm told. She's pure and innocent."

Dr. Sprague sat up. "Bullshit, she set you up, there's your first suspicion, and she was peddling here for you, too. Innocent doesn't work. Find out about her."

"Dr. Sprague, the Chinese are the eyes and ears of the world. They take each other's pulse hourly, I swear. She couldn't get past them. Her family's prominent; they're well known and well respected. They'd know if she was leading another life."

"Is her father paying for her reputation?"

"I doubt it. I like him, he seems honest and honorable."

"I'm glad you didn't go into law, you're making a lousy case for yourself."

Peter sighed. "Boy, I know it. Her life's been lilywhite and mine," he shrugged, "mine was a mess."

"You're sure it can't be yours? You'd be surprised how many OB students get caught."

Peter shook his head. "It's not mine. I didn't lose control. I was exhausted. I'm not bionic and there was no evidence. I checked."

Dr. Sprague leaned back and rubbed his face. "Okay, then how do we prove it? She's Miss White and you're Mr. Black. What do we do without causing a Chinese uprising?"

"I got her family to agree to tests. She's only done a dime store deal. I want to determine what stage the embryo's at. This all happened a week ago."

Dr. Sprague sat forward, coming to life. "Good man, you got us that much." He took a pad and made notes. "I'd like to have Dr. Gurstfeld handle it. He's sharp and tight-lipped. He's seen it all and gotten some good men off the hook."

Peter was encouraged. "If you'll list the tests, I'll have my grandfather contact her family. The Chinese have their own way of handling things, pride and all that."

Dr. Sprague shook his hand. "No, I'll call Gurstfeld. Have your grandfather give the family his name. Like I said, he's seen it all. He has a sixth sense about these situations. And Peter, find out about her. Miss White's having fun behind daddy's back."

Peter fidgeted. "Dr. Sprague, that's tough to do. I don't know anybody in the community anymore and if I poke around then the Chinese dignity and honor get messed up. My guess is it's a college kid who can't afford her, but even then her father would help." Peter shrugged. "I don't know what to think. She's got this beautiful innocent face and I hear that story and I even have trouble believing I'm innocent."

Dr. Sprague scowled. "Peter, if you're not sure."

"No, I'm sure, I just mean she doesn't look the type to fool around and set me up for it. Damn, she looks like a nice kid. I feel bad for the family."

"Peter, the girl's done you dirty. Get mad and stay mad or you'll drown in her lilywhite lies. She got pregnant somewhere, Peter."

"I know, I know," Peter answered. "It's just hard to believe. Her sisters were totally straight. The family's totally straight."

Dr. Sprague shook his head. "Peter, read my lips, the girl got pregnant somewhere. Get mad." Dr. Sprague thumped his pen on the desk. "What's this doing to you and Jeneil?"

"She believes me."

Dr. Sprague smiled. "I'll call Gurstfeld. Let's bury this fast."

"Thanks," Peter said, standing.

Dr. Sprague extended his hand. "For what it's worth, I believe you, too."

"I appreciate that," Peter answered, and shook his hand and left.

Peter was glad he had taken Steve's advice about telling Dr. Sprague. He felt more comfortable even though nothing favorable had been proven or resolved, and it helped his confidence to have someone else believe him. It was difficult for Peter to imagine Dr. Gurstfeld to be the steel-spined sleuth Dr. Sprague described. Seeing him around, it always looked like he was lost and suffering from amnesia but Peter trusted Dr. Sprague.

*****

Peter washed his hands for dinner. Jeneil had seemed distant when he got home, not mentioning anything about Uette. She had listened quietly as he told her about his meeting with Dr. Sprague and he had been surprised to find that Dr. Gurstfeld was her gynecologist. Jeneil had a lot of faith in the doctor's ability and professionalism, and he had taught her a lot about her body. Peter had trouble picturing Dr. Gurstfeld as a hero to women, but Jeneil sang his praises.

Jeneil was sitting at the table when Peter got to the dining room. He kissed her cheek and sat down. She hadn't felt like cooking so they were having leftover roast beef. She ate quietly and he was getting concerned. "Honey, don't let it get at you, okay?"

She looked up, looking surprised he was there. "Peter, how is your mother handling this new twist?" He wondered why she asked and swallowing his mashed potatoes he cleaned his mouth with his napkin.

"She's behind Uette because she saw us in bed. She thinks I'm a low-life and should be grateful this happened with Uette and not Lin Chi. Why?"

Jeneil found it interesting his mother hadn't mentioned her. "I'm just curious. I'd like to know how much of a hand your mother and Karen have had in this."

"What do you mean?"

She clasped her hands over her plate. "It seems strange that Uette knew when to be at the house, that's all. It's unlikely that she managed it alone."

"She knows a lot about me from Karen. I know that much."

Jeneil nodded. "I thought so."

Peter sat back. "Honey, you've given me an idea. I need to find out about Uette's private life. Karen might be the answer." Jeneil watched as he got up and went to the telephone. "Karen, it's me."

"Hi, Pete," Karen answered softly.

"I guess you've heard about your friend, Uette."

"Yes, I did, Pete. My father raged about my involvement. He said Uette told him."

"What is your involvement, Karen?" Jeneil got up and went to the sofa. Karen didn't answer. "Karen, I know you didn't come to the hospital just to give me brownies. How did Uette know I'd be home alone Thursday night?"

Peter heard Karen sniffle slightly. "I told her, Pete. She wanted to get you away from the hospital. But Pete, she didn't set you up. Uette's not like that. She's crazy about you."

Peter was surprised. "Why, Karen? Why me? I never encouraged her, so why me?"

"Peter, she knows you. She knows your background and she still thinks you're great. She's not like her sisters at all."

"Karen, how does she know me?"

"From her father, I guess. She laughed when she told me that her older sister had nightmares from his warnings about you."

Karen's answer made Peter more curious. "Then how come Uette isn't afraid of me?"

"I don't know. She thinks for herself. She's smarter than her sisters, I guess. She bought herself a gorgeous corvette from a modeling job. Her father can't hold her as tightly as he does her sisters."

"Oh, really," Peter's curiosity was peaking, "who does she hang out with in school?"

"No one really. She sort of drifts in and out of all the groups. The kids don't trust her."

"Why not?"

"They think she's superficial. They feel like she's doing research on them. She wants to be an actress so she observes things like she's studying everything around her. I like her; she's been nice to me. She feels awful about what happened and the trouble she's caused you. She understands your attitude. She knows you're shocked."

"I am that, Karen. Tell me something. Was she dating anyone?"

"Oh, Pete, that's low. You think she's blaming you for someone else's...." Karen sighed. "Poor Uette, that's awful. She really doesn't date."

"That's a surprise, isn't it, with her looks?"

"But I told you, the kids don't like her. She's not interested in our interests. Anyway, she seems above it all. She's different, Pete. She just doesn't fit in."

"Karen, give me an honest answer. What's the word on her morally?"

"Pete, you're bad. She thinks the world of you and you're looking for dirt on her."

"Karen, answer my question."

Karen sighed. "She's a Wong, Pete. Do you know what that means? The guys have a joke about the Wong sisters. They say those girls never do anything Wong."

"Karen, you told me she wasn't like her sisters. What does that mean really?"

"You're making me mad, Pete. It doesn't mean what you think. She's not a snob like her sisters, that's what I meant. Boy, you're desperate to get out of this, aren't you?"

"Karen, do you like being blamed for something you didn't do?"

"No."

"Neither do I. Karen, think. Isn't there a guy she hangs around with a lot?"

"Yeah, he's in the drama club, but he's gay and makes no secret about it."

"Then what the hell does she do for fun?"

Karen thought for a minute. "She likes movies and plays. She reads a lot. She's a loner, Pete. She works and goes to school. That doesn't leave too much time for anything else, trust me. I'm familiar with that kind of schedule."

Peter could tell it was useless. "Thanks, Karen."

"Pete, are you going to marry her?"

"Karen, you'll hear it first, I'm sure. Thanks again." He hung up and went to the sofa. Lying down, he put his head in Jeneil's lap.

"Nothing?" Jeneil asked.

"Nothing that makes sense; she's a loner, doesn't date much, keeps to herself mostly. Goes to the movies or plays and reads a lot. She doesn't fit in."

Jeneil stared at him. "That sounds like me in college."

He chuckled. "You fooled around with wind and sunsets. They don't get a person pregnant."

"Only with ideas."

He smiled and touched her cheek. "You're cute." She kissed his hand. "Then what can't her father tie her tight from?"

"What?" Jeneil asked, not understanding his question.

Peter sat up. "Karen said Uette's father can't tie her too tight. No dating, movies, reading. What's to tie her from?" He got up and went to the telephone and dialed. "Karen, me again. What did you mean Uette's father can't tie her too tightly?"

"I don't know. That's what she told me."

Peter hung onto the telephone cord, hoping. "Her life sounds dull as hell; I just wondered what her father wanted to tie her from."

"She didn't say, Pete. She just said he allows her toys like the Corvette, which he thinks is too showy, and her modeling job."

"Oh." Peter was disappointed. "Okay, Karen, thanks again."

"Pete, give it up. She's decent."

"Karen, the girl is pregnant. You don't get that way from movies and reading."

Karen sighed. "She told me that you couldn't remember that night. She hates this having happened to you and she's worried about your career. She really is flipped out over you. She's more concerned for you than for herself."

"Thanks for sharing that. She knows which button works the loud speaker, doesn't she?"

"You're tough, Pete. You really are. I think she's crazy."

"Well, we certainly agree on that."

"Bye, Pete," Karen snapped, annoyed by his remark about Uette.

"Bye, Karen."

Jeneil was kneeling on the sofa, leaning against the back. "Anything?"

"No, the girl's weird. She a loner; leads a quiet life reading, movies, and plays. She wants to be an actress, owns a Corvette, and has a modeling job."

Jeneil wrinkled her brow. "She's two people, opposites. What do you and Karen agree on? I heard you say that."

Peter grinned. "That Uette's crazy."

"Karen thinks she's crazy?" Jeneil was surprised.

"For a different reason."

"What's her reason?" Peter hesitated and shrugged. "What?" Jeneil insisted on an answer.

Peter was embarrassed. "Karen said Uette's flipped out over me."

Jeneil put her head down on her arms. "We're dead."

"Why?" Peter asked, gently rubbing Jeneil's back.

Jeneil stood up and paced with her arms folded. "I'll do the dishes now." She began clearing the table and he went to help her. "No, Peter, I want to be alone."

He took her arm. "Baby, don't pack it in now. What will happen when the screws get tighter?"

She looked at him surprised. "I'm not. I just need to think. There are odd pieces in this and they're racing through my mind all mixed up." She kissed him.

He sighed. "You scared me, honey."

Jeneil's telephone rang and she answered it.

"Hi, sweetheart, how's it going?"

Jeneil smiled. "I'm okay, Steve. I apologize for collapsing last night."

"You don't have to. Is Pete home?"

"He's right here, hold on." She handed Peter the telephone and went to the kitchen.

"Steve," Peter answered.

"Pete, did you see Sprague?"

"Yeah, he set up a doctor for the tests."

"Good. Pete, I found something very odd. Last night after I left, I called a girl I once dated who knows people who know everybody or can find someone who does. I asked her to put the word out on Uette. She called me a few minutes ago."

Peter held his breath. "Steve, make it good news."

"I don't know if it's good or bad, just odd. She told me her cousin 'rapped' all day on Uette and hit brick walls. Then, at the end of the afternoon, he got a call from a guy who told him to drop it. The guy was a good friend, he said Uette's untouchable. I asked Rayna what that meant, she said it could mean she's clean or surrounded by money and power that the streets won't mess with."

"They didn't say what money and power?"

"Pete, Rayna advised me to drop it. She said her cousin's connection is huge and he wasn't poking around for anybody on it again. She said whatever it is, they're important enough for the street to avoid them."

Peter was puzzled. "Her father's that powerful? Man, I know they have money, but I didn't know he held such a big stick."

"I guess he does, Pete. Boy, when you tangle, you do it big."

Peter sighed. "Isn't that the truth? Thanks for trying, Steve."

"It's okay; I just wish it was more. Have you been able to uncover anything?"

"I asked Karen and she said Uette's a loner who leads a quiet life, drives a Corvette and models. She's studying drama at college."

Steve groaned. "Wonderful, an actress. Well, she's got this role moving nicely."

Peter rubbed his forehead. "Then it looks like my only hope are the tests."

"Who's the doctor?"

"Gurstfeld."

Steve chuckled. "Oh shit, now I feel sorry for Uette."

"Why?"

"The guy is so thorough, it's almost obscene."

"Jeneil likes him. She thinks he's very professional."

"Sure, she's straight. For her, he'd be a kindly figure. Word is he got nailed early in med school by a coed. He claimed the baby wasn't his but he never proved it. That marriage ended in divorce, but it left him obsessive-compulsive about embryonic research. I don't think he'll die happy unless he can match chromosomes from an embryo to its biological father. When he gets a case like yours, he acts like he's reliving his own experience. You can count on Uette being given every test except a polygraph only because he couldn't explain the relevance to a medical board." Steve laughed. "Boy, Sprague is tough as nails when he's riled. And, I heard Gurstfeld doesn't need to give polygraphs. He has this built in divining mechanism that can spot a setup three states away."

Peter smiled. "You're cheering me up, Steve."

Steve laughed. "Well, don't get too comfortable. He doesn't bat a thousand, but he's close to it. The joke is he has the girl return for test after test, one at a time, until she's ready to confess just to be left alone and the whole while he treats her like he's going to help nail the son-of-a-bitch. To be fair, he does, if the guy is the one shittin' in the case."

"Oh great, one look at Uette's innocent face and I'll be the son-of-a-bitch. She's shrewd and lies like she believes her story. You should have heard her. She even looked me right in the eye, crying huge tears, and asked me how I could lie like that in front of her!"

Steve whistled. "I wish I was Gurstfeld's assistant on this one. Sounds like the clash of two pros. Gurstfeld and Uette."

Peter sighed. "I wonder how long this all takes."

"He's fast, Pete. A girl sometimes spends a whole day waiting for tests or going through them. I think you'll know in a week. I'm telling you, Gurstfeld has done more for birth control than the pill. You can count on a girl pulling a trick like this only once in her lifetime when he's done with her."

Peter watched Jeneil brush her hair slowly before bed. She had been quiet since doing dishes, sitting in the living room chair with an open book on her lap that she never looked at. Her mind was elsewhere and Peter was afraid he knew where. She got into bed and turned off the bedside lamp. He turned, facing her, kissing her shoulder. "Honey, don't shut me out."

She patted his hand. "I'm just thinking."

"Talk to me. Tell me what you're thinking."

She sighed. "I'm wondering what Uette's motive is. When Karen said she was flipped out over you, I realized we were in deep trouble. If that's her motive and she's pregnant because of it then she'll be tough to oppose. She's operating from love not hate or fear or desperation."

"Jeneil, the bottom line is the baby's not mine. What kind of love is that?"

"Peter, the bottom line is you have to prove it."

He turned a strand of her hair around his thumb. "You don't sound very hopeful." She was silent and he kissed her cheek.

"Peter, I need to know what will happen if you can't prove you're not the father."

"Jeneil, if I was the father, I'd marry her. I wouldn't do that to my child. I know what it's like."

She looked at him steadily. "You didn't answer my question."

"I don't need to think about it."

"I do," she said. "I'm involved, too. I'd like to know."

He looked at her. "We're married. I can't just leave you."

"We're not married legally, we have no rights. We haven't even been together long enough to qualify for a common law marriage."

"Well, you've done some research on this." He lay back on his pillow.

She folded and unfolded the sheet hem. "I had to, Peter. I don't like surprises. I need to face things and direct as much of my life as I can. I've made myself face the possibility that you'll have to leave me." She choked on the pain and wiped her tears as they fell.

Peter got up and paced. "Jeneil, can't we face this, if it happens at all?

"I'm not made that way," she said, and he sighed as he paced. "How was the meeting left? What will happen next?"

"Her father and grandfather agreed to the tests. We'll have another meeting."

"Even if you're proven innocent?"

"I guess so. The Wongs will need to apologize."

"Do the Wongs believe Uette?"

"Yes, but they would, don't you think?"

"What do the Wongs want if you're not proven innocent."

Peter stopped near the bed. "Baby, can't we stop this already? Please?"

"Please answer my question."

"They agree with Uette, a marriage for family honor then a divorce because the situation is so unusual. There's no love in this."

"What is your grandfather's answer?"

Peter held his breath. "Jeneil, please."

She sighed. "Peter, I know what his answer was. He didn't have any choice. If you can't prove you're not the father, you need to protect the family honor for the Wongs and the Changs. You'd have to marry her."

"No!" he said, hitting the bedpost. "I won't. I can't do it, Jeneil."

Jeneil's heart ached for him. She felt his insult and as she analyzed the situation, she realized the principle of honor and duty. She understood saving face. This was a situation beyond justice and one thing life had taught her early in her growing years was that injustice was something you didn't necessarily recover from or change into justice. Most times it was something you endured. Life wasn't always fair. She thought about that as she watched Peter pace and wondered if maybe life was meant to be fair, but people had weaknesses and that caused the injustice. Was injustice doled out by chance?

The questions created by that one thought seemed endless to her. Was life a game of chance run by luck? Like the big bang theory? The right set of circumstances and elements and bang, an explosion, a resulting planet breathing life as complicated as it was? Something deep inside of her resisted but she didn't know why. She wondered where the answers would be. She sighed. Life wasn't an accident. It couldn't be. She sighed again from the frustration of not having answers and wanting to avoid thinking about Uette. She got up and went to Peter, who was standing near the desk having drifted into thought, too.

"Hold me," she said. "I don't like damp fog."

She moved closer to him and he grabbed her, holding her tightly against him. "Jeneil, you belong to me," he whispered. She heard the desperation in his voice and realized the cold, damp fog had reached him, too.

"I always will, Peter," she answered. "I always will."

Fifteen

Peter and Jeneil awoke in each other's arms the next morning. He smiled at her and she snuggled to him. He held her, not wanting to let her out of his sight. Their passionate love had calmed them both. The alarm rang and Peter groaned. Jeneil yawned. "Good morning, Friday."

The routine of a new day sent them into the dim light of morning. They met for breakfast, which was eaten standing in the kitchen.

"Honey, I picked up the results of our blood tests yesterday. Let's get our license today. My mother had all my papers in a metal box. Meet me at the municipal building at five."

Jeneil looked stunned. "Peter…."

Anticipating her thoughts, he kissed her. "Baby, I want to continue with our plans. When this mess is over, we'll at least have our license and we can be married." She understood; continuing with their plans gave her a feeling of security, too. She nodded, agreeing with him. He smiled and kissed her again. "Thanks, baby."

Taking the lunches she had prepared for him and Steve, he left. Jeneil began dancing with a vengeance. She needed the adrenaline; it helped her endure injustice.

*****

Peter headed back to work, buoyed up from their visit to the municipal building. They had gotten their marriage license and he got back to the hospital wanting to tell the world the news. Steve was at the medical charts when Peter returned.

Peter straightened his shirt and tie. "Is everything quiet here?"

Steve nodded. "The hip patient was having some discomfort."

Peter looked at her chart. "I wish I could give her to Jeneil." Steve looked puzzled and Peter laughed. "She's having trouble healing."

Steve smiled. "Did everything go okay at the bureau?"

"Yeah." He sighed, smiling.

"Congratulations," Steve said, patting Peter on the shoulder.

Steve replaced the chart. He was sincere about his feelings. Having seen Jeneil's reaction to the news about Uette, he had come to accept that she was Peter's. He wanted things to work out for them, for Jeneil's sake. He was concerned about her and didn't want to see her get hurt. He was surprised how quickly objectivity had engulfed him. Yet, as he studied his feelings about both Jeneil and Peter, he knew he was the one expected to protect the triad. She needed security, Peter needed help. Somehow he felt he was the answer. Jeneil was his main concern now. Having gone a step beyond love, whatever that step was, had changed him. He was devoted to her and always would be, no matter where life took him. He was puzzled by his feelings, but grateful for the resulting objectivity. Being around them was bearable. He was calm inside, almost peaceful. It felt good and he liked being in control of himself. His panic over losing her earlier had worried him.

"This is your last day, isn't it?" Peter asked, smiling

Steve nodded. "Yep, now I go on to earn the platinum tongue depressor." Peter extended his hand to Steve. Steve shook it. "Don't you say goodbye."

Peter shook his hand, feeling his emotion building. "No, I wasn't. I was going to say thank you. They call me Dr. Chang because of you."

Steve smiled. "Shit, you still don't understand that if you hadn't wandered into med school I'd have quit myself, or gone crazy. Getting the two of us through to prove you don't have to be a snot-nosed Morgan Rand to make it in medicine was a high for me." He laughed. "And that son-of-a-bitch has had the nerve to become human on me. Now I have to admit that he's an incredibly gifted surgeon. All those years of hatred, wasted."

Peter laughed. "He may be gifted, but I notice you're the one finishing a half year ahead."

"The marker system, Pete."

Peter grinned. "Markers, shit. You're still shocked to learn that you're brilliant."

Steve smiled. "No, I knew I was a brilliant pickpocket, but I have to admit finding out that my brain could understand all this still overwhelms me." Peter laughed.

A group of hospital staff had gathered around the nurse's desk, and Peter and Steve turned as the group called, "Paging Dr. Steven Bradley." Someone had brought in a cake and put a Fourth of July sparkler on it. Steve choked up. He was familiar with the farewell ceremony but it still surprised him that it was his turn to receive it. The hospital had been home and these people had been his family for so many years that the separation wasn't easy for him. He held tight to the thought of Jeneil and was calmed knowing he had her to go to and to talk to. He liked the way she looked at life and had meant it when he told her she made life a career. She made sense of it and he loved that. Somehow having Jeneil and Peter made the end of this year less painful. He accepted the backslapping and handshakes and words of farewell and congratulations cheerfully.

Barbara Stanton came up to Peter. "You have a phone call."

Peter went to the desk and picked up the receiver, recognizing the voice. "Uette, I'm on duty."

"I know, but I think we need to talk privately."

"I don't," Peter answered quickly.

"But I'd like to know what will happen to me. I'm very frightened." Peter heard her voice catch from emotion.

"Uette, your father will handle this. Talk to him and he'll see my grandfather."

Her voice got a pitch higher. "It's not their lives, it's ours!"

"I like the way they're dealing with it," he answered quietly. She began to cry and Peter sighed. "Uette, I've got to get back to work." He hung up. His stomach was tight. He rubbed his forehead and exhaled. She left him tense. He noticed she had that effect on him, encounters with her leaving him torn between rage and compassion. He could tell she was frightened and he wondered what the story was on her pregnancy. Why the hell couldn't she say she was raped and save her own honor. Why drag him through it? His rage began to take over his compassion. He turned and joined the festive, happy group hoping to recapture the feeling of celebration that had followed him from the municipal building.

*****

The following days each seemed like they were a month long. Peter called his grandfather to report Uette calling him and to ask that her father tell her why Peter wouldn't deal with her. His grandfather understood, Uette's grandfather understood, and her father understood. Uette cried bitterly when her father explained Peter's shunning was to show his contempt for having been so insulted by her charge. Uette became more frightened when she realized her father accepted Peter's attitude as understandable and acceptable. The only man she seemed to find sympathetic was the doctor she was told to visit. Dr. Gurstfeld had a calming effect on her and she enjoyed going to see him.

The waiting wasn't easy on Jeneil either. She was very quiet and spent a lot of time thinking, and had gotten in very late one night after going to the ocean to face the wind. After that night she cried easily, but seemed steady and resolute otherwise. She made life between them absolute bliss and Peter was stunned by the extra care and attention. He assumed she was trying to ease the tension that filled him almost constantly while he waited for word from Dr. Gurstfeld. It was nearing a week and he was anxious to hear something. He hated the feeling of being in limbo and wanted to get on with his plans to marry Jeneil.

Peter saw Dr. Sprague get off the elevator and was surprised to see him. It was after hours for the administration staff. He came to Peter carrying a large manila envelope. The realization that the envelope contained the reports seized Peter and shock stunned his body. Finally, he thought, and he felt his heart beat a little faster.

"Peter, I got someone to cover for you. Let's go to my office. I have to see Dr. Campbell on one small matter. I'll meet you there in fifteen minutes."

Peter got to Dr. Sprague's office a few minutes early. The door was locked and the lights were off. He leaned against the wall, struggling with excitement and fear. The elevator doors opened and Dr. Sprague walked toward him. He looked serious and Peter became concerned. Dr. Sprague unlocked the door and left the lights off in his waiting room. Making sure the door was locked again he went to his office and turned on the lights. Peter waited in semi-darkness.

"Come in, Peter," Dr. Sprague said, standing in the glaring light of his office. Peter walked in and sat down. Holding the manila envelope, Dr. Sprague sighed. "Dr. Gurstfeld has completed a battery of tests. These are the results." He cleared his throat, obviously upset. "It's not good, Peter." Peter sank in his chair and stared. "She was barely over a week pregnant when she was tested. I guess you were hoping she would be farther along?" Peter only nodded, his voice having disappeared. "There was one test Dr. Gurstfeld felt you should know you have available if you wanted to convince the girl. The other of course is the routine DNA test after the baby's born. She is pregnant and about two weeks along now."

Peter felt like he was going to be sick to his stomach. He got up and paced. "I can't believe it. I wasn't drunk. I would have known." He ran his fingers through his hair.

"Peter, I told you Gurstfeld was very shrewd. We had a long talk. Some of what he told me I won't repeat because of doctor-patient confidentiality, but I'm going to stretch ethics as far as I can because of his findings and the nature of the circumstances involved. I think you have a right to be aware of a few things."

Peter stopped pacing and looked at Dr. Sprague. Dr. Sprague was sober. "Dr. Gurstfeld's complete tests can be subpoenaed if you should go that route. He gave you only what is pertinent to you at the moment, which is the reality and term of the pregnancy."

"What aren't you telling me?" Peter asked sitting down, getting the feeling Dr. Sprague was circling an issue.

Dr. Sprague sighed. "Peter, what I'm going to tell you now is inadmissible in a court of law because it's only Gurstfeld's opinion. I told you he's seen it all, cases where the girl is ignorant about her own body or cases where the girl is negligent about protection for a variety of reasons. But, in your case, he thinks the girl is, and I'm quoting him, 'One of the shrewdest bitches he has ever encountered.'" Peter watched Dr. Sprague; he was angry and grasped his pen tightly. "Peter, you've been set up by a pro." He rubbed his mouth. "She's not lilywhite, believe me. Listen to me carefully; there is evidence to support that in Gurstfeld's findings which can be subpoenaed. Understand me, Peter. Dr. Gurstfeld said to look past the beautiful face and the innocent eyes, and that you'll need the information when you begin to struggle with what you know is real but can't prove. He said to cling to the evidence, it will keep you sane." Dr. Sprague exhaled then breathed in deeply. "Now, this next part is a pip and Gurstfeld's going on shear instinct, but he told me to let you know that the records he'll have in his files will be copies."

Peter was confused. "I don't understand."

Dr. Sprague shook his head. "Neither do I, but like I said, Gurstfeld has seen it all. He's keeping the originals in his private safe out of the building. He told me that in the last case like this several of his case files disappeared from his office."

Peter raised his eyebrows. "What the hell?"

"Peter, the girl involved in the other case was connected to real power, organized crime. The break in went undetected until the records were subpoenaed and were found to be missing. But what Gurstfeld found interesting was that the other patient records for the same day as hers were also missing, which made it look like his office screwed up. There was never a screw up like that before that day or since."

Peter sat back against the chair. "That's the second time it's been hinted about her being connected to power. I've tried to find out about her."

"What does her father do?"

"He's an importer."

Dr. Sprague closed his eyes. "I'm afraid to ask what he imports." Peter was stunned by the remark. "Is there money in the family?"

"Yes, but they're honest people."

Dr. Sprague shook his head. "Peter, daddy's able to buy a shiny reputation for her. She's not lilywhite."

Peter rubbed his forehead . "Okay, so what I have here is a piece of trash everyone thinks is snow white, but she's pregnant and I can't prove it's not mine." He sighed.

"You did tell me that she said you don't have to stay married."

Peter nodded. "Yes, why?"

Dr. Sprague looked uncomfortable. "Because I'm worried you've been selected because you're a doctor. If daddy's importing things like drugs, you might be handy."

Peter was bordering on shock. "Dr. Sprague, these people are decent. I'd stake my life on it."

"Peter, you have to be very careful. You don't know what the hell you've been snared for, but you have been snared."

Peter rubbed his chin. "I can't believe it. They have money but they're not swimming in it, and the kind of power we're talking about would have enormous money, wouldn't they?"

Dr. Sprague shrugged. "Then, I don't know, Peter. This is all supposition anyway. We're building all this on Gurstfeld's instincts."

Peter looked up. "Which you trust quite a bit." Dr. Sprague nodded. Peter took a deep breath. "If I decided to sue, how would that affect my career?"

"Not favorably, Peter. I'm going to tell you something. You and Bradley were screened very carefully before you were allowed in here. You especially because of your connection to a gang called the Dragons. When we looked closer, we found they were...," Dr. Sprague searched for a word.

"Scum," Peter helped him out.

Dr. Sprague nodded. "It was a conversation with Dr. Danielson that turned things around for you. He told me the whole story of the war that took place and how you were almost killed opposing the takeover. He got affidavits from the police and everybody he could think of who could prove you were straight. I have to tell you the information about the Dragons will probably come out in a trial, as well as you living with Jeneil at the time this girl got pregnant, along with the bitch's story of being drunk, etc, etc. Peter, you're knee-deep in shit. You've got to tread carefully. We could get you a truckload of praise on how you changed your life, but all that will be passed on and remembered is the sensational dirt and lies. Like skunk spray, the smell lasts and lasts. I'm not saying don't fight her legally, I'm just letting you know the reality of the situation."

Peter nodded. "It isn't anything that hasn't passed through my mind." He sighed heavily. "Well, that's it then." He stood up. "Thanks, Dr. Sprague. At least I know what I'm dealing with."

Dr. Sprague studied him. "I don't think you do. You're getting conflicting stories and that's not easy to handle. I want to be kept up to date. I'd like you in here once a week."

Peter looked at him. "I'll handle this."

Dr. Sprague loosened his tie. "Peter, it's unofficial. Actually it's for me. I'm...you're one of my favorites. I'd like to stay in close touch through this."

Peter shrugged. "Maybe you're right. I've lost Steve as a crying towel."

Dr. Sprague got up and put his arm around Peter's shoulder. "Trust me; we'll see you to the end of your residency and into your career. Bitches can't kill good surgeons. We're the tough, we're the few." Peter smiled at Dr. Sprague's words of enthusiasm.

*****

Peter went to the telephones at ten-thirty and called his grandfather. The old man was pleased to hear from him. "Grandfather, I got the results of the tests. Uette's pregnant and only two weeks into term."

"Oh." Peter heard the disappointment in his grandfather's voice. "I'm sorry, Peter. What now?"

"Her family has to be told."

The grandfather sighed. "They'll want to meet with you again."

"I know. I'm off duty Saturday morning if they're free."

"What will you do, Peter? How will you handle this?"

Peter's throat tightened. "Grandfather, I don't want to marry her. I can't leave Jeneil. She's my wife."

"I understand, Peter. I don't know what their reaction will be."

"Not pleasant, I'm sure of that."

The grandfather was quiet. "I don't understand the girl. Why is she doing this?"

Peter decided to ask his questions. "Grandfather, is her father straight?"

"Straight?"

"Yeah, honest and really what he seems to be?"

"Yes, he is, Peter. He takes pride in family name. Lu has done well with his sons and his daughter. They're all good people. Why?"

"Because...," Peter hesitated. "Grandfather, this stays between us, okay?"

"Of course, Peter."

"I was told unofficially that Uette...," he hesitated again, not knowing how to soften the terms for his grandfather. "She's not the young innocent she wants us to believe."

"Oh?" His grandfather seemed surprised. "I assumed since the baby isn't yours but this sounds more serious."

"Grandfather, I've tried to get some word on her and was told to drop it, that there's money and power behind her. I don't like the sound of it. I don't want to be around it. All I know is that she is not Miss Innocent."

The grandfather was concerned. "You make it sound dangerous. What will happen to you if this money and power decides that you have to marry her? It sounds evil, Peter, and the Wongs are decent people. This isn't making sense. Our people know them well. Their lives are open and honest. There must be some mistake."

Peter sighed. "That was my reaction, too. I know how the community can be. You can't slip a hangnail past them. It might be a whisper, but it's whispered."

"Not with the Wongs, Peter. People look for something to bring them down because of jealousy. They're above it all. There's no dirt there."

"What can I say, Grandfather?"

"Are the people giving you this information Chinese?"

"No."

"Then I hesitate to accept it as truth."

"Why?"

"Because the community watches over its own. It all ties in to honor and pride. You earn your reward or punishment. Even your name has improved since you left the low side of life. The network is honest. They watch themselves closely so no one is deceived."

"Well, they slipped up in this case. She's pregnant and I'm not the father."

His grandfather sighed. "That's one big hole in this."

Peter remembered Gurstfeld's warning, *'cling to the evidence, it will keep you sane.'* He was beginning to understand. "Grandfather, I've got to get back on the floor."

"Okay, Peter. I'll call the Wongs."

"I'll be in touch."

Peter was amazed to hear his grandfather's reasonable explanation of the gossip network in the Chinese community. It had felt like a strangling net while he was growing up, but he could understand his grandfather's explanation of its protection. He just had serious doubts about its accuracy now. He sighed and dialed again.

"Hi, honey." It felt good to hear her voice. He had wanted to talk to her since meeting with Dr. Sprague.

"Hi." Jeneil was quiet.

"Will you wait up for me?"

"Okay."

"I want to talk to you," he added, surprised she hadn't asked why.

"I know."

"You know?"

"Yes, it's about a week now. You must have heard from Dr. Sprague. I'll wait up."

"Thanks honey, I've got to get back on the floor but I'll be out of here as fast as I can."

"I'll be waiting," she said quietly. He walked back to work wondering why she hadn't asked about the results.

*****

The apartment was dark except for the bedroom. Jeneil was going over some papers when Peter walked in. Putting them in a file folder, she smiled at him. He couldn't figure her out. Tossing his jacket in the chair, he eased onto the bed and kissed her. She felt warm and soft and honest and clean. At the moment, that felt comforting to him.

"Your lips are freezing." She fixed the strands of hair the wind had tossed out of place. "I have some Ovaltine keeping warm."

He lay on his back. The room felt comforting; the apartment secure. These were things he could trust. Jeneil returned and handed him a filled mug. "Thanks." He smiled, sipping it. "I enjoy my Ovaltine breaks." Propping the pillows, she pulled her robe around her and sat against the headboard. "How come you haven't asked me about the tests?"

"I know what the results are," Jeneil answered quietly.

"How did you know?"

She shrugged. "Instinct, intuition, the wind, she's pregnant and only two weeks probably, maybe a little less." Peter stared at her, and she smiled slightly and kissed him gently. "How are you taking the disappointment?"

"I'm tired and numb, but I've decided that I don't care anymore. She's not my worry. The baby's not mine."

She was silent then asked, "When do you meet with the Wongs?"

"Saturday morning."

"Have you thought that decision through completely?"

"There's nothing to think about. The truth is the baby's not mine. That's it right there."

Jeneil finished her drink and put the cup on the bedside table. Turning to face him, she kissed his cheek. She followed his profile with her eyes. She had always loved his features. "You had mentioned that Dr. Gurstfeld has a sixth sense about cases like this. Has he shared his opinion or is that unethical?"

"He's given his opinion." Peter put his cup aside.

Jeneil began to unbutton his shirt and noticed him watching her. "Aren't you going to bed?" she asked quietly, explaining her actions.

He grinned and pulled her to him. "Wouldn't miss it for the world." She had been subtly aggressive lately, being very seductive, and he enjoyed it.

When Peter awoke in the morning, the bedroom door was closed. He pulled his mind awake, trying to grasp what day it was. "Why is the bedroom door closed?" he asked himself, groggily. "It's Friday, I think."

He hadn't slept well. Turning onto his side, he stretched and pulled Jeneil's pillow to him. It smelled good. He remembered her and smiled. He heard the door to the microwave snap open and he looked at his watch. "Nine and Jeneil's home?" Finding his robe, he got up to see what was happening.

"Hi," she said, smiling as she arranged a plate with food.

"Baby, you're supposed to be at work."

She shrugged. "You need me more."

He grinned. "Well, I do like that."

She arranged plates, juice glasses and mugs on trays. "I have breakfast ready."

"In bed?" he asked, noticing the lap trays. She nodded. He sighed. "If I'm dreaming, don't wake me." He kissed her cheek and, taking a tray, went to the bedroom with her. "Honey, this is great. I'm starved." He drank his juice. "Why did you really stay home? Is the corporation making demands?"

"Always." She smiled. "But I really stayed home to be with you."

"Why?" he asked, puzzled.

She looked at him cautiously. "Finish your breakfast."

"Okay." Taking the lap trays and putting them on the floor by the bed, he then put his arms around her. "Now, you sexy sneak, what's really happening?"

"If your meeting with the Wongs is tomorrow, we really need to talk."

He kissed her lightly. "There's nothing to talk about. I'm not marrying Uette. She's pulling or thinks she's pulling a fast one on me. I've been told she's not shy or innocent. She's a pro. She'll have to find some other sucker."

Jeneil studied him. "Is that Gurstfeld's evaluation?"

"Unofficially, yes. He said she's a shrewd bitch. Well, damn it, why me?"

Jeneil sighed. "Because she's very attracted to you. In her own way, it's love."

Peter chuckled. "Then her love is diseased."

"It is, but I think she's gotten caught in a combination of crazy circumstances." He looked at her, puzzled. She nodded. "I really think she's two people. She stays home and reads, leading a quiet life, and the other drives a Corvette, works as a model, and wants to be an actress. I recognize the two lives because I'm doing the same thing."

"Honey, you can't compare yourself to her."

"Peter, she is like me. Trust me, she has two lives; one that her family can accept and the other is what she wants or wanted."

"Wanted?"

Jeneil nodded. "Yes, wanted, until you. Let's assume she's getting bored with her other life or lives. Karen comes along and offers to have her meet you. She's very attracted to you. You are now what she wants. You don't show any interest. She decides she'll try to see you away from the hospital. That's the iffy part because that's difficult to do alone."

Peter stared in disbelief. "It's not iffy, honey. Karen set it up with Uette to be at the house alone with me."

Jeneil sighed. "Karen will never know what she's done to our lives then." She shook her head. "If Karen helped her, it means Uette knew the schedule. Well that would explain Uette's confidence that night. You ignore her again so she decides to be more aggressive and get into bed with you. What I had trouble figuring out was why she didn't wake you up if you're what she wanted, but I realized why." Peter listened, fascinated by Jeneil's observations. "She didn't have time to wake you up. Your mother arrived to wake you for work. Uette was trapped so she pretended she got drunk to excuse the whole thing morally. If she's been leading two lives, she's good at covering herself with alibis."

Peter smiled. "Jeneil, this is another one of your Camelot episodes. It's too crazy. It's fiction. Then, let me hear you explain the baby."

"Well, this part is bizarre."

Peter laughed. "I doubt it, but let's hear it anyway."

"What if after the incident with you on Thursday night, she has a chance to slip into her other life and decides to get pregnant. You can't ignore that. Morally she's covered, you and she were drunk, it just happened. It's a shame, but more forgivable than getting pregnant sober."

Peter laughed and hugged her. "You and your love for reading are too funny."

She shrugged. "I know it sounds like something that would make Agatha Christie hysterical, because that would make Uette a very cold person. It's difficult to believe she'd do that to you knowing that we're living together and planning to be married."

Peter stopped laughing. "She didn't know. She found out at the family meeting."

Jeneil stared at him. "Then why is my version so fictitious?"

Peter smiled. "Stick to being sexy. You're better at that." He kissed her cheek.

Jeneil sighed. "I know; it really is a bad mystery plot. It's so full of holes." She shrugged. "And it took me days of thought."

Peter hugged her. "She's just a bitch. She got caught somewhere and I'm just her target. Now, that's the biggest mystery. Why me? I have a lousy reputation among the Chinese. Her father gave his daughters nightmares in order to have them avoid me, yet she doesn't avoid me."

Jeneil snuggled to him. "I know. It's contradictory to her behavior pattern of making sure she pleases the family."

Peter laughed and squeezed her. "Honey, you're so cute. You're trying to find something good in Uette. You'll never cover her with romance."

Jeneil looked at him. "There is some good. Look at the story she's telling. She's not making you a villain. She's excusing the both of you. Even explaining giving her the drink, she made you sound like a boy scout. Oops, sorry, no insult intended. There are good boy scouts somewhere I'm sure. I know I'm prejudiced about them."

Peter sighed. "I really think Uette's crazy."

Jeneil shook her head. "No, she's leading a double life, she's probably afraid of gossip, too. That can make you off-center."

Peter laughed. "You're insisting she's like you. You won't be happy until you've made her a romantic person. Honey, she's a bitch."

Jeneil became quiet then looked up at him. "Peter, what about saving face and family honor." She felt him tense up.

"Jeneil, don't pour that romantic shit on this situation. The baby's not mine."

She rubbed his chest gently and kissed his cheek softly. "I'm not, honey. Really, I'm not. What I've been pouring over lately is cold reality."

He looked at her. "What do you mean?"

She sighed and touched his face lovingly. "You're trapped. You're in checkmate. If you fight her legally, the publicity will be so damaging to your career that you won't have one. If you don't fight her but refuse to marry her, you'll have a trial anyway in the gossip courts. The story that you got a girl with a decent reputation drunk and pregnant then refused to marry her will be passed on because it's sensational, and gossips love the sensational more than the dull truth. Are you forgetting there are Chinese working at the hospital as doctors, in maintenance, in office jobs? Your story will be passed on at all levels and it will reach the hospital administration, and because you can't prove your story, you can't win."

Peter covered his eyes; he hadn't seen what Jeneil had just put before him and he knew she was right. "Oh shit!" he gasped as panic struck. He felt trapped and held onto her tighter. "Jeneil, I'm adding up what you're saying and I must be adding wrong because it sounds like you want me to marry her."

She felt the pain, too. "No, Peter, I don't want you to marry her. I'm saying you don't have a choice, you have to marry her. It has nothing to do with want. We don't always get what we want." He let go of her and got out of bed, pacing furiously.

"Peter, swallow all the bitterness at once so you can face things squarely. There is more to realize here." Tears were forming in her eyes. "If you don't marry her, that shame will hang over you and your family, your mother, over us in our marriage and it would get passed on to our children. They'll hear it, Peter. Gossip never stops. I understand what the Chinese mean by saving face. If you marry her and it ends in mutual divorce, that's an acceptable shame, preferable at least to her story of dishonor." Peter leaned on the desk, rage building as he realized the complete injustice of it. Jeneil began to cry. "Think about it, Peter. Her baby will grow up thinking you're his father and that you got his mother drunk and pregnant then refused to marry her. The passion was intense. Remember how your father's reputation affected you."

"No!" he said in pain, his stomach knotted from rage and tension. He hit the desk with his hands. "Shit!" he gasped. "Oh shit!" He could feel Chang rage. He grabbed some of the books and papers on the desk and threw them to the floor. "That lousy bitch has it all her way!" Jeneil went to him, putting her arms around him, crying from the pain she felt for him and the injustice of the situation. He held her. She sobbed and he began to feel his rage decrease as he concentrated on her and her need to be comforted. He sighed. "Baby, I can't marry her. What about us? We're already married."

"Not legally." She took a deep breath. "Peter, get this mess handled. I'll wait. I belong to you."

"You don't mean that." He stared at her, dazed.

"Yes, I do, Peter. I can't face the damage her story would do to you and our children. The only way to stop the injustice is to save face and marry her."

He let go of her. "Oh shit, Jeneil. I can't. Everything in me is in a rage because the baby isn't mine. I can't say it is by marrying her. I can't. I can't stand to think about her, how could I live with her? I'd go crazy. I would."

"But think, Peter. Maybe married to her, you could find out who the father is."

He held her again. "Jeneil, you're into fiction. Life isn't that romantic. I'm not a hero. She's not a maiden in distress. She's a piece of trash."

She looked at him sadly. "We're people, Peter, all of us caught in a monstrous mistake. The solution isn't fiction or romance; it's reality. Marriage will save face. Yours, hers, our future"

He let go of her. "You've flipped out. Think about what you're saying! It's crazy! I'll marry Uette and you'll sit patiently by and wait for me. That's straight out of fairytales, baby, wake up! How the hell will that save face? Tell me how you'll explain it to your uncle. What Uette's father won't do to me, your uncle will, and I wouldn't blame him. He'd have a right to. I'd let him."

"I'll tell him the truth, Peter. I'll explain saving face. No more hiding from life for me. It might just be the jolt that helps me find Jeneil. No hiding, no fears, no fiction."

He shook his head. "Jeneil, you're scaring me. You're making yourself believe what you're saying. Stop it right now. Baby, I don't want to be separated. You belong to me. We were married forever. That was real to me."

Jeneil fought back tears. "That's our strength, Peter. That's how we'll survive saving face. We are married forever. We won't be separated forever."

He threw up his hands in surrender. "Geez baby, you're being so thick. No. Hear me? It's that simple. No." He sat down on the bed, thinking. He stood up again. "No," he said emphatically. "The baby isn't mine. She's a piece of scum for trying to pass this off. That baby will not have my name. It's not mine." He paced angrily. "If I marry her, I'm saying it's mine." He stopped before Jeneil. "Honey, believe me, if I thought the baby was mine, I'd marry her. I'd even stay married to her. It would kill me, but I'd do it. Why can't you see my side of this?" Jeneil was silent, unable to bring herself to tell him that she felt he didn't have a side in this because he didn't have a choice.

She sighed. "Let's go to your grandfather about it."

Peter stretched his back and rubbed his neck. The tension was eating him up. "I told him I wouldn't marry her. He said he understands."

Jeneil was surprised. "Then let's just visit him. It'll get us out of the house. He's such a peaceful man. We need to get some fresh air. My head is spinning from the confusion."

He put his arms around her. "I'm sorry about this mess, honey." He kissed her. "You don't deserve this craziness. You're a lady, a lady who believes in love and civilized behavior."

Jeneil leaned against him for comfort. "Every pedestal I've seen had a cold, lifeless statue on it. Please don't put me on a pedestal. I like being with people. They're alive and warm. We make mistakes; that's how we know we're human. We're human and it hurts sometimes."

He smiled and held her closer. "How the hell did I wake up and see you? I'm not that bright."

She smiled. "We met going under for the third time in a sea of anesthesia. We saved each other."

He kissed her passionately and she responded equally. At times when life refused to be reasonable, being physical could be a haven. The normalcy helped to survive the chaos because it was natural and that could feel reasonable. It was more than just a physical need at a physical level.

Anxious to visit with Peter's grandfather, Jeneil went to pack a lunch for the three of them while Peter took a shower. She and the picnic basket were ready when Peter walked from the bedroom buttoning his shirt.

He smiled. "A picnic?"

"Yes, a winter picnic in the greenhouse."

"I called my grandfather. He's looking forward to the visit."

Sixteen

Peter's grandfather finished feeding the finches then went to the parakeets. The water dish was empty. Going to the kitchen, he filled a jar with water and headed back, wondering about Peter and Jeneil's visit. He was very worried about them and deeply concerned for Peter. There was no way he could see his grandson winning in this situation with Uette. If he married her, he'd lose Jeneil and if he didn't marry Uette, he could lose, too. The old man saw it; he was concerned that Peter hadn't. He felt that Peter's reaction was natural though. Peter loved Jeneil deeply.

"The lovebirds are in deep trouble," he told the parakeets, who chirped at the sound of his voice as he filled their water dish. "I wonder what all this has done to them already."

The greenhouse door opened and Peter and Jeneil came in. The old man turned to see Peter put his arm around Jeneil's shoulder. They were both smiling. He was surprised and pleased that they still showed a devotion to each other. He had worried about Jeneil's reaction to hearing the test results.

"Are you going on a picnic?" the grandfather asked, seeing Peter put the small basket on the bench.

"Yes, here with you and your birds. Jeneil had me stop at the pet shop. She bought a cuttlebone for Chin Su and Chu Ling."

The grandfather smiled and went to her. He hugged her, which surprised Peter. "Jeneil, how are you?" He studied her eyes. There was tension, she seemed weary.

She smiled slightly. "Fair to middlin', but you seem much recovered from your bout with the flu."

He shrugged. "As you say, fair to middlin'!"

Peter took the cuttlebone from the box. "You can put it in the cage, Grandfather. Chun Su and I understand each other. He stays in the cage and I stay out of it."

Jeneil smiled and went to the birds. Taking the cuttlebone, she explained that she had brought it for them. "Let me put it on your cage, okay?"

"Honey, watch the vulture," Peter cautioned, as he watched her open the cage slowly. The birds flew to the highest perch. Jeneil attached the clip quickly and closed the door. Chun

Su was the first to examine the new addition. Peter smiled then kissed Jeneil's cheek. The grandfather watched, surprised they were still so close. Both Peter and Jeneil seemed weary, but they were still affectionate toward each other.

The grandfather sat down. "I have my lunch around noon because I have breakfast very early. Would you mind if we eat now? Since getting the flu, my system is still weak."

"Of course," Jeneil said, going to the basket. She poured creamy tomato soup into a mug and gave it to him along with a sandwich. Peter and Jeneil sat on the bench together and the conversation was pleasant. The grandfather was encouraged; they were doing well as a couple in spite of the serious problem that had come into their lives. Again, he was surprised and very, very pleased. They finished their picnic with grapes and cookies.

The grandfather was glad and encouraged they had visited. "Jeneil, how come you have the day off?"

She hesitated. Peter noticed and slipped his arm around her shoulder. "To be with me, Grandfather," Peter answered for her. The grandfather was puzzled. "When I'm on the second shift, we hardly see each other. Since I got the test results yesterday, she stayed home today to be with me."

The old man smiled, pleased at her level of consideration and caring. "It's good to see you two so together on this." Peter and Jeneil looked at each other.

Peter kissed her cheek. "We're not, Grandfather." The old man studied them more closely. "Jeneil thinks I should marry Uette to save face."

The grandfather stared, completely stunned by the admission. "Jeneil," he said, "can you tell me why?"

The subject was an emotional one for Jeneil and she had to concentrate to remain calm. "When I add up the problems the marriage would prevent, like damage to Peter's career, our future, Peter's reputation with our children and Uette's baby," she shrugged slightly, "there really doesn't seem to be a choice. Peter can't win because he can't prove he's innocent." The grandfather was amazed how thoroughly she had considered the consequences. Jeneil swallowed. "But I can understand Peter's anger. This is a deliberate injustice and that's infuriating. I see the long range damage it will do and Peter doesn't deserve that. He's worked so hard to get where he is and I can't see any other way to stop the injustice quickly except marriage." Tears ran down her face and she reached for her purse to get a tissue. Peter took her hand and sighed, lowering his head.

The grandfather saw their suffering and his heart ached for them. He understood their anger since he struggled with this own. Jeneil would always be special; she seemed like a granddaughter to him and he was very proud of her. He waited then asked, "Jeneil, you've considered everyone else in this. What about you and Peter?"

She nodded. "Peter has the greatest struggle. He has to bear the dishonor and its damage if he doesn't marry her and the injustice if he does. He can't win." Peter squeezed her hand to let her know he loved her.

"That brings us to the damage to Jeneil," the grandfather said, with quiet concern.

She shrugged. "Uette has told him they don't have to stay married. I would wait for him." The grandfather looked at Peter, who had his eyes closed and looked in pain. Jeneil sighed. "But it has to be Peter's decision."

The grandfather wondered. "Will you accept him no matter what his decision may be?"

Jeneil hesitated. As seconds passed without her answer, Peter opened his eyes and looked at her. She stared at her clasped hands. Peter sat up slowly, wrinkling his eyebrows. "Gotcha," Jeneil said, as she quietly poked his arm with her elbow.

Peter sighed deeply, leaning forward and resting his elbows on his knees. "Oh, baby, you scared me that time."

She leaned against him gently and rubbed his back. "I'm sorry. I couldn't resist. You were looking so serious."

The grandfather smiled. Their harmony in spirit touched him as he noticed how well suited they were to each other. "Jeneil, where did you get the idea for a spiritual marriage?"

"From being in the wind on the beach shortly after I had fallen in love with Peter. I think there are dimensions to life than just the one we call reality. In fact, I honestly feel this dimension is very narrowly limited in what is actually real. But somehow the ceremony didn't feel quite complete."

Peter sat up quickly. "It did to me."

Jeneil smiled. "Oh, it was very real to me, but not quite complete. I really don't know what was missing." She sighed, looking very concerned. "I know it wasn't the right time, but I was frightened about this situation."

The grandfather sat up straight, becoming very curious. "Your ceremony seemed out of its natural time?"

Jeneil nodded. "I don't know why it should or what time is right, but I'm glad we did it." She slipped her arm through Peter's. "I feel calmer inside, like I've been granted a promise. It's that feeling that helps me to accept the idea of saving face. I know I belong to Peter and we'll be together. Our vows are blended with the energies of life somewhere written in the wind."

The grandfather watched her. It was obvious she believed what she was saying. Her childlike faith surprised him. The old man took a breath. "Peter has mentioned you interact with two energies."

"Interract?"

"Harmonize," the grandfather explained.

Jeneil thought. "Do I?" She looked at Peter.

"The wind and the sunset," Peter answered.

Jeneil sat in thought. "Not really. The sunset is a…," she struggled for an explanation, "it's a lifeline, a connection to my…," she struggled again, "to my life force."

The grandfather held his breath. "Jeneil, you learned this on your own from being with the elements?"

She nodded. "But the sunsets only feed me. What I usually harmonize with is the wind." The grandfather smiled. "And the Earth."

The grandfather's heart stopped. "Both?"

She nodded again. "The Earth's virility, in the sense that it's forceful and strong, is comforting to me. It's odd to sense the quality in an element thought of as feminine."

"Yin and Yang, Jeneil."

"In all things, Mr. Chang? Masculine and feminine?"

He nodded. "Fire can be forceful and fierce, or warm and something comfortable."

"Yes." Jeneil smiled, understanding. "Yes, of course, Yen and Yang, a balance and harmony. Of course, it makes sense."

"If you find the Earth's forcefulness comforting, what do you sense in the wind?"

Jeneil thought about the question. "Life," she replied, thinking out loud. "Yes, life, a steadiness and continuity I can't connect to the sun and my life force without the wind. Well I can, but not intensely."

The old man smiled broadly and relaxed. Her answer pleased him and had shown her level of sensitivity, which totally impressed him. "Your sensitivity must make life difficult for you." She smiled, appreciating his, and then nodded. Peter watched them, not quite grasping their level of communication, but enjoying the closeness which was very evident. He liked to see that; it made him see Jeneil as part of the family.

"Mr. Chang, how do you know about Yen and Yang if your family is Christian?"

The grandfather grinned. "From my great grandfather. He wasn't Christian and demanded equal time in our training. My mother worried about it, but my great grandfather was a very wise man. He told her the philosophies harmonized and would give broader understanding."

"That's wonderful. He must have been very peaceful from such strong faith."

The old man shrugged. "Wisdom brings its grief, too."

"Yes, I can understand that, Yin and Yang again." Jeneil smiled, and the old man nodded. "I can't imagine knowing my great grandfather. What an opportunity it must have been to learn from him. I never knew my grandparents either but I think I would have enjoyed knowing them. My parents were interesting to me. They were my friends and saw me as a person of value. That was something my peers didn't offer. They actually fascinated me; they were so close to each other. I want a marriage like theirs seemed to be. I think that's why my father didn't survive long after my mother."

"Well, it's obvious they taught you to love."

She smiled. "Mr. Chang, who taught Peter?" Peter looked at her and smiled. The old man was taken aback by the question and gave it some thought.

"Peter was a loveable baby and his mother spent hours with him. She was completely fascinated by him and he thrived on the attention. Then, she went to work and my wife and I looked after him. I worked nights so again we had a lot of time for Peter and we enjoyed it. His Aunt Malien loved him and fussed over him, too. Risa did too, but Malien was younger and home more. As babies, he and Ron were opposite. Ron was unyielding and tense, while Peter was gentle and quiet. Ron was always into mischief while Peter would find a toy and concentrate on it all day. It was when they went to school that each changed. Ron settled down and Peter became unyielding."

Jeneil smiled at Peter. "We don't have to worry about a Mogwai. Chang reacted to what was around him. It wasn't a natural action."

Peter took her hand. "You've been covering him with romantic dust since you met him. He's still reacting to his peer group, you. You're a nicer peer group, that's all. He's still a bit rebellious."

Jeneil squeezed his hand. "White Fang, Peter."

The grandfather watched, enjoying the romance they shared when a thought came to him. "Risa didn't want to burden us with Ron when she went to work. My wife was getting weaker and Ron was energetic. She had him stay with her husband's cousin who had two children of her own. It seemed to work out for him. He had two active children to help use up his energy. Ron and Peter were both curious, but Ron would get into mischief then struggle to get out, while Peter watched. School was different for Ron. His parents had already moved here. Peter didn't like school and we watched him get tougher and tougher and into more and more serious mischief."

Jeneil smiled. "Learned the important things, didn't you?"

Peter looked at her. "Yeah, like my father was white and there was a name for kids like me who had no father. The kids were quick to tell me my father was scum and everybody waited for me to be just like him." He leaned forward, sighing. Jeneil heard the obscenity he mumbled and she swallowed from pity for the loveable little boy who went into the world and learned how to hate himself. She wiped the tears that fell. The grandfather stared at the floor and felt his heart ache as it had throughout Peter's growing years over the cruelty he had to endure. Peter stayed silent then shook his head. "Damn it! How do I get that bitch to stop saying that baby's mine? I don't want its future on my conscience!" He got up and paced, and his grandfather saw his pain.

"By saving face, Peter," Jeneil answered calmly.

Peter was annoyed. "No, that's like saying the baby's mine. The bitch is hiding behind tradition. She's a pro. It's taken me years to hold my head up and she's just kicked me back into the shit."

"Peter," the grandfather leaned forward, "in saving face, you would make your protest clear in that you are only saving face by marrying her, not accepting the moral stain. The question of her personal honor is then challenged."

Peter stopped pacing. "Does Chinese law tell you how to keep your sanity? How would I keep from killing her if we lived together?"

The grandfather sighed. "It's a test of endurance, Peter. You would be under no obligation to her as a husband or even have feelings toward her. You certainly can't physically abuse her, but I don't think you want to. It's a loveless marriage and the trial is on both people involved. If the woman gives in and asks for a divorce or the man gives in and becomes her husband, the liar is usually uncovered in the end and the wronged person has the injustice corrected. Honor wins out because the desire to prove one's honor gives a person strength. It's a very difficult life, but I've seen truth come from it."

Peter shook his head. "I understand how both are protected from scandal, but truth comes from it? I doubt it, Grandfather. I sat across from her right here in this house and she lied to my face. She doesn't know what honor is."

The grandfather shrugged. "I'm only telling you what I've seen happen and what I've heard."

Peter returned to pacing. "Saving face," he said, and exhaled. "How easy it sounds. I'm caught in that, too. If I marry Uette, Jeneil's uncle will find me dishonorable."

Jeneil clasped her hands nervously. "I'll explain it to him, Peter. You're not abandoning me. It's a short separation."

Peter shook his head. "A short separation to marry another woman and that's not dishonorable? I just bet Hollis would love that. Civilized is too damn complicated. Chang's way is easy. He'd tell Uette to go peddle the blame somewhere else."

Jeneil was filled with compassion. "Peter, I can't believe Uette would even accept those conditions. I think her motive is a genuine attraction for you. When she hears the conditions of the marriage, she might be encouraged to tell the truth."

Peter stopped pacing and turned sharply. "Nobody seems to be listening to me. There's no such thing as Uette and truth together. She can lie to a person's face. To me, that means she has no conscience. If she has no conscience then the word honor is meaningless to her, too. And, Jeneil, tell me what the hell is a short separation, huh? I'm the one who'll be tied into hell with her for who knows how long. Will you wait a year, maybe two?"

Jeneil's mind reeled. "I never thought in terms of years...."

Peter interrupted. "No, you're not thinking at all, that's for sure. It still shakes Chang up to hear you tell him to marry that bitch of a shark." He put his head back and exhaled, then paced again. The grandfather's stomach knotted seeing his grandson's anguish. Every way he turned, he seemed to face a dilemma with its resulting tension and frustration. Peter stopped before the parakeet's cage. "I know the feeling. And if Chang's locked in a cage he'll have that cuttlebone into fine powder in minutes." He could feel tension building in the center of his chest. He turned to Jeneil. "Honey, let's go. I'm pacing in circles here and its making me crazy. I'd like to run before I go on duty."

Jeneil looked stunned as Peter put on his jacket. "Run? It's in the teens outside!"

"Then, I'll go to the exercise room but I've got to keep moving. Okay?" he replied sharply. The grandfather watched, saddened by the draining affect the tension was having on them.

Jeneil buttoned her coat and then smiled, punching his arm gently. "Hey bud, I ain't a kickin' your dog aroun', so don't go spittin' fire at me, Dragon. I'm your woman, Warlord, not your rug."

Peter looked at her. She grinned, Peter smiled. "Oh yeah, my woman, huh?" He playfully scooped her into his arms. She screamed, shocked by the spontaneity. "Pick up your picnic basket, Princess from the Land of Leprechauns."

"Bye, Mr. Chang," she said, lifting her basket. The grandfather stood up, smiling at the playfulness that seemed to ease the tension.

Peter turned to him. "What time do I face the firing squad?"

"Eleven," the old man replied with a sigh.

"Can I come by at ten to be fitted for a bullet proof vest?"

The grandfather nodded. "Of course." He patted Peter's shoulder.

Peter kissed Jeneil's cheek. "Okay, Princess, to your coach and castle, I'll show you that Chinese warlords know how to deal with a lady."

The grandfather was impressed with Peter's ability to show Jeneil respect. It wasn't something he had shown many girls and the old man was grateful to Jeneil for that, too.

Peter turned to face the door and saw his mother standing before him. "Peter, put me down," Jeneil said, gently but seriously.

"What, and let a beautiful princess escape? Not on your life. You're mine. You belong to me." He looked at his mother. "Mrs. Lee, since you're closest to the door, will you open it for me? I have to take this princess to the enchanted forest where she lives." Jeneil couldn't believe Peter's boldness and she chuckled. She turned her head to avoid his mother's look of disgust and waved to Peter's grandfather, who was smiling broadly. Peter walked through the door carrying Jeneil proudly past his glaring mother. "Thanks. Mom, can you close the door, too? She's a lady. I can't just throw her over my shoulder and carry her home," he said, and continued walking to the car with Jeneil in his arms.

The mother closed the door, shaking her head. "Does anything reach his conscience? He gets a girl pregnant and acts like nothing is wrong. And I guess it doesn't bother her either. She's still clinging to him. Poor Uette." The grandfather watched Peter put Jeneil down near the car and kiss her gently, and then he held the door for her and closed it. Getting into the car, Peter kissed her cheek. The grandfather loved watching them, the life force between them healthy and refreshing. The mother watched them and shook her head then turned to her father.

The old man looked at her. "Whatever it is, Lien, don't say it. Just don't say it, please." He walked back to his chair in the greenhouse.

*****

Peter got to the exercise room and put on gloves. Batting the bag felt good. He hit it again and again until his anger was wasted. Leaning on the bag like a tired opponent, he sighed and thought about the meeting with the Wongs. He hit the bag again then went to the rowing machine. The rowing machine was the greatest for him, always seeming to loosen the muscles he had tensed without realizing it.

It was still early when Peter got on the floor. Getting a cup of coffee, he went to the viewing room for privacy and peace. He clipped an x-ray to the viewer and sat back staring at it. His mind wandered to Uette. He finished his coffee realizing he had to get on duty and put Uette behind him. Steve knocked gently and walked in. Peter turned and smiled. "Well, look at this peacock that used to guzzle beer with me in sweatshirts."

Steve grinned and sat on the table. "Laugh sucker, you're turn's coming."

Peter looked at the grey vest and tie. "Oh, you look every bit the pro, Steve. It's weird."

"Weird." Steve laughed. "Try sitting behind a desk in this. I miss my scrubs."

Peter stood up. "So what brings you around here at this hour?"

"I'm making rounds and checking on patients in Recovery. I thought I'd stop by and check on you. What's happening with that Uette shit?"

Peter sighed and crushed his cup. "She's had tests. She's just the right amount of days pregnant and I'm tiptoeing through shit."

Steve couldn't believe it. "Pete, it can't be!"

Peter shrugged. "Oh, it is, Steve. It is and I meet with her family tomorrow morning."

"Whew!" Steve exhaled. "That's not what I expected to hear."

"Me neither." Peter threw the cup into the metal wastebasket.

Dr. Sprague opened the door. "Peter, I'm on my way to a meeting and dinner. I'd like to hear what's happening before I go."

"Nothing," Peter answered. "I'm meeting with her family tomorrow."

"What are you going to do?"

"Tell her she's full of shit."

The older doctor sighed and nodded. "Want tomorrow off?"

"No," Peter answered. "I don't know."

"We'll see about it tomorrow then," Dr. Sprague said compassionately.

"Can I cover for him?" Steve asked.

Dr. Sprague grinned. "You've been C-sectioned, big brother. The cord's cut and knotted. You'll get your tie dirty."

"Yeah, I guess so." Steve answered.

Dr. Sprague smiled pleased the two of them were still friends. "Play psych coach. That helps, too." Steve nodded. "Well, I've got to get to the meeting. I'll check with you soon, Peter." He handed him a business card. "My home phone's on that. Use it if you need to, okay?"

Peter took it and nodded. "Thanks." Dr. Sprague closed the door and walked away. Peter sat down. "He's been really great about this mess."

Steve nodded. "Yeah, he's really okay to have in your corner." He stood up. "Well, I have to make rounds." He patted Peter's shoulder. "I'm in your corner too, Pete. How's the kid doing since she heard about the tests?"

Peter smiled. "She's being Jeneil."

Steve smiled. "Did I even have to ask? She knows how to stand in people's corner, too. She's crazy about you, Pete. She really is." Peter looked at Steve. It was good to hear, especially coming from Steve since Peter knew how he felt. Peter could see Steve was being the good friend that Jeneil had claimed.

Peter grinned. "We don't agree on how to handle this, but she's letting me decide. I love that about her."

"What does she think you should do?" Peter took the x-ray off the viewer. Steve noticed Peter's reaction. "Bad question?"

Peter nodded. "She wants me to save face and marry Uette."

Steve was stunned into immobility. He wrinkled his brow as he absorbed the impact. "She's not kidding?"

"No." Peter sighed. "She sees it as my only choice. She said she would wait for me."

Steve shook his head and gave a cough-laugh. "She's totally crazy! I mean...," he laughed. "She crazy!"

"There's a lot of merit in Jeneil's point of view, but my stomach gets sick when I even consider doing that."

Steve was shocked. "Merit?" he asked incredulously. "Merit in marrying another woman? The kid's from another universe altogether. I knew she wasn't from this century, but to ask you...and accept your...geez, the kid's not real. She's more than lopsided Pete, she's into flake now.

Peter smiled. "Saving face means I challenge Uette's charge by marrying her but not being her husband. It's a gunfight at high noon really."

"I still can't believe Jeneil agrees to that."

Peter sighed. "Neither can Chang. I'm having enough trouble keeping him from raging over Uette's accusation. My Dragon blood boils hotter every minute I think about it. I feel this explosion coming right from the center of me and I know Chang's behind it. There won't be any logic behind what happens, just Chang's sense of honor. He hasn't been this strong since Jeneil...," Peter stopped before he said seduced Chang. "Jeneil likes Chang," he said. "To her, the street kid streak in me is romantic, if you can figure that." He chuckled. "She is crazy, she's keeps him alive. She insists on it. I hope we're both not sorry we did."

Steve stared. "You two aren't normal. You really are not normal. She's lopsided from playing with helium and she's got you tilted now." He held his chest and breathed deeply. "I'm going to start rounds. That's normal, that's sane. Good luck, Pete. You're going to need it. One woman accusing you of getting her pregnant and the woman you live with is telling you to marry her. It's right from the ninth floor psych ward." Steve stood at the door. "I'm in your corner, Pete. Maybe you should let Chang rage. He'd probably tell Uette to go to hell and sling Jeneil over his shoulder and whisk her off to a judge to get married. That sounds sane to me." Steve laughed. "Turn Chang loose, Pete, tell him to go for it!" He opened the door and left.

Peter watched him walk away. It was a complete surprise to hear Steve's advice and he was consistent with it; take Jeneil, marry Jeneil. Peter shook his head. "Steve, you're not normal either. I saw the look on your face, I know how you feel about her and yet you keep giving her to me. I know I couldn't give her to you that easily, no way." He put the x-rays into the envelope and sat down to make a notation on the medical chart.

Steve finished making rounds and was looking over some charts. Slipping the last one into the slot, he picked up his jacket and overcoat and headed for the doctor's parking area. He passed by one phone booth and then the next. Stopping, he walked to the third and reached inside his pocket for change. He dialed wondering why he was but he never put the receiver down.

"Steve," Jeneil answered, the pleasure her voice indicated making him glad he called.

He leaned against the wall, smiling. "Hey, kid, I just thought I'd call."

"I'm glad you did," she said. "You're becoming such a stranger. Where are you now?"

"At the hospital."

She giggled. "No, I mean are you into your apartment yet? How does the painting look in your office?"

"No, and great," he answered. "Dr. Sprague liked the painting." Steve's voice got serious. "He recognized your name."

"It doesn't matter." She sighed. "I'm about ready to step into the sunlight on everything anyway. Having seen Uette, my two lives feel dirty, like I'm lying and I've never felt that before. I thought I was protecting Peter and me."

"You were, kid. You had a great start because of it," Steve said. "How are you doing?"

She paused. "I guess it depends on the minute you're asking. Sometimes I feel positive and other times I want to scream in anger. Sometimes those feelings are only minutes apart." Steve was glad to hear that; it was closer to what he felt was normal. "So what have you been up to, Dr. Bradley?"

"Getting established, fitting into a routine, which means nothing really. I can't get used to all the time I have on my hands."

"Well, that's good isn't it?"

"Once I fill it with something, I guess so." The operator interrupted for more money and Steve inserted a quarter.

"Steve, why are you paying to talk to me? Why don't you come over for dinner? Are you free?"

"Yes."

"Then hang up and come on over. Really, I'd like that. I wasn't looking forward to facing the evening alone. Peter's meeting with the Wongs tomorrow and I'm a wreck."

"I'm on my way," Steve answered, wanting to see her.

Seventeen

Steve walked to the front door and it opened, setting him back a step. Adrienne and Charlie smiled at him on their way out.

"Dr. Bradley, how are you?" Adrienne asked.

"It's Steve, I don't make house calls," he joked.

Charlie laughed. "Go on up, Jeneil's home."

"Thanks," Steve said, stepping into the warm hallway, making sure the door was secured behind him. Ringing the buzzer, he studied the Camelot sign while he waited for Jeneil. Her world wasn't so perfect right now he thought sadly. Jeneil opened the door and Steve looked her over as he walked in, loving the long brown print European dress she always wore. "Wow," he said, smiling.

"Wow," she said, looking him over as well. "You really are a doctor, Doctor. It's good to see you. I miss you at the hospital." She hugged him and he held her gently.

"You used to try to miss me at the hospital by at least a corridor."

She stepped back, laughing at his pun. "I know. Isn't it nice Peter helped me to grow up? What a great friend I'd have missed." She smiled as Steve kissed her cheek. "Dinner's ready, let's get to it."

"Sounds good to me," he said, taking off his overcoat and suit jacket.

Steve began to relax as the conversation flowed easily. Jeneil went to get dessert and he struggled with the feeling of how right this all felt to him. Jeneil placed a dish of ice cream with strawberry sauce before him and sat down.

"When are you moving into your apartment?"

"John's gone already. He gave me a month's free rent. He said it felt good to be able to do that after years of counting pennies. I just need to clean it. He wanted to have the cleaning woman do it, but with a month's rent already it didn't seem right to me."

"Then let's finish here and go clean your apartment," she offered, smiling.

He looked at her completely taken by surprise. "You'll go with me to my apartment? Jeneil, some people from the hospital live there."

She shrugged. "It's my new open door policy. I'll just use the service elevator," she snickered then patted his hand. "I'm kidding. I'll have the furniture delivered sometime next week. The model apartment is being painted so the furniture is in storage right now. It's all yours."

He squeezed her hand. "Thank you is beginning to sound very empty."

"We'll stop at the discount store and get cleaning supplies. Is that okay?" she asked, and he nodded as he stood up. Jeneil looked at his neat vest and tie. "And we'd better get you some cleaning clothes. Peter's kick-around jeans and sweatshirt are in the bedroom."

Steve smiled. "You're bossy."

"It's part of my charm," she said, wrinkling her nose, and she got up and began clearing the dishes. "If you'll take these to the kitchen, I'll get Peter's clothes for you."

Steve came from the bathroom with his suit on a hanger. Jeneil came from the bedroom in old jeans and a top. Steve wondered if she ever looked bad.

"You'll need a jacket," she said, going to the closet. "We're ready to go." She handed one to him and put her toggle coat on.

They reached his apartment without seeing anyone they knew. Steve dragged the vacuum cleaner in and Jeneil looked around. "John's a very neat person. This is light cleaning. Shall we work together?"

Steve smiled. "Sure, so we can talk."

Taking the bag of cleaning items, Jeneil headed for the kitchen. "I'll fill the bucket with water. We can start in the bedroom. That should be easy."

"It would be for me," Steve mumbled to himself.

She turned. "What?"

He held his breath. "Sounds okay to me," he answered quickly.

"Be right back." She continued on.

"Mess up, Bradley, and I'll kick your ass," he lectured himself, and went to look at the condition of the bedroom. He flipped the wall switch turning on the light. In the center of the room was a small white paper bag with his name written on it. Steve was puzzled and picked it up. Opening it, he shook his head and smiled. "Cute, John," he said, seeing the package of condoms.

"What did you find?" Jeneil asked, coming into the room. Steve jumped and tore the bag trying to close it. Fumbling from embarrassment, he nearly dropped it. "What is it?"

Holding the whole mess behind his back, he cleared his throat. "Gag gift."

She smiled. "It worked, you're gagging." Holding the bucket, she stopped before him and soaked a sponge in the soapy water. "Women give house plants," she said, grinning as she walked to the closet to sponge down the shelf. "You can put your gift there until the bureau drawer arrives." Snickering, she went to the window to clean the sill and frame.

He put the package on the closet shelf and watched as she enjoyed his embarrassment. "Smart mouthed kid, aren't you?"

She stifled a laugh. "Another one of my many charms."

They cleaned quickly. Steve sponged the door and the frame while Jeneil vacuumed and the bedroom was finished. Standing at the door, Jeneil looked around. "What are you going to do about drapes? Do you have a bedspread?"

Steve leaned against the doorframe and sighed. "I don't have anything. No, I have a pillow you made."

She patted his arm. "Not to worry. We'll go shopping. Before I leave I'll measure the windows. You're not interested in custom drapes yet, are you?"

He shrugged. "I don't know what they are, but my guideline is inexpensive. My career is costing money right now. That's top priority."

She nodded understandably. "I'll have my crew in here Monday to do your rugs."

"You don't have to. I'm not down and out."

"I know, but I have the crew. Let me help you get started. I really should make a list of what you need." She went to her purse for a notebook and pen. "Linens, blankets, bedspread; I'll contact the company that supplies my motel, the price might be better." She went to the living room.

"Jeneil," he called, and she turned. "You're great," he said, appreciating having some of the details handled by someone who knew what was needed.

"You're welcome." She smiled warmly and continued to the living room. "Just drapes in here." Looking around at the walls, she added more notes to her book. "This will be easy cleaning, too. The kitchen and bathroom are always tougher. Ready to start in here?"

"All set," he said, and picked up the bucket.

Each taking a wall, they met in a corner. Steve left the apartment while Jeneil vacuumed and he returned with soft drinks from a machine in the laundry room. Jeneil had emptied the bucket and was filling it again to begin the kitchen.

She looked around. "Goodness, this is your expensive room. You need dishes, a set of cooking pots, glassware."

"I can't even cook."

Jeneil grinned, looking into the bucket. "Doctor, doctor," she said, rotating her hands above it, "I see your future in my crystal bucket. There will be a long line of beautiful women asking for the chance to be chained to your kitchen."

He laughed. "Find me just one and I'll marry her."

Jeneil added cleaning liquid to the bucket. "I'll bet you you'll be married within a year," she said, swishing the sponge in the water and starting on a wall.

Steve laughed. "I'll take that bet. By the first of next year, if I'm not married, you'll come here and cook for a week."

"That's a deal. What do I get if I win?"

Steve chuckled. "You'll get to bring Pete with you. You'll need to feed your husband, too." Steve heard her sniff. "Is the cleaning solution too strong for you?" She shook her head, not answering. Walking over to her, he saw her tears. "What did I say?" he asked, feeling bad. She waved her hand gently, trying to pass the situation over lightly, but only cried harder. Steve understood. Putting the sponge down, he put his arms around her. "Jeneil, he's yours. You'll get married."

She leaned her head against his chest, trying to stop crying. "His birthday is in three weeks and I'm afraid I won't even get to share that with him." She cried harder.

Steve felt her shaking and he rubbed her back gently. "Come on, kid. He's going to tell the bitch to take a hike."

Jeneil shook her head. "He can't, Steve. He doesn't have a choice. He hasn't realized it yet." She sobbed as she clung to him and he sensed her fear. Compassion filled him, her pain all too real to him.

"Honey, don't cave in yet. Wait until all the votes are counted." He kissed her temple, sighing as she cried softly as he held her. "Maybe I should marry her. She deserves to be chained to this kitchen. I'd love the chance to teach her not to lie." He kissed her cheek.

Jeneil laughed lightly, enjoying his attempt at humor. "She wouldn't accept that, Steve. She wants Peter."

"You know that for sure?"

She nodded. "No tangible proof, but she got herself pregnant to trap him. I know she did. That's why she's the right number of days pregnant. She's out to win."

"You think she's that cold-hearted?"

"No, Steve. She sincerely wants him. To her, that's equivalent to love. There was a girl in my hometown just like her. Amy Farber would do anything to get a boy simply because her hormones had no conscience. Uette didn't know Peter and I were living together. Now she's caught in a mistake and she's desperate. She'll get vicious to keep him. Amy Farber did. I was always grateful Billy wasn't her type."

"Billy was yours, huh?" Steve asked, smiling. Jeneil nodded and he felt her relax against him. She hiccupped. "Drink some soda." He flipped the can open for her and she sipped, her hiccups stopping. Steve opened his soft drink and drank some, enjoying the coolness. "Jeneil, she can't win. You can't trap Peter and win. It makes him crazy."

Jeneil sighed. "What a disaster from a foolish combination of mistakes."

"What do you mean?"

"Peter's mother and Karen didn't want me for Peter. Karen introduced Uette to Peter then set him up to be in the house alone with her."

Steve almost gagged on his soft drink. "Karen set him up? Holy shit," he said, leaning against the counter.

Jeneil rinsed a sponge. "The right place, the right time, and the right circumstances." She shook her head. "I never knew a person's destiny could be so precarious. It's a frightening thought that your life could be so drastically changed by someone else's chance mistake. Yet it's all around; assassinations, bombings, terrorism, all effect people, ordinary people who were in the wrong place at the wrong time."

Steve watched her. "Jeneil, you can't lead a healthy life letting sensational stories that make good news coverage be your philosophy. Life may be precarious but it has its securities, too. You said it in your film, *Hope*. You don't quit, you don't give up; you keep running on hope."

She sighed and smiled slightly. "I know; Yin and Yang. Steve, I can't fully understand up if I haven't experienced down. There seems to be a need for opposites."

He kissed her forehead. "You're into helium, sweetheart."

She smiled. "Peter calls it right angled thinking."

"That, too." Steve chuckled, rinsing his sponge and going back to the wall.

Jeneil began on the cupboard shelves, finishing the first section. She turned and watched Steve stooping to wash the baseboard. Slipping quietly off the counter, she stepped behind him, putting her arms around his neck. She kissed his cheek and hugged him. "I think you're terrific."

Steve smiled and continued cleaning. Jeneil went back to the cupboard and he watched as she climbed onto the counter and began scrubbing shelves. He turned away and concentrated on washing a small red glop off the wall. He took a deep breath hoping the electrical charge in his chest would go away. Oh kid, he thought, you have no idea what I think of you.

Jeneil checked the stove. "John must have eaten out a lot."

"Very smart man," Steve said laughing, and Jeneil smiled.

"I'll give you some easy recipes. You won't want to eat out once you learn to cook."

"Only if it's your pot roast."

Cleaning the bathroom went quickly, too. Jeneil got her notebook and tape measure to size the windows. Packing the cleaning supplies in cupboards, she joined Steve, who was lying on the living room rug. "Early surgery?" she asked, and he nodded and yawned. "TGIF," she said, stretching out next to him.

"Uh-huh," he answered. "Aren't you tired?"

She turned onto her side to face him. "No, I'm getting tense. I'll wait up for Peter in case he needs to talk. He must be in torture about tomorrow. Poor Peter." She sighed.

Steve smiled, thinking how nice it would be to have her wait up for him. He turned his head to look at her, aware how close she was. She was staring blankly into space. She looked beautiful. He loved it when her hair fell in wisps from her hairpins. She looked at him, aware that he was watching her. She smiled that quiet, gentle smile of hers that always made him want to kiss her passionately. His heart pounded in his chest.

"I'd better get you home," he said, sitting up.

She yawned. "I'll make Ovaltine and defrost brownies in the microwave."

"That sounds good," he said, standing up, holding his hand to her. She took it and got up. "Thanks for helping me put this together."

She smiled. "It helps me, too. I didn't spend the evening thinking of the chaff that comes into life." Steve grinned, noticing how she avoided vulgar words.

"That's not chaff, kid. That's chit, sometimes spelled with an 'sh.'"

"Ya calls dem as ya see's dem don't cha, Ebenezer?"

"Damn right, kid. When it's chit, its chit, ain't no mistaking it for anything else."

She sighed. "That's for sure. We better get going."

*****

Taking the brownies from the freezer, Jeneil put them in the microwave oven and set the button to defrost. She waited for the buzzer thinking how man had made great strides in technology, but in humanity the oldest and dirtiest tricks were still being cruelly perpetrated. They were taking giant steps backwards in some ways. She sighed. The buzzer sounded, startling her from her thoughts

Steve had changed to his suit and stopped at the kitchen door. "Need help?"

She smiled. "Just stay with me while I put this on a tray. I need your company."

Her words raced through him and he realized what he found so attractive about her; she reached out to give love and to ask for it in return. It felt healthy. It made her soft and warm. He watched her setting the tray and he knew she was a woman he wanted to touch, to hold.

"What are you staring at?" she asked, looking up, and then she laughed. "Do I have to ask? My hair is always falling out of its pins, my lipstick disappears into my pores, and my eye makeup must be smeared from crying." She shrugged. "Be kind, some of us weren't born feminine, we have to work on it."

He smiled, not answering. Taking the tray, he went to the living room. She had no clue. Feminine, she breathed it. Finishing a brownie in silence and pouring more Ovaltine, he sat back and looked at Jeneil curled up next to him. "This is really none of my business, but I have to ask or die of curiosity. Peter told me you think he should marry Uette."

"Not should," Jeneil corrected, "has to."

He stared, still not believing it even after hearing her admit it. "Jeneil, why? I don't understand."

"To save face, Steve. He can't win otherwise. He can't prove his story. She can't either really, but she's closer to it than he is with his mother as her witness. If he doesn't marry her, gossip will fly through the hospital halls. His family, especially his mother, will hang it over him forever and the ugliness is sure to reach his children. And Uette's baby will think he's the father and is total scum. If he marries her, he gets the chance to save face on the streets and with her family because he would marry her protesting her charge."

Steve put his cup down. "And you can take that?"

"I would have to, Steve. It would be a marriage in name only anyway. I belong to Peter."

Steve felt his heart drain, but the fact she could still think that about Peter with the charge against him made her more beautiful to him. "You're incredible," he said, staring at her.

"If that means brave or shining bright in honor, forget it, I'm not either. I want to smack Uette, but saving face is the only way Peter can win and I want him to win. So you see I'm really unforgiving and super competitive," she pouted.

"You're okay in my book," Steve said, grinning, thinking she was incredible for saying she belonged to a man in their liberated era in the history of relationships and she said it convincingly. She believed it. Steve decided he'd like a woman to say that about him. He'd like to have a woman feel she belonged to him. If that was chauvinistic then chauvinism was deep in his gut and tied to his libido.

She smiled wearily. "Thank you for coming tonight."

"I'll check with you tomorrow. It sounds like a tough day."

She nodded and bit her lip. "Dinner?" she asked, through a tight throat.

"We'll see how it goes, kid. Maybe we'll drag in dinner," he said, and she nodded as tears rolled down her cheeks. His heart ached for her and moving closer he put his arm around her and she leaned against him. "What can I do to help?" he asked, frustrated.

"Make tomorrow go away, Steve. It feels like an ending and I'm scared."

She cried gently and it got to him. She was so fragile and he worried about the next day for her sake. If it was hurting her now, what would it bring tomorrow? He held her tighter as he shared her pain. He couldn't remember ever feeling so deeply for a woman. Not even Marcia. He wished he could make tomorrow go away and all the other yesterdays that he had overlooked her at the hospital. He wished he had Peter's insight and had taken the time to look more closely at this girl-woman with extraordinary devotion and loyalty, love and generosity.

He closed his eyes, enjoying holding her. "I love you, Jeneil." He kissed her forehead tenderly.

"I love you too, Steve," she replied softly.

He opened his eyes, shocked he had said the words out loud but knew his words were meaningless to her. It was just as she had said, she belonged to Peter, and her love for him was as a friend. It was very clear to her and he even loved that about her. He smiled, holding her closer. Loving her, being there for her, even feeling the pain with her, felt good to him. He felt alive and he liked feeling alive, and for whatever crazy reason he was meant to do this for her.

*****

Peter finished his shift and headed to the exercise room to work out his anger. He felt trapped and Chang hated feeling trapped. Putting on gloves, he attacked the bag. He wanted to hurt something and it felt great to hit it and hit it hard. Chang was so close to the surface now and it scared Peter. Exhaling as he finished another barrage of jabs at the bag, he took a jump rope and worked himself to a soothing rhythmic pattern. Ki had cut several clothes lines into jumping ropes for the Dragons to use and the exercise used all the muscles in the body. It strengthened leg muscles and helped to build coordination and control. Peter had always found it soothing. He stopped, bending slightly as he exhaled. He felt drained. Standing up, he was surprised to see Steve at the door.

Peter smiled. "What's with you? Can't you cut the cord from this place?"

Undoing his tie and vest, Steve walked over to Peter. "I had dinner at your place then Jeneil and I went to my apartment to clean it. I stretched a back muscle. I thought I'd loosen it here before not going to bed."

Peter watched as Steve walked into the locker room to change into sweats. Leaning against the wall, he sighed. There were two good reasons to not marry Uette. One was he was crazy about Jeneil and two was Steve was crazy about Jeneil. Feeling tired and loose,

Peter walked into the locker room to shower. He had a feeling Steve was there to work off the effect of Jeneil, not a back muscle.

"Did you finish cleaning the apartment?" Peter asked, after he'd showered and dressed.

Steve nodded as he tied his shoes. "She's great to have around. She knows all about setting up a life."

Peter smiled. "Yeah, she has a strong nesting instinct."

Steve looked up at him. "You won't marry Uette, will you?"

"I think I'd learn hara-kiri first," Peter replied, surprised by the question. "Why?"

Steve sighed and stood up, relieved to hear Peter's confidence. "She thinks you should marry Uette, but it would hurt her. I know it would. She belongs to you, Pete. What would happen to her? You're the center of her life." Peter watched Steve closely, wondering where he was coming from. "Go home, Pete. She needs you. She's so damn fragile right now."

Peter studied him and decided Steve loved Jeneil enough to want whatever Jeneil wanted. "Yeah, I think I will. Take care of that back."

Steve nodded. "I will. It's nothing I can't handle, believe me."

Peter looked Steve steadily in the eye. "Yeah, I believe you. I know you can handle it." He paused. "You're a great friend." Steve hit Peter's arm lightly and smiled. Peter sighed. "I'll get home to Jeneil."

Steve nodded. "Good. I'll call you tomorrow."

"Steve, I'm going to be at the mother's house at ten tomorrow. Can you stay with Jeneil? I know this isn't easy for her."

"Sure," Steve answered, "I understand."

"Thanks." Peter walked to the showers.

Steve sighed and shook his head. "No, it isn't easy for her, Pete, not at all. How the hell could you have left her for even one night? Her type you protect like something rare and valuable. If she was mine...." He stopped. "She's not yours, Bradley, so let's get in that exercise room and remind your body of that fact."

*****

Peter unlocked the apartment door. Steve's observation about him being the center of Jeneil's life cemented his confidence that she was really his. Franklin, Danzieg, Dennis, and now Steve. She did belong to him. He closed the door as Jeneil came from the bedroom. He went to her and held her. As she clung to him, Peter could sense she was fragile. "Are you okay?"

"Not quite, fair to middlin'," she answered, clinging to him.

He kissed her head and held her close. "We'll get through this, baby."

She nodded. "I love you, Peter. I always will." Her words were music to him and they gave him strength.

"Let's go to bed," he whispered, and she nodded.

Eighteen

Morning came too soon for Peter. This was one day he wouldn't mind avoiding. Jeneil was snuggled against his arm and he moved slightly to kiss her head. She looked up at him.

"You're awake?" he asked, and he kissed her lips.

"I've been waiting for you to wake up." She smiled and moved against him seductively, and smoothed her hand across his forehead gently fixing his hair. "While I was lying awake waiting for you, I had a chance to think. I'm ready to face all this now. I had allowed myself to struggle between what I wanted and what has to be. Ambivalent feelings and mixed emotions won't achieve superlative. You are a superlative." She smiled and kissed him. "I've got to remember that if I'm going to make it through this."

Peter smiled. "Can you put that in terms I can grasp?"

She looked at him steadily. "Turn Chang loose today, Peter. Let him deal with Uette. Jeneil and Nebraska will try to stay out of Irish's way so she can keep up with him."

He laughed. "That's clearer to you, huh?"

She touched his face lovingly. "Irish is crazy about Chang. They belong together. The ocean, the beach house, the meadow, the ceremony, it was all Irish and Chang." She snuggled against him. "Let go of Chang, Peter," she whispered, and kissed him passionately.

Chang was so near the surface as it was, thrilled by the call from Irish, that Peter had no choice in the matter. His passion for her was unleashed, the freedom she allowed him feeling great after being so trapped by the situation. They were fantastic together. They knew they belonged together. The wild freedom unleashed combined with their passion and physical desire resulted in a superlative level of love. They held each other, breathless from the ecstasy they had experienced, not wanting to let go of the moment. They were beyond the physical where soul had only taught them to begin. As they drifted back down to the level others called reality, they held onto each other not wanting to let go of soul, knowing that each needed the other.

"Irish, you're fantastic." He smiled, still slightly breathless.

"Remember that." She smiled, regaining her normal breathing.

"Count on it." He kissed her.

She looked at his watch and then at him. "It's time to be getting up."

He lay back on his pillow and sighed. "Something deep inside of me doesn't want to go."

"It's Peter," she said quietly. "Let Chang handle it. Go and take your shower."

Peter nodded and reached for his robe. Jeneil lay back thinking for a few minutes and then reached for her robe feeling determined and confident. Peter returned to the bedroom drying his hair.

"I've laid out clothes for you."

Peter was surprised. "Do I look that helpless this morning?"

She smiled. "Not Chang."

Looking at the clothes she had chosen, Peter laughed. "Irish, you're smart. Make me look so tough it'll scare the hell out of her." He picked up the black shirt and laughed again. "Shit, I'll look so much like Chang, the Wongs will be afraid to talk to me." Peter kissed her cheek. "You know costumes, baby."

She smiled and raised her eyebrows. "I'll take my shower now." She left, calmed that he had accepted her choice in clothes.

Jeneil made the bed while she waited for the coffee to brew and for Peter to finish shaving. The front doorbell rang and she went to answer it. Steve leaned against the doorframe with his jacket collar turned up against the wind.

"I brought breakfast," he said, smiling boyishly. "It was hot when I left the fast food place. Geez, sweetheart, can I come in? It's freezing out here!"

Jeneil laughed and stepped aside. "Yes, of course, I'm sorry. I'm just surprised to see you." He kissed her cheek, his lips icy cold. Jeneil shivered and closed the door tightly.

The apartment was warm and Steve stood near the baseboard heater to thaw out. Jeneil had taken breakfast to the microwave to keep warm. Peter walked into the living room and Steve turned and stared. Peter's outfit made him look different. "Hey, pretty tough there Chang, I'd let you borrow my switchblade but I left it home."

Peter took a deliberately tough stance. "Don't need the blade, dude. I've got my bare hands."

Steve laughed. "Shit, if you don't look like that kid I met in med school called Peter Chang, only tougher."

Peter waved his hand. "Bah, that wimp," he sneered. "Today calls for the Dragon Kid. We need cool and tough." He jokingly exaggerated the way he had walked on the streets.

Steve laughed, shaking his head. "Pete, you can still do the best damn street kid I've ever seen. I had to wear white shirts and crew neck sweaters so I looked least likely to be a pickpocket in a crowd. I had a studious preppie look. I envy your gut level living. It was honest. Remember how shaken Morgan Rand would get when you did that routine in the dorms?" Steve asked, laughing hysterically.

Peter chuckled. "I swear he thought I was regressing."

Steve did an impression of Morgan Rand. "Well, really Chang, maybe you should consider trade school." They both laughed remembering the dorm life and how they hadn't fit in.

Peter turned his collar up. "Damn if this doesn't bring back memories even without the stud bracelets and sweatband." He sighed. "I don't know, Steve; sometimes I think there was a lot of dignity in that street kid." Peter held his hands at his waist and spread his feet. Pointing his hand like a gun, he growled, "The name's Chang. Don't like it, don't look."

Jeneil stood by the kitchen door watching. Hearing Peter's words, she grinned slightly, raised her eyebrows and nodded. The oven buzzer rang and she slipped back into the kitchen unnoticed, convinced she had chosen his outfit well.

With the three of them sitting at the small kitchen table eating the biscuit sandwiches Steve had brought for breakfast, the triad seemed rejuvenated. Jeneil enjoyed the moment, knowing it was only a flashback. Too much change had come into their lives and the triad was part of the past, resurrected for a brief moment by the memories each shared. She smiled as she watched Peter relax. It was nearing ten and he noticed her watching him and touched her cheek lovingly.

Finishing his coffee, Peter sat back and sighed. "I've got to go."

Jeneil felt the panic in her stomach and forced herself to concentrate on what had to be done. Deep inside she knew the inevitable was immoveable and fighting it would be disastrous. Oddly, that knowledge calmed her and helped her accept what she had to face. She recognized the feeling from when she had faced the deaths and funerals of her parents and Mandra. Those experiences had left her with a strength and knowledge that life at its lowest had to be lived through. She understood survival and it was an instinct that pulsed deep within her. She got up and went to the closet for Peter's jacket.

Peter was surprised to see her bring the leather jacket instead of his winter parka and he smiled. "Bring me my tire iron and chains too, woman, and I'll be ready for this brawl."

Steve put his head back and laughed. "Good luck, Peter," he said, picking up the coffee cups and going to the kitchen.

Peter put on his jacket and Jeneil's heart fluttered; he looked so much like Chang. They went to the door together and Peter put his arm around her and kissed her strongly. She took a deep breath, forcing the lump in her throat to disappear. "Do what you have to do, Chang. Irish will understand."

He touched her cheek. "Then you understand that I can't marry her? You can accept that even if the story reaches our kids?"

She watched him. "I know you'll do what's ever necessary in order to survive, Chang. No one can ask you not to. What more can anyone require of you?"

Not quite grasping what she meant, he looked at her. "You've been very lopsided this morning."

She shrugged and smiled. "I'm still only eccentric."

He kissed her and then smiled. "Boil lots of water and get out the antiseptic, I'll be back."

Jeneil leaned against the door after he had left. "I'll do that, Peter. You're going to need it." She sighed softly and closed her eyes, hoping she would be able to face his return. She concentrated on what was necessary; it wasn't easy. Her emotions were active and she could sense Nebraska stirring as Irish lost courage. Come on, Jeneil, you're the civilized one, get us through this, she thought. She opened her eyes to look at her ring and saw Steve watching her. She smiled weakly.

"Let's go to the discount store for enamel cooking pots and then the secondhand store for some odds and ends and dishes. Maybe we'll be lucky and find four plates that match. That's enough isn't it for you and three girls?" she teased. "I like to win my bets so I have to make sure you're married by the end of the year." She smiled. "I'd like to introduce you to Charlene. You'd make a great couple, you're both so beautiful. I'll get my coat. I'm talking non-stop here and saying nothing." She sighed and Steve continued to watch her. As she walked by, he put out his arm and drew her to him. "Don't let me cry, please," she struggled with the words as she melted into his arms. "I can't face what's coming if I cry."

"What's coming?" he asked quietly.

"A speeding train and I'm stuck on the track."

He looked down at her. "Then you'd better get unstuck and get off the track, kid."

"I can't, Steve. There's no time. My only hope is to concentrate really hard and become invisible."

He smiled. "You're a flake."

She put her head against his chest and sighed. "Tell me there's a place in life for flakes. Tell me that what flakes think and feel is reality, too. Tell me I'm invisible and the train won't hurt me." She shivered.

He touched his lips to her forehead and kissed her gently. "You're not invisible, you're very real and the train won't hurt you. I won't let it." He chuckled. "That's me, defender of truth, justice, and flakes."

She smiled and hugged him. "Thanks for not letting me cry."

*****

Peter got to his mother's house and sat in his car for a minute. He sighed and got out. Wanting to avoid going into the house, he went to the outer door of the greenhouse. His grandfather was putting fresh paper on the bottom of the cages and looked up as Peter came in.

"Peter, you look...," his grandfather searched for the word.

"Tough?" Peter asked, smiling.

"No, different."

Peter sat on the bench. "Is the house empty?"

"Tom and your mother are home. Tom insisted that John and Karen leave."

"Good." Peter sighed.

His grandfather sat in his chair. "You look very strong and masculine in that shirt and jacket. It reminds me of when you were a Dragon."

Peter smiled. "Jeneil's crazy about Chang."

The door to the house opened and they could hear Tom talking to Peter's mother. "Leave him alone, Lien."

"He's my son; I won't stay out of this." Peter's mother walked to the back of the greenhouse and stopped to face Peter squarely. "I want to talk to you. I can't stand by and let you do this." She was shaking. "You can't get a girl pregnant and just ignore it." Peter looked down at the earth floor. "You have a responsibility to...to...do something. Think of Uette! How will our family face the community?" She began to cry. "Peter, for gosh sake think of somebody besides yourself. The shame is on us, too."

Tom took her arm. "Lien, please."

"No!" she snapped. "He can't think past that piece of trash he lives with." Peter stood up and faced away from her, trying to stay calm.

"Lien, that's enough!" Tom said strongly. "Don't go beyond your bounds."

"My bounds, my bounds!" she screamed. "I saw him in bed with Uette. The girl is pregnant! He's my son! What are my bounds? He can't ignore this. It's her, she won't let him go. He's never been this bad. It's all since her. He never lived with a girl until her. She's trash and I don't care if he doesn't want to hear it. She sure knows how not to get pregnant. Trash know about that. Poor Uette has been wronged. You should have let me call Jeneil. She's the one who can get him to do anything. I should have told her what I saw when I went to wake him."

Peter spun around surprised his mother had thought to drag Jeneil into this. His grandfather put his hand up indicating to Peter to be silent. Peter rubbed his forehead, wondering what his mother would eventually say to Jeneil.

Tom was resolute. "Jeneil stays out of this, Lien. It's not her doing."

"You're not his father," she shouted. "He's my son."

"I am his father in this."

"You're not," she responded, staring at her husband. Peter had never seen them argue before. Quibble, even discuss loudly, but this was serious.

Tom went to touch her arm. "Lien, you are not thinking rationally right now. He needs some time with Liam before they get here."

His mother pulled away. "What he needs is someone who'll tell him the damage he's doing by not marrying her. The Wong family are decent people. He can't shame them like this. He would know that if it wasn't for that trash. She even has him convinced they're married. A godless marriage, can you believe it! It's not even legal! Tell me how this isn't her doing. He would marry Uette if it wasn't for her. She's beautiful. Who wouldn't want her? But that white trash speaks his gutter language." Peter held his hand against his stomach.

His grandfather stood up and faced his daughter. "Lien, I want to talk to Peter…alone."

"Father, I have to talk to him. Someone has to plead with him for Uette."

"Lien, you've made your feelings clear. I want some time with Peter. Now!" His voice was adamant.

"Peter, please." She began to sob, holding her chest.

His grandfather took her firmly by the shoulders. "Lien, leave us alone now. You'll make yourself sick again."

"Sick again?" Peter caught the phrase but no one answered. Tom put his arm around his sobbing wife and led her from the greenhouse. Peter watched, feeling his throat get tighter and tighter as the door closed and his grandfather sat down sighing. "Sick again?"

"Yes, she began raving after Karen described the tests Uette had taken. Uette told Karen about one she had refused because it was so dangerous." The grandfather shook his head. "Your mother insisted she call Jeneil. Tom and I told her to leave Jeneil alone and she had an anxiety attack." He put his head back sighing, rubbing his eyes from exhaustion.

Peter sat down heavily and put his head back sighing. "So Jeneil's back to being white trash?"

"Peter, she's upset. She sympathizes with Uette in this situation. She's been through the gossip and the hurt. She's felt the shame."

Peter got up and paced. "Yeah, I know." He drummed a dowel on the potting table absentmindedly. He turned to his grandfather. "Have the Wongs talked to you at all about my decision?"

"No, they were pleased the test results supported Uette's story. They never asked about your decision."

"What about you, Grandfather? You must have an opinion about any decision."

"I do, Peter, but it is your decision. What about Jeneil? Has she changed her mind?"

Peter shook his head. "No, she's still leaning toward saving face but she said the same thing as you before I left this morning, do what I have to do to survive, she'll understand."

"She's quite a girl." His grandfather sighed again. "I call her a girl but she is a woman. She's childlike but behaves like a woman when the situation requires responsibility."

Peter went to the side of the greenhouse facing the street and stared at life passing by unaware of the turmoil within. He felt alone. Decisions were easy at the hospital. This decision unnerved him and he could see the damage Jeneil had described already beginning. His mother would rage and keep on raging.

Peter watched the Chis get into their car and drive off and he realized his mother's upset over the situation. She was surrounded by the Chinese community. It wouldn't be long before everyone on these streets for blocks heard about Peter Chang getting that decent Wong girl drunk and pregnant. The thought stirred his rage because it wasn't true, and he could feel Chang tensing and the feeling of the explosion inside of him activated again.

More than anything he wanted to stay calm, to deal with this as an adult. It was difficult enough to accept not being able to prove he wasn't the father, but he didn't want to add anymore embarrassment to his grandfather and the years the old man had stayed by him in his scuffles like the time he was pulled into the police station along with several young boys for suspicion of robbery. He hadn't done it, but he was in the alley when the boys ran from the backdoor of the appliance store. He remembered the hours it seemed to take sitting in the precinct waiting to be questioned and waiting for results. His grandfather had asked only once if he was guilty and then sat with him to see the ordeal through. He had forced Peter to thank the shop owner for being honest, who could have easily implicated Peter but had told the cops Peter was with the boys but didn't seem to know what was happening. It supported Peter's story and he was released. His grandfather had only said, "Peter, if you live your life in the streets some of its filth will rub off on you and you don't deserve that kind of life. You're a Chang." He had only been eleven, but it was still vivid in his memory.

Peter thought back realizing he hadn't been guilty of that robbery, but he had been guilty of others. He was good at jimmying coin operated machines in laundries and restaurant hallways. He remembered sitting at the precinct waiting for his mother to come and get him. His grandfather had been at work and he dreaded having his mother come down. She always screamed at him no matter who was around. That was the night he had met Ki, who was there because one of the Dragons had been picked up for drugs. Ki couldn't do anything legally, but he came down because the kid had called him. Ki was there with two guards waiting with the boy because he was one of them. Peter remembered sitting on the chair watching the four boys together. Ki was laying into the kid for his stupidity, reminding him that other gangs were just waiting for the Dragons to show weakness.

"You can't do drugs," Ki had said, "it messes up your thinking and survival is thinking. Do you want the cops hassling the Dragons because you're on junk? Think of the rest of us. You're one of us. Your dirt gets us dirty. We don't need the problems from poppers; we've got our hands full holding onto our streets. You get busted for doing stuff and the Bashovas can plant poppers all around us. Then how can I convince Halley that it's not ours when one of my men got popped and caught at it?" Ki had pushed the kid against the seat. "Wake up and think man. Protect your brothers." Peter had watched, fascinated because even the police captain talked to Ki like he was somebody important and hadn't treated him like trash. Ki had noticed Peter watching and sat down next to him to find out why he was there. Peter had been surprised Ki seemed to know who he was. "You walk through my streets; I like to know who walks through my streets," Ki had explained.

Peter smiled thinking how much like Robin Hood and his gang the Dragons were. He had thought gangs were stupid. His mother had dragged him to a boy's club because Risa had told her that Ron loved it. Peter hated it and avoided gangs. He only changed his mind when his mother got to the station and started in on him. She had dragged Ki into it, accusing him and his filthy bunch of using younger boys to do their crimes. Peter was embarrassed by her yelling but something clicked inside of him that night as he watched Ki stare at his mother as she berated him, then standing up, he pointed at her angrily, which stopped her cold. Ki had stayed calm but stared right at her and said, "Listen you screaming banshee witch, you want to treat your kid like an animal that's your business and his, but you leave me out of it. I'm a Dragon and nobody shits on Dragons." He then turned sharply and walked away from her like she was dismissed. She had grabbed Peter and pushed him through the station saying, "You live with filth and you grow up filth."

Peter checked out the Dragons after that. They didn't sound like filth to him. He had already learned not to do drugs from his grandfather. After sniffing around the Dragons for a while he joined. Life made sense to him after that, not everywhere but with the Dragons at least. Ki had stopped the names Peter was called to his face and especially amongst the Dragons. It took no more logic and reasoning than telling the group to layoff. "He passed his test. He's as good as you. He's your brother now and the Dragons need strong men. You don't like him, don't look at him, but he's earned his spot here. Can you prove your old man's really your old man? Then shut up about it."

Watching the Ling boy ride his bicycle on the sidewalk, Peter thought of how much like the boy's club the dragons were, even more so. They had trained hard physically and had been tied together by a very strong fusing agent—survival. Ki had taught them they needed to trust each other to be strong, to prove they could be trusted by being honorable and showing respect to each other, and to protect the Dragons and their name. Ki had been into Chinese up to his eyebrows, he had breathed it.

Bringing himself back to the moment, Peter closed his eyes and sighed thinking how far he had fallen from the pride and honor he had felt as a Dragon. He choked up imagining what Ki would say about his situation. He remembered the look of disgust Ki had for the boys who got caught by a skirt and never allowed them to blame the girl. "You're in charge," he'd say, "in everything you do. Don't give me the, 'I trusted the skirt.' The only one you trust is you. You know if you get a girl pregnant. She doesn't surprise you and if you let a skirt shit you I'll bruise you bad myself." A couple of the guys ended up marrying girls because they were pregnant. Ki never felt for them. "If it's yours then grow up," he'd tell them. "If it's not then don't let the girl shit you. Fight her. You don't want scum on your name." It was always outside of the Dragons though. Ki made sure the groupies understood if they got pregnant all the Dragons would swear that all had her that night. No groupie ever got pregnant or sick. Some of them never slept with any of the Dragons and no one was allowed to force them to.

Peter was amazed thinking how well ran the Dragons were but it all made sense. You trusted the guys and your name meant something. Peter shook his head thinking what his name meant now, especially to his mother and to himself, for having let a girl shit him. Rage flared again and he struggled for control, Chang so near the surface. In the Dragons, you fought for your name and your honor because you had worked hard to make it mean something. It was valuable. That's why the cops looked up to Ki, they trusted him. He handled justice within his gang and he insisted on the Dragons being honorable so he could defend them when necessary. Many times Ki won on his word alone. Even the head of the Caucs and the Bashavas trusted Ki's honor. Peter sighed and rubbed his face with his hands. He felt the conflict inside of him and it unnerved him. He felt like he needed more time to think. The rage was stronger and the explosion was moving slowly to the surface. Peter turned to face his grandfather who had been watching him closely.

"What's your struggle, Peter?" he asked, studying Peter's face intently. "Do you have doubts?"

Peter sensed something in the questions. "Not about the baby, I'm not the father."

The old man nodded. "What is it?"

Peter rubbed his forehead, trying to stay calm. "I resent this whole situation. It's making me crazy."

"You have to have honor to be honorable. If you're of no value in your own mind, you won't allow yourself any value to others." They heard a car in the driveway and Peter looked up. He could see the Wongs getting out of the car. His grandfather stood up slowly. "Peter, remember you're a Chang, most especially remember what you've achieved to add honor to that name."

Tom walked into the greenhouse. "They're here," he said quietly. "Lien is resting. I thought we should meet in the dining room. The atmosphere is warmer and more comfortable than the kitchen and more formal than the living room. I hope it'll help to keep things calm."

Peter's grandfather nodded. "Thank you, Tom."

Tom turned to Peter. "I'm with you, Pete. I wish I had a solution for you." He held his hand out and Peter shook it. "Good luck, Pete." Peter just nodded, choking on rage. The doorbell rang and both older men looked at Peter.

His grandfather touched his shoulder. "We have to greet them."

"Can I have a couple of minutes alone?" Peter asked.

His grandfather looked at him. "Not many, Peter. It could look like weakness and that's a small step to guilt."

Peter nodded and his grandfather and stepfather left him standing alone. His mind was in complete confusion. He began to feel warm and started to remove his jacket. He thought of Jeneil as he did. Slipping it back on, he swallowed. "I'll keep it on, baby. It keeps you near me. You're what matters to me, Jeneil. I'll just keep that in mind." He put his head back. "Oh, Chang, behave. Irish is counting on you." Straightening his jacket, he headed for the door aware that the pain in his throat was Chang raging for freedom.

*****

The only voices Peter heard as he approached the dining room were his grandfather's and Uette's grandfather talking about someone they both knew who was recently released from the hospital. Peter stopped at the door. Uette looked up and looked him over slowly. Jeneil was right about Uette's attraction, he saw it in the look. He also realized that kind of look wasn't coming from a beginner. She acted like someone who had tasted the physical side of life and had learned to enjoy its pleasures. The lying little bitch his mind raged and he glared at her as he walked into the room. Both of the Wong men stood up and the grandfather extended his hand and Peter shook it. The father waited and shook his hand, too. That surprised Peter. The men took their seats and Peter sat after they did.

Peter's grandfather cleared his throat and looked at Uette's grandfather. "Since we all know the results of the tests it seems we should work from there. We thank your granddaughter for allowing the tests to be done. We are sorry to hear that she suffered so much," his grandfather said, and Peter rested his ankle on his other knee. Suffer my ass, he growled in his head. "We apologize for the indignities she suffered and we thank you for understanding the necessity of the tests. What's left now is to hear what you are requesting." Peter felt Uette watching him and he avoided looking at her

Uette's grandfather nodded. "Thank you, Liam. I have to tell you that my son and I have spent hours talking and agonizing over this situation. We have tried to see all sides. We really have. We even considered the girl Peter's living with."

Peter bolted upright at the reference to Jeneil. "Hey, you leave her out of this. She's innocent. She hasn't done anybody any dirt. I won't allow mud on her."

Peter's grandfather touched his shoulder. "There was no offense meant, Peter. I'm sorry, Lu. Jeneil is very special to Peter. He loves her deeply."

"It's all right, Liam." Uette's grandfather turned to Peter. "I was going to say my son and I feel compassion for her in this, too. We feel for the hurt she must be experiencing."

"Then I apologize," Peter said, settling back against the chair.

Uette's grandfather accepted the apology and again turned to Peter's grandfather. "We want your family to know this hasn't been easy for us. We know it isn't easy for anybody, but we have tried to be fair. Since my son has dealt with so many issues in this I think he should explain what he's gone through." Peter's grandfather nodded that would be acceptable.

Uette's father sat back and sighed. "Well, once the tests were completed and we got the results, we decided it was Uette who we had to consider. She is the one who is pregnant and she has been wronged, even if accidentally." Peter's rage pulsated as he realized to the Wongs the test results meant that he was guilty. "I've contacted my lawyers to see what legal rights were involved." He paused and fidgeted with his tie. "Peter is not legally married. Uette asked Karen how long they had been living together and my lawyer said it doesn't subscribe to the definition of common law marriage. I say that only to show how we have tried to be fair by being thorough." Peter's grandfather nodded and Mr. Wong took a deep breath. "To us, that means Peter is free to correct his mistake." Peter felt his chest pounding as Chang raged but forced himself to remain silent. "Our request is that Peter marries Uette so she doesn't bear the full burden. She has told us she feels very sorry for Peter. She is quite taken with him." He cleared his throat and Uette kept her head bent contritely. "Trying to see it from Peter's side, it is a dilemma. We can certainly see that, but again he's not the one who will bear the shame nine months from now. Uette will, and since Peter's as much responsible, our lawyer has advised us to consider a court case so that Peter has to acknowledge his responsibility morally and by child support if he doesn't feel he can take on the responsibility of marriage."

Uette began to cry and Chang raged furiously as the words, 'You're guilty, the baby is yours,' kept ringing through Peter's head. He heard it over and over again throughout Uette's father's speech. The explosion was near his throat. He sat back as he thought of Jeneil. She knew it all along and he had called her lopsided. His throat was so tight he couldn't speak. He remembered her words at the door that morning, 'Chang, do what you have to do. Irish will understand.' She knew it then. His body was tense from rage.

Mr. Wong folded his hands. "Mr. Chang, it seems all that's left is to hear Peter's decision." Peter's grandfather nodded slightly.

Uette's grandfather spoke again. "Liam, we can understand Peter wanting to think about this. We only ask that something be decided quickly. We need to begin planning Uette's future."

Peter's grandfather cleared his throat. "I understand, Lu. Peter has already given a lot of thought to his choices. He doesn't choose to marry Uette." Uette put her head down and sobbed. Her father patted her arm.

Peter looked at the people around the table. He watched Uette sobbing and he felt the explosion spill through him. He stood up. "Grandfather, I'd like to say something."

His grandfather looked at Uette's grandfather. "Of course," the man replied, and Peter could see he was badly shaken by the decision.

Peter looked down hoping his feelings would come together so his mind would be able to form words. "I've been sitting here listening to all this and one thing keeps being said that I can't accept."

"What's that?" Uette's father asked.

"That the baby is mine."

"But Peter," Mr. Wong began.

"No," Peter interrupted, "let me finish." Uette's father shrugged and shook his head. "Mr. Wong, I understand how you think the baby's mine but I want this said and made very clear. Your daughter is not carrying my baby and she knows it." Uette cried at his words and the Wong men looked angry. "I'm so sure she's not carrying my baby that I'm prepared to save face to prove it." Uette's father and grandfather looked at each other.

Uette looked up hopefully. "What does that mean? That he'll marry me?" Both of the Wong men sat back obviously taken completely by surprise. "What does this mean?" Uette pleaded for someone to answer. Tom stared at Peter in shock. Peter's grandfather sat with his hands folded on the table and dealt with the lump in his throat.

Peter sat down as the impact of his own words hit him. "I'm furious about her accusations," he continued. "I feel filthy from them. I can't even understand how I'll live in a marriage with her."

"He's going to marry me?" Uette asked her father excitedly.

"Uette, please, yes but there are conditions. This is serious Uette, very serious." He looked at her angrily. "He's charging you with deliberately lying."

She sighed. "I don't care as long as he marries me!" Her grandfather closed his eyes and shook his head, covering his face with his hand, shamed by his granddaughter's words and obvious lack of honor. She got up and headed for Peter. "Thank you, Peter."

Peter got up quickly. "Sit down you lying bitch. Just stay away from me." She was stunned by his words and her face showed it. Her father stood up and took her arm.

"Sit down Uette and stay there. Don't open your mouth unless you're asked to." Uette sat down still in shock over Peter's words.

Peter rested his hands on the table, leaning for support. He bent his head. "I'm sorry," he said in agony, "that's what I mean. How can I marry her? I can't stand being in the same room with her." He looked up at Uette. "For gosh sake, tell the truth now."

She glared at him, infuriated by his words. "I'm pregnant because of you."

Peter stood up straight. "Uette, if that's your final word then we'll go through with saving face and you'll wish you had told the truth when you had the chance." She sat scowling at him and the four men looked at each other. Peter sat down. "Grandfather, it seems all that's left is to have the rules of saving face explained to us." He looked at Uette and pointed. "And listen to the rules carefully you piece of trash so you'll get it straight, bitch." He spat out the vulgarity. Uette's father and grandfather sat back, shocked by Peter's attitude toward Uette.

Peter's grandfather touched his arm gently. "Peter, there's dignity and honor in saving face. Stand tall, please."

"No, there isn't, Grandfather. She stole dignity and honor from me with her filthy lie." The Wong men bent their heads and were silent, shamed by the counter accusation.

"Peter, saving face is your opportunity to regain your honor. I'm asking you to remember that now."

Peter sighed deeply. "I'm sorry, Grandfather. I apologize to both Mr. Wong and his son." He sat back in his chair feeling beaten, but noticed that Chang was quiet, the explosion inside of him gone. All that was left was a pulsing rage that passed through his heart in time with its beating.

Peter's grandfather sighed. "Lu, can you accept my grandson's request?"

The old man was stricken. "Liam, I'm sorry, I don't know what to say. We have to accept his request. We've requested marriage, he's honoring our request. He's certainly being honorable but this is such a shock. I hope you understand."

Peter's grandfather sat tall in his chair. "I understand Lu, but I'm sure you can understand Peter's side."

"Of course, of course, I certainly didn't mean any insult. This is new to me. I've never seen it happen in my family. Give me a moment to steady myself."

"Maybe we can have tea now," Tom offered.

"I'd like that," Uette's grandfather replied.

"It's ready. I'll get it." Tom got up and left the room. Peter stood up and paced near the door then leaned against the doorframe staring into the living room facing away from everyone.

Uette looked at her father. "May I be excused for a minute?"

"Yes," he said quietly, deeply stricken himself by the situation.

Uette got up and her father watched as she stopped by Peter. "I'm really sorry." Peter turned his back to her.

Her grandfather looked up, watching her and Peter. "For gosh sakes, Roland, doesn't the girl have any sense of dignity? Why does she insist on insulting him like that and us?"

Her father sighed. "Uette, you asked to be excused." She nodded and left. "I'm sorry. She doesn't seem to grasp Chinese ways. I accept the blame for her behavior. I should have insisted she accept the family ways. She thinks I'm too old fashioned. She's very strong willed." Tom brought the tray with tea and Peter went to the kitchen for a glass of water.

Uette's grandfather looked at Mr. Chang. "How did Peter learn the old customs? He was very head strong when he was younger."

Peter's grandfather shrugged. "I wish I knew. Sometimes children take the wrong doors and still end up in the right room, and other children look like they can take all the right doors and end up in the wrong room. It isn't old China here."

"Don't I know it," Uette's father answered. "As each of my daughters started dating I saw a difference in the boys, degeneration and they were all good boys. There's just something missing that used to be in all the children; a steadiness, a respect, a sense of pride. We seem to have lost the rules to civilized living."

Peter's grandfather smiled. "Not everyone. I know a young woman who seems to understand the necessity for a civilized society."

Uette's grandfather sighed. "That's good to hear. I'm wondering if all our efforts are wasted."

Peter's grandfather stirred his tea. "After meeting this young woman I've realized that she sings the same words I remember from my training, but the music is different. I guess what matters in the end is how the fruit develops on the tree."

Uette's father sighed. "Maybe it's America. Maybe here where so many different kinds of people are trying to live together it's impossible to achieve unity and common rules."

Peter's grandfather smiled. "I don't think it's America because the young woman I know has parents who are Irish and English and they taught her the same things I was taught in China. I am still stunned by that."

Uette's father smiled. "English and Irish in a marriage together; they must have learned peace before teaching her anything at all."

Peter's grandfather looked up. "Roland, you may have just found the secret. We can't teach what we haven't learned ourselves."

"Then how do you explain my daughter, Uette? Her sisters all understand the ways of family honor, but Uette can't seem to."

Uette's grandfather looked at his son. "You and your wife are different people from the ones who taught your oldest daughter."

"Are we?" his son answered. He shook his head. "Well, I take Uette's lack of understanding personally. I see my failure with her in this."

Peter's grandfather smiled. "Don't Roland, not completely. Like I said, you can't know what door they'll take. Peter didn't find the right door until he opened all of them. That was his way."

Uette's father smiled. "Well, I can tell you, Mr. Chang, the fruit from that branch of the tree is a total surprise. You can be proud. He has courage, dignity, and a sense of honor."

Peter's grandfather thought for a moment. "You know, I'm almost tempted to say he learned it on the streets, but the streets are too civilized and the Dragons were not boy scouts." All four men smiled, all having heard about the Dragons.

Uette's grandfather sighed. "Liam, to be honest, I don't know how saving face will work in this. Life is different now. Will it even work?"

Peter's grandfather sat in thought. "I have thought about it, Lu. We can stay close to the original principle. You and I are the grandfathers. The problems they encounter will be reported to us then you and I can put the pieces together. I want the truth in this either way. I'm sure you know that."

Uette's grandfather nodded. "I know that, Liam. That fact keeps me calm. Your honor is my inner peace. But what do we do about the actual marriage? Should they live with one family or the other?"

Peter's grandfather shook his head. "No, I think they should be by themselves. It will be a marriage in name only and any plans should protect that. I'd like to see what will develop if they're left to everyday existence. Truth might surface faster than if they lived amongst their elders who would guide them and even hold them back. What do they call it now, inhibit? Alone it will be Uette, Peter, and truth."

"The test seems fair. Let's let them work out the details when they return. The principle is sound, it can survive modern life. What do you think Roland?"

Uette's father sighed. "My daughter isn't ready for marriage or life. Her head's still in the clouds. I'm worried her lack of ability in making a home will get in her way. It's sure to cause problems and friction."

Peter's grandfather looked at him. "Roland, the lie is causing friction. The test is about friction."

Uette's grandfather nodded. "I agree. They made their life now let them live in it so we can see what develops. What else is fair?"

Uette's father sighed. "But Peter is no match for Uette; he's older, more mature, certainly more educated. How can Uette hope to keep up with that?"

Peter's grandfather stood firm. "Roland, let's not forget Peter carries the bigger burden; a marriage, he has to prove he's not the father, and he's facing a struggle in having to leave Jeneil. Considering his disadvantages, they seem equally matched."

Uette's grandfather nodded again. "I agree with Liam."

Uette's father shrugged. "I bow to your combined wisdom. How will we handle it from here on?"

Uette's grandfather looked at Mr. Chang. "Your grandson has chosen saving face. I feel the rules should be yours, Liam. The boy has put forth an attempt at honor."

"Thank you for that respect, Lu. I would like to have each one report to the family. The women are to report all they hear. Nothing is passed over as unimportant; everything gets reported to you about Peter and to me about Uette. We take our places as patriarchs. I feel that should keep tempers between the two low if we referee. We can come together to discuss what we hear. As far as the details of their lives, I feel we should open that to them and see what they do with it. Let's see how they begin before we leave here today."

"That sounds fair to me. We can deal with anything that doesn't fit as it comes along."

Peter's grandfather hesitated. "I'd like to ask that the truth about this marriage be told in the community if it comes up. We don't need to shout it. I don't feel we can't expect to get to truth if we hide either side. Both sides should be known."

Uette's father sighed from concern. The older Mr. Wong looked at his son and saw his reservation. "Roland, you can't worry about pride now. Honor is at stake and truth is necessary. She put her pride in jeopardy when she and Karen set Peter up. Truth will restore honor and pride will follow for whichever one has been wronged and eventually for both."

Peter's grandfather rubbed his forehead. "I think it's wise not to tell them we're gathering information and observing them. That will at least eliminate having the situation manipulated. We want a natural development in this." Both Wong men nodded and Peter's grandfather sat back. "We should get them in here so we can finish."

*****

Peter stood at the kitchen door watching some birds fly into a small area under the garage eaves carrying bits of grass and string in their beaks. He then looked at the birdhouse that stood empty by the bushes and wondered why they'd chosen an area more open to the weather. He turned his thoughts to Jeneil. She loved watching nature and had learned more lessons by doing so than any two people he knew. She thought nature was extremely shrewd and was impressed with instincts, and had come to believe that civilization was degenerating because life was soft and human instincts were smothered resulting in a façade of social interaction. She insisted all of nature was different; it kept life simple and at its basic level. It was honest.

Peter smiled to himself. Maybe nature was too uncivilized. The birds would be more protected in the birdhouse but their savage instincts directed them to the eaves of the garage. Hey you twits, he directed his thoughts to the birds, move into the house, get civilized. Peter shook his head, laughing to himself, realizing how Jeneil had gotten him to start talking to birds. His eye caught a movement below the bushes near the birdhouse. Looking carefully, he saw the neighbor's cat half hidden under the junipers staring at the birds. Survival, Peter thought, impressed. Those damn birds knew the cat was there and that the birdhouse was well built but a death trap. They would be easy prey once they were inside.

Peter grinned as he heard Chang shout, "Peter's too soft! He's the cause of this mess. He's too far from the streets. He got caught because he's soft. Now I have to bail him out. Irish is better at survival than he is. I always thought she'd be a great Dragon."

"Pete." Tom came to him. "They want you in there again."

Peter sighed and nodded. "Yeah, I know; civilization." They walked toward the dining room as Uette walked in from the living room. She had touched up her makeup and had pulled herself together. "The actress is ready for scene two," Peter mumbled.

Tom patted his back. "You're looking good, Pete. I'm proud of you."

"Oh, thanks," Peter answered, "it only cost me Jeneil." They walked to the table and took their seats.

Peter's grandfather looked at him. "We've decided the plans and details of your life should be left to the two of you. We thought it would be wise since we're all here for the both of you to discuss how each of you sees the future together." As hell, Chang raged in Peter's mind. "The Wongs have said that since you're the one saving face, we should begin with you."

Peter sat up straight as Chang settled in for a peace treaty. "To me, saving face means I'm her husband in name only."

Uette looked at her father. "Have you negotiated the right for me to talk or do I bow down before all my elders here?"

Her grandfather turned quickly, pointing at her. "You watch your tongue, is that clear? The shame of an accidental pregnancy was enough for the Wongs and Changs. This charge against you is very serious and we'll discuss it at home. For now, you'd be wise to see the charge as seriously and as shameful as it is. I demand respect from that viperous tongue of yours and an apology to your elders." He mocked the word as she had.

Her father took her wrist. "Don't push me, Uette. Your grandfather is right, behave or you'll see ancient Chinese laws enforced that you never dreamed existed. Now offer the apology you owe."

"I'm sorry," she said quietly, lowering her head.

Her father was furious. "Stand up and face your elders, girl." He also mocked the word. "Speak to their faces and show your sincerity for the offense. Humility will be forced down your throat if it isn't flowing in your veins." She stood up, embarrassed by the berating as she faced the men. Peter was enjoying every fraction of a second of it.

"I apologize to all of you," she stammered, shaken and feeling very foolish standing there. "And I apologize to my father and grandfather for the embarrassment." She stayed standing with her head bowed, obviously humbled by the embarrassment.

Her father glared at her. "Now sit down. We have you here because your elders assumed you were intelligent enough to deal with it. Prove us wrong and you'll be removed." She sat down, keeping her head lowered.

"Continue Peter," her grandfather said.

Peter was close to laughing and cleared his throat. "If she comes with a dowry, I hope it's a whip, a chair, and a muzzle." Tom quickly put his head down and covered his mouth to hide the broad smile he couldn't hold back.

"Peter," his grandfather cautioned.

Uette's grandfather spoke up. "It's all right, Liam. Believe me, Peter; right now I'd like to see that arranged along with my son's permission to use them."

Uette's father smiled. This man who he first had dreaded to have connected to his family by marriage was proving to be a great surprise. He was beginning to like him and he thought it was too bad the relationship had such a sour beginning. Peter seemed to be exactly what Uette needed and he hoped against the odds that the two could work out a real marriage. He'd like to have a son-in-law who knew he was a man and was not afraid to be Chinese. He wondered what the girl he was in love with was like. It surprised him remembering he'd been told she was white and he wondered how Peter, so strong in his customs, was living with someone who must be so foreign to them.

Peter's grandfather looked at Peter. "Peter, before you continue I'd like to hear what you mean by husband in name only."

Peter was beginning to understand his grandfather's approach to this whole meeting. He understood that 'we' meant Uette with her father and grandfather as witnesses. He pulled his thoughts together, glad his grandfather understood survival. Chang was pleased. "A husband in name only means there won't be any physical or emotional relationship."

Uette looked up. "You mean…." She stopped talking, not sure of her place. Peter looked at her realizing her confusion. He didn't want her confused about anything in this meeting.

"Uette," he said calmly, "you don't need permission to speak. You were reprimanded for being smart mouthed, not for speaking." The Wong men looked at each other and smiled. They both liked the way Peter handled Uette. His coolness complimented her fieriness.

Uette looked at him, encouraged by his kindness. "I guess you mean we'll need an apartment with two bedrooms."

Peter choked at the thought of sharing an apartment with her. "I'd rather have two apartments, but yes. I'm offering you my name, that's all, not me."

"What will that prove?" she asked.

Peter's grandfather studied the girl who had trapped his grandson. He didn't like what he'd seen so far. Even if she was a Wong, she was a viper. The older men were uncomfortable, wondering why she needed to have things explained so explicitly.

Peter was grateful for his training as a doctor, knowing to treat her like a patient who needed to have details explained simply and plainly. He could see she wasn't as comic a character as she thought she was. He could look past the face and the innocent eyes, and he reminded himself how deadly she really was. He understood how she used her look of innocence to nail a person. Looking so innocent, she could ask almost any embarrassing question and get away with it. He saw her shrewdness and he stood his ground and decided to be as direct as she was.

"It proves I don't love you. Get it clear that the marriage is to save face, to lessen the shame, that's all. There is nothing romantic about it. Is that clear?"

She shrugged, looking innocent. "Sort of."

Peter sighed. "What isn't clear?"

She bit her lower lip. "Will you come home for dinner and things like that?" The older men lowered their heads. It wasn't easy watching two people try to publicly establish a personal life.

Peter looked at her. "Uette, don't use the phrase 'things like that.' I want you to be specific." Peter's grandfather was pleased. The Wongs took sideward glances at each other and with Peter, too. He could handle Uette; few could. Peter shook his head. "Uette, worry about yourself. Consider me a boarder who'll rarely be there. My schedule is very difficult as a doctor."

"Well, how does Jeneil manage it?"

Peter was annoyed. "Don't compare my marriage to Jeneil with the situation we're in. They're not similar. Not even close."

Uette stared at him steadily. "What happens to Jeneil after we're married?"

Peter glared at her. "Get off the subject of Jeneil, will you?"

Peter's grandfather interrupted. "It's a fair question, Peter."

"I agree," Uette's grandfather added. Uette grinned slyly. Peter noticed and kept himself in check, sensing she was out to throw mud.

"What are you driving at Uette? What's your problem?" His stern directness made her withdraw; she didn't want to risk another berating or make her awful beginning with Peter worse.

"I'm concerned for her, that's all. She must be very upset and hurt. I just wondered what your plans are after we're married. She'll be shocked to hear it, won't she?" Her eyes got all innocent and gentle.

Chang wanted to let her have it. "Uette, Jeneil believes the baby isn't mine. In fact, she encouraged me to marry you and save face. When I clear my name I'm going to marry her. She's going to wait for me. We talked all this over before I came here today."

Uette's innocent eyes grew darker as anger filled them. "Will she be your mistress?"

The question hit Peter's stomach hard; he hadn't thought about the details of him and Jeneil. He hadn't thought of leaving her until this meeting. He switched positions in his chair uncomfortably as he took a deep breath. "None of your business," he said calmly, pleased he didn't rage at her. He looked at the men. "That's not a fair question. I'm marrying Uette to give her a husband during this pregnancy. That's all that involves her. I don't want her to look after me or perform any other duty a wife would perform. We'll be strangers sharing an apartment. I hope it doesn't even last long enough for me to unpack. That's how I see this marriage. I plan to clear my name and get a divorce. If that's not how anybody else is seeing it then let's hear it now. In fact," he sat up straight, "I'd like a vote on that. Is it acceptable in this saving face business?"

Uette's grandfather sighed. "All things considered, it's acceptable to me." He looked at his son.

Uette's father shrugged. "We don't have any delusions; we have hopes, but no delusions. It seems like an acceptable beginning in this mess." Peter sat back satisfied. Tears filled Uette's eyes and she cried softly.

Peter became exasperated. "What are you crying about?"

Uette dried her tears. "I wanted us to have a church wedding and a reception."

Peter was struck senseless and stared at her as he regained his balance. "You're pregnant! You really want to walk down an aisle in a white dress and all that stuff?"

Uette became defensive. "The white dress is only a tradition, it doesn't have anything to do with being pregnant or not."

Peter couldn't believe her taste for what he called nonsense. "Then why don't you save it for your next wedding. You'll be in love and everything will be perfect."

Tears streamed down her cheeks. "I'm in love with you." The older men lowered their heads at her remark.

Peter bolted from his chair, upset. "This won't work. She's got crazy ideas." He paced. "Oh man, what a screwy kid." He ran his fingers through his hair.

"I don't have crazy ideas. I know you don't love me." She sniffled and wiped her tears away. "But I want to know what happens when you can't prove the baby isn't yours. And you won't either!"

This was all so personal that the witnesses weren't looking up at all. They were hardly breathing. Peter's grandfather listened carefully, absorbing every word and how it was said. Peter stopped pacing and went back to the table. Grabbing the back of his chair tensely, he looked directly at her. "You're wrong, Uette. If it takes me all my life, I'll find out who the father is. I intend to clear my name. You can count on it. Now let's get anything else that's necessary straightened out. I want to leave."

"When do we get married?" she asked.

"I don't care," Peter said. "Let my grandfather know the date."

"Your grandfather!" Uette was shocked.

"Yes, you'll call him, not me."

She sighed and shook her head as more tears fell. "This is a nightmare," she sniffled.

Peter looked at her. "Hey, it started with your pipedream, not mine. Is there anything else?"

She shrugged. "I'm so confused. I can't think anymore. Do you care where we live?"

"I have to stay close to the hospital or you could live in an apartment and I'll stay at the dorms."

She stared at him angrily. "That's a violation of this arrangement. Don't get funny, I'm not stupid."

Peter grinned. "Neither am I. Neither one of us is being fooled, trust me." She lowered her head and he looked at the men. "I'm on duty today and I'd like to spend some time with my wife. I owe her that. Actually, so much has happened here that I wasn't expecting to be the one who needs her. I need to talk to her. She's my lifeline." Uette watched him as tears rolled down her cheeks. He sighed heavily. His sentiment was genuine; he had been bruised by the meeting. The realities of his decision were hitting him and he felt rattled. He needed to be with Jeneil, to hold her. He stared at the seat of the chair thinking about everything that had happened. As the men watched, not one of them missed his genuine sadness and they understood. Peter looked up. "Is there anything else?" His grandfather looked at Uette's grandfather.

"No, Peter," Uette's grandfather answered compassionately. "We can deal with anything else as it comes along. I want you to know that I'm sorry about all this. I really am. I thank you for what you've done here for the Wong family. I know it's to save face, but in making that choice you've also given us our dignity. I'm truly grateful to you for that."

Uette's father stood up and came to Peter. He extended his hand and Peter shook it. "I'd like to add my thanks to my father's on behalf of the Wong family." He paused. "I haven't been one of your greatest fans in the past, but I'm glad I had a chance to see that I need to change my opinion of you. Consider it changed. I'm very sorry I had to get to know you better under these circumstances. I was telling your grandfather that he can really be proud of you. I mean that."

Peter felt drained, but the respect he was being shown by the Wongs felt good. He could hold his head up in the middle of the filth he was in and that felt right somehow. Uette was watching, completely surprised her father showed Peter such respect and Peter became even more desirable to her as a result.

Peter looked at her. "Uette, I'm sorry, no big church wedding." She frowned. "It's too hypocritical considering the kind of situation this is. Get a judge." She felt resentment but assessed the situation and stayed silent, neither arguing nor voicing her disagreement. She waited, having learned early in life that if she waited life seemed to change things her way. Peter looked at his grandfather. "I'll be in touch." His grandfather smiled and Peter could tell he was pleased with him. Peter even saw pride in the smile. Tom watched him with concern. Peter sighed. "I'd like to make sure my mother's okay. What do you think?"

"Sure," Tom answered.

*****

Peter knocked on the closed door and heard his mother's quiet, "Come in." She was surprised to see him. He sat down next to her on the edge of the bed. She looked rough and wrung out. Peter strongly identified with the feeling.

"I'm concerned about your attack. Has Dr. Slater seen you?" Peter asked, feeling bad about her suffering.

She nodded, staring at the white handkerchief she fidgeted with nervously. "I'll be fine. Is the meeting over?"

"Yes."

She sighed. "Well, I'm surprised by the quiet. I expected shouting, maybe even gunfire."

"I'm going to marry Uette," Peter said quietly.

His mother looked up quickly, not quite trusting her hearing. "You are?"

He nodded. "I couldn't stand them thinking the baby's mine. It isn't. I decided to save face."

She put her arm around his shoulder. "Peter…," she choked up, "never have I been so proud of you as I am right now, never, not even med school." She kissed his cheek.

He stood up, shocked by her display of emotion toward him. "Mom, you have to understand it's a marriage in name only. I intend to clear my name. The baby isn't mine."

Compassion filled her as she understood he was having trouble accepting the truth because he loved Jeneil so much. "Peter, I'm sorry for the names I called Jeneil. I was so upset. I feel so sorry for Uette."

Peter felt his resentment for Uette surface; he ignored it. "You were wrong about Jeneil, you know. She wasn't keeping me from marrying Uette. She told me to marry her."

The news totally shocked his mother. "That's very odd, isn't it?"

Peter smiled. "Not for Jeneil. Her normal is our lopsided."

"What happens to her now?" she asked, even more confused as she considered the effects of Peter's decision.

"She's going to wait for me."

"She said that?"

Peter nodded. "She's really special, Mom. She is, and I've got to get home. I'm on duty this afternoon."

"Yes, of course," his mother answered, still somewhat overwhelmed by all of Peter's news. "Jeneil must be sitting at home worried right now."

Peter went to the door. "She and Steve were going shopping. She's helping him put his apartment together. She's probably back by now. Take care of yourself and stay calm."

"Yes, I will," she answered, and then stared at the closed door after Peter left. "You get a girl pregnant, Jeneil tells you to marry her, and instead of being at home in a panic over the meeting she's out with Steve." She sighed, shaking her head. "Oh, Peter, wake up. Uette must be the out Jeneil was looking for."

She felt bad for her son. He loved Jeneil so much. This marriage wouldn't stand a chance. Why didn't Jeneil just make a clean break? Why say she'd wait for him? Was it spite? Anger because of his betrayal? Was that her plan, to leave her memory in him so it destroyed his chance in this marriage? Tears rolled down her cheeks. "What a complete mess and poor Uette's in the middle of it. Uette's the one who really loves you, Peter. Wake up."

Nineteen

Steve watched as Jeneil paced. She had looked at her wristwatch several times within minutes. "Why don't I go to the deli for some sandwiches?"

She turned to him and smiled wearily. "That's not necessary, I have turkey here. You brought breakfast. We don't have to wait for Peter if you're hungry."

Steve shrugged. "I'm okay."

Jeneil returned to pacing and Steve continued to watch. He had seen her tension increase all morning. He admired her attempt at bravery and it surprised him that they had gone shopping. She had stayed at it cheerfully and he had seen the looks of sadness only when she thought he wasn't watching. He couldn't understand why she was so upset; Peter could endure the jabs he'd get for telling the bitch to hike. The front door opened and closed and Jeneil turned, listening for footsteps. They stopped at the apartment door. Steve saw Jeneil swallow as she wrung her hands nervously. Peter walked in and he looked awfully low. Steve guessed the Wongs really raged. He watched Jeneil study Peter for a second. She closed her eyes tightly and took a deep breath. She looked pretty low, too. Then, she held her head up and walked toward Peter.

Peter choked up as he stood watching her. "Baby…," he couldn't finish the sentence, swallowing hard. Steve was concerned. Something felt very wrong, but he didn't know why it should.

Jeneil slipped her arms around Peter's waist and he grabbed her quickly, holding her against him, burying his face into his shoulder. "You had to, Peter. You had no choice. I understand."

"Baby, how can you understand? I don't. The whole thing shits. I must be crazy."

Steve stood up slowly. Something was definitely wrong. Peter looked beaten, totally done in, and Steve watched as he smothered himself against Jeneil. Tears streamed down her face. "Pete, what happened?" he asked with dread, his stomach in a knot. Peter groaned and Jeneil held him tighter. "Pete, what happened?" Steve repeated, really worried.

Jeneil looked at Steve. "He's going to marry Uette."

Steve laughed nervously. "No, he isn't. Pete, what happened?" He moved closer, not liking the feel of the whole situation.

"Steve, he's upset right now," Jeneil explained, holding Peter.

Steve didn't like Peter's silence. "Look at me, Pete."

"Steve." Jeneil looked at him, concerned about his attitude.

Steve bristled and pushed Jeneil away from Peter, completely shocking her. Holding Peter by the coat collar, Steve tried to control his anger. "You said you wouldn't do it, Pete. Damn it. Why? Why!"

"I had to, Steve," Peter answered quietly.

Steve felt anger swell within him. "No, you lousy son-of-a-bitch! What about Jeneil!" he shouted, and before he could think his fist hit Peter with a full blow sending him backwards against the wall.

"Stop it, Steve! Are you crazy!" Jeneil cried, going to Peter, who was bleeding.

Steve shook his hand as the pain from the blow hit him. He grabbed his jacket. "I'm outta here!" he said angrily, heading to the door.

Jeneil turned quickly, leaving Peter, and ran to the door to block it. "No, you can't just leave things like this," she pleaded. "He's your friend. What's wrong with you?"

"He's nobody's friend!" Steve snapped. "He's a gutless, spineless son-of-a-bitch. He doesn't deserve you."

"Shut up!" Jeneil shouted, shocking herself, stunned by Steve's response. She covered her face and sobbed.

Steve was surprised and he put his arms around her. "I'm sorry, kid," he said quietly, holding her.

Peter walked over to them wiping his bleeding lip with the back of his hand. Jeneil pulled away gently, trying to calm down. "Oh please," she cried, "we're all we have. We're family. We can't let this craziness ruin that. We've got to keep a clear head or we won't survive. I'm sorry I yelled." She hugged Steve and kissed his cheek. "Please don't leave." She turned to Peter and touched his face gently. "Are you okay?"

He nodded. "Thanks, Steve. I needed that. Oh shit, I wanted so bad to get into a fight. Now I'm satisfied."

Jeneil stared. "This is incredibly bizarre." Steve went to check Peter's lip and Jeneil noticed his hand. "Is that your blood or Peter's?"

"I'm not sure." Steve laughed lightly. "I think we need ice packs, Jeneil."

She nodded. "I'll get the first-aid kit."

"The cut isn't deep," Steve said, and then he sighed. "I'm really sorry, Pete. Shit, that was blind rage. I can't believe I did that to you." He shook his head.

"It's okay, Steve. Like I said, I really needed that. I did. I know you're upset for Jeneil."

Steve studied Peter's face. "What the hell did they do to you? Threaten to sever your head from your body and send it to Jeneil? What?"

Peter shrugged. "You had to be there." He sighed. "I sat there across from the bitch with everybody believing the baby's mine. I just couldn't live with that. Then, I heard myself accuse her of lying about me being the father and I chose saving face."

Steve shook his head. "I don't understand how giving the bitch what she wanted helps you feel better."

Peter exhaled and dried his lip again. "If I think about it, I get confused. All I know is the blind fury I had has lowered to rage since I made the decision. I don't have to be her husband." He gritted his teeth. "And I can tell you right now she's going to be sorry she said I'm the father. Divorce will sound like heaven when I'm through with her."

Jeneil stopped in the hallway outside the bathroom. "Dr. Chang, Dr. Bradley, ER is ready for you." Steve laughed and Peter grinned, and they went to join her.

Peter and Steve sat with makeshift ice packs that Jeneil had put together. Having made sandwiches for lunch, Jeneil called them. Lunch wasn't cheerful, but there was a closeness amongst them that was calming. Jeneil looked at them as family. Steve remembered that and he held onto it since it explained his place in her life. He accepted it eagerly and it justified the deep concern he felt for her since Peter's news. Peter held her hand throughout the meal and stayed close by, hovering like a man living on borrowed air. His telephone rang and they all looked at each other. Peter got up to answer it.

"Peter, its Dr. Sprague. I was wondering how your meeting went."

Peter sighed. "I'm going to marry the girl."

Dr. Sprague sighed. "Are they forcing it?"

"No, I had the choice of marriage or court for admission that the baby's mine and child support."

"Shit," Dr. Sprague mumbled.

"That's why I chose saving face."

"What's that?" Dr. Sprague asked.

"I'm marrying her but under stated protest. I lodged a counter accusation that she's deliberately lying."

"I didn't know you had that option. You still have to marry her though?"

"Yes, but it's not a real marriage. I'm buying time to prove I'm not the father."

Dr. Sprague smiled. "I like the sound of that. Peter, would you let me contact my lawyer? That marriage deal sounds like it's ripe for a contract. You could save yourself some headaches by having a premarital agreement signed. I'm sure the decision to marry her is eating at your gut, but it does quiet the fireworks for a court case."

Peter paced. "I never thought about a contract."

"Think about it," Dr. Sprague advised. "You don't want the bitch on your ass and dipping into your career."

Peter understood. "Okay, let's see what a lawyer thinks. Thanks, Dr. Sprague."

"And how about a private detective to help you find the father?"

Peter gasped. "Wow, you're talking big money, Dr. Sprague."

"I'd like to help, Peter."

"I can't accept that," Peter said. "It's…thanks a lot, but I'm hoping to drag some truth out of her as this circus we call marriage begins. I'm not going to be a wonderful husband so she'll want out fast. The girl's life is fiction, she lives fairytales. She even has herself convinced that she loves me. Let's leave a private detective as a last resort."

"Okay," Dr. Sprague agreed. "Now what about the weekend off?"

Peter brightened. "I'd like tonight if I could. I haven't had a chance to talk to Jeneil. There are details that need to be ironed out."

"I'll see what I can do," Dr. Sprague answered. "What was Jeneil's reaction to your decision?"

"She told me to marry the girl. She said she'll wait for me."

"Oh, wow." Dr. Sprague smiled. "Peter, I expected bushels of shit when I called, but you've given me a marriage agreement and a girl whose loyalty leaves me speechless. We're lucking out." He sighed. "Let me call Dr. Fisher. I'll get back to you about the night off."

Peter went back to the living room. Steve was pacing and Jeneil was sitting in a chair listening to some music with her eyes closed. Peter bent down and kissed her lips, and she smiled. "Sprague's trying to get me the night off."

"That would be great," she said quietly.

Steve turned. "I should leave. I know you two need privacy but this thing has me so rattled I'd rather be with people. This beats a singles bar. Pete, what about contacting a lawyer?"

Peter sat on the hassock he had pulled to Jeneil's chair and held her hand. "Sprague's contacting his lawyer."

"Good." Steve smiled and then sighed. "I'm going to go." He picked up his jacket.

Jeneil looked at him. "Has the swelling on your hand gone down?"

Steve flexed his fingers. "Yeah, the cut is closed, too." He looked at her with boyish embarrassment.

She smiled. "You're a hot head."

He grinned. "I feel stupid about it."

Peter lightly laughed. "Don't, it helped me a lot."

Jeneil looked at Peter. "The corner of your mouth is still swollen. How will you explain that at the hospital?"

"I walked into a door." Peter shrugged. "At least it felt like one." He laughed. "Ouch," he said, the healing cut reminding him to not laugh. His telephone rang. "Sprague," he said, getting up to answer it.

"Peter, I called Dr. Fisher. Stanton and Ludlow we're rear-ended this afternoon. Stanton has whiplash and Ludlow's wrist is sprained. He was scheduled to cover ER surgery. I hate to ask, but we need you here."

Peter was disappointed. "I understand. Don't worry about it, I'll be in."

"I'm sorry, Peter. You're sure you are together enough?"

Peter sighed. "Yeah, not knowing what was going to happen was worse. Oddly enough, I'm calmer than I thought I'd be."

"I'm proud of you, Peter. I am. That comes from a man who's watched you work your ass off to get where you are. The situation stinks, but I'm really glad you didn't risk your career."

Putting the receiver back, Peter sighed. His decision seemed to be great for everybody and everything in his life except Jeneil. He thought about her attitude and her strength overwhelmed him. He didn't know about his Songbird needing his protection. She was always holding him up through the messes he brought to her; his background, his mother, and now this. After this he needed to bring his life into line and give her the kind of life she deserved. Jeneil looked up as Peter walked in. Steve was doing up his jacket. "I have to go in, honey. Two residents are out. They need me."

She nodded. "We can expect to swim upstream through this, Peter. Once the current washes against you, the only thing to do is wait for time to swing the pendulum in the other direction. Don't expect things to work our way. We're in a Yin cycle." She sighed, and Peter and Steve watched her. She looked up and smiled wearily. "But at least the pendulum does swing the other way. The trick is to grit your teeth and bite the bullet until it does." She stood up. "I'll get your dinner packed for work."

Steve was shocked Peter could do this to her and he was worried. He wanted to be with her. He was upset; Steve had promised he wouldn't let the speeding train hurt her and it had. He choked up thinking how much the situation had cost her and she was completely innocent. The tidal wave wasn't her doing, but she was the victim of the backlash, almost its only clearly innocent victim. "Pete, I'd like to stay. Damn, I feel so bad about this. I want to strangle the bitch."

Peter put his head back, sighing. "Steve, the girl is lopsided, she's definitely lopsided." The word was familiar to him as he realized that's how he and Steve described Jeneil. "Jeneil is too, but she's a different kind of lopsided. She's fun. Uette is….," Peter searched for a word.

"Not funny," Steve offered, "not funny at all."

Peter nodded. "You know, I looked at her and begged her to tell the truth and she looked at me straight in the eye and said, 'I'm pregnant because of you.' She has no conscience." Jeneil had come into the room and overheard his comment.

"She said it that way? Those were her exact words?"

Peter turned around, surprised she was there. "Yes, that's what she said. Why?"

Jeneil shrugged. "That's an interesting way to say it. Why didn't she just say you're the father? She said she's pregnant because of you."

"What difference does it make?" Steve asked.

Peter agreed. "Yeah, it's only words. We know what she meant."

Jeneil pinched her lower lip in thought. "Words are very revealing," she said. "Think about it. She's at a serious meeting and truth was demanded of her. I'm pregnant because of you was her reply when she was asked for truth."

"You've lost me," Steve said.

"Me, too," Peter agreed.

Jeneil smiled at them. "Don't you think it's interesting she didn't say you're the father but she blames you for the pregnancy?"

Steve looked at Peter and wrinkled his eyebrows. "Let me know when she's speaking English."

Peter shook his head. "Jeneil, you are lopsided."

"Don't you see," she said excitedly, "she has her own concept of truth. She's two people. She wants to tell the truth, but she's up against something that's preventing her from doing that. She's caught in something. I can feel it. There's a conflict and she's caught in the crossfire."

Steve shook his head. "Helium overdose, Jeneil."

Peter smiled and put his arm around her shoulder, kissing her temple. "She's a bitch, honey. Don't sprinkle romantic dust on her. Don't waste your kindness."

"Peter, you've just been given an ace." Jeneil smiled. "The very thing that caused this problem for you is the very thing that can save you."

"What's that?" Peter asked, curious about her excitement but not following her reasoning.

"Her attraction for you. She loves you."

Peter was shocked. "Jeneil, you sound just like her."

Steve smiled. "Maybe Jeneil's right if they're both lopsided."

Jeneil sighed, frustrated. "Ooo, you guys are not grasping this."

Steve touched her cheek gently. "Kid, play back your words, you'll see why."

"No," she insisted, and then thinking better of continuing she shrugged. "It's not time yet I guess, but I know I'm close. I can feel it. My father taught me to listen to words and Uncle Hollis taught me to watch words when dealing with contracts. They haven't been wrong. What else binds the whole world together except words? No, I'm wrong, it's love and music. They're more international because they interpret more easily."

Steve shook his head. "She can follow that thought pattern and not get a headache. That's amazing."

Peter hugged her. "But her lopsided is cute."

Steve nodded. "And harmless."

Jeneil grinned. "You'll see," she insisted, "I'm not living in fiction; you guys are because you're not multi-ddimensional."

Peter kissed her cheek and laughed. "I'm changing my shirt for work. She's into right angle thinking. Just let her talk to herself, Steve. She eventually wanders out of it." Peter went to the bedroom and Steve smiled as he watched Jeneil settle into her chair again, lost in her right angle thoughts.

"Hey, want some company tonight?" Steve asked, sitting on the hassock.

His question brought her to the moment. "Yes." She smiled. "Thanks, let's take all the things we bought to your apartment and settle them into place. If you'll get the bed sheets from your car, I'll put them in the washer now to remove the sizing from them. They'll be dry by the time we leave."

"That's a lot of work, Jeneil. You don't have to."

She patted his hand. "Yes, I do. I need to keep moving in order to survive this. We can drive to the motel and pick up the bedspread and drapes. Then, you'll just need your bed.

Monday, the crew will be in to do your rugs and floors. You'll have furniture in on Wednesday then that's it for you, Dr. Bradley. Life begins."

"That easy, huh?" He laughed.

Peter came from the bedroom carrying his parka. "I've got to go."

Steve stood up. "I'll get the stuff from my car," he said, leaving Peter and Jeneil alone.

Peter sat on the hassock. "Wait up for me, baby."

She nodded. "I will. We need to spend the night talking."

"We can't, honey. I'm on first shift tomorrow. Remember?"

She sighed. "Swimming upstream against the current isn't easy. I wonder how salmon manage it."

Peter smiled. "Strong motivation."

She grinned. "I can equal that."

"Sexy wench." He grinned and went to kiss her passionately, but his lip reminded him it wasn't completely healed. He pulled away and sighed.

She touched his face lovingly. "Things just ain't goin' our way lately, Jaspah."

"So I've noticed." He stood up and took her hand and pulled her to him. "If salmon can swim against the current, so can we."

She smiled broadly. "You bet."

He held her close, leaning his head next to hers. "Jeneil, you are being incredible about all this. I promise you that when this whole mess is over we'll get married and settle into a very normal, quiet, dull life and yawn each other to sleep."

"That sounds wonderful."

"In case I haven't said it, I love you for standing by me in this and in our whole relationship. It's been pretty crazy at times."

She squeezed him. "Growing pains, love. Just growing pains. This one is the crazy situation."

He sighed. "I can take this marriage as long as I know you'll wait for me."

She kissed his chin. "I don't have any choice, I belong to you. So we'll just keep walking through the fog until it disappears."

"I love you," he said, choking with emotion. "I always will."

"I know." She smiled, holding up her right hand and pointing to the wedding ring. "I live in your soul now. You'll never be free of me."

He kissed her gently. "That's fine with me."

She hugged him. "Go to work, Dr. Chang."

"Yeah." He sighed, pulling away. "Nothing stops, does it?"

"Life doesn't care what's going wrong. Get onto the conveyor belt and hang on." She handed him the bag with dinner in it.

"What are you and Steve doing?"

"Getting his apartment humanized."

Peter smiled. "He really appreciates the help."

"I know and it keeps me busy. We're a good blend together."

Peter watched her, becoming a little concerned. "Miss me, okay?"

She nodded. "Like crazy, Chang."

He hugged her. "I'll be back here as fast as I can." He kissed her cheek then opened the door and left. The sound of the door closing vibrated through Jeneil. Tears filled her eyes as she reminded herself that one day soon he'd have to walk out that door and not return, and she went to the bedroom sobbing.

Steve waited at his car until he saw Peter open the front door. Going upstairs, he found Jeneil lying across her bed crying. Feeling awkward about going in, he stood at the door, compassion filling him. He went to her and lay next to her, rubbing her back gently. "I thought you were being too brave, kid. You have a right to scream and throw a fit."

"That won't change anything. At least crying makes me feel better." She sniffled.

His throat tightened and he felt her suffering. "I'm sorry, Jeneil. I really am." He kissed her shoulder. "I didn't do well protecting you from the moving train." He kissed her cheek. "I wish I could make it go away. Tell him you've changed your mind. He'll stop the crazy wedding. He will for you, honey."

She shook her head. "No, he has to live with himself, Steve. He has to prove the baby isn't his. Marrying her is the only way to keep it from destroying every part of his life."

"But it's destroying you," he argued.

"No, it isn't. This is just a weak moment. I'll survive, you'll see."

He took her hand. "Well, I have to tell you that I admire your spunk. Your loyalty overwhelms me."

"I belong to Peter. It's that simple."

Steve swallowed. "Yeah, I know. To you, it's that simple." He squeezed her hand gently.

She smiled as she watched him. "You are a very sensitive person. I like that in a man. Thank you for caring about me. I just realized you hit Peter because of me."

He looked at her, wondering what she had figured out. "What do you mean?"

"You didn't expect him to marry Uette. You're my friend. You were upset because of me and you hit him. You really should get married. You have all the right ingredients for a good husband."

He smiled and kissed her forehead. "Except a wife."

She smiled and sat up. "Let's get your apartment put together then you can look for a wife." She stood up and took his hand, pulling him off the bed. "Who knows, this nightmare will end and then maybe we'll both be married by the end of the year."

"Who knows?" He smiled, following her out of the bedroom.

*****

The evening flew by for Jeneil and Steve. The ride to the motel was pleasant and they stopped for dinner before going to his apartment. It began to look a little more put together after everything was put in place; shower curtains, bars of soap, towels, all the small indicators that someone lived there. Jeneil smiled and closed the kitchen cupboards after washing the dishes and putting them away as Steve dried. "We were lucky to get those mixing bowls at the secondhand store. And those old glasses for a nickel each. Now you can save the set you got on sale for when you have people in to visit."

Steve laughed. "Pete's right, you do have a strong nesting instinct."

She laughed, too. "I know. It gets embarrassing. I really can nestle right in." She cleared the counter of paper, putting it in the wastebasket. "It's how I gauge myself. If I'm not nesting, I'm depressed or out of touch. If I'm hyper nesting, I'm ready for a change, ready for more in life."

"You're such a flake."

"Eccentric," she corrected. She looked cute to him; he liked her here in his apartment, in his kitchen. He liked watching her nest. She looked around. "It seems to me that all you need for now is a toaster, a blender, and a coffee pot and you're ready to put your kitchen to work." She thought for a minute. "You know, the Fairview Apartments has a box for items left behind by tenants. We save them in case they were left by mistake. There are really good things sometimes. I'll bet you could get a toaster there. I'll check it out." She made a note in her book and then tossed it into her purse haphazardly, exhaling a sigh of exhaustion.

Steve watched her. "Come on, kid. You've just about reached your limit."

She stretched her arms in front of her. "I'm drained," she said. "And that's good, I'm too tired to feel."

He got her toggle coat and held it for her. "Home, sweetheart."

She turned to him as she did up her coat. "I tease you about getting married, but I really want to see you happy. Your life is opening up now."

He smiled. "Oh yes it is. Tomorrow, I'm going to dinner at the Sprague's and I'm going to learn to play bridge. Now that is worth years in med school."

Jeneil looked at him, surprised by his sarcasm. "But you like the Spragues."

"Yes, I do," he said. "It's bridge I really don't care about or bridge parties. And there's going to be a fourth for bridge, too." He shook his head wearily. "Now it starts, Bradley on parade, get the guy married, and it's tough to have to say I really don't care for her. I hate the pressure."

She laughed. "Hey, at least I'll win my bet."

He snickered. "I love your compassion."

She kissed his cheek. "You get grouchy when you're tired. Let's lock up here."

Steve closed the door behind him wishing they could have locked up the outside world and stayed in a world of their own inside the apartment. He pushed the elevator button thinking how life played stupid tricks. There he was with a girl he knew he could be ecstatic with and never let out of his sight and he was taking her home to a guy who would be marrying someone else while she waited for him to come back to her. Damn, he thought to himself, he hated that button marked 'Shit.'

*****

Peter left the hospital as soon as he could. Since deciding to marry Uette, he had a deep feeling of wanting to have Jeneil close to him and had changed his mind several times about going through with it. Besides not wanting to marry Uette, he was concerned about leaving Jeneil alone. He knew the feeling stemmed from his insecurities and the thought of Robert Danzieg's interest in her began to gnaw at him. He touched his lip, the swelling nearly gone. He sighed, realizing the enormous feeling Steve must have for Jeneil to have exploded like that. Steve was a talker; he talked in to and out of situations. Peter had seen it all through med school. Steve kept his cool and talked through whatever he faced. It was a quality he admired and tried to duplicate in himself. It wasn't easy, he had learned that much. The punch that afternoon was definitely out of character. Pulling into the parking lot, he turned off the ignition and lights. Opening the car door, he got out and headed quickly through the cold to the front door. Running up the stairs, he promised himself that he would keep Jeneil near him. No way was he letting her out of his sight. He heard her in the kitchen and could smell something baking. Undoing his jacket, he went to the kitchen and grabbed her around the waist.

"Ooo, you're cold," she said, shivering.

He pulled his jacket off and dropped it to the floor then pulled her to him. "I'm home," he said, kissing her several times.

She laughed. "Yes, it would be tough to miss that. Quick, change for bed. Ovaltine's ready and I defrosted cinnamon rolls, they're still warm." He took one and went to the bedroom.

Jeneil followed carrying a tray with two mugs and a plate of rolls balanced on it. She handed it to him and climbed under the covers then held the tray while he went to his side of the bed and got in. She put the tray between them and spread a napkin on her lap.

"No, no, no," he said, lifting the tray, "over here, beautiful. You're too far away." He fixed the pillows so they could sit against the headboard.

Jeneil moved over, studying him. "Has something happened? Do you have news?"

"No, why?" he asked, as he moved closer to her.

"You're being very attentive. I just wondered."

"Why, do I usually ignore you?" He laughed.

She smiled. "No, but this is different."

"Geez, the meeting was only this morning. What could happen?"

Jeneil shrugged, breaking a cinnamon roll in half. "She's going to move fast, Peter. She's already two weeks pregnant."

He drank some Ovaltine and didn't comment. He sighed. "She asked me what will happen to you."

Jeneil was stunned. "Oh really, conscience or fear?" she replied sarcastically. He looked at her and she lowered her eyes, embarrassed. "I'm sorry," she said softly. "I can't afford sarcasm. It's a waste of my energy flow. If I were a nice person, I'd say she is a person after all but I don't feel like being nice to her."

Peter smiled. "It's okay. I'll even answer your question. It's fear. I told her I'm not giving you up."

Jeneil looked up quickly, surprised. "What do you mean?"

"She knows I'm not going to stop seeing you after we're married," he said, and the thought twisted Jeneil's stomach and she turned and picked up her drink. Peter noticed her reaction. "What's wrong?" Jeneil took another sip to avoid answering. "Jeneil, talk to me."

She rubbed her temple. "I just didn't see myself as being your mistress."

"You're my wife," he said strongly, "not my mistress."

She shook her head. "Peter, in the dimension of this world she'll be your wife, not me." Her throat began to hurt. She sipped more Ovaltine and swallowed hard, but the pain wouldn't ease up. She reached for her robe and got up. Pacing helped.

He watched her, becoming concerned. "Jeneil, what were you thinking? A complete separation for us?"

"Well, yes," she said, holding her throat. "I was thinking you wouldn't be married long. I mean, you'll be married to her."

"In name only, Jeneil. In name only."

"I know that, but…." She stopped as shock began to take its toll. Words weren't forming easily. "I…I thought the honorable thing would be for us to separate."

Peter was annoyed. "Her lie is shit and you care about honor in that stupid marriage."

Jeneil had trouble breathing normally. "Well, I…but…our honor, Peter, yours and mine. Somehow it doesn't seem right." She saw him grip his mug and tighten his jaw. "Peter," she said, sitting on the bed, "how would you manage the time to see me anyway? We rarely run into each other when you're on second shift. You should be asleep right now. You're going in tomorrow morning." Jeneil could see he was angry. "Peter, I don't know what you're angry about."

He looked at her with fire in his eyes. "Jeneil, I have trouble understanding where honor was all these months that I've been asking you to marry me and we've been living together. Now I get honor thrown at me like I'm a real low life for assuming we'd continue seeing each other."

She shook her head. "I didn't mean that," she insisted sincerely.

"Oh please, Jeneil, get out of fiction will you," he snapped.

"I don't see it that way. At least neither one of us was married."

"I'm not going to be her husband."

"But you will be legally."

He shook his head and sighed. "Then I'll call the bitch tomorrow and tell her it's off. This isn't how I saw this shittin' mess."

Jeneil was stunned. "You can't do that!" she gasped. "Think of the damage to your career alone!"

He looked at her steadily. "Would you like to explain to me how marrying that lying bitch and separating from me is coming so easy to you?"

The remark hit Jeneil like a physical blow. She stood up slowly, staring at him angrily. "I'm afraid to ask what you're implying because if we're all the way back to Steve and infidelity then we have a much bigger problem here than Uette." Tears ran down her face.

"I didn't mean that," he said quietly, regretting the remark.

"Odd that your denial isn't as strong as your charge was," she said, holding back more tears.

He took the tray and put it on the floor. "Get back in bed."

"I don't want to," she answered, reaching for a tissue.

"Jeneil, get back here now," he said more strongly, but she ignored him. "Jeneil, don't do this to me. The only thing keeping me sane right now is the feeling that you belong to me, that you'll stand by me."

She turned around quickly. "Well, you were certainly quick to start implying that I wasn't a second ago."

"Shut up, Jeneil," he said calmly. "This is getting ahead of us. Get back to bed now." She stared at him as unleashed anger and hurt raced through her. The arrogance in his non-apology annoyed her. "I'm sorry," he said sincerely. "I just can't believe all this. You want me to marry her and you want me to stay away from you. That hurts Jeneil and it scares me." She watched him, his admission beginning to dissolve her anger. That was more than he had ever revealed.

"You brainless baboon." She sighed. "Nothing in this situation is what I want, it's what I've been handed. I'm hurt and scared, too. We're in this mess because you wanted me to decide if I really wanted you. Didn't I prove that when we were married spiritually? Why do I have to keep proving it?" She paced. "Ooo, I'm so angry at myself. We should have gotten married months ago just to settle your doubts, but no, I had to find Jeneil." She sighed again and turned to him. "I'm sorry, Peter. I've contributed to this mess, too."

"Please come back to bed, baby," he pleaded, and she slipped off her robe and settled in next to him. Feeling his arms around her, she wondered how she could tell him to marry Uette and stay away from her. She sighed, hating the turmoil in their life.

"Peter, I think we should make our move before she arranges our life. That would put us in control of us."

He looked at her. "What are you saying, move out tomorrow?"

"Don't say it that way," she pleaded.

He shook his head looking at her steadily. "No, baby. Listen to me carefully. We will live together until the day before I marry her and I will continue to come here after I'm married to her even if it means you quit the hospital so we can be together."

She stared in disbelief, unable to bring herself to tell him about the resentment she felt for his plan robbing her of her dignity. He went to kiss her but she couldn't. She turned away.

"What's this, a headache?" he asked, and lay back on his pillow.

"No," she answered, tears spilling down her cheeks.

"Jeneil, what is it?" he asked, sighing.

"Your plan doesn't leave me any pride. For the first time since we've been together, I feel dirty," she cried softly.

"Shit," he mumbled. "I'm so damn sick of the words honor, pride, and dignity. All I know is the only thing that means something to me is being taken from me, you."

Jeneil dried her tears and turned to face him. "She can't take me from you. We are married forever. If we're ready to deal with the problem she's dealt us then we're the ones in charge, not her. If we wait until the day before the wedding then she is the one separating us. If we brace ourselves now then we're planning our lives, not her."

He kissed her forehead. "I can understand that. I don't like it, but I understand." He sighed and put his arm around her. "I'm sorry, baby; my plan had only me in mind. I want to hang onto you at any cost. I couldn't see that the cost was your self-respect." He rubbed her arm. "I knew I wouldn't like leaving you, but it's really bad now. Not seeing you at all scares me. Jeneil, we could lose touch with each other. I don't like it."

She snuggled to him. "Peter, you have to remember that I belong to you. Our marriage was real to me, too. I really don't believe you'll be married to her that long. I couldn't give you up. If there was any thought in my mind that I'd lose you, I would never agree to saving face. Never. I'll wait for you. You'll come back to me."

He held her. "Jeneil, when you're in my arms and saying the words, I'm okay. When I'm away from you, I panic."

"We can't panic, Peter. Not if you want to get to the truth. I love you, Peter, remember that. Life wouldn't work for me with anyone else. It just wouldn't."

Peter smiled at her. "I know what you mean; Chang breathes because of Irish." She kissed him gently and he continued the kiss, enjoying the closeness that returned. She cuddled to him and that made him feel more secure. She never could fake being physical. He loved that about her. Trust between them had been restored, love and physical desire evolved. The comfort of sharing their love brought peace between them and they held onto each other through the night not wanting anything to be over.

Twenty

Jeneil stood at the apartment door still feeling the light lingering kiss Peter had given her. Her heart ached thinking of how close their separation was to being real, knowing Uette would be setting the date soon. Going to the laundry room, she picked up one of the three boxes she had collected to pack his things. Taking it to the bedroom, she began with his medical books. Tears filled her eyes and she decided not to fight them. There were times in life when tears were allowed, even expected. To her, this definitely qualified as one of those times. The doorbell rang as she finished filling the box. Drying her eyes, she opened the door to a smiling Adrienne whose smile faded quickly.

"Jeneil? What…something has happened?" she asked, walking in. Jeneil nodded, biting her lower lip as tears spilled again.

Adrienne sat on the bed trying to absorb the story Jeneil had just told her. The second box was already half filled. "This is incredible!" She heaved a sigh. "It just doesn't happen these days. I don't believe it! You two are so right for each other. This can't happen!" Tears rolled down Adrienne's cheeks and she reached for a tissue from the box Jeneil was quickly emptying. "Isn't there anything he can do besides marry her?"

"Not without a lot of damage to a lot of people." Jeneil sniffled and set aside the second filled box.

Adrienne sighed. "Well, I pity the girl. What man responds to a woman who has trapped him? She's chosen a very strange path. How could she even hope to pass a lie off to someone like Peter or any man?"

Jeneil sat on the bed. "I've asked myself that question over and over. The only thing I can think of is she smelled the bourbon on Peter's breath and assumed he had more than he did and decided to use that as his excuse for not remembering. He can't deny he had a drink. What else is a reasonable explanation for her bold lie?"

Adrienne sighed. "Jeneil, this whole situation isn't reasonable, are you really trying to explain it rationally?"

Jeneil nodded. "I believe everybody has reasons for doing things. Their behavior may not seem reasonable to anyone except themselves. I wish I could understand where she's coming from. You have to be desperate to force a man into a no-win situation like this. What could be making her so desperate?"

Adrienne held her forehead and shook her head from side to side. "Girl, I'd be hair-pulling mad right now and you sit there wondering why she's so desperate. You're incredible."

"No, I'm not Adrienne. I feel like strangling her but I know it won't help. Our only hope is to uncover the reason for what she's doing and I can't do that if I'm raging."

Adrienne looked at the boxes. "Is Peter leaving already?"

"He should in order to stay in control. She's sure to have the wedding soon and I have to be in Nebraska next weekend." Jeneil shrugged. "The clock is winning the race."

"Do you really have to go to Nebraska?"

"It's best really. I'll be away from here. I think that's what will be the most difficult, living with all the reminders of him and I can't afford self–pity, it's negative. Survival will require positive energy. I know that from experience. Being near my roots at the cottage will be good for me."

Adrienne stood up to leave. "Well, I admire you. The only thing that would make me settle down is a good caterwaulin' brawl with the bitch. You are too civilized." She hugged Jeneil. "Lean on me when it gets tough. I want you to. Is that clear?"

Jeneil nodded, touched by her friend's sincere caring. She smiled thinking some people may complicate life, but others made you feel you had some time at living because you had a chance to know them well.

*****

The afternoon seemed to be over before Jeneil realized it. She had dusted, cleaned, and polished thoroughly to use up energy. The vegetables were ready for dinner and the steaks were defrosted. She changed into a long dress and wandered around the apartment already aware of its emptiness. Her stomach knotted and tears stung her eyes, but she held herself together. Peter would be home soon. Inserting a cassette into the stereo, she sat in a chair with a book she was reading. Soon the loud, angry classical music had swirled through her and she sat back giving herself over to the vibrations, her anger draining from her. She was startled when Peter leaned down and kissed her. She looked at her watch. "I lost track of time," she said, getting up. "I'll put the steaks on."

He took her hands. "A kiss first." He smiled, pulling her closer. He looked around. "You've been busy. I smell furniture polish and cleaning fluid."

She smiled and leaned against him, loving the feeling of him holding her. "I had extra energy."

"I noticed from the music," he said, kissing her temple.

She kissed him lightly. "I'll put the steaks on."

He went to the bedroom concerned having noticed her eyes were puffy even though her eye makeup was flawless. He sighed. The whole situation was hitting her so hard and it would get worse as time got closer and plans were made. "Shit," he grumbled, undoing his jacket. He turned from the closet and saw that his medical books were gone from the shelf. It hit him solidly in the stomach. Going to his desk, he saw the two packed boxes on the floor. His stomach knotted as reality hit him. He understood why she had been crying. He sat on the edge of the bed numbed by the message that was before him.

"I fixed the homemade steak sauce you like," Jeneil said, smiling as she came into the room. She stopped when she saw Peter sitting on the bed facing his packed belongings. She sat down next to him unable to speak and he put his arm around her.

"You really have been busy." He sighed.

"We don't have much time, Peter. You'll see. I expect that phone to start ringing very soon. I don't want her to take you from me. Maybe I'm being silly, but I can accept you leaving here and moving to the dorms more easily than I can take you leaving here and moving to her apartment."

He nodded. "I can grasp that," he said, rubbing her back. "When?" he asked, totally discouraged.

"Never if I had my desire." She leaned against him, wiping away her tears. "I'm going to be in Nebraska next weekend." He looked at her and she swallowed. "I'll need to get away by then anyway I'm sure."

He nodded. "Yeah, I can understand that, too."

She sighed. "I've decided the best way to deal with this is to not treat it like a goodbye. Let's make sure we don't say goodbye. This is only temporary."

"When?" he asked again; she had obviously given the separation some real thought.

"Tonight," she answered softly.

"Oh shit." He leaned forward. "Jeneil, no, that's too sudden. No!" His throat was in pain.

She rubbed her hand over his back. "My plan is to have you start sleeping at the dorms tonight and we can see each other every night this week while you're on first shift. Thursday would probably be our last night together since I leave Friday afternoon and you'll be on second shift the week after that so we won't be able to see each other. I don't think Uette will go past two weeks. I really don't. I think that would be easier on me. But this feels less like goodbye and more like it was when our relationship began." There was silence between them. "I have to turn the steaks over," she said, getting up and leaving.

The awkwardness continued as they did dishes together. Jeneil put her head back and closed her eyes as the tension got to her. "Peter, we need to keep a positive energy between us. Remember, it's not goodbye."

Peter stacked the dessert plates on the dinner plates and looked at her. "Jeneil, I can't find anything positive in this even if it isn't goodbye. I don't like it. I understand it, I really do, but I don't like it at all. My stomach's in a complete knot."

"I know," she agreed, putting her arms around him. "Mine is too, but at least this way we can see what problems and insecurities might develop from a separation and deal with them before you're married."

"You like to plan, don't you?" He forced a smile, kissing her gently.

She nodded. "I think it's part of my nesting instinct."

He sighed and rested his head against hers. "I'm secure when I hear you talk about the plan. It's living through it that has me worried."

She kissed him. "It's temporary. I promise we'll be together again and married."

He smiled. "Hey, a promise, now that's what I like to hear."

"It's almost nine," she said. "Why don't you put your things in the car now so when you leave it won't feel like goodbye?"

He squeezed her. "Every detail is worked out, isn't it?"

"Even our reunion," she beamed.

He smiled and shook his head. While it felt strange, he began to really understand what Jeneil was doing with her plan. Not saying goodbye left them together and united. That feeling calmed him for the rest of the evening and he enjoyed lying with his head on her lap reading a magazine while she read her book.

*****

As Peter carried his things into the dorm he marveled at how Jeneil had been right. Their final kiss had been emotional, but the tension was low. That kid had a knack. He smiled and unlocked the door to his dorm room. Steve was lying on his bed reading. Seeing Peter, he bolted upright.

"What?" Steve asked, seeing the garment bags Peter carried. "What happened?"

"Jeneil has a plan, it involves separating tonight before the screwball bitch and I...," he trailed off, hating the words, "get married."

"And you're buying it? Damn it, Pete, what the hell is with you? For a tough street kid, you sure let women run all over you."

Peter looked steadily at Steve. "Back off," he said strongly. "Jeneil's not here to stop punches this time and I sure in hell won't stand still while you swing. So ease up. I'm not exactly enjoying this but it's what Jeneil can live with. I owe her that."

Steve nodded. "You're right. I've been a real son-of-a-bitch lately. I'm sorry." He took two garment bags from Peter and went to the closet. "Any word on when you get hanged?"

"No, but Jeneil seems to think it won't go past two weeks."

Steve agreed. "That's a safe assumption. The little bun in the oven keeps getting bigger every day. She's under pressure. Is this all your stuff?"

"No, I have two boxes in the car, some luggage and my pillow."

Steve nodded. "I'll be moving out soon. What happens to the dorm room?"

Peter shrugged. "We're paid to the end of the quarter so who gives a shit. I can store some of my things at my mother's if I have to."

"And you're always welcome at my place," Steve offered. "My place," he repeated, laughing. "Imagine, at twenty-five-years-old I finally got my own place. It was dorm rooms in the home, dorm rooms in college and med school, now Steve Bradley has his own place. I was beginning to think crowds were my appendages; I was part of a Siamese public all attached and entangled. My probation has made me realize that I like having my own life." Peter smiled, enjoying the milestone in Steve's life. Steve got his jacket. "Come on. Let's bring your stuff in here."

Peter awoke in the morning feeling low. He didn't like the way life was moving and he felt it deep inside. Steve came from the bathroom. "I have early surgery so I'm leaving now. I'm sure there's something for breakfast around."

"I'm not hungry," Peter answered quietly.

Steve watched Peter as he did up his shirt. "Sorry you made the move, aren't you?"

"Of course," Peter answered, staring at the ceiling.

"So change your mind."

"I can't. Jeneil's right. I can't."

Steve sighed. "Must be the view from this side of the fence, I can't see in there."

"I'm tired of even thinking about it," Peter growled.

Steve chuckled. "Shit, I'm sure glad I'm moving out. You're mean and ugly today. What will you be like on Friday?"

"Go to work," Peter replied, feeling as mean and ugly as Steve had observed.

*****

Peter headed to the hospital feeling only half alive. His life had been dissected and an important part was missing. As he put on his lab coat, he was glad he at least had medicine. It was a part of his life that was steady. He went to the floor knowing Jeneil was right. If he let Uette destroy medicine for him, he'd be no good for Jeneil. "You have a knack, Songbird." He sighed as the word Songbird reached his chest, bringing the empty feeling again.

Jeneil turned over in bed as she heard the alarm. The bed felt empty, the apartment lifeless. She sat up and slumped forward in a heap. "Keep your routine moving, Jeneil," she lectured. "Remember what Mandra said, 'Make sure your life has purpose.'" She sighed and dragged herself into a standing position. "I will survive," she said, "I will survive. The pendulum will swing in my direction again so I'll keep surviving." She went to change into leotards before dancing. "Keep moving Jeneil, just keep moving."

Jeneil packed her lunch, missing having to do Peter's. The empty feeling filled her. "It's only temporary," she spoke to the tears that were threatening to attack. "I belong to him. Our souls are married. She can't top that. She won't. Feel sorry for her, not yourself. The man she's going to marry calls her ugly names. That's very negative energy." She smiled as she snapped the lid onto the cold vegetable container. "Now there's a new thought. Uette is also swimming against the current." She smiled broadly. "Thank you life for making injustice a little more tolerable, at least I'm not alone in the sea of despair."

*****

Jeneil worked hard to make their evenings together special. They talked about their feelings and Peter admitted that he was worried about Danzieg. He never mentioned Steve. They were reaching an understanding, a bond they could work from. Jeneil had admitted all she was going on was Peter's insistence that the baby wasn't his. Peter had told her that if he knew the baby was his, he'd marry Uette and stay married to her, especially having brought counter charges. Jeneil was reassured seeing how insistent Peter was that he was innocent.

The days passed too quickly. Peter received a call from his grandfather; Uette had scheduled the wedding for a week from the coming Saturday and wondered if he could take a week off for a honeymoon. Peter had nearly stopped breathing and exploded angrily. No had been his reply, which resulted in Uette pleading about how strange it would look. Getting married so quickly had already raised questions which she answered by saying Peter and her father were never compatible and she wanted to get married before the current peace wore off. Peter noticed how skilled she was at lying and told her a honeymoon was out of the question. She had hung up angrily but began spreading word that Peter was in his last year of residency and it was vital that he not take time off now.

The wedding was going to be held at Uette's house and she was annoyed that he wouldn't cooperate with rehearsals. He told her about his hospital hours and to plan everything without him, asking her to have him stand in one spot and leave it at that. Steve had told Peter he'd rather not be invited; it was more pretending than he could handle, having trouble believing the wedding was really going to happen, and he wanted to spend that day with Jeneil. Peter's mother suggested Ron be best man. Peter couldn't care less about the issue so she asked Ron for him, becoming very concerned about Peter's attitude.

Wednesday was followed by Thursday and Peter found himself dreading that day more than the wedding day. He headed for Jeneil's apartment right after work wondering if he could possibly get her to change her mind about this being their last night together. It was the thought uppermost in his mind as he kissed her warmly, holding her to him tightly. "Baby, do you really have to go to Nebraska?"

She nodded. "Let's stay with the plan, Peter. I can see a strength between us already from this week's trial. I'm very encouraged."

"But now it's over, honey." He choked on his words

She looked at him seriously. "No, Peter, don't use those words. Don't even think them. We are not over. We can never be over. Never. We promised each other forever. Don't let go of that. I know I won't." He sighed and a sense of dread crept through him.

Jeneil brought dinner to the table, surprised to find that Peter had rearranged the place settings. He had them sitting together at the long side of the table. She smiled as she put the chicken platter on the table.

Peter grinned. "I've noticed we've had my favorite meals this week and this one's my all-time favorite."

She shrugged. "Well really, should I give the Sultan what he doesn't like? He'd get rid of me."

"Are you playing Harem?" he asked, smiling.

She looked at him steadily. "I'm not playing. I'm dead serious."

He put his arm on the back of her chair grinning. "Then how the hell do you expect me to live without all this?"

"Us," she reminded him. "You're not alone. I'm going to live without this, too. Remember that so you won't get angry at me." She kissed him tenderly.

"I'm not hungry," he whispered, kissing her neck, smoothing his lips across her ear.

"Dinner will be ruined," she said, tilting her head to the side, enjoying his kisses.

"It's impossible to ruin this dinner," he argued. "Let's go to bed. I'll prove it to you."

"Ooo Chang, what are you going to prove to me?" she cooed.

He smiled. "Playful makes me crazy, baby. Playful is a terrific memory."

She turned and put her arms around his neck, kissing him sensuously. "Then let's go to bed and make memories," she whispered in his ear and smoothed her neck along his jaw, enjoying the excitement his beard caused.

They lay together appreciating the memory that had been created. Jeneil reached for her robe and got up. "Where are you going?" he asked, enjoying lying there totally relaxed.

"Dinner," she answered, smiling.

"Don't worry about it, honey."

"Oh, I'm not, Chang. I'm lopsided right now and loving every offbeat second. I just don't want it to end."

She disappeared and Peter smiled as he shook his head. "Irish, you're something else."

Jeneil returned minutes later with a dinner cart, smiling as she spread a tablecloth on the bed. Getting under the covers, she pulled a plate of chicken from the cart and reached for dinner rolls. "Dinner is served," she chuckled, setting the plate on the bed between them.

Peter sat up. "Oh, baby, you're terrific. I love chicken this way. That stuff on it tastes so good and I'm starved."

Jeneil smiled. "Wet washcloth and hand towel, Sire." She handed them to him. "And because of the sauce, a finger bowl." She put a bowl of water on a tray beside them.

"I love you, kid." He smiled and kissed her warmly. "Hey, no vegetables?"

"This is lopsided, Chang, offbeat. You only eat what you like."

"What's under the silver dome?"

"A surprise dessert."

He took a piece of chicken. "Now this is fun, great chicken, no vegetables, and dessert eaten in bed with my harem. Those sultans knew how to live. I'm glad somebody wrote a book of instructions."

Jeneil laughed, taking a piece of chicken, too. "When I malfunction, I malfunction."

Peter took a piece of dinner roll and dabbed the sauce that had dripped onto his plate. "I think I like the sauce more than I like the chicken," he said, putting it in his mouth then cleaning his fingers from his feast. "If I don't like dessert, can I just have more chicken?"

Jeneil nodded as she wiped her fingers on the towel. "This is my malfunction. You can do anything you want to do." He smiled his approval and she put a tray with two wine goblets and a small cluster of green grapes between them. "This is to cleanse your palate for dessert. Grapes and wine seem redundant so that's good malfunction food, I guess." She chuckled, putting a grape in his mouth and then held up her goblet. "We need to make a toast."

He sighed. "Just don't make it tomorrow. I don't want to think about it."

She smiled. "But we have to think about tomorrow. How else can we make a toast to our reunion?"

He looked up and smiled broadly. "You're damn good, Jeneil. You have a real knack. I mean it."

She tossed him a kiss. "Hold up your glass, Sire, and let's make a toast. Because our souls are married forever our reunion will feel like we were never apart. The Princess of the Land of the Leprechauns has decreed it to be so."

He smiled and touched his goblet to hers gently, then leaned over and kissed her. "I'll make you keep that promise."

She grinned. "It will happen. You'll see. All my magic spells come true. That one I've given to the wind to handle." He smiled and sipped his wine. She reached for the silver dome after she had cleared everything from their picnic. "Now close your eyes," she ordered, "and make a wish while my magic powers are raging strongly." Peter laughed and closed his eyes. He heard her lift the lid and he smelled lighter fluid.

"What are you doing?" he asked, curious what she was up to.

"Shush," she answered, "concentrate on your wish."

"I made my wish already," he said. "I wish that we could get married."

"Aw, Peter," she said, disappointed. "I thought you were going to make it a tough wish to fulfill." He laughed, opening his eyes and was startled by the burning candles on a cake. "Happy Birthday." She smiled warmly. "I had to move the calendar ahead so we could celebrate it today. See the kind of magic powers I have. Now do you doubt that your wish will come true?"

"No," he said, choking up. "I believe you can do anything."

"Blow out your candles and keep concentrating on your wish." The smoke swirled from the twenty-five candles as Jeneil and Peter waved it away. Peter looked more closely at the chocolate cake. She had written, *Happy Birthday Chang, I'll always love you,* in white frosting.

He looked at her. "Boy, you're damn good. This whole night will never be forgotten."

"Exactly." She smiled and kissed him. "I have two birthday presents for you." She reached to the cart and then handed him two envelopes. "One's a card. The other envelope is a gift."

He opened the smaller one. She had made a card of a silhouetted man and woman walking together. *Love is really a journey through days that are given in which we create memories. Our love has been a wonderful journey filled with beautiful memories for me. Thank you for that gift. I hope this birthday is a special gift of a beautiful memory for you. With all my love forever, Jeneil.* He was afraid to talk, choking on emotion.

"Open your gift envelope," Jeneil said excitedly. "I want to see if you like that, too."

Peter swallowed and smiled at her, appreciating the fact she wasn't requiring words from him. He opened the envelope and removed the letter finding an important looking certificate. He was puzzled. The letter explained that she had been left a municipal treasury bond which had matured. She had taken that money and put it into a market certificate for him that would mature at the end of his residency when he'd be needing financing and could best afford the dividend for capital gain taxes.

He looked at her and smiled. "Every detail," he said, shaking his head and taking the certificate from the envelope. "Holy shit!" he gasped. "Jeneil, where'd you get this kind of money?"

She shrugged. "My father bought two municipal T bonds when I was born. The city flourished and paid good dividends. He had them mature on what would have been my college graduation."

"But they were for you," he insisted.

"Peter, since then he's left me Alden-Connors Corporation which Uncle Hollis handled really well. I don't have a career. You do. You take it. I know my father would be pleased to help his son-in-law out."

He exhaled. "Oh, baby, you're heart attack material, you really are. Geez, I never dreamed…," he exhaled again.

She smiled. "I should tell you I gave the other bond to Steve. With all that happened since that night I forgot. I'm so impressed with the both of you and what you've achieved. You guys are both superlative."

"Uh-oh," he said, staring at her. "What did Hollis say about this?"

Jeneil snickered. "He grinned and asked me how come he never met any coeds like me when he was in college and law school. I told him because he was a snob and never dated drop-outs."

Peter lowered his eyes. "Honey, what was his reaction about this mess?"

Jeneil sighed. "He doesn't know, Peter. I'm torn about telling him at all. You could resolve this in a month or two. I don't want this ruining you with Uncle Hollis. If he should uncover it, I'll explain it to him. If not, then who is really hurt?"

He took her hand and kissed it. "It's tough to turn a frog into a prince, isn't it, beautiful princess?"

"I'm not listening," she said. "The evil witch didn't turn my prince into a frog. She doesn't have magic powers, I do." She smiled and leaned to him for a kiss. He kissed her powerfully and she pulled away breathless. "I almost forgot the cake was between us."

"Put it on the cart," he said. She smiled and cleared away the cake and tablecloth, then snuggled to him in a passionate kiss that they each gave in to.

Peter was discouraged as the evening moved on and he faced the final moments. They walked to the door together and Jeneil smiled. "I hope the third shift isn't busy tonight."

He put his head back and closed his eyes. "Jeneil, I can't go through with this. It won't work. Everything in me is screaming to forget it all. I've made the wrong decision."

"You made the decision you had to make, Peter."

"No," he said, looking at her. "No, we could move away, just leave."

She was concerned. "Don't do this, Peter, especially at this moment. We can't move away from it. It would follow us because it would be on your conscience and mine. This way, we'll be able to stand tall and face ourselves and each other besides everyone else." She handed him a paper bag. "The rest of the chicken. And please take that chocolate cake. It'll look better on you and Steve."

He put the bag down and put his arms around her. "Jeneil," his voice cracked.

Jeneil choked up. "Don't say it, Peter, please. Just I love you, that's all nothing else. Save anything else for our reunion. Please keep remembering our reunion." Tears started and she wiped them away quickly. "I have some things for you to take with you." She went to the hutch and came back with a book. "Jack London's *White Fang,* I put it aside to make sure you took it with you. Find time to read it. I think you'll see a message in it." She reached into her robe pocket and held up his silver ID bracelet.

"You had it!" he said, relieved. "I was afraid I'd lost it."

"I had it inscribed on the back."

He turned it over and read, *Chang and Irish.* He recognized the date inscribed as the day their souls were married. He held her to him and she heard him swallow.

"Now this last one is important," she said, pulling away gently, "it shows the kind of trust I have in you, so don't let me down." She reached into her robe pocket again and pulled out a glass unicorn. "Take it on your quest. When the prince returns it, the princess will keep her promise to marry him."

He looked at her sadly. "Oh, baby, this isn't fiction. This is real. It's zero hour." He took a deep breath to calm his emotions.

She nodded. "I know, Peter, but I want to be with you so much and the only way I could think of doing that was with these three things. The book is advice you'll probably only understand when you're ready to, the ID is a reminder of our wedding ceremony, and the glass unicorn is my hope for us. Giving them to you makes me feel like I'm going with you." She took the glass unicorn and kissed it gently, then handed it to him. "Now you'll always have my kiss with you, too. I feel better already."

He took the unicorn and put his arms around her. "Crazy kid," he said lovingly.

"Eccentric," she corrected, "blue sky on top, green grass on bottom." He smiled, looking into her eyes and he kissed her with all the love he had for her. She understood and he knew she would. Irish and Chang never needed words. She smiled and pulled away, opening the door. "It's late. Those sick people need a responsible doctor." She smiled, tears rolling down her cheeks. "Don't look back Peter, just like you're going to work."

He nodded and kissed her lips gently. "I love you, Jeneil, beyond words," he said, choking up.

"I know, Chang. Me, too. Forever."

He put the unicorn in his pocket and picked up the cake and bag of chicken. He kissed her cheek and walked out the door unable to speak or swallow. She closed the door gently and gave into the tears that fell.

Peter stood at the top of the stairs and turned around. Looking at the Camelot sign, he remembered the first time he'd seen it. His throat was in pain. He reached into his jacket and took out the unicorn. "Don't worry," he said, looking at it, "I'll be back to claim the beautiful princess. That's a promise."

The next day was a struggle for Jeneil. The women she worked with asked if she was sick. She certainly felt like she was. She was glad to be going to Nebraska, the thought of spending the weekend in the apartment depressing her.

*****

She went to the estate after her meetings on Saturday. Taking a can of soup, a saucepan, and a spoon, she had dinner in front of the hearth at the guest cottage where she had spent years reading and thinking. She fell asleep exhausted from crying and awoke chilled. The fire had burned to red embers that glittered from igniting fibers. She sighed and sat up feeling stiff and stuffed up. "Well, Jeneil Alden-Connors," she said, stretching, "this is a fine way to survive."

She sighed again and putting a small log on the fire wondered what to do with herself. She hadn't notified the caretakers she would be there so the house wasn't ready. The water had been turned off and pipes drained for the winter. She sat closer to the fire to keep warm wondering where to spend the night. She knew she could stay in the big house but it frightened her. Having spent her life there with Mandra after her father died, she had come to look on the enormous house as a mausoleum because Mandra seemed buried by it and the demands her money made on her. Jeneil shivered and put a bigger piece of firewood on to warm her. She heard footsteps crunch on the snow and stomp on the porch. She waited. The door opened and Bill stood there tall and unsmiling.

"Hey, this is why you broke our dinner date?" he asked, walking over to her and sitting down. He saw the saucepan and empty can of soup. "Well, I could have done better than that and what's with the low fire? Afraid the scouts will detect your camp?"

She chuckled. "I'm sorry. I wasn't in the mood for being sociable."

"I heard," he said. "Hollis called me thinking we were together. He doesn't like the way you look. Seeing the smoke from the chimney, I came over to see what he was talking about." He touched her face, turning it to look at her. He sighed. "Hollis tends to worry over you at times but not this time. What is it, dipstick?"

Jeneil laughed, hearing the nickname he'd given her as a kid. "Dipstick," she said, sighing, "takes me back." Tears rolled down her cheeks.

"Jeneil doesn't live here anymore so why are you trying to?"

She shrugged. "Sometimes when the path gets foggy I need to see where the path began."

"You're losing the path often, aren't you? Seems to me one of your other visits you spent curled up here. What's happening in your life to make it foggy?"

Jeneil put another log on. "It's a two log story." She sighed and sat back. "Promise not to tell Uncle Hollis?"

"If it isn't dangerous," he said, and moved closer to her and held her as she cried through the details. "When life kicks you in the ribs, it seems to use steel-toed boots. Cry, dipstick, you've earned it."

She leaned against him, crying softly. "Don't tell Uncle Hollis."

"Jeneil, you're sure of this guy?"

She nodded. "He's a great person, Bill, honestly."

"Well, I know his grandfather thinks so. Hollis said you settled a sizeable bond on him."

Jeneil pulled away, annoyed. "Uncle Hollis goes beyond his limits."

He took her hand. "Hey, your father hired him to look after you. He understood that to mean more than your money. He loves you like family."

She nodded. "I know, I know. It's just that he and Peter had a bad beginning. This could, what do I mean could, it would make things worse. Please don't tell him."

"Who's the other guy who got a bond?"

Jeneil looked at him. "I think I should talk to Uncle Hollis."

Bill squeezed her hand. "Come on, dipstick. It's me. Hollis and I cut you up a lot."

Jeneil sighed. "And I was here feeling alone." She hugged him. "The other bond went to Peter's friend."

Bill raised his eyebrows. "Darlin', you're bright but not swift about men. Are these two really okay for you?"

"Well golly gee, Billy, they's my good buddies. They flatter me and make me feel real good."

"Aw, Jeneil, that's nasty."

"No, Bill, your question was. Give me credit for having some ability to judge people intelligently."

"Okay, okay, consider me put in my place. Now let's go to my house where there's heat, electricity, and running water." He got up, pulling her to him.

"I wasn't trying to put you in your place. I was just trying to protect mine."

"I know, dipstick, and I'm glad to see that because if you're doing that with me then you're probably doing it with them, too. We're on the same team. I'm trying to protect you, too. So is Hollis. You're going to be a very rich lady soon. We have to be careful."

"Oh no I'm not," she insisted, stepping back. "See what's happening already? You're suspicious of the men around me because of that foolish money. Mandra went through it. Her father thought everyone was after her money and the one person equal to her in wealth wasn't the right race." She put on her jacket. "Not me," she said, going to the fire, "that kind of conveyor belt would strangle me. I don't want it. I have enough money. My own investments are fine, too." She separated the glowing chunks of wood to help the fire go out. Picking up the dinner things, she took her purse and stood before Bill. "Let's go to your place." She smiled warmly. "Are the servants on duty tonight or can we have fun and go to the kitchen and make our own hot chocolate and cinnamon toast?"

He smiled. "You have a definite nasty streak, dipstick. I hardly call one man running my home servants. He's not even a butler. His name is Jake and I'd starve and never find clean clothes if I didn't have him and his wife to help me. Where's the beautiful sweet girl I had fun with growing up?"

"She grew up struggling to survive in a man's world," she said, standing at the door.

Bill broke into laughter. "Oh damn, a liberationist. Not you, Jeneil. Not you."

Jeneil smiled. "We all need freedom and equality, Bill." She locked the door behind them.

"Yeah, but your idea of freedom and equality used to be sitting in the home of your choice, side by side in front of the fire with your husband. What happened to that girl?"

"Life made demands on her, Bill; the foundation, the corporation. Life is trying to pull her into the jai alai game and she's struggling to stay a spectator. Men don't want us to be dependent on them anymore, they want freedom, but they never counted on us being so good at independence and intelligent enough to point out the flaws of male dominated freedom. You men are reaping what you sowed so now live with your harvest."

"Ooo, what right wing propaganda," he teased, laughing.

"Reality," she said, smiling as she stood by her car door, "reality. Oh, you're good for me. The path is already less foggy since you showed up."

Bill leaned against his open car door. "You know, Hollis thinks I am, too. Did you know that I'm his choice to be your husband?"

She laughed. "Do you and I get to vote on that? Poor Bill, don't panic. I'll meet you at your back door."

Bill smiled. "Want to chicken on Crazy Corner?"

She laughed again. "Are you kidding? Rasmussen is probably on duty by the big elm tree."

Bill laughed. "Yeah, but he's too old now. He spends his duty sleeping behind the wheel of the squad car. That's why I told the chief to assign him to this road. I haven't had a speeding ticket in almost a year now."

Jeneil shook her head. "You're what's bringing America down, Bill. Repent!" she teased.

He laughed. "Sure you ingrate, criticize and then drink my hot chocolate and eat my toast."

She spun a snowball past him. "Last one home fixes the snack." She jumped into her car and started the engine feeling better for having come back to where the path began.

Twenty-One

The weekend took a turn for the better for Jeneil. Sunday morning's meetings were pleasant, her flight back was uneventful, and her high spirits lasted until she got to her apartment. She expected that. She even planned for it by making a list of things she wanted to achieve. The doorbell rang. "Adrienne, come in," Jeneil said, opening the door. Adrienne studied Jeneil as she walked in holding a foil package. "Mmm, smells like ribs." Jeneil smiled as she touched the foil. "And they're warm. You're a great friend. I was going to make a sandwich. I like this much better."

Adrienne smiled. "How are you doing?"

Jeneil nodded and shrugged. "Sometimes okay, sometimes not. Normal, isn't it?"

Adrienne grinned. "I think so, as long as the ups and downs are equal. Isn't that the gauge?" She handed the package to Jeneil.

"Sounds right to me." Jeneil smiled, sniffing the aroma. "You know, I use your mom's rib sauce on chicken, it drives Peter crazy. I think it's an aphrodisiac."

Adrienne laughed. "Honey, there are some men who don't need aphrodisiacs. I think Peter's one of them. And who's this Dr. Bradley?"

"Peter's best friend, why?"

Adrienne winked. "No sauce for him either. For having such a pretty face, he oozes Je ne sais Quai."

Jeneil smiled. "Most of the women at the hospital think so, too. I'm going to introduce him to Charlene. Can you even imagine the stunning children they would have?"

Adrienne shook her head. "Not to be, Jeneil. Charlene's current is living with her now. It looks serious."

Jeneil sighed. "Too bad, she's so nice. I'm sure Steve would have really liked her."

Adrienne smiled. "I don't think Charlene's Dr. Bradley's type. She's formal, almost tight. He goes for the more natural type."

"No, he doesn't," Jeneil replied. "You should have seen what he was going with at the hospital. They were women, there was no doubting that. He and Rita were reportedly neon together and Rita is drenched in je ne sais quoi."

Adrienne shrugged. "Maybe. You know him better, but I think you're his type."

"Me?" Jeneil laughed. "Not hardly. He likes me and we're good friends, but when it comes to neon he definitely drifts to Rita's type. Why would you even think of my type?"

Adrienne thought about it. "I guess from when you had your accident. He hovered." Adrienne thought again. "I don't know there seemed to be something more." Jeneil stared at her. "What's wrong?"

"Peter thought there was more, too. Maybe we're too close. I'd like to stay friends with him but I certainly wouldn't want his date or his wife thinking that. How do these things get started? Wouldn't I know if that was true? I just spent the weekend with Bill. He's like Steve is to me, and we're good friends."

"Don't panic." Adrienne smiled. "It might have been his reaction to your accident."

"I'm sure it was," Jeneil replied. "We were polar opposites before Peter refereed."

"Then don't listen to me. I was pretty shaken that day, too. See how gossip starts? We see something that isn't really there. Boy, I sure like getting down into the pecking with the rest of the hens, don't I?"

Jeneil laughed. "Me, too, Imagine trying to find him a wife? Like he needs help." Adrienne and Jeneil both laughed.

After Adrienne left, Jeneil decided to have dinner. Opening the foil packet, she took a rib and wandered around the living room while she ate. It wasn't pacing, it was restlessness, and a feeling that hadn't surfaced since the Uette incident broke loose. It was back now that she was alone and open to her inner feelings. Taking another rib, she sat at the kitchen table and looked at her to-do list. She sighed. "I should add finding Jeneil to the top of this list. I'm so tired of being unfinished." She thought of Peter. "Boy, now I'm really unfinished. At least I knew that part of me was with him and happy to know it."

She got up again as her restlessness stirred. She put her finger in her mouth to clean the sauce from it. Her thumb was covered, too. She put it in her mouth and sucked on it. She shrugged, taking it out. "No big deal," she said, "maybe it only works if you're really young. It's even awkward or am I just too entrenched in the role that's expected of me. Adults don't suck their thumbs."

She hated restlessness; it sent her into the unknown. She had gotten restless her junior year of college and look at her now, a harem with no sultan. She sighed. Restlessness brought change, change she didn't need right now. She was surrounded by change and she'd like some, she paused in her thinking, some what? She hated that about restless, she couldn't make up her mind. Turning quickly, she stomped her foot.

"Go wash your hands. There," she laughed, "a decisive move, a decision." Walking to the bathroom, she giggled. "Uh-oh, Jeneil, I think you are swinging from the 't' in eccentric."

*****

Peter looked at his watch. She should be back from Nebraska. He sighed and closed his eyes. He missed her. He didn't like her belonging to him and not being able to see her, not being able to talk to her. He went to the telephone booths and stopped. He turned to walk away then went to a telephone and dialed.

"Adrienne," he said. "It's Peter. Is Jeneil back?"

"Yes, she is, Peter. All safely unpacked. I took her some ribs."

"How is she?"

"Okay, but missing you."

He sighed. "She's not alone, believe me."

"Peter," Adrienne began, "I'm sorry about this mess. I was looking forward to…."

"Being a witness at our wedding?"

"I'm sorry, that was thoughtless of me," Adrienne said, embarrassed.

Peter sat down. "It's okay, Adrienne. You'll still be our witness as soon as I take care of this screwball bitch."

Adrienne laughed. "Well, I'm glad somebody's mad at her. Jeneil is impossibly civilized about it. She said it won't help to rage. Somebody should teach her that sometimes it just feels good."

Peter laughed. "But then she wouldn't be Jeneil."

"That's true." Adrienne chuckled. "Boy, her parents must have told her that her name means peace. Do you want me to give her a message?"

"No," Peter answered. "This call is a violation of her plan. Don't even tell her about it."

"I hope she knows what she's doing." Adrienne sighed.

"That makes two of us," Peter answered. "I've got to get back on the floor, Adrienne. Thanks for looking in on her. It makes me feel better."

"Sure, Peter, and take care of yourself, okay?"

"I intend to," he replied. "I've got a princess in that Camelot tower who I'm anxious to get back to."

Adrienne laughed. "Her sense of romance has rubbed off on you, Peter. That's cute."

He laughed. "I'm finding out how much she's a part of my life. Watch her for me."

"I'll do that, Peter. She's special to me, too," Adrienne said. Peter went back to work feeling calmed that Adrienne was looking after Jeneil.

*****

Jeneil went to work Monday grateful that Peter was on second shift. She missed him and it was one of her insecure days and was afraid she would weaken if she saw him. Thinking of the wedding on Saturday, she knew she couldn't. Hollis had called to see if she'd arrived home safely. He was suspicious, his questions about her life and Peter too obvious. She had lied to protect Peter without her conscience bothering her, which surprised her. They had always shared an honest relationship and she hoped he would never know; she didn't want him to be hurt either.

Dinner with her lawyer was easy enough and then she went home. Steve was coming by for a toaster and kettle she had claimed from Fairview. Peter's telephone was ringing as she got in. The sound made her stomach tense up and it knotted as she recognized Peter's mother's voice.

"Jeneil, I'd like to stop by and talk to you tonight. Can you spare some time?"

"Well, yes," Jeneil answered, totally surprised.

"I can be there in fifteen minutes. It won't take long."

"That'll be fine, Mrs. Lee." Jeneil hung up still surprised by the call. She changed into a long dress and waited. The front doorbell rang and Jeneil jumped to her feet. Going to the apartment door, she saw Jeff open the front door and walk in.

"Jeneil, a visitor for you," he said, looking up at her.

"Thank you, Jeff. I was on my way down. Mrs. Lee," she said, as Peter's mother walked in.

Jeff stopped at her door. "Dennis is crossing his fingers that we'll have you at the playhouse this season." Jeneil smiled and nodded. "Hey, great news," he said, and continued on.

"Come in, Mrs. Lee," Jeneil said, stepping aside. She noticed Mrs. Lee look the apartment over as politely as her curiosity allowed.

"I expected an apartment building."

Jeneil shrugged. "I like the atmosphere and warmth of a home. This is a good compromise."

"This is very pleasant." Mrs. Lee smiled surprised her son was capable of maintaining a relationship with someone who had the amount of good taste the apartment showed.

"Let's sit down," Jeneil said, going to the sofa. Mrs. Lee sat on the other end. Jeneil waited, the woman seemed uncomfortable. "Can I get you some tea?"

"No thank you, Jeneil." Mrs. Lee looked down at her hands.

Jeneil could tell it was awkward for the woman, whatever it was. Jeneil clasped her hands nervously, hoping to calm down. "Mrs. Lee, I know what Uette is saying, but…."

Mrs. Lee interrupted. "No, Jeneil. I saw them together."

Jeneil caught her breath. "Do you mean you saw them together intimately or lying next to each other."

The woman stared. "Oh, Jeneil, you really do love him," she said sympathetically. "He doesn't deserve you. I never imagined how deeply."

Jeneil's throat was tense. "You didn't answer my question."

"I woke both of them when I walked into his room."

Jeneil's mind zeroed in on a fact. "Uette was asleep, too?"

"Yes, she sat up very confused when I screamed. She had a drink to get warm."

"Yes," Jeneil answered, "I heard. Did you call to Peter before you opened the door?"

"Well, yes, I usually do once or twice. If he doesn't answer I knock and go in and shake him," Mrs. Lee said, and Jeneil nodded. "Why?"

Jeneil shrugged. "I have a mind that likes details, that's all. Uette drove off in her car after all that happened?"

"Yes."

"And was she sober?"

"She seemed to be. She never said she was drunk. She said things were fuzzy. You don't want to believe Uette's story. I can see that."

Jeneil didn't want trouble. "Mrs. Lee, it seems to me there isn't any real proof on either Peter or Uette's part, so those who listen can choose either one equally. I believe Peter. You don't. Can you tell me why you don't?"

"Yes," Mrs. Lee said, looking down at her hands, "because this is Peter's history. Girls. He joined that horrible gang and he was different after that. He always looked older. He was taller and girls found him attractive at an indecently young age. There were all kinds of girls hanging around that gang and God only knows what else. He was always in trouble because of them and fathers were always raging. It was embarrassing. But most of all, Peter never had a conscience about it. His defense was always that he never twisted their arm."

Jeneil sighed. "And that's why you feel he's guilty now because he was then."

Mrs. Lee grasped the meaning. "Well, when faced with Uette's reputation and Peter's." She shrugged. Jeneil nodded understanding, seeing that Peter was a victim of past crimes.

Jeneil sighed. "Well, we can only see how this will turn out then."

Mrs. Lee fidgeted. "Jeneil, I'd like to ask you to not wait for him."

Jeneil was shocked by the directness and boldness. "Mrs. Lee, that's not fair. Peter has asked me to."

Mrs. Lee shook her head. "I know, but I'm hoping you'll see my side." She fidgeted and straightened a strand of hair that didn't need to be. "This isn't easy for me." She sighed as she struggled with emotion, opening her purse for a handkerchief. Jeneil was struck by the show of pain and softness, the woman always seeming to be strong and formidable. Mrs. Lee took a breath. "Jeneil, all of Peter's life he has been in trouble with the Chinese community. The Wongs thought of him as filth. Their girls thought of him as an animal." Jeneil noticed the woman's struggle to hold back tears. "When he entered college, he was still tough but not crazy. That's the only good thing Lin Chi did for him. We doubted he would make it and then he met Steve. Steve seemed to help Peter make sense of college and med school. He pulled his life together and even gave up Lin Chi. This situation with Uette will ruin everything he's worked so hard to achieve."

"But he's marrying her, Mrs. Lee."

The woman shook her head. "Oh, Jeneil, you should see it. It's pathetic. He's the same belligerent kid I had to deal with while he was growing up. He's not cooperative at all."

"Mrs. Lee, it's understandable, she trapped him," Jeneil argued.

"No, Jeneil, he made a mistake, so did she, but she's at least trying to make the best of it. She's going out of her way to please him and he refuses to."

"And you think if I'm not waiting for him, he'll be different?"

"I know he would be."

Jeneil shook her head. "I doubt it. He's insulted and enraged about her accusations."

"Jeneil, he can't accept the truth because he loves you. The baby's his. He was attracted to Uette that night. He could make this marriage work if it wasn't for you. You'll have other men who'll be interested in you. Peter…Peter doesn't have too many choices since the attack. His damaged body and his background make him undesirable to the Chinese. The Wong family are good people. This is Peter's chance to have what he deserves."

Jeneil was getting annoyed. "Meaning I'm less than he deserves?"

"No," Mrs. Lee spoke quickly, "but you're not Chinese. What if you two don't work out, then he's given up a chance to be in a decent marriage that would be good for him."

Jeneil stood up. "Mrs. Lee, this isn't fair. It really isn't. I'm even looking past the insult and seeing it from Peter's side. You don't have a right to manipulate his life and I certainly won't be a part of it. You're overlooking something here. If he was attracted and she's the one married to him, then she's got a pretty good beginning right there. She'll be living with him, not me."

"But you'll be his mistress."

Jeneil stood tall, holding back her rage. "Mrs. Lee, you're wrong. I know what you think of me but never have I even thought of being Peter's mistress." Jeneil walked to the door. "You really should have talked to Peter before coming to me. As usual, Uette is a little mixed up about her facts and she's using you as a weapon against your son. Someday you'll regret that. Right now, I want this made clear, leave me alone, I'm tired of feeling contaminated."

Mrs. Lee stood up unsure of the situation, torn between anger and embarrassment. She hadn't reached Jeneil and had uncovered facts she should already have known. Jeneil was asking her to leave. That was clear and nothing had been accomplished. In fact, she found Jeneil's attitude somewhat insulting and obviously hostile. She walked to the door and stopped. Jeneil looked at her.

"Don't say anything, Mrs. Lee; I'm struggling with all of this as it is."

"I'm sorry."

"Are you?" Jeneil asked. "Sorry for what? That Uette put you in this embarrassing position? Well, Mrs. Lee, whatever you may think of me morally, at least I never got pregnant to force a man to marry me."

Jeneil saw the woman's eyes turn to fire and her hand move quickly upward, feeling the slap burn the side of her face, sending her against the door. Jeneil regained her footing and opened the door without speaking, stunned by the pain. Mrs. Lee walked out in a rage. Jeneil closed the door trying to figure out why she had been slapped.

Opening the front door quickly, Peter's mother met Steve coming up the stairs. They were both surprised to see each other. "I thought Peter didn't live here anymore," she snapped angrily.

"He doesn't," Steve said, shocked by her anger. "I'm here to see Jeneil."

"How interesting," she said, with a sneer. Steve stepped inside as she walked out and closed the door.

You foul-minded bitch, he raged to himself as he headed for the staircase. Then, remembering her anger, he became concerned and ran up the stairs, skipping some as he went. He buzzed the bell several times. Jeneil opened the door and he walked in looking her over. One side of her face was bright red and he sighed and ran his fingers through his hair. "The bitch hit you, didn't she?"

Jeneil nodded. "I made a smart remark about Uette and she exploded. I had reached my limit. Honestly, I must have 'RUG' imprinted on my forehead." She paced angrily. "Really, the things that woman thinks I'll tolerate scare me."

Steve shook his head. "What the hell was she here for anyway?"

Jeneil stopped pacing. "I suspect she was here on an errand for Uette who armed her with a lot of false information. She wanted me to stop being Peter's mistress so Uette would have a chance. Peter was attracted to her that night. If I'm not satisfying him, he'll turn to Uette. And I should tell him I won't wait then he'll accept the truth that the baby's his and make a decent marriage and please the Chinese clans. After all, this is his chance to have a decent grade A Chinese wife instead of just a white one."

Steve stared in disbelief. "She said that?"

Jeneil sighed. "Oh really now, Steve. She's Chinese; it was all said with humble diplomacy. I was almost ready to apologize for being insulted." She folded her arms and angrily paced. "She's very good; very, very good. If she hadn't been so embarrassed about not knowing Peter wasn't living here she'd have been tougher."

He took his jacket off and threw it on the sofa. "Well, shit. I've just about had it up to my chin with this whole mess. This will stop." He went to the telephone and dialed quickly.

"What are you doing?" she asked, going to him.

"Peter Chang, please. Steve Bradley calling."

"No, Steve," Jeneil pleaded. "Don't upset him. What can he do? He's at work."

Steve covered the mouthpiece. "Damn it, Jeneil. He got his ass into this. He's got to handle it. He's not a kid." Jeneil sighed and shook her head. Her throat was tight and she fought tears caused by anger and hurt.

"Steve?" Peter answered.

"Yeah Pete, I'm here with Jeneil. I met your mother storming out of here on her broom."

"Oh shit," Peter groaned. "What the hell was she doing there?"

"For starters, Pete, she belted Jeneil."

"What!" Peter shouted. "She hit her? Let me talk to Jeneil, Steve."

Steve sighed. "Pete, get this shit stopped."

"Let me talk to Jeneil, Steve," Peter repeated. "And of course I'll stop it. I don't need you to tell me that. Put Jeneil on, damn it. She's still mine as far as I know. Have you gone into law now and become her attorney?"

Steve was insulted. "I'm tired of it, Pete. It's a mess that she doesn't deserve."

"Fine, Steve, I apologize for doing it deliberately. How's that? Feel any better now?"

"Lousy attitude, Pete, really."

"Yeah, well I'm having trouble swallowing yours, too. Now do you want to stay on the extension while I talk to her so you can monitor my attitude?"

Steve began to laugh. "Your tongue is as sharp as your scalpel, buddy. We're ganging up on you, huh?"

Peter laughed. "Aw, the whole thing shits. Every time I turn around it's something else. And the screwball bitch wanted to take a honeymoon. Can you believe that bullshit? Let me talk to Jeneil. I need to."

"Sure," Steve said. "I'm sorry, Pete. I really am."

Peter groaned. "Thanks for understanding why my attitude stinks."

"Here's Jeneil." Steve handed the telephone to her.

"Peter, I'm sorry." Jeneil sighed, biting her lower lip. Peter grasped the receiver tightly as he heard her voice.

"Honey, what happened?" he asked, filled with concern.

"Your mother called me. She came over to ask me not to wait for you. She feels you'll accept the truth that the baby's yours if I wasn't waiting for you."

"Shit." He sighed.

"She thought I was going to be your mistress and feels that you were attracted to Uette that night and would be again if I wasn't your mistress. I think Uette's behind it all."

"Why did she hit you?"

Jeneil sighed. "I got annoyed and I asked her to leave me alone from now on."

"Good for you."

"I went to the door to let her know that the visit was over. She must really like Uette because when I told her at least I never got pregnant to force a man to marry me, she exploded and hit me."

Peter sighed heavily. "What the hell is all this? I chose saving face so this mess could be handled sanely. And since then I've had nothing but madness from my mother and the bitch. I'll report it, honey. I'm sorry, I really am."

"Report it to whom?"

"My grandfather and Mr. Wong, they're in charge. My mother and that piece of shit are out of line. These are not the rules we discussed at the meeting. Are you okay, baby?"

"I'm confused and hurt and angry, but I'll be okay. Peter, I just want some peace. I've done all I can do. I'm out of it now. I want them to leave me alone."

"That's a promise. I made that clear at the meeting, too. There have been some major screw ups. I'll handle it, honey."

"I love you."

"Say it again, honey," he said, choking up.

"I'll love you always," she repeated. Steve was watching her and shook his head slowly, not believing her loyalty and devotion to the relationship even after getting dumped on.

"Baby, I miss you so much, you'll never know how much, but I intend to show you when this is all over."

"That sounds good." She smiled. "Get back on duty. I'll see you soon."

He chuckled. "I keep hoping that."

"Me, too." She rubbed her temples after replacing the receiver. Exhaling, she then stood up straight and smiled at Steve and joined him on the sofa just as her telephone rang.

"What next?" She reached to the shelf behind her.

"Jeneil?"

"Yes?"

"This is Uette Wong. We haven't met."

"Uette?" Jeneil repeated, totally surprised. Steve sat up in shock and listened carefully. "Oh you are wrong, Uette. We have met. One day at the hospital you were lost and wandered into my office. You even thought I looked like someone's sister. You asked me my name. I remember that very well. I know exactly who you are." Uette had been in near panic after hearing Peter's mother's story of what happened, but hearing Jeneil's directness and stern tone, she realized the mousey girl had more fire to her than she had guessed. "Uette, why are you calling?"

Uette was thrown off-guard from Jeneil's display of strength. Things were going badly as it was and her fear of Peter's reaction to this new development all rushed at her. She began to cry. Jeneil was taken aback by the tears but she understood, Uette's desperation was noticeable, so she waited and took the time to assess the snip of a girl who had caused a major earthquake in her life.

"I'm sorry, Jeneil." Uette tried to control her crying.

"Why are you apologizing to me?" Jeneil asked unemotionally. Steve raised his eyebrows.

"Peter's mother told me about her visit."

"Why are you apologizing to me?" Jeneil asked again.

Uette sobered quickly hearing Jeneil's tone. This mousey girl was not a mouse now, she was two people. "She was trying to help me and I feel responsible for the way the visit ended. I'm concerned about you, that's all." Uette brought out her most innocent inflection for the sentiment.

Jeneil realized the purpose for the call. "Uette, there's really no need for you to concern yourself about my welfare. I'm trying to be fair to everyone in this situation because I consider myself to be civilized, but I'm not sophisticated enough to be able to chat pleasantly with a girl who claims my husband is the father of her baby. It's more civilized than I've grown to be at this point, so I'd appreciate it if you wouldn't call me again. You have enough to worry about right now. I can look after myself. Thank you for calling." She replaced the receiver gently on its base.

Steve held her face and kissed her gently. "I'm proud of you." He kissed her again. "That's for Peter. He'd be proud, too." He sat back, sighing. "Yes, that was very nice to watch, very nice." An unformed thought had circled Jeneil and she stared at the telephone as the thought took shape. Steve watched her. "What's wrong?"

"How did she get my telephone number?" Jeneil asked, puzzled.

He shrugged. "From Peter's mother probably."

"No, Steve. They had Peter's number. My telephone number is unpublished and private." Steve watched her, wondering about Uette and her power, but never replied.

*****

Peter inserted coins and dialed as soon as he finished talking to Jeneil. He waited for John to get his grandfather.

"Peter, how are you?"

"Furious at the moment," Peter answered.

"Why?" his grandfather asked, concerned.

Peter tried to calm himself. "My mother went to Jeneil tonight."

"Oh no," his grandfather sighed. "What did she want?"

"She asked Jeneil not to wait for me. She said the baby's mine and if Jeneil wouldn't be my mistress, I'd turn to Uette because I was attracted to her that night and might be again." Peter heard his grandfather gasp.

"That's disgusting, poor Jeneil."

"Grandfather, its Uette's doing. I'm sure it was. I'm out of it. Saving face is off. I made it clear that Jeneil was to be kept out of this. If I'm getting violations before I'm married, what the hell will she do after the ceremony? It's off. Tell her that. They had no right and Grandfather…." Peter stopped to catch his breath. "She hit her. She slapped Jeneil!"

"Oh my goodness!" The grandfather closed his eyes. "Is Jeneil all right?"

"Yes. Steve called me. You know what makes me the angriest? Jeneil is the only one I've seen trying to act honorably. I moved out of the apartment the night after the meeting, Jeneil's idea of propriety. We won't be seeing each other until this is settled, Grandfather. Because of honor and dignity she got slapped! I'm furious, Grandfather, furious."

"You have a right to be, Peter. I'm angry about it, too. I'll talk to your mother. Did she say why your mother slapped her?"

"It's stupid, Grandfather. Stupid! Jeneil had been insulted as it was and told my mother at least she never got pregnant to force a man to marry her. That's no reason to hit her, Grandfather. She had no right to lose control like that! I'm so mad at her. I don't want to talk to her. I'm honestly afraid of what I'd say. I want Uette and my mother stopped."

"This is serious, Peter. They have violated saving face. You can back out now. They'd sue I'm sure, but your honor has been violated."

"Grandfather, I will back out, I mean it. I'm trusting you to let them know how furious I am and how wrong they were to take matters into their own hands. No more warnings. I'm doing this more for Jeneil than anyone else, so they'd better leave her alone."

"I'll handle it, Peter. I'll tell them you wanted to cancel the marriage and you're only taking time to cool down because I asked you to."

Peter sighed. "Whatever will stop this craziness. Grandfather, please, Jeneil doesn't live that kind of life. Violence isn't her way. It wasn't my mother's either. She was a screamer. I've never known her to slap."

The grandfather understood his daughter's reaction as much as he didn't approve. "I'm really sorry, Peter. Poor Jeneil must be so confused and hurt." He paused. "Peter, you and Jeneil won't have any contact with each other during this?"

"Jeneil can't accept anything else, Grandfather. She's a decent person who operates on pride and self-respect."

"I'm worried, Peter. The Songbird will be unprotected. I'm very worried."

"I can't help it, Grandfather. She can't accept any other arrangement."

"What about telephone calls?"

"No. She thinks I'm going to settle this mess quickly so she's not too concerned about our separation. Why? Are you worried because of Steve?"

"No, Peter. Steve has been a good friend. It's just circumstances I'm concerned for. When a bond isn't maintained, chance becomes a strong influence. I don't like the Songbird left to chance."

"She promised she'd wait for me," Peter insisted.

"I know. I'm just an old man, Peter. Ignore my anxieties. Let me handle this right now. I'll get back to you."

Peter began to relax. "It would be better if I call you tonight from the dorms. I've been away from the floor too long now."

"That's fine, Peter. I'll wait. And Peter, I'm glad you called me."

"It's the rules we agreed to," Peter replied simply.

"I know, but thank you anyway." The old man stayed by the phone, smiling after he'd hung up. "Thank you, Peter. Your behavior shows your understanding and respect for honor and your word, and Uette's lack of honor and a lack of regard for hers. You're both showing us what you're really made of. Your story will prove more believable based on your behavior." He was proud of his maverick grandson who had learned honor and dignity.

Peter sat back against the phone booth and sighed. His life felt as cramped as the booth, narrow and suffocating. "I'm worried about the Songbird too, Grandfather, and I'm worried about Steve. He's becoming more and more of a Lancelot to Guinevere and less of a friend to Arthur. Oh, baby, I don't like this plan at all. Guinevere probably didn't intend to fall in love with Lancelot." He rubbed his forehead, then getting up slowly, he went back on duty.

*****

Peter didn't wait to go to his room and take off his jacket after getting in from the hospital. He went directly to the telephone. His grandfather answered immediately for which Peter was grateful. He wasn't looking forward to talking to his mother.

"Grandfather, it's Peter."

"I know," the old man answered. "I think Uette and your mother are aware of your anger now. Lu Wong was very upset. He can't believe his granddaughter would do that. I think he's waking up to her, Peter. And I have to tell you that Uette told him she called Jeneil to apologize but Jeneil hung up on her. Uette and your mother are beside themselves with fear that you'll back out. I've never seen Tom so angry at your mother. Both the Wongs offered their apologies."

Peter sighed. "Grandfather, apologies are so empty. My whole life is upside down from her and people can only apologize."

"I understand, Peter, but don't weaken now. When it's over and you have full honor and dignity restored, you'll know the sweetness of saving face."

"I hope so," Peter answered, very discouraged, "because it tastes pretty awful right now."

"That's understandable, too," his grandfather commiserated.

Peter sighed. "Thanks for handling that for me. I'd better get to bed. I'm assisting Dr. Maxwell in early surgery and I'm meeting my lawyer. He received an approval on the prenuptial agreement he sent to Uette's lawyer. I guess you can call her tomorrow and tell her I'll continue with the plan to get married."

"I'll do that and Peter, I'm proud of you."

"Thanks, Grandfather, but right now honor, pride, and dignity taste as bad as saving face."

"I feel for your suffering. Call me soon, Peter."

"I'll probably be by Wednesday, Grandfather. Ron and I are going in for my suit."

*****

Peter stopped at Dr. Sprague's lawyer's office to sign the agreement with Uette. He noticed her dawdling behind as he sat and waited until she had left the office. After what he considered a safe length of time, he left. Uette had waited at the elevators for him and came toward him quickly.

"Peter, avoiding me is ridiculous. We've just signed a prenuptial agreement. We'll be married in two days. You can't keep avoiding me. Can't we at least talk about your anger?" He glared at her and took the stairs, leaving her watching him walk away. Uette pushed the elevator button totally discouraged, tears close to the surface.

Peter met Ron at the tailor's. The suit was from his mother and Tom. He thought about how Jeneil had gone with Steve to get a suit and his heart sank. He missed her. Ron sat across from him at lunch watching him closely. "Come on, Peter. Cripes, cheer up. You look really low. Shit, fate deals you a bouquet of hot house orchids and you act like you'd rather be shot. Damn, the girl's a knockout and her name opens doors. She's ideal."

"For what?" Peter asked.

"For crying out loud, at least she's not like her sisters. She's got fun in her."

Peter drank his coffee. "I'm not impressed."

Ron sat back. "Okay, so I heard what you're accusing her of, but Peter, she chose you. You, Pete."

Peter couldn't believe what Ron was saying. "Do you think I should be grateful because she lied to get me to marry her? That my name is filth again? I was going with someone who's twice the woman she'll ever hope to be. Believe me, Ron, gratitude is not what I'm feeling."

Ron sighed. "I just meant that it could be worse. She's not a dog and she wants you, and she's Chinese."

Peter picked up the check. "Lunch is on me. Thanks for the help and all the details you've covered for me this week. How the hell did you survive a large wedding?"

Ron smiled. "Survive is the word all right. But the women get all caught up in it so you survive. Enjoy it because that's as dazzling and as excited as you'll ever see them again. It's their trip back to fairytales. They're all romantic and feminine while they're planning the wedding and then its life as usual after that."

"Jeneil was always romantic and feminine and she wasn't planning a wedding."

Ron sighed. "Pete, you'd better put your memories away or you'll be miserable."

Peter laughed. "Are you kidding, my memories keep me going. It's facing reality that makes me miserable."

"You're tough, Pete, really tough."

"I have to be, Ron. I'm marrying a screwball bitch in two days."

Twenty-Two

It was tradition in the Wong family to have a family dinner the night of the wedding rehearsal. Peter insisted that he couldn't get out of work. He and Uette had argued, but the dinner and rehearsal were held without the groom. Uette's grandfather absorbed the lies Uette told of how hard working and dedicated Peter was and that's why he was missing the tradition. She was acting like the understanding and caring bride. Her grandfather absorbed it all becoming very concerned about the situation. He wished his granddaughter would have just been silent, not liking how easily she lied.

Dr. Sprague forced Peter to take Saturday and Sunday off to protect his image. Peter hadn't cared how it would have looked for him to work the day after he was married. Dr. Sprague insisted he'd need the break anyway just to get his new life together.

Uette was always sending word to Mr. Chang that Peter hadn't moved into the apartment yet and he was beginning to grow tired of the girl. He found her very manipulative and irritating to deal with, and he felt even more compassion for Peter.

The living arrangements surprised both grandfathers. Peter insisted he'd pay only as much as his budget allowed. Uette's father was paying the rent on the beautiful and expensive apartment Uette chose, and the furniture was a gift from her parents as well. Peter disapproved and insisted on paying Mr. Wong what he could afford and would have paid for rent. Both Wong men and Peter's grandfather were impressed, Peter insisting a budget be maintained and that he didn't want a lot of handouts.

Peter arrived at the dorms on Friday night feeling very low. He wanted to talk to Jeneil just to hear her voice. He needed reassurance that she'd wait. Steve had told him that he was spending Saturday with her to keep her busy. They were going shopping in Boston then to dinner and a play. Peter hung his jacket in the closet and sighed. He heard the hall telephone ring; no one answered.

He went to it. "Pete, its Steve. Jeneil and I had dinner tonight. She's sorry to break the rule, but she wanted you to know that she's thinking of you. She said to tell you that she loves you. She said she always will."

Peter rested his head against the wall. He was choked up. Chang and Irish had never needed words. She was spooky like that. She knew him. She could read him so well.

That's why she had Steve call. He cleared his throat as he realized what it must be doing to Steve to deliver that message and he began to relax about Steve. "Thanks for calling, Steve. I needed to hear that. Jeneil must have known it."

Steve's voice got real serious. "Don't let her down, please. She's attached to you. It's almost frightening how vulnerable she is. She's like a kid who's counting on Christmas. Don't let her get hurt, Pete. She could be very badly hurt. She's crazy about you."

Peter absorbed it all like a man in desperate need of a drink of water after facing a walk through the desert sun. The words renewed him. Even Steve's word of caution shored him up, mostly since Steve was acknowledging that Jeneil belonged to Peter. Tension drained from him. "Steve, I won't hurt her. I can't live without her. This week's been the pits. Tell her that the ID bracelet won't come off. I've had it riveted to my wrist."

"That'll make sense to her?" Steve laughed.

"Yes, it will," Peter answered.

"Okay, I'll tell her. And Pete, good luck."

"Thanks, Steve." Peter paused then decided to say it. "Steve, I'm glad you're watching over Jeneil. You're a great friend."

"You're welcome, Pete. She loves you. I know that. I'll help her get through this. I owe her a lot, and you, too. You've been there for me."

Peter sighed. "I wish it was the triad going to Boston tomorrow."

"Trust me, Peter; you'll be there with us."

"Thanks for calling, Steve. Thanks a lot." Peter walked back to his room slowly, enjoying the warmth that filled him. Irish could get to him even through other people. "Songbird, you're beautiful."

The telephone rang again and he went back to answer it. "Peter Chang, please."

"This is Peter Chang."

"Peter, it's Uette. Please don't hang up."

The effect of the Songbird was still with him and he resented the intrusion. "Listen you screwball bitch, I'm being executed tomorrow at four. I'm still a free man so leave me alone." He hung up and walked back to his room basking in the glow of Jeneil's message. Getting into bed, he smiled thinking about how she had Steve deliver the message and he wondered if it was her way of letting him know he shouldn't worry. She could have written a note but she didn't. She had Camelot deliver a message to Arthur from Guinevere. He liked that. He liked that a lot. He drifted to sleep feeling calm and relaxed.

*****

Peter heard the knock at the door like it was part of a dream. He pulled himself awake. The knocking had stopped. The room was grey and dismal. He looked at his watch. Twelve-fifteen; he'd slept twelve hours. Sitting up, he tried to remember what he had to do. He was starved and the cupboards were empty. Standing up, he went to the shower and didn't hear the knocking at the door. Dressing, he looked at his watch. In three hours he would be married. His stomach knotted. Taking his luggage, he packed enough clothes for a week. He planned to maintain the dorm room just in case he couldn't stand being around her. Taking his parka, he suddenly remembered he was supposed to be at his mother's at eleven for lunch. He and Ron would leave from there. Someone knocked on the door. Peter opened it and saw telephone messages stuck to his door.

Joe Bartelli smiled. "Geez, I thought you were dead. Nothing wakes you up." He handed him another message. It was from his grandfather. The ones on his door were from his mother and Uette. Anger stirred as he called his grandfather. She was going to be a pain in the ass. She didn't listen to what he told her.

"Peter, everybody's worried. You were due here at eleven. It's one-fifteen."

"I slept in, Grandfather, and we have a rule here. We knock five times, if there's no answer, we leave a message."

"Well, at least you're all right."

"Well, I wouldn't say that," Peter replied, "but I'm awake and I'll be right over. I hope there's food left, I'm starved. I have a call here from Uette. Why is she pestering me?"

His grandfather laughed. "You're marrying her today. That's the arrangement. Now she'll call you and you report problems to me."

"After we're married, Grandfather. I'm not married yet. Do you know what she wants?"

"Yes, she'd like you and Ron at her house at three to rehearse since you haven't been available to be there."

Peter was annoyed. "Oh please, I'm due there at three-thirty, that's soon enough. Ron will be right by my side. He'll tell me what to do. He's been to rehearsals. I owe him for this whole week."

"You do, Peter. He's been great at explaining your absence."

"I'm on my way to your house, Grandfather. I just finished packing."

"Fine, Peter. At least we know you're all right."

Peter went back to his room and closed the zipper on his luggage. Taking the garment bag in one hand, he looked around. The room felt gloomy. The day was cold and rainy, and the wind was raging outside. "Great!" he said, picking up his luggage. "It's how I feel, too."

*****

Peter got to his mother's feeling chilled. The weather was miserable. So was he. He walked in the kitchen door and his mother turned from the stove. "Peter, for heaven's sake, you're hours behind schedule!"

"Is there any lunch left?" he asked, ignoring her, still annoyed at her for slapping Jeneil.

"There's some soup and I have sandwiches made." She put a bowl on the table before him. His grandfather, Tom, and Ron watched him as he took his jacket off. "Where's your suit!?" his mother shrilled, putting the sandwiches before him. "Honestly, your attitude is awful. Did you forget your suit?"

Without looking up, he answered, "Get off my back. The suit's in my room downstairs."

His mother sighed and went to answer the ringing telephone. "It's Uette for you."

"Go to hell," Peter mumbled. All three men looked at each other and Ron shook his head. Tom and his grandfather understood.

"Peter, telephone!" his mother called insistently.

Peter slammed his hand on the table. "Tell that piece of scum I don't want to talk to her until four or I won't be there. Both of you get off my back!" he shouted, standing up.

Uette had heard him shout and ended the call quickly. His mother stared at him angrily. "You are disgusting."

He turned quickly, facing her. "Why the hell didn't you convince her of that? She sure hasn't changed her mind about marrying a man who's disgusting."

"She doesn't have any choice," she snapped back at him, then left the room.

He sat down to finish his lunch, looking at Ron. "Explain the details of this circus. What do they want the clown to do?"

"Aw, Pete, come on," Ron began in a pleading tone.

Peter interrupted. "Ron, don't lecture. Explain what the bitch has planned." Ron sighed and explained the details of the wedding to his belligerent cousin.

His mother returned dressed for the wedding. "It's nearly three," she said. "She wants you and Ron there at three." Peter ignored her and poured more coffee, then sat down and added cream and sugar to it. "Peter, you're not even dressed." She sighed. "You don't have time for coffee! Please don't embarrass the family at this wedding. They can't believe you haven't invited anyone from the hospital to the...."

Peter interrupted her. "Why would I want them there? I don't even want to be there."

His mother sighed heavily. "He's going to ruin this. I know it." She sighed again. "Peter, if you embarrass her at this wedding, you'll embarrass us, too," she said pleadingly. He ignored her and she threw up her hands in frustration. "It's three. I guess you're not planning on being there for rehearsal." Peter continued to ignore her. "Father, please. Get him to start dressing. He won't even be there for three-thirty. It's a twenty-five minute drive with traffic."

His grandfather touched his arm. "You really should get dressed. We have to leave soon."

"You all go on ahead. I'll change and be there."

His mother gasped. "Don't leave him alone! He won't show up!" He stared at her angrily. She shook her head and sighed.

Ron smiled. "Hey, it's traditional for the best man to assist the groom."

Peter finished his coffee. "That's for weddings, Ron. This is an execution. Ride over with the rest of them. The prisoner will show up. He's saving face, remember." His mother groaned and he ignored her. Ron sighed, and his grandfather and Tom looked at each other with compassion.

*****

The house sounded empty, it felt empty. Peter knew the feeling. He fixed his tie and slipped into his suit jacket. The overcoat Jeneil had bought him was in the car. Peter gathered his jeans and shirt, and for an instant he wanted to drive to Boston to find Steve and Jeneil. He gathered everything else quickly and headed for the car. He couldn't afford to concentrate on Jeneil or he wouldn't show up for the wedding, but go to her apartment and wait for her instead. He concentrated on his reason for saving face. He had to prove the baby wasn't his or he couldn't face Jeneil. He knew that now. He didn't want that hanging over his head. He put on his overcoat and got behind the wheel of the car determined to see this through. He got to the house at three-fifty. Ron was posted at one window and his mother at another, both relieved to see Peter walk toward the house. Going to the kitchen as he had been instructed, he rang the bell.

"Yes," one of the catering staff asked, standing before him.

Uette's father came to the door. "It's okay," he said to the woman. "He's expected." Mr. Wong showed him to the den. "You can leave your coat here. Everyone is expecting you." Peter combed his hair quickly, straightened his tie and buttoned his jacket. He looked at his watch. It was three fifty-seven.

Ron walked in. "Okay, cuz. Everything's set. The rings are here." Ron patted his pocket. Peter stayed silent.

"I'll go to Uette now," Mr. Wong said, excusing himself.

Ron watched him leave then turned to Peter. "You scared the shit out of Uette. She burst into tears ten minutes ago. Man, you're making this tough on all of us."

Peter grinned. "Gosh, my heart's bleeding, Ron. I'm broken up that she's crying." He shook his head.

A man with a camera walked in. "Bride's ready. I'd like a picture of the best man fixing your tie," he said, positioning himself. Peter headed for the door and the flash went off. "Hey!" The photographer looked up. "You ruined the shot."

"Oh, did I?" Peter grinned. "I'm really sorry."

Ron was shocked. "Shit, Pete. Cooperate for crying out loud."

Peter turned at the door. "Look best man, shut up and carry the rings or you'll swallow them." He walked out.

The photographer was shocked. "Wow, major attitude problem. He's gonna be tough."

Ron patted his back diplomatically. "Do the best you can. I'll keep after him."

The photographer was puzzled. "If this is a happy day, what's he like when he's upset."

"Its nerves," Ron explained, leaving the room. The house was buzzing with the sounds of people talking and laughing. Ron took Peter's arm in the hallway. "We have to wait for the prelude music then we walk out and stand near the big window where Judge Miller is. When you hear the traditional music, we'll turn and face the stairs as Uette comes down. That's easy enough, isn't it?"

Peter shook his head. "And that's why she wanted me here at three. You just explained it to me in two seconds. Geez, what a screwball she is."

"Pete, that screwball is about to become Mrs. Peter Chang." The name stung Peter's chest. To him it was Jeneil's name and it shocked him to hear Ron call Uette that. He put his head down and sighed. He had wanted Jeneil to be the only one to ever have that name. Anger began to filter through him as he thought how Uette had ruined that. He clenched his fists. "Relax, Pete. You look angry."

"Do I?" Peter pretended to be shocked.

Ron shook his head. "Oh, Pete, you've got me shittin' scared. I have to tell you that."

"Hey, I'm here, aren't I?"

"But don't cause a scene," Ron cautioned.

The prelude music began and the photographer approached them. Peter turned his back to him as the flash went off. "Thanks," the photographer growled. "You're gonna cost me the profits on this job."

"Concentrate on the bride," Peter replied coolly. "Better still, how much can I pay you to break your damn camera and disappear?"

"Pete!" Ron whispered loudly. "Let's go. Keep time with me. Don't walk faster or slower."

The photographer watched them walk into the living room and grinned. "Oh, I get it, shotgun wedding. There go my profits. Poor guy, I feel for him." He followed them into the living room to position himself for the bride's entrance. The music began and everyone faced the stairs behind them.

"Pete, turn and face the stairs," Ron whispered.

"Why? I know what she looks like." Judge Miller heard the remark.

"Pete!" Ron groaned softly, but Peter didn't turn.

Uette looked toward the large window as she stood at the top of the stairs in her white gown and veil on the arm of her father. Her heart was beating furiously and then discouragement followed as she noticed Peter deliberately shunning her as she made her entrance. She swallowed so she wouldn't cry and held onto her father. People were admiring her and smiling, pleased with her entrance. To her, it was all wasted since the one person she wanted to impress was the only one not looking. Her father positioned her next to Peter and as she went to put her arm through his, he pulled away subtly.

"Pete!" Ron gasped. "Don't."

Judge Miller cleared his throat and looked from the bride to the groom and then, stepping closer, whispered, "If anyone would like to change his mind, now's the time." Uette's eyes widened in fear and she looked at Peter, panicked that he would. "Mr. Chang?" The judge waited. "Is this wedding your choice, too?"

"Not really," Peter answered.

"Oh my gosh!" Ron groaned.

"But let's continue with the circus anyway." Uette closed her eyes to stop from shaking.

"Are you sure?" Judge Miller asked.

"Yes," Peter answered.

"Very well." The judge stepped back as the guests looked at each other, wondering what was happening. The mothers of the bride and groom were crying softly. The grandfathers had their heads lowered.

Ron leaned over to Peter's ear. "The soloist will sing now. You'll take Uette's hands and look at her while the song is being sung."

"Like hell," Peter answered. The first note began from the organ and Uette turned to Peter. He clasped his hands tightly in front of him, holding his arms close to his body so she couldn't slip through even if she wanted to.

"Oh shit," Ron whispered. "Pete, you're crazy."

Peter ignored him and stared out the large paneled window behind the judge and watched a tree branch scratch at the glass, pushed into a wild motion by the raging wind. Peter thought of Jeneil and their ceremony. He remembered her words, 'Whenever you feel or hear the wind, you'll think of me.' He grinned to himself. Great protest Jeneil, I'm with you, baby. Come on wind, break the damn glass. He'd love to see that happen.

The singing ended and Peter was relieved. The tension and the smell of flowers were making him sick. He forced himself to listen to the judge so he could repeat the words. He went to put the ring on Uette's finger and dropped it. A gasp went through the guests. Karen put her foot out quickly and stepped on it, keeping it from rolling past her. She bent down and handed it back to Peter. Uette was shaking as he put the ring on. He got the words out through a very dry throat and heard himself say, "I do," in answer to the question of taking her as his wife. "In name only," he added, only loud enough for the judge and witnesses to hear. Karen and Ron looked at each other, shocked.

The judge stared at Peter momentarily, shocked by the addition, and then pronounced them man and wife. "You may kiss the bride," the judge said softly, watching Peter, curious about his reaction.

"I'll pass on that," Peter said calmly, softly enough to be heard by the judge. Karen and Ron gasped as they saw Uette lean toward Peter. Karen reached for her and Ron slipped around Peter to help Karen with a crying Uette. Peter never made a move toward her. The guests stood up, looking at each other and at the sick bride and uncaring groom.

The judge looked at the organist. "Play something for goodness sake, something loud to quiet people down." He looked at Peter. "Can I talk to you, Mr. Chang?" The mothers of the bride and groom wept openly at the sadness that surrounded what should have been a beautiful moment in the lives of their children. Peter stepped aside with the judge and the man sighed. "I guess you know what was happening here didn't escape me, especially you're remark of husband in name only. I should tell you that it isn't legal if it wasn't prearranged with the bride."

"It was," Peter answered, "in a prenuptial agreement."

"Good," the judge said, and extended his hand. "I could see the protest from you. I'm glad it's legal. I marry more people I think shouldn't be getting married and then worry about their future. I could see this shouldn't be taking place, but I'm satisfied that whatever's behind it has been discussed and handled legally. Best of luck to you."

"Thanks."

"Pete," Ron called. "She's shaking badly."

"Have her lie down then unless she'd like to go to the emergency room. I could call an ambulance."

Ron and Karen stared at him, amazed at his lack of concern. Uette's father came to her. "Shall I call a doctor?"

"I feel very weak," Uette cried softly.

Peter studied her. "I could give her a sedative, but she'd miss the reception and probably wake up tomorrow at noon. It's up to her."

Uette was stunned at his suggestion. "I'll be fine," she said softly. "I haven't eaten all day. This will pass as soon as I've eaten some food I'm sure."

Concerned guests gathered around relieved it was just nerves. Uette's older sister, Phyllis, sighed. "I broke out in hives the day I got married. I was so nervous." Peter smiled, remembering Phyllis. She was the one who was nearly hit by a car running away from him.

"I'm glad this wasn't a large wedding," Peter said, smiling. "I couldn't handle it. I'd probably break out in hives, too."

Phyllis smiled warmly. "Is that right? I wondered what was happening up there, nervous bride and groom." She extended her hand to him. "Welcome to the family."

He shook her hand. "Thanks."

She shook her head. "I can't believe you're a surgeon. I think that's wonderful."

Peter shrugged. "Didn't want to waste all the training I had with knives on the street."

She laughed, enjoying the joke. "That's funny."

Peter liked her; she wasn't the snob he remembered. He grinned, remembering one of the guys saying years ago that she'd be okay once someone taught her how to have fun. She was so concerned about her virginity it made her a nervous wreck around boys.

Phyllis's husband came over and extended his hand. "Jeff Chu," he said, smiling, "pleased to meet you and congratulations."

"Same here." Peter smiled, shaking hands.

Uette watched dumbfounded as Peter spoke to her sister so personably. She was encouraged and went to them. "I see you've met Phyllis and Jeff."

"I need to talk to Ron." Peter nodded to Phyllis and Jeff and walked away. Uette watched him.

"He's very nice, Uette. I was shocked when I heard Peter Chang was going to marry my sister, but he's okay, really."

Uette sighed. "I think so, too." She watched Peter talking to Ron and her heart turned over. "He's so gorgeous."

Her sister hugged her. "Ooo, you are off the deep end about him, aren't you?" Uette nodded as tears filled her eyes. "Well, don't cry, silly. Want some advice? Don't think about tonight. Concentrate on the party. I broke out in hives worrying and ruined my wedding for myself. Relax. Everything will be fine. He seems so quiet and sensitive. I can't believe he's the same Peter Chang, although he wasn't noisy just so darn tough looking and ran with a wild bunch. Peter Chang a doctor. Wow!" She put her arm around Uette's shoulder. "Come on, let's get you fed. This is not a day to be sick. The weather was bad enough. I'm glad you didn't have to leave for a church. That wind would have totally destroyed your dress. It's like it wanted to get in and destroy the place. I thought that tree would crash through the window during the ceremony. Come on, a nice hot cup of coffee will perk you up."

"Okay." Uette smiled weakly, the thought of putting anything in her stomach making her stomach turn. "But I need to be excused. I'll meet you in the dining room." She left quickly, heading for the bathroom as the new experience of morning sickness introduced itself even though it was four-thirty in the afternoon.

*****

Jeneil and Steve waited at the counter of the department store as the clerk went to ring up the transaction. Jeneil glanced at her watch and Steve put his hand over it gently to distract her. "It's over." She sighed. "The world now has a person called Mrs. Peter Chang as a part of humanity."

Steve smiled. "I'm looking forward to dinner and the play. Let's stop for a drink afterwards someplace where we can dance. I haven't danced for weeks. We'll get home really late."

Jeneil smiled, understanding he was changing the subject. "I love you," she said softly.

He looked at her steadily. "I'm crazy about you, kid. You're something special. You really are."

She sighed. "Keep telling me that. I need to hear it today."

He slipped his arm around her and kissed her temple gently. "That's a deal, beautiful. You are special." She looked up at him and smiled that luscious, gentle smile of hers. The clerk brought her package and Steve watched her thank the clerk and take her purchase. Wisps of hair fell over her ear. He smiled to himself. He'd love the chance to show her just how special he thought she was. Steve took the package from Jeneil and she slipped her gloved hand into his.

Another sales clerk joined the one watching them walk away. "Wow," she said. "How do you get a guy to look at you like that?"

"By not noticing, I guess." The clerk smiled. "Oh, is she ever in for a surprise."

"High voltage," the second clerk said, and the first nodded in agreement.

*****

Uette kept turning up at Peter's side. It was annoying him. Going to the kitchen with his cup of coffee, the staff was shocked to see him. He went to the back hall and watched the storm from the door. The photographer turned up and Peter looked at him and turned away. "Don't give up, do you?"

The photographer grinned. "It's my job. Her album will look strange if the groom is missing. They're looking for you now. It's time to cut the cake and coo to each other."

Peter looked at him. "How the hell did such stupidity ever get started?"

The photographer laughed. "Hey, don't complain. There was a custom long ago where the groom took the bride upstairs then would bring the bed sheet back to the party downstairs to prove he had been with her and that he was her first."

"Oh geez." Peter shook his head, disgusted at the thought. "Man is so intelligent."

The photographer laughed. "Could be worse, cave men didn't even have separate rooms for sleeping."

Peter looked at him, smiling. "You're full of cheer. You're nuts."

The photographer laughed again. "I'm nuts? You're the one hiding from your wedding."

Peter grinned. "Craziest groom you've ever met, huh?"

"No, actually the craziest was a guy who married Attila the Hun's sister who nagged him through the ceremony. She had to be good in bed because her face was twenty miles of bad road and her mouth was power generated and stuck in high speed." Peter laughed and the photographer studied him. "I hope you know what you're doing. I was married once. I've been divorced for a year now. It's not fun. Kids get mixed up. I was expecting to live happily ever after on my wedding day. Man, you're starting off like my ex and I were at my lawyer's five years later. Now I take pictures of weddings to earn pocket money. I'm a news photographer for the Evening Gazette but the ex gets most of that paycheck. She'd probably take the wedding money too if she found out. I give her name to every single guy I meet hoping she'll get married again so I can have some money of my own. Divorce is no fun." The photographer sighed. "What the hell is the answer? What causes the magic to disappear?"

Peter shrugged. "You've seen more of it than I have. Do you always cheer up grooms like this?"

The photographer smiled and then they heard Uette in the kitchen. "Has anyone seen my husband?" Peter groaned.

The photographer punched Peter's arm gently. "Smile for the camera. I'll try to retouch out the frosting smeared all over you."

"Peter, what are you doing?" Uette asked, coming into the hall. She looked at the photographer questioning the camaraderie she sensed between the two. Peter didn't like the way she looked at the photographer like he was servant.

The photographer shifted his bag. "I was trying to talk him into some stills. He's camera shy."

"Then take shots of the guests. Good grief, don't offend the groom," she said, dismissing him.

"Right," the photographer replied.

Peter was irritated. He extended his hand. "You didn't offend me. I enjoyed the talk." The photographer smiled, looked at Uette, and left them alone.

"Do you enjoy watching storms?" Uette asked in a gentle voice.

He looked at her with a sneer. "I came here to be alone."

"It's time to cut the cake," she said, becoming more formal.

"Why does that take two people?"

"It's tradition."

Peter folded his arms. "I'm not letting you stuff cake into my mouth and vice versa."

She sighed. "People are wondering where you are. We didn't have a toast." She shook her head. "It's been a strange wedding."

"Tell me about it," he answered sarcastically.

She shrugged. "Okay. I'll explain about the cake, you're conservative, but would you at least mingle? People are noticing your absence. My family has never met you before today and they find that totally odd. None of your friends are here, which is odd, too." She began to walk away. He stayed at the door. "Please, Peter."

"I'll be there." He continued looking out the window. She watched him for a second then sighed and walked away. Peter hated the thought of returning to the party. Uette's mother glared at him whenever they were in speaking distance from each other. His mother glared at him whenever he was in speaking distance to her. Karen wouldn't speak civilly and Ron had given up. Everyone else was treating him like the happy and proud groom. He was nauseated by it. He heard footsteps. Turning, he saw Rick and smiled. His cousin's spiked hair and black leather shirt and pants were outrageous.

"Sorry, Pete," Rick said. "I was looking for a spot to call my own. I'm tired of breathing carbon dioxide."

"Join me," Peter insisted. "We can open the door and breathe in carbon monoxide from time to time."

Rick smiled at him. "Well cousin, I'm glad to see you haven't lost your humble roots. I figured you wouldn't appreciate me since being in medicine and money now."

"Money?" Peter questioned.

"The bitch who said I do," Rick answered.

"You don't like her?"

Rick shook his head. "It's your business, Pete, but the lady's a reptile."

"How do you know?"

"I've been watching her. She's a different person when she thinks no one is looking. Chameleon clear through."

Peter smiled. "How old are you?"

"Sixteen," Rick answered. "So that means my observation isn't valid? Humph, sleep facing her, Pete. She's a reptile. Trust me."

Peter grinned. "How'd you get so bright at sixteen?"

Rick smiled. "Well, don't tell me you know that these spikes don't pierce my brain."

Peter laughed. "Hey, Rick, people don't understand different let alone odd."

"Tell me about it."

"Then why do it?"

"To experience negative," Rick answered simply.

"Negative?"

Rick nodded. "That's why I only wear black. I'm experiencing negative."

"I know a girl on your wave length. Blue sky on top, green grass on bottom."

Rick laughed. "Hey, she doesn't get sucked into black holes. That's great!"

Peter was stunned. "You understood that?"

"Yeah," Rick answered. "She knows dimensional reality, but can she spacewalk? I can't, I still get woofed, tweeted. Is she floating?"

"Floating?" Peter asked.

"Yeah, available, free, or is she looped, tied to a guy?"

Peter smiled broadly, enjoying the language. "She's looped."

"Figures." Rick sighed. "Space fems are rare. They get looped fast because they can't be cloned."

"Well, I know this one can't be."

Rick shrugged. "Too bad, I wouldn't mind a tether. I'm tired of the clones' festival."

"You're also younger."

Rick raised his eyebrows, smiling. "Are we talking a decade here?"

"Not quite but close."

Rick closed his eyes with enjoyment. "Oh shit, forget a tether. I could deal with a full orbit. Is the loop welded? Is she married?" Peter shook his head and Rick brightened. "Is she nuclear fusion?" Peter wrinkled his eyebrows, not understanding. "Does she split from the atom? Is the loop open? Can she go with other guys?" Rick sighed from the struggle to make himself clear.

Peter smiled. "No, she's into formulas to fuse herself to the atom, welded or not."

Rick whistled. "A real orbit; that would be ultra-nutritional. Too, too bad."

Peter chuckled. "No wonder your mother is worried about you."

Rick grimaced. "My mother, Malien, lives in ground station zero."

"Hey, she helped me grow up,"

Rick laughed. "Ooo, cuz, I'm turning green. Maybe Malien will help me so I can grow up like you and slice human flesh and rewire bones, too. But you can keep the reptile." Rick laughed again. "Hey, Pete, maybe if you weren't so grown up you'd be with the space fem who's looped and orbited instead of a reptile."

Peter stared at Rick seeing how close he had gotten to what was happening in Peter's life. "You're too bright for sixteen, Rick, too, too bright."

Peter's grandfather joined them. "Peter, people are asking where you are."

"Pete, what he said, that's nice ancient speech, translated it means Reptilia slithered to your grandfather and complained." Rick broke into laughter and hit Peter's shoulder. "This is some wedding, you've got the loop so oxidized already and suffering from rust."

Peter grinned as he watched Rick leave laughing. "Watch him, Grandfather. He's too bright for sixteen."

The grandfather smiled. "He's promised to write a dictionary for me so we can talk to each other."

"Do you know that he's wearing black to experience negative?"

"So he's said. Does that make sense to you?"

Peter laughed. "Grandfather, it means his clothes are not costumes, it means something to him and he's being up front with everybody. He sounds like Jeneil."

The grandfather laughed. "I understand Jeneil. I don't understand Rick. The wedding needs a groom, let's go."

Peter met his mother as he returned to the party. "Well, the missing groom," she said, and he walked past her, shocking her. "I feel very sorry for Uette," she said to her father.

"So do I," he replied, "but I'm sure it's for a different reason."

Everyone gathered around as the bride and groom prepared to cut the cake. Peter kept his distance and had to be told to place his hand on Uette's as she made the first slice. He could feel her shaking. He looked away as the camera flashed. The photographer smiled and came to him. "Could I ask you to just lower your head to your chest to avoid the flash then it looks like a groom is reluctant and not the photographer's a klutz."

Peter smiled. "Thanks, I can live with that." The photographer winked and walked away.

Uette put a slice of cake on a plate. "Peter is very civilized," Uette announced. "We're going to use forks for the cake."

"What a spoil sport," someone said.

Phyllis turned to the heckler. "Hey, he's a doctor. He understands about hands and germs. He's used to scrubbing for surgery." Peter smiled, appreciating her defense. She smiled in return. Uette held the cake on the fork for him. He took it noticing the flash go off. He held the piece of cake for her. She put her hand on his as she put it in her mouth. He withdrew his hand as soon as the cake was safely in her mouth.

"Are there any more of these traditions?" he asked, fighting irritability.

"Yes, the garter and the bouquet," Amy answered. She was the sister after Phyllis and Peter remembered her, too.

"Shut up, Amy," Uette said swiftly.

Peter picked up on it. "Why should she shut up?"

Ron was beside him. "The bride throws the bouquet to the single women and the groom throws the garter to the single men." Uette watched closely.

"That sounds easy enough," Peter said. "Where's the garter?"

"On her leg," Ron answered.

Peter wrinkled his brow. "She gives it to me to throw?"

Ron fidgeted. "You take it off her leg."

"In front of everybody?" he gasped, shocked. The crowd laughed at his sense of modesty. "Uette!" he said, glaring at her.

She smiled. "Relax, darling. I'll hand it to you. You are such a wreck today. You dropped the ring. You'd probably break my leg trying to get the garter off anyway." She slipped her arm through his as everyone laughed.

"I need some coffee," he said, moving away from her quickly. "Geez, how do men survive these weddings?"

Everyone laughed again loving the groom's embarrassment. It all added to the festivity of the moment and the electric atmosphere preceding the exit of the bride and groom who would leave and begin their first night together. Uette was caught up in the frenzy and pleased with the way Peter handled it. She couldn't stand near him without feeling faint from the electrical charge that raced through her. The thought that he had been without Jeneil for two weeks now had her very encouraged about their night together. She had planned well for it and the apartment was ready. Peter poured himself a cup of coffee, totally annoyed with the whole reception.

His grandfather went to him. "You handled that very well in spite of your shock."

Peter groaned. "Grandfather, what's all this for? Throwing things, taking garters off legs in public." He shook his head. "I'll never be civilized. I don't understand the rules."

His grandfather smiled at his grandson whose sense of decency would have made his ancestors proud. "Peter, I can understand your attitude. Chinese weddings didn't have traditions like that. These are modern traditions."

"Well, it feels cheap and degrading," he scowled. His grandfather smiled proudly at the unruly boy who had grown up to become a man of honor and decency, knowing he would grow to be a good patriarch, too.

"I'm proud of you, Peter. I'm comfortable leaving the Chang name to you."

Peter looked at him. "I need to hear that, Grandfather, especially today. I feel cheap and degraded enough without the stupidity of wedding traditions adding to it." He sighed.

His grandfather patted his back. "You can stand tall, Peter. Saving face is not for wimps. You're a man, a strong proud man."

Uette came to Peter, smiling. "We need to throw the bouquet and garter now then we go upstairs to change."

Peter was puzzled. "What do you mean 'we'? What's wrong with my suit?" he asked, and his grandfather held back a smile.

"Nothing's wrong with your suit." She laughed. "It's just tradition that we go upstairs and change our clothes to leave. The groom is supposed to help the bride do the snaps and zippers on her gown." Peter's grandfather held his breath, waiting for Peter's reaction, seeing him tense up.

"Uette, listen carefully to me will you please. I'm finished with traditions once the garter is thrown. This isn't a traditional wedding. I have a prenuptial agreement in my pocket that says that. You signed it. Did you read it at all? You've been getting yourself undressed and dressed for years now. Continue that tradition."

She looked stricken. "I didn't mean anything," she said, looking innocent. "You could wait out of the room. It's just to keep up appearances."

Peter sighed and shook his head. "Grandfather, do I speak in plain English? Maybe I should yell and throw a fit. Do you think she'll understand that?"

Uette's eyes widened in fear. "Okay, okay, I understand. I'll change and then the garter and bouquet." She walked away quickly.

"What's with her? Is she young, stubborn or stupid?" Peter asked. "She's going to be trouble."

His grandfather watched the new Mrs. Chang walk away. "Peter, be on guard," he said softly. "She's not young, stubborn or stupid. Remember that." His grandfather tightened his jaw resenting the degrading wife who was married to his grandson. She wasn't the wife of a patriarch. He frowned to himself. She wasn't an honorable wife.

Peter grinned. "Rick called her a reptile."

His grandfather watched the girl talking to guests. "Rick is very bright for being sixteen," he replied, as a look of anger crossed his face.

Ron came over to them smiling. "Aren't you going to help her change?"

His grandfather was losing patience. "Ron, some traditions border on stupidity if not impropriety. In China, the attendants helped the bride change not just to coordinate a color scheme. The groom was allowed dignity and self-respect and not made to look like a weakling of so little self-control that he'd be willing to take on the duties of the bride's maid to get near the bride. He didn't joke about his responsibility. He waited for his bride to be ready and then brought her proudly to the home he'd worked hard to provide for them. He shared his life with her not just his bed. He was taught that his wife was specially chosen for him. Together they would create life and continue what was good and honorable. He needed her and he knew it. She did, too. We accepted that of each other. We didn't abuse it."

They heard applause from behind them. Turning, they saw the photographer clapping his hands. "Fantastic! I've always wanted someone to make sense of a wedding day for me. Thank you, sir. Being at so many weddings, I wondered if the groom should wear a clown suit instead of a tux. That's beautiful." He walked away to await the bride's return.

Uette returned wearing a dress and walked directly to Peter. "We should be leaving."

"Why?" he asked. "I haven't eaten yet. There's no reason to leave so soon."

"Peter, it would look strange to stay much longer. Besides, you haven't moved into the apartment yet."

"I have my stuff in the car."

She sighed. "Peter, please. I'm begging you. The guests will be expecting us to leave."

Peter shook his head. "More tradition shit, right?"

She shrugged. "I guess so. Please get your coat."

Peter went to the den for his overcoat and sat thinking. It was zero hour, he knew that. Now it would be the two of them. He knew the apartment had two bedrooms, but he couldn't imagine himself alone with her. He sighed. The wind moved the bush outside the window and he smiled and thought of Jeneil.

Uette fussed with her hair in front of the hallway mirror wondering why Peter was taking so long. He was working so hard to avoid being near her. She wondered if he felt the same electricity she did. He must be near starvation after two weeks of celibacy. She'd changed her mind about Jeneil, who was stupid to leave him on his own. He was a man, a sexy man with a healthy appetite. She grinned and fixed the collar of her dress. Jeneil was either stupid or had the most inflated ego ever created. "Well, thank you anyway, Jeneil. You made my job easier."

Peter came from the den and she turned and smiled. "Ready to throw the garter?"

"Oh gosh, Uette, I'm all a flutter about it," he mocked.

She sighed. "Why did I ask? Let's go." She took his arm and he pulled it away.

"Can I make something perfectly clear? We're married in name only, remember. No touching, no romance. Got that?"

"I understand," she said gently, "but I keep forgetting. I'm just the type who holds hands naturally. I'll learn. Be patient with me."

He gave her a weary look and walked away. She caught up as he walked into the living room. Everyone applauded. Peter wondered why but then remembered that not much made sense to him that day so he stopped wondering. The garter and the bouquet toss were over and a picnic basket of food was handed to them, and more shaking hands and kisses. Peter sighed, wanting to shout and run off. He caught sight of his grandfather watching him. Peter met his stare. His grandfather nodded slightly. Peter grinned and nodded slightly in return. Peter opened the front door and the wind nearly tore it from his hand pulling him with it. He stood in it and smiled. The elements were angry. Peter enjoyed thinking that even if he didn't believe it. The wind matched his fury. They were equals. Peter wasn't allowed to show his fury so he fully enjoyed letting the wind say it for him while he stood in the middle, feeling a part of it.

"Peter, bring the car to the door," Uette called to him. He looked at her vacantly, still in the wind then nodded and walked away.

"He has a thing for windstorms," she said, closing the door. "Every time I've seen him today, he's been watching it."

"He's odd, Uette," Karen said, hugging her. "You'll need to retrain him. You know who has spoiled him rotten. They're both weird. She encourages him to go back to his black leather jacket days. You're living with the result of that little game. His behavior is just like when he was a kid. He was nicer than this before her."

Uette smiled. "I'll handle it." She heard the car horn and opened the door, waving to Peter to come to the house.

"What now?" He sighed and got out, walking to the door. "Now what?"

Uette smiled. "Everyone wants to throw confetti at us."

He stared at her, not believing that's why he had walked through the storm again. People had put their coats on and stepped outside. Uette stood by Peter and faced the smiling crowd. Peter saw the photographer and lowered his head as the flash went off. He looked up. The photographer smiled and gave him a thumbs-up. Peter smiled at him. The wind kept whipping the confetti away from them sprinkling over the lawn beside them.

"Uette, this is so stupid. It's not even reaching us. Let's go," Peter growled.

"But I want confetti in my hair. It's all part of it."

Peter stared at her, stunned by her remark. "You are a screwball, I mean it."

She pouted. "Darn this wind."

Peter shook his head. "Hey, I'm tired of this shit." He ran up to one of the guests who was holding a bag of confetti. "Can I take this? She's disappointed. She wants confetti in her hair." The guest smiled and handed it to him. He ran back to Uette and turned the bag upside down, spilling confetti over her head.

She looked shocked and then laughed. "Thank you," she said, smiling at him. The guests smiled thinking how anxious the groom was to please her and thought he wanted to leave with her quickly. Peter's gesture left a mellow feeling in them of their own wedding day and the nights that followed. The groom headed toward the car as the bride ran to catch up to him. He held the door for her and slammed it as soon as she was inside then went to his side and got in. He started the engine. "Wait, I want to wave. Let the photographer take our picture."

"Oh geez." Peter put his head back sighing. "Will this shit ever be finished?" He lowered his head as the bulb flashed. Uette raised the window trying to fix her ravaged hairdo.

The photographer headed back to the house grinning. "Boy lady, you ain't seen nothing yet in this furious windstorm. Wait until you taste married life with him." He smiled broadly thinking it couldn't happen to a nicer lady. She was a real snake, one of the worst bitch brides he'd ever seen. He followed the guests as they went back inside.

The woman next to him smiled. "You have a nice job. I love weddings. Nothing can ruin the feeling of people in love. Not windstorms or mistakes in the ceremony. You are so lucky; you get to see it all."

The photographer looked at her and grinned. "Yeah, I do. I really do see it all." He turned his head and caught sight of the car heading down the street. He shook his head and walked into the house saddened by the results of mistakes people made in their lives.

Twenty-Three

Uette looked at Peter studying his profile as he drove. He was gorgeous. And she belonged to him now, her, Mrs. Peter Chang. Her heart fluttered. "Is this all your luggage? One bag?" she asked, surprised.

"Shut up," he growled. "My head aches and my ears hurt from the noise of that crazy circus. I feel like an animal just let out of a cage. So shut up and let me enjoy the silence." She was stunned by his reaction but she shrugged and stayed quiet.

Peter gritted his teeth as they rode up in the elevator. The building was expensive and he hated it. He hated that he was living in a place he couldn't afford. He didn't want to owe anybody in this marriage. Not a dime. He reached into his pocket for the key as they walked toward the apartment. He hadn't seen it yet. He opened the door to darkness. Uette walked in and turned the switch filling the room with soft light. Peter groaned inwardly; ultra-modern and in black and white. Hospital rooms seemed warmer to him.

Uette smiled. "I still need to add finishing touches like paintings and things, but there's been so much to do. Even unfinished I love it!" she said, turning around to take it all in.

"Where's my room?"

She looked at him and smiled. "They're all your rooms. This all belongs to both of us."

He sighed. "Okay, I'll try again. Where's my bedroom? I want to put my luggage down."

"I'm sorry." She headed toward a hallway and smiled as she opened a door and turned on a switch. "I don't know your likes and dislikes so I didn't decorate. You have the basics."

"That suits me fine," he said, walking past her into the room. She followed him in. There was a double bed and a dresser with a mirror over it, and a small nightstand and lamp.

"I'm sorry, Peter. It seems so drab."

"It's fine, Uette." He put his luggage on the bed.

"Do you want to see mine?" she asked, and he looked at her suspiciously. She shrugged. "You have to let me know if you like it or not so I'll know how to decorate yours."

"This room is fine like it is. Don't add anything to it. There's a place to sleep and a place for my clothes. That's all I need."

"But it looks like a prison cell." She sighed.

"That's what this marriage feels like to me anyway. Leave the room as it is." He walked out of the room and into the bathroom across the hall. Turning on the switch, he opened the medicine cabinet. It was empty.

"Do you have anything for a headache?" He turned, surprised to find her there with him.

"No, I can't take any medication because of the baby. Is it a very bad headache?"

He rubbed his forehead. "I'll be okay." He went back to his room and she followed him. He began to unpack.

"I'll let you settle in," she said, and left.

He sighed and shook his head. "She's a pain in the ass. I just knew it." He threw his undershirts into a drawer. His stomach reminded him that he was hungry and he finished unpacking quickly. His head ached. Going to what he thought must be the kitchen he turned on the light switch. The kitchen was black and white, too. He went to the refrigerator. There was a bottle of champagne in it, nothing else. He thought of the picnic basket and went back to the living room. He was starved. One thing about the Wongs, they knew how to put out the food. He remembered the potato salad looking really good and the sandwiches small but fresh. He opened the basket and took out a plastic container, opening it quickly. "Pastries?" He took out another. "More pastries!"

Uette walked in wearing a black dress that dipped very low in the front and the back, turning to show him. "My grandmother gave me money for a whole new wardrobe. She's a sweetheart. She's an in-the-now person. I love her."

"Uette," Peter hung onto the basket weakened from stomach pain, "where's the food? There are only pastries in here."

She stopped fussing with her dress. "Oh, that's all I asked them to pack. I thought it would be elegant to have champagne and dessert. Have you ever tried that?"

Peter got annoyed at her condescending tone. He felt like she was insinuating that he was just new off the streets and she was going to civilize him. "Yeah," he said, "I have at an exclusive hotel in Vermont with a fantastic balcony and a view of the sunset. Jeneil likes champagne and dessert, only we ate real food first." Uette bristled at the news and the name that rattled her to the core. He looked at her. "Uette, how old are you?"

"I'm twenty-one," she said. "I'll be twenty-two at the end of summer."

"You're still in college?"

"Yes, I took a year to model then decided I'd rather be an actress. Why? I guess you think I'm stupid because we don't have real food. Well, I've been very busy. I had a lot to do in only two weeks. Give me a break."

Peter grinned. "Hey, you're right. After all, you did find time to pick up champagne. You handled the necessities. I apologize." He shook his head and walked toward his room.

"I don't like your attitude," she snapped.

He turned around. "I don't give a damn. You eat the pastries and get drunk on champagne for all I care. That's really good for the baby. I don't drink." He turned and walked away.

"Ha!" she sneered. "Don't give me that. You were drunk the night I got pregnant."

He stopped and spun around and walked back. "Listen bitch, I know you've rehearsed that story until you can say it backwards in your sleep, but don't lay it on me. I was there, remember? We both know what the truth is, so peddle your shit somewhere else."

She glared at him. "And you listen to me you foul mouthed oaf. Stop calling me vulgar names. I don't like it and I don't deserve it."

Peter grinned nastily. "There's nothing that'll cover up a shitting bitch and make her smell like a lady so don't try. The masks are off here, you screwball bitch, so stay off my back about your sensitive nature or get a divorce." He turned and walked to his room.

She paced trying to calm down. He came back wearing his parka and jeans. "Where are you going?" she asked, surprised he was leaving.

"To get some real food, I'm starved."

She raised an eyebrow. "Oh really? Where? At Jeneil's place?"

Peter studied her. He had found her Achilles heel. Jeneil's name alone made her rage. He grinned. "You'll never know, bitch. You'll never know so eat your heart out." He zippered his jacket and headed for the door.

"You're totally disgusting. You're boorish and pigheaded, completely uncivilized."

He stopped at the door. "Hey, the name's Chang, you don't like it, don't look." He opened the door. "Or get a divorce," he added, and walked out.

She stomped her foot growing furious at how Jeneil would laugh hysterically because she couldn't keep him in the apartment alone with her for an hour. She burst into tears as rage filled her. "Don't push me, Chang. You won't like it if I get mad." She paced, raging at an absent Peter. "We're in this mess because of you and I owe your mousey mistress, too. You're both uncivilized. I called her to apologize and she treats me like a servant she can dismiss. I know your weak spot, Peter Chang. Jeneil's your big weakness, that's obvious, so don't push me. Just don't. Who do they think they are? I hate this mess, too. They're not the only ones suffering." Sitting on the sofa, she sobbed. "This doesn't seem fair." She punched a cushion and stood up quickly. Going to the telephone, she dialed and waited then asked to speak to her grandfather. He was talking to Peter's grandfather and being concerned both went to the telephone. "Grandfather!" she sobbed.

"Uette, what's wrong?" her grandfather asked, and Peter's grandfather tensed as he prepared for bad news.

"He…he's…awful, just awful," she sobbed.

"What do you mean he's awful? What happened? You'll have to calm down Uette, I can't understand you," her grandfather said, and Peter's grandfather took a deep breath. He had hoped Peter would have lasted longer than this before exploding.

"He's not even nice to me and he's already gone," she wept bitterly.

"He's gone? Gone where? Shall I come over?"

"No. Well, maybe. What should I do?"

"About what, Uette? I still don't understand. Where is Peter?" he asked, struggling to make sense of what she was saying.

"He's gone to Jeneil's probably. If he doesn't stay away from her, how can I make this marriage work? He won't even give me a chance. He's so mean to me. We had an argument and he left."

"What did you argue about?"

She sighed. "Oh, you know arguments. One says something and the other adds to it until its way out of control."

Her grandfather furrowed his brow. "Well, if you've argued then he's probably gone to cool down."

"With Jeneil!" she shouted, and began crying again. "What an awful wedding night! I can't believe this!"

Her grandfather was surprised. "Uette, you didn't really expect any romance, did you?"

"Well, I didn't expect an argument either. Can't you do something?"

"Like what?" he asked, puzzled.

"I don't know," she cried again.

"Why don't you calm down, pull yourself together so you can be in control of yourself when he comes back. I'll call you in a little while to check on the situation."

"That makes sense. You're right. I look like a horror story right now." She sighed. "Thank you, Grandfather. I don't feel so alone now."

Her grandfather felt compassion for her. "Good, Uette. You sound like you're more in control of yourself. Now think before acting."

"You're right," she said softly. "I should know that. I guess I'm just so frustrated with his mistress there to comfort him. Grandfather, I'd be a good wife to him if he'd only give me a chance. I really love him."

"Then you'll have to prove that, won't you?" Her grandfather was touched by her sincerity, hopeful that this high-strung granddaughter of his might be able to succeed.

"Yes," she said. "Thank you, Grandfather. What I need is a husband like you, but they don't make your kind anymore."

He smiled. "I'll call you later." He sighed after hanging up.

Peter's grandfather was afraid to ask for details. "What is it, Lu?"

"Oh, Liam, they argued and Peter left. She's disappointed. This is such a mess. I'm wondering if this was wise."

"It was necessary, Lu."

Uette's grandfather sighed again. "I suppose, but there's so much unhappiness."

"It's living with the harvest, Lu. One of them is lying and the other is suffering an injustice. We need to remember that."

Uette's grandfather nodded. "You're right, you're right."

Peter's grandfather sighed glad he had offset Uette's affect. "Shall I call Peter later and bring him into line?"

Uette's grandfather shook his head. "No, Liam, the plan is I take complaints about Peter and you take complaints about Uette. I'll call Peter. I just don't know what to do. I can't make him stop seeing Jeneil."

Peter's grandfather was stunned. "Seeing Jeneil?"

"Yes," Uette's grandfather replied. "Uette is convinced that's where Peter is now."

"No, Lu. Something's wrong here. Jeneil isn't even in town."

"She's not?" Uette's grandfather was surprised. "But Uette sounded so certain."

"Lu, believe me, Jeneil is in Boston and she has told Peter that they are separated until he settles this. She is honorable. My life would be safe gambled on her word. I know her."

Uette's grandfather studied him. "You like the girl, don't you?"

Peter's grandfather choked up. "I do. She's a very rare breed and I pain for her hurt here."

"That's enough for me. I won't hear of her name mentioned again. She has been degraded enough. This is between Uette and Peter."

"Thank you, Lu. Jeneil was the first one to act honorably in this mess. She encouraged Peter to save face."

"Oh, the victims that this lie has caused."

"Victim, Lu. Jeneil is the only clear and innocent victim; she isn't responsible for any of the cause yet is sharing the result. That's an injustice she won't ever be repaid for and I worry how much damage she'll suffer. I'm worried about her like she's my own. She's a gentle, sensitive girl."

Uette's grandfather shook his head. "I thought Uette was, but this situation has turned her into someone I don't recognize. She's always been different from her sisters, strong-willed, but this Uette is new to me. I'm worried about her too, Liam."

Peter's grandfather patted the other man's shoulder. "Let's hope truth will be good for all people involved."

*****

Peter sat in the parking lot of a fast food restaurant finishing the coffee he'd bought, the cheeseburgers having settled his stomach. He sighed and stretched, tired from the tension of the day but too keyed up to relax. He had been to the market and bought basic food items, and had decided to swing by the dorm to pick up some of his books and magazines to pass the time. He thought about Jeneil. It was hard for him to believe she was only two years older than Uette. Jeneil was always in control of herself. She knew how to make a home, to protect her life, her health, and to care for a man as well. She was in business reluctantly, but she saw to those details. She was trusted enough by Mandra to be put on the board of the foundation, and she had even managed to grow up in a few months and become sexually and emotionally mature enough to be Chang's equal if not his superior.

Peter shook his head thinking of the person Uette was. "Pregnant and bringing in pastries and champagne, an actress who has trouble being real in reality. It has to be more than the two years Jeneil has on her." He sighed and reached into the grocery bag for the aspirin. Taking two with the rest of his coffee, he pushed the trash into one bag and started the engine and headed for the dorms.

A redone and touched up Uette was sitting on the sofa browsing through a magazine when she heard Peter. She sat up straight, watching as he walked in carrying a box and two grocery bags. "Want some help?" she asked, standing up.

"Yes, take the bag from my hand," he said, and she did and took the one on the box, too. "Just basics; milk, bread, that stuff. Can you cook?"

"Sort of," she answered indignantly. "And I can read so that means I can learn to cook by reading a cookbook. It doesn't require a PhD."

"Do you have a cookbook?"

"My mother gave me one but I bought one that I've seen advertised. I think I'll like it better. Really, what's to domestic life? Is there a mystery to cleaning and vacuuming?"

"That depends, so I've heard."

"On what?"

"On whether you want to make a career of it or you want it done quickly."

She wrinkled her brow. "Domesticity is boring."

"Life's full of details that demand attention," he cautioned.

She shrugged. "So life gets lived. What's the big deal? Do you want me to make something for you? I can scramble eggs. Did you buy eggs?"

He nodded. "But I stopped and ate."

"Then I'll just put these away." She headed toward the kitchen then stopped. "I'm sorry I got nasty," she said gently.

Peter went to his bedroom with the box and Uette sighed and went to the kitchen. He was feeling better since having eaten and taken aspirin. The telephone rang but Uette didn't answer. He picked it up as she rushed from the kitchen.

"Peter, this is Uette's grandfather. Is everything calm now?" he asked, and Peter was confused then realized Uette must have called him.

"Seems to be," Peter answered.

"Uette told me you two argued and that you left. Have you settled the problem?"

"Yes, I went out to get some food. She had only pastries and champagne here. I told her I was going out to get food. I was starved."

Her grandfather sighed, embarrassed realizing his granddaughter had used him. "She's not very skilled in domestic life I'm afraid."

Peter raised his eyebrows. "She not only lacks skills, she lacks the instinct for it, too. She concentrated on a completely new wardrobe from her grandmother and never thought past pastries and champagne. Her balloon doesn't land, Mr. Wong."

"What new wardrobe?" her grandfather asked.

"The one her grandmother gave her the money to buy."

Uette's grandfather groaned. "That must be my son's mother-in-law."

Peter grinned. "The one who's a totally in-the-now person?"

"That's her." Uette's grandfather sighed. "How can I help?"

"Everything's fine. I bought some food. I'll go shopping tomorrow and pick up some things for the week. I don't have time to teach her so she's on her own. I can help by looking after myself. She doesn't lack confidence. She thinks there's not much to domestic life so she'll have it mastered by Monday I guess." Peter chuckled.

Uette's grandfather smiled. "I like you, Peter. I'll let you get back to what you were doing. It sounds like you've gotten things under control."

"I'm sorry you were called."

"It's okay, Peter, it's all part of it I'm learning. Goodnight."

"Goodnight," Peter answered, and hung up. Uette stared at him anxiously. Peter shook his head disgustedly and went to his room.

Uette's grandfather dialed Peter's grandfather immediately. "Liam, I've just talked to Peter. I owe you an apology. I'm sure you've been concerned since Uette called."

"Then is everything settled?" Peter's grandfather was hopeful.

"Yes, thanks to Peter. He only left to buy food. My granddaughter had only pastry and champagne in the house so he went to the market. Liam, she knew that. He told her he was going for food." He sighed heavily. "How could she even think that meant he was with Jeneil? Uette isn't stupid so what's happening to her?"

Peter's grandfather wanted to tell him she was getting caught in the web of lies she'd weaved but he held back. "Lu, I think it's the tension of the day. It's an odd marriage, we can expect odd behavior."

Uette's grandfather nodded. "Liam, this is teaching me a lot of things. Now I understand why grandfathers are patriarchs."

"Why's that?"

"Because grandfathers are usually retired, they're the only ones with enough time to handle the pettiness."

Peter's grandfather laughed. "That's funny, Lu, and probably full of truth."

Uette's grandfather laughed. "Well, it can't be my understanding and wisdom. My granddaughter knew how to manipulate me too easily. Liam, I'm very impressed with Peter. It isn't looking too good for Uette, but I can't help enjoy watching what's happening from Peter. He's a man, Liam. The kind we don't see too often anymore. I only wish his marriage to my granddaughter was a natural one because he looks like a wonderful choice for a husband."

"Thank you, Lu. That's really good to hear under the circumstances. Thank you for calling. I was concerned."

Peter's grandfather sat thinking about his grandson after the call ended. He hoped Peter would finish the trial with as good a beginning as he had. This was only the first night in an ugly situation and he hoped the nights were going to be few. Who could tell what kind of damage would result from it and to how many people.

*****

Peter stretched out on his bed and took a medical magazine from the box but none of the articles caught his attention. He traded it for a textbook but he couldn't zero in on that either. He put it back in the box and spotted the book, *White Fang*. He smiled and picked it up. Holding it against him, it made Jeneil seem closer. He touched the ID bracelet and undid the clasp so he could take it off to look at the inscription. He remembered the ceremony at the beach house and the love and unity he had felt. Now that had been a real wedding ceremony, not a circus. It had involved a man who had found life and the perfect woman to share it with. It was perfect; they had even fit into the universe around them. The warm memory filled him and he smiled thinking of how Jeneil's lopsidedness always seemed to make sense when he was living it with her. He enjoyed living at tilt and she lived at tilt when she slipped off the conveyor belt and free floated. He chuckled thinking Jeneil would have just smiled and said, "You are waxing poetic, Chang."

"Comes from living with a lopsided lit major, Irish," he said, half aloud. He smiled and held the book closer as if it was Jeneil then he opened the hard cover and began to read. He wondered what message Jeneil thought he'd get from a story about two men sledding a human corpse through the frozen wilderness, but the adventure caught his attention and he continued reading. There was a gentle knocking at the door. He was annoyed by the interruption as the story was taking an interesting twist but he called to Uette to come in.

"Oh, you're reading." She smiled warmly. "What book is it?"

"*White Fang*."

She thought for a moment. "Oh, the wolfdog; I had to read that in school. I think they threw it on the list to keep the boys happy. It didn't keep my interest and I was glad when it was finished. It's a boy's book. I like books where I can imagine myself in the part." Peter found her remark interesting since Jeneil was impressed with the book enough to want him to read it. She had enjoyed it and found messages in it.

"What do you want?"

"I wondered if you would like to have dessert and champagne," she said, doing her best to look innocent.

"No thanks. I'm not hungry and I really don't drink. I'm relaxing here with my book."

She shrugged and backed out the door. "Okay, I just thought I'd ask. Good night," she said, slightly awkward and closed the door quietly.

He shook his head. "She's going to be a pain in the ass." He returned to the story.

Uette turned off the apartment lights feeling discouraged and alone. She walked to her bedroom slowly and stood outside Peter's room for a second. This marriage could be very damaging to her self-image; the great Peter Chang alone with her and he reads a book about a bunch of savage animals. He wasn't normal. Maybe Karen was right; Jeneil might have really messed him up. She sighed and continued to her bedroom. Peter Chang was a fool. They could have had some real fun. She turned on the lamp and looked around at all the candles she had in place to create an erotic evening.

Undoing the zipper on her dress, she grinned. She could wait. Eventually she'd undo the damage Jeneil had done and he'd enjoy an evening in a room full of candles. She'd bet Jeneil had never done that with Peter, even in that hotel in Vermont. She giggled at the thought. Oh, not Miss Mouse and candles, she'd be too afraid it would damage the dull routine of sex with her. A sunset? Oh, Jeneil, you get Peter Chang alone and show him sunsets, you wouldn't hold onto him anyway. Sunsets weren't for Peter Chang. She'd bet Jeneil even dragged him to classical music concerts. Poor Peter, what kind of damage had she done to that marvelously savage animal? Now he just read about them instead of being one. She sighed. Boy, what damage people could cause to other relationships.

*****

Jeneil and Steve climbed the stairs quietly and slipped into her apartment. The building was hushed. "It's two-thirty in the morning!" she whispered, looking at her watch.

"You don't have to whisper." He chuckled. "There's no one asleep."

She smiled. "This was crazy fun, a semi-malfunction. I love dancing with you."

"Dinner and the play were fun, too." He smiled and helped her off with her fur jacket.

"Yes, they were, but the dancing used up energy and I needed that." She sighed. "Let me put my jacket away." Since looking at her watch that afternoon and realizing that Peter was married to Uette, she had to struggle against the empty feeling inside of her. Now that she was standing alone in the darkened bedroom, she especially felt discouraged and alone. It drained her of the high spirits the fun evening had provided. She put her jacket away quickly and returned to Steve.

"I'd better leave."

"Oh, really?" she answered. She smiled but Steve sensed her disappointment. "Be careful going home." She put her arms around him for a hug. He held her and felt her clinging and he knew she was fragile.

"What burst your balloon?" he asked, holding her closer to comfort her.

"I'm feeling discouraged and alone. It'll pass. This is a tough night for me," she said, trying hard not to cry.

"Then we'll stay up all night," he said, kissing her temple tenderly.

"We can't," she said, pulling away. "That's too crazy. You'd never catch up with your sleep. You can't go into surgery tired on Monday." She shook her head. "No, we can't."

He looked at her. "Then I'll sleep here and we'll get an early start on tomorrow's fun."

She smiled and touched his cheek lovingly. "The care and attention you show me leaves me stunned. You're so good to me."

He took her hand from his cheek and held it, squeezing it gently. "Returning favors, beautiful. You're very special to me."

She gave him a quick hug. "I'd like you to sleep here, I really would. I don't want to be alone tonight."

He smiled, loving it when she reached out for love. Her honesty about her feelings got to him. "Then it's settled," he said. "Let's fix up the sofa bed."

Steve took off his overcoat and Jeneil put it in the small living room closet before helping him prepare the sofa bed. There was always an extra robe and pajamas she kept in case Hollis or Bill got stranded there on a visit. Steve lay in bed thinking how natural it was to be here in the apartment with her. The feeling that she belonged to him wouldn't go away. He had spent weeks lecturing himself about how foolish it was to give words to the feeling, but nothing worked. In his mind, she remained his. That's what made it so difficult to understand Peter's neglect of her for the week he was at his grandfather's. He thought about that week and sighed. He knew he'd never be able to leave her alone like that. Never. He couldn't leave her unprotected. Something deep inside of him knew that instinctively and strengthened the feeling that she was his. He understood her life like she was a part of him. What incredible damage had been caused in their lives during that week by such a strange set of circumstances. He felt for the pain she was suffering. She didn't deserve to be hurt like that. She was gentle and caring. She lived in love. It was her fuel. He smiled thinking about her as he drifted to sleep.

*****

Peter felt slightly disoriented as he opened his eyes. He couldn't place his surroundings and then he remembered. He groaned and turned onto his side. The apartment was quiet and then he heard rushing footsteps to the bathroom. Uette was sick. Peter grinned. Hormone imbalance, welcome to motherhood. He got up and put on his robe then went to the bathroom door. The doctor in him surfaced automatically knowing of the complications of what people considered simply throwing up.

"Uette do you need help?" he asked, through the door. "Why are you crying?"

"Why is this happening?" she groaned, and Peter wondered if he understood her question, it seemed so ignorant. "Oh my gosh!" she shouted, opening the door and flying past him to the kitchen where smoke was coming from the stove. He watched her push at the smoking skillet sending it crashing to the floor, spilling food as it tumbled and rolled. She jumped back then gave out a scream, stomping her foot as well. "I hate all this. I hate it." She began to cry. "Why is this happening?" Peter took a towel and picked up the hot skillet, putting it into the sink. He looked around then took a plate and spatula and scooped up what looked like strange eggs.

"Where's the trash can?"

"I don't know. I don't have one." She sat down at the table feeling weak.

Peter put the plate on the counter. "Is there a sponge or a mop to clean the floor?"

"No, I don't have those either." She sighed, wiping tears. Peter shook his head wondering what else she had overlooked. The floor needed to be cleaned.

"Do you have any cleaning fluids?"

"There's a bottle under the sink. It was left here. Maybe it's cleaning fluid." She put her head down on the table. He got the bottle; there was a half inch of floor cleaner in it.

"No bucket either?" he asked, and she shook her head. "I should have known," he said to himself as he went back to the bathroom which smelled of vomit. In her haste to save the kitchen, she hadn't flushed the remains of her morning sickness. Her violent convulsions had caused her to miss the bowl. That needed cleaning, too. Peter leaned against the sink and rubbed his forehead. "I think her middle name is catastrophe." He sighed and picked up the small wastebasket he had gone there to get and flushed the bowl.

Carrying the wastebasket back to the kitchen with hot water in it, he added the cleaner. Taking the kitchen towel, he tore it in several places to indicate it was now trash and he used it to clean up the floor. He headed to the bathroom and began cleaning it. Having finished, he washed his hands. "Well, she remembered soap anyway." He looked into the mirror; the shower looked strange. He looked around, no towels. He went to his room for one of his that he had packed. What was it about the shower? Going back, there were frilly curtains held back by ties. He shrugged then realized the curtain you close while you shower was missing. He began to laugh. She was a total screwball, he thought as he laughed hysterically. She moved into sight near the door and Peter stopped laughing.

"What's so funny?" she asked, and he looked at her. She was wearing a light blue satin nightgown and a matching robe that wasn't closed. It didn't look like it was designed to. Peter got the distinct impression it was supposed to be alluring. She had grease splattered near the hem and morning sickness had destroyed the alluring quality of the lacy top.

Peter cleared his throat to keep from laughing. "I, uh…I just realized that the shower's not complete."

"I know but it isn't my fault. I went to Bed and Bath Boutique and chose what I liked and told the stupid sales girl to put whatever I'd need for a complete bathroom together matching the colors I chose. There was no tank top and the shower curtain was missing. She completely bungled my order." Uette looked at the bathroom. "You cleaned up?" He nodded and she sighed. "I'm sorry. I don't understand why this is happening. I'm not a klutz. I'm fairly intelligent yet I'm not bringing this all together."

Peter shrugged. "You're out of your natural element."

"Oh now really, any animal walking upright can be taught to keep house. It's hardly skilled labor."

Peter shrugged again. "Have it your way. I've heard it mentioned at the hospital that unsalted crackers settle a sick stomach during pregnancy."

Uette smiled. "High tech, huh?"

"Hey, if it works why knock it?"

"That's true and after this morning I'll try anything." She looked at her outfit and gasped. "Oh, how disgusting and the shower curtain is missing." She groaned. "Why is my luck so lousy?"

Peter suddenly realized he hadn't helped put the apartment together; life could be hell with problems and mistakes. "Uette, let's go through the apartment and find out what's missing so we can buy what's needed."

"But there are wedding gifts. We could end up buying what's been given as a gift."

"Okay then let's bring the gifts here and get organized. I have the envelopes from the wedding. I'll go through them and mark the amount on the card. We'll use that to go shopping."

"You'll help me?" she asked, very surprised and very touched.

"I'll help you get organized," he said, uncomfortable with her reaction.

"Thank you, Peter. You've been very decent about the horror this morning." She noticed his robe. Somehow she hadn't pictured him in a robe but she liked it. It suited him. She noticed the pocket. "A preppie robe? Alligators, too?"

"It's a Dragon," he corrected. He didn't like her looking him over. "I'll get dressed so we can move out." Uette was encouraged by the sound of 'we' and went to change, too.

Peter paced in the living room waiting for Uette. He hated to sit down. The white sofa made him uncomfortable. At least Jeneil's was dark so he could sprawl out and not worry. Yeah, he grinned, even wrestle. He sighed and looked at his watch. "Uette, let's move out."

His voice thrilled her and she liked hearing him call her name. She checked her outfit in the mirror. Oh, how she loved boots. He stared at her as she walked into the living room.

"Why are you so dressed up?"

"I like dressing up."

"We're going to a discount store. You look like we're going out to dinner. I haven't even had breakfast."

She smiled. "Then let's eat breakfast out."

"Fast food."

"Ugh, I hate that stuff." She wrinkled her nose.

"No restaurant," he said, determined. "They're too slow and I'm not dressed."

"Then let's eat at my family's house. They always have food around."

"No, you take your car to your house, open the gifts and make a list then pack them up. I'll take the shopping list and go to the discount store for cleaning things. I'll meet you at your parent's house and pack what doesn't fit in your car in mine."

"But," she looked disappointed, "we were going to have breakfast."

"You eat at your parent's and I'll stop for fast food, then we can have what we want."

"But," she said, thrown off guard.

He ignored her stammering. "I've marked the cards. The checks are with them. I'd like to put the receipts in an envelope so you know where your money went."

"Our money," she reminded him.

"No." He shook his head. "All this stuff is yours. I just don't want the money squandered. I'm leaving with what I brought. I don't think it was fair to have people spend money on gifts knowing the wedding was a phony. This is all your stuff. I don't want to touch it."

She sighed. "You sound as old fashioned as my father."

Peter smiled. "Don't try to flatter me. My mind's made up."

"Flatter you! Not hardly."

"I'm leaving. I'll meet you at your parent's house." He opened the door and left.

She shook her head. "You're impossible, Peter Chang. Just when I think the wind is blowing my way, you cross current and change directions." She sighed and went to get her purse. But at least he was helping. That was an improvement. He must care a little. She smiled. Now really, her ego would be inflated to think that he'd be that easy. He was tempered steel; she didn't want to change him, did she? Jeneil had done enough damage. Offer him the freedom to be himself and he was hers. She headed to her parent's home feeling very cheerful.

Uette arrived in time for family brunch. Her sisters were surprised she was alone; her mother was surprised by her cheerfulness and new clothes. Her father watched and listened, absorbing the fact that Peter was helping her set up the apartment and had helped her after she'd been so clumsy in the kitchen. He watched his daughter closely having called his father earlier and learned how she had tried to manipulate him into taking action against Jeneil.

*****

Adrienne went to ring the apartment buzzer and was surprised to hear laughter. Jeneil answered smiling and Adrienne walked in trying to switch her approach. She had come to cheer Jeneil up thinking she'd be really down after Peter's wedding. She smiled at a shirt-sleeved Steve Bradley and noticed the sofa bed was unmade and had been slept in.

"Excuse the mess, we had a late night and slept in this morning."

Adrienne noticed 'we' and it sounded so natural. She was slightly surprised. "I'm family," she answered, "spit and polish is for strangers."

"Want some coffee?" Jeneil asked.

"Yes, I think I will have some." She joined them at the dining table wanting a closer look at 'we.' She remembered Jeneil telling her that Peter thought there was more on Steve's part than just friendship. The cheerfulness around the table caught her off guard and she decided Steve was good for Jeneil. He had a quick wit and that was charming, and Jeneil was a good audience and opponent for his wit. Adrienne liked him and decided to relax. Jeneil seemed cheerful and at this point in the craziness that was fine with Adrienne. It was deserved as far as she could tell. He was Peter's good friend and he showed real concern for Jeneil. The 'we' looked very healthy. "What are you two doing today?" she asked, finishing her coffee, curious about how they filled their time together.

Steve shrugged. "It's Jeneil's choice."

Adrienne looked at Jeneil and smiled. "He's a rare breed. He's in service to a woman."

Jeneil smiled at him impishly. "I've decided on the fun. Now that Dr. Bradley is Dr. Bradley, let's tour the sports car circuit."

Steve smiled broadly. "Are you serious?" he asked, and Jeneil nodded. He raised his eyebrows hopefully. "Do you think you could put up with the car expo at the Civic Center?"

"Sure, I think I'm mature enough now to be introduced to the delights of cam engines and fuel injections."

He smiled at her and squeezed her wrist. "We'll stop by my place and I'll change."

Adrienne saw how close they were; they really liked each other. She knew husbands and wives who weren't that sensitive to each other. The thought that their closeness could be dangerous crossed her mind, but Jeneil seemed so cheerful that she dismissed it.

*****

Peter headed toward the fast food restaurant near the discount store to kill some time since it was so early. Finding himself near Jeneil's neighborhood, he couldn't resist the desire to drive down her street. He wrestled with the idea to stop by and say hi. The house was coming into view; he slowed down fighting with himself. The new apartment and having Uette around made him feel disconnected. He just wanted to see Jeneil, maybe just hold her to settle his mind. He looked in the lot; her car was there and then he noticed the burgundy Lynx next to it.

"Steve?" Peter drove past the house. "What the hell is he doing here so early?" He remembered that Steve always parked on the street unless he slept at the apartment. His stomach tightened. "That son-of-a-bitch slept there. Boy, he's enjoying looking after her." He sighed as anger began to fill him. "Shit, this mess is going to cost too much. I know it. I can feel it!"

He pulled away from the corner and reminded himself to slow down, but an uneasiness had settled inside of him that couldn't be rationalized away. The uneasiness stayed with him after he'd done his shopping and had gotten to Uette's house. Her cheerfulness irritated him as he thought about Steve with Jeneil. He felt strangled and imprisoned by the situation. He was sullen and silent. Uette's mother managed not to glare at him, but she wasn't cheerful either. It was rather like she tolerated his intrusion into her normally quiet life. He got up and paced in the living room needing to keep moving.

Uette and her sisters were oooing and awing. Mr. Wong watched Peter closely. He could see that Peter was elsewhere. His father's words about the dessert and champagne Uette had provided and how Peter had handled it impressed him, along with Uette's cheerfulness about Peter's help in setting up the apartment. She had told her father about being sick and how Peter had offered to help and even cleaned up after her. He agreed with his father that it was a shame the marriage wasn't real.

"Can I get you anything, Peter?" Mr. Wong asked. "Coffee?"

"No thanks," Peter answered, continuing to pace.

"Peter, Uette told me about the help you're giving her. Thank you."

Peter stopped. "Don't thank me, Mr. Wong. I'm helping to organize the apartment because life can be a living hell with everything she has overlooked."

"Well, I'm glad you don't want it to be a living hell."

Peter looked at the floor. "Mr. Wong, I'm not a hero. If I found out who the father was tomorrow, I'd be gone."

"I understand that, Peter. I'm talking about you caring that the quality of life with her will be civilized at least."

Peter shrugged. "She's pregnant. I saw what that involves this morning."

Mr. Wong smiled. "We can't give you any blue ribbons, can we?"

Peter smiled. "I don't like being a hero to anybody." He looked into the dining room. It was a hen party. He realized he'd be waiting for hours at this rate. "Maybe I should pack the gifts in my car and get that job done."

Mr. Wong smiled. "The Wong women like to visit with each other."

"That's fine," Peter replied, "but this Chang is getting rattled sitting around waiting. I'll get the gifts packed."

Taking the most unbreakable gifts, Peter packed them into his car until it was full. He drove to the apartment and took them inside. He was scheduled for a hip surgery and he wanted to review some points of procedure so he went to his room to look over some of his notes and research. He looked at his alarm clock and wondered what Jeneil was doing. The uneasiness about Steve returned. Going to the kitchen, he made a sandwich for lunch and returned to his room. The anger had returned. He worked out a budget for the apartment expenses and listed what Uette would be able to spend. He resented her spending his money. He resented being married to her while his real wife was being looked after by his friend. The budget irritated him and he was glad to have it finished. He heard the door open. Uette called but he didn't answer. She knocked on his door.

"Yeah?" he called softly.

"Can you help bring the gifts up?" she asked, and he sighed and threw the medical magazine across the bed.

Putting the last of the gifts with the others, he took off his jacket. "I have lunch ready," Uette said, smiling cheerfully.

"I've had lunch," he answered, and went to his room.

Uette frowned and shook her head, exasperated by the way he had avoided her since the morning. She ate slowly and decided she wasn't going to be the floundering female in this marriage. It was a role she wasn't used to playing. She decided to attack the apartment and take charge of this new life. It was a matter of pride to show Peter that she wasn't the screwball he thought she was. She wondered if that had been Jeneil's attraction; the perfect little homemaker. "Well, I can manage just as well and still leave lots of time for living. I'm not a mouse, Peter, and I'll change your preference for nondescript women of low IQs. Jeneil's going to be a passing thought. I've decided that's how it will be and that's that." She nibbled at a potato chip and grinned.

Twenty-Four

Uette threw herself into organizing the apartment. Putting away the wedding gifts, she decided to go to Bed and Bath Boutique to get her order straightened out and after that a trip to the market to get something for dinner. Peter liked real food, she thought, putting on her leather gloves. Steak, baked potatoes, and salad should be real enough for him. She smiled and went to his bedroom. She heard music and she knocked.

"Hi," she said. "You've been caged up in here most of the afternoon. Would you like to go with me for some air? I'm going to get the bathroom order taken care of."

Peter shook his head. "I have some studying to do."

She nodded. "That's important but don't eat anything. I'll get some steaks for dinner."

He looked at her. "Do you work?"

"I had a modeling job but I quit that a month ago. Why?"

"Because this is the budget," he said, picking up a sheet of paper from the nightstand and handing it to her. "The circled figure is what's available for food and other necessities. Steak isn't cheap."

"Okay," she said, smiling, "I'll manage but we'll have steak tonight at least."

He shrugged. "Just stay within the budget."

"No problem. I'll be back in an hour or so. Okay?"

Peter sighed as Uette closed the door and he wondered if he should have been more specific and explained that other necessities meant gas money. He was concerned. He and Jeneil managed because her apartment was inexpensive and she was willing to cooperate. She had three jobs really. The corporation and the foundation gave her a small salary and her car lease and upkeep were part of a deal from the corporation. She had a thing about avoiding money and would rather be paid in fringe benefits. Peter smiled thinking about her. She lived at tilt but life ran smoothly knowing how to avoid trouble and manage life well. He missed her and the thought of Steve staying at the apartment overnight hit his chest again. There had to be a reasonable explanation.

Getting up, he went to the telephone and dialed her number. "Her rules shit," he said out loud. "When I get an answer about Steve, I won't call again." He let it ring several times but there was no answer. He sighed and hung up, sprawling across the bed wondering where they were, becoming more irritated realizing in his mind they were now a couple.

"Shit," he said, sitting up and rubbing his face. Opening the nightstand drawer, he took out the small brown box. Pushing aside the ragged washcloth, he lifted out the fragile glass unicorn. "When the prince returns this, the princess will keep her promise to marry him." He smiled thinking of Jeneil's words and he remembered the kiss she had put on the unicorn. *Now you'll always have my kiss with you,* she had said. "Guinevere is fine but I'm worried about Lancelot," he said, and then felt guilty about the way his friendship with Steve was going. Holding the unicorn in one hand, he picked up the textbook again and found himself concentrating on the words. Studying went well after that.

The apartment door opened and Peter heard the rustling of paper bags heading toward the kitchen. "I'm back," Uette said at his door before disappearing into her bedroom.

"Oh wait," he said, half aloud, "let me light the skyrockets I was saving." Sarcasm surfaced and he put the unicorn on the nightstand and rested the textbook on his lap. She knocked at the door but he didn't want to answer. "What is it?" he asked reluctantly.

"May I come in?"

He sighed. "Okay." The door opened. She was wearing a long silk dress that plunged in the front. He was sorry he had let her in. She smiled warmly and sat at the foot of the bed.

"I got the bathroom order straightened out," she said, smiling proudly. "Aren't you claustrophobic yet? You've been in here for hours." She shrugged and her neckline revealed more of her, something Peter felt she had rehearsed.

"I have early surgery tomorrow. Studying is part of it."

"Gosh, that's a really ugly way to start a morning. It sounds disgusting."

"It's a part of life," he said unemotionally.

"Ooo, not mine, that would annihilate me. I had no idea your life was so ghastly." She noticed the unicorn. "Oh, how cute!" she said, moving toward it.

"Don't touch it," he said quickly, wishing he had put it up. He didn't want her ruining Jeneil's magic on it.

"Someone gave it to you?" she asked suspiciously, looking at him closely.

"No, I bought it at The Glass Menagerie. It's a good luck charm. It helps me to study."

She began to laugh. "You're a riot, a surgeon who has a good luck charm. That's too funny."

"What can I say?" he replied. "I can't take a rabbit's foot into surgery. The patients need to trust me, so I think of my unicorn."

She smiled as she studied him. "You're more sensitive than you let people see," she said quietly, sitting by his legs.

"Uette, I really need to study," he said, not believing how forward she was by sitting so close to him.

"Okay, I'll put dinner together." She smiled, leaning forward slightly to use her neckline to its best advantage. "I bought real food."

"Good," he answered, "but Uette watch the spending. That circled figure is for food and car expenses. I do my own car repairs but I won't touch your Corvette, it's too pedigreed, so that money has to cover your car, too."

"Money, money, money." She grinned. "I like it better when you're studying with your unicorn." She patted his knee and stood up slowly. "I'll make dinner. You must be hungry by now." He watched her as she went to the door and turned, leaning against the frame. "You really should relax a little. You need to be careful of your health, Doctor." She smiled and closed the door.

Peter continued staring at the door as anger began to stir. Jeneil was right, Uette was two people. The lying little bitch, did she really think he was that easy? He knew what hunger she was thinking about and hell would freeze over before she'd get to him. She was skilled in displaying herself and she could bet he was going to find out exactly where she'd been performing that little act. He threw the textbook down on the bed and picked up the glass unicorn.

"She almost touched you. She won't even see you from now on. She's not clean enough. Her heart's not pure. Nothing about her is. I'm convinced of that." He sighed. "Baby, unless I'm seeing wrong, she's a pro. A lying pro, but how the hell has she gotten past the community? How far can she have them believing she's an innocent?"

He took the brown box and nestled the glass unicorn in the washcloth and put the box in the deeper drawer of the nightstand. Going to the box of medical magazines, he took a few and put them in the drawer over the box. He paced and remembered his grandfather's warning about Uette, the game he was involved in becoming a little clearer. She was two people; the one at the Wong house with her sisters and the other a seductive lying bitch who was in the kitchen making his dinner.

He wondered how to play his hand. It was obvious she was skilled around men; he had caught a glimpse of that a few minutes ago. He was tempted to go to the kitchen and play her little game to trick her into revealing some facts about herself but he thought better of it. He had never liked women like her and avoided her type. They always made him feel like they thought he was weak and could be easily had, like he was a joke of a man who could be manipulated.

Ki was the one who could handle them and had said the subtly seductive type fell into two categories; those who were inexperienced and had learned the wiggles from movies and the real bona fide pro who was usually wiggling her ass for something. Most times it was for more than just sex. He also said you go to bed with that type hiding a knife along your jaw bone. Both girls like that Peter had seen in the groupies had turned out to be plants from other gangs. Ki always tightened security when new girls showed up and he would plant false stories then listen for echoes on the streets.

Peter smiled wishing he had let Ki teach him how to squeeze the truth out of them, but he hadn't been that interested. He never liked being around girls he felt he couldn't trust. That's why he had his rule; you smile at anyone else and you're his. He wished now that he was less rigid about relationships and then laughed thinking how he had Uette compared to the groupie spies. While he didn't think she was an innocent playing at sophistication, he couldn't believe she was that much of a pro. The Chinese community was too tight to miss it and they had her on the straight and level. But she wasn't and the confusion wore him down and he had other things to concentrate on.

He wished he had Steve's ability to grasp things quickly. It was Steve who got him through math, even making sense out of it. He sighed. This bitch was going to be tough and he didn't have time to play games. He was annoyed at her for putting him in this spot. Lying across the bed, he thought about Jeneil. He loved her simplicity. She had no tricks in her life. He could trust her. She didn't lie. He remembered the beach house and how she hadn't told him the full truth about owning it. And Mantra's estate, she had kept that from him, too. But that was different. Her privacy was important and she didn't think the money was hers. She was protecting her simple lifestyle. He smiled remembering the car for three-hundred dollars he thought about buying and why he had accepted Jeneil's offer and how Uette's made him furious.

"They're not even alike," he said, sitting up. "Jeneil would never hurt anyone with a vicious lie."

Uette knocked at the door. "Dinner's ready, Peter."

He was hungry and steak sounded good. Opening the door, he went to wash his hands while she waited for him. Damn it, what a haunt, he thought, and he smiled remembering how he loved Jeneil watching him shave. He loved Jeneil watching him do anything. He could see the difference love made. Love had to be protected. It was the magic that made a relationship work and he wondered what made people love each other.

The dining table was set with candles and flowers. Peter saw the champagne and caution signs began popping in his mind as he sat down. She wouldn't have the nerve to suggest a toast to the two of them.

"Will you uncork the champagne?" she asked, smiling as she sat across from him. He did and she held up her glass for him to fill it.

"You're pregnant," he reminded her.

She frowned. "Oh please, Peter, in a few months I'll be bloated and misshapen. While I'm still feeling human, let me enjoy myself." He filled her glass and put the bottle back in the ice bucket. "You're not having champagne?"

"I have early surgery tomorrow."

"Yes, I know, a hip case, so what?"

"I'm assisting. It's like being in training for the Olympics or pro sports."

"Get real," she laughed, "you're putting me on."

"Would you like a surgeon working on you with a hangover?"

"You won't get drunk on a glass."

"It's in your blood. What difference does the degree make?"

"But you were drinking the night...that night I was at your house," she said, watching her words.

"I had a shot of bourbon, less than a shot really, and I needed to sleep. I wasn't in surgery, I was on floor duty and I was living on coffee."

She stared at him. "Your life is so rigid."

"Did you think being a doctor was glamorous?"

She shrugged. "Well, people oh and aw when you tell them your husband's a doctor."

Peter laughed. "They probably feel sorry for you."

She smiled. "I find your humility charming."

"Can I eat now?"

"Of course," she answered. "What would you like to drink?"

"Water's fine," he said, lifting his steak knife. "I'll get Ovaltine later."

"Ovaltine? That's a kid's drink."

"I like it," he answered, trying to cut his steak. Uette was trying to cut hers and having the same trouble.

"What kind of steak is this?" she pouted.

Peter cut a sliver. "It's easier to cut in thin slices."

She sighed. "Wonderful, the potato will be cold and the salad wilted."

"I don't care, I'm hungry," he said, continuing to eat.

She laughed. "You are so gallant."

"I'm hungry," he answered, "don't make it more than that." The steak was tough and chewy; he missed Jeneil's steak sauce. The potato was fine and there was something missing in the salad. Jeneil's had all kinds of things in it. Uette's was lettuce, tomato, cucumbers, and the tomato was slimy. He decided he didn't like bottled salad dressing, but it was food and he was hungry. "Do you have any questions about the budget?"

"Oh no, we're not going to talk about money again, are we?" She wrinkled her nose.

He looked up. "Uette, you know what I earn. You don't have a job. Face reality. There won't be much money. We're lucky your father is helping."

"Well, how did you and Jeneil manage?" she asked curiously.

"Are you kidding?" He sat back. "The apartment was cheap, she made her clothes, and she knew how to manage money. She can live on almost nothing."

Uette raised her eyebrow. "Why did I even ask, I was sure it had to be nothing short of a miracle. Jeneil walks on water." She looked at Peter distrustfully. "Wait a minute. Didn't Karen tell me that her father left her a small business or something?"

"That's one of her jobs. She has to work hard at it." Peter grinned boastfully.

Uette smiled a false smile. "Well, of course, what else would Miss Perfect do? Nothing average, I'm sure of that."

"No, she's not average," Peter said, enjoying the thought.

"Could we just not talk about her? It's hardly fair." Uette stood up to clear the dishes.

"You're the one who asked."

Uette was annoyed. "Next time I'll know better." Then, she smiled wryly. "But isn't she the type I hear about all the time? They kill themselves putting husbands through school and then get dumped."

Peter grinned, staring directly at her. "No sane man would ever dump Jeneil."

Uette became more annoyed remembering that Steve was supposedly crazy about Jeneil, too. She held up her champagne. "Oh goodness, a toast to the one and only perfect woman ever created. May she teach the rest of us inferior women how she does it."

Peter smiled broadly. "Hey, you asked for it."

"Oh, shut up." Uette stomped into the kitchen carrying her dishes. Peter cleared his and took them to the kitchen, surprising Uette. "You help with dishes?"

Peter grinned realizing it had become a habit. "Hey, don't all liberated men?"

She leaned against the counter pretending to be near fainting. "Oh my goodness, a liberated man, be still my heart."

He watched her. "Pull that again and you'll do the job alone." He turned and walked back to the dining room.

She followed quickly. "Peter that was a compliment, I've only found men who say they're liberated but they only mean they want women to work, too. They like two paychecks but don't do dishes."

"Okay, drop it," he said. "What do you want to do with the champagne?"

"Pour it down the sink. I hate flat champagne."

"Watch the waste, Uette. I mean it." He took the bucket to the kitchen.

"Oh, yes sir," she answered after he was gone. "Count on it. Anything your perfect woman can do, I can do better."

"Are you going to stay in school?" Peter asked, after Uette rejoined him.

She rinsed the dishes for the dishwasher. "Yes, I am. The semester is paid for and then I'm finished. Well my goodness, there's something I did that Jeneil hasn't. Karen said she's a college dropout, can't find herself so I hear. She's a little old for that, isn't she? It's amazing that all I hear about from you are her wonderful achievements. It's nice to know about the failures, too."

"Oh, shut up," Peter replied, and walked away.

Uette grinned as he left the room. "I hope she finds herself while you're away from her, Peter. Yeah, I really do. I hope she finds herself right in Steve's arms. What an interesting thought. I'll bet if I can hang onto this marriage for a while, Steve and Jeneil will gravitate toward each other. She's my only hurdle, I can see that. Whatever she did to him, he enjoyed it." She threw the sponge into the sink, irritated and tired of Jeneil, and now he'd go into his cave and study. She sighed. She had made that room so depressing; she thought for sure he'd be out of it. He was going to be tough but he was going to be very interesting, too. He had bought himself a unicorn. She would have thought that was something the mouse would have given him as a reminder of her. He didn't add up. A unicorn, an ID with Chang inscribed on it larger than life, and he reads, too. Be still my heart was right, sensitivity all wrapped up in that fantastic body of his. She'd wait. She'd wait patiently. He was hers without trying as soon as Jeneil and Steve found each other.

Peter went to his room irritated with himself for not following his first thought to eat dinner in his room. It was stupid to think he'd find out anything about her. Sneaking around wasn't his style and he wasn't skilled in dealing with women with words anyway. He hadn't steered it right and had ended up dumping on Jeneil. He sighed and sat down, wrestling with his textbook until he felt himself getting sleepy. Getting his robe, he took a shower and then opened the door to the bathroom only to find Uette in the hallway.

"I do like your robe," she said, grinning as she looked him over. He was tired of games and he missed Jeneil.

"Uette, why the hell are you doing this? You've snarled our lives up over this thing. Why?" he asked, his voice indicating his discouragement.

"Peter, I know it's difficult for you to accept the truth, but the baby's yours. I can wait. I'm in love with you."

He shook his head. "How the hell do you think any man could return the love having you push another guy's baby off on him? Can't you realize what an insult that is? Why do this? You can probably have your pick of guys. Why do it this way? Shit, you must know I'm crazy about Jeneil. Uette, I always will be. Why didn't you marry the baby's father?"

She sighed. "I have, Peter." She paused. "I really love you, Peter. I do. I don't have any choice. I'll wait."

He was tired and discouraged so her words didn't incite anger. "Uette, we both know I'm not the father. Don't wait for me because I know I could never trust anyone who'd pull something like this and I can't love anyone I can't trust."

Tears rolled down her face. "Goodnight, Peter." She turned and walked to her room, then stopped. "What time should I have breakfast ready?" she asked, wiping away the tears with her hand.

He shook his head. "I don't eat before early surgery."

"Okay, goodnight then," she said quietly, closing the door to her bedroom.

He put his head back and closed his eyes. "Why is she doing this? Why?"

*****

Surgery went very well and Dr. Maxwell had allowed Peter to perform quite a bit of the operation. Peter had expected that; that's why he had studied so well. Dr. Maxwell was pleased and Peter felt good about the operation, leaving the OR tired but confident.

"Tired?" Dr. Maxwell asked.

"Very," Peter answered. "Aren't you?"

"No." Dr. Maxwell grinned. "Handball and farm work keep me toned. Once you're living a normal life things pick up. Residents flirt with exhaustion."

Peter smiled. "That's encouraging."

Dr. Maxwell gave Peter's shoulder an appreciative pat. "You're damn good, Chang. Damn good."

Peter took his mask and cap to the laundry cylinder and saw Steve come out of OR2. Taking a clean gown, he changed leaving the soiled one. Steve sat on the bench near the wall and Peter went to him and sat down.

"Hi, Pete." Steve sighed. "Maxwell got you in early?"

"Yeah," Peter answered, watching Steve closely. "You seem to have early hours regularly."

Steve nodded. "Rookie duty, standard cases, part of the corporate medicine system. How's everything?" he asked, feeling bad for Peter. "Was it rough?"

Peter shrugged. "Missing Jeneil is worse."

"I can understand that," Steve said compassionately.

Peter swallowed. "What did you do over the weekend?"

"I told you about Saturday," Steve said. "We went dancing at Cappy's after the play. Sunday we went to the car expo in town." Steve smiled broadly. "Jeneil taught me to cook. I'm impressed; I didn't know steak, baked potato, and salad were so easy to put together. She took me to the market and taught me about the different cuts, too. It's not like restaurants. It's nice to know I can do more than heat soup now."

"That was your whole weekend?"

Steve chuckled. "Well excuse me, but it wore me out."

"I mean that's it? All of it?"

Steve looked puzzled. "Was I supposed to do something else?"

"No," Peter answered. "I just wondered."

"Hey, Pete." Dr. Sprague walked in suited for surgery. He extended his hand and Peter shook it. "How's it going?"

Peter shrugged. "What's to say?"

"Dr. Maxwell said you were great this morning."

"I was prepared."

Dr. Sprague smiled. "He noticed; your steadiness, too." He extended his hand again and Peter knew he had pleased the surgical staff. "Ready there, Dr. Bradley?"

"Yep." Steve got up. "Take it easy, Pete." He patted Peter's shoulder.

"Yeah, I will." Peter nodded. "Thanks, Steve."

"Sure." Steve smiled and went to scrub with Dr. Sprague.

Peter rubbed his forehead and got up, going to his locker for his lab coat before heading to the floor. He was checking medical charts when he saw Jeneil get off the elevator and walk toward the nurse's desk. She looked beautiful and the blue sweater she made was a great outfit on her. She looked warm, gentle, and soft. He thought about Steve and wondered why he hadn't mentioned staying over. He wanted to know. He wanted to hear it. His life was full of lies and he wanted truth desperately. Jeneil never looked up at him.

She left the envelopes then turned and headed back to the elevators. He needed to see her, to hear the truth. He dropped two charts on the counter and a nurse looked at him.

"Something wrong?" the nurse asked.

"I'll be right back," he said, heading for the elevator.

Morgan Rand walked out of the medical room from where he had seen Peter watching Jeneil so intently. "Did he get married yet?"

"Yes, Saturday," the nurse answered. Rand watched Peter run to catch the elevator, catching the door and slipping on with Jeneil. Rand raised his eyebrows and wondered.

Jeneil smiled, shocked to see him. "I didn't know you were coming toward the elevator."

"Jeneil, why did Steve sleep at the apartment?"

"How did you know that?"

"I drove by Sunday morning. His car was in the lot. Why?"

She put her head down. "I asked him to." Peter's heart sank. "I was feeling discouraged and alone. I hated facing an empty apartment so I asked him to stay. Why did you drive by?"

"Because I was feeling discouraged and alone and I wanted to see you. I fought with myself about stopping."

Jeneil was shocked. "Peter, you can't!"

"I know."

She smiled. "But I'm glad you wanted to. You thought about me then?"

"Are you kidding? You're hardly ever out of my thoughts." Tears filled her eyes and he touched her cheek gently. "Baby, I miss you so much," he whispered, and leaned forward and kissed her lips. The elevator slowed and they could hear people talking. Peter backed away from her as the doors opened and she got off. He sighed and got off, too.

"Peter!" she said, shocked to find him beside her.

"Baby, don't get discouraged."

"Peter, this is reckless!" she said, trying to look casual.

"I don't give a shit!" he said. "Are you listening?"

"Yes," she answered, "and you shouldn't worry either."

"I won't," he said, smiling. "I just needed to hear the truth. I feel better now." He stood so his back was to the nurse's desk. "Jeneil, I love you, remember that, okay?"

She nodded and smiled gently. "Me too, I really do. I'm finding out how much." He wanted to kiss her. That smile of hers always made him crazy.

"I have to get back on five."

She nodded. "Thanks for catching the elevator."

He smiled. "Made my day."

Peter walked back to the elevator and signaled for a car, electricity filling his chest as he watched Jeneil walk to her office. After that, he tried to make sure he was around when she delivered afternoon envelopes. He couldn't believe that one of the highlights of his day was watching for her. Morgan Rand was having trouble with the situation too, making it a point to watch the two, trying to evaluate what was happening.

Twenty-Five

Uette decided to make life pleasant. Remembering how easily Peter talked to Phyllis and Jeff, she asked them to dinner. She was tired when she got home from classes, but made meatloaf and baked potatoes and put a salad together. She had even stopped for a bottle of wine. Dinner was almost ready at six. Phyllis and Jeff arrived and they waited for Peter. Uette couldn't understand why he was so late since she had heard him up at four-thirty that morning. By seven, she was getting irritated, wondering where he was and why he hadn't called. Phyllis became concerned. The marriage didn't seem normal and she worried for her sister who had worked so hard at an evening that wasn't going to happen. Uette called the hospital at seven-ten and was told that Peter had signed out. Uette failed to ask when. She had no idea that a twelve to fourteen hour day wasn't unusual for a doctor. Totally infuriated, she went ahead with dinner for the three of them.

Peter left the hospital and found himself driving to his mother's house. He didn't want to go home to Uette. He saw the light on in the greenhouse as he drove by. Glad his grandfather was home he parked in the driveway and went to the door.

"Come in," his grandfather said, surprised, watching Peter closely. "You look tired."

"I had early surgery today."

"Are you just getting out of work?" his grandfather asked, and Peter nodded and sat down on the bench. His grandfather waited and wondered about his visit. "Why are you here?"

Peter shrugged. "It's been a tight day for me. I wanted to relax."

"You can't do that at home?"

Peter sighed. "I can't go home. Jeneil won't let me."

"You mean Uette," his grandfather corrected.

Peter looked up. "No, I mean Jeneil. That's my home. I live in a room at Uette's apartment."

"How has Uette been?"

"She's improving. I thought I was in trouble when she hadn't finished the apartment; I thought she didn't know how but she's getting her act together now. She spends money too easily though. She's saying she's in love with me."

"I know." His grandfather sighed. "That makes it very difficult. If love is passionate then it's quite a force. Uette is a very strong energy so I understand your concern. You'll have to trust the Songbird while you settle this with Uette. I don't understand your lack of trust in Jeneil."

Peter sighed. "If you knew her better, you'd understand. She's not quite together, Grandfather. She's like a kid and she doesn't know men. She's missing a natural instinct. She'll take the hand of a stranger and walk with them."

His grandfather smiled. "You can't keep the cage locked on a Songbird."

Peter shook his head. "But even you keep your birds in cages when you're not around. I can't. The greenhouse door is open and I worry about the cat getting in."

"Then you'll have to trust that Songbird's instincts."

"She doesn't have some in a few areas," Peter argued.

"Nature is strong and clever; it provides what's necessary for survival. You're used to controlling your women. Life isn't that easy and now life has introduced you to a woman who controls you through your love for her. Your rules are demanding and she has been able to satisfy them so far. Now we'll see how you've both affected each other as life opens for the two of you. Passionate love is a strong force, Peter. Passion isn't. Even love alone isn't. Passionate love is nature's force; it's more enduring in all things."

Peter shook his head. "I wish it was that easy with people. Life gets complicated when people start messing with it. Ask me, I'm living with the result of that theory right now."

His grandfather sighed. "It's a strong person who can taste life properly."

Peter nodded. "That's why I worry about Jeneil. She's gentle, sensitive, and caring. She's not equipped to handle real life. She lacks strength and toughness."

His grandfather smiled. "Peter, life's going to teach you what real strength is. I've said that survival is life's first law. Survival is a balance of instincts and intellect. Look after your own survival right now. The Songbird will continue singing."

"I can't do anything else," Peter replied. "Have you eaten?"

"You're hungry?" His grandfather got up and Peter nodded. "I'll get you something."

*****

It had been an awkward and embarrassing evening for Uette. She had no explanation to give her sister and brother-in-law for Peter's absence, although excuses were forming in her mind now that they were gone and she had time to think. "Jeneil," she sneered the name. "What else? He must have seen her at work today." She called her grandfather. "Something has to be done about him seeing Jeneil."

Her grandfather braced himself. "Uette, he doesn't see her."

She was irritated. "He works with her. He'll see her every day this week. Where would he be this late? I won't have it. We get along until she's around."

"Uette, Mr. Chang told me that the girl is being honorable. He trusts her."

Uette paced. "She has him hypnotized, too. Karen told me that."

"That's ridiculous, Uette. Mr. Chang is intelligent."

"She's crafty, Grandfather. She makes a big announcement that they're separated to impress people, but she sneaks around with him."

"Uette, I don't believe that and you signed a prenuptial agreement. If you're dissatisfied then divorce might be your solution."

She was shocked. "I've only been married for three days!"

"Then make your decision and stand by it."

"Thank you, Grandfather." She backed off, realizing no help would come from him. "I'll handle it," she said, sounding cheerful. "I'm a married woman now, I'll deal with it."

"Very good, Uette, that's a more positive attitude."

Hanging up, Uette paced as anger grew inside of her. Hearing the key in the lock, she turned and studied Peter as he walked in. He took off his jacket and headed for his room.

"Wait a minute," she said. "Do you have any idea what you caused tonight?"

"No," he answered, stopping. "What did I cause?"

"I invited Phyllis and Jeff to dinner. They finally left when you never showed up."

"I didn't even know about it."

"Why didn't you come home from work?" she asked angrily.

"Because I didn't feel like it," he snapped, resenting her, resenting the marriage.

She raised an eyebrow. "And I'll just bet I know where you felt like going."

Peter smiled. "You guessed it. That's exactly where I felt like going."

Uette clenched her fists. "And the little liar has told people you're separated."

Peter glared at her. "Watch who you're calling a liar. I told you not to treat me like a husband. I work odd hours and sometimes I work a double at the last minute. And above all," he pointed at her, "don't think your little games are going unnoticed. Don't include me in your little dinners. Don't cook for me. Leave me alone. I'm not your husband. I'm in love with Jeneil. If you can't stand to hear that then too bad. She's more woman than you'll ever be." He continued to his room.

"How would you know?" she flared, seething with rage.

Peter stopped and turned around smiling. "Well now, what was that, an admission that I never touched you?"

Uette caught her breath and gathered her wits. "I meant that you were too drunk to know anything. You can't even remember."

"Bullshit!" Peter sneered. "I've never been that drunk in my life. I never touched you, we both know that. And here's a news flash, I never will so you can stop putting yourself on display for me. I've never been that desperate and I never will be." He went to his room.

His words enraged her. Taking the pillows from the sofa, she threw them on the floor and paced furiously. "It's her," she fumed. "He saw her today and it's ruined us. He was doing better yesterday." She threw a pillow at a chair. "Ooo, that vapid little mouse, I could strangle her. She has manipulated everyone into thinking she's not seeing him. Ooo," she growled, and stomped her feet. "We'll see how desperate you get." Grabbing a pillow, she hit the sofa again and again until she was worn out. She sat down on the sofa arm and breathed deeply. "She won't win. I won't let her."

Peter sat on his bed reading the book Jeneil had given him. He was tired and he had early surgery again, so he knew he had to go to bed soon but the book relaxed him. There was a knock at the door and he glared at it but didn't answer.

"Peter," Uette called softly.

"Leave me alone."

"I want to apologize."

"I don't want you to," he snapped.

"I'm opening the door," she said, waiting a second before opening it. She stood holding a cup and saucer. "I made you some Ovaltine."

He got off the bed quickly. "You don't listen, do you?" He took the Ovaltine and rushed to the bathroom sink and poured it down the drain. "Now get out of my room!" he shouted at her. Tears rolled down her cheeks and she ran from his room crying. He slammed the door furiously. Then, going to the phone, he dialed his grandfather.

"Peter," his mother said, "you sound upset."

"I'd like to talk to my grandfather."

"I'll get him." She didn't try to find out more.

"Peter, what's wrong?" his grandfather answered, sounding like he'd been running.

"I'm sorry to do this, but the rules of this idiotic saving face require it."

"What's wrong?"

"Uette's in her room crying because I yelled at her. She refuses to listen to me. She's playing house. I'm not her husband and she acts like I am." Peter paused not sure how to explain his next complaint. "Grandfather, she's trying to interest me physically. I've let it pass and each time she gets more open about it. At first, I thought I'd be nice to her and find out about her, but I can see that won't happen without getting myself in bed with her. She's a pro, Grandfather. She's not innocent. There won't be any faking and tricking without it turning physical. I don't have time for games. This is the last year of my residency and I have demands that require my full attention. This is a mess, Grandfather. I can't handle it the way I had hoped. It's a pretty sure bet that I could get somewhere fast if I played her game." He paused. "But the thought makes me sick. I don't want to sleep with her. This is a huge mistake. I can't pull it off on my terms."

"Peter, follow your instincts. You have a prenuptial agreement. Keep to that and see what happens. It won't be easy, but you expected that. Do what you feel you have to do. Now I have to talk to her."

"Why?" Peter asked. "I don't want you to."

"I have to, Peter. It's part of it."

"Well, shit." He sighed. "I feel like a kid running scared to his mommy."

"Peter, those are the rules."

"Damn it, then I'm sorry I called."

"Peter, please call her," his grandfather said, and Uette came to the telephone surprised she was asked to. Peter's grandfather cleared his throat. "Uette, Peter has said you're not keeping the prenuptial agreement."

"Well, neither is he," she pouted. "One day he's nice to me and the next day he's yelling." Peter was embarrassed, hating this ridiculous arrangement. "I try to be nice and he accuses me of trying to seduce him."

"Are you?"

"No, but I'm in love with him and if he decides he wants me then I'm not going to care about a stupid piece of paper," Uette said, and Peter shook his head. "We get along fine until he sees Jeneil. That's what happened tonight. I made dinner, my sister and her husband were here, and Peter never came home. I can't see what this arrangement will prove if he's able to be with Jeneil like he was tonight." Peter started to laugh. "Hear him laughing? He thinks it's funny. How can I have a chance with Jeneil around?"

Peter's grandfather sighed. "Uette, Peter was with me tonight. He got out of work at seven and was here at seven-fifteen or seven-thirty. He wasn't with Jeneil."

"Well, I didn't know that," she replied defensively. "He tells me he loves her and that I'm dirt. It infuriates me."

"Uette, it's the harvest of the mistake that was made."

She sighed. "I can understand that, I guess. I'll have to be more patient and loving. It'll work. I'm sorry you had to be involved."

"Those are the rules, Uette."

"I know," she replied quietly. "The marriage is only three days old. I can improve."

The grandfather could see what Peter was up against and he was concerned. "Then I'll let you get back to your evening."

"Thank you," Uette answered politely, and replaced the receiver and kept her hand on it while she thought. Peter hadn't been with Jeneil. He was celibate. His pride must be killing him having to run to his grandfather. She took a deep breath. Turning, she looked at Peter. "I hate this arrangement. I feel so petty complaining to others." She sighed. "When you get tired of the situation making you feel like a wimp let me know. I meant what I said to your grandfather. Anytime you're interested in living by our own rules let me know and I'll tear up the stupid agreement. I love you. I don't know how she can stay away from you. I know I couldn't."

Peter stared in disbelief as Uette left the room. "Holy shit! What have I gotten myself involved with here?" He went to his room determined to avoid her. He was convinced she was such a haunt that she'd soon tire of not getting near him and with early surgery his schedule would make it easier to disappear.

*****

Surgery ran later than expected and Peter left as fast as he could, hoping to see Jeneil. She had gotten discouraged and asked Steve to stay overnight; that worried him. He had to be sure she didn't stay discouraged. As he walked onto the fifth floor, he noticed the stack of envelopes. He sighed, realizing he'd missed her. At lunch, he ran down to the gift shop and picked up a small bouquet of spring flowers then raced to her office. Morgan Rand got off the elevator and saw Peter with the bouquet.

"Very romantic Chang, but they'll probably wilt before you get them home to your wife."

Peter fidgeted. "I'll put them in a glass of water."

"Anniversary?" Rand asked, studying him.

"Not really, she just likes flowers."

Peter backed onto the elevator and Morgan Rand watched until the door closed. He raised his eyebrows and walked to the cafeteria. "A changed man, a very changed man."

Jeneil looked up and smiled as Peter walked in with the flowers. "What's this?" she asked, going to the counter.

"I love you." He leaned over and kissed her quickly.

"Peter, we're being careless. We shouldn't be doing this."

He took her hand. "I don't want to hear it, baby. I love you." He gave her the flowers.

She smiled as she held them. "I'm ready for spring. It'll be a nice change. I miss you," she said, and her voice cracked. She bit her lower lip.

"Don't get discouraged, honey. Please." He kissed her cheek.

"I'm okay."

"What are you doing tonight?"

"Robert asked me to go to a party with him."

Peter's heart flipped. "Does he know about us?"

She nodded. "Karen reads the legal notices. She saw our license listed, and then yours and Uette's. She showed it to Dennis and he told Robert."

"How did you explain it?"

"I didn't. They just assumed you changed your mind and married someone else."

Peter sighed. "Has Dennis called you?"

"Yes, I'm on the playhouse staff this season." She smiled. "He and Karen got married a month ago."

"Married? He's married?" Peter smiled.

"Karen got pregnant."

"Deliberately?"

Jeneil shrugged. "Robert didn't say. He just said they were quietly married with no frills. We're taking them to dinner to celebrate this Friday."

He took her hand. "Honey, watch Robert, okay?"

"Peter, we're friends."

He squeezed her hand. "Honey, please."

"Okay." She smiled. "Don't worry; Chang taught me all I know."

Peter stifled a laugh. "He didn't teach you enough to be able to survive out there, Songbird."

She smiled. "That doesn't matter. I belong to him. That's enough to help me survive."

He leaned closer and kissed her lips. The kiss felt warm and soft. "I love you," he said, kissing her neck gently.

She backed away. "Peter, I'm not made of granite. We really are getting too casual about this separation." She looked at the clock. "You'd better get something to eat or your stomach will be in trouble."

"The line's too long. I'll get something from the vending machine."

"Oh, Peter. You're not watching your health." She went to her desk and got her lunch. "It's my hungry week, a turkey sandwich and an apple, take it. I'll get a salad on my lunch break."

He smiled. "I miss your fussing."

She touched his arm lovingly. "Will it be easy to settle this mess? I know it's only been four days, but how do you see the situation so far?"

He shook his head. "She's a nut. She looks straight at me and tells me it's my baby."

She sighed. "Well, it's only four days. I guess it'll take five." She grinned.

He smiled and kissed her. "You're beautiful."

"Thanks for the flowers. You'd better go. Jerry Tollman stops in after lunch every day."

He frowned. "Watch yourself with all these guys."

"Please, don't worry. I'm not the kid you met in here a year ago."

"I know," he said, smiling wryly, "and other guys suspect it too, that's what worries me."

She shook her head. "No need to worry. Nebraska's still shy, Irish hangs tough, and Jeneil is cerebral." She looked him steadily in the eye, her voice becoming serious. "Besides, I'd never do that to Chang. I promise."

His heart pounded at her words. "Boy, I'm crazy about you." He kissed her again then backed to the door and left. She smiled and went to get a vase for the flowers.

The door opened and Morgan Rand walked in. "Hi, Jeneil. Are you free to give me printouts on two cases? I'd like to do a comparison." He handed her the request slip.

"Sure." She smiled, putting the bouquet in the vase and taking the slip.

"Special occasion?" he asked, nodding at the flowers. They looked familiar.

"No, I just like flowers and I'm feeling ready for spring." She went to the computer.

"Dr. Chang, what are you up to?" he mumbled to himself.

Jerry Tollman walked in smiling. "Hi, beautiful." He brought out a red rose from his lab coat. "Happy Tuesday."

Morgan Rand smiled. "Well, she'll have a garden in here soon. Really Jeneil, I feel guilty about coming in empty handed." He reached into his lab coat and brought out a pen. "Here, I picked this up from someone along the way. It says, *'Sunsets are good teachers.'* I haven't figured out why, but anyone who feels ready for spring is probably poetic enough to unravel the paradox."

Jeneil smiled, recognizing the pen. She had put several of them in Peter's box of medical books. She folded the printouts thinking if the pens could find their way back to her then so could Peter.

*****

Peter's schedule got busier. He had asked Dr. Sprague to get him out of the house as much as possible, who was more than willing to help after Peter had explained he hoped Uette would get so discouraged about his hours that she'd want out of the marriage. Peter avoided her when he was at the apartment eating his meals in his room when he was home for them or he would go to his grandfather's and eat there. He noticed angrier looks coming from Uette and he felt encouraged. He stopped in often to see Jeneil when he worked day shifts and he went to work earlier to see her any other time. He found himself feeling calmer whenever she said that she and Steve had been together. Steve had said she had taught him to make stew and Peter could see that Steve really enjoyed learning to cook. That relaxed Peter, too. He felt Steve had the situation under control and was dealing with her as a friend.

Peter was assigned more and more complex operations and for the most part he was in charge with Dr. Maxwell assisting except in cases with variables. His hours were difficult but they kept him away from Uette. It was hard to believe a month had passed already. He grinned as he drove home feeling an explosion from her was inevitable. Her looks were getting angrier every day. As he got off the elevator and went to the apartment, he hoped she'd have his bags packed and at the door. Opening the door, he heard the TV in her bedroom and walked quickly toward his room. Her bedroom door opened as he got to his own. She was wearing the long, loose fitting, plunging silk dress.

"I want to talk to you," she said seriously.

"Okay," he answered, hoping this was the end.

"Let's sit down," she said, heading for her bedroom.

"The living room, Uette," he said, and she shrugged and followed him. He sat on a chair and watched her pace. "Uette, I have early surgery and I need sleep. Talk if you're going to talk."

She looked at him steadily. "I want to talk to you about our situation."

"You mean the baby isn't mine?"

She looked displeased by his remark. "No, this game you're playing; the absent husband."

"This isn't a game," he said. "I'm serious."

"I want it stopped," she said, folding her arms and leaning against the sofa.

"Go to hell." He started to get up.

"Sit down," she snapped.

He stood up. "Hey, bitch, package it for fertilizer. I'm going to bed."

"I said sit down," she yelled.

He stopped and pointed at her angrily. "You don't give me orders, you screwball bitch. Don't push me."

"Oh, I have some orders for you," she scowled, "because you have pushed me too far. You and that mousy mistress of yours may have everyone else fooled but I know better."

He shook his head. "Oh, give it a rest. Geez, you're a nut. Besides I told you, I'm in love with her and you signed a prenuptial agreement."

"I'm unsigning it," she said seriously.

He smiled. "Good, does that mean this marriage is over?"

"Not hardly," she said, "it hasn't even begun. You will honor your responsibility to me, that's what will begin."

"You're flipping out," he snapped.

She ignored him. "You will have meals with me and we'll work from there. You will also stop seeing Miss Mouse."

He grimaced. "You're crazy. I haven't seen her."

"Lie to your grandfather and mine. Peter, I want you to stop going to her office at noon. I want you to stop bringing her flowers and I want you to stop getting on the elevator with her." He stared at her, not believing she could guess all that. She raised her eyebrows. "Ooo, I caught your attention."

He shook his head. "You're still crazy. You're guessing and thinking it's true."

She stared at him menacingly. "I'm not guessing and you know it. I want it stopped. And I'll know when it's stopped. I've got my connections."

Peter was thrown hearing she knew someone at the hospital, but he didn't let her see his shock. "So you know somebody, big deal. I don't give a shit. That doesn't scare me," he answered calmly, and turned to walk away.

"I'm not trying to scare you. I'm more interested in how scared Jeneil will be."

Peter stopped and turned. "Uette really, what are you trying to do, have one of your Chinese janitors shake a broom at her." He shook his head. "You're pathetic, even resorting to extortion now. Do you think that will make you more appealing to me or any man, you shittin' bitch?"

"You'll stop calling me names, too," she said, still giving orders.

"I'm tired of this. I've worked a double and I have early surgery," he said, and started to leave. "I don't know why you're into this."

"Peter, my friends aren't janitors and I'm into this because I've made some surprising discoveries. Your mouse is quite a character. She's very misleading. No one at the hospital would ever guess she's as loaded as she is. She has a whole other life she's living. But then you know that, don't you? I think I found out what her deadly attraction is." Peter stared and Uette smiled. "Imagine, that drippy little girl in Records is president of Alden-Connors Corporation, a little group of businesses here she plays at and the mother lode in Hadley, Nebraska that she oversees once a month. And gosh, she's director of the board for the clout-carrying Mandra Foundation. Oh yes, and this must be her big attraction. The entire estate of Amanda Pike just sitting there waiting for the mouse to decide if she wants it. Those bonds she dropped on you and Steve are pocket change compared to what she's got in Nebraska." Uette sighed dramatically. "And she works in the records department pretending to be a humble clerk."

Uette glared at Peter. "I don't like being made a fool of. I thought she was a nothing, a college dropout trying to find herself. Well, I don't care how much clout and muscle she has behind her, I've decided she can't have you. Maybe I can't either, but she's not going to sit in the middle of all this and laugh at me. No wonder she told you to marry me. What is she, a spoiled brat who got bored with her caviar and champagne? I can promise you something, Peter. She won't like my friends. Get used to living without her one way or another." Peter stared, not daring to breathe, shocked she was able to get such detailed information and wondering about this girl he called a screwball. He walked past her to the telephone and dialed. "What are you doing?"

"Tom, it's Peter, I'd like to talk to my grandfather."

"Peter, it's nearly midnight, he's in bed."

"Wake him up, Tom."

"It's really serious then?" Tom asked, hearing Peter's tone.

"Yes, it is," Peter answered, trying to calm down while Tom went to get his grandfather.

"Bad move, Peter, you'll see," Uette said, and then she walked away.

"Peter? What's wrong?" his grandfather asked.

Peter ran his fingers through his hair. "I've got a beaut for you this time, Grandfather. I got home from work and Uette issued an ultimatum. I have to have meals with her for starters and I'm not to see Jeneil at work like I have been or else Uette's going to have her friends scare Jeneil. Now this part is an exact quote, Grandfather. She told me to live without Jeneil 'one way or another.'"

"Oh my heavens! Was that a threat?" His grandfather sat down. "This is incredible. What friends?"

"You tell me," Peter replied dryly.

"Let me talk to her," his grandfather said angrily.

"Okay," Peter sighed, and held out the receiver, "your turn." Uette stared at him steadily as she walked to the telephone and the anger that had been building rushed at Peter and he grabbed her wrist. "Deny you said any of that and I'll tear your tongue out, you lying bitch. I've had it with you." He released her and handed her the receiver. His grandfather closed his eyes, concerned about the level of anger he had just heard.

"Mr. Chang, I'm sorry," Uette said, "you must have heard him. You can tell Peter is overreacting. He's worked a double and he's too tired to be rational. I said those things but certainly not in the way he's taking it. You know my family; we don't associate with thugs. I don't think it's too much to ask him to have a meal with me."

Peter's grandfather was shocked at her defense. "Uette, that's a violation of the agreement. You signed it. You can't issue orders to change that."

Uette sighed. "Then what sense is this arrangement going to make?"

Peter's grandfather was annoyed at her innocent act. "That should be clear, Uette. You have a husband to cover the pregnancy, which is what you and your family requested. Peter honored that request by saving face."

"I'm sorry, Mr. Chang," Uette said apologetically. "When you explain it, it makes sense but when I'm here alone I get confused." Peter's grandfather looked at the receiver in disbelief and Peter put his head back and closed his eyes not believing how she had squirmed out of the situation.

"Is everything clear now?" Peter's grandfather asked.

"Yes, very. Thank you. This isn't easy for me. I think I'm getting too emotional being pregnant and all." She began to cry. "This is a strange way to live. I just wanted my baby to have his father." Peter rubbed his forehead beginning to understand as he watched the act play out; this girl was far more dangerous than he first thought and he sensed a need for some kind of therapy.

"Try to stay calm, Uette," Peter's grandfather suggested finding it difficult to be civil.

"I will," she said quietly. "I keep having to say I'm sorry for bothering you. It's embarrassing."

Peter's grandfather shook his head disgusted by the false sentiment. "Get some rest, Uette. I'd like to talk to Peter." She smiled at Peter and handed him the telephone.

"What is it, Grandfather?" Peter asked.

"Peter, what's happening with her? If I didn't know better I'd have you here yelling after what she said."

"Grandfather, I just realized something. She needs professional help. I know I've called her a screwball, but I didn't know she was really sick."

"Shall I tell her grandfather?"

"I think so," Peter replied. "I'll call you tomorrow." He hung up and sighed then heard a noise. Turning, he saw Uette covering her mouth with her hand trying to keep from laughing.

"Oh, Peter. I can't believe you're the great Peter Chang, man of raw courage and steel nerves. You're going to try to convince my family that I need therapy after your mother saw us together and your grandfather heard you threaten to pull my tongue out if I called you a liar." She laughed openly. "Why am I so crazy about you? You're so arrogant. You call me all sorts of names and you're no prize, Chang. Your body's pretty badly scarred and your mother had you out of wedlock. You should show more gratitude for my interest in you; a Wong girl, Peter, the cherished prize of the Chinese community."

Peter watched her closely. She was definitely off. It was barely discernable but detectable to a trained eye. He wondered if it was stress related. Was she paying for her lie? "Maybe your sisters are prizes," he said, "but not you. You're not even Chinese. You're a genetic mutation. All races have them. Cancerous blights on civilization."

She laughed again. "Ooo, sticks and stones won't chase me away. Is that what you're hoping?"

Peter shook his head. "It's over for me. I didn't sign on for a cuckoo's nest. Get help, Uette." He went to walk past her but she stepped in front of him.

"I'm trying to," she said, tears rolling down her cheeks. "I even married a doctor." She put her arms around him, and his back stiffened and he pushed her arms away.

"Don't touch me," he said, and she cried harder as despair filled her. He sighed, feeling compassion for the confused girl before him. "Uette, I'm going to do both of us a favor and get out of this marriage. If we stay together I'm going to do a lot of raging because of your lie. You need help and I need to clear my name. That kind of confrontation leaves scars. You're not well enough to handle it if we're living under the same roof." He went to pass her but she stepped in front of him again.

"How can you think I'm crazy for telling your grandfather what I did? Wouldn't it be crazier to say yes, Mr. Chang, I threatened the mouse mistress because he's my husband. He's mine, not hers. She's trying to take what's mine?"

Peter sighed. "Uette, you're doing it again. You're confused. I'm hers. This marriage is not real."

"But it could be," she said pleadingly. "I could be a wonderful wife. She was supposed to marry Steve."

"Where the hell did you get that?" Peter asked, shocked.

"Karen told me. Jeneil must have changed her mind and now everything's messed up. She doesn't want me to have you. She wants you and Steve. She's a rich, selfish mouse and I should teach her a lesson."

Peter stared at her as another symptom revealed itself. "Uette, are you on anything?"

She grinned. "Not so you'd notice."

"Oh geez," Peter said, putting his head back. "Oh shit, a catfish with a cold nose." He held his stomach as the shock hit him. "Hey, it's over for me. Your nose could cost me my license. Let's hope it's only your nose."

She laughed. "Are you sure you're Peter Chang, the mighty and powerful Dragon? You are such a coward." She grinned. "I only take enough to wash the edge off at the end of the day. Some people drink less than a shot even." She winked.

He sighed. "Consider me gone." He stepped past her.

She turned. "No, no, Mr. Dragon. You can't go or my friends will hurt little white mouse." She smiled. "And I know you wouldn't want that. I'm not stoned, Peter. I'm feeling nice and easy, but I never leave reality. I know what I'm saying."

He stopped. "What friends? You told my grandfather the Wongs didn't have 'friends.'"

She shook her head. "Wow Dragon, you're way off the streets now but I love it. I totally love it. You are what's called awesome, totally awesome."

He sighed. "You're drowning in snow. Don't tell me you're not stoned."

"Try getting out of this marriage," she said, walking to him, "and you'll see how stoned I am. Call my bluff, doctor man, and the white mouse gets flushed. Swoosh, right through the big black hole."

"What friends?" he asked, not knowing if he could trust what she was saying.

"You not only think I'm crazy but stupid, too. What friends?" she mocked his question and laughed. "Oh wait, I'll get their names and addresses for you so you can send Christmas cards. What friends?" She laughed louder as she walked to her bedroom. "And he thinks I'm crazy." She stopped at the bedroom door and turned. "Goodnight, doctor man. Remember, dinner here tomorrow night at seven-thirty and if you get the urge to buy flowers make sure you bring them home. Is that clear?"

He looked at her. "What's your bedtime snack costing you?"

"Not nearly as much as it used to darling," she said, and looked at him steadily. "I love you, you know. I really do." She smiled warmly and closed the door.

"She's a fruitcake," Peter said, taking a deep breath.

Sleep was impossible so he paced watching the clock move slower and slower. Going to the kitchen, he got out the milk and a pan. He opened a jar of Ovaltine and put a spoon inside. He stopped, wet his fingers, touched the crystals and tasted it. It was just Ovaltine. He sighed. He couldn't turn his back on her. He couldn't trust her at all. What was it Rick had said? Sleep facing her, she's a reptile. Geez, a sixteen-year-old kid spotted her and he hadn't. She was right; he was far from the streets. But he was going to check them out. He was going to find her little friends. The bitch could count on it. He thought about Jeneil and his stomach tightened. He wondered if Uette's threat was only empty words. Were her friends two dirt connections with cold noses, too? He felt sick that he had brought such trash so close to Jeneil. She didn't deserve it. It wasn't her lifestyle.

Peter poured his Ovaltine into a mug and went back to the bedroom with it. Opening the book, he read about the wolfdog with which he could identify. He bet she knew that. He put his head back. Where the hell was this all going? How could he protect her? How the hell did saving face become saving her life? Was this all just more of the shit? He drank his Ovaltine and got under the covers. He could feel his body relax, but his mind wouldn't turn off.

Twenty-Six

It seemed like the alarm rang just as Peter fell asleep. He sat up and felt dizzy. Standing, he stretched. His head was fuzzy. Turning the shower on, he stepped in, alternating the water between hot and cold like Jeneil had done when he was getting sick. He wished he had her herbs now. Dressing, he felt off-balance as he tried to put on his shoes standing on one foot. He drove to work and decided to run a half block to see if that would help. Taking the stairs instead of the elevator, he went to scrub. Taking a scalpel, he practiced aiming at a fine line. He missed by a hair, but he missed. He sighed as Dr. Maxwell walked in and joined him at the sink.

"Dr. Maxwell, were you planning on me taking this case?"

Dr. Maxwell nodded. "Problem with procedure?" he asked. "You sound like there's trouble."

"Not with procedure," Peter replied. "I'm not physically up to it. I've tried everything. I even ran a half block. I was off when I tested my hand. I can assist. I'm sure of that."

Dr. Sprague looked up from the other side of the sink and Dr. Maxwell looked at Dr. Sprague with a raised eyebrow. "What caused it?" Dr. Maxwell asked. "Party?"

"No," Peter said. "I couldn't get to sleep."

"What have you taken for it?"

"Ovaltine and hot milk," Peter answered, and Dr. Maxwell turned his head to look at him and grinned. "Well it worked, just not fast enough."

"Take OR," Dr. Maxwell replied. "I'll assist and take over if I have to."

Peter was determined to perform a successful operation but felt himself get weak after the second hour. He paused and did cleansing breathing like he had seen Jeneil do. He then made sure he breathed with his mouth closed. His head cleared and he felt stronger. He finished and an intern closed. He felt wrung out but pleased. Dr. Sprague had slipped in and observed after which he and Dr. Maxwell went to a corner of the OR and talked.

Dr. Maxwell walked to Peter as he changed his surgical gown. "Peter, that was terrific. You were right to report your doubt, but you never hedged." He hit Peter's arm. "That's the stuff surgeons are made of. I've suggested that you be given an hour or so to sleep. You've got ER later today."

"Thanks," Peter replied, and Dr. Maxwell went to the anteroom.

Dr. Sprague came over to Peter. "I'd like to know why you didn't sleep. Too many hours?"

"No," Peter replied. "I've got to talk to you."

Dr. Sprague looked serious. "Okay, be in my office in half an hour."

*****

Dr. Sprague handed Peter coffee and sat back with his. "You were terrific in OR." He smiled. "Did you feel it, too?"

Peter nodded. "Yeah, it surprised me since I felt so off-center."

Dr. Sprague nodded. "I'm glad Maxwell decided to handle it that way. You learned that you're better trained than you think you are. There's a finer edge to your ability that you should know about and count on." He got serious. "Talk to me," he said, sitting back. "It must be about Mrs. Peter Chang."

Peter sighed. "That name still doesn't sound like it's hers."

"What is it, Peter?"

"Last night I found out she's popping something. What does that do to me?"

"Nothing if you don't supply her. There are doctors whose wives are drug addicts. There are doctors who are drug addicts themselves. We can't kid anybody. Encourage her to rehab and keep your prescription sheets locked away."

"I hate this. I didn't want this in my life. Her habit messes up my medical image."

Dr. Sprague nodded. "I know the feeling. It tore me up when I found my youngest son bouncing off the walls. You shake your head and tear your hair out. Luckily, he grew up and put it behind him without a jail sentence. So Lily-White isn't so innocent."

Peter fidgeted. "She also needs therapy. There's a few beats missing from the tune."

Dr. Sprague stared. "Well, she's a mess. She's the one who kept you up?"

Peter was embarrassed to have to admit the next fact. "Not her, just her threat. I have to avoid Jeneil or she'll bring out these thugs who'll...," Peter had trouble getting it out, "scare her for starters."

Dr. Sprague's eyes widened. "I don't like the sound of that. She can use Jeneil to muscle you into doing anything now." He stood up and paced. "Write a prescription or Jeneil's in trouble. Oh, Pete, that's not good. Who are the muscle? Are they real?"

Peter shrugged. "I'm going to check the streets."

Dr. Sprague sighed. "That doesn't sound good either. I don't like the idea of one of my surgeons poking around in the gutters. We see that level of life seep into the ER."

Peter nodded. "I understand but I think it's my only hope. That has to be where she got pregnant. I've got to get rid of this marriage. I'm worried sick about Jeneil."

"Have you told her?"

Peter shook his head. "I'm not sure what to do. I don't want to scare her, but I'd like her to be able to take precautions and protect herself." He groaned. "I can't believe all this. That kid is completely innocent and she's being dragged into this shit."

Dr. Sprague scratched his head nervously. "Maybe your wife's bluffing."

Peter cleared his throat. "She knows every move I make here at the hospital."

Dr. Sprague was surprised and drummed his pencil on the desk. "I don't like this. I don't like it at all. Peter, maybe it's time for a detective."

Peter shook his head. "Not yet, that could make waves sending every piece of news deeper into the street. I know somebody who might know what's happening. Let me try her first."

"Peter, watch yourself. We're moving into areas that are new to me. The guy who lives at the end of my street is supposedly connected to organized crime. He's a nice guy, maintains his property and lives a quiet life. The only clue we have is that our street never has potholes and it's the first plowed in a snowstorm. Street crime is different, that's a whole breed of animal that I don't like to have around. They try to infiltrate hospitals because of the access to drugs. They're bold, ugly, and uncaring."

"I was there." Peter smiled. "I know the breed."

Dr. Sprague shook his head, disagreeing. "Not anymore, Peter. You've been away from it for almost ten years now. Your instincts aren't as sharp. They can't be. Even jungle animals lose their survival instincts after being in captivity."

"Yeah, I'm reading *White Fang*. I think it's pretty clever the way the author crawls into the wolf's mind."

Dr. Sprague smiled. "What made you pick up that?"

"A Christmas present from Jeneil. She said there were messages in it and good advice."

Dr. Sprague thought about it and smiled broadly. "That girl is a sweetheart. Now and then they come along and she's definitely one."

Peter got up. "I think so, too. I'd better get back on duty. I'm glad I came in."

"Me too, Peter, keep me informed."

Peter nodded. "Thanks for the advice."

"Peter, don't let her muscle you into anything illegal for any reason. There's always a way out. Come to me right away if things get tight, at home too if necessary."

Peter nodded. "Thanks again."

Jeneil was returning to the elevator when Peter saw her. He looked around, no one was in sight. The administrative floors were like that, people were usually in an office. He ran to the elevator and hugged her.

"Peter!" She looked around for witnesses. "You're getting crazy." The doors of the car opened, he pushed her inside and kissed her passionately as soon as the doors closed. She pushed herself away breathless. "Peter, we shouldn't."

"Yes, we should." He pulled her to him, holding her close and then kissed her again. She returned his passionate kiss until the car slowed to the signaled floor. "I love you, baby." He smiled and gave her cheek a quick kiss.

"I love you too, Chang." The doors opened and Jeneil stepped out. Peter waited for another floor to avoid being seen with her.

*****

Peter went home for dinner, staying silent and avoiding looking at Uette. She had tried to make conversation but he refused to participate. He reminded himself to taste a small amount of food before eating. He had come to distrust her even more and barely ate what was before him. His grandfather called and asked for Peter to stop by; the Wongs had been invited to discuss Uette. All three men were shocked to hear about the drug use, Uette's father visibly shaken. Neither her father nor grandfather could understand why she would even suggest that she knew people with muscle, certain she was only joking. It was a habit since early childhood; she imagined the most outrageous things.

Peter returned to the apartment more relaxed since being reassured her threat was empty. The mail had accumulated; he took it to his room and sorted through it. It surprised him that she was staying within the budget allowance for food. Her father had given him a check for the rent, the remainder was in the mail. He opened the credit card envelope quickly not realizing she had one other than the gasoline card. The amount due nearly choked him. He shook his head not believing the staggering amount. Opening his door, he heard the TV from her bedroom. He knocked sharply on the door.

"Come in."

"I want to talk to you," Peter replied.

"Then come in."

"In the living room," he said, and turned and walked away.

She came to the living room wearing something blue and revealing. Sitting on the sofa, she smiled. "I'm here."

"Uette, I thought you understood about the budget?"

"I do," she said, looking puzzled.

"Then why is this gas credit card still being used?"

"I ran short," she answered, shrugging.

"Why didn't you tell me?"

"You were never around. You've just started getting meals here." She grinned.

He studied her eyes. "You haven't had your bedtime snack, have you?"

She laughed. "I like that, bedtime snack."

"Uette, answer me."

"No, I haven't." She put her head back on the sofa, bored by the subject.

"Then listen carefully. The money I gave you is for food for the house and gas for your car."

"It wasn't enough." She sighed and brought her feet up under her gown.

"Then you're wasting money. I don't know where you're getting the money for your kicks, but it can't come from what I give you. I refuse to pay for your habit."

"I haven't bought any since we've been married and I won't when I run out. I don't use it every night. I'm not hooked."

"Then food is too expensive. There's almost a whole meatloaf in the refrigerator. Why did you make chicken tonight?"

"Because last time I tried to reheat a meatloaf, it got cremated or close to it. I hate leftovers anyway."

Peter sighed. "Well, why did you make such a big meatloaf?"

She laughed. "Well, I can see you don't know how to cook. I followed the recipe and that's the size it makes."

"But you can divide it into three meals. You can make a meatloaf the size of my fist. That's enough for two people. Some of the recipe can be meatballs and the rest you put on a plate and cover with vegetables and cheese like a pizza."

"Meatballs from meatloaf? My cookbook has meatballs made differently."

"Trust me; a meatloaf recipe can make meatballs, too. And you can slice that meatloaf, heat it in sauce with peppers and onions and serve it with rice. It's good."

Uette looked at him. "Oh, I get it. These are mouse ideas, aren't they?"

"So what?" he asked, sitting in a chair. "If it saves money, who cares? Jeneil got the idea from a Spanish neighbor."

Uette pouted. "Well, I don't like cooking. I'm not made for the kitchen."

"Jeneil didn't like to cook either, but she understood it's an area where you can save money. It's a flexible expense."

"Oh, Jeneil, Jeneil. I'm tired of her. You call me a screwball. With her money, why is she cooking anyway?"

Peter shook his head. "Then check with Phyllis. She must know how to cut corners. They're not rich."

"Phyllis?" Uette laughed hysterically. "Oh please, she gets high on dull and has tomato soup for blood. She lives in her kitchen and her hips show it. I don't need to gain weight from food; I'm already adding pounds because of the baby." Tears rolled down her cheeks.

Peter sighed. "I'll have to take your credit card and instead of giving you the whole allowance I'll give you a weekly food and gas budget. How did you make ends meet last month?"

She pouted. "I took money from my savings. You're treating me like a little child giving me an allowance."

"Uette, where money's concerned, you are a little child."

"I'm not stupid!" she shouted.

"I didn't say you were. You just lack training in cooking and budgeting. I'll give you smaller amounts to work with while you learn. I don't have money to waste."

She watched him scornfully. "What, are you sentimental about that bond mouse gave you? Those certificates are giving you a nice amount of interest monthly. Why do we have to live on the ridiculous amount from the hospital?"

He stiffened. "I'm not touching that money. I'll have loans and financing to face when I'm finished. Jeneil managed on what I make."

"She worked!" Uette replied hotly.

Peter smiled. "Jeneil knew it was a macho thing with me that we live on my money, not hers, and she accepted it. She saved her earnings and only used it when we splurged for dinners and entertainment."

"Then you're both screwballs," Uette pouted. "Money is boring."

"Jeneil grew up understanding that people get rich by not spending money. It's a fact of life. Rich or poor, people have to watch what they spend. I'm sure your mother does. Check with her."

"My mother!" Uette giggled. "Who do you think made Phyllis? Boy, the only woman I know is my grandmother. She scrimped like a pauper, watching every penny, and when my grandfather died she couldn't believe how much money he had in the bank, plus the insurance. She's still mad at him for making her live like she did for all those years." Uette smiled. "Now she's a woman who understands money and its powers. She blames my grandfather for my mother's attitude about money. He made them all watch their pennies." She shook her head. "She thought they were poor and she feels cheated. She's making up for lost spending and I don't blame her. I don't see why we can't increase your income with the interest from the bond."

Peter stood up, getting angry. "Look you, get this clear. That's my money for education costs and my career. I covered that in the prenuptial agreement. I don't want you using your savings to make ends meet either. Your father's helping us with the apartment, Uette. How many people do you want to drain? We can live on my income. I know it can be done, Jeneil and I managed."

"There's Jeneil again. Maybe she'll give me her recipes so I can be perfect, too."

Peter grinned. "I can ask her."

"Don't you dare!" Uette snapped. "I'd rather live on sardines than have her think she's better than I am."

Peter shook his head at her attitude. "I just realized a major difference between you and Jeneil. You don't want to learn. She doesn't care who teaches her. She's a sponge."

Uette laughed. "Well, personally, I think she's a mouse afraid to reach out and experience life, but if you think she's sea life that's okay with me, too." She grinned nastily at him.

Peter sighed. "You're hopeless. Let's talk about this other credit card. What did you buy? The amount due is incredible! Your semester tuition must be less."

Uette was getting tired and irritated with the conversation. "Oh, Peter. You need a course in economics. Credit spending is twenty-first century life. Get with it. The whole amount isn't due. You make monthly payments. Don't you?"

Peter shook his head. "Boy, Uette, you've mastered the science of half-truths. Okay, so the whole amount isn't due now. I'll make a monthly payment using the money from the food and gas budget. They're the only flexible expenses. That's all we have available."

"What!" Uette sat up quickly. "That's almost my whole budget. You can't do that!"

Peter raised his hands and smiled. "Hey, she woke up and can now see the problem of twenty-first century credit spending. You have to pay it back. What a gyp to mess up a beautiful fantasy with reality."

"Don't get smart," she replied, annoyed by his mocking.

Peter grinned. "One of us has to."

She glared at him. "I'm not stupid."

"Then you're a great actress."

"That's enough," she yelled. "I'm tired of you calling me names."

"And I'm tired of your attitude. What did you buy that made this account so high?"

"Look around you. These sofa pillows, the lithos, towels, sheets, a coffeemaker, the bathroom accessories, two clocks. Who knows?" She sighed, falling back on the sofa. "I'm getting a headache."

"You are a headache," he said, and stepped aside to avoid the pillow she threw at him. It hit a vase on a small table behind him, knocking it to the floor. He picked it up and replaced it, and tossed the pillow back at her. "Be careful, Uette. You don't want to break all this evidence that you understand twenty-first century credit spending." He laughed. "The economy loves you. You should check out the interest they're making on you for this month alone. That isn't as clearly shown as the monthly payment is, but it's there, Uette. I like Jeneil's idea of economic stimulation. The interest on the bond is going into my pocket, not into some corporate office."

Uette covered her face with the pillow and screamed, "I hate her!"

Peter pushed the sleeves of his sweater up to his elbows. "Okay, Uette, here's how we're going to handle this." She uncovered her face and looked at him. "The previous balance on the credit card will come from your savings. Its stuff you bought for you. Can you cover eight hundred-fifty dollars from your savings for both cards?"

"Yes," she replied quietly.

"Good, then the amount you spent last month for all these twenty-first century necessities will come from the checks that were gifts at the wedding."

"Oh no, Peter!" she pleaded. "I thought we could get a big screen TV and home entertainment center with that money."

He stared at her. "You're incredible! They should put a bronze plaque dedicated to you on the federal treasury building. Being married to me, your drop in spending will be noticed in next month's statistics. They'll think you died."

"I might as well be dead," she said, slumping against the sofa arm, sighing. "I can see how Jeneil managed and it's not fair to me."

"What do you mean?"

"She at least got to sleep with you. That probably made everything else worth the sacrifice. I get all of the hassle and none of the fun."

Peter wished he hadn't asked. He folded the bill and put it back in the envelope. "Discussion's over," he said. "Stay in your budget and give me all your credit cards."

She looked at him seductively. "I could give you all I've got."

"Take it to the guy who got you pregnant," he said, walking past her.

She knelt against the sofa arm. "You are the father, you imbecile," she called, irritated by his rejection. He turned and came back grinning. Stopping, he leaned toward her. She could smell his cologne and electricity spun through her.

"Tell the truth about the baby and we'll talk about your offer."

She loved the shape of his mouth. "I did," she whispered, leaning closer to him. "Your bed or mine?" She grinned, pleased with her answer.

Peter studied her face then touched her cheek gently with his hand. "You're very beautiful, Uette," he whispered, and leaned closer to her. She felt faint. He put his lips near her ear. "Uette," he whispered seductively, "handle it yourself and pretend I'm there." He stood up quickly and walked away.

"That's filthy, you disgusting animal," she yelled.

"So get a divorce, Lily-White," he called, and slammed his bedroom door.

She put her arms on the sofa and rested her head back. "I must be crazy," she cried softly. "This is not a healthy way to live and it's all her fault. I'm so tired of the name, Jeneil."

*****

Since feeling the threat was empty and Uette was harmless, Peter continued checking on Jeneil. They had both come to enjoy the noon visits and Peter remained calm. His only frustration was not being able to hold her and touch her the way he wanted to. He continued to go to the apartment for dinner when his schedule allowed to keep Uette quiet and to check on how she was doing with the budget. She was trying hard and he increased her gas allowance when she began crying about school and visits to the doctor and being able to visit her parents often or she'd go crazy. She seemed unhappy and looked tired, and morning sickness was taking its toll. He felt sorry for her, but felt he had no choice but to continue living the rules of the prenuptial agreement even though some of them seemed too stringent now. He also didn't want to back down feeling she was the type who'd take your elbow too if you offered your hand.

Peter called Uette's father to ask if he could send less toward the rent in order to increase her household budget and was surprised to hear her father was giving her a weekly allowance. They both felt certain the extra money was going for drugs since it wasn't showing up on the table, and her father was disappointed and discouraged wondering why it was happening since being married to Peter. Peter strongly resented the blame and told her father that. Taking the problem to the grandfathers, her father had to admit Peter was doing his best and had tried to find a way to increase her money. Uette wasn't looking too good as truth began eroding the veneer of lies. The marriage was slightly more than a month old and it was an ugly mess. It had seemed like an eternity to Peter.

Peter was determined to find out about Uette's other life and had tried to find Lin Chi, who always knew what was going on in the street. His problem at the moment was trying to remember the name of the man she was living with; he wasn't Chinese so the community hadn't heard. He had asked a Chinese man working in Housekeeping feeling he might know but all he knew was that she had moved in with a black man on the east end of town. Peter couldn't help but marvel how the community knew everything he and Lin Chi did when they were together, but now that she wasn't their responsibility and had moved into the black community she wasn't of their concern. Peter also wondered who Uette's connection was at the hospital and made his questions as casual as he could, asking the man one day when he saw him in the hallway.

A new concern was surfacing though. Steve had asked Peter what he was doing with Jeneil to make Morgan Rand ask so many questions and had cautioned him to be careful. "Rand's a bulldog," he had said. "He'll birddog the situation until he gets what he's looking for." Peter took Steve's advice and was more careful around the hospital. He felt Steve was right as he began to notice that Morgan Rand watched him a lot, especially when Jeneil was around. Jeneil had gotten concerned when he told her and suggested their visits should stop. Peter disagreed and refused. The visits had become necessary to his mental health. She had agreed without much argument; they were good for her, too.

The lack of progress had them concerned. They couldn't remember Lin Chi's man's name; Jeneil had heard him called Bo but nothing else. So Peter took a telephone book during lunch hours and breaks and began looking for anybody named Bo, sure he'd recognize a last name or any first name that could be shortened to Bo but nothing came of the search. They came close once but the address was in a small town in the southern end of the state. The search had been slow and once past the T's Jeneil hadn't been very hopeful but continued through the whole book. Peter tried contacting people he could remember who knew Lin Chi, but they led transient lifestyles and he ran into dead ends.

Uette had fussed and made a special dinner to celebrate the second month anniversary of their wedding. Her determination both irritated and impressed him. He couldn't believe she hadn't caved in yet. He was as absent and as silent as he dared to be, and she seemed to adjust to whatever their life together brought. Peter wondered about her motivation for the marriage. He couldn't believe it was passionate love since he wasn't responding to her. How would love survive? He wondered about the father of the baby. Didn't she love him? She was three months pregnant now and most of the morning sickness was past. She had gained some weight and Peter noticed the amount of diet soda cans in the refrigerator had increased. He cautioned her about watching her diet. She had smiled and said, "Why Peter, are you watching my body, too?" He had watched her for the symptoms of stress he'd seen earlier and except for a high from popping she seemed to be in control, although he wondered how normal any woman could be trying to pass another man's baby off in a tricked marriage. That in itself indicated the need for therapy.

The concern uppermost in Peter's mind was Jeneil. She was confused that the situation was continuing for so long. It was beyond her understanding why Uette would accept the kind of mental abuse the marriage had to be causing her. Peter had no answer, he had only kissed her passionately to remove the sadness from her expression, and he began to bring her flowers and small gifts to make sure she stayed cheerful. She was the only girl he knew who could smile at a roll of tropical flavored hard candies, but she liked the tangerine flavor. He put his own discouragement aside as he worried about her. He missed her and seeing her at noon wasn't enough. He accepted it reluctantly and resented Uette all the more every time he and Jeneil experienced frustration from their separation, which was often. He was beginning to dislike the day shift because it meant he had to go home for dinner. Uette had been unusually quiet all week and he would catch her staring at him angrily from across the table.

Three more days then back to the second shift, he thought as he washed his hands for dinner. Uette was especially sullen and he reminded himself to check his food carefully. Sitting at the table, he began eating, avoiding looking at her. He was aware that she was staring at him. He looked up, irritated by her silent anger "Uette, what's your problem? I'd rather eat in my room or at my grandfather's than sit through this."

"Or at Jeneil's?" she asked, glaring at him.

He sighed. "Shit, here we go again. Okay, damn it. Yes, I'd love to be having dinner with Jeneil. Why is that such a shock?"

She put her napkin on the table. "Oh, it's not a shock, Peter. The fact that you ignored my warning is."

"What are you talking about?" he asked, annoyed by her word game.

She continued to glare at him. "I thought I made it clear you were to stay away from her."

"Uette, go to hell. I'm sick of this shit. I don't like games."

"Except as Jeneil as a partner?" she asked, and as he looked at her a feeling of caution penetrated his chest. She rested her arms on the table. "You're still visiting her. She's still getting flowers. I guess you didn't believe me. Well the game is over, Peter. If you two want to play hardball that's just fine but now I've changed my demand. I want her out of the hospital because I can't trust you," she said calmly, staring at him with a deadly serious expression. He wondered where she was going with this and he stayed silent until he had the whole thing before him. "You can ask her to leave or my friends will."

"I can't do that," he said, hoping she had popped something and her threats were empty.

She shrugged. "Fine, then my friends will."

Peter had had it and tossed his napkin on the table. "Uette, I'm really sick of the 'my friends' threat."

She stood up slowly and walked to the buffet and opened a drawer. Taking out a manila envelope, she turned. "I thought you might not believe me about my friends, so I decided to give you some proof." She put the envelope on the table near him. "Open it," she said, folding her arms. He took the envelope and opened it. It contained photographs. The first one was of him and Jeneil standing at the elevator together. He felt his chest tighten. "Those pictures surprised me, Peter. Has she been to a beauty specialist? This isn't the same drab girl I saw in the record department the day I stopped in." He looked at her, surprised to hear she'd been to Jeneil's office. "Look them over, Peter. She made interesting copy." He looked at the next one of Jeneil leaving envelopes at the nurse's desk. Morgan Rand was talking to her. "She turns heads so I hear, not only yours. The mouse is a surprise to me. I like the next one, Peter."

He turned to the next photo and his heart stopped. Jeneil was in the elevator with whoever was taking the picture. She had no idea she was being photographed. He turned to the next and swallowed hard, his chest pounding. It was of Jeneil getting into her car in the parking lot, again unaware of whoever was taking the picture. She was alone and looked vulnerable. His stomach knotted. He hesitated then turned to the last one. Jeneil was unlocking the front door of her house. The photo was taken in the dark. This was a pro taking the photos, a stalker. Peter paused before taking a deep breath.

"What do you want?" he asked, through a tight throat.

She smiled. "I can see they were convincing enough for you; very good."

"What do you want?" he shouted.

"I told you, I want her out of the hospital. She doesn't need the money anyway. I want her out of your life. Is that clear enough?" Uette watched as he took another deep breath and put the pictures back into the envelope and put the envelope on the table. "Peter, I didn't hear your answer. Is my request clear enough for you?" He nodded and pushed his chair back, standing up slowly. "Oh, I hope you're not going to call your grandfather because I'll have to tell my friends that I'm mad."

Peter walked over to her slowly and stood close to her. He stared directly into her eyes. "I want you to listen to me closely, you piece of filthy shit." She began to protest his vulgarity. "Shut up," he shouted, grabbing her shirt collar with both hands, holding it to her chin. "If I find out Jeneil needs so much as a Band-Aid because someone has closed a door on her finger, I'll leave my mark on your face so bad you'll wish I had left you ugly. That's if I leave you one eye to see from, you filthy bitch." He was shaking with rage. "And your buddy with the camera will be picking pieces of lens out from where I've shoved the camera up his ass. I want him. I want him so bad I can taste his blood and I'll get him. Count on it. You've gone too far with this one, you shithead. Did you really think

I'd sit still and let you mess with her? The name's Peter Chang, bitch. You're going to hear it in your nightmares where you'll see me finishing the job I'm starting now."

"Peter!" she gasped hoarsely as he squeezed his fists against her throat.

"Shut up!" he growled, shaking her. "You slipped up on your research. You see, what you didn't realize is if anything happens to her then I don't care what happens to me, so killing you will be a necessity just to calm down. Would you like the Dragon oath on that? It's usually written in blood. Yours." He released his hold on her, shoving her away. She rubbed her throat and coughed, glaring at him. He pointed at her angrily. "You and I are now at a face-off. It's downhill from here on in. Walk the straight and narrow, you piece of trash, because if I come home and you're buzzing around the ceiling I'll turn you in and I'll keep turning you in as many times as your father buys your freedom like he's bought your spotless reputation too, probably. If you think life was unpleasant before, you've just kissed the good times goodbye."

She began to cry. "I have nothing else to lose, so go ahead. It would please me to have her flushed." He went to his room and got his jacket. Snapping it quickly, he headed for the door. "Where are you going?" she asked, and he slammed the door behind him without answering.

*****

Peter pushed the elevator button angrily and then ran down the stairs to his car too inpatient and angry to wait. He headed for the east end, his rage surfacing an idea. If Lin Chi was sick then she must buy medication regularly. He decided to check every pharmacy in the area until he located the one she used. He had to find Lin Chi. It was the only way to find out about Uette. She'd know who to ask. He felt sure of that.

He stopped at the first pharmacy he came to as he began a street-by-street check on the east side. They hadn't heard of her or Bo, but they told him where the other pharmacies were located. There were only three in the area. The second one hadn't heard of them either. He headed for the third hoping his luck would change. The houses began to look more expensive and he felt discouraged; it didn't look like Lin Chi's usual neighborhood. The pharmacy was in a group of stores. He ran in and headed for the counter.

The pharmacist looked up. "The pharmacy is closed. If you'll leave your prescription, you can pick it up in the morning unless it's a real emergency."

"I'm looking for a woman named Lin Chi Deng. She lives with a man named Bo. I was told they live in this area. Do you know them?" Peter pulled out his hospital ID. "I'm a doctor at Cleveland."

The pharmacist smiled. "I guess I know them better than you do. Bo owns the diner across the street."

Peter was so relieved he could hardly speak. "Oh man, that's great news." He looked across the street. The diner was dark. "What time does it open? I've got to talk to them."

"Bo's usually in there at six for the breakfast crowd, but you won't find them for a while. They're in Alabama visiting his folks. He goes there for Christmas and comes back in the spring. He does the circuit down south."

"Oh shit." Peter sighed. "When will they be back?"

The pharmacist looked at his calendar. "Geez, where did March go? Bo comes back the first of April. He calls himself the April Fool for coming back." The man laughed.

"What's his name?" Peter asked. "I've been trying to find him in the telephone book."

"Robert Calves. He was called Bobby, but everybody in his neighborhood was named Bobby after Bobby Kennedy was shot so he changed it to Bo. He's a nice guy, him and Bobby Kennedy."

"Thanks for your help," Peter said, smiling, and he went back to his car feeling a lot better than when he had gotten out. "April first, it's only four days."

Peter headed back to the apartment relieved having found Lin Chi but still furious with Uette. He felt Chang rage and it felt good. He wondered where all this would go now. He couldn't let Uette muscle him or she'd make outrageous demands and that wouldn't protect Jeneil. Uette would only use Jeneil more and more as a club to get him to submit to her orders. He knew he had to stand up to her, but he wondered about the strength of her friends. As he thought about the photographs, he realized any good private detective could have taken them, which he hoped was the case. It was difficult to believe that was as low life as she was indicating with her threats. Her family was well known in the community. How could she get all the junk past them? And yet she had. The drugs were a complete surprise to her family. She knew street slang, but she could pick that up dealing for drugs alone. Peter sighed as he waited for the elevator to reach the apartment floor. He knew it could go either way. Uette was either bluffing or she wasn't. The safest solution was to tell Jeneil so she could protect herself, but he hated the idea of scaring her like that. Anger and resentment filled him. The fact that Uette obviously needed help was almost forgotten as Chang joined the war and made Jeneil's protection his top priority.

Uette was talking on the telephone and crying as he walked in. He stood at the door with his hands in his jeans pockets waiting and listening.

"He just walked in, Grandfather. Okay." She held up the receiver to indicate Peter should take it.

"Mr. Wong?" Peter asked, taking the receiver.

"Yes, Peter," the old man said and cleared his throat, obviously upset.

"Is something wrong?" Peter asked, wondering what Uette had told him. He felt Chang rising in him and was surprised how close to the surface that part of him was now.

"Don't you think so?" the old man asked.

"What do you mean?" Peter asked, pretending ignorance to uncover what Uette had said.

"Uette told me that you grabbed her by the collar and nearly choked her if she didn't stop haunting you about Jeneil. Peter, really, I can't allow physical abuse. I'm very upset."

"Mr. Wong, I'm very concerned, too. I told you the other day at our meeting about my concern for her." Peter looked at Uette. "Come here a minute, Uette," he said calmly, with kindness in his voice. Uette stared, frightened and confused. "Come here," he said quietly. "She is frightened, I can see that." Uette walked to him and he checked her eyes. "Mr. Wong, she's on something."

Uette's mouth dropped open in shock. "That's not true!"

"Mr. Wong, I went to the dorm for a textbook and then made a quick check on a patient while I was in the neighborhood. I don't understand why she'd say those things." Peter looked at Uette, who was still in shock. "Uette, why would I get angry about you haunting me? Since the last threat, you haven't even mentioned Jeneil." Her eyes widened in disbelief of his outright lie. "Mr. Wong," Peter continued, "this is exactly what I meant when I said she needed help. The drugs aren't helping but I feel the core of the problem is stress from her lie about the baby. This marriage is uprooting a lot of trouble that indicates Uette isn't as innocent as everyone had thought. The drugs, her lack of conscience enough to make threats, even empty ones. She's not the Uette I thought I was marrying."

"Well, I can hardly disagree with you there," Mr. Wong replied. "This situation becomes more incredible every day."

"I agree," Peter said, "and I'm very concerned. If I'm frightening her like this, even if it's imagined, I don't think it's wise to stay married. Do you?" Uette covered her mouth with both hands, not believing the trap Peter had set.

Mr. Wong shook his head. "I can't disagree there either, Peter. She sounded so convincing when I talked to her."

"That's the psychosis, it's very real in her mind," Peter explained, his stomach tightening as he realized the violation of his medical oath.

Uette grabbed the telephone. "Grandfather, no. I don't want the marriage to end."

Mr. Wong was shocked. "Uette, you just told me that he threatened you. Why would you stay married to him? Why?"

"I love him, Grandfather." Tears rolled down her cheeks.

"Uette, the marriage isn't healthy. It isn't working. I agree with Peter. It's time to end this before you're hurt, or either one of you for that matter."

"No!" she cried. "No, I was lying," she sobbed.

Her grandfather was silent, stunned by her words. "Uette, how can you tell such vicious lies about him and say that you love him?" Compassion filled him as he realized the instability of his granddaughter.

"I don't know, I don't know," she sobbed, worn out, her mind too tired to scheme.

Peter took the receiver. "Mr. Wong, do you see what's happening?"

Mr. Wong choked up. "Yes, Peter, I see it clearly."

Peter nodded. "I'm sorry. This isn't right. My gosh, what a mess. I'm not good for her. I could leave tonight."

"No!" she screamed. "No, you can't!" She grabbed the telephone. "Grandfather," she pleaded through tears, "please make him stay. I need him! He has to stay! Oh, please. I'll kill myself. I will. I'll do it," she sobbed.

Peter watched her listening carefully to her words. He was confused about her real panic over him leaving. It didn't make sense. She was out of lopsided again and in to real tilt. He knew his diagnosis was close, if not exact. Psychology wasn't his field but he knew enough to see that she was sick.

Her grandfather gasped. "Uette, please! My gosh, calm down! Let me talk to Peter!"

"Yes?" Peter answered.

"Peter, will you stay? What's happening to her? Stay with her, Peter, please. If she doesn't calm down, I'll come over and we'll hospitalize her."

"That's fair enough. I am concerned." Peter meant that. His medical training wouldn't allow him to lack that much compassion.

Her grandfather sighed. "Thank you, Peter. Is she beginning to quiet down at all?"

"Yes," Peter answered, watching her closely as she pulled herself together.

"Oh, Peter, what a nightmare this is. I'm sorry. I don't even know why I'm sorry. I can't decide if the marriage is causing all this or just exposing what was already there. I'm confused, I really am. This is beyond anything I've ever faced. I feel sorry for her suffering and I'm angry at all the lies we're uncovering. My mind's not well from the situation, I don't know how you two are dealing with it. I'll talk to your grandfather tomorrow. We'll be in touch."

"Okay, Mr. Wong," Peter answered, and hung up. He looked at Uette.

She scowled at him. "You think you're pretty clever, don't you? Well, just try to leave me and the mouse will get squashed even if I have to do it myself."

"Nobody shits on Chang, you bitch." He made an obscene gesture and went to his bedroom.

Sitting on the edge of the bed, he sighed. He didn't like himself very much. He was too much of the old Chang and he was disappointed he had violated his oath. She was sick and he had set her up. It was unethical. He felt dirty. Opening the lower drawer of the night stand, he took out the brown box. Holding the unicorn, he smiled at the memory of giving it to Jeneil. Were those days real? This nightmare made him wonder what was real anymore. This was the Chang he had been afraid to show Jeneil. He never surfaced during all the months they were together and in only two months Uette had him unleashed and raging. Chang didn't like survival anymore. Both he and Peter believed in fiction and fairytales now, and they couldn't wait to return to Camelot. Camelot, he smiled thinking of the apartment; the coolness of its rooms and plants, the quietness and order, her gentleness and caring, her love. He thought about Jeneil's love. He could feel it. She cared, she showed it. He thought of Uette sobbing to her grandfather that she loved him. It couldn't be, he thought, it wasn't like Jeneil's. It wasn't even close. He could understand her grandfather's confusion since he was struggling with it, too. Putting the unicorn on the night stand, he settled back against the headboard and picked up his book. The wolfdog was him now. The book could be his autobiography and the author gave insight into himself he had only feelings about. The book gave him words. He smiled. But then you knew that, didn't you, Songbird?

Twenty-Seven

Peter stayed in the marriage for many reasons, Jeneil being the motivating force for most of them. Having seen Uette's panic attack, he felt leaving might cause her to overreact and since finding Lin Chi he felt his chances had improved one hundred percent in discovering Uette's other life. The final reason was to find the baby's father so he could clear his own name. The nonsense had to be buried so he could return to his life with Jeneil, being in such a turbulent marriage making him crave their normal, peaceful life. Having seen Steve in the scrub room made him realize how much he envied Steve's life. Steve looked and sounded professional, not from any specific phrases or mannerisms, but more an air and an attitude. He was in control of his life and Peter envied that.

The thought to warn Jeneil about Uette's ravings disturbed him. Having thought about it the previous night, he decided to have her meet him in the records storage room. It would be private, which was necessary since the exact words and how to say them wouldn't form in his mind. Jeneil showed up to deliver the morning envelopes and he went to her, surprising her with his openness around witnesses. Taking the envelopes, he browsed through them as if looking for something particular.

"Meet me in the storage room at twelve-thirty," he said, under his breath and he handed the envelopes back to her. "Thank you, I'll check on it later." Morgan Rand was watching, puzzled by Peter's open attraction to the quiet girl in Records.

Jeneil went directly to the storage room at twelve-thirty wondering what Peter wanted to talk about and hope began to stir. Maybe there's finally been a breakthrough she thought as she unlocked the door and went inside. Peter knocked gently and Jeneil opened the door quickly, waiting for him. Locking it behind him, she left the lights off.

"Please make this good news," she said, smiling at him.

"Why?" he asked, his chest tightening, wondering if something else was wrong.

"This has already gone on so long without a hint of anything positive being uncovered. Mentally, I had braced myself for a shorter siege. My nerves are frayed." He put his arms around her. "Peter, we shouldn't," she said, holding herself away from him with her hands against his chest.

"Jeneil, I want to hold you. I'm going crazy without you. I'm a raving maniac around that creature I'm with. I can't stand myself half the time." He pulled her to him and she released her wedge and leaned against him, enjoying being in his arms after so many days of separation.

"Oh, Peter. I miss you," she whispered into his chest.

"Baby, I'm barely alive without you. I miss us. I miss our life and Camelot." He kissed her temple and smoothed his mouth across her cheek, continuing the kisses to her lips.

"Peter, be care…." He kissed her passionately interrupting her caution to be careful. Both forgot caution as they got lost in the electricity their kisses caused. She turned her head and caught her breath. "Peter, we're getting out of hand here."

He kissed her neck and her perfume filled him with memories of being with her. "Jeneil, I love you, I want you." His words filled her whole body with a strong feeling of love and she felt his hand undoing the buttons to her blouse. Pulling her lips from his, she backed away slightly to allow him more freedom. Seeing the wedding band on his finger, her throat tightened as reality sobered her.

"No, Peter," she said, beginning to cry.

He stopped, jolted by her tears. "Honey, what's wrong?"

"We shouldn't," she sobbed. "I can't." She pulled away and went to her purse for tissues. She pulled her blouse around herself and folded her arms to keep it closed. He put his hands on her shoulders as he stood behind her, listening to her cry.

"Jeneil, baby, don't cry. Please don't cry. I'm sorry." He rubbed her arms lightly.

"I'm sorry!" she sobbed. "I can't be your mistress! I can't turn what we had into this! I just can't," she cried, leaning against a storage file bin.

Her words sobered him and he understood what she meant as his mind absorbed the rows of metal file drawers in a dark, locked room. He kissed her shoulder lightly. "I understand," he said. "I'm sorry, baby. This isn't what I had intended, believe me. It just happened." He kissed her shoulder again.

She nodded and dried her tears. "I believe you, Peter." She sighed. "What did you want to tell me?"

Peter closed his eyes and massaged her shoulders. The words stuck in his throat. He couldn't bring himself to scare her after what had just happened. "I found Lin Chi," he said, avoiding the real issue. She turned quickly and faced him, and he saw what he had done to her. Her silk blouse was partially unbuttoned adding to the shoddiness of the situation. He felt angry at himself for doing that, feeling he was adding to the trash he and Uette had already brought to her life. He kissed her cheek. "I'm sorry."

"For finding Lin Chi?" she asked, puzzled.

He smiled. "No, beautiful." He began to button her blouse and she let him, hardly noticing what he was doing as her mind grasped for the hope of Lin Chi's help.

"What did she say? Can she help?" she asked excitedly.

"I just found her, I haven't talked to her," he answered, continuing to do her blouse buttons. "She and Bo won't be back until April first. They're in Alabama."

She looked down at his hands having become aware of what he was doing. "Thank you," she said, as tears filled her eyes. "I want you to know that I miss you. I really do in every way. Please understand that."

He nodded and smiled, brushing his finger lightly across her cheek. "I understand. I've got to get back on duty but I want you to understand something. To me, you're my wife not my mistress." He pulled the wedding band off his finger. "I wasn't wearing it but people asked where it was so I put it on to shut them up. It feels like a noose." He threw it angrily and Jeneil's eyes widened as she heard it hit something, ricocheting onto the floor with a pinging sound.

"Peter," she began. He kissed her lips tenderly, being careful not to undo the soberness her tears had caused in him.

"What, Mrs. Chang?" He smiled and for the first time since the wedding two months earlier the name sounded right.

"I love you," she said softly.

"Remember that, okay?"

She nodded. "Always, Peter." He kissed her lips lightly then moved away to leave.

"You belong to Chang."

"I always will." She smiled. "It's like breathing to me."

He smiled broadly. "I needed to hear that," he said, and then sighed. "I'd better get back. Dan's covering for me." She nodded and he closed the door behind him, leaving her in the darkened room.

She took a deep breath to hold back tears. "I hope so, Peter, because I don't know what to do about the restlessness inside of me. If I don't act on it soon, I'll go crazy. It's pulling at me like some magnet in the center of my entire being and my mind keeps shouting to follow it and find Jeneil."

*****

The encounter with Peter left Jeneil unsettled. Mixed feelings stirred within her, which added to her restlessness and she was glad when the day was over. Unlocking the apartment door, she stepped inside and sighed. Emptiness filled her. Going to the bedroom, she changed into a long dress and lay on the bed. She turned and faced Peter's side, touching the pillow lovingly. "Peter, I need you right now. I'm afraid of the restlessness. It's so strong. If I follow it, I know I'll change and if I don't, I won't survive." Hearing the words aloud, she sat up quickly. "What am I talking about?"

Annoyed at herself, she sighed and undid her hair. Everything she did was a chore now, even the simplest of tasks like taking down her hair. The time and the waiting seemed endless. She tried to fill the hours, but there seemed to be so many to fill. And at the root of the restlessness was the knowledge that she was ready for a change. She wanted a change. She thought about the encounter with Peter earlier in the day. She missed him and the longer his marriage went on, the sharper her pain became. It was unavoidable, his memory everywhere in the apartment.

She sighed knowing time was running out. She could feel change in the air and in some ways it was a necessity. She was marking time, waiting in limbo for Peter. That had to change; she was losing her grip on her life. "Come on spring," she said into the darkness of the room, "at least predictable change, you're not tied to restlessness."

Her telephone rang, startling her. She hated the thought of answering it, but she reached out and pulled the receiver to her ear.

"Jeneil!" The loudness of the voice surprised her and she hadn't even said hello.

"Uncle Hollis?" she questioned, not believing it was him, his tone so strong.

"Jeneil, I hope you're free right now because you and I need to talk."

She sat on the edge of her bed, concerned. "I'm free. What is it?"

"First off," he said, "have you applied for credit or are you making a deal we're not aware of?"

"No, I'm not. Why?"

"Ron Chatfield just notified me that inquiries have been made about you and I'm getting the same here. What's up?"

"I don't know," she answered. "What kind of inquiries?"

"You name it. Whoever it is, is probing deep. I expect to hear from your dentist next with questions about your molars. You haven't done anything to cause the probing?"

"No," she answered. "I don't understand."

Hollis sighed. "Well, as long as it isn't you. Ron was concerned; he thought you were mastering a major sale on your own."

"Of what?" she asked, puzzled.

"We can't be sure, Jeneil. You haven't been yourself lately. You've been unavailable for important meetings and you missed your trip this month. I've never known you to do that." He paused, hesitating.

She rubbed her temples. "I know I've been disconnected, I'm sorry. I'll pull it together next month, you'll see."

"What's the problem, Jeneil?"

She choked up as his gentle tone reached the Nebraska in her, making her become emotional. "Oh, just restless I guess," she answered, holding back tears.

"When were you planning to tell me?" Hollis asked after a brief silence.

"About what?"

"About your man, and I use the term loosely, getting married to Uette Wong?"

"Oh," she replied softly, covering her eyes with one hand. "How did you hear about it?"

"Ron mentioned that might be why you've been screwed up lately. He thought I knew about it. He said your marriage license notice appeared in the newspaper and about a week later another one for Peter to someone else. What the hell happened? Like I can't guess; the bond was enough for the bastard so he left to marry his childhood sweetheart. I want to kill him. I want you to know that. I'm damn upset right now. I just heard about it and I'm mad you didn't tell me, and I'd like to kick that son-of-a-bitch all over the state. I'd like you to give Ron the okay to institute an alienation of affection suit against the bastard and get back your bond, and a sizeable chunk of his flesh as well to hang on the side of the barn."

"Uncle Hollis, please. Let me explain." She paused, sighing. "I don't know where to begin. Uette Wong has accused Peter of being the father of her unborn baby."

"Oh my gosh!" Hollis gasped. "The filthy bastard."

"Uncle Hollis, listen please. The baby isn't his."

"How do you know that?"

"Peter told me."

"Oh shit." Hollis sighed.

"It's true, Uncle Hollis. I believe him."

"Well, the girl can't be pulling at thin air, Jeneil, or he wouldn't have married her. Those cases take some real hard evidence to tie a man up in matrimony. Think about it, there must have been some reason she thought it was his. Even if the baby isn't his, he must have been unfaithful to you for her to accuse him. Jeneil, think, please." Jeneil saw the flimsiness of Peter's story and she didn't dare tell her uncle Uette's witness was Peter's own mother. There was no way she could successfully defend Peter to her uncle.

She sighed. "Uncle Hollis, I know this looks bad for Peter, but I believe him, I really do."

"Oh, Jeneil, you really are a babe in the woods when it comes to men. But it doesn't matter now anyway. I guess he's married and out of your life."

"No, he isn't. He got married to save face. He's going to prove the baby isn't his. I'm going to wait for him."

"What!" Hollis yelled. "Jeneil, if that son-of-a-bitch is using you as a mistress I really will kill him. Damn it, why are you so blind about him?"

Jeneil stood up and paced. "Uncle Hollis, Peter and I are separated in every way. We're being honorable." Deep inside she was grateful the statement was true. It felt like her days back in Loma. She could face it knowing she wasn't lying, glad nothing had happened between her and Peter earlier in the day.

Hollis sighed. "I think you should be even more separated. Jeneil, I think it's time to come back home. It's over a year now since you dropped out of school. Your personal life is going from bad to worse at a faster and faster pace. Look at yourself. Come back now. I think it's time. I really do."

"No, Uncle Hollis. I have a company here that can't be abandoned." She could feel panic stirring inside of her.

"Jeneil, you've all but abandoned it these past few weeks. You're not holding up. You can live here and fly back once a month until you sell off what you have there."

"No!" she insisted. "No, I can't do that! I won't do that!"

"Jeneil, listen. I feel responsible for you; you're like family to me. This situation you're in with Peter isn't healthy. I want you out of it. I want you away from him. You're at the hospital every day. You're there because of him. That's not good. Honey, he's married."

"In name only, Uncle Hollis. They're not man and wife. He has a prenuptial agreement."

"Oh great." Hollis sighed. "Then it's only a matter of time before the two of you collide or he gets entangled with his wife for real leaving you hurt again. Damn it, that's it, Jeneil. I'm flying out there and you and I will go a round about this and you'll either come back with me or find a new lawyer because this isn't healthy. You've lost your grip."

Jeneil was shocked. "You wouldn't really give up on me, would you?" Her eyes filled with tears; she had never known her uncle to give up. She wiped the tears that fell and grasped for a way to stall the change she faced with her uncle's ultimatum. She sniffled and cleared her throat. "Uncle Hollis, give me a month, okay? I'll turn this around. Let me think about it. I understand your worry and concern. I really do. You've rushed at me with this and I need time to find solutions that are acceptable to both of us. I haven't lost my grip. I'm floundering, I know that, but it's not out of control. Give me time to pull it together, okay?"

There was silence and then a sigh. "Only a month and that's just because you've done so well in the past, but I'm watching you and taking a firmer stand on your personal life."

"That's fair," she answered, feeling like an errant child facing a scolding. "I just want a chance to live my life my way."

"As long as it makes sense, Jeneil."

She stopped pacing and smiled. "Now we might have a problem there. My sense doesn't seem to be what most people call sensible, but as long as I can prove I know where the blue sky and the green grass are then we'll negotiate. How's that?"

Hollis sighed again. "Blue sky, green grass sure sounds part lopsided, Jeneil. A month and we'll talk about everything along the way. Fair enough?"

"Fair enough. Thanks, Uncle Hollis. Thank you." She began to relax having bought herself some time to steady her life.

Jeneil paced in the darkness of the bedroom feeling pressured on all sides. "If I don't make the change myself then I'm open to whatever change is the strongest force against me." She sighed. "Face the wind, that's all I can do," she said, sitting on the bed. "Winnow—let the real kernels in my life land and let the wind take what isn't real away." She sat thinking of her choices and realized she had to give in to the restlessness.

*****

Monday arrived slowly for Peter. He hated weekends because he couldn't see Jeneil and this weekend had been really tough waiting for the days to pass so he could contact Lin Chi. He made some Ovaltine and toast. He was scheduled for surgery but not early. Uette rushed in, drank some juice, and took a vitamin.

"When will you be home?" she asked. He shrugged, not answering. He hated to even talk to her since their explosion on Thursday. "You've made this so difficult for me." She sighed then left the kitchen and he heard the apartment door close.

"Then get a divorce, you screwball bitch," he muttered, and finished his Ovaltine then rinsed his cup and went to put it in the dishwasher. It was full of dishes. He took one out. They looked clean but he wondered if they were. He shook his head. She was a walking disaster going in twelve directions at once. He put his mug on the counter and left the kitchen to shave. The bathroom tap was covered with soap. He grimaced at the blue glop oozing and caking around the porcelain. Remembering a package of sponges he had bought, he cleaned the bathroom sink and placed the sponge under the bar of soap when he was finished. The method had worked well for Jeneil; she was right, it took longer to clean than to grab a soapy sponge and swish the sink. He loved her simplicity.

The elevator opened to the lobby and Peter saw the mailman. He wondered what disaster they'd been billed for the month as he went to the box and unlocked it. The box was full. He browsed through the envelopes quickly, stopping at the one for the credit card. Zero balance! He smiled. She did it. He browsed through looking for the gas credit card. Zero there, too. He felt relieved. His eye caught the return address on the next letter from a modeling agency in New York addressed to Uette Wong, not Chang. She worked in New

York? Was that how she got past the community? She took it out of town? Betcha that's where daddy was, too. Taking his pen, he copied the name and address in his notebook and smiled not believing his good luck. Lin Chi had connections in New York, too. Peter felt hopeful as he put the mail in his jacket pocket and left for work.

*****

Scrubbing for surgery, Steve joined Peter at the sink. "What's happening with you?" Steve asked, taking a brush.

Peter could hardly keep from telling. "I've located Lin Chi and this morning I found out Uette has a modeling job in New York."

"Hey, that's good news. The kid's really low about low about how long this is taking."

"I know. Maybe we're finally getting a break. Did you see her this weekend?"

"No, I didn't get an answer whenever I called. She must have been out of town." Steve looked across the sink. "Hey, Tollman, you look really low, watch those parties."

"He's been jilted," the intern next to him said.

"Well, I still say it's strange," Jerry answered, shaking the water off his hands. Dr. Fisher came for them and the interns walked away.

Steve smiled. "Two timing bastard, I thought he was still maneuvering for Jeneil."

"Think I'm going to complain?" Peter asked, smiling.

Steve laughed. "Now you're in big trouble. He's on the rebound. Better lock her up."

*****

Peter finished in OR near noon and headed for the records office. Opening the door, he was surprised to see Mrs. Sousa there instead of Jeneil with a girl he'd never seen before.

"Hi, Dr. Chang." Mrs. Sousa came to the counter. "How can I help you?"

"New help?" Peter asked.

Mrs. Sousa sighed. "She's temporary. I've lost Jeneil."

"What does that mean?" he asked, trying to stay calm, shock passing through him.

Mrs. Sousa shrugged. "All I know is she quit. Administration accepted her notice and waived the two week working agreement. I was told that she gave up two weeks' vacation salary in exchange."

"What happened?" Peter asked, almost breathless.

"I don't know. She left word to say goodbye and thanks to all of us. They said it was sudden and the short notice couldn't be helped. They had a temp here for us this morning. I feel bad, I really liked her. I went to her desk to pack her things and there weren't any.

Other than her nameplate, she never had any personal things here. Just a pen that said, *'Sunsets are good teachers.'* Makes me wonder if I really knew her. She hasn't looked like herself lately, puffy eyes, things like that. I wonder if she's in trouble." Peter could barely breathe as Uette's threats came to him, his heart pounding rapidly. Mrs. Sousa smiled. "Well, what can I do for you?"

"Oh, I, uh, I was going to look up something on one of my reports but I think it's okay, you catch it if it isn't right."

"I guess so. Are you feeling alright?" Mrs. Sousa asked, looking puzzled.

"Uh, yes," Peter replied, heading for the door.

Mrs. Sousa watched as the door closed behind him. "Boy, he looked like Dr. Tollman did when he found out Jeneil was gone." She returned to her desk. "But he's married."

Peter rushed to the telephone booths wondering if Uette had called his bluff about Jeneil leaving the hospital. He dialed the apartment. There was no answer after several rings. He dialed the corporation. "Is Jeneil in?"

"No, she isn't. Can anyone else help you?" the receptionist asked.

"Will she be in?" he asked, sensing a hesitation on her part.

"Sir, I'm sure one of the staff can help you. Why don't you explain why you're calling and I'll transfer the call to someone."

"It's personal," Peter replied, getting more nervous. "How about Adrienne?"

"Whom may I say is calling?"

Peter sighed. "It's Dr. Chang."

"Oh," the receptionist said, "I have a message for you from Jeneil." Peter began to breathe again. "It's right here," she said. *"Peter, I had to leave. When the situation is resolved, leave word at my office. "*

"What does it mean, she had to leave? Where did she go?" Peter asked, not satisfied.

"That's the complete message, Dr. Chang."

"Will she be calling in? Can I leave a message for her?"

"I didn't take the message, Dr. Chang. Adrienne left it for me. Oh, here she comes. Hold on, maybe she can help you." Peter inserted another coin as he waited for Adrienne.

"Peter?" Adrienne answered.

"Adrienne, what the hell is happening?"

"I was hoping you could tell me." She sighed. "I found a list of things she wanted me to handle and the note to you on my desk. I haven't seen her since Friday. She left a note that there was a major upheaval and not to panic, to continue as usual and she'd be in touch, that there was no time to explain. I called her uncle and everything hit the fan. He's flying in. I hope I haven't made everything worse. Apparently he talked to her Friday and told her to get her life together or move back to Nebraska. He thinks she bolted. He said she was upset, but he didn't think she was that upset. Boy, he's furious with you. Apparently he just found out what happened. He thought you might be involved until I gave him her message to you. He told me to tear it up and disconnect you if you should call."

"Oh shit." Peter sighed and panic grew inside of him. "Where the hell is she? Does her message mean I shouldn't call her anymore?"

"It sounds like it, doesn't it?" Adrienne sighed. "Peter, I'm going to trust her. She said she'd be in touch. I think Hollis is overreacting. He's so upset about you leaving her that I don't think he's seeing things clearly. She doesn't bolt. It isn't like her."

"Then where is she, Adrienne?"

"I don't know, Peter. She's been neglecting the business. That's why Hollis pressured her. I think he's scared he caused this."

Peter sighed, hoping Adrienne was right and that Uette hadn't been the one to cause it. "I'll call you again to see if you've heard anything."

"Call me at home, Peter. Hollis is due in soon and there'll be trouble if you call here. He's furious. He wants you out of her life."

"How the hell can I blame him? Look at the mess I'm in and dragging her into."

Adrienne sighed. "This is crazy, Peter. It's not like Jeneil."

Her remark hit his stomach and he wondered if someone was making Jeneil do this. "I'll be in touch, Adrienne. I'll check with the motel, sometimes she goes there. I'll also check the beach house."

"Okay, I'll wait to hear from you."

*****

Peter left the hospital and drove to the beach house. It was locked. He checked the windows. There wasn't any evidence of anyone having been there let alone living there. He sat in his car concerned about Jeneil. He didn't like this and now he felt separated from her. He started back to town, driving through the east end to check on Bo's diner. It looked open. Driving around the block, he stopped and went to the door. There were boxes on the counter and the lights were on. He knocked and Bo came from a room at the end of the diner. Seeing Peter, he smiled and went to let him in.

"Hey, Pete." Bo extended his hand, surprised to see him.

"Hi, Bo. How's it going?"

"Not bad," Bo answered. "What brings you to my diner?"

"I need to talk to Lin Chi. It's important. I need her help."

Lin Chi came from the backroom carrying a box. She stopped, surprised to see Peter. "Hey, dude." She smiled, put the box on a chair and sat beside Peter, patting his back.

"He needs your help," Bo explained.

"Great, and me fresh out of scalpels," Lin Chi said.

Peter laughed. "Assisting me in surgery might be easier for you than what I need."

"What is it?" she asked, looking his face over closely. "Trouble?" Peter nodded. "First, tell me about the white princess."

"That's why I need your help," Peter said, and Lin Chi looked puzzled.

Bo leaned against the counter. "Is this private or can I stay?"

"Stay," Peter replied. "I'll take all the brain power I can get." He sighed. "I'm married, Lin Chi."

"Hey!" She smiled then wrinkled her brow. "Why ain't you smiling when you say it?"

"I got nailed on a paternity thing. The bitch is holding all the aces. She resents Jeneil and she's threatened to have some friends visit her."

Lin Chi stared in disbelief. "Who the hell did you marry?"

"I know you won't believe it, but she's a Wong."

"Not Uette?" Bo asked, standing up.

"You heard of her then?" Peter asked.

Lin Chi's mouth stayed open from shock and then she swallowed. "Oh, Pete." She took his hand. "Oh, man, Pete, you're soft dude, you're too far from the streets."

"Everyone on the street knows her," Bo said, sighing.

It was Peter's turn to be shocked. "What's she into?" he asked. "Does she really have people? How did she get past the community?"

"Pete, worry about the white princess if she's been threatened. Uette's crazy. I swear she is." Lin Chi wiped a tear that spilled down her cheek. "Oh, Pete, she has friends. She's not talked about except in whispers because she's involved somewhere in the scum that took over the Dragons."

Peter felt his head go numb as the news hit him. He stood up, holding his stomach. "What?" he gasped. "How could I miss that?" he added, still overwhelmed.

"Nobody wants to even whisper the name Dragon let alone anybody connected to it."

Peter rubbed his forehead. "Shit," he said quietly, heaving a sigh. "Well, I've got to shake the tree. The father of her baby is in there somewhere."

"You can't!" Lin Chi gasped. "You've lost touch with what's out there. It takes know how to stay alive. The strings behind the Dragons are cold blooded, Pete. You'd never make it past your first question."

"I have to," Peter said. "I'm not getting nailed for the baby. I want my name cleared."

Lin Chi shook her head. "Pete, honey, if they let you live, you won't be a surgeon when they're done with you." She got off her chair and hugged him. "Stay away from it, please."

"How far into the group is she?"

Lin Chi shrugged. "She's running around in a Corvette, you know that's not second string."

"That's not from her father?"

Lin Chi shook her head. "She lies so much, I don't think she knows what truth is. My advice, accept the baby and then get a divorce."

Peter sighed. "I can't, Lin Chi. I'm not made that way." He kissed her cheek and turned to Bo to shake hands.

"Better listen to her, Pete," Bo said. "You're not from the street no more. Life on the street is cheap. It means nothing to them."

"Thanks, you two." Peter smiled. "I got information faster than I expected to."

Twenty-Eight

Peter drove to work wondering what to do first. Lin Chi's information about Uette being connected to the Dragons made him worry even more about Jeneil. He had to find her. He had to know that she was okay. Uette's filth changed everything completely. He called Steve's office and was told he was making rounds at the hospital. Walking on to the floor, he spotted Steve at the nurse's desk.

"Got a minute?" Peter asked, as he got near him.

"Yeah, I'd like to see you, too," Steve said, following him to the viewing room and closing the door. "Pete, what's this about Jeneil quitting? The whole hospital is talking about it. I called the apartment, there's still no answer."

Peter sighed. "Steve, I need your help."

"Where's Jeneil?"

"I'm not sure. Steve, please listen to me, okay?" Peter was getting anxious.

"Okay. Is it about Jeneil?" Steve asked, and Peter nodded and leaned against the table worn out from worrying.

"About a month ago, Uette told me to stop seeing Jeneil here. I've been going in at noon to see her and any other chance I had. Uette hinted that she'd get friends to talk to Jeneil if I didn't. Last Thursday, Uette showed me some photographs she had taken. Jeneil was completely unaware she was being photographed. Uette decided she wanted Jeneil out of the hospital and said I should tell her or her friends would." Steve's face showed concern and Peter saw anger in his eyes. "Steve, her family assured me there was no way she could have such friends. I believed it. I wanted to believe it. I didn't tell Jeneil. I didn't want to scare her." Steve stared intently in angry silence. "Today, I found out Jeneil quit. She left a message at her office that she had to. I'm not sure what that means. Her uncle was pressuring her to leave, too." Peter sighed. "Today, I saw Lin Chi and Bo. They told me Uette has connections to the garbage who took over the Dragons."

"Holy shit!" Steve gasped, and turned away shaken. He turned back quickly filled with anger. "Pete, you were supposed to keep the shit away from her, damn it!"

"Steve, don't waste time getting mad at me. Find Jeneil, please. I can't make a move, not now that I know who Uette's muscle is."

"Will her office tell me?" Steve asked, pacing.

"No," Peter replied. "I don't know."

Steve sighed, running his fingers through his hair. "Where do I start, Pete? Where?"

"Get a detective, Steve. I'll pay for it, but my name can't be connected to him. That's why I'm asking you."

Steve nodded. "You're right. Okay, I'll get on it right away." He rubbed his chin. "Pete, I don't have to tell you that I hate this. It's not how she lives and if that kind of muscle is behind her leaving here, I'll kick Uette's ass. Tell her she can count on it."

"Get in line, Steve. I've already told her what to expect if Jeneil gets touched. You can have the pieces that are left over."

Steve exhaled deeply. "I hope she's okay."

Peter nodded. "She left a note for Adrienne. It didn't sound like she was scared. My concern is that Uette is connected to worse shit than even I imagined. Be aware of that. I intend to stay away from Jeneil until this mess is cleared up to protect her." Peter looked at Steve. "Are you free to watch her for me?"

"What do you mean free?"

"Any serious relationship in your life right now?"

Steve shook his head. "No, but I'm being introduced to every eligible girl in the state. Mrs. Sprague wants me married, I guess. She's rounding up all kinds of girls for me. I'm dating, but nothing serious. I'll watch Jeneil for both of us."

Peter sighed and put his head back. "This is going to end. I can't take much more."

Steve could see Peter's suffering and he patted Peter's shoulder. "Jeneil is probably safe somewhere and I'm leaning on you. It must give you nightmares worrying about her."

"If I lost her, Steve, I think I'd just give up. There'd be no reason to live."

Steve smiled weakly. "When you fell off the mountain, it was straight down for you."

Peter nodded. "It's beyond me. She got into my blood and all through my system." He looked down at the floor wondering if he should tell Steve since the moment seemed right. He looked up. "Steve, I have to tell you that I'm worried about you looking after Jeneil." Steve held his breath and never asked why. Peter stood up and walked away then returned. "You and Jeneil are good friends. She's the type who gets into your blood. She can't help it. I'm worried about you."

Steve was stunned by Peter's directness, his honesty reaching him at a level of a trusted friend and he felt Peter deserved honesty in return. He struggled to find the right words. "Pete, I'm not going to tell you that I'm not crazy about Jeneil. In fact, I'm wondering about your remark. You wouldn't have said it without a reason but you have to understand something, she's yours, I know that. She doesn't see past you. It's incredible. I hope I can find someone who can be that attached to me because I'd marry her whether I'm in love with her or not. Jeneil's devoted to me as a friend. I know I'm special to her and I'm crazy about that. I'll take that kind of love because to be able to manage that kind of relationship with a woman was beyond me or so I thought. Jeneil has unlocked feelings I thought were locked away under deep scars. You're right; she gets into your blood. I'd get married and I'd be happily married because of Jeneil. I owe her for that if nothing else, but I'm not kidding myself. To use her words, she belongs to you. That's it right there, Pete. You don't have to worry because of that. I love her enough to want what will make her happiest and that's you. Enjoy it, man. I guess there are times when people are just destined for each other like it's written in the stars and you've got it."

Peter sighed. "Boy, am I glad I spoke up."

"Me, too. We'd sort of lost something between us, hadn't we?"

Peter nodded and extended his hand. "But it's not trust, Steve. I know that."

Steve smiled broadly and shook Peter's hand. "So what are you planning now?"

Peter shrugged. "What can I do? Somewhere in the shit is the guy who's the real father. I've got to get to him."

Steve was concerned. "But why? He probably didn't want to marry her, that's why she nailed you. So why find him? In fact, he'll eat your flesh if you try, you must know that."

"Because I want the truth, Steve. I can't live with the shit she's dumped on me."

Steve shook his head. "You might have to, Pete. You're marching against sealed doors and armed men. How many times will you need your head smashed in before you quit? Look at what it cost you. I know you married the bitch to save face, but who the hell figured on the shit that's involved. Mess with them and you'll be lucky to save your fingers, let alone your face, and then its goodbye surgery. I can understand why Uette's lying. She knows what telling the truth would cost her. And we haven't even begun to discuss the fact that you don't know the streets anymore. That's a double disadvantage."

Peter shrugged his shoulders. "So I'll play it by ear until I learn it again."

"Great, your ears will be the first things they send to you bronzed. Hang in there long enough and they'll send you enough bronzed pieces of yourself to complete the statue."

Peter smiled. "Ki used to say that everyone's got a weak spot. You have to find it."

"Oh, Pete, please. That didn't work for Ki. Geez, they spilled his guts all over the damn street."

"Yeah, but Ki trusted Reed. That was his weak spot. I'm not trusting anybody in this."

Steve stared at Peter as a thought flashed through his mind. "But your weak spot is Jeneil. They'd muscle her to shut you up. Think about what you're doing. Give it some thought."

Peter smiled. "That's why I want you to watch her for me. Be seen with her Steve; switch the gossip here to you and Jeneil."

"What?" Steve asked, almost blown over by the words. "Pete, you're crazy."

"It's ideal, Steve. Jeneil's gone now, the gossip won't hurt her. Nobody knows about Jeneil and me. It's the safest route. Let the bitch think you and Jeneil are together. Then Jeneil's protected."

Steve shook his head. "Shit, you're more naive than I thought. Even Uette won't buy that. It's a risk. It might make you feel secure thinking they're buying it, but Jeneil's the one who'll get hurt if they don't. They'd muscle her just to teach you not to mess with them."

"Steve, this is the safest risk I have. Uette wants Jeneil out of my life, that's the best way to do it and convince the bitch. I can't turn this around in a week. I know that now. But I'm going to move fast in order to surprise them all. That gives me a slight advantage. I want Jeneil away from the backlash."

Steve sat down and rubbed his neck. "Geez, I didn't know this is what you meant about looking after her for you. What the hell happens when it's over, assuming you survive with workable parts, and you and Jeneil get married? Won't that shake up the gossip line quite a bit?"

"Do you care?" Peter asked. "If it protects Jeneil?"

Steve stood up and took a few steps. "No, of course not, but I still think you're wrong. You and Jeneil could both get hurt. I say dump the whole idea. Divorce the bitch."

"I don't have too many choices. I really don't," Peter said thoughtfully.

Steve sighed. "Oh shit, what a mess this is."

"Will you do it?"

Steve paced. "Will Jeneil know about all this?"

"No!" Peter answered emphatically. "No, the less she knows, the safer she is. Just find her and be seen with her. The gossips will take it from there."

"I'll find her, Pete. I want to know she's okay, but as for making us look like a couple, I don't know, it sounds impossible."

"Just watch her, Steve. She expects me to stay away. Her uncle wants me out of her life and there's my reason to prove the baby isn't mine. I'm not dragging anymore shit into my marriage to Jeneil."

Steve shook his head. "Man, you crept into a suit of armor when you flipped out over her and you can't get out of it. It's welded on."

Peter smiled. "I told you. She gets into your blood."

*****

Encouraged by the talk with Steve, Peter went to the telephone and called Adrienne. There was no word from Jeneil and Hollis had arrived taking charge like a five star general. Adrienne was worried; Hollis had threatened to place Jeneil on the next flight to Nebraska as soon as she was found. That concerned Peter and then he realized how much safer she'd be there. He told Adrienne he'd call again the next day and he returned to work. His job required his full and undivided attention, and he was glad for the mental relaxation it provided.

Arriving home, he felt tired and drained. Uette opened her bedroom door as he reached his. "Peter, can I talk to you?"

He stopped, struggling with a strong urge to hit her for the filth she'd brought into his life and into Jeneil's "What about?"

"Us," she answered simply.

"There isn't any us. What do you want to talk about next?"

"I'll wait." She sighed. "It'll take more time, I guess."

Peter remembered the mail. "Oh, I got the bills from your credit cards. Both had zero balances. Very good," he said, pulling the envelopes from his pocket. "By the way, there's a letter for you from a modeling agency in New York." He watched as panic filled her eyes. "I didn't know you worked in New York."

"Where's the letter?" she asked abruptly. "Give it to me." He handed it to her; she grabbed it and went into her bedroom, closing the door quickly.

"Well, I know where to start looking for daddy." He grinned, going into his bedroom.

Peter awoke to the sound of Uette's bedroom door slamming. Putting on his robe, he went to the kitchen and made toast. He had mid-morning surgery with Dr. Maxwell. Uette stomped in looking disgruntled. Peter watched as she poured some juice and took a vitamin. She didn't look pregnant. Peter counted mentally. She must be in her fourth month by now. Going to the table with the plate of toast, he put it before her. "Have a piece of toast. You should be careful of your nutrition."

"I'm taking a vitamin every day," she said, looking at him suspiciously because of his show of concern.

"Nutrition's more than that. Are you eating a good lunch and dinner?"

"Do you really care?" she asked sarcastically.

"Uette, you wouldn't believe the damage prenatal neglect can do. The refrigerator has more diet soda in it than anything else. If that's all you're getting then you'll be in trouble, along with the fetus."

Uette glared at him. "It's a baby, Peter, call it that. A fetus sounds like a malignant growth. You and I are having a baby."

"It's just a word." He shrugged.

"But it indicates your attitude. I had hoped you'd have accepted the baby by now." Tears filled her eyes.

"We're talking about your nutrition."

She picked up her purse. "I have to get to class."

"What was the letter from the modeling agency about?" he asked, wondering what answer he'd get.

She stared at him suspiciously. "Nothing."

"Businesses don't send letters for no reason," he persisted.

She raised her eyebrows. "What's with all the questions and concerns? Last night I had typhoid, this morning you're spreading honey on my toast."

"I just wondered if you owed any money, that's all."

"Well, don't worry about it. I'd take care of it if I did. I wouldn't spend your money on me, my goodness, I know better now." She dramatized her words.

"Uette, there's very little food in the house. Where's the money going?"

She sighed. "Get off my back. You're never home to eat anyway, so what do you care?"

"Are the dishes in the sink dirty or clean?"

She closed her eyes. "I'm not sure."

"I'll put them through a cycle then. No problem."

She wrinkled her eyebrows, surprised by his consideration. "You cleaned the bathroom sink," she said. "That sponge under the soap dish was a good idea. I hate cleaning that oozy soap. It's disgusting." She shivered. "Is that something they do at the hospital?"

Peter wanted to avoid Jeneil's name at all cost. "In the doctor's lounge."

She smiled. "Thanks for helping."

He nodded. "It's okay. Do you need my help with the modeling agency? I forgot what you said they wanted."

"I didn't say," she replied, watching him, "but thanks, I'll take care of it."

"Fine." He shrugged nonchalantly and drank his Ovaltine.

"I've got to go," she said, still watching him closely.

"Take a piece of toast with you," he suggested.

"No thanks, too many calories."

"Watch your diet, okay?" he said, concerned for her health. "You must be somewhere near your fourth month and you don't look pregnant. You're not gaining weight and you look too pale. Who's your doctor?"

Uette was surprised by his sincerity. "Nelson Vandiver."

Peter didn't know him. "Are you keeping your appointments?" She nodded, not believing his genuine concern. "Isn't he worried?"

"He said to watch my diet and worry about my figure after the baby is born. But it's not easy having a new husband to impress while the baby is making you bloat."

Peter shook his head. "Uette, get your priorities straight. That baby's doing what it's supposed to do. Pregnant women are not ugly. In fact, most women bloom with beauty when they're pregnant."

She smiled warmly. "You're so sweet when you're being human."

Peter felt he might have shown too much concern. "Toxemia's not funny, Uette. Watch your health."

"I will," she answered, charmed. "I've got to get to class." He nodded, and she walked to the door and looked back for a second before she left.

He shook his head. She was flirting with trouble. She was no more ready to have a baby than he was. He sighed worried about the damage she might be doing to the life growing inside of her. She was a selfish bitch in everything she did. And damn slick, too. She was shrewd. Just the type he avoided. He sighed again. But he hadn't avoided her nearly well enough. The telephone rang interrupting his thoughts.

"Grandfather, how are you?"

"Worried, Peter. You're just lucky I happened to answer the call that came for you."

"Oh, what is it?" Peter asked, concerned.

"Lin Chi wants you to call her and said not to use your home phone and make sure you didn't use the same public phone all of the time. Peter, what's going on? What is she doing in your life again? Don't you have enough trouble to handle already?"

"Grandfather, relax. I went to Lin Chi for help finding someone who knew about Uette. She knows Uette, Grandfather. Lin Chi and her man, Bo, have heard of her. Uette's a...a...one of the women used by the filth who took over the Dragons."

"What?" his grandfather gasped. "That's impossible. That has to be wrong."

"It isn't. I wish it was because I have to worry about her threat to Jeneil and Jeneil has disappeared." Peter heard silence and knew the concern it indicated.

"Oh my heavens, Peter, you don't think."

"At this point, no, not based on Jeneil's note and Uette's behavior. The bitch would be grinning from ear to ear if she had been behind it, but she acts like she doesn't know."

His grandfather sighed. "Then where's Jeneil? Why did she disappear?"

"Her uncle wants her back home. He heard about me getting married. That's probably what's happening."

"That's almost as bad," his grandfather replied sadly.

"I think so, too." Peter sighed. "I'm in big trouble with him now and it's certainly understandable."

"Of course," his grandfather replied. "There doesn't seem to be much honor for you in saving face, Peter. Uette's grandfather called. The doctor contacted her father. She's not eating properly or looking after herself. The Wongs are worried that you don't give her enough money."

"I won't buy that guilt," Peter answered sharply. "I've given her ideas for food, but she's not listening as usual. The refrigerator is stuffed with diet soda and not much more. This morning she told me she's watching her weight because it's hard to impress a husband while the baby's making her bloat. She's living a fantasy and I refuse to be blamed. I'm not going to sleep with her to cheer her up. I warned her about her health. I even offered her some toast but it had too many calories, so she had juice and a vitamin and went to school. You tell the Wongs if the problem's that serious then she can go home so they can look after her. I'll be glad to move out. I can't watch her with my hours. I'm seldom at the apartment."

"Has she lost control again like she did last Thursday?"

"No, I've hardly seen her. Make it clear to them that this screwy marriage is causing the stress. I'm not out to hurt her or the baby, but I refuse to play house. She signed the agreement. I've told her that I'll never be interested in her, but she keeps waiting for me to accept her and the baby. We're at a stalemate. I don't even know if she's doing drugs anymore or if the doctor knows. And being honest, I really don't care. I've warned her, there's not much else I can do."

"I understand, Peter. I think the Wongs will, too. They're seeing her failings in this, they really are. I appreciate how fair they are trying to be by listening to your side. You hold more of their respect than she does. Your word is stronger. I can see that."

"You can tell them that her doctor will only take her neglect for so long before hospitalizing her. That's procedure. She'll wake up or get hospitalized."

"I'll tell them, I'm sure it will help. I feel better knowing that. What do you think Lin Chi wants?"

"I don't know," Peter replied. "She's worried. She doesn't want me poking around."

His grandfather gasped. "You're not going to, are you?"

"Grandfather, how else can I find who the father is?"

"But Peter, even people who are not on the street know about the Chun family. They're vicious, ruthless people."

"I don't have any choice, Grandfather. My wonderful Chinese wife brought a strange dowry to the marriage."

His grandfather sighed. "Peter, please think about what you're planning. It's more than dangerous, it's foolish."

"I have to go, Grandfather. I'm scheduled for surgery. Tell the Wongs I'll pick up frozen diet meals and keep them here for Uette. The apartment has a microwave. It's better than nothing. Maybe she'll eat anything labeled diet. I'll get some fruit. After that, I can't do more," he said, getting annoyed. "Damn, she's such a screwball. She's a lousy doctor's wife. She can't manage her own life let alone a baby's and a husband's."

"You're being fair, Peter. I'll report that to them."

*****

Peter called Lin Chi; she wanted to see him. They couldn't work out a time to meet at the diner around his surgery schedule so she said she'd be at the hospital after the dinner crowd at the diner. Steve stopped by the hospital to tell Peter he'd found a private detective who would start on the case immediately. They both missed Jeneil and were hopeful they would find her soon. Peter mentioned that Uette seemed unaware of any change which could mean that Jeneil was just taking time off somewhere.

Lin Chi arrived during early evening visiting hours. Peter came from the ICU and met her in the hallway. "I can find a private spot."

"No!" Lin Chi replied quickly. "Right here, man, in the middle of everything and out in the open." She took some papers from an envelope. "Pretend you're looking at medical reports, Pete."

"Why are you so nervous?" he asked, wondering about her behavior as he took them from her.

"Man, you are soft. You must be being watched for her to know about you seeing Jeneil."

"Oh, right." Peter nodded. "Why are you here?"

"Because I want to help. Bo and I talked it over. We want to help you by shaking the tree."

Peter was shocked. "I can't let you do that, Lin Chi."

She smiled. "Sure you can, honey. I owe you big. You pulled me off the ceiling quite a few times. You were there when I OD'ed and you took the muscle a few times when my dealer got itchy about his money."

Peter smiled at her. "I was returning from Lin Chi."

"Like hell, dude. I owe you and you never asked for nothing."

"You helped me to grow up."

She laughed. "You did that yourself once you saw what real craziness could do to a person, and I was real crazy."

He put his arm around her shoulder and hugged her to him. "But this is different," he said, releasing her.

"No, honey," she said. "Bo and I talked a lot about it and there are a few question marks."

"Like what?"

"Well, she's been in the game a long time, so how come she wants a baby? She's never been into mothering. We were thinking she got pregnant and the guy didn't want to bother with it. But when Bo and I thought about it, that's not the tune that bunch sings. So she must have gotten herself pregnant just to nail you."

"Why?" he asked, puzzled.

She smiled. "Because you're a sexy son-of-a-bitch and a doctor besides."

"That's not cutting it with me."

She grinned. "How about she wants out of the shit but everything on the straight street bores her. That is until she came across you. You offer her the toughness of the street and a straight life. The 'rappin' on her wondered how she was going to fake much longer."

"How long has it been?" he asked, very curious about the innocent face.

Lin Chi shook her head. "She was a kid, Pete. I heard she wanted to be a model. They own a modeling agency that fronts for other things, too." Peter felt sick. "She was always a little crazy, different from her family, so she thinks she's sharp shit and slips into a fake life for them. They're so decent, who the hell would have the guts to tell them. Well, son-of-a-bitch if she doesn't find a way out. She's out slicked them if Bo and I are seeing this right, and she still has the Corvette. Now that's interesting because they usually strip you of everything when you want out. It helps the girls want back in, but she's getting old."

"Where do they find all the Chinese girls?" Peter asked, surprised she called Uette old.

She wrinkled her eyebrows. "Come on, Pete. They're not bigots. White, black, mulatto, they're equal opportunity. Race doesn't matter at all."

Peter sighed. "Lin Chi, I'm worried about you two doing this."

"Honey, it's safer if we do it. We got people out there. You don't. We know where to look. There's no talking between us on this. It will take time though; we're not going to be foolish. You just watch the bitch. If we're not reading this right then she'll be a cobra. So watch her and watch yourself around her until we get some echoes, okay?"

Peter hesitated. "Lin Chi…."

"No," she interrupted. "No thanks either. I'll get a chance to pay you back. I like that."

"Be careful, please." Peter sighed.

"You know it." Lin Chi smiled, pleased with the crusade she was about to begin, pleased Peter was overwhelmed.

*****

It was Wednesday, an early surgery day. Uette had been sleeping or at least silent when Peter had gotten in from work the night before and he was surprised to see her rush into the kitchen as he drank his juice. Uette sighed. "Oh good, you're still here. Can you take me to my parent's house so I can get my mother's car? I have an early class."

"Where's the Corvette?"

"I'm having trouble with it," she said, and headed toward her bedroom. "I'll put jeans and a top on. It won't take long."

Peter chuckled. He'd just bet she was having trouble with it. What was in that letter, he wondered. He got his jacket and waited, the thought she had been just a kid when she got tangled into the mess settling in his mind. Compassion filled him as he pictured her as an inexperienced girl trying to follow a dream and uncovering a nightmare. She walked into the room and he smiled at her, still saddened by the thought. His smile surprised her and warmth filled her heart.

*****

Peter called Adrienne. While he didn't believe Uette was behind Jeneil's disappearance, he was concerned that too many days had passed without a word from her.

"Peter, has she contacted you?" Adrienne asked.

"Then you haven't heard from her yet?" He sighed.

"No, but Hollis has."

Peter stood up straight. "She's okay then?"

Adrienne sighed. "I don't know, Peter. He's seen her. He's even more upset. I heard him call Bill Reynolds and ask him to fly in. Hollis is shaken, that's for sure. Something's odd because I heard him tell Bill that he wouldn't believe it. Whatever it is, he blames you because he said, 'this is his fault, that son-of-a-bitch. You should see her, that beautiful girl ruined. It'll break your heart.' Hollis is really low. I can tell he's really worried."

Peter felt his heart skip a beat. "You don't know what he meant or why he's worried?"

"No." Adrienne choked up with emotion. "I wish she'd call. I don't understand why she hasn't."

Peter sat back. What had happened? What was wrong with her? He sighed as the operator signaled for more money. They ended the call and Peter was left wondering what could be wrong. He went back to work and calmed his worries by concentrating on the fact that she had at least been found. He missed her. He missed seeing her. The empty feeling stayed with him now and he had come to accept that as normal.

*****

Uette explained the disappearance of the Corvette by saying it was too expensive to maintain. She was driving an economy car now that her father had bought for her. Peter couldn't resist and had asked why her father had bought the car and why she hadn't bought it with the money from the sale of the Corvette. He watched as her mind spinned into action. She explained that the car was leased by the modeling agency and they had asked her to pick up the lease now that she had left. Peter realized she may have been an inexperienced girl when she arrived in New York, but she was in total charge of her lying now. He didn't trust her and he knew he never would. It was a feeling that emerged deep from within just like the emptiness over Jeneil's absence. The distrust lasted side by side with the emptiness.

Peter continued to check with Adrienne and there was still no word from Jeneil. Bill Reynolds had arrived at the office and he and Hollis had gone to visit Jeneil. They returned and locked themselves in her office with deli sandwiches and a pot of coffee, emerging two hours later. Not being able to stand the suspense any longer, Adrienne asked them if Jeneil was all right. Hollis had just sighed; Bill smiled and told her that Jeneil was fine for Jeneil. "She's a butterfly, that's all. She's always had her own drummer. She has just taken the week to readjust to her surroundings." That didn't make sense to Adrienne since Jeneil hadn't been at the apartment since a week ago Friday.

"She's quit her job and a lot of change has come into her life. She needed to go to the center of herself," Bill explained, smiling broadly, obviously quite taken with whatever Jeneil was into. Hollis had shaken his head and insisted there was nothing wrong with the beautiful girl Jeneil was. Bill laughed and patted Hollis's back. "It's a natural part of life for beautiful young girls to merge into beautiful women." Bill had said Hollis's problem was that he didn't see Jeneil changing daily and since she was so skilled at costumes, he was surprised by her life. "It's more like a thrust than emerging," Bill said, "but that's Jeneil," and he laughed. Adrienne still wasn't sure what it all meant, but the tone after they returned from visiting Jeneil had been more cheerful. Hollis still had reservations and insisted that he was going to keep a close watch on her. Bill handed him his briefcase and reminded him, "I didn't give her the name of dipstick for nothing."

Bill was taking Hollis back to Nebraska with him, but not Jeneil. They wished the personnel a good weekend and said Jeneil would be in touch. Adrienne was hopeful, but still puzzled. Tony was, too; he felt like Hollis about Jeneil. Peter felt a sense of loss as he realized something was happening in Jeneil's life and he wasn't sharing it with her. The emptiness turned to pain then returned to emptiness as he became entrenched in work. His grandfather kept telling him the Songbird needed protecting, but Peter found that he needed the Songbird more. Her song was missing from his life and it left a noticeable gap.

Peter looked up as Steve walked into the medical room smiling broadly and closed the door. Peter grinned. "I still can't get used to you in a suit and overcoat, Dr. Bradley."

Steve looked down at himself and shrugged. "You get used to it." He hit Peter's shoulder. "I heard from the detective. He found Jeneil!" Steve beamed with excitement.

Peter sighed. "Don't tell me where she is because I know damn well I wouldn't stay away from her and that would mess everything up. Are you going to see her?"

"You bet, first thing tomorrow morning. I have a meeting tonight with Dr. Sprague but I'll find this place early tomorrow, I promise. Boy, the guy is thorough. He gave me detailed directions. Dr. Sprague's lawyer said he was the best." Peter enjoyed Steve's sense of relief. "I have to be going. I feel better now that I know I can find her. I'll be in touch. Are you on duty this weekend?" Peter nodded. "Okay, I'll check in with you," Steve said, and went to the door.

"Thanks."

"It's okay. Feels good to breathe again, doesn't it." Steve grinned and left whistling.

The emptiness turned to pain again as Peter realized Steve could whistle. He'd be seeing Jeneil tomorrow, sharing whatever was new in her life. He'd be seeing her, talking to her, and watching her smile. Peter heaved a sigh and returned to his medical report, hoping the pain would again return to emptiness.

Twenty-Nine

Steve awoke the next morning feeling very cheerful even though the day was dismal with a fine misty rain. His telephone rang as he put his jacket on.

"Hi, Steve, it's Pete."

"Well, you just caught me. I was heading out."

"Could you tell her I've been crazy with worry this past week?"

Steve smiled. "I'll tell her you love her and that you miss her and that her idea of separation shits. Does that about cover it?"

"Just about," Peter said quietly then sighed. "I'll let you go."

"Okay, Pete. I need to start early; this is new territory for me. I'm glad it's daylight. I'll get back to you tonight."

"Thanks, Steve. Thanks a lot. I mean that."

Steve could almost feel Peter's discouragement. "She's okay, Pete. Don't worry."

"I know that," Peter said, "I just wish I was seeing it for myself. This is another reason to find Uette disgusting. I'll wait to hear from you, Steve. My grandfather, too. Send his love to her also."

Steve laughed. "Want to go along?"

"What I want is for this to be over. I'll let you go."

"Okay, Pete. Call you later."

*****

Steve headed toward Weeden. All he knew about the town was it was small and somewhere near the ocean. Thistle Lane sounded small, too. It was off Route 20, which he'd never heard of. But they all sounded fine to him because that's where he could find Jeneil. As he entered the center of town, he began to feel anxious about seeing her. Why hadn't she called him? He was disappointed about that. Passing Gilend Road, he began noticing how remote the area was. Briar Patch Lane was next. It was exactly that, a small road, almost a path. Houses were fewer and farther between, and he became concerned about her safety and reminded himself to wait until he saw her before worrying. Looking to his left, the roads led toward land. To his right, the roads looked like they led toward water. Pulling over, he checked his directions; three more lanes to go. He felt his heart beat faster and he continued driving. A sign marked Thistle Lane was nailed to a thin post at the end of the road. It didn't look very well-traveled. He turned his car onto the small path, surprised it was so rugged. He wondered where she was living; there were no houses in sight. The lane turned left and he saw the roof of a house coming into view, the house itself obscured by high shrubs. There were no other houses.

It must be hers, he thought, pulling up to the driveway. Her car was there. He smiled and pulled in beside it, getting out quickly. Looking around, the small house was weathered and broken down and it puzzled him that she'd be living there. The yard was unkempt and weeds had claimed what looked like flower beds near the base of the house. "What's she doing here?" he asked, looking at the window shutter hanging from one hinge. He rang the front doorbell and not hearing any sound, he knocked on the paint-peeling door. There was no answer. He walked around the back. The yard was overgrown with long clumps of dead grass. He could see the inlet of water at the end of the yard. The ocean smell was unmistakable and seagulls screeched their familiar call. The wind swept across the yard, sending litter from abandoned garbage bags rolling across the yard into the shrubs growing along the side of the house. "Jeneil, what are you doing?"

A fine mist had begun to fall that combined with the wind made Steve feel chilled. He walked back to his car and was glad to be out of the dreary weather. Where was she, he wondered as he looked around. This was the only house and, looking farther down the lane, he could see it led to a large area of water. Realizing that she was living in such a remote area began to worry him. She was too vulnerable. There was no one to help her if she should need it. If anyone wanted to get to her without warning, they could. She was a sitting duck, alone and unprotected. He was getting more worried as he considered the threat of danger from Uette's friends. He sighed and began wishing she'd turn up.

Deciding to drive the rest of the lane, he put the key in the ignition and turned his head to back out. He caught sight of something green moving in the lane. It was someone in a bright green rain slicker. He turned off the engine and waited. It had to be Jeneil. He watched as the figure got closer. It was carrying a bucket in one hand and had something held in the other balanced on its shoulder. It looked like a tool of some kind. The hood of the slicker was pulled forward to keep out the rain so Steve couldn't see who it was. He thought it was an odd way for Jeneil to be dressed, army green rubber boots flopping near the knees. And what the hell is that thing she's carrying?

Steve got out of the car and walked to the other side of the driveway to wait. The figure must have seen him because it stopped and then began walking quickly toward him waving. It was Jeneil! His heart beat rapidly and he choked up at the relief of actually seeing her. The bucket slowed her down and he saw her struggle with it as she tried to walk faster. He ran the short distance to her and put his arms around her, tightly holding on to her without talking. He could feel her clinging to him.

"Oh, you crazy kid," he said, laughing. "You scared me sick." He released her and looked at her. She looked different somehow. Her cheeks were bright from the cold, along with her nose and chin. "What're you doing here?"

She smiled her gentle half smile. "Getting dinner."

"Dinner?" he asked, looking into the bucket. "For what, your pet shark? What is that?"

"The black things on top are mussels and there are clams underneath," she answered. "How did you find me?"

"Private detective," he answered. "And now that you've mentioned it, why didn't you call me?"

She shrugged. "I haven't called anyone except Uncle Hollis. Things rushed at me. I needed to change my surroundings. Everything at the apartment reminded me of Peter."

"He's worried sick about you."

"I left him a message," she answered defensively. "Has the situation there changed?" Steve shook his head and she sighed. "I'll carry the clam rake if you carry the bucket."

Steve looked at her, thinking she looked different. Jeneil put her hand in his and they walked back to the house.

"Why are you staring?" she asked.

He laughed. "You look like a storybook character."

She smiled. "Who?"

"I don't know."

She squeezed his hand. "It's so good to see you. It feels good to know that you care."

"Peter hired the detective."

"Oh gosh, he doesn't have that kind of money to spend. I guess I shouldn't have been so selfish but it was a survival thing, me against negative forces." They reached the driveway and she ran to put the clam rake in the broken down garage, and then joined him to walk to the back door. Sitting on the steps, she pulled off her boots. "It's unlocked," she said, standing. "Just go on in."

Steve worried about her lack of security. The kitchen was small and the inside of the house smelled of fresh paint. There were pegs on a board nailed to the wall by the back door. He took off his jacket. Jeneil took off her gloves and began unsnapping the rain slicker. "Where do you want the bucket of shark food?"

"In the sink," she answered, laughing. "I'll scrub them and let them sit in water with oatmeal. That makes them 'spit grit' so the chowder isn't crunchy."

"Oh geez," he said, as he lifted the bucket into the sink and turned around to look at her. His eyes opened wide in shock as she took off her rain slicker. "Jeneil!" he gasped. "Your hair! What happened to your hair?" He walked to her, staring at the short strands of hair that waved and curled around her face.

"I cut it off," she answered, running her fingers through it awkwardly. "It must be a mess right know from the slicker."

"Oh, Jeneil," he groaned. "Why, honey? Why? All that beautiful hair." He stopped and looked at it. "Wow, I can't believe it!"

She shrugged. "I don't know why I did it. I just felt like changing, I guess. I really like it now." She smiled gently. "I feel sort of set free." He put his arms around her and held her. She leaned against him.

"What are you doing kid? Why are you living in this dump?"

She pulled away and laughed. "Dump! It's a sad house. It's not a dump."

"A sad house?" he asked, not believing he heard her right.

"Yes," she said, sitting at the kitchen table. "I was looking through some real estate books and this house was in one of them. I felt bad for it. It looked like it was sad. I came to see it and I'm living here rent free in exchange for fixing it up. You should feel how cheerful the house is already now that painters and exterminators have been here. It's a cape cottage, the windows are small and the interior was dark. I did everything in white to pick up what light does come in. There are flower beds all over the place and I think there's an herb garden out back. There was love here once. So I decided to stay and cheer it up."

Steve looked around. The small kitchen looked clean with fresh paint. Everything was white except the floor, which was linoleum in a grey and beige pebble pattern on a cream background. There were no curtains, just white shutters at the windows. He smiled and shook his head. "Wait until Pete hears that's why you disappeared, you're cheering up a house." He laughed, went to her and kissed her cheek. "From you, that makes sense."

"It's a partnership." She smiled. "It needed love and I needed to love something." Steve smiled, understanding, having felt seriously what her love could do. "Are you hungry?"

"Not for anything you've dredged in from the ocean."

"I've been living on turkey all week. I dredged it in from the market," she said, getting up. "Turkey soup sounds nice and warm."

"Don't fuss," Steve said.

Jeneil washed her hands and put a blue enameled pot filled with water on a burner. Taking a foil-wrapped lump from the refrigerator, she cut off pieces of meat and added them to the pot, along with seasoning cubes and celery she had chopped quickly. Taking a plastic pan, she took out the clams and mussels and scrubbed them, putting them in the pan with fresh water. She poured oatmeal over them and set the pan aside on the counter. The soup water boiled and she added rice. Steve watched as she put the meal together with what looked to be little effort or thought. Scraping a carrot, she grated it over the pot of soup and washed the grater and scraper.

She turned to him, drying her hands. "I'm going to do the bedroom floors after lunch. Feel like helping?"

"What are you doing to them?"

"A second coat of polyurethane. They're hardwood and the sanding has brought them back to life. I think the day should be a drier one, but I don't have much choice, I'm going to work Monday."

"Where do you work now?"

She stirred the soup with a wooden spoon and replaced the cover. "In the corporation, but I'm going in full-time for only a week to catch up then I'll cut back my hours. The playhouse begins its season soon and I'm joining it."

"Hey, you finally made the big jump."

She smiled. "I'll be a gopher, but I like being around all of the areas. I intend to find out what its fascination is." He looked at her, fascinated himself having watched her hair dry and curl up as she worked in the kitchen. Her hair was thick and full, and she was still beautiful. He smiled as she got two bowls, two mugs, and two spoons. She made toast, cut it diagonally and put it on the table then sat down across from him.

"Damn, you look so healthy," he said, looking at her apple red cheeks. Her hair had no particular style. It rambled across her head in waves and curls, doing its own thing as if it was happy to be set free from being tied up and pinned for so many years. She looked relaxed and tousled and incredibly feminine, even in a ragged sweatshirt and paint-speckled jeans.

"Soup must be ready," she said, getting up and filling the bowls. She put a steaming bowl in front of Steve. It smelled good and looked colorful and healthy with bits of green celery and orange carrots.

"Mmm, it's good," he said, tasting it.

She smiled. "My father said to never lose my taste for humble soup. 'You can get used to eating roast beef and steak,' he'd say, 'if you have money, but if soup is a treat for you then you'll feel rich no matter what.' He wasn't alone in his theory. I once read an interview of a great actress who was full of spunk and zest at seventy-three. She said she liked life simple. To her, life was good when the soup was, too. I can understand that. I really can." She ate a spoonful of soup.

Steve wasn't sure what Jeneil, her father or the actress meant, but he felt warm and comfortable sitting there with her eating soup and toast. He relaxed, aware that the wind was churning outside, but he was content right there. He smiled at her. "That haircut makes you look even younger."

"I hope Peter won't mind it," she said, taking a piece of toast. "I'm into such a self-centered syndrome. I can't think past me right now."

"You're loving a house back to health, that's how your life works, sweetheart. You're used to giving love in order to survive." Electricity passed through him and he looked down at his bowl, concentrating on being content.

They went to do the bedroom floors after dishes were done and Steve was surprised at how easily he accepted the work. They talked and laughed, and the chore seemed to move quickly. The bedrooms were painted white with white shutters at the windows. While he enjoyed being with Jeneil, he still didn't like the house. The rooms weren't very big and the house felt too small to him. They sat together on the hallway floor drinking apple juice from mugs after they'd finished.

"Thanks for helping," she said, smiling. "I'd have had to do the other one tomorrow. I did the dining room yesterday and the living room the day before."

"Is everything white with white shutters?"

She nodded. "I know it looks like I lack imagination, but the rooms are small and dim. I thought it was the most practical thing. Summer must be hot in here so I decided on shutters that can be tilted for privacy but still let in some air. I hope I'm not here that long." She sighed. "I miss Peter and Camelot." She smiled. "And you, until you fell down the rabbit hole into Wonderland." She kissed his cheek.

He laughed. "I guess this is Wonderland because I wonder how the hell you'll save the outside of this place. It's the pits."

She laughed. "The house will tell me. It must be about four o'clock, daylight is slipping away. I'll get dinner." She finished her juice.

"Let's eat out, my treat," he insisted.

"But I don't have dresses here."

"So we'll eat somewhere casual. Come on, I insist." He bumped her arm with his.

"Okay," she said, getting up. "It'll be good for me to get into makeup. I'll get showered. Cleaning and painting are taking their toll, I feel pretty drudged."

Steve waited at the kitchen table reading a magazine. The paint on the table was chipped and the chairs were mismatched and in the same condition. He shook his head. This was really Wonderland and he wondered how she could stand it after living in Camelot. He had gotten the magazine from the living room and had seen the folding bed she was sleeping on. It looked like a prison cot. Boy, she was at full tilt. Settling back to read, he caught a glimpse of her passing into the living room and the scent of her perfume wafted faintly to the kitchen. He smiled. The perfume was familiar even if she seemed a little different. He looked up as she walked into the kitchen carrying her toggle coat. Her hair actually looked very nice. She had on a white long sleeved blouse with a plum colored short sleeved sweater over it and grey slacks.

"Did you have your hair styled?"

She grinned. "You're very diplomatic. No, I chopped it off. One side was always uneven and it kept getting shorter."

"I'm getting used to it," he said, standing up and taking her coat to hold for her. Standing behind her while she slipped it on, he could smell the shampoo in her hair. He wanted to hold her; he wished she was his and he felt glad that at least he had found her. He felt sorry for Peter having to stay away from her and he was angry at Uette for threatening her. He wondered if Jeneil should be told about the danger she might be in. His worry filled him and he put his arms around her as she was buttoning her coat, surprising her.

"What's this for?" she asked, smiling.

"Honey, do you think it's safe living out here all alone?"

She nodded. "This is a very nice town. It's mostly retired people. That's what happened to this house. The elderly people who owned it died. They hadn't been able to afford the repairs. They had a small mortgage for their roof and their children wanted it. They couldn't sell it so it was left to foreclosure. It's really very sad, but the area is so remote and all the jobs are north so the younger people go elsewhere with the cost of gas and travel time." She shrugged. "It's a farming community. People don't become farmers anymore and that tells you the state of civilization."

He knew she wouldn't understand his concern without being told about Uette's threats and he couldn't bring himself to tell her. "Okay," he said, kissing her cheek. "Let's get some dinner."

*****

Steve sat across from her as they waited for their order. "The quiet life must agree with you. You look great even under those conditions."

Jeneil laughed. "Those conditions? You sound like Uncle Hollis. The house is warm and dry. I have a place to sleep and food to eat just like you. I just got rid of all the extras. I think Jeneil will surface faster if I get rid of the extras and just face the necessary. Society and I are at a Mexican standoff."

"Don't knock it," he replied. "You make your money from society."

"I'm not knocking society or its lifestyles. I just insist that I want my life my way and I want the chance to see what that way is. It isn't unreasonable to ask for the same rights I allow society, is it?"

"When you say it, it sounds like it makes sense. When I see you living it," he paused, "it looks off-center."

"You're used to mainstream. I'm into alternate lifestyles. That's hardly bizarre or eccentric."

"I'll toss you bizarre maybe, but eccentric, well it does fit."

She shrugged. "I'm not afraid of eccentric."

"I guess rich people aren't."

"I'm not rich," she replied quickly.

Steve laughed. "Hey, you don't have to work. That's not poor."

"I got into trouble with my uncle because I wasn't working. Don't tell me I don't have to work. Rich people work even harder. It's only the people on an assembly line who can leave work behind them. The owner is there long after closing time. Mandra was always into something or other simply because of her money. I'm not rich and I never will be. I don't want to be." The waitress brought their orders.

Steve smiled. "You're colorful, Jeneil, and cute." She smiled and cut into her steak.

*****

It was decided that Steve would spend the night at Jeneil's motel to spare him traveling since he wanted to spend Sunday with her. They stopped in to make arrangements and Steve thought he should call Peter, thinking he must be completely berserk by now. He waited as they connected him.

"This is Dr. Chang," Peter answered. Jeneil watched as Steve smiled.

"Dr. Chang, this is Dr. Bradley."

"Steve!" Peter all but shouted. "Where are you?"

"Right here with Jeneil."

"Really, she's there? What's happening with her?"

"Pete, talk to her." Steve looked at Jeneil questioningly. She smiled and nodded, going to the phone

"Hi," she said.

Peter's heart caved in. "Honey, oh baby, what have you been doing? You scared me. Your message was so vague."

She tugged at a strand of hair. "Hollis wants me devoting more time to business. Considering everything, I decided to leave the hospital. I don't trust myself around you," she said quietly. Steve looked up, surprised by her directness.

Peter smiled broadly. "I've been in touch with Adrienne and she said that Hollis was worried about you."

Jeneil sighed. "There's no reason for him to be. I'm okay, really."

"Why aren't you at the apartment anymore?"

"I need a change, Peter. I'll be working in the corporation starting on Monday."

Peter held the telephone tightly. "Honey, this past week has been hell not knowing where you were."

"I'm sorry, Peter. Everything rushed at me. Was Lin Chi able to help you?"

"She's working on it." Peter didn't add any detail. "It looks like it will take a little time."

"Oh," Jeneil replied, sounding disappointed. "How is life with Uette?"

"I'm rarely at the apartment," Peter reassured her. "I hate the separation, Jeneil. I hate it."

"I do, too." She sighed.

"Honey, if things rush at you again please don't freak, call me here at the hospital, please."

Jeneil smiled at his concern. "I'll be okay. The new change is keeping me occupied."

"I'm being summoned, honey. ER wants me."

"Okay, I love you, Peter."

Peter smiled. "Baby, I'm crazy about you. When this is over, let's take a century and go away somewhere."

She laughed. "That's a deal."

"My grandfather says hello. He was worried. He'll be glad to hear you're all right. I've got to go, honey. Love you."

"Bye, Peter." She listened to the sound of the dial tone for a few seconds and then replaced the receiver, sighing. Getting off the bed, she paced. "Have you ever felt out of synchronization with something?"

"Yes," Steve answered quietly, thinking of how he had missed having her in his life.

"Well, that's Peter and me. We were close to the brass ring, it was at the tip of our fingers, and now we're on separate carousels trying to spin past the ring at the same time. And so far it ain't a workin'!"

Steve got off the other bed. "The trick is to keep spinning. You're okay as long as you keep spinning to the music, and when the music stops, you buy another ticket in order to stay on the carousel. That's the tune life plays, kid."

Jeneil stared in amazement. "Will you teach me to understand the music at the prom?"

"I just taught you," he said. "Keep moving to the music. Don't stop to figure out which instrument you should be playing and why. Just keep dancing, kid."

"Even if it doesn't make sense?"

He shrugged. "Sometimes we get out of step then catch up, but only if you keep on dancing."

She smiled at him. "You're a surprise, Steve Bradley. You're not as mainstream as you pretend to be."

He grinned. "And your problem is you want to write the music that you're dancing to."

She put her arms around him for a hug. "Is that really so bad?" She sighed, and he held her gently.

"Only at the prom, most people won't understand the music being played and life doesn't work that way. Life doesn't mind a few not understanding, but it needs most of the people to keep in step."

She chuckled. "You know, that's making sense to me."

"Oh geez," he said. "Now we're both in trouble."

She laughed and lifted her head from his chest. "You're quite a puzzle."

He guided her head back to his chest to avoid kissing the lips that smiled so gently and asked so many unanswerable questions. Fragile was getting to him. "I love you, Jeneil."

"Now that music I understand." She smiled as she leaned against him.

He grinned, thinking no, you don't, honey. No, you don't.

*****

By the time Peter got home after work, he was discouraged about his separation from Jeneil. The emptiness inside of him was a dull ache and he missed her more since hearing her voice. She belonged to him and he wanted her in his life; he wanted to be responsible for her and to be there to share the changes in her life. He resented the separation and Uette for causing it. Turning off the apartment lights, he went to his bedroom. Uette opened her door and stopped at Peter's. She was wearing a modest robe, which surprised him. He had come to expect revealing outfits. She leaned casually against the doorframe. Her hair was different, less professionally styled. He watched her as he undid his jacket.

"Something wrong?" he asked, slipping it off.

"No." She smiled. "No, not at all. I want to thank you for getting those diet meals for me."

"Did you eat any of them?"

She nodded. "They're not too bad for a frozen meal and the portions are so small my conscience feels okay about them. You're really sweet." He wondered about her conscience, thinking it should be worried more about the baby's health.

"Your family was worried." He went to the closet and hung his jacket. Taking the coins and keys from his jeans pockets, he put them on the bureau along with his wallet. "Was there something else?" he asked, wondering why she was still standing there.

"I understand that Jeneil has left the hospital."

"Yes, she has," he answered calmly, even though he felt anger rise through his center.

"Did you ask her to?"

He breathed a sigh of relief that she hadn't done anything to cause it. He turned to face her. "No, the businesses she plays at need her attention."

"Then you haven't seen her lately, have you?"

He didn't answer. "I have first shift tomorrow; I need to get some sleep."

"I wish you and I could be less hostile."

"Less hostile?" he asked not believing she suggested it. Sarcasm ate at him. "Who knows, Uette, maybe it's possible once I get over being separated from Jeneil and resenting you for it. And the spying will take some time to swallow. Then, there's the lie about the baby."

She sighed. "I'm not lying."

He stared at her steadily. "Do you really believe that story or are you trying to psych me out?"

"Forget I mentioned it." She moved to leave.

He laughed sarcastically. "I'd like to forget you mentioned it, believe me, there's nothing I'd like more, but your lie is stuck in my chest and choking me. Forget? Not a snowball's chance in hell of that happening. You think we're hostile? Well, we're hopeless, too." She went to her bedroom and closed the door, and he shook his head wearily and got his robe.

Thirty

Steve arrived to take Jeneil to breakfast. The clams and mussels were steaming in a pot. "Gonna make the best chowdah you evah ate, Abner." She buttoned her toggle coat, smiling.

"I'll have to be unconscious, sweetheart," he said, laughing as he pushed her out the door ahead of him. They took her car because it was larger and she needed things from her apartment.

"Did you smell spring?" She sighed as they headed north. He smiled at her appreciation of nature. "The crocuses are out and green shoots are popping up, but spring is closer and the conditions are right. The earth is awakening from its hibernation. Good healthy earth. Maybe that's the smell of spring before it's overpowered by the heady scents of summer blossoms growing profusely." She sighed again. "It feels good." She opened the car window an inch as if wanting to be closer to the smell and feel of spring. He smiled, enjoying being with her in the sunny weather after a dreary Saturday.

Jeneil packed some clothes in garment bags and picked up her blender, slow cooker, and microwave oven. Her doorbell buzzed several times indicating an anxious visitor. Adrienne rushed to Jeneil and gasped. "Oh my gosh, your hair." She covered her mouth in shock. "Oh my gosh," she said, walking around Jeneil several times. "I like it. Yeah, I really like it. Where the hell have you been?" she scowled, remembering why she stopped in. "You had me scared blue. Damn, you're crazy. You really tore Hollis up. That's not too bright." Adrienne tried to look stern.

Jeneil grinned. "Hollis wasn't supposed to know until I was floating instead of treading water, my dear sweet friend. You panicked."

Adrienne closed her eyes. "Oh boy, I wondered if I had bagged you."

"I'm lucky he sent for Bill, at least he accepts my strangeness. He always has."

Adrienne laughed. "Yeah, I heard dipstick." She noticed Steve. "And how come you're here? Did you know where she was?"

"No, I found Wonderland yesterday."

"Wonderland?" Adrienne looked at Jeneil, confused.

Jeneil smiled. "I'm moving from Camelot for a while to Wonderland. You and Charlie will love this house."

"Excuse me?" Adrienne asked. "What house?"

"Adrienne," Steve said, "Jeneil is cheering up a house in Weeden. That's where she's been and she's dragging shark food in from the ocean to eat."

"Ugh," Adrienne grimaced, "that is strange."

"You were smart to not make a career of PR work," Jeneil said, raising an eyebrow. Steve shrugged and walked away grinning. "Adrienne, I think this could be the house for you and Charlie."

Adrienne was shocked. "Honey, I can't afford a house even with the money I'm making now and they'll run us out of Weeden if we try to buy property there. Are you kidding! I can see the white sheets and smell the burning cross already."

"I don't think so, Adrienne. The town is in trouble. It might be the right time to buy and there are all kinds of ways to buy a house. Anyway, you'll have to come and look at it. It's got land around it just like Charlie has wanted. Good farmland." Steve smiled, realizing Jeneil was being Jeneil. He knew there must have been more behind the house deal than just fixing it up and abandoning it again.

Adrienne shook her head and grinned. "You're a kick, Jeneil. You really are. So what will you do now? I heard you quit the hospital."

Jeneil nodded. "I'm in the office starting tomorrow and I've decided to get involved with the playhouse."

Adrienne sighed with relief. "Tony and I have been biting our nails all week." She hugged Jeneil. "It'll be good to be working with you. You really are needed here."

Jeneil nodded again. "I have put off the move for too long. Uncle Hollis was right to be annoyed with me."

"Any word about Peter?" Adrienne asked.

Jeneil shook her head, sighing. "No, and it's going to take more time than we thought."

Adrienne looked at Steve. "And so you're playing John Alden for Miles Standish."

"Who?" Steve asked.

Jeneil laughed. "Wrong story, Adrienne."

Adrienne wondered if it was, but she smiled. "So where are you two going today?" They both shrugged and Adrienne laughed. "Very decisive people."

"I don't even know what our choices are," Jeneil said. "I jumped off the conveyor belt a week ago and I haven't looked back."

Steve smiled at her. "That's one of the things I like most about you, being with you is a relaxing vacation."

"Thank you, Sir Steven." Jeneil curtsied and Steve laughed at the title. Adrienne watched; they were close, there was no doubting that, and she wondered where all the new changes were heading with Jeneil.

*****

Steve met Peter in the anteroom of the OR. "Got a treat for you." Steve smiled, handing Peter a brown paper bag. "Best chowdah you evah ate, Abner," Steve mimicked Jeneil's studied New England accent. Peter smiled, recognizing Jeneil's twist. "You're lucky, you didn't have to see her drag it from the ocean and open them up. She came walking down the road in a rain slicker, heavy boots, carrying a bucket of shellfish and a clam rake. She's a sweetheart though, no bellies in the chowder."

Peter took the bag. "I remember the days when I brought you food."

Steve saw Peter's discouragement. "Those days will be back." He smiled sincerely.

"What did you do over the weekend?"

"Polyurethaned two of her floors Saturday, moved some things from Camelot Sunday, and we went to a florist because she was narcissus hungry."

"She's near the ocean then?" Peter mused.

Steve nodded. "Well, the bay actually, and she's cheering up a house, Pete. Although I have my doubts about the yard because it looks like it's suffering from chronic depression. What a mess!"

"Why is she doing that?"

Steve shrugged. "Because she's Jeneil, I guess. She's got Charlie and Adrienne chosen as its new tenants."

Peter smiled. "Crazy kid, you can never figure her out."

Steve rubbed the back of his neck. "Uh, Pete, there's something else I should tell you." Peter waited, not knowing how to prepare himself. "She did something else that she can't explain either. The beautiful thick hair is gone. She chopped it off herself and is running around in short hair that looks as happy to be changed as she does."

Peter's mouth opened in shock. "Why?"

Steve shrugged. "She just said she needed a change. It looks cute though, it makes her look even more like a kid. She can't ruin her face no matter how she surrounds it."

"Damn it." Peter sighed. "She is caving in."

"I thought that too, but she's on an upswing trend, all positive energy and determination. It's nice to watch really. She's full of life and excitement." Steve laughed. "She claims she's exploring alternate lifestyles. She is changing. It's not a major change except for the surroundings, but she just seems sort of determined about herself." The news made Peter uneasy as he wondered where all this change was going. Steve hit his arm. "Hey, enjoy the chowdah, Abner. I've got to scrub."

"Yeah, Steve, thanks." Peter put his name on the bag and hid it in a corner behind a bench for protection. He loved her soups. It was a winter enjoyment they shared. He headed to the scrub room wondering about her changes.

*****

Jeneil was in the office at six a.m. As the others arrived, she walked to the reception area causing Tony and Charlene to stare in shock at her short hair making Adrienne laugh. "Now I know what I looked like when I first saw her new style."

Tony hugged Jeneil. "Oh my gosh, what did you do that for?"

Jeneil smiled. "One day I was brushing it and I felt like I was in a cocoon all wrapped up in it, so I got the scissors and aimed for my shoulders but got closer to my ear lobes instead."

Charlene walked around her. "You did a decent job for having chopped it off yourself."

"Well thanks, Charlene, but I'm going to make an appointment if I can find a hairstylist daring enough to patch it up."

Charlene smiled. "You're lucky to have good skin. Your face can stand the attention."

Adrienne nodded in agreement. "And your hair waves and curl on its own. That helps."

"We'll see," Jeneil said. "How is that salon in the Blinden building?"

"Upwardly mobile." Adrienne laughed.

"Ugh," Jeneil groaned. "Does that mean lots of lacquer? I haven't been inside a beauty salon since Mandra."

"No, I think it's more mousse," Charlene explained. "Upwardly mobile people don't have time to fuss with hair."

"That's for me then," Jeneil said, smiling.

"I still think the long hair was sexy." Tony frowned, and Jeneil hugged him and kissed his cheek.

"Tony, don't tell me that I've lost my sex appeal, not on Monday anyway."

Everyone laughed and Tony gave her a quick hug. "Never." He smiled and followed that with some words in Italian.

"Be nice, Tony, be nice," Jeneil cautioned.

He chuckled. "I just said that you're a beautiful woman who is made for love."

"Ooo." Jeneil raised her eyebrows. "Are we paying this wonderful man enough?" She smiled, slipping her arms through his. He kissed her cheek and patted her hand, smiling. "Now listen everybody, I've been here since six this morning and I've poured over what was on my desk, so who has me in the first hour meeting, Adrienne or Tony?"

Adrienne shrugged. "It doesn't matter to me."

"Well, I have to wait for the mail before I meet with you," Tony answered. "Arnie is sending in the latest reports from The James Gang and I'd like to go over those with you."

"Okay, then I'm yours Adrienne, put me to work." Adrienne and Jeneil headed for Jeneil's office and settled in for a conference. Although office hours began at eight-thirty, the public didn't usually begin to stir until nine.

At nine o'clock, the door to the corporation office swung open and a man rushed in boldly standing before Charlene with his hands in his pockets. He looked at her nameplate. "Okay Charlene, do more than just grace this office with outstanding beauty and get Jeneil for me."

Charlene was stunned by the man's approach, but proved herself to be well trained. "May I give her your name?" she asked pleasantly.

The man raised his eyebrows. "Oh good, then she is here and no you may not give her my name. Just get her for me."

"She's in conference. Maybe someone else can help you?"

"I don't want anyone else, only Jeneil, and I'll stay here until I see her," he replied loudly, and then began pacing.

Charlene persisted. "Sir, I need you to calm down. Can I get you some coffee?"

"No," he answered flatly. "Just get me Jeneil."

Charlene sighed and picked up the telephone. "Jeneil, there's a man here who insists on seeing you. He won't give his name and he seems very upset." Charlene looked at the pacing man. "Jeneil wants to know why you are upset."

"She owes me something," the man snapped.

"You owe him something," Charlene relayed the message more pleasantly than it had been delivered. "Thanks, Jeneil." Charlene replaced the receiver. "She's interrupting her conference for you."

"She should, the damn wench." He studied the paintings hanging in the office and Charlene studied him as he did, wondering why he looked so familiar.

Jeneil's office door opened and she and Adrienne came to the reception area. "Robert!"

Robert Danzieg glared at her. "Don't you smile at me…," he stopped as he noticed her hair. "Holy shit, what the hell happened to you, brain surgery? Is that a wig?" Charlene looked at Adrienne, shocked at the man's rudeness. Adrienne grinned. "That's the only excuse I'll take from you is brain surgery," Robert continued his tirade. He walked over to her and pushed her toward her office. "Get some bandages ready folks, I'm gonna bruise this little bitch real bad."

Tony had come out of his office when he heard the shouting and saw Robert pushing Jeneil. He hurried to the reception desk with his crutches. "What the hell are you doing standing there? Call the cops!"

Adrienne laughed. "No need, that's Robert Danzieg, the man behind those paintings. He's been a regular visitor to Jeneil lately. Colorful, isn't he?"

"To say the least." Charlene sighed, relieved. "I thought he looked familiar. Boy, Jeneil is a total surprise. He is so flamboyant. Are they dating?"

Adrienne nodded. "Jeneil's style of dating, that is."

Tony was shocked. "What? Where's Peter?"

"Who's Peter?" Charlene asked.

Adrienne sighed. "There have been some changes in Jeneil's life lately people."

Robert closed the office door. "What the hell is this?" he asked, walking around her, checking her hairstyle more closely. Jeneil folded her arms and waited for him to land. "Shit! What the hell have you done?" he growled.

She smiled. "I've decided to live in this century."

"So?" he snapped. "Did you lose your hair in a time warp? This is because of your buddy, the surgeon, isn't it?" He sighed. "Damn that guy. I could wring his neck."

"Robert, stop." Jeneil touched his arm gently.

"No," he snapped. "Did you count the number of messages I've left for you? Not one was returned. Not one!"

"Robert, I found them yesterday. I've been away. I'm living in Weeden for a while."

"Weeden? That's all people do there."

Jeneil wrinkled her nose. "Bad pun, Robert. Don't be angry. I'm touched that you've found me. How did you find me?"

"I was at the gallery yesterday at a party I've been trying to invite you to and I mentioned you to Phil. When I told him I was shocked because I knew so little about you and I've known you for so long, he smiled and said he still can't get you to explain what your company does. Well, you can imagine my surprise when I heard you owned a company. He gave me the address from your account card. What the hell is all the secrecy for?"

Jeneil looked apologetic. "Looking back, I'm not sure. It was for protection I think. I want people to know me for me, not the trappings around me."

Robert shook his head and grinned. "You can't ruin that face." He kissed her gently. "I've been worried about you."

She smiled and hugged him. "Thank you for falling down the rabbit hole, too."

"Are we in Wonderland now and not Camelot?" he asked, and she nodded. "Can I find truth in Wonderland?" he asked, and she nodded again. "I think I like Wonderland better. And I like the new hair. The eyes have still got it, baby; deep, dark and smoldering." He hugged her as he looked around the office. "You are a surprise, my executive."

"Early Robert Danzieg." She laughed, explaining the display of his works on the walls.

"Yeah." He smiled, very pleased. "Are you taken with the guy, I hope?"

"He's bold and dynamic."

"Oh yeah?" he asked, kissing her cheek. "Is that good?"

She moved away from him. "On canvas, it's exciting. In life, it's intimidating."

He laughed. "Do I really scare you?"

She tilted her head from side to side. "You overwhelm me sometimes."

He walked to her and held her arms at her elbows. "You need to be overwhelmed so you'll wake up and release the you that's inside." He looked her over sensuously. "I'd like to see you ignite and skyrocket."

She moved away from his hold. "Robert, you are skyrockets. I can't breathe at that level. I like life slower."

"Sure you can breathe and I'll prove it," he answered. "You're just suffering from the result of Peking Man, the Scientific Wonder. He was a good beginning lover, but you're ready for real life now."

She raised her eyebrows slowly, shocked by his directness. "Robert, you're starting it again. You're trying to overwhelm me with your boldness."

"I am not," he answered defensively, and went from a grin to a smile. "I'm responding to your changing life form, you sexy creature. It's exciting and invigorating. I like it. You're finally going to live enveloped in the quality I first saw in you. That's great!" He moved closer and hugged her.

"Cosmic?" she asked, surprised, moving away from him.

"Yeah, that's what you call it, cosmic. Hell, you'll be deadly!" He smiled with delight at the thought.

"You mean like you painted me?"

"That's it, precious." He grinned.

She laughed. "Robert, that was surrealistic and I think you projected some of your boldness onto that canvas. I'm not bold. I can't be. I don't recognize myself when I am."

Robert put his arms around her. "Baby, ready or not, it's rising to the surface. You're heading for neon, sweet darlin'! Neon and skyrockets, and it's delicious just being around it." He kissed her temples and pulled her closer.

She pushed away. "Robert, really, you're too bold."

He grinned. "You move away from me an awful lot, sexy lady."

She understood his meaning. "I am not sexually suppressed. I'm overwhelmed, that's all."

He smiled a seductive half smile. "Fine, have it your way." He moved closer to her. "But I'm glad Wonderland insists on truth." He bent closer and kissed her lips gently. "I've decided to launch a campaign to remove Scalpel Sam from your memory," he whispered, and kissed her again.

"You're outrageous!" she said, moving away, shaking her head. "You really are completely irresponsible."

"That's part of my charm, woman, and I intend to make it contagious. Just for you. I'm going to show you how to catch fire."

She wrinkled her eyebrows. "Are we back to S-E-X again?" she asked, having lost his drift.

"No, baby!" He shook his head. "The fire that's in you for life, kid. That's what I want, unrestrained and floating free." He grinned slyly. "Of course, I guess I should warn you that S-E-X is usually a way of expressing the energy that results from the inner blaze."

She shook her head and smiled. "How did I know that already?"

He laughed and hugged her. "You're so damn cute. Come on," he said, putting his arm around her shoulder, "walk me to the door. I'll leave now, but have dinner with me tonight."

"Only if you calm down."

He squeezed her shoulders. "Sure I will. I told you I'm reacting to the new you. Shit, I thought the Camelot hairstyle was a turn on, but this Wonderland haircut is sassy and sexy. It makes me hyper." She shook her head as they got to the reception desk. "What time for dinner?" Adrienne, Charlene, and Tony watched fascinated that their shy and quiet boss could deal with this man who loomed larger than life.

Jeneil shrugged. "I'm out of here at six tonight."

"Okay, my coach will be here at six. What's it going to be, Boston for seafood or Hartford for beef?" He grinned. "Or we could raid my refrigerator and eat on my swing." Adrienne, Charlene, and Tony looked at each other and raised their eyebrows.

Jeneil smiled. "Robert, anytime I've looked inside your refrigerator, I've only seen penicillin experiments."

He kissed her cheek. "So, I'll have Tiel's cater dinner."

"How about the Green Door here in town? My treat as an apology," Jeneil suggested.

He made a sour face. "Honey, the Green Door is so public. I want more ambiances for us."

Charlene smiled. "The fountain room at the China Bay is very romantic."

Robert glared at her deliberately. "Charlene, thanks a bunch, I'm allergic to anything Chinese; it makes me break out in anger."

"Oh, I'm sorry." Charlene shrugged timidly. "I didn't know." Adrienne was amused by the sly grin on Jeneil's face remembering the China Bay was owned by Peter's family.

Robert looked at Jeneil. "What are you grinning at you lady executive? You don't fit that role either, you know. You'll burn your desk down." He ran his fingers through her hair briskly causing strands to pop and curl and sprawl all over her head. He smiled, pleased with the new style. "That's your look, sweetheart, unleashed. That's more you." He kissed her lips quickly. "See you at six." He rushed out as abruptly as he had rushed in, Jeneil's assistants still aghast that he had touched her hair.

Jeneil turned and sat on the edge of the reception desk, sighing. "A woman needs to date early in life in order to have enough experience to repress his type. I can't win." She ran her hand over the strands of hair trying to restrain what Robert had unleashed, her three assistants smiling at each other, watching her reaction to the havoc the man had brought to her appearance.

"Gosh, he's right, Jeneil. Tousled is a good look for you," Charlene commented.

Adrienne grinned slyly. "Charlene, I think the term he used was unleashed. There's a big difference." She stared at Jeneil, who just shook her head wearily and sighed wondering when her quiet life with Peter would return. Change wasn't warm, soothing, and comforting. Life with Peter was and deep within her she knew that unleashed was part of the restlessness that was causing the change in her life.

Thirty-One

Not wanting to go home, Peter dawdled at his locker. The day had been difficult but rewarding. Dr. Maxwell had him in for several tedious surgical cases and he had performed well and the accolades felt good. The sense of achievement was exhilarating but now, facing his own personal time, he wanted to be with Jeneil. He had come to enjoy sharing moments like this with her. She always knew when he was high and she'd get dinner over and done with and they'd go to bed early. She usually asked questions that required more of an answer than whether or not the operation had been a success. It surprised him that she could ask such detailed questions from just thinking about what he was explaining. He liked that about her; she really listened and he knew from her facial expressions that she was picturing it in her mind. Sometimes she'd ask what bone the graft was on and he'd get his textbook to show her. She had built up a tolerance and while the procedures made her wince he could tell she was fascinated. It was her sense of pride in him that made his success complete. The emptiness was a dull ache now as he missed her and the closeness they had shared. He could almost smell her perfume from the vivid memory in his mind.

Peter sighed and put his lab coat in his locker and closed the door. Putting on his jacket, he decided to visit his grandfather. He needed to share some time with someone he liked. The thought of going to the apartment left him cold. Uette was getting emotionally clingy and her tactics had changed. She no longer wore clothes that exposed her body, and her style was less false and made up. She was more natural and she was harder to dislike when she was normal, and if she hadn't messed up his life so much he felt he could probably be very decent to her. But the memory of her lie was never far from his mind along with the reminder that because of her Lin Chi and Bo were on the streets asking questions that could easily get them beaten, if not worse, by some of the lowest scum walking the Earth. He couldn't be sure of who she was at the moment, so he didn't want to find out what she was pretending. He kept things peaceful to protect Jeneil since he couldn't be sure of her influence with Dragon muscle.

He noticed his mother's car was gone and that relaxed him even more. She had been a haunt since he got married, always calling and checking on things. He had even found food in the refrigerator that looked like it was from either China Bay or from her own kitchen. He hadn't asked Uette about it because he didn't want to know.

The greenhouse was dark so he went to the kitchen door and knocked before going in. His mother came from the hallway, surprising him. "I didn't see your car," he said limply, hoping to explain his expression.

"Tom has it. He's taking Grandfather to visit a friend." She looked at him closely. "You've lost weight and you look tired."

"Tough schedule," he replied. "It's been a long day for me."

"How come you're not home?"

He shrugged. "I wanted to check on Grandfather."

"Have you had dinner?" she asked, and he shook his head. "Is it not fair to your wife to not go home and eat?"

"She's not supposed to cook for me. It's in the agreement."

"Agreement!" she answered disgustingly. "She wants to cook for you because she loves you." She sighed. "You are a complete fool for treating her the way you do."

"Yeah, well I like you too, Mom."

"Peter, I can see a big change in her since you've been married. She doesn't look well either. Why are you doing this? Is it so hard to be decent to her? She is trying so hard to please you. No woman I know would put up with what Uette is, not even your perfect Jeneil."

"Been talking to Uette lately, huh?"

"Oh, Peter, give her up."

"Who, Uette? I'd love to."

"Don't be smart mouthed. You know who I mean."

"I haven't seen her lately," he said, hoping to cover all the bases in order to protect Jeneil.

"Then work at your marriage before it's too late."

Peter sighed. "Mom, you don't understand so please don't start, okay?" He headed to the door. "I'll call Grandfather another day. Take care."

His mother was surprised by his abrupt visit. "Peter, I'm not finished. Don't you want some dinner?"

He stopped at the door and turned. "The refrigerator at the apartment is full of food donated by you. I can eat that. I'll see you." He opened the door and left.

His mother sighed and shook her head, disappointed that she wasn't able to reach him. This was since Jeneil had been in his life. He just ignored people he didn't want to deal with. He had become as aloof as she was. Poor Uette.

*****

It was a strain to unlock the apartment door and Peter had to remind himself that he could barricade himself in his room and read. He went to the kitchen and opened the refrigerator. Taking out some aluminum foil packages to see what they were, he selected his dinner. Turning to go to the microwave, he saw Uette at the door.

"I expected you for dinner," Uette commented.

"Why? The agreement says that you won't cook for me and why did you cook anyway? My mother's sending enough to feed at least four people."

Uette sat at the table. "What's her problem?" she asked, annoyed.

He looked up at her. "What do you mean?"

"Does she think I'm incapable of cooking for you?"

Peter was surprised; he thought Uette and his mother were close. "She's probably trying to help us out."

"Well, I find it irritating."

Peter shrugged. "It saves us money and its food that would have been wasted anyway." He ate a piece of cold chicken. "Take the money that's saved and go to a hair dresser."

"What's wrong with my hair?" she asked sharply.

"Nothing except it doesn't look as professional as it used to. I just thought you couldn't afford to have your hair done. My mother thinks you don't look well since we married."

Uette stood up quickly. "That woman is exasperating, a royal pain. Why doesn't she mind her own business?"

Peter grinned at the great opportunity he'd been handed. "Because you tell her your business, that's why. Stop using her to peddle your messages. She's the type who tries to help." He took the food from the microwave oven and put it on his plate. Pouring some milk, he put everything on a tray, cleaned up the kitchen and started to leave for his room.

"Can't you eat at the table?"

"No," he answered flatly.

"Are you sulking because Jeneil's gone?"

He stopped. "You're a drama major, stay out of psychology. You wanted her out of the hospital and my life. She's gone. Now leave it alone. I don't even know where she is. That should please you."

"You really don't know where she is?" she called to him as he headed to his room.

"Not a clue," he replied.

"How come, is she mad at you?"

He smiled, his back to her, realizing that he was building a beautiful protective story for Jeneil. "Don't know, she just disappeared," he said, and he went into his room grinning, pleased he'd begun his defense of Jeneil and that it was going so well. Taking the glass unicorn from its place of hiding, he sat on his bed and ate feeling better about spending the evening in the apartment than he thought he would.

*****

Peter found himself living for weekends, or at least Mondays, so he could hear about Jeneil's weekends from Steve. He had reported that Jeneil would be cutting back on her hours at the corporation to join the playhouse and that she had surprised him by taming the yard. It had taken a professional with a bushwhacker to get it to a manageable length for a lawnmower. The flowerbeds had been weeded and spring bulbs were growing making the backyard pleasant. Steve seemed impressed she had accomplished all she had in only three weeks. Carpenters and professionals had come in for the muscle work, but Jeneil had done the flowerbeds herself and was starting on an herb garden with plans for a vegetable garden, too. She was delighted to find two apple and two pear trees growing on the property as well as berry bushes. All were in blossom. She had pulled some blossoms hoping to improve their development wondering if growing untamed had damaged the growth. Steve had become impressed with her love for nature and nurturing, and for her love of being in the yard surrounded by the life going on there.

Adrienne and Charlie had stopped in to see the house. They loved it. Jeneil was right, it was exactly what they had always dreamed of owning but they couldn't. Charlie had asked if he could repair the garage just to be around the place. Jeneil had grinned and told him that she had a plow coming to furrow the two adjacent fields which belonged to the house so he could put a market crop in if he wanted to. Charlie was beside himself with joy. Since summer was his busy season in construction he began making plans to camp out in the field to save travel time.

While Adrienne took a calmer approach to the idea, she was ecstatic as Charlie spun his dreams and they began looking into the possibility of buying into Weeden. They were skeptical since they knew of a fourth generation Italian couple who bought a home in town and were asked to leave several times by residents. The town was closed to outsiders and they considered anybody an outsider if they weren't white, Anglo-Saxon, Protestant, and knew someone in town. The town was dying and abandoned houses were not uncommon, the remaining residents narrow-minded, stiff-necked, and prejudiced against anything different and almost nothing could survive on that alone. Political power was held by a reactionary elitist group of people who didn't want change and they accepted the town's decline as proof that civilization in general was in trouble for leaving American values behind. They were determined to hold off against invading inferiority in order to protect what was good in America.

The town's one small school was now closed and the few children left were bused to a nearby school where they interacted with different nationalities and races, and who if they followed the previous generation would leave Weeden and move to a bigger town nearby. Those who did stay developed the same love and devotion to American values and ideals. The ancestors of the older residents had come over on the Mayflower or on the next two ships and that fact alone gave them the determination to keep their America free from foreign influence.

Jeneil had smiled as she told Steve and quoted her mother who had believed strongly that the attitude was a problem of breeding and that the Mayflower was full of dissidents and social malcontents from England, Great Britain glad to be rid of them. Jeneil couldn't help but notice the current generation of descendants behaved as badly as the political power those on the Mayflower were rebelling against. She sighed, hoping the best for Adrienne and Charlie. Steve had been stunned not realizing such bigotry existed in the north. He had always associated that kind of narrowness as a southern peculiarity. Jeneil had shaken her head and commented that she was beginning to think the ignorance of bigotry was a problem of small towns in general. She had laughed and called it too close an interbreeding of ideas and thoughts.

Steve brought Peter up to date on the art show they had attended where they didn't meet anyone they knew. Peter suggested Steve take Jeneil to dinner closer to the north end where more of the hospital staff lived since no gossip would start if they weren't seen together. Steve then smiled, reached into his inside coat pocket and handed Peter an envelope. Peter opened it quickly. It was a card with a unicorn drawn on the face of it.

Dear Chang, Just a note to share a moment in history. What seems like forever, but was only a year ago, a lonely girl was dancing in the wind on what she thought was a deserted beach where she ran into a handsome and charming prince standing tall and strong in the wind. She fell deeply in love with him. An evil curse befell the prince and caused the girl to live in exile. The girl walks on a different beach now waiting for her prince to return. She's still lonely and misses him like crazy. All my love, Jeneil. P.S. I love stories with happy endings so move it, Chang, and get this story happily ended.

Peter smiled broadly enjoying the surprise. He thanked Steve then went to his locker where he hid the note on the shelf. It smelled faintly of her perfume. He missed her like crazy, too. He had trouble believing they had been separated since early February and it was now almost the end of April. He took the envelope again, smelled it, and returned it to its corner on the back of the shelf. Closing the locker door, he sighed and thought, baby, I want a happy ending as quickly as you do. He smiled, pleased that she had sent a note. All the changes in her life were making him nervous, but the note let him know she still belonged to him and as he walked onto the fifth floor her words echoed in his mind, *I always will, Chang. I always will.*

*****

At break, Peter called Lin Chi at the diner. "Not here, honey," she had said quickly when he identified himself. "Give me your booth's number and stay there two seconds."

He waited for her call anxious about the tone of her voice. The phone rang and he answered quickly. "Lin Chi, what's going on?"

"Pete, you can't call me at the diner, it's not smart. We're getting close to something."

"How do you know?"

"Hot vibes are shakin' on the tree, man. Bo and I are going to slow down for a week or two so stay away from us. Okay?"

"Why?"

"Man, I can't believe how much street sense you've lost. We don't know which way the wind is blowing about Uette; I don't want to get hit by crossfire. If you come around then I'm tied to her. Savvy?"

"Yeah." He sighed. "I'm sorry, I didn't think. Why is it taking so long?"

"Honey, I've got some bad news for you."

He held his breath. "What is it?"

"We've gone through the whole army. That's not her playground. Pete, that means she was somewhere in the traffic division or higher, and shit if it's higher we can all get screwed damn good just for asking questions."

Peter heard the panic in her voice. "Lin Chi, then drop it. Please! It's not worth seeing you hurt."

"No, Pete. I'm okay. Shittin' scared, that's for sure, but I'm okay. Bo's got a good brain. The guy is as smart-assed as anything I've ever come across. He wants to slow down now for a few days or even weeks. She's an untouchable, so she's private stock. I thought I had heard that but the vibes are strong and the air gets thinner when we ask about her. That's what makes me think something's up because her name's too hot."

"She doesn't have the Corvette anymore."

"Ooo, then maybe they're leaning on her. Shit, what a piss pot mess. Pete, watch yourself, some of those dudes are really twisted and I mean knotted. I've heard stories that would make your flesh bump about some of the upper level."

"You mean the Chuns?"

"That's the ones. I heard one of them got a short wick and a huge ego. He'd pull out a thumbnail for looking at him weird."

Peter groaned. "Damn it, Lin Chi! Then I want you and Bo out of it!"

"No, Pete, we didn't count on this being easy but we didn't expect to reach the traffic division either. It's okay though, we'll slow down and inch our way. We need to be sure about who we're talking to. I'm only anxious, honey. I wanted it to end fast, but it can't. We ain't no good to you dead, so we'll slow down."

"Lin Chi, I want to go directly to the Chuns and ask them myself."

She gasped, horrified. "Are you shittin' me, you screwball? Don't you dare! If you walk in wanting to try something, they'll make you pay with your doctor's kit. Oh shit, Pete, don't scare me like that. Stay put for crying out loud."

Peter sighed. "Does any of this mean that Uette has connections to muscle?"

"I don't know. It's hard to tell which way the wind's blowing. I'm not kidding. People are checking their own pockets for bugs before talking. Something's definitely happening and if the Corvette's been repo'd then the tree could fall either way. I've seen these people lean to get them back and to get them to leave so I can't say for sure, and if she's private stock, who she knows, especially at traffic on up. Pray its traffic, Pete. If the rooster wants her back in the coop then he could give her muscle just to please her like others give diamonds, boxes of candy or flowers. Right now, I can't be sure what her game with you is all about, so hang loose and stay out of her way. Stroke her nice so she don't get nervous, savvy?"

"Yeah," Peter answered, "I'm savvy."

"What is it, honey? The white princess?"

"Yeah." Peter sighed. "I don't want her spilled on."

Lin Chi sighed. "Then break it off, honey. It's the only sure way."

"I'm doing that."

"I'm sorry, Pete. I liked the way you two looked at each other. You must be hurtin' bad."

"It would hurt worse to see her muscled," he answered, rubbing his forehead.

"I know. She's quality stuff." Lin Chi sighed again. "Tough break for you, honey."

"Lin Chi, thanks for all this and you know I'd want you to back off if you see a wall, right? Don't hit it. Please don't get heroic for goodness sakes."

"I hear you dude, but let me see what cards we're holding. No sense folding if you've got four aces, is there?"

Peter shook his head. "Come on, Lin Chi, you really think you'll find four aces in this can of shit?"

"Can't tell, it depends on who's the rooster and why he's crowing. I'll get to you in a while. Just hang loose, okay."

"Thanks, Lin Chi. Really, I mean that."

"It's okay, kid. I still love you. You always did have the best damn heart I've ever seen. I want the white princess for you, so let's dump the barf bag. Deal?"

Peter grinned. "You're the gutsiest skirt I've ever come across, you and the white princess. You two could be twins."

Lin Chi laughed. "Imagine me in her league. That's something."

"She'd say the same about you and be just as impressed."

"Pete, take care. I've got to face those damn dishes now. I tell you, washing dishes is cleaner work but my last job I did without moving so many muscles. I'm too old to be honest."

Peter laughed. "I love you, Lin Chi."

She smiled. "I know you do, kid. Take care, honey, and I'll call you real soon I hope."

The call left Peter more determined to protect Jeneil. He wanted to get the gossip started about her and Steve as fast as possible convinced it was the only way to keep her safe.

Thirty-Two

May began and the longer daylight hours combined with the warmer sun took people and nature from the drowsiness of winter hibernation to the stirring of summer activity. Spring injected it's headiness into its boundaries and the feeling of new life became an intoxicant.

Steve arrived at Wonderland as quickly after rounds on Friday as he could. He hadn't felt spring as early as Jeneil, but it was flowing in his veins now. He had missed being with her and was anxious to see her after not being able to all week due to their schedules. The playhouse was due to launch its summer season and Jeneil was in the thick of it, and he had several medical seminars and private dinner invitations. His interest in dating waned as he found himself preferring to spend his time with Jeneil and there was a relaxing quality at Wonderland he liked being near.

He could feel the temperature drop as he got closer to the coast and that in itself was worth the trip. Opening his window wider, he breathed in the air's sweetness which Jeneil had said was the scent of apple blossoms. Pulling up to the driveway, he saw the red Porsche parked next to Jeneil's car. He sighed as he parked on the other side and got out, disappointed she wasn't alone. The smell of barbeque was in the air as he walked to the backyard and noted new additions. The deck she had built onto the back of the house was partially screened, the other half open, and a huge telescope was aimed skyward. A pan was balanced on a group of rocks in a barbeque pit and was gently smoking. Another addition was a square screen house closer to the water. It was exactly that, all screen supported by 2x4 posts. Jeneil and Robert Danzieg were sitting inside. She was working with some wood and Robert was slouched in a lawn chair watching her.

Jeneil looked up surprised to see Steve coming toward them with his suit jacket over his shoulder. She smiled. "Hi! You're here early. I expected to see you after dark." Robert turned slightly to see who she was talking to and Steve noticed Robert looking him over carefully. "Come on in," she said cheerfully, "the door's facing the water."

"You've been changing things around here," Steve commented, sitting on a free chair.

"She can't help herself. She's a cross between Mother Nature and Daniel Boone. She's lashing a chair right now. Chopped down dem pieces of log with her own brawny little hands, she did, and now she's a tie'n dem wet strips of rawhide to the joints as fasteners. Don't believe in nails, too new-fangled," Robert teased.

Jeneil smiled good-naturedly. "I guess you two know each other," she said, holding the end of rawhide with her teeth as she finished lashing the post.

"You look familiar," Robert answered, "but I don't have a name, sorry."

"Steve Bradley," Steve answered.

Jeneil put her project down. "Can I put some chicken on for you? The coals are still hot."

"No, you look busy, don't fuss."

Robert watched Steve steadily. "Fuss?" He laughed. "She can't spell the word. She keeps partially cooked chicken in the fridge and just throws it on the fire to finish barbequing."

Jeneil shrugged. "Wonderland's a no fuss place. I planned it that way."

"Then why are you building furniture?" Robert smiled and kicked her foot gently with his shoe.

"I'm a nestin' person. It keeps me busy. I like doin', I don't like fussin' Jaspah," Jeneil said, grinning. Robert smiled at her warmly obviously enjoying her lifestyle at Wonderland. Jeneil stood up. "Lettuce is growing fast so I made a big salad. Dinner won't take long. Did you bring some sprawlin' duds?" she asked Steve.

"I sure hope so," Robert commented, studying Steve closely. "You look strangled by citified life in that suit."

Steve found Robert very irritating sitting there in cutoff jeans, shirtless and sockless, and wearing deck shoes. Steve wondered why he was undressed and why he didn't look like an artist should with long messy hair and protruding bones from starving in a garret with a preference for the same sex. This guy was well-developed in the chest and arms and proud of it.

"Well, it seems too cool here to be dressed the way you are," Steve replied.

Jeneil chuckled. "Steve, this is conservative for Robert. He's from California and I can't believe he's adapted so well to the climate here. He's a member of the Polar Bear Club. You know the ones who put on bathing suits and take a dip in the ocean on a freezing New Year's Day."

"What are you proving?" Steve asked, unimpressed.

Robert grinned. "That I can do it." They eyed each other suspiciously. "It's invigorating."

"Life is invigorating for you, Robert. All of life." Jeneil smiled, zipping her sweatshirt and pulling it over her jeans as she walked by. Robert put his foot out and she jumped it, turned and made a face at him, then left. Steve loosened his tie not liking the fact that they were so playful.

Robert watched him. "Well, you have an uptight job. I can see that. What do you do?"

"I'm a doctor," Steve answered, trying to keep from getting more annoyed.

Robert's face became serious as he thought. "Oh yeah," he said, with a smile, "my New Year's party. You're a friend of the Taiwan twit blade man." Steve's back stiffened and he forced himself to stay silent for Jeneil's sake. Robert glared at him. "And what do you want? Are you here to finish the damage he did to her?"

"Mind your own business," Steve answered through a clenched jaw, near boiling over.

"She is my business. I'm making it my business."

"Does she know that?" Steve snapped.

"She's too unspoiled to know what's good for her."

"Oh, and I suppose you do? What do you think is good for her, you?" Steve answered.

Robert leaned forward angrily. "Why don't you give the kid a break damn it. She's amongst her own kind now. At least we won't use her and toss her away like your buddy did. Leave her the hell alone." The screen door opened and Jeneil went to the barbeque pit and added dinner to the fire before joining them in the screen house. Robert got up and put his arms around her. "I wish I didn't have to go."

"Do you want Section A started on Monday?"

He nodded and kissed her cheek. "Walk me to the car," he said, slipping his arm around her shoulder.

Steve watched them walk away not liking the moves Robert made toward her, watching as he slipped his arm down to her waist then squeezed her to him as they walked. Steve's throat tightened from annoyance and he undid his tie completely with one good pull trying to calm down. He looked up in time to see Robert kissing her. Anger started at his stomach and spread upward. They turned the corner to the driveway and were out of sight. He sighed heavily and slouched in the lawn chair.

Jeneil reappeared and went to the fire then to the screen house. She stood quietly and then sat down. "Did something happen between you and Robert?" she asked, concerned.

"Why?" Steve asked, wondering what Robert might have said.

She shrugged. "Things seemed tense between you and Robert never spoke to you when we left. That's not like him."

"It didn't get past alley cat," Steve replied, uncomfortable having to confess.

She wrinkled her brow. "What happened?"

Steve shook his head. "It doesn't matter."

"It does to me," she said, watching him steadily.

"He connected me to Pete and he's not one of Robert's favorite people."

She sighed. "I know and I don't know how to change that. It's so difficult to make Peter's story understood. It seems easier to let them think he married someone else by choice."

"Jeneil, what's he talking about? What damage has Pete done to you?" Steve asked, and Jeneil put her head down obviously embarrassed. "Jeneil?"

"Well, it seems when one ends a relationship, one is expected to begin another."

Steve grinned, understanding. "And this one isn't?"

She shook her head. "Poor Peter can't win. Robert blames him for everything from war to pestilence."

"Does he kiss you like that all the time?"

"No!" Jeneil answered quickly. "That kiss was my real clue there was trouble in here. I think that was for your benefit because he and I have an understanding."

Steve was still curious. "What understanding? How have you explained your lack of interest in a physical relationship?"

She shrugged, reluctant to answer. "I used the truth really. I told him that my love for Peter didn't end with the relationship and that I can't be interested in anyone else."

Steve became sober. "Honey, that's like waving a red flag at a bull. Now it's a challenge to him to help you get over Pete."

She nodded. "I'm finding that out. You know I don't mean to be dense and I'm even embarrassed that I am, but what else should I do? I'm telling the truth. What is life all about, the art of lying? It isn't fair that my feelings aren't accepted and if I said that I don't want to have sex just to have sex I'll bet that wouldn't be accepted either." She sighed and leaned back in her chair. "It was easier when I was with Peter. I was normal. I had a sex life, society was satisfied. Whatever happened to the days when women weren't expected to be physical before marriage?"

"You were all liberated," Steve answered, understanding her dilemma.

She looked up. "But our freedoms as women meant the right to make the choice ourselves like men do. We don't have a choice. You can't be a prostitute, that's too much, and you can't be a nun, that's not enough. I get the distinct feeling that my choice to be celibate is seen as odd, very odd."

Steve smiled. "So is mine."

"You're celibate?" she asked shocked, and then grimaced. "I'm sorry, that's none of my business."

He laughed. "You see, even you find it odd."

She covered her eyes with one hand and shook her head, embarrassed by her narrowness. "Equality isn't easy to achieve, is it?" She bit her lower lip and turned red, and Steve understood more clearly why Peter hovered over her so closely; she really lacked relationship experience which was odd for her age. "I think I'll check on the chicken," she said, quickly getting up and going to the fire. "You should change. Smoke can really cling to clothing." Steve went to get his luggage from the car and Jeneil was in the kitchen taking bowls from the refrigerator when he returned in jeans and a shirt.

"Can I help?" he asked.

"Yes, the thermos jug and plates over there please."

"Are you eating, too?"

"I'll have more salad. It's driving me crazy and I think Adrienne, Charlene, and Tony will quit if I bring in anymore for them. I'll have to start eating it for breakfast too, I guess. Even the rabbits can't keep up with it."

Steve smiled realizing he liked that he never had to wonder about relationship pressure with her. They had gotten to know each other as people, as equals. Really liking her as a person was what had eventually turned him on. He held the door for her and they sat and talked and ate as the daylight dismissed and evening shadows began to surround them.

"I like Wonderland," he said, relaxing after cleaning his hands. "It's a nice summer lifestyle."

Jeneil nodded. "I'm leaving things that I'll keep in my winter lifestyle, too. I get caught up in trappings. Wonderland gives me a chance to understand Thoreau's simplified theory a little better. I agree with his statement that when we own something, it possesses us. The possession has to be mentioned or we lose our investment in it causing us to worry or concern ourselves with this thing we possess and thereby become a slave to its demands on us."

Steve smiled. "You won't be happy until life makes sense, will you?"

She shrugged and smiled. "I'm the happiest when I'm trying to figure it out. Thoreau also believed people were living lives of quiet desperation. That's really sad if it's true. Gosh, at least Christian teachings and most religions believe that life is to be a song of joy. I like the sound of that much better."

"What's the telescope for?"

"To study the sky."

"What for?" he asked, amused.

"Because it's there, oh man of science. That's not a very scientific question. Where would you be if no one wondered what was in our bodies?"

"I know that, I meant why are you studying the sky? How will it fit in with your plans for life?"

"Because that's what I do. I collect bits of knowledge. It's a hobby that seems to have become a career." She shrugged and put her hands in her sweatshirt pockets. "Actually, it's part of cerebral. You know, that telescope came with a map of the sky. I used to be so smug thinking the cluster of stars I'd see was Pleiades. There are other clusters called Delphinus and Sagitta and probably more than those. What you see in the sky is affected by what time you're looking at it. It's seems easier to find your way through traffic in Upton. NASA has new luster in my book."

"How far can you see?"

"On full power, the moon's surface is visible."

"You're kidding?"

She sat up straight, surprised. "You're really interested?'

"Yeah, I'd like to see the moon's surface."

"Oh great, let's sit on the deck. There's a lantern we can use to read the map."

Jeneil was surprised to see Steve actually get in to reading the map. She was even more surprised at how easily he grasped the directions. She read the compass, but he navigated the map with such ease that she could only stare in amazement.

"I guess I was locking my mind to those instructions because you made it seem easy."

Steve smiled watching her pivot the telescope to his reading points. "The mosquitoes are fierce here," he said, slapping his arms for the third time in response to another bite.

She swished mosquitoes away from him. "I know but I don't want to have the marsh sprayed. I'm bringing in a Purple Martin house and probably an electronic bug zapper if it gets worse. I have an herbal mixture you can rub on as a repellent."

He followed her to the screened deck and took the gauze she wet for him to rub his face and arms. They had an easier time at the telescope after that and Steve was truly impressed with what the lenses were able to magnify. Time passed quickly and left them still looking for Jupiter at ten o'clock.

"I think it's beyond us," she said, sighing as she stretched her back. Steve looked at her, grinning at her remark. She smiled. "I wasn't being funny. I know it's beyond us in space, but I meant it's beyond our ability to read it on the map right now. Let's go inside," she yawned. "My nose is getting cold and if my feet get cold, I'm done for." Having had Steve put the telescope in the living room, she got two bowls of sliced strawberries in sweetened juice. "Do you want to snack here or in the living room?"

"There's no furniture in the living room."

She smiled. "Steve, those big cushions make great chairs. Wonderland is no-fuss remember?"

He sat at the kitchen table. "Hey, you painted it." He smoothed his hand across the shiny royal blue surface and noticed the chairs were freshly painted, too.

"Yes, I did. The chipped paint wasn't cheerful," she said, joining him.

"Tell me about your job."

"The corporation?" she asked, surprised.

"No, the playhouse."

"That's my hobby," she said, chuckling. "Their budget wasn't large enough to afford a gopher so I'm a volunteer."

"Nice of them to tell you before you took the job."

Jeneil shrugged. "I cut my job from the budget when Dennis and I were reviewing it." Steve was concerned about Dennis remembering how he had scooped her into his arms and carried her off after his play and he wondered how Peter was able to deal with all the guys in her life who had obvious interest in her. "Poor Karen wants to help out but being six months pregnant limits her. She comes to the playhouse and does what she can. The pregnancy has her aglow but she feels fat. I guess it's important to be emotionally ready for a baby. She really gets down about how she looks and without reason. I think she looks great. So does Dennis, which is most important."

Steve listened carefully. "Dennis is committed to Karen then?"

Jeneil smiled. "I hope so, they're married."

Steve relaxed. "That sounds committed to me."

Finishing the last of her strawberries, Jeneil sat back. "I watch Karen and think of Uette who's a month behind her."

"Uette doesn't look pregnant," Steve commented.

Jeneil was surprised. "You've seen her?"

He shook his head. "Pete told me. She was living on diet soda. He bought her some frozen diet dinners so she'd eat. She graduates next month and she's concentrating on that and staying thin."

Jeneil nodded to indicate she was listening but words wouldn't form as she compared her own life's drifting pattern to Uette's pattern of making life fit her plans. What concerned Jeneil the most was Peter being part of Uette's plans and the thought of Peter looking after Uette by getting frozen dinners lingered deep within her. She got up and washed her bowl and spoon feeling uneasy and thinking being honorable could really choke a person.

Steve lay awake in the second bedroom. He had noticed Jeneil's quietness as they went to bed. The situation rambled through his mind and he shook his head having trouble believing what had happened to Peter and Jeneil. He sighed and turned to watch the wall instead of the ceiling. In thinking seriously he could understand why they had made their choices. Realizing Peter's loneliness and Jeneil's quietness was probably the same thing his love for her was overshadowed by the thought of her pain from missing Peter. He sighed and listened to the night sounds of birds and insects, which eventually lulled him to sleep.

*****

Steve awoke late Saturday morning wondering why the house was so quiet. A note on the table explained that Jeneil had a volunteer group at the theatre and expected to be home for lunch at twelve-thirty. She had also listed some things he might eat for breakfast. Having found the lawnmower in the garage he began mowing the grass. Charlie pulled into the driveway at noon and began working in the garage. True to her word, Jeneil arrived at twelve-thirty just as Steve was gathering the grass clippings. She looked nice in her outfit but he had noticed she didn't wear dresses much anymore. The khaki pants and red top looked good on her but she seemed more like Jeneil in dresses.

"What have you done?" she asked, walking to him carrying a pale green box. "This is time off for you. You're already burned." She brushed something off his forehead.

"I need the exercise," he said, concerned that he liked being shirtless in front of her.

She looked around. "You've done the whole yard. Well now, I'm glad we're going to dinner so I can repay you for all this."

"No," he said, "no, I'm taking you to dinner. You don't wear dresses anymore," he heard himself add, not believing he had said it.

She smiled. "I do at the office and lounging here, but the yard work and the theatre seem to need slacks or jeans. Why?"

He shrugged. "You're changing so much. I just want you to know that I think Jeneil is okay the way she was."

"She's unfinished, Steve. That's no way to go through life."

"Fine, but don't get rid of all that's good either."

She grinned and tapped the green box. "One dress to be worn to dinner; how's that?"

He smiled his approval. "Danoli's Garden, okay?"

"But that's at the north end! There's an Italian restaurant down here."

"I like Danoli's. I don't mind driving."

She shrugged. "Fine with me then. Would you mind if we stop at that big sporting goods store since we'll be near there? I'd like to get a small inflatable boat for the water."

"That's a nice compromise."

"I'll get lunch together," she said, and Steve watched her head for the house and he hoped Peter was right in insisting that gossip be started. He sighed knowing that Danoli's Garden was a favorite with a lot of doctors and nurses from the hospital.

The afternoon passed quickly and Jeneil had to get Steve from the garage where he was helping Charlie so he could get ready. He was adjusting his tie in the mirror when Jeneil stopped at the door. "Hey, you look sensational," he said, smiling.

She turned to model the dress. "It feels light and summery. I knew there was a dress in that boutique for me. I heard it calling to me as I drove past on my way to the playhouse."

He smiled as he leaned against the door frame watching her, knowing that dresses and Jeneil were a natural combination. "Very nice," he replied, "very nice. This is the Jeneil I recognize. Don't change her."

She smiled, studying his eyes. "You mean that, don't you?"

He nodded. "Yeah, I mean that."

"Thank you." She smiled warmly. "I needed to hear that."

The dress draped gently around her, falling softly at her shoulders and elbows. Her hair had been styled and framed her face softly. Steve could feel objectivity slipping away from him. "Let's get on the road, Princess."

"Don't call me princess. I deal in reality now," she said softly but seriously.

"Not with me," he said, smiling. "To those of us who remember the triad you'll always be a princess." He saw the emotion in her eyes as she stared at him, the mention of the triad releasing a flood of memories she had been holding in check. "No," he said quickly, holding her shoulders and kissing her cheek. "Come on beautiful, dinner is waiting." He rushed her to the door distracting her from the thoughts of the lost days of the triad.

*****

They arrived at the restaurant during the crowded dinner hour. Steve had made the reservation deliberately so they'd be seen just as Peter had suggested. Scanning the room quickly he didn't recognize anyone and relief filled his chest. Deep within him, he didn't want anyone from the hospital to know about him and Jeneil. She was special in his life, a fantasy, and he didn't want that trampled. The idea of gossip never had made sense to him and he was just as glad to see it put off.

Steve suggested the veal scaloppini and ordered the proper wine and Jeneil had trouble remembering him as the Steve Bradley from the early days at the hospital. She enjoyed the Steve Bradley she had gotten to know so well. He was comfortable and comforting; she enjoyed that most about their relationship. She could relax and be herself, he wasn't after more in their relationship and he understood her feelings for Peter. Steve, Dennis, Tony, and Charlie were the only men in her life at the moment.

"Why are you smiling?" Steve asked, looking up to see her watching him.

"Because I love being with you," she answered quickly, not hesitating with the sentiment. He smiled and felt electricity pass through his chest. He squeezed her hand gently and drank some water. They settled back after dinner with coffee and listened to the classical music being played by a chamber group.

"Dr. Bradley, how was your scaloppini?" Both Steve and Jeneil turned quickly surprised to see Jane Simpson, a nurse on the first shift, standing at their table smiling. Jeneil crumpled the cloth napkin in her clenched hand and tried to stay calm. Jane looked at Jeneil. "Don't I know you? You look so familiar but I can't place you." Then she smiled as Jeneil's face became familiar. "Oh my goodness, you're Janette from Records, aren't you? Your hair! You've cut off your hair! What a transformation. It looks very nice. What happened to you? You left the hospital so quickly our heads were spinning."

Jeneil's throat was dry and she fought panic. "There was a job offer I couldn't ignore and the hospital understood about the notice in exchange for my vacation wages." Steve smiled as Jeneil told the truth but not the details.

Jane looked from Steve to Jeneil. "And how did you two get together?"

"We're friends," Jeneil answered quickly. "I'm a neighbor of a grandmother to a girl he once dated and we ran into each other through another mutual friend."

Jane smiled broadly. "That's right! I remember now. You're the one who got him off the hook with that ugly gossip. Well, it looks like you two were destined for each other having so many people in common."

"We're only friends," Jeneil insisted, and Steve remained silent.

"I understand," Jane said, "just friends. Well, my husband's waiting for me. Dinner here for an hour or so and a babysitter is all our budget allows for but I'm so glad to know you're okay. We wondered and thought you had gotten married and moved away. Jerry Tollman will be thrilled to hear that I've seen you. You really look so different! You're absolutely glowing and you look so tanned." She smiled sincerely. "Enjoy your evening together. Nice seeing you again, Janette, and I'll see you again I'm sure Dr. Bradley."

Jeneil stared at Steve as Jane walked away and he could see the panic in her eyes. "Steve, this will be all over the hospital by tomorrow. I'm worried about Peter hearing the story told wrong."

"I'll tell him about it," Steve reassured her.

Jeneil took a drink of water. "The scaloppini was good but was it worth the gossip?"

"There's no problem with me and Pete's finishing his residency soon anyway. The hospital becomes a smaller part of your life after that. Don't worry about it."

Jeneil sighed heavily. "When will this nightmare end? I can't believe I might miss Peter's graduation. I missed his birthday. What else?" She sighed again as she placed her napkin on the table. Steve could see the warm mood of their evening had changed and he sighed knowing the gossip had already taken its toll.

"Well, this makes espresso in the garden impossible. I'll take you home," he said, signaling the waiter.

"No," Jeneil replied, "I need to see it. I've heard it's spectacular. I'd like to be surrounded by something beautiful that a human created. It'll restore my faith in mankind."

The garden overwhelmed Jeneil and the evening's pleasant mood returned. Steve had been there before but seeing it with Jeneil was an experience. The plants had interested her, the work of sculpture had impressed her, and the atmosphere of the lush green garden had restored her spirit. She had carefully poked into all the areas enjoying the visual beauty offered there. He went to get drinks at the small café smiling over the fact that she couldn't drink espresso because it was too heavy and she didn't drink wine or liquor because she was allergic. He got her mineral water with a slice of lime thinking how much like the delicate plants in the garden she was, requiring extra care.

Steve stopped to watch Jeneil by a waterfall. A big leafy plant grew beside the waterfall, letting its dinner plate sized leaves droop slightly. She was nestled amongst them and was standing with her eyes closed, letting the spray from the waterfall breathe on her as the huge plant held her lovingly. Steve was stunned by the sensual pleasure she was experiencing in that moment. Even before knowing who the girl in Peter's life was he was sure she must be sexy because of the change in Peter, and having met and gotten to know her he had seen glimpses of that sexuality. Watching her now was the most sensual and personal moment he had ever witnessed. He walked closer fascinated by her interaction with her surroundings and he could see that she was lost in the moment, her expression serene. The moment wasn't erotic for her, it was restorative, an elixir, and he wondered about her level of sensuality if this wasn't a turn on.

The garden became more beautiful as he watched her draw a personal quality from it. He had seen beauty before but until this moment he had never felt the beauty of surroundings. She reminded him of a delicate bird the plant welcomed to rest amongst its leaves. She was in surroundings that were natural to her and he was fascinated that she could snuggle to things of the earth and extract comfort from them. Now he understood why she had left Camelot and created Wonderland. She seemed less lopsided when he considered the way she looked at life and he smiled watching her, loving her gentleness and sensitivity.

She was quiet during the drive home but there was a restful peace between them. She thanked him for those qualities before she went to bed after which he sat shirtless on the screened deck thinking of how she appreciated the comfort and quiet peace of their relationship while he waited for a quality she inspired in him to pass. He closed his eyes enjoying the cool night air and waited for the stirring passion within to disappear.

*****

They inflated the boat the next day and took it down to the water. The shore near the house was too rocky so they set it afloat in the bay where Steve got his first glimpse of Jeneil's fear of water. She stayed close to land getting out of the boat in the shallow water explaining she needed to get to know her relationship with the boat and water better. He thought it was cute and stayed in the boat letting the tide buoy it along. Lying on the floor of the boat as it drifted was a soothing sensation and he wondered if drifting in life was what made Jeneil such a soothing person to be around. She wasn't caught up in the stampede; she stopped to smell the flowers. He smiled thinking about her and her life at tilt; he liked it. Arriving at the house after their fun, they found Charlie, Adrienne, Dennis, and Karen there.

"We came to see Wonderland," Karen said. "Robert's been talking about it so much that we had to see it for ourselves. You're certainly isolated here. Are you capturing Walden, Jeneil?"

Jeneil smiled. "No, he had only one chair for visitors. I have a bunch of cushions. Does that make me more extroverted?"

Steve wondered and grew more curious as he became aware of Dennis watching Jeneil. He decided he liked Dennis better as the flamboyant playwright who openly swept Jeneil off her feet. The quiet, silent, watchful man wasn't easy to read. Also, the fact that Karen was enormously and uncomfortably pregnant made Steve wonder how much of Dennis's attention was unsatisfied needs. Uneasiness stirred within him as Jeneil brought lemonade out. Everyone sat in the screen house on the stools that she had lashed except Karen who took a lawn chair for back support.

"Are you arrested in a youth camp flashback?" Karen asked, smiling at Jeneil. "Why are you doing this?"

"Because the butterfly is now transforming," Dennis answered, drinking lemonade while he watched Jeneil. He smoothed his tongue across his lips slowly. Steve wondered if his suspicions about Dennis were imagined. Was the look Karen gave Dennis filled with anger or had Steve imagined that, too.

"Actually I just needed a break," Jeneil explained.

"A break?" Karen laughed. "A break is a week or two on a tropical beach."

Jeneil chuckled. "I have a strong nesting instinct. I'd probably spend two weeks building grass huts along the beach." Dennis laughed heartily and Steve watched Karen sigh.

Adrienne smiled. "She'd probably rent out the huts and earn the cost of her plane fare, too. She has a strong business sense as well."

"That she does. You're a tightwad, beautiful. We're going to stay in budget this year with you around," Dennis said, stretching his legs, and Steve noticed Karen grip her glass.

Jeneil laughed. "Now listen people. Just because you're drinking my lemonade doesn't mean you have to sing my praises, too. I've heard enough about Jeneil."

"So do I at home," Karen mumbled, sighing. "And when Robert's visiting it's Jeneil in stereo from him and Dennis."

Dennis got annoyed. "Karen, she's good and we're lucky to have her full-time this season. Stop being pregnant and start being human, geez."

Steve looked at Jeneil who was studying Dennis and Karen. "Shut up, Dennis," Jeneil said, getting up and going to Karen's side. "Look at her. How can she stop being pregnant? She's a wisp of a woman carrying a tummy full of baby that keeps pushing at her ribs. Her small frame looks barely able to carry her own body let alone a second person's who's moving around inside." Jeneil squeezed Karen's shoulder. "I think you deserve a trophy. How would you like the Crab Monique you said you were craving?"

Karen looked at Jeneil completely surprised by her outburst at Dennis. "How do you know the baby is doing that?"

"You told me," Jeneil said sympathetically, standing up. "I picked up some Crab Monique at Tiel's yesterday. I was going to bring it to the theatre for you, but now is a good time for some pampering."

"I don't need the calories," Karen said, her eyes getting moist.

Jeneil patted her arm gently. "Give me the lemonade and I'll bring you ice water with zero calories. You know Tiel's portions fill a thimble. I have a neighbor who is an authority on pregnancy. She has six children and said when the pregnancy is all in the stomach, the weight comes off with the delivery. With some toning, you'll be back to your normal size again. Besides, Mrs. Rezendes said that a pregnant woman should satisfy her food cravings even if it's just a taste. I'll get the Crab Monique."

Jeneil headed to the house as tears rolled down Karen's cheeks. "She listened," Karen said, touched by Jeneil's attention. "I can tell most people are looking right through me when I talk about the baby. She actually listened to my petty complaints. I can hardly stand them myself and she listened."

Karen wiped her tears on her wrist and Dennis slipped his arm around her shoulder and kissed her cheek gently. Steve noticed Dennis watching Jeneil, who was heading to the house, and he didn't like the set of circumstances he was seeing. Adrienne and Karen talked about being pregnant until Jeneil returned with food for everyone, but Karen alone got the Crab Monique and a flower Jeneil had picked on her way to the screen house. Karen smiled enjoying the fussing.

Dennis smiled at Jeneil. "You made me feel like a mean man."

"No, Dennis, you're just a man and you've never been pregnant," Jeneil said, smiling as she sat on her chair again.

"Thank heavens!" Dennis said. "Because I know I couldn't handle it as well as Karen is."

Karen looked up pleased by his words. "Do you really mean that? I feel like a bitch most of the time."

"Only since the kid has been kicking," Dennis said, smiling at her.

Steve looked at Jeneil who was watching them and smiling. At that moment, he wished he could have put his arm around her shoulder and kissed her cheek. He loved her compassion and he loved her being able to put Dennis in his place.

Charlie ate a few strawberries and then got up. "I'm getting stiff. I'll get back to the garage before I seize up completely."

Jeneil stood up. "Charlie, I know you consider that fun, but would you mind if I had some workmen do the shell and you do the customizing inside. You can't spend every weekend hammering. That's too much work." She grinned. "And as a favor, would you put a stake near the water to dock my boat?"

Charlie smiled. "I don't mind the work."

"I know you don't but have you checked your fields? The rabbits like the butternut squash better than the lettuce. It needs some help."

"Oh no," Charlie groaned, and headed out of the screen house with Jeneil running after him talking about fencing.

Adrienne smiled. "That girl is a total kick in the head."

"Yeah, she is," Dennis said, smiling as he watched Jeneil keep up at a running pace to Charlie's long strides as they disappeared into the field. Steve drank some lemonade and was surprised to feel electricity pulsate through his chest, but he liked what she had done for Karen; he liked it a lot. It left its mark on him and Dennis too from what he could see.

Jeneil returned stomping mud from her shoes. "I'm going to Vernal Hall at State this afternoon. Senator Prescott is flying in for commencement and he's agreed to appear before a student group in an open forum. Everyone is welcome to go with me or stay here and relax. There's chicken in the fridge that needs to be barbequed or beef patties. Help yourself to what's there."

"Are you joining the political arena?" Dennis asked.

"No, I enjoy the interaction between people. It's interesting to observe what issues are emotional. Except for street brawls and bar fights, student groups and town meetings are the best arenas for open debating. I like to hear people speak. I can almost hear Ben Franklin and Patrick Henry applauding if I concentrate hard enough."

Dennis laughed. "I'll pass. It sounds too much like playhouse director's meetings. They give me nightmares." He looked at Karen. "Want to float the kid in a boat?"

"Oh yes!" Karen answered, her eyes sparkling. "My back would appreciate the feeling of being in a sling."

Adrienne shook her head. "I'll stay and relax. I'm dying to look through the telescope. I brought ribs and potato salad and everyone's welcome to share it."

"Oh, save a couple for me," Jeneil pleaded.

Steve stood up. "Count me in, Jeneil. I'll tag along. Being able to say I was at Senator Prescott's forum will make it sound like I have a life when I'm scrubbing at five a.m."

Jeneil laughed. "Well, just for choosing door number three you get an added bonus of having a New York style wiener at the vendor's."

Steve laughed. "Oh, will my luck never run out."

Dennis watched Steve. "Teacher's pet, huh?"

Steve grinned. "Wouldn't you try for straight A's if they looked like her?"

Dennis laughed. "I can't argue there."

Jeneil pushed Steve gently. "You'll get nothing extra for flattery, so don't try."

"You're tough," Steve said, bumping her arm and then holding the door for her aware that Dennis was watching. He felt good about that because whether Dennis was watching for himself or Robert, the men of science had just edged out the men of arts by a nose. He beamed knowing that Peter would be proud of him.

Steve appeared in dress slacks and sport coat with Jeneil by his side in a sundress and sandals. She looked really good and Dennis took it all in. Steve smiled and held her hand as they walked to the car feeling sure that Dennis's eyes were glued in their direction. Sunday with her at Wonderland had been relaxing and he was sorry to have to leave for home, but he had some studying to do for a case he had in the morning. The whole weekend lingered with him and thoughts of her filled him with contentment.

Thirty-Three

Peter parked his car in the lot and clenched his jaw noticing Steve's Lynx. Word about Steve and Jeneil had swept through the first shift on Sunday. He hadn't expected his stomach to knot when he heard about it since he had pleaded with Steve to get gossip started, but the comments about what a nice couple they made and how they looked up and smiled at each other got to him. His jaw had pained hearing about Steve gently squeezing her hand and he wondered how much of it was really true since he knew how distorted gossip could be. He had finally calmed himself by thinking that Steve had probably pulled out all the stops to make it look convincing. Peter had to trust him, but the empty feeling pulsated through his chest. He was looking forward to OR in order to put it all behind him and relax.

"We were seen Saturday," Steve said quietly.

"I heard," Peter replied, and then added, "thanks."

"Jeneil felt bad. She wanted me to explain to you."

"It's okay, Steve. I understand gossip."

"I sure hope you're right about this, I really do," Steve said, sighing. Peter looked at him and smiled glad his attitude wasn't more cheerful.

Jerry Tollman stopped at Steve's side. "I heard you and Jeneil are dating." Dr. Sprague looked up surprised by the news and he looked at Peter, who seemed unaffected. Jerry hesitated uncomfortably. "She broke up with her boyfriend unexpectedly, didn't she?" Steve nodded. "Yeah, I thought so. Cut her hair off doing a tailspin, didn't she?"

"I didn't ask details about her ex, Jerry," Steve answered.

"Shit," Jerry fussed, "I thought something was going wrong in her life. I should have spoken up. I thought you were hovering close to her the day she came in to the ER."

Steve never looked up. "I'm sorry," he said, hoping to end the conversation and Jerry's growing agitation.

"Sorry?" Jerry sneered. "Sorry is what you'll really be if you pull a Steve Bradley. She's not the White Stallion's speed so don't mess with her or you'll face me with scalpels at ten paces." Steve looked up annoyed and about to respond.

"Tollman!" Dr. Sprague snapped in as loud a whisper as he dared. "You're out of line and insubordinate as well, apologize!"

"Like hell!" Jerry answered.

Dr. Sprague glared. "My office at nine-thirty."

"Yes, sir," Jerry answered, walking away angrily. Dr. Sprague snapped the water off his hands and walked away shaking his head.

Morgan Rand stopped behind Steve on his way to OR-1. "That goes for me too, Bradley. I'll stand behind Tollman with a club if you ruin her."

Steve looked at Peter, who was staring in shock at Morgan Rand's back as he walked away. "You didn't tell me this job would be dangerous to my health," Steve teased.

"Your health?" Peter asked, chuckling. "Can you imagine what would happen if they find out I'm the ex who caused the tailspin?" Steve struggled to keep from laughing but Peter got caught up in the silliness. "Sure, laugh White Stallion while the Chinese Stud sings soprano. Ten paces for you and a two sec amputation of the future Chang heirs for me."

Steve turned his head and gritted his teeth to hold back a laugh. "Oh geez," he sighed, "she really causes hormones to rage."

Peter groaned. "Nice Steve, I needed to hear that this morning besides Rand's and Tollman's problems."

Steve lost control and belly laughed. "Oh shit," he said, and threw his brush into the sink, "now I'm contaminated and I have to start all over again."

Peter laughed. "You contaminated my hands, too. Come on, Bradley, we've got sick people in here paying top dollar for responsible surgeons."

Steve sighed from laughing. "I'm going to use another sink. When we got to starting like this Rand would lock us out of the dorms because we couldn't stop."

They looked at each other and smiled. "Seems like yesterday," Peter said, and Steve nodded.

"Too bad some things have to change." Steve sighed and went to the next sink.

*****

Jeneil got in her car at ten and drove south toward the playhouse. She had gotten to her office at six-thirty intending to leave by nine. "What a Monday," she sighed, grabbing her briefcase and purse. Locking the car door, she raced to the playhouse office. Tossing her purse on the desk, she sighed again. "I raced here thinking I might be holding up progress and I find you leaning back in your chair sleeping. Dennis, why are you goldbricking?"

Resting his hands on his head, he smiled. "That's what's nice about creative work. Prove I'm not working."

Jeneil slipped off her suit jacket. "Use that on the budget chairman, I happen to know what needs to be done." She opened her briefcase. "What is it, Dennis? Spring fever?"

"Give me a blood transfusion. What are you on?" He stood up and yawned.

Removing a file folder, she closed the briefcase and sat with the open folder before her. "I went over the script again. These are suggestions for Act Two," she said, and held a sheet of paper out to him and he took it and returned to his chair still showing a lack of enthusiasm. Jeneil watched then went to the office door and pushing it shut quickly, she turned to him. "Dennis, this is getting serious. Your lack of interest is beginning to penetrate this whole play. What is your problem?"

There was a knock at the door and Jeneil opened it. Karen stood there smiling. "Hi, I brought coffee," Karen said, and Jeneil smiled and stood aside. Karen handed a coffee mug to Dennis. "How's it going?"

"It's not," Dennis said, sighing. "Jeneil was about to kick my ass."

Karen looked surprised and then uncomfortable. "It's me, isn't it?"

Dennis shook his head wearily. "Karen, worry about being pregnant. Just have the baby."

"Sure." Karen nodded and went to the door. "I hope it goes better for you. Don't be too hard on him, Jeneil. I'm sure it's me." Jeneil watched Karen leave and Dennis signaled with his hand to close the door.

"You just saw my problem," Dennis said, getting up to pace. "She's strangling me."

Jeneil wrinkled her brow. "Dennis, she was here for all of two minutes. She brought you coffee, wished you good luck and left."

Dennis sat on the edge of the desk. "Ever since she got pregnant I've heard the same guilt routine over and over."

"It wasn't planned then?"

Dennis shook his head. "Neither of us wanted children. That's why I thought we were a good combination."

"Well then, why didn't you take more permanent precautions?"

Dennis smiled. "You've changed, Jeneil. You didn't even blush saying that."

"And don't answer the question either. It has nothing to do with the problem at hand anyway," Jeneil said. "Dennis, we have to pull this together. This can't go on."

"Don't I know it," Dennis said, sighing. "I feel bad because she looks so damn pregnant. It can't be easy but she wanders around with an aching back and muscle cramps. I don't know what a good night's sleep is anymore."

"You give her mixed signals, Dennis. Yesterday you told her to stop being pregnant and start being human and just now you told her the opposite. Maybe she's confused. She could be responding to you." She sighed. "I don't know, Dennis. I'm just guessing."

Dennis paced again. "Actually, it feels good to just talk about it."

Jeneil watched as he drank his coffee and she got up quickly, taking the mug and surprising him. "Dennis, turn your life around. Inject fresh air into it."

"What?" he asked confused.

She went to her purse and poured some juice for him from her thermos. "Here, get away from coffee for a while. It'll be a change."

"I hate grapefruit juice," he moaned.

"Good, it'll be punishment. Whip that lethargic flesh into submission. Drink!" she insisted, smiling. "And here, take some vitamin C. The spa is having a special this week, a month of treatments for half price. Let me give you a membership for Karen. The pampering will be good for her blues. You've infected each other with lethargy. You're both strangling on the umbilical cord."

Dennis laughed. "Boy, you're one bossy bitch when you get started. But I understand what you're saying. We're both insecure about the baby. We know we can live like vagabonds in the theatre, but can a kid?"

Jeneil put her arm through his. "Dennis, kids grow up everywhere. Not everybody lives in a white house with a picket fence. It's my understanding the magic ingredient is love. I think you and Karen are terrific, why wouldn't your child?"

Dennis smiled. "I've caught your energy flow." He kissed her cheek. "You're right, I'm just drifting."

"Watch your health," she cautioned. "You always did worry me living on black coffee the way you do. Even the coffee growers don't want you to do that!"

"You have an odd way of looking at life."

"Odd?" she replied. "Watching your health is odd? You can't move a sick body, so it's odder to be developing one."

Dennis laughed having caught her positive energy flow and he hugged her. "Do you think Karen will be insulted about the spa?"

"She's an actress, it's a necessity and she'll be in her eighth month when her membership is finished and the play will be in full production."

Dennis grinned. "You're a manipulative wench."

"No," Jeneil disagreed, "I'm not hiding my ideas from you, am I?"

Dennis shook his head. "No, you just burst into my life with enthusiasm and fire taking my breath away." He sighed and held her in his arms. "And it feels great."

She smiled as she rested her arms on his shoulders. "Your muse needs freedom."

He nodded. "You're a good diagnostician. My muse is suffocating from a snag in the umbilical cord."

She kissed his cheek. "You can't do that, Dennis. Your talent is your life force. Interrupt its natural flow and your life will suffer."

"How come the world isn't as impressed with the greatness of my talent as you are?"

"But it is, Dennis. At least the limited world that has seen it. Do you think the board would have accepted the poor level of work that you put in the last production if they didn't feel you have talent?"

He laughed gently. "Jeneil, you're changing. At times, your tongue has the snap of a bullwhip."

She grinned and the closeness between them became more intense. She pulled away gently. "Now Mr. Blair," she said, going to her desk, "if you'll look over the list I just handed you, I'll see that Robert's staging has begun and then check our volunteer group. After that, we'll sit down and work on Act Two."

She walked past him with the clipboard aware he was silently watching her. She continued out of the office and down the hall. Dennis took a deep breath and sighed as he walked to his desk.

*****

Jeneil left the theatre at seven-thirty feeling tired but hopeful. A lot of work had been accomplished but watching Karen and Dennis go home together made her aloneness feel more acute. She had begun to worry about Peter's marriage and that it was lasting so long. There were hundreds of unanswered questions in her mind. But most of all, she missed Peter and their life together. It wasn't easy to divide a life into one after having multiplied it into two. She envied Karen's and Dennis's increase to three even though it was a struggle to make the numbers work.

She sighed and turned on the light locking the door behind her. Putting her briefcase and purse away, she showered quickly and changed to a lounging dress. There was food in the refrigerator but nothing appealed to her. The restlessness was stirring again; she could sense it in her indecision about dinner. She had learned a little about the restlessness; it had to be satisfied not ignored and it was usually satisfied when she focused some thought on herself. It had no definite shape or direction, arriving and fading as a head cold would with minor annoying symptoms. Finishing a slice of cantaloupe, she cleaned the counter and turned out the lights to the kitchen.

The bedroom fan hummed soothingly. Sitting on the cot, she wondered what she should feed her restlessness. She chuckled half aloud wondering if she'd developed a new medical formula; feed a neurosis and starve a psychosis. She laughed openly feeling she'd probably be tongue lashed for making light of mental health. Taking the picture of Chang from the fabric-covered corrugated box that she used as a nightstand, she smiled. "You're too small," she said to the 4x6 shot. "Tomorrow I'm bringing in the poster of you and hanging you on a wall in here. After that, it's just the life-sized real you left." She sighed. "Oh, Peter. When? What's happening? Why can't we get anywhere in freeing you? And why isn't she huge and suffering in her pregnancy like poor Karen? Uette doesn't look pregnant; that's unmotherly."

Putting the photo down, she dragged the box of her father's research to the cot. It was a job she kept starting to sort and then would become distracted. It didn't have order, she thought. Maybe if she sorted through all of it and put it into categories she'd be inspired. There was so much research that she should be doing something with it. But what? She sighed and began lifting the loosely bound manuscripts from the box, setting them on the floor in a pile. There seemed to be more manuscripts than other papers and she was impressed with her father's passion for history to have spent the hours it must have taken to put the material together. Why hadn't his clear-sightedness passed on to her genetically? Both her parents knew what their life's work was.

She picked up a thick manila envelope and undid the clasp. It was filled with letters to her father from his family in Ireland and from her mother at an address in France and then in Boston. She sorted through arranging them according to sender. Finding one different from the others, she noticed the envelope was unopened and addressed to William Alden in Devon from her mother. Devon? Devon was only an hour and a half or so away. Her mother had family that close by? The envelope was marked, *Return to Sender*. She thought for a minute and then opened it.

Dear Father, It has been so many years now that I'm writing with the hope the situation between us has changed. I wonder often how you and mother are doing. Neil and I have a lovely daughter. We've named her Jeneil Serena. Jeneil was startled to learn about a middle name and that she was named for her maternal great grandmother. The letter continued. *She seems to be exactly like her name, Serene. She's pleasant and smiling and an absolute wonder to us and our friend, Mandra. You'd think no other child had ever learned to walk or talk the way we fuss over her achievements. Neil considers her a miracle and that in itself is miraculous considering his disbelief in such things. I won't go on about her or I'll never stop writing. It would be nice if we could repair the damage between us. Life seems too short to live with anger. I'd like the chance to be reacquainted with you and the family and to introduce Jeneil to her grandparents. We have changed our last name and are now known as Alden-Connors.* It was signed, *Sincerely, Jennifer.*

Jeneil sat on her cot completely baffled. What damage had been done to have separated a daughter from her father? Going to the telephone, she dialed information. There was no number listed for a William Alden. He'd probably been gone for years now and she became more curious about not having been told about a disagreement so serious that a man would return a letter sent to him by his daughter unopened. It was so contrary to what she had been told about her mother's family. She had never heard of an angry silence, just a lack of closeness. As she sorted through the other letters, her curiosity grew. There was one to William Alden from her father notifying him of her mother's death. It too had been returned unopened. Was her grandfather still alive at that time? That seemed impossible. Why hadn't anyone else in the family written? Didn't her grandmother care? Jeneil remembered Serena Randolph, her great grandmother. The four poster bed and bed jackets were from her. But where was her grandmother?

Amongst the letters was a sheet of folded parchment. Opening it, Jeneil found a drawing of a tree with names written amongst its branches. One half of the tree was her father's ancestors and the other half was her mother's and was incomplete. Jeneil again wondered about the anger that separated her mother from her roots. She glanced over the names on her father's side. Connors became O'Connor as she went back further; Leary, Lynch, and Smith. Jeneil stopped as she read the non-Irish name but there it was. Doolen Lynch had married Martha Smith. "Good for you, Doolen and Martha. Good for you, and in Ireland, too. That took courage."

Jeneil continued through the papers. There was another envelope which contained legal documents; the court document legalizing Alden-Connors, the marriage certificate for Neil Connors and Jennifer Alden, and a birth certificate for Jeneil Serena Connors. "Well, I'll be." Jeneil smiled. "I'm glad I didn't know or I'd still be in kindergarten trying to write Jeneil Serena Alden-Connors."

Putting each category in a separate envelope, she repacked the box feeling better for having put it in order. Keeping the legal documents aside to be kept in her files at the office, she got her things ready for the next day. Lying on the cot, she completed some work from the office and made a list of things she wanted to accomplish at the theatre. The restlessness had been appeased and Jeneil got into bed feeling relaxed, but missing Peter. She laughed as she thought that she missed him because she wanted to tell him her middle name. "Let's have a daughter too, Peter," she said, thinking out loud, "Serena Chang for the lady who for some reason was the only person to not disown my mother. It has to be Serena Chang. The poor child would never forgive us if her name was Serena Alden-Connors Chang and her camp clothes were initialed SACC. It doesn't seem fair to have your initials spell SACC." Jeneil chuckled. "Having children gets complicated." She yawned exhausted from the day's schedule, snapped on the lamp and smiled at the picture of Chang, and then turned off the light and gave in to sleep.

*****

Peter sat in his bedroom eating dinner. His mother had sent all his favorites. Uette seemed animated about something, but he was feeling down after all the talk about Steve and

Jeneil. He missed her and he wanted to talk to her just to hear her voice. The soft knock at his door irritated him.

"What?" he asked, setting his plate on the bureau and cleaning his fingers.

Uette opened the door. "I'd like to show you something."

He sighed. "Uette, I'm tired. I'd like to be left alone."

She folded her arms and grinned. "Peter, you poor sweet idiot."

He spun around annoyed by her words. "Beat it," he scowled.

"No, I have something to show you," she answered, shaking her head. "You sit here all broken up missing Jeneil and she doesn't even care." Peter wondered if she had heard about the gossip. "Come on," she said, "I have some interesting things to show you."

He followed her out of the room and toward her bedroom. He stopped in the hallway. "Okay, Uette, play it straight. I'm too tired for games."

"It's on my TV."

"What?" he asked, getting more annoyed.

"Oh, Peter, really. I'm not going to rape you. Look, I even have a chair for you to sit on. This is all I need to help me." She inserted a video into the VCR and then sat on the bed.

Peter sat on the chair thoroughly irritated by her games and then jumped off the chair as he saw Jeneil's car drive into view on the TV. "What is this?"

"Sit down, Peter. The story gets better I hear." Uette grinned. "Sit down." Peter stood staring at the TV, panic growing in him as he saw Jeneil get out of her car, stunned by her short hair. Uette giggled. "Oh my, she cut off the rat's nest. I haven't seen this yet either."

Peter wanted to hit her, but he remained silent and slipped into the chair not trusting the weakness in his legs. "They found her!" he breathed shallowly.

Uette picked up a sheet of paper as Peter watched two men walk into view. The film was spliced. He wondered why. Checking the paper, Uette laughed. "Oh my goodness, there's no car in view because they arrived by plane using a meadow as a landing strip. The jet is owned by a William Reynolds who has his money in everything, he's the man in the mustache, and the other man is Hollis Wells, a lawyer from Nebraska."

The film was spliced again and showed Jeneil walking with the two men near her car. Peter was surprised that Hollis was so young and Bill could easily star in movies. He hardly looked the role of the wimp from Jeneil's childhood. Hollis held Jeneil in his arms and kissed her forehead. Bill put his arm around her and kissed her lips. They walked out of sight and Jeneil was left alone waving to them. Peter's heart beat rapidly from seeing her and from fear for her safety. His mind kept trying to figure out where the guy with the camera could be, but the surroundings weren't familiar.

"William Reynolds is filthy rich, Peter," Uette added. "I can't imagine our poor little rich girl waiting for a penniless surgeon with a sexy looking owner of a jet flying in for a visit. He brought in a heavy construction crew and turned the meadow into an airstrip. You don't do that if you only visit at Christmas."

Peter tuned her out desperately making note of the angle of the camera and a description of the background so he could tell Steve. The film spliced again and a red Porsche drove into what looked like a driveway. Peter grasped the arm of his chair. He hadn't known Robert Danzieg was seeing her. He held his breath wondering what the camera had picked up. Robert got out of the car in his favorite outfit, cutoff jeans and no shirt.

"Ooo," Uette remarked, "look at this guy and a red Porsche, too. Miss Mouse likes fast men." Peter closed his eyes as anger toward Uette surfaced. Jeneil and Robert stood near his car talking and Peter noticed Robert's body language toward Jeneil. He swallowed. Uette checked her paper. "This heavy breathing macho man is one Robert Danzieg, an artist with roots in California and to money. And look at that body. He sure likes showing it off for her, doesn't he?" Peter bit his lip to keep from yelling. Uette shook her head. "My, my, Miss Mouse, how do you keep him in line? That is one very anxious cat she's got there." Uette looked at her paper. "Oh dear, it says here that Mr. Danzieg is a frequent visitor." Peter's heart sank. "Are you sure she's waiting for you, Peter?" Uette taunted.

Peter's throat was dry from his anger at Uette and he bolted back in his chair as he saw Robert move closer to Jeneil and put his arms around her. "I'll kill him!" Chang raged inside of Peter and his body tensed rigidly. Jeneil turned her head avoiding Robert's kiss; Robert pulled her against him holding her tightly. Peter pushed himself against the chair afraid he'd get up and put his foot through the TV screen.

Uette turned to look at him. "Peter, Miss Mouse has an interesting life, don't you think?" Peter ignored her and watched the TV in angry silence, stunned as Jeneil broke Robert's hold with a fast arm thrust. He wanted to laugh as he watched her spin around completing a full performance of footwork toward Robert's chest and face, missing him deliberately. It shocked Robert and then broke him up, bending him over in laughter. "I don't believe it!" Uette gasped at the screen with shock, wide eyed. "She's too tough for words! What do you see in her! She's not even feminine! What does she have that attracts you guys?"

Peter was glad he was too angry to talk because he wanted to answer her question in graphic detail. He knew it would give him the greatest satisfaction to describe exactly how feminine Jeneil really was, but he remained silent as hatred for Uette choked him. He remained silent to protect Jeneil. He watched as Robert leaned against his car and shook his head, smiling broadly. He said something and moved toward her slowly, protecting himself like a prize fighter and kissed her cheek. Jeneil laughed. Robert got into his car and rolled down the window. Throwing her a kiss, he backed out and drove away.

"I don't believe it! He loved it!" Uette gasped. "This is incredible. It must be her perfume!"

Peter remained silent as Jeneil's car pulled into the driveway followed by another car that he didn't recognize. Four men got out and Peter held his breath as he recognized Dennis Blair. They joined Jeneil and Dennis put his arm around her shoulder and walked around the corner of the house with her followed by the other men. His heart drained and his mind screamed, "Dennis Blair! Damn it! Damn this whole mess and this shittin' bitch for keeping me here while those guys muscle Jeneil. Damn it!"

Uette turned off the VCR and grinned. "Well Peter, Miss Mouse isn't very lonely is she? Does she know any women? Those last four are Director, Assistant Director, Staging Manager, and leading man at the playhouse. Miss Mouse is playing at show biz now. She's a volunteer, full-time, a gopher to the director, Dennis Blair. I wonder what he has her go-fer, Peter. Are you sure she's waiting? It doesn't look like she's sitting around counting the days until you return dear heart. Is your brooding worth it?"

Peter stood up forcing himself to remain calm. He went to the bedroom door and turned to her. "Uette, you could have saved yourself and your friends some time and money. Was that supposed to hurt me? Well, you're a little behind schedule because I told you she left without a word to me. I got the message through gossip that Steve and Jeneil are dating, at least that's what I heard when I hit him with the question. So laugh Uette, laugh all you want. You were right, she's not waiting. I read her all wrong but that film didn't hurt, having my best friend deliver the Dear John letter did." He turned and went to his bedroom leaving Uette standing by the TV completely stunned. He closed his door and gritted his teeth as the anger he was holding back raged through him thrusting Chang to the surface.

Uette knocked. "Peter, let's talk."

"Go away!" he shouted.

"Peter, please. I'm sorry. I didn't know she had done that. She's a bitch, Peter. You were too good for her," she said through the closed door.

"Shut up!" he raged. "Shut up and leave me alone!" He wanted to destroy something, to beat on something. His anger was strangling him. He looked around the room wanting to overturn the bed and tear it to splinters with his bare hands. He snapped open the closet door and grabbed a pair of old jeans from the hanger, pulling at it and swinging it wildly, slamming it on the bed until he was totally wasted of strength and empty of rage. The jeans were beyond use, shredded and torn to pieces at the seams. He lay on the bed and sighed heavily. "They found her!" He sat up. "I've got to get to Steve!" Opening the door, he headed out of the apartment.

"Where are you going?" Uette asked, coming from the kitchen.

"I need some air," he said, slamming the door behind him. Running the stairs, he stopped at the telephone booth in the lobby and dialed Steve. "It's Pete," he said, breathless.

Steve's heart pounded hearing the tone of Peter's voice. "Pete, what is it?"

"Steve, I just sat through a video tape of Jeneil at her house. It must be her house; I could only see a corner of it. It was brown and there's a driveway with some kind of shrubbery protecting the backyard."

"Oh shit," Steve gasped at the accuracy of Peter's description. "Oh shit, they found her! Peter, do something!"

"I think I have, I slipped the rug from under her by saying you delivered a Dear John letter to me."

"Did she buy it?" Steve asked, almost shaking.

"I'm pretty sure."

"Pete, be more than pretty sure, please," Steve pleaded.

"Steve, whoever it is has the camera across the street from the driveway. The angle looks like it might be coming from the second or third floor of a building."

"That's impossible, there's absolutely nothing around her. She's the only one living on the road and there are no buildings across the street. She's completely alone there, Pete. Totally, it's blackness after dark except for a full moon. She's completely isolated."

"Oh shit," Peter moaned. "No neighbors?"

"Maybe a half mile away," Steve answered, beginning to pace.

"Holy shit!" Peter said. "We've got to get her out of there. She has to go to Nebraska."

"Great, how do we convince her?"

"I don't know." Peter sighed, discouraged. "I don't want her to live looking over her shoulder."

"Pete, if Uette believes your story then what would be her next move?"

"I don't know, Steve. I just saw the damn video and swallowed my panic through it. Then I went to my bedroom and acted like a gorilla. After I calmed down, I called you. Shit, I can barely think. I'm so scared for her. Where the hell is she living?"

"In Weeden," Steve answered. "There's nothing there but farmland and water."

"Then where the hell is the camera? What's across the street from her?"

"A landing strip."

"The angle was high and across the street so what's there? There has to be something. A tower maybe? A barn in the distance?"

"Nothing, Pete. All she's got is her house and the bay. She's lucky to have power lines."

"Power lines!" Peter replied. "Is there a pole across the street?"

"Maybe." Steve struggled to remember. "Yes, there is. I had to park my car further in the driveway and when I backed out I had to remind myself about the pole behind me."

"Then that's where the camera is. It has to be."

"So what now?"

Peter sighed again. "If we destroy the camera it'll tip them off that I'm in touch with her."

"Is that all that was on the video, just her driveway?"

"Yes. Why?"

Steve hesitated. "Then what's the immediate danger?"

"I don't know," Peter replied. "I don't like them knowing where she is and watching her."

"I don't either but Uette's the key, right? She's the one who pushes the muscle button so what did she use the video for?"

Peter hesitated. "To show me that Jeneil isn't sitting around waiting."

"Oh shit." Steve sighed. "Pete, Danzieg is….well he's…."

"I know. I saw him on the video."

"Don't hold anything against her. He's as subtle as an eighteen wheeler bearing down on her at ninety miles an hour. He irritates me. His name alone makes my blood pressure rise. Every time I see his name or picture in the social column I make sure I use it for the coffee grounds." Peter laughed at Steve's remark. "Pete, what's with Dennis Blair?"

Peter's face got serious. "Why, have you met him there?"

"Yes, and Karen's very pregnant, hugely pregnant. Follow my thinking?"

"Yes," Peter answered, sighing. "How is he with Jeneil?"

"In a word, possessive, watches her like the father of a girl on prom night."

"Damn it." Peter breathed in a long breath of air and then exhaled. "I think he's with Karen because he couldn't have Jeneil. Did he try with you around?"

"Yes," Steve answered. "She's deadly, Pete. I mean it. The kid's a killer."

Peter stared at the wall in front of him thoughtfully. "I know. That body combined with her trusting, innocent face causes a hormone riot."

"It's what she does with your mind that's the megaton bomb," Steve added.

"She can't help it, Steve. It's how she lives. It's intense and passionate. It's not her fault."

"So what do we do?"

"We're not running this show, the screwball bitch is. Right now, she wants to be my shrink and hold my hand. I can get a few days out of that and then I'm on the second shift." Peter sighed. "Hell, if this mess doesn't end soon I won't know what normal is, but now that I've had a chance to think about it and talk to you I'm certain that Jeneil is probably okay for now. The Dear John worked, I'm sure of it."

Steve sighed. "I'm going to be grey-haired before this is over from worrying about hidden cameras, homicidal bitches, guys on shark attack, and the kid who's in the middle of it smelling flowers and living like life is wonderful. I watch her and I tell myself not to wake her up. It's so nice to watch her live at tilt. It's like fresh air."

Peter smiled understanding completely and adding one more grey hair to Steve's list; a good friend who was deeply and sincerely in love with her. Peter saw the kind of love Steve had for Jeneil and he could understand Steve's feeling because that was how he felt about Jeneil. He sighed, leaning against the telephone booth wall after hanging up. "Songbird, can you survive all of it or will it wake you up? Oh baby, my grandfather's right. Songbirds need protecting."

*****

Getting out of his car, Peter headed for the kitchen door to his mother's house. The lights in the greenhouse were off, but he hoped his grandfather would be home. Knocking, he opened the door and walked in. His grandfather, his mother, Tom, and Karen were all standing in the kitchen and they all stared uneasily at him.

"What?" he asked, feeling the odd man out.

"How are you?" his mother asked, looking upset. Karen came to him and gave him a hug, which totally shocked him, but he had no patience for any of it.

"Grandfather, can I talk to you?" he asked, and his grandfather nodded sadly and they headed to the greenhouse. Peter felt he was missing something that was happening.

"Peter," his grandfather started, "Uette called just before you got here and told your mother that Steve and Jeneil were seeing each other. She's not waiting for you?"

Peter shook his head then leaned back sighing. "There are so many lies in my life now that I'm meeting myself coming around corners. Grandfather, I told that story to Uette to protect Jeneil. Uette had a video tape of Jeneil at her new address. Uette's having her watched. I told her that so she'd leave Jeneil alone. It was the safest thing to do."

His grandfather covered his mouth stunned by the level of deceit. "Peter, I can't believe Uette would hurt her."

"Grandfather, she's crazy. I'm not taking any chances."

"Then end it, Peter. End it now. Lies, deceit, spying, danger, it's not what saving face is about. This is way out of hand. It's gone beyond honor and dignity."

"I can't get out now, Grandfather. For some reason, Uette panics when I threaten to leave. I'm afraid she'd hurt Jeneil if I left and I haven't gotten the truth yet. I can't face Jeneil's people if I don't clear my name."

His grandfather sighed. "I'm very worried, Peter. You and Jeneil are living at different levels now. It's too easy to get lost."

"I'm stuck with it, Grandfather. It's here and it's what's happening. In my mind, the situation is reduced to finding the truth and protecting Jeneil. That's all of it for me."

*****

Uette was waiting for Peter when he got in. Standing near him, she touched his arm gently. "Peter, I feel bad about the video. Honestly, I wouldn't have shown it to you if I had known."

"Uette, why did you even have her spied on?" he asked, the sincerity in her voice surprising him.

She lowered her eyes in embarrassment. "I can't compete with her. For some reason, she has you totally infatuated. The way you talk about her doesn't match what Karen says about her. I guess I couldn't imagine a woman waiting for a man who had gotten someone else pregnant."

His back stiffened. "I'm not the father of your baby and you know it." He walked past her annoyed.

"Peter," she called, turning quickly. He stopped and turned around. She walked to him. "Why is it so difficult for you to accept being the father? Am I so repulsive that you can't bear the thought of being with me? Jeneil has found another life with Steve. Why can't you at least give me a chance? I really love you and I find that so crazy because you're so horrible to me, but I do love you. Give me a chance to prove it to you."

"Do you really mean that?" he asked, watching her. "You really want a chance to prove that you love me?"

"Yes." She smiled, encouraged by his question.

At that moment he wished he could trust her. "Then prove it by coming clean with me. Who is the father of your baby and why have you nailed me for it?"

She sighed and her shoulders dropped from discouragement. "Peter, you are the father."

"No, Uette. I wasn't unconscious that night. You don't love me, you're using me and I find that repulsive." He turned and went to his room, leaving her staring sadly at his closed door. He was tired and worried about Jeneil. His grandfather's concern for the two of them worried him. Jeneil's safety worried him. The marriage was lasting much longer than he had expected it to.

Sleep eventually calmed his mind and he drifted off with dreams passing and fading before him. They were vivid dreams. He felt the coolness of the room with Jeneil in Camelot, the peace of their life together and her gentleness. Her hand smoothing his hair and the softness of her voice calling him were pleasant and stirred deep feelings in him. He felt her hand on his shoulder and he reached for it smiling.

"Hey, baby," he said, half awake. The sound of his voice woke him and the reality of the hand he was holding shocked him. "What!" He raised himself on an elbow quickly and was horrified to find Uette behind him in bed. "What the hell!" He moved quickly to the edge of the bed and turned on the lamp. "Uette! What the hell do you think you're doing?" He got up and grabbed his robe, wrapping it around himself quickly.

"I'm trying to prove how much I love you," she said, smiling, and Peter stared at her not believing what she was doing. "Don't look so shocked poor darling. Ease on back into bed. Come on." She moved to make room for him, letting the sheet slip so he'd have a chance to see her. Anger pulsed through him and he had to tell himself that he couldn't risk annoying her or Jeneil could be hurt. He forced himself to calm down and think. "Peter, I know I can please you. I know I can." She sighed, rubbing her hand gently on the bed where he would be. "Let me prove it."

He could hardly focus due to rage. "Uette, don't do this," he heard himself answer. "Get out of here now. Look at yourself. Where's your pride? Where's your dignity? You don't need to throw yourself at a man. Play it straight! For crying out loud, look at yourself!" He could tell she was on something. "Uette, get out of my bed."

"No, Peter. I want a chance to be your wife. I'll be a good wife for you."

"Not as popped as you are," he growled, "and what about the baby? Shit, think of that kid. It's as high as you are right now. Uette, you'll get the baby hooked, too." Peter was disgusted. He sighed and shook his head.

Tears rolled down her cheeks. "It moves inside of me." She wiped her tears with an unsteady hand. "It feels ugly. I don't want it moving inside of me like some horrible parasite," she cried. "I hate it."

Peter rubbed his forehead. "Uette, you need help. It's time to get some therapy. You need to talk about these feelings with a doctor."

"You're a doctor," she cried. "If you'd talk to me, we could be happily married. The stupid baby is going to get in the way soon and you won't want to be near me at all. I'll be so huge," she sobbed. "Please come to bed, Peter."

He felt sick to his stomach. "Uette, if you don't get out of my room, I'm leaving. This is a violation of saving face."

"Saving face?" She giggled. "Saving face, what the hell do you know about saving face?"

He watched as the drug worked on her. "Why, do you know more about it?" he asked, wondering how much she'd reveal in her condition.

"Ooo, dignity and honor," she taunted, trying to focus on his face and then cried. "I'm only teasing, Peter; I think you're terrific for caring about dignity and honor. And you care about me, too. You got those frozen dinners for me. I love you. Please come to bed."

He closed his eyes and drew a deep breath, hoping to settle the feeling of nausea. "Uette, please don't. Go to your room now. Don't force me to get mad."

"Why aren't you mad at the mouse?" she asked. "She's making it with half the men in the state and you sit and pout about not having her. I'm willing to be faithful to you." Peter was infuriated by her remark but realized it was senseless to even try dealing with her sanely. She smiled at him, obviously completely controlled by whatever she had taken. She wrinkled her nose. "Well, if you won't come to me, I'll just have to come to you. I know all kinds of ways so stay there if you want to." She moved across the bed clumsily, uncovering her naked body.

He was torn between repulsion and compassion for her. He leaned on the bed and covered her. "Uette, don't do this. I mean it, please. I can't make love to you. I feel sorry for you right now. You need help." He took her arm gently. "Come on." He wrapped the sheet around her as she stood up unsteadily before him.

"Are you going to turn me in? You said you'd turn me in if you found me high." She swayed to the left and he put his arms around her.

"No," he said. "No, I'm going to take you to your bed." He lifted her into his arms securing the sheet around her.

"Peter," she said groggily, "I love you. You're so nice to me. Even when you're being mean it's not as bad as...." She stopped.

"As bad as who?" he asked, as he took her to her room.

Tears rolled down her cheeks. "I really am sorry, you know."

"About what?" he asked, hoping for information but she was going under. Putting her on her bed, he left her wrapped in his sheet and covered her with her bedspread. Turning off the lights, he closed the door and returned to his room sighing with relief that the situation hadn't been worse.

*****

Peter scrubbed at six the next morning trying to decide if he should report the incident to his grandfather and the Wongs. He felt he should because it was a rule for saving face and he believed truth would be uncovered if the rules were followed, but he was worried about Jeneil. Steve walked into the scrub room stopping by Peter.

"Hey, you look rough. Is everything okay?"

Peter nodded. "I found her in my bed last night totally popped and ready to swing. She could barely see let alone anything else."

"Holy shit," Steve said, sighing. "What happened?"

"She slipped into the snow zone and I put her back in her own bed. She is one sharp bitch though. Even popped she wondered why I wasn't angry at the mouse."

"What mouse?" Steve asked.

Peter smiled. "That's what she calls Jeneil."

Steve choked on a laugh. "Mouse, huh? Boy, does she read things wrong."

Peter nodded agreeing with Steve. "She does and it constantly puts her in trouble. She lives in a world of half-truths and fantasy."

"Have you noticed that she's like Jeneil?"

Peter was shocked. "Get real."

Steve smiled. "No, really, they both play with helium."

"Steve, Jeneil plays with helium but deals in truth. Even in helium, she knows its helium." Peter smiled at the memory. "Besides, she gets high on life and that's fun."

Steve smiled agreeing with Peter. "You won't believe her latest. She's got an inflatable boat and the water near her house is full of rocks, so she bought a wheelbarrow and she runs down to the water every chance she gets to move the rocks to make a place for the boat. She's killing herself lugging all those rocks to the garden." Steve laughed. "But get this; she's afraid of the water. Is that lopsided or what?"

"But ask her to explain why she's doing it and I'll bet it makes sense."

Steve laughed. "That's what I'm afraid of. I begin to wonder about myself when I understand her. It absolutely fascinates me that she runs a successful business and lives at tilt."

"I used to think she lived at tilt. I don't anymore. Uette's at tilt. Jeneil has found a magic door in life where she goes to make Camelot real. And she makes it real, Steve. I sure miss it."

Steve patted his shoulder. "I didn't mean to bring back memories."

"Memories?" Peter repeated, chuckling. "They're how I get through the screwball bitch's idea of reality. I remember Camelot. I'm beginning to think Jeneil's the only completely sane person in life, her and my grandfather."

"I know what you mean; she circles the stampede on the expressway so you think she's part of what's happening, but when you look closer she's really in a rest stop watching the stampede race past her."

Peter nodded. "Yeah, and she picks up people who get thrown out of the stampede. They're her friends. She really is like some storybook princess who lives a life that she creates magically."

Steve laughed. "Boy, you fell through the rabbit hole, too."

"What?" Peter asked, not understanding.

"Jeneil calls her new place Wonderland. When I found her, she said she was glad I fell through the rabbit hole and found her. But you don't even ever need to be at Wonderland, she cast a spell on you, buddy." He slapped Peter's back gently. "Swoosh, right off the mountain." He walked away laughing.

Peter finished scrubbing. Steve was right; she had cast a spell. Maybe Steve fell through the rabbit hole, but she lived in Peter's soul and she got there deliberately while he watched and called her crazy the whole time. She wasn't crazy, the rest of them were.

Later that morning, Peter called his grandfather to report the incident and pleaded to not l

et the Wongs do anything for Jeneil's sake promising he'd keep talking to Uette about getting some help. His grandfather was aghast at the kind of life Peter was living. It was like his era with Lin Chi, but the Chinese community approved of his relationship with Uette, glad he had straightened out his life and had married someone decent.

His grandfather opened the bird cages and watched them fly happily into the potted trees. He wished he could open a door and as easily free his grandson from the cage that held him. Peter was in a cage and his songbird was flying in the trees unprotected. He shook his head worrying about the damage that could result from such a delicate balance. Were they strong enough to survive it? He looked at the garden blooming outside his window and he remembered that there was snow on the ground the day the Wongs came to meet with them. The days were passing into seasons bringing changes. He sighed sadly wondering if Peter and Jeneil would find their way back to each other.

Thank you for taking the time to read
"The Songbird / Volume Two - Author's Limited Edition."

In The Songbird/Volume One we introduced the main characters of the story. Jeneil and Peter were able to keep their relationship private and a secret and as such were able to establish a firm foundation with promises for a bright future together.

In The Songbird/Volume Two outside forces have loomed it's ugly head. Protecting the Songbird is not easy for Peter as Jeneil continues to expand her search for superlative in her life. Is Peter up to the task? And what about Steve? Is he really Peter's best friend? Will Peter and Jeneil survive?

In The Songbird / Volume Three we are introduced to a new character, an "Evil" girl named "Uette". In the dictionary "Evil" is defined as *adj.* (1) morally bad or wrong; wicked, (2) harmful; injurious, (3) unlucky; disastrous - *n.* (1) wickedness, sin. (2) anything that causes harm, pain, etc. Is Uette really an "Evil" person or is she just plain desperate???

Read on.....

Please, if you haven't read The Songbird / Volume One and Two, it is recommended that you do. It will add so much background and your understanding to Peter, Jeneil and Steve and the direction of the path that brought these three society's misfits together.

Your views would be most welcome and appreciated. Feel free to post your thoughts and comments on our website at:

http://www.TheSongbirdStory.com
OR
Search "The Songbird Story" on Facebook

"The Songbird"

by
Beverly Louise Oliver-Farrell

Author's Limited Edition / Five Volume Series

This unedited version of "The Songbird/Volume Three" is as the author intended it to be read. Only a limited numbers of copies will be available for the family and her friends. (A more condensed offering of "The Songbird Story" with be made available for the public at a later time along with a screenplay version.

We invite you to visit "The Songbird Story" website at:

http://www.TheSongbirdStory.com

Register your Email address to receive information on upcoming Volumes.
(The Songbird /Volume Four will be available in April of 2012.)

For Further Information and Inquiries Contact:

Brian B. Farrell
4844 Keith Lane
Colorado Springs, CO 80916

Tel: (719)380-8174 / Fax: (719)380-8365

Email: farrell_family@usa.net

BUY DIRECT FROM THE FAMILY AND SAVE
Volume One, Volume Two and Volume Three are now available at Discount

Made in the USA
Charleston, SC
04 October 2013